D1084398

Nor the Battle
to the Strong

For

The Sons of the Revolution
in the State of Georgia
February 18, 2011

Nor the Battle to the Strong

A Novel of the American Revolution in the South

Charles F. Price

With Maps and Illustrations by the Author

*For Ed,
Best Wishes
Charles F Price*

FREDERIC C. BEIL
SAVANNAH
2008

Published in the United States of America by
Frederic C. Beil, Publisher
609 Whitaker Street
Savannah, Georgia 31401
beil.com

LIBRARY OF CONGRESS CATALOGING-IN-PUBLICATION DATA
Price, Charles F., 1938–
Nor the battle to the strong : a novel of the American Revolution in the South /
Charles F. Price
p.   cm.
ISBN: 978-1-929490-33-2 (alk. paper)
1. United States—History—Revolution, 1775–1783—
Campaigns—South Carolina—Fiction.
2. Greene, Nathanael, 1742–1786—Fiction.
3. Eutaw Springs, Battle of, S.C., 1781—Fiction.
4. South Carolina—History—Revolution, 1775–1783—Fiction.
I. Title.
PS3566.R445N67   2008
813'.54—dc22

2008001005

Manufactured in the United States of America

First edition

To the memory of
Nathanael Greene (1742–1786)
James Johnson (1760–1850)
and to
Lee F. McGee for his tireless assistance

Whatsoever thy hand findeth to do, do it with thy might; for there is no work, nor device, nor knowledge, nor wisdom, in the grave, whither thou goest.

I returned, and saw under the sun, that the race is not to the swift, nor the battle to the strong, neither yet bread to the wise, nor yet riches to men of understanding, nor yet favour to men of skill; but time and chance happeneth to them all.

Ecclesiastes 9:10–11

Contents

Illustrations

Chronology

December 2, 1780: Major General Nathanael Greene assumes command of the Southern Department of the Continental Army.

January 17, 1781: Battle of Cowpens. Brigadier General Daniel Morgan, maneuvering in the South Carolina back country under Greene's orders, decisively defeats Lieutenant Colonel Banastre Tarleton and an army of British regulars.

March 15, 1781: Battle of Guilford Court House. Charles Lord Cornwallis, with an inferior British force, defeats Greene's much larger army, but suffers such serious losses that he must withdraw to coastal North Carolina for refitting. Greene turns back to South Carolina.

April 25, 1781: Battle of Hobkirk's Hill. Greene advances on Camden against a British force under Francis Lord Rawdon, who attacks with an inferior force. A panic of the First Regiment of the Maryland Line forces Greene to abandon his position, but British and American casualties are about even.

May 8–12, 1781: American troops under Lieutenant-Colonel Henry Lee and Brigadier General Francis Marion capture Fort Motte on the Santee River in South Carolina.

May 20, 1781: Cornwallis, having invaded Virginia, assumes command of combined British forces there, maneuvering against inferior American forces under the command of the Marquis de Lafayette; panic ensues in Virginia.

May 22, 1781: Greene besieges Ninety-Six, a Loyalist fortress strategically located in the South Carolina back country.

Late May 1781: Runaway indentured servant James Johnson enlists in the First Virginia Battalion commanded by Lieutenant Colonel Thomas Gaskins, Jr., at Point of Fork Arsenal in Virginia. Baron Friedrich Wilhelm Augustus von Steuben, the famous Valley Forge drillmaster of the Continental Army, assumes command of the Arsenal.

June 5–19, 1781: Steuben's force, including Johnson, evacuates Point of Fork Arsenal at the approach of British troops under Tarleton and Lieutenant Colonel John Graves Simcoe, and after a roundabout march joins Lafayette's army at Dandridge's Plantation in Hanover County, Virginia.

June 19, 1781: Greene hears that Rawdon is marching from Charles Town with fresh British troops to relieve Ninety-Six. After a failed attempt to take the fortress by storm, he abandons his siege.

June 21, 1781: Rawdon relieves Ninety-Six.

July 11–16, 1781: Greene maneuvers against Rawdon in an effort to bring him to battle before he can be reinforced. However, troops under Lieutenant Colonel Alexander Stewart succeed in joining Rawdon. Greene withdraws to a camp of repose on the High Hills of Santee.

July 12, 1781: Brigadier General Thomas Sumter, with a mixed force of partisans and Continental cavalry, begins an expedition into the South Carolina Low Country around Moncks Corner. The expedition meets with mixed results.

Late July 1781: At Chickahominy Swamp on the Virginia Peninsula, James Johnson enlists in the First Continental Light Dragoons commanded by Colonel Anthony Walton White. He enters training at a dragoon camp at Manakin Town on the James River above Richmond.

August 6, 1781: The British execute South Carolina militia colonel Isaac Hayne in Charles Town.

Mid-August 1781: James Johnson leaves Manakin Town as part of an escort for a wagon train of clothing commanded by Lieutenant Ambrose Gordon of the Third Continental Light Dragoons. The clothing is destined for dragoons serving under Lieutenant Colonel William Washington in Greene's Southern Army.

August 21, 1781: Rawdon leaves for England; Stewart assumes British field command.

August 23, 1781: Greene leaves the High Hills of Santee to take the offensive against the British force under Stewart.

August 25, 1781: *The Records of the Moravians* record the passage through Bethabara, North Carolina, of Lieutenant Gordon's clothing train of eight wagons and its escort, including James Johnson.

August 28, 1781: Lieutenant Gordon, in Charlotte, North Carolina, learns of Greene's offensive. He leaves the clothing wagons there and hastens with his small dragoon detachment, including James Johnson, to join the Southern Army.

September 1, 1781: Greene's army encamps between Orangeburgh and Eutaw Springs. Stewart's British command has moved to Eutaw Springs.

September 7, 1781: Greene's camp is now at Burdell's Plantation, seven miles from Eutaw Springs. Gordon's detachment, with James Johnson, joins late in the evening.

September 8, 1781: Battle of Eutaw Springs.

Nor the Battle
to the Strong

Part ye' Firſt

In Which a Young Man Takes the Shilling
of the Continental Congreſs

FOR A DAY AND A NIGHT THEY LAY HIDDEN IN THE newly green thickets at the edge of the woods above the joining of the waters. The whole of that first day they watched the ox-drawn wagons and the crowds of people hurrying past below them along the two yellow-dirt roads that passed by on either side of their hilltop to converge on the promontory at the fork of the river. Then, in the evening, a long file of dusty men came tramping down the left-hand road, led by four or five horsemen who parted the crowds with sharp words and forced the wagons to turn aside to make way for the column, while in the other road the people and wagons and carts kept pressing on with the same frantic urgency that had been amazing and frightening James and Libby all day long. The bustle on both roads continued as night fell; and even after dark, when the lights in the buildings yonder on the promontory began to glimmer, they could still hear the noise of the people and the beasts and the wagons going past unseen, a great scuffling and clattering and sighing, as if the whole of the country were on the move.

They hid in the bracken that day and then through the long cold night. Their fear made them wait. Then, early on the second morning, hunger and weariness overcame their fear and they decided at last to go in. James led the way out of the forest and across the wedge-shaped field of fresh grass that sloped and narrowed between the roads toward the flat ground at the point a mile or so on, where the roads met. Beyond the point the river wound its wide flat coils between low timbered headlands on its way to the faraway sea.

Going down, James chose an old cow-path. Soon he grew sorry for the choice. There had been no cows in the field for a long time, and the path was grown up in weeds and in prickly nettles that snatched at Libby's skirts and tore them worse than they were already torn and scratched her already bloody shins and bare feet. Once again she began to cry. James wanted to comfort her, but knew by now that he could not. The most he could do was try to redeem the promise he had made to her. Grimly determined, he led on.

Ahead, the sun cleared the tops of the trees beyond the point and bathed them in a slanted light that seared their eyes and cast their shadows behind them. There was some warmth in the light. Still, they blew plumes of vapor when they breathed and they ached from the chill that the night had set deep in their bones. But the light felt good anyway, and James stopped and took it gratefully on his face, and after a moment Libby too stood with arms outstretched as if to embrace it and draw it to her; she shut her eyes and lifted her own face in a way that made him think of a flower blooming. She had stopped crying. After a time she turned to him with a weary smile and said, "It *will* be better. Won't it?"

"Yes," he answered at once. At that moment, with the fear overcome, he had never been more certain of anything in his life. But life had also taught him how fragile every certainty could be, and as soon as he'd spoken his spirits began to ride on a dim air of apprehension.

They went on. They neared level ground. Ahead of them the roads met at a compound lined with buildings, and on the other side of the buildings the new light struck the big river that the two smaller rivers had come together to make; and the water beyond the point shone roughly, as if it were a big wrinkled sheet of tin laid down there. The roads to left and right were sunk between snake-rail fencing, and now as James and Libby descended they could see only the oddly disembodied tops of what was passing on them—the hoods of the wagons and the horns of the oxen that drew the wagons, the heads of all the people who were hastening toward where the roads met, and sometimes the heads of horses or mules that the people were leading or riding. There were no more files of men as had passed the evening before. Thick drifts of dust blew off the roads and across the flat and out over the river.

As they drew closer to the compound they saw that a low wall of stone hemmed part of it in. At a gap of this wall two soldiers lounged leaning on their muskets. One wore an old blue coat with red facings and the other a newer brown one, but the lower legs of both were clad in splatterdashes crusted with dried mud. The men were unshaven and dirty. Behind them stood a long low shake-roofed building of two stories, rock below and log above, the top level penetrated at intervals by shuttered windows that gave the place a pent and forbidding look.

Back of this were a range of forges and several cabins covered with clapboard and some stables and stock pens and then, just at the tip of the point overlooking the river, a brick shot tower and a squat stone building with a cupola on top that James suspected might be a powder magazine. Smoke came from the chimneys of the cabins and blew out over the river. The smoke, together with the dust raised by the people who hurried along the converging roads, joined over the water to make a thin haze that darkened the new sunlight in some places and brightened it in others.

They passed between the two sentries and through the gap in the rock wall. The sentries, who smelled strongly of rum, took no notice. In the center of the compound a flag dangled from the peak of a peeled pole. Because the flag hung limp James could not see its device, only some red-and-blue stripes and a bit of white flecked with blue eight-pointed stars. It was not a flag he had ever seen before. All about it was turmoil.

Two uneven ranks of men, mostly men of James's age though some were younger and many older, stood before the closed-up building and gaped about them as if bewildered by what they saw while a fellow in faded blue yelled at them. James suspected these must be soldiers, or men like himself who wished to become soldiers, though strangely they bore no arms and were dressed in common garb. Off to the right of the magazine, beyond the rock wall, a few parties dressed in the same civilian drab were idling about some campfires in the trampled farmhouse meadow dotted with tents and several huts of brush and leaves. Nearby, a hundred or so of their fellows, under the eye of a man on a prancing white horse, were trudging up and down in a scraggly line. James thought it possible they were marching, though appearances were decidedly against it.

Upcountry, the farm people had told him this was an important army station; it was why he had come. He had also heard folk were hastening here because the war had taken a turn for the worst. But the war was always taking bad turns, and even setting that aside, the place did not appear fit at all to be a station of the army. Its mad disorder did not seem in any fashion military, as he had imagined the military to be. Several times since the war began he had watched columns of blue-coated Maryland troops march past the farm where he was bound. They had marched in step to the music of fifes and the rattle of drums. Their ranks had been straight, their shouldered muskets had all sloped at the same angle. They had seemed the picture of discipline.

Here he stared disbelieving at bands of children dashing hither and yon as wild as wolves, geese waddling self-importantly, wives with infants at suck, a pair of dogs snarling over a bit of bone, a woman so big with child she cupped the bottom of her belly in her hands, pigs drowsing in mudholes, gangs of Negroes digging vaults, a donkey hitched to a post pissing in contentment, a milkmaid on a stool pulling the teats of a cow, a group of fiddlers sawing away in a corner of the yard, a flock of goats by the powder magazine. "It stinks," Libby declared, wrinkling her nose. *By God*, thought James, *I hope I've done right by us*. But his apprehensions deepened; his certainty of a few minutes before commenced ever so slightly to waver.

Near the magazine he spied a man seated at a table under a large maple tree just coming into leaf. And a splendid figure he was, loafing at his ease on a folding camp chair, one leg thrown across the other, his left hand resting languidly on the raised knee. He wore a large black cocked hat and a soft-collared linen shirt of spotless white, with a stock of black leather wound loosely about his throat. His brown coat had facings of scarlet, and his smallclothes and britches were a gleaming white. His fine black boots had oxblood tops. At his side hung a straight sword in a leather scabbard trimmed with brass. There were papers on the table, and he had laid his spontoon over them to hold them down. The blade of the spontoon glared brightly in the low fresh light that came through the boughs of maple; it made a nimbus, like a halo, about the lazing man.

A clerk hunched next to him scribbling in a book with a quill; nearby, a big soldier dressed in the same brown stood with crossed arms in an attitude of patient waiting. With a gush of relief James drank in the sight of the confident fellow in the cocked hat. Here at last, in all this bedlam, was a proper man of war. Here, surely, was authority. As he watched, the officer—for he was such, without a doubt in the world—flicked an eye over the hurly-burly in the yard, raised a pewter cup to his lips with a gesture of regal negligence, and drank an ironical toast to the commotion in whose midst he was such an island of repose.

James caught Libby by the hand. "There," he said, pointing to this vision of inspiration. He drew her behind and they crossed the crowded compound toward the commanding figure. Approaching the table, James let go of Libby's hand and made a small obeisance, dragging off his cap to show a proper submission. "Beg pardon, Your Honor," he said, regretting the tremor in his voice. "Is this the army?"

The clerk and the big soldier in brown ignored him, but the young offi-cer—no older than himself, James thought—glanced up with the same air of royal boredom he had shown in proposing his toast to the confusion in the compound. He fixed on James a hard hazel but bloodshot eye; his rud-dy and well-formed face took on an expression of amused disdain. "Does it seem an army?" he inquired archly. "Is it dressed in regimentals? Does it stand in ranks performing the evolutions of the school of the soldier? Is it armed? Does it march? Do drums beat? Fifers fife? Bugles blow?"

James blushed to be thus mocked. "No, Your Honor," he stammered, looking down at his cap, which he now turned nervously this way and that.

Crisply the officer nodded. "No. No, indeed. It's no damned army at all." He flourished his free hand toward the chaos surrounding them. "'Tis but a mob—a rabble, a congeries. Whoresons, defrocked pastors, absconded redemptioners, bounty-jumpers, cow-keeps, dog-whippers, dilapidated macaronis, emptiers of mingos. The scrapings and offscourings of the province." He stopped of a sudden, evidently in need of further refresh-ment, for he treated himself to another generous quaff from his cup—it was brandy, from the nose-numbing smartness of it—and James took note of the nearly empty bottle at his elbow. Martially splendid the officer might be, the very embodiment of the high-born commander of men; yet it had to be confessed that he was also as fishy as an Irish tinker.

"Why have they come, Your Honor," James ventured, "if they be not an army?" He was truly puzzled.

"Why?" the officer demanded, slamming the cup on the tabletop with such force that a quantity of brandy leapt out and splashed over the papers that lay under the spontoon, drawing to him the offended scowl of the clerk. "You ask why? Are you the only two persons in Virginia not to have heard the tidings?" He leaned at James, feigning a shrewd and complicit air. "Then I must divulge to you a terrible truth. Why, my gosling, we are overrun. Overrun by the dreaded Briton."

He made a contorted face of pretended horror. "Bloody Tarleton rav-ages the land. Simcoe plunders. Cornwallis, Scourge of the South, is upon us." He wagged his head with a rueful chuckle, drained the last of the brandy from his cup, caught up the bottle, turned it to his mouth, emptied it in one swallow, waved it in air like a baton. "All these wretches you see milling about us are recruits. Recruits due for eighteen months' service in the Line. If God favor us, they are the *stuff* of the Continental Army. The stuff, I say, but hardly the thing itself. Nor may they pretend to be—not for a fortnight at the soonest."

James was alarmed. "Pray, Your Honor. Who might Corn Wallace be?"

The officer put by his empty bottle and sank back in his chair with a laugh that this time was not unkind. He made an impatient motion to the clerk, who thrust aside his wetted papers and with an immediacy born of long custom bent and fetched up from beneath the table another bottle and gave it over. "Corn Wallace, as you so drolly name him, is a great lord of Britain," the officer explained. He drew the cork with his teeth, spat it forth, and drank. "He's a general in its terrible vast army," he went on, "and has come upon us from the country below, which he has laid waste with fire and slaughter." He favored James with a supercilious smirk. "Are you perhaps acquainted with the fact that we in the Confederated States are at *war* with England?"

"Yes, Your Honor," James replied, drawing himself up to seem as tall as he might. "And if this be the army of America in truth, why, I wish I may join the war."

"God rot me," cried the officer, "I believe you. You radiate a most beguiling sincerity. But why in the name of Bacchus do you *wish* to join it? Most young men of sense hope to avoid the service. It's true, scores have scurried here in terror of the British and will *pretend* to enlist; but as soon as they fancy the danger's past, they'll melt off like the morning dew. Some will fetch their enlistment bounty only to creep away before the musters are made up and enroll again a month hence in some other regiment, and jump from that one too in time, richer if only by a penny or two. Many were compelled into the ranks by draft. No one *wishes* to join. At least, not since Philadelphia was took back." He paused to shape a facetious smile. "No one, it seems, but your most unlikely self."

"I came hither, Your Honor, because I thought this place a fort of the army of America, and I hoped men in authority here would let me set down my name and be enrolled a soldier."

"It *is* an arsenal of the army, if not strictly a fort," the officer shrugged. "And one *may* be enrolled." He drank; he had forgotten his cup and continued to take his dram direct from the bottle. "In fact, I myself am empowered to do the enrolling. Indeed, it is my very purpose in so conspicuously sitting here." The reddened eye focused narrowly on James again. "You desire to be enrolled though you do not even know we are invaded?"

"I didn't know we are invaded, only that there was a great stir among the people. But me and my sister, we've not been much abroad. Not lately, I mean."

The officer peered past James to Libby, and his look lingered while she put one foot on top of the other and plucked up and closely examined the frayed end of one of her pigtails. "Your sister?" the officer inquired, disbelieving. His face waxed even rosier. "Is this not instead your bunter? And a comely one at that, I may say. Not poxed and battle-hammed as many are."

James did not like his words nor the tone he said them in. But James also knew how to behave before his betters. "No, Your Honor," he murmured deferentially. "She's my own sister in blood." Sometimes it put them off the scent if you reminded them in a pitiable way that persons of privilege were thought to know best what was right and what wrong, and that in consequence they were obliged to deal the more fairly with the common ilk. He guessed the officer thought sufficiently high of himself to respond to this.

He proved right. But in turning his attention from Libby the officer now grew stern and peremptory. "I suspect you, my young rustic," he declared. "You and this lass have about you some of the disheveled and starveling air of the fugitive. You carry no plunder. Are you not a kid? Have you broke your indenture and escaped your master? Do you mean to join the army to shirk a lawful servitude?"

James considered before he spoke. Gentlefolk set much store by virtues they flattered themselves they alone possessed. But on occasion they could be brought to admire these virtues in persons of the lower order who were not generally thought capable of having them. It made them approve of themselves as broad-minded and liberal. Honesty was one such virtue. Accordingly, he returned a robust answer, "I'll not lie to a gentleman, Your Honor. I have indeed run off from my master, just as you say. By no pledge of my own, I owed him more service than was just. Our Ma and Da died of fever on the voyage from Campbelltown, and the supercargo of our ship the *Edinburgh* sold us to him. Bound me fourteen years on their accounts and seven more on my own. Slavery, it was. And the master a cruel beast of a man that treated me ill and used my poor sister shameful. Six years we had of him. So I cracked his head for him with a pair of iron tongs and we run off. We've run a long while and are weary. We hunger. Three weeks we've hid in the fields and forests, eating wood-mint and birch-bark, grasshoppers and the legs of frogs, drinking out of brooks on our hands and knees like cattle, sleeping on beds of pine-boughs and moss. We've come to the army where we shall be fed and clothed. I'll always tell truth to a gentleman, sir."

Indulgently the officer smiled. His manner had softened; he seemed almost affectionate now—drunken men were given to odd changes of temper, James reflected; he remembered to hold himself wary lest affection turn as swiftly back to mockery and contempt. "And an artless truthteller you are too," the officer declared, sounding genuinely pleased. "And a Scot to boot, eh? The Scots are damned ferocious fighters, and I'm sure the Congress longs to see you hewing up the Redcoats with your Glaymore—though I see you've not got your Glaymore about you just now. But you apply in vain if it is in your plan to feast on tasty viands and wear a fine uniform. In the army of the Congress 'tis carrion beef or salt pork to eat and no more than a hunting-shirt to cover your nakedness—and that little about as often as Christmas comes. And you must know it's law that the army can't enlist an indentured man, lest his master pay him forth as his substitute."

James was guarded. "I ain't indentured. Not no more, Your Honor."

"I warrant not. Can your master advertise for you?"

"No, Your Honor. Not as I left him."

The officer laughed. "For a small sprightly thing it seems you wield the ironmongery right nimble. Batterers and murderers I am permitted to enroll, so long as they be free men. And I guess your freedom's fairly earned. What do they call you?"

"I'm James Johnson, Your Honor."

The clerk found a dry sheet of paper. James saw that it was a printed form with three blocks of text, each followed by a blank line. The clerk dipped his quill and commenced to write, filling in the empty spaces. "And your baggage?" demanded the officer.

"Elizabeth, Your Honor. Libby's how she's known."

"Are you of age?"

"As best I know, Your Honor. I'm twenty, I believe. Or thereabouts."

"Very well, Master James Johnson. Put up your right hand and swear to be true to the Thirteen United States of America, to serve them honestly and faithfully against all their enemies or opposers whatsoever, and to observe and obey the orders of Congress, and the orders of the generals and officers set over you by them."

"I swear it."

The officer nodded. He got to his feet—a bit unsteadily—and clapped a companionable hand on James's shoulder. "You are duly enrolled a private soldier in my company," he intoned in elaborate fashion, blowing brandy fumes in James's face. "I," he announced, "am Captain John Harris; Harris' Company be your abode from this moment on." He shoved his inflamed face close and confided in intimate guise, "*I'm* your Da now, in all matters public and military."

Taking a pace backward, he tripped over his sword, almost fell but managed to recover his balance with a lurch to leeward. "Your obligation's one year and six months' service," he continued, carefully pulling down the points of his waistcoat and passing a hand along its buttons in an effort to restore the portion of his dignity the stumble had cost him. "Make your mark in the places given on the form. Get your bounty from the clerk there—an interest-bearing certificate worth twenty dollars in Continental bills, a scrap of miscellaneous paper so utterly worthless that you may use it to wipe your backside and have far more advantage of it than if you were to pass it in any sort of commerce—though speculators do abound, defying logic, who'll buy it off you at a discount of some percentum of nothing.

Oh, and by your enlistment you've also got the pledge of Congress they'll give you a hundred acres of land at war's end, provided you ain't killed first, or Congress itself all hanged for traitors."

Captain Harris sampled his bottle as James took the pen from the clerk and proudly signed his full name to show that he was not as ignorant as some might think, then took the greasy lump of paper the clerk handed him. As he straightened from the table, the Captain once more took him by the shoulder and held him fast. "Listen now, Little James," he declared in the solemn vein of a preacher. "You have involved yourself in paradox. You have done violence to your master to win your freedom. But by enrolling to fight for the liberty of your country, you have entirely yielded up your own again. You are now once more sunk down to a creature lower than the meanest cur, and with as many rights. Any arbitrary man of greater rank can freely abuse you and you must abide it. You have no redress as you did with your master. You must welcome all the shit they drizzle on you.

"There is, however, this one great comfort—the knowledge that who-ever abuses you cringes under the abuse of one greater than he. You, my poor ruben, are the absolute least in Lieutenant-Colonel Thomas Gaskins' First Virginia Battalion of the Continental Line. But the whole of the army being governed by inflexible principles of subordination, I myself am but Gaskins' running dog and Gaskins is but the worm of our commander, Major General von Steuben, who in his turn must lick the boots of the Marquis de Lafayette, who even on his lofty perch is obliged to bend and kiss the hairy arse of His Excellency the Commander in Chief. And even the great Washington must tug his forelock to the Congress. Take from that what solace you may."

Releasing James, he stepped back and tilted his bottle high, and James watched as his adam's-apple rose and fell five times by actual count. Then he flourished the bottle in the direction of the big soldier in brown who had stood by silently all this time. "Now," he said, "here's a sergeant who'll get you fitted out and settled in your camp. He wears a frightful aspect, I grant you. He lost that eye on the terrible field at Camden and before that was among the blessed few in the Second Regiment of Foot that 'scaped the fall of Charles Town. He's seen the lions and can teach you how they're bearded."

But before the sergeant could advance and take James in charge, Captain Harris once more drew fondly near and, throwing an arm about James's shoulders, walked him a few paces aside. At a distance from the others, putting his head close, he gave a confidential wink and spoke intimately in James's ear. "But before you go," he said, "here's a piece of wise counsel from your new Da: From this day treat your Libby as your sweetheart, or better yet, as your wedded wife. If she's your sister as you claim, I reckon 'twould be best not to go so far as to be a-rogering her. But keep her cozy in your pallet of a night and now and then make such motions as will counterfeit a flourish or two. Else your messmates will covet her oyster basket, steal her off from you, and outrage her worse than ever did your late master."

———

The big sergeant whose face was so disfigured that James could not bring himself to look at it led them across the compound and over a stile in the rock wall toward the meadow. The drilling had ended now, and the men who had been making shift to march were dispersing to the fires to join their fellows, and the officer who had instructed them was turning his white horse with a jerk of the reins to come riding back toward the compound. He approached at a brisk canter. James saw that he was just past middle age, short and portly and with a long nose and heavy chin and a small delicately formed mouth just now bitten tight and turned down at the corners in a show of displeasure. He wore an expensive powdered wig. His face was crimson and congested. On his left breast he wore a huge medallion of silver, as big around as a dinner plate, embossed with an eight-pointed star. The sergeant gave him a salute, which he acknowledged with an absentminded flick of a hand. He rode past trailing his palpable air of disgust and also a slight whiff of what might have been perfume. They also smelled the powerful odor of his horse and felt the thump of its hooves in the earth under them.

They walked on. After a time the sergeant surprised them by speaking a word. It sounded like "Waxhaws."

James was unsure what he had said. "What's that, Your Honor?"

"'Twas the Waxhaws," answered the sergeant, "not Camden like he said." The voice was harsh and scraping as if his throat were sore from too much loud talk. "And don't call me Your Honor. Call me Sergeant."

"Like who said? Sergeant."

"The Captain. He said it was at Camden. Where the damned Green Dragoons took my eye." He turned a thumb toward the face that James had dared not study. "But it was the Waxhaws."

"What's the Waxhaws?" James wanted to know. "And who are the Green Dragoons?" He was getting exasperated. The mass of new information being heaped on him seemed too great to be taken in. His head was already dizzy from everything Captain Harris had told him, and now the sergeant was telling him even more. He had not expected the army to be so confusing.

The sergeant gave a snort. "The Waxhaws is a waste place down in the black jack and piney woods of Carolina, full of Ulster Scots, New Lights,

12

and every other stripe of nonconforming shit-sack, that I was passing through when Charles Town fell—me and Captain Catlett what was carrying dispatches to the Governor of Virginia. We thought ourselves lucky not to be took like the rest of them poor beggars. The British bagged near about the whole of the Virginia Line in Charles Town, save us few that was out in the country. Tossed 'em in a fleet of prison hulks in the harbor, left 'em to rot. In the end, though, 'twas the prisoners had the luck. For *we* was with Buford, at the Waxhaws."

James sighed at the sound of yet another strange name. "Who's Buford? And you never said what a Green Dragoon was."

The sergeant came to a halt and turned to James with a laugh that was even ruder than his former tone. James had no choice then but to observe that face. He felt himself blanch, and from behind heard Libby—who had kept her eyes averted till now also—gasp aloud in pity and horror. "You don't know a goddamn thing, do you, son?" the sergeant demanded, oblivious of their dismay, or perhaps hardened to all dismay by now. Indeed, he pushed his face down on James as if proud of its effect. "You never heard tell of Colonel Buford or the Waxhaws or the Green Dragoons *or* Tarleton's Quarters?"

"The Captain said the name of Tarleton just now, I remember that," James blurted, displaying a bit of the irritation he felt despite the fierceness of the sergeant. "He said Tarleton was with Corn Wallace. But I never heard of a Buford or the Waxhaws or of a Green Dragoon neither. And why does it matter where this Tarleton's quartered?"

"'Tain't *that* kind of quartering that's meant, son," explained the sergeant. He drew back his terrible countenance and James thought his temper turned milder. Perhaps he was more tender of heart than he had wished at first to appear. "It don't signify where the fellow lived," he went on. "It speaks to his fashion of making war. He's an English officer, leads a pack of bum-fuckers he calls the British Legion. Tories. Half cavalry, half infantry, and all as mean as the spawn of Satan. Wear green jackets, they do—it's why they're named the Green Dragoons."

He resumed walking as he spoke and James fell in stride beside him while Libby followed. He seemed in a mood of reverie now, as if pondering pleasant remembrances. "Buford's a Virginia colonel," he continued, "commanded a detachment that was on its way down to Charles Town, but turned back for Virginia when he heard the place was took. We was marching with him, passing through the God-blasted Waxhaws. Tarleton caught up with us. Pitched into us like a cyclone. Licked us good and proper. We figured to quit. When you want to quit, you ask for quarters. It's like mercy. 'Quarters!' you cry, and the enemy's supposed to do you no more hurt. So we cried quarters."

Then James realized the sergeant's mood was not one of mellow memories after all. Instead he was meditating on some unpleasant experience that seemed to have left a deep mark on him. James was innocent of any knowledge of the ways of armies, but he was not unacquainted with the darksome deeds of men and knew something himself of how such doings could quiet the soul with horror as the sergeant's had been stilled. "But they never stopped," the sergeant continued in that brooding, almost wistful tone. "They come at us with them goddamned sabers—hell, I can see 'em flashing yet, them curved blades, ground sharp as razors, hewing and hacking. Cut through bone like it was turds. Killed my captain, slashed poor Stokes till his own mother wouldn't want to look at him. Cut off arms and legs and heads—heads was bounding in the road like footballs. And poor wretches a-begging for their lives all that while. The whoresons gave me this face, that affrights the toads. My damned eyeball fell out in my hand just like a grape. *That's* Tarleton's Quarters."

He stopped again and turned and this time James did not flinch to see him. In fact there was something in his one good eye that James now wanted to see, and knew that the sergeant wanted him to see too. The sergeant wanted him to understand about the bewilderment one had to feel when the cruelty of the world exceeded all bounds. It touched James that the sergeant did not know he already understood this, that the sergeant had hoped to prepare him for it. "That same whoreson Tarleton's headed this way just as fast as he can ride," the sergeant was saying. "Bloody Ban, they call him. So here's your lesson, son—if you're up against Bloody Ban Tarleton or any of his murdering devils, don't you *never* try to surrender."

The sergeant led them across the field of flattened grass among the dozens of campfires, some smoldering and some still fully burning, but all sending up in greater or lesser degree the dense white smoke that spoke of green wood cut and committed to flame before its time. And looking about, James saw that in all the sweep of land running up to the distant farmhouse, not a post or rail of a fence remained. Every stick of finished wood had long since gone into the fires and now the soldiers had started to burn the living trees too. Judging from the number of raw stumps to be seen, all the woods on the place would soon be cut. It seemed to James that war might be a kind of wholesale pestilence that killed not men alone but the beauty of the world as well.

Another thing he noticed—the air smelled of the tart smoke only. No fragrances of roasted pork or boiling peas or hot stews came. The faces gathered round the fires were drawn with want. With his own hunger raging, he knew a moment of alarm. Would he and Libby not be timely fed after all? He recalled with foreboding Captain Harris' portentous words about carrion beef, and how seldom it was served out.

They approached a fire where six persons crouched or reclined or squatted before a little arbor roughly fashioned of tree boughs. Suddenly these burst out a chorus of complaints: "Where's our tents? We was promised tents. 'Twas so damned cold last night I couldn't find my own pecker." "What about our rations? We ain't et so much as a handful of beans since yesterday noon, and force-marched all the way from Carter's Ferry." "Muskets too. Where's them? The goddamned British come, we supposed to fend 'em off a-throwing rocks? I been in this army a week now and ain't laid hands on a firelock yet. Or even *seen* one."

Disgust contorted the sergeant's marred countenance and made it even more appalling. He came to a stand and doubled his fists at his hips. "Stop your swearing," he thundered. "There's women present."

One of the men lying on his side with his head propped on the heel of his hand gave a deriding laugh. "There's *chickabiddies* present. And punks too." He was cribbage-faced from smallpox, and thin of frame and knobby of bone, with swatches of red hair sticking out from under his knitted cap. He had on checkered trousers and a dirty workman's jacket. Oddly, he clutched a shoat in the crook of his free elbow, which kept poking its narrow head into his armpit as if it thought a cache of acorn mast might be hidden there.

James knew him for the one in every company who had to be brooked before any other business could be done. He stepped up and told him stoutly, "This here's my good and lawful wife, and anybody names her doxy'll answer to me." He had not known till then that he would take Captain Harris' advice and pretend for her sake that Libby was his wife. Of course it made no difference anyway—wife or sister, he wouldn't abide a slur. He beckoned to the caitiff. "Stand up, you."

The sergeant cocked his head at the redhair in a signal of warning. "You'd best think on that a spell, afore you do it, Sides," he smiled. He winked his good eye in James's direction. "I'm told this little nit, dainty as he looks, has broke a fellow's noggin for playing rude with his light-o'-love."

Sides stroked his piglet and gave James a study. "He don't look so capable."

"Stand up and see," invited James.

Sides made a negligent flapping motion in the air. "I'm give out," he explained. "That Dutchman's had us marchin' all morning. Let's do it later." The others laughed, even the sergeant in gruff fashion, and James saw now that this fellow Sides was a harmless puffer. Even so, he thought it necessary to finish what had been started. It was always best to drive a good point home.

"It's now or nothing," he said. "And if 'tain't now, then you must make your manners to my Libby or bear the name of coward."

Sides made his pushing-off motion again. "You've lugged the wrong sow by the ear, Mister. Sue a beggar and catch a louse; I'm a coward all right." But he sat up then and let the shoat go and gathered his feet under him and stood. Turning to Libby, he gave her a long moment's study, then pulled off his cap, clutched it to his breast and spoke with apparent sincerity, "I meant no disrespect, Missus . . ."

"Johnson." Libby furnished the name with a blush and a curtsy as the piglet explored her skirts for something to eat. "Libby Johnson."

"And who's your pocket hero?" Sides inquired with a mischievous squint. The lout, James saw without surprise, had a bruised and swollen jaw; clearly he was the sort who often wanted thrashing.

James identified himself and the ginger-hackle came to him grinning and grasped his hand and shook it warmly. "Well, James Johnson, I'm Poovey Sides and I like the cut of you. Why, I expect we'll be fast friends."

For the moment James elected to hold himself distant. "We'll be," he nodded, "if you can keep a civil tongue in your head." He eyed the shoat suspiciously as it returned to Sides and rubbed against his bony shanks like a cat.

"I doubt if he can hold civil for long," one of the others spoke up. "Sides's tongue's his worst enemy. But he's as craven as a dunghill fowl, I'll testify to it. So you can plague him all you want and he'll only make a joke." This one got up too and came and took James's hand. "I'm Blan Shiflet," he said. "Orange County's my home." Shiflet had an unruly shock of auburn hair and bright brown eyes and was nearly as large as the sergeant; his grip was tight and hard and callused from labor, as were Sides's and James's own.

A third man stood, approached, and gave his hand. He was nearer to James's size and tow-headed. "Charlie Cooke," he said. "I'm from Orange too. We was all drafted, and mustered together at Charlottesville."

"Eighteen damned months in the regulars," Sides sneered in scorn. "Why, I've done four terms in the militia already. What about all them engorged platter-faced landlords and great swollen arbitrary rascals squatting on their fat arses, dodging any kind of service, whilst poor culls living in huts has to turn out?"

"You got your division's bounty, didn't you—same as all of us?" the man Shiflet retorted.

"Oh, I got a hunk of grimy papers all right, looking something a crow coughed up, that they said was a payment on some thousands of dollars coming due one time to come—on Judgment Day, I guess. Money's down so, what they gave won't buy this pig of mine a poke of shelled corn."

"There's the land they gave," Shiflet insisted.

Sides honked his contempt. "Three hundred acres in the western country? Find me that much ground ain't already took up by the same gross high-flyers running this damned war."

James noticed this piece of seditious talk passed unremarked by the sergeant, as did Charlie Cooke's reply of weary sarcasm, "They've got to look after their big goddamned estates. Keep their niggers close. Hire substitutes, or send the folk they've got indentured." The sergeant continued indifferent to their grumbling, no doubt hardened by now to every lamentation a recruit might offer. Cooke recalled his manners then, and pointed to a nondescript figure who sat prodding the embers of the fire with a stick. "This here's my Janet." Janet favored them with one furtive look of her black eyes like chips of coal and went back to poking at the fire. She was plain and had mouse-colored hair, and James would have thought her a man had Cooke not told him differently. She looked angry. "Sides has spoke ill of her already," Cooke said. "That's why he's bruised up."

Sides gave a shrug of aggrieved innocence. "Yes," he acknowledged, "they all make free with me." He resumed his place recumbent by the fire and again drew the pig to him; greedily as before, the little creature nosed at his armpit. It was very skinny, nearly as skinny as Sides himself.

"I'm Dick Snow," said the fourth of the party, who reached up from where he lay at fireside. "I'd stand and greet you proper, but I've rubbed a blister on my heel a-trampin' about for that damned Dutchman." He wore a sleeved waistcoat and breeches and a pair of half-gaiters. He had a harelip. James took the thin strong hand. "Can you cook?" Snow asked with some urgency. "Either one of you? We're in sore need of a cook. Iffen we ever get aught to eat. Janet here's got her good points, but cooking ain't amongst 'em. We had one ration of fish and rice awhile back and she burnt it to charcoal."

"God blast you for a poxed bastard," Janet hissed, not glancing up from the fire. But nobody paid her any heed.

"I'm a house joiner by trade," James informed them with more than a hint of pride, "and no cook at all."

"*I* can cook," Libby said.

"Hell," Sides blurted, "it don't matter; they ain't never going to give us nothing *to* cook."

"Cook a baby," Janet muttered, shaking her mass of grayish hair. "Cook a baby and eat that." She vented a sudden alarming squeal of laughter and drove her stick savagely into the fire, stirring forth a burst of sparks and flying ash. James and Libby stared aghast, but the others ignored her as before.

The fifth man came to James, shook hands, and offered the unlikely name of Samuel Ham. At once Sides fell into a convulsion of derisive laughter. From Ham's expression of woe it was evident Sides had the habit of ridiculing the name whenever Ham uttered it. But James—always sensitive to the feelings of others—greeted the unlucky Sam Ham with a studied formality, which he hoped would stand in contrast to the rudeness of Poovey Sides—one man upon earth, James reflected, who ought not make sport of ridiculous names. It was James's opinion that no person should be made to suffer for a thoughtless choice of one's parents, be he Sam Ham or Poovey Sides, or even such an ogre as Corn Wallace. Sam Ham was dressed in a slouched hat, a linen frock, britches buckled at the knee, and stockings stuck full of beggar-lice. He had a moody air, perhaps a result of the effect his name so often had on others. James wrung his hand with special emphasis, to make up for his hurt feelings.

"Well," the sergeant said to James, "this'll be your mess, son."

Here was yet another vexing term James had not heard before. He frowned. "What's a . . . ?"

This time the sergeant anticipated him. "A mess is a gang of soldiers that agrees to eat together and take turns toting the camp kettle on the road." To the others he said, "Listen to me now, my sprats. As to tents, you ain't getting none." He held up his hand to still their groans. "But the weather's mild and you've made yourself a snug little brushwood booth here, and anyways, 'lessen I miss my guess, we'll be a-marching in a day or two, the British being as they are, coming on to Petersburg, and Richmond likely to be given up."

"I thought we was going into South Carolina," Charlie Cooke protested.

"We *was* wanted there, with General Greene. But with Cornwallis jumped up in Virginia, they may keep us back to stop him."

"*Try* and stop him, you mean," sneered Sides.

The sergeant ignored him. "As to rations, each of you'll get his pound of salt pork, a gill of rice and one of peas, and a pint of good spruce beer—the women too." This fine news heartened James, and he and Libby exchanged happy looks. "They'll pass it out afore noon," continued the sergeant. "Muskets also. We've had a shipment of firelocks from Charlottesville and Philadelphia—Brown Besses mostly, and some French ones and Committee of Safeties. We've no cartridges boxes yet, so when you draw your rounds, dump 'em in your pockets. Tomorrow the Baron'll give another drill and show you the manual of arms and teach you some light infantry tactics." He allowed himself a whimsical smile. "Hell, by this time tomorrow, you'll all be so fierce and smart and proper the Bloodybacks'll take to their heels at the sight of you."

"Speaking of appearances," Shiflet spoke up, "what about uniforms?"

"There's some clothes here at the Arsenal," answered the sergeant. "Don't know if they'll be shared out, though. They're State stores, and by the law of it, you're Continentals, and ain't eligible."

Charlie Cooke sighed. "I was wanting one of them fine regimentals, and a three-cornered hat."

"Then you should've enlisted afore this," the sergeant retorted, turning to go. "Now you'll likely march in your own linsey-woolsey and halfthick, or in nothing at all."

"We'll see his little prick a-hanging down," Janet warned them with a sly grin, and this time the comment was so unexpectedly canny that everyone burst out laughing—everyone, that is, save Charlie, who darkened with mortification.

With the sergeant gone, James came to the fire and stood watching as Poovey Sides toyed and cuffed with his piglet. Finally he asked, "How can a soldier have a shoat for a pet?"

"'Tain't no pet," the red-hair answered brightly. "It's a remedy. I'm indifferent to the brute itself." Seeing James's frown of puzzlement, Sides endeavored to explain. "I may not look it, for I've been druv hard these past days and have got soilt, but I'm of a right finicky disposition. I fancy cleanliness and I do hate like fury to have any sort of crawly chats about me, and I've been in the militia and understand enough of armies to know how they abound in fleas and wood ticks and lice and every kind of revolting pest, which I can on no account abide. So early this morning I crept up to yonder farmhouse and stole me this weanling shoat, to keep it close, so the varmints'll all leave me and go to it. I mean to tote it in my knapsack—soon as I *get* a knapsack—the whole duration of this war, and so keep myself free of biting and itching creepers for all time."

"It'll be fun," Blan Shiflet observed, "watching you haul that damned thing about. By the time the whole war's finished, it'll have growed to a right smart of tonnage."

"There's another flaw in your reasoning," James told Sides. "You carry that shoat, the cooties and such will exchange back to you, in time."

"Not by the lights of my old Daddy," Sides confidently declared. "My old Daddy always slept with his pig—a great bristly hog it was, too—and that man was as clean as a whistle, at all times and in all weathers. All loathsome blood-sucking critters went from him to the pig, then from off that pig to somewheres else."

James pursed his lips in doubt. "We'll see, I guess."

Sam Ham glimpsed an opportunity to exact a measure of revenge for Sides's ridicule of his name. "Your Dad slept with a hog," he slyly remarked, "but not with your Ma. Is that it?"

But the slur lacked the effect Sam intended, for Sides blithely answered, "Oh no, the pig slept in *betwixt* 'em, y'see." He smiled. "My Mama," he added, "she was a clean 'un too."

While awaiting the promised deliveries, they got to know one another better. The harelip Dick Snow was a Charlottesville cooper and cabinet-maker; Sam Ham, a tanner from Culpeper; and Blan Shiflet and Charlie Cooke were tenant farmers from Orange. Sides claimed to be a farmer too, from Fluvanna, but when pressed, showed himself unable to offer much convincing proof that he knew the finer points of husbandry, save of course in the keeping of hogs. James suspected the red-hair of being no more than a stroller. Charlie Cooke's Janet was, regrettably, a madwoman. She hadn't always been. Once she was a respectable seamstress of Cumberland. But a scoundrel of an itinerant Presbyterian preacher had had his way with her and the child that was born of the union had died and she had been shamed into a degraded life. Cooke had taken pity on her and brought her with him to the army in hopes she might prepare the food of the mess. But because of her derangement she could not manage even that, and now spent her time alternately having fits and lapsing into trances. Libby, who had a soft heart, spent the afternoon with her, crooning to her, untangling her heap of mouse-colored hair, and brushing it out with a horse's curry-comb that Charlie had found near the stable of the farmhouse, while Janet murmured and sang her weird melodies and jabbed her stick into the fire.

The rations came at last—in a single kersey poke stuffed into an iron camp kettle full of clashing utensils, dropped by a Negro off the back of a two-wheeled cart that trundled past—and Libby left Janet to her lunatic tunes, stirred up the fire, and soon had the kettle on a boil to ready their meal. The pork and rice and peas were still bubbling in the pot when a steer wagon arrived and the one-eyed sergeant stepped down to supervise a pair of sweaty slaves in the distribution of muskets and attendant gear. "You'd best not get used to having all this truck," he warned them. "We're at an arsenal of the State of Virginia, is the only reason, and Virginia's loaning it. By and by, you'll be loading your firelocks with nails, and chewing your belt-leather for breakfast."

James's musket was as long as he was tall and so heavy that he could barely hold it level against his shoulder. It had brass mountings and a steel ramrod and brown walnut stocks fastened to the barrel with metal pins. It felt remorseless and lethal. "She's a Rappahannock Forge," the sergeant told him. "A good honest Virginia gun, seventy-five caliber, made by our own James Hunter at Fredericksburg. Treat her decent. She'll stand up for you, so long as you do right by her."

Clearly the piece was well made. It was even pretty, with its shiny barrel and brass fittings and dark rubbed wood and its finely curved cock with a knobbed screw holding the two steel jaws that clamped the flint in place. James believed what the sergeant had said about it being a worthy weapon. But even so, holding it inspired in him an unaccountable feeling of guilt. It seemed to make him complicit in something larger and more destructive than he had counted on. He had joined the army chiefly to warm his chilled bones and feed his pinched belly and soothe his fear, and to get away from the tyranny of his master and save Libby from further ravishment. But the musket—and, even worse, its bayonet, with its wicked-looking right-angled socket, its seventeen inches of narrowly tapering shaft, its point of impermissible sharpness—spoke to him of murder; and a part of his soul recoiled from it.

Of course he was no stranger to powder and shot. One of his former tasks had been to take the master's fowling piece and hunt quail and wild turkey for the table. But the prospect of shooting a man was a matter far more dire than the downing of game, and so seemed to him utterly wrong. He told himself that the men to be shot were brutal oppressors who, if given the chance, would readily shoot him. He reminded himself that he well knew the purpose and meaning of war; that yes, war was indeed a terrible offense, but that the hearts of men were so evil that sometimes only war could burn it out of them, and so was justified, even in the eyes of whatever God passed judgment on such matters. Whence, he wondered then, came this suspicion that by taking a musket in his hands he had somehow involved himself in a kind of wickedness that might be irredeemable?

Along with the muskets there were bayonets with scabbards, and in place of the cartridge boxes the sergeant had said were lacking, a jeans sack heavy with some ready-mades as well as the lead bars, bullet moulds, powder flasks, packets of paper and twine that would be needed to assemble more cartridges for the muskets of odd caliber. James gazed helplessly at these last items till the others, all of whom had done militia service, showed him how to make a cartridge by winding the stiff paper around a dowel of wood called a "former," pouring in the proper amount of powder, tying one end with twine, and crimping the other into a twist. There also were knapsacks, blankets, haversacks with linen slings, canteens, a bag of gunflints for general use. James handled the exotic implements reverently, much as a wilderness heathen might when shown artifacts of a civilized world. *But these is hardly civil tools*, he thought.

They talked, lying close in the cramped arbor, till late. Then Blan Shiflet and Sam Ham, who'd fetched hatchets from home, chopped down and cut up a blighted poplar nearby, which no one else had thought worthy of trying to burn, and stacked the wood by the fire for use during the night.

Stinking smoke from the burning of the poor wood made its way into the arbor to smart their eyes and give them sieges of coughing, and they were annoyed by the disagreeable odors of everyone's unwashed bodies and soiled clothes; but since there was no help for this they soon grew resigned to the rude conditions. Poovey Sides retired with his piglet. James chose a spot as far from Sides as he could get, close to Charlie Cooke and his Janet; and for a while after they all bedded down, Libby lay holding Janet by the hand, talking to her in a tender gibberish. Janet tossed and twitched, whimpered, now and then uttered some foul oath; but at last quieted and fell asleep.

Then Libby crept to James and he gathered her close under their blanket as he fancied a good husband might. But he was in a misery of embarrassment, and Libby did not help matters by breaking into fits of giggling. Presently, though, she turned serious. "What a strange day it's been," she mused. "Think how hungry and afraid we were, only this morning, hiding in the woods, all alone, as timid as hunted beasts. Now we're fed and warm and safe—or safer than we were, at least. And we've met good friends."

James nodded but said nothing. He had not yet made up his mind about the wisdom of what they had done. He was not sure how good these new friends might be, especially the coaster Sides. And he knew that he and Libby were far from safe—it was not possible to *be* safe, not in any army, not in wartime. For James there would be the dangers of the march and the battlefield. For Libby there would always be the special kind of danger that Captain Harris had warned him of. And dangers of the soul were lurking too; he knew that from the sinister message his musket had passed to him. Dangers of all sorts crowded in on them, and James knew that he must be shrewd and vigilant if he were to stave them off. But it was true, as Libby said, that they were warm, that their pangs of hunger had been appeased. He would permit himself to be thankful for that.

Still, he gathered from the campfire talk he'd heard that had he been a Virginia man, drafted into the army of the Continent by his militia fellows like Shiflet and Cooke and the others, he'd have earned a greater bounty of land and money. Even if it were true, as Sides so cynically maintained, that wartime extremities had much reduced their value, such state bounties might have lifted him and Libby at a stroke from a mean condition to a middling one. It vexed him to think he'd sold himself into service for a pittance of money and ground instead. The thought made him squirm with disquiet, forcing Libbby to shift her position under the blanket.

From the compound beyond the rock wall they heard the blare of a bugle and the rattle of a snare drum; and sitting up, propped on his elbows, James watched the alien striped flag slide slowly down its pole in the yard, to be gathered in by some soldiers standing there in a flare of red light from the forges. One of them folded the flag and gave it to another, and this one carried it before him in his two hands like an offering and entered a lower door of the big two-storied building of rock and log that had been closed up earlier, but whose many windows were now unshuttered, dispensing a smoky glow of lamps and candles. Horsemen—couriers, James guessed—came and went with a clatter of hooves on the hard-packed ground. The forges uttered a constant clangor of hammered iron.

He lay back, resting his head on the knapsack he had been fortunate enough to grab when the Negroes flung them out of the wagon; his and Shiflet's and Dick Snow's were the only three in the mess; Poovey Sides, Sam Ham, and Charlie Cooke would have to make do rolling their goods in their blankets, to be thrown over the shoulder, tied at the ends and worn that way like some vagabond's budget—it would be interesting to see how Sides managed to carry his shoat that way. James had been lucky about the knapsack. Granting his misgivings, it was also possible he had been lucky about his choice of joining the army. With all its inconveniences it was far better than the abasement of servitude or the blind terrors of flight.

He sighed and crossed his hands behind his head on the knapsack and gazed up at stars that flecked the night sky. All about him in the dark he could sense the hundreds encamped on the broad triangle of land between the forked waters settling at last into rest and slumber, and in the quiet that came then he could hear the low deep rushing of the two rivers coming together into one. The massy sound made him think how all America was astir in this war and how huge that motion was. Till now he had not taken much thought of the war or of its meaning. He had heard men talk of liberty—Captain Harris had talked of it today. The war *was* about liberty, he supposed. But in his servitude, the idea of liberty had never meant much. Now that he was free, he guessed it might mean more. The notion made him feel expectant, and involuntarily he gave a peaceful little grunt. Libby snuggled closer. She put her lips to his ear and drowsily whispered, "Speak of home, James."

It was an old ritual with them, but they had not practiced it in some time. They had been too busy running, hiding, shivering with fright in black woods. Now as she asked for it again he realized how much he had missed it. "Yes," he said eagerly, "all right." He paused, summoning it, remembering. Then he began. "There's the firth and the cliff above it and the long flat sands. The gray sea and the mist clinging to it. The roar of surf like faraway storms. Rocks showing shiny dark in the breakers—purple or lilac or black from the wet, and the white water streaming off after the waves pass, the sea boiling all about. Gulls wheeling over. The smell of brine in the chill of the haar that blows, sometimes even on the sunniest days. Drizzle that pricks your face like needles.

"Westerdale in its cove, its roofs of thatch and tile. The smoke of chimneys streaming back. The hundred lochs scattered over the moorlands, every one agleam like a shard of looking-glass. The long-haired cattle in the fields, some as red as copper. The hills so green it makes your heart want to break. The oak woods. Cairns and standing stones set up by the folk in the old time, the moss and lichen over 'em. The River Thurso turning down its woody ravine. Dirlot Castle with its rock foot in the river. Strathmore. The cottage."

He had seen it all, of course, when a very young boy. But in fact he remembered very little of it. He had lost the greater part. His life since had wiped it out. He thought perhaps he could actually recall a few vestiges— the way the lochs had resembled pieces of broken mirror, the rumble of the surf, maybe the cries of the wheeling seagulls. But nothing more remained. He was telling Libby what his Da and Ma had told him day after day and night after night in the dank hold of the *Edinburgh*. Libby had been but a babe then. Over and over as the ship wallowed with the heave of the ocean, his Da had repeated it to him, telling of Dunnet Head and the firth and the moorlands and the Thurso and Westerdale and Strathmore and the cottage. He was telling it so James would remember it—remember the words if not the scenes themselves. And the sicker James's Da became, the more often and the more urgently he had repeated the telling. And after his Da died, his Ma began to repeat it too, telling it again and again and again as she grew weaker and weaker in her turn, till in time she also passed away. But between them, they had given it to him. It was his now. He possessed it. He held it in his mind's eye as clearly as if he could remember it all himself. Now he gave it to Libby, as his Da and Ma had given it to him.

Part ye Second

In Which General Greene Purſues ye Siege of Ninety-Six

DEEP IN THE PINE AND HARDWOOD FORESTS OF the South Carolina backcountry, the General stood behind a heap of gabions on an embankment of fresh-turned dirt and peered through his spyglass. He leaned forward and rested his elbows on the yielding wicker-work of one of the big round baskets to steady his view. The lens fetched the earthen walls of the Star Fort so close that he could see the patches of fresh mint-green grass on its ramparts; the tiny pink and white faces of new wildflowers; and little amber pebbles and russet clods of clay lying on the banks themselves. Beyond the fort he could see the big stockade from which the smaller fort projected and a portion of the covered way that connected the two, and the twin log blockhouses guarding the nearest corners of the stockade, all these standing flatly one against the other, without perspective, like so many cutouts of stiff paper.

The spyglass showed him the coarse red-brown cladding of the bark on the vertical timbers of the stockade and the axe-marks on their sharpened points and even the rosin that had run down their sides from the trimmed points, congealing in white streaks and shiny transparent beads that made the rough wood look as if it wept. *Perhaps it does*, he mused; *perhaps all the world does*; but then he pushed the notion aside; it was one of those maundering sentiments that sometimes sprang up unbidden from his old life, that could have no place in the deadly work he did now.

Much too often he found it necessary to force himself from meditation to action; it irked him to have to do it now, with so much at stake. He made a petulant purse of his mouth and pressed the eyepiece harder against the socket of his eye, as if its little "o" of discomfort would help discipline his mind. He swept his glass along the parapet, concentrating. None of the garrison was on show. *They're digging*, he told himself. *Ditches, traverses, probably even a well. To shelter themselves from the artillery, to give cover to the civilians, to have water for the time when we take their spring.* He was digging too. They were all digging. They were two armies of moles digging away at

25

each other. He thought of all the reading he had done—Sharp's *Military Guide*, Saxe, Turenne, the Comte de Guibert, everything he could find on strategy and tactics. But he had neglected siegecraft, had not opened his copy of Vauban in years. Though he'd long believed in the efficacy of simple earthworks, this elaborate business of parallels and saps was something else again, far outside his compass. The brilliant Rufus Putnam had designed the entrenchments before Boston. Here, unwisely, he'd relied on Kosciuszko; and Kosci, his diploma in military engineering from the Royal School at Warsaw notwithstanding, left much to be desired. Nothing had prepared the General for this war of moles. He blew out a small gibing gust of air. *All this time, it turns out I should have been reading about moles.*

He twisted the brass tube and sharpened its focus on the British flag stirring on its pole within the fort, its reds sun-faded to pale pinks, its royal blues to ghostly grays. He could distinguish its frayed edges and dangling threads. A few yards to its right, the closest of the blockhouses offered its irregular corner of notched logs, a crooked vertical like the tongue-and-groove work of a craftsman far gone with drink. He could see the coarse weave of the sandbags piled along the edge of the gun platform, and a sparrow perched in the black mouth of a bronze cannon, meticulously grooming a wing.

The illusory nearness of the images on the lens mocked him; he lowered the glass, thrust it impatiently aside—Captain Pendleton, one of his aides, took it—and the star-shaped redoubt, restored now to its true distance, stood as before, defiantly, behind its ditch, its fraising and its tangled skirt of abatis, on an immense mound a quarter of a mile away across a cluttered expanse of dead brush and old stumps and downed trees, backed against the even larger stockade that enclosed the village of Ninety-Six. Behind it all, the vast dark forest rolled to the horizon, a leafy sea that had no apparent end.

He turned to his engineer. "Kosci," he said, in a tone far more amiable than his anxious mood might have predicted, "how soon do you expect the second parallel to be finished?"

Before them yawned a six-foot-deep trench, the first parallel, a narrow slash in the ocher clay that ran off southeast several hundred feet before angling sharply back northwest and stopping short, the whole affair making a rough V of ditching with one truncated leg which was to be, when completed, the second parallel. The works spanned nearly the whole stretch of ground between the hillock where they stood and the stockade with its fort and blockhouses. There might have to be a third parallel, to complete the system of entrenchments and approaches by which the troops could at last assault the fort and capture it by storm. But if they were lucky, and if the British did not send up reinforcements from Charles

Town in time, Greene could summon the enemy to surrender as soon as the second parallel was complete; and if the fortress yielded, there would be no need of a third. His question to Kosci, then, was an important one.

Kosciuszko observed with a seemingly practiced eye the fatigue party of Negroes digging at the head of the shorter leg of trench. He fell to considering with his customary air of shrewdness and confidence. He plucked his lower lip between thumb and forefinger while the General waited. Finally he answered, unequivocally, in his broken English, "By fall of night today." But still Greene waited—he had learned to know the Pole well these last weeks—and after a moment or two, sure enough, Kosci tugged his lip again and reconsidered. A slight frown now wrinkled the lofty brow. "Morning of tomorrow," he declared, though the new and contrary opinion was uttered no less conclusively than the first. But once more Greene waited; and indeed, after another pause, Kosci gave an eloquent European shrug and delivered his third, and finally most realistic, estimate. "Maybe, day after."

The General rolled his eyes but spoke no rebuke; Kosci's heart was in the cause even if his head often wasn't. Besides, his looks were so dramatic that Greene sometimes thought them worth at least a company of Continentals. His upturned nose seemed eagerly to sniff the air in hopes of scenting a fight; the square chin jutted with determination; even in repose the sensuous mouth was always clamped as if desperately resolute; his bounty of dark hair swept romantically back from his forehead like some warlike poet's. His dark eyes flashed fire. He could inspire if he could not think.

But yonder under the walls of the Star Fort were two flattish mounds of bright red upland dirt—a pair of filled-in trenches, melancholy reminders of the folly into which the Pole's rashness could tempt him. Nine days ago, on the rain-soaked night of their arrival from Island Ford to invest the place, Kosci had insisted on opening parallels a mere seventy yards from the walls, insultingly near according to the elaborate protocols of siege warfare, Greene had since learned. Enraged, the defenders had mounted cannon on a gun platform of the Star Fort and next day, under covering artillery fire, had sallied out to bayonet the working parties, dismantle a covering battery, and collapse the trenches. Kosci had been apologetic. Since then he had supervised with scrupulous care the digging of the new parallels, begun this time at a proper distance of four hundred yards, covered by two regiments of infantry and a pair of light guns in timber batteries. Now, divining the tenor of the General's thoughts, he sought to reassure. "In three day," he pledged, "I give you second parallel. Then you summon garrison."

Greene nodded his indulgence. He drew a long breath in through his nose to give himself time to muster a new fund of patience, smelling the new-dug soil that formed the embankment and filled the gabions. Anxious though he was, he had no wish to tread harder on his engineer's feelings, already tender from the blunders of that first day. Besides, he had allowed that first day to happen. He had been as impulsive in his own way as the Pole had been in his—perversely, he was as prone at times to impulse as he was to meditation. He had been angry about the failure at Hobkirk's Hill and had wanted to scoop up Ninety-Six quickly, in recompense. It had been his mistake as much as Kosci's. And the delays since hadn't all been Kosci's fault. There had been repeated nighttime attacks from the fort; the digging had often been interrupted.

Indeed, even as he turned from Kosci, the gates of the Star Fort flew open and out rushed a party of twenty or thirty green-coated Provincials, the sun gleaming on their bayonets. They dipped from sight into the ditch that surrounded the fort and stockade, reappeared on its outer rim, scuttled between the downsloped poles of the fraising, and came plunging through the abatis of felled trees whose thicket of sharpened limbs bristled outward. Not since the first day had they sallied in daytime; to do so now was next to suicide, yet they were doing it; that was the mettle of Cruger, their commander. Kosci swore—what he blurted was in Polish, but Greene assumed it was an oath of the same wonder and rage he himself felt. Retrieving the spyglass from Pendleton, he trained it on the scene.

The nearest soldiers guarding the parallel—some of Colonel Gunby's Marylanders—clambered over their makeshift breastwork of pine-trunks and brushwood, briskly formed a skirmish line, and opened a sputtering fire; but still the Loyalists came dashing headlong, though three or four fell. At the head of the parallel they divided, some to make a wild, hopeless bayonet charge on the Marylanders, others plunging over the lip of spoil into the ditch itself to assault the fatigue detail. Some of Gunby's men had been at Stony Point. They knew the use of the cold steel. They made short work of the forlorn hope.

It was different in the parallel. Only a corporal's guard protected the luckless diggers. Greene turned his glass that way in time to see a soldier in dusty blue clubbed down by musket-butts. One of the green-coats, shoulder-deep in the pit, sank a bayonet in the belly of a Negro worker and used it to lift the poor creature off his feet and heave him bodily out of the trench, as a farmer might toss a forkful of hay. Greene's stomach rolled over to see it. Another stabbed downward again and again and again, at something in the trench that Greene thankfully could not see. Two pistol shots popped. Another. White puffs of smoke rose. An American in a fringed smock reeled and fell. Faint huzzas came on the hot breeze. Or perhaps they were jeers. Several Negroes scrambled out of the ditch, flung away their picks and spades, and ran back toward the camp with the mad energy of terror.

Kosci shook his magnificent head in disgust. "I go," he said, saluted, clapped on his enormous cocked hat, and went to see what could be done to resume the digging. As his horse clattered off, the General watched through the spyglass while the green-coats emerged one by one from the head of the parallel and hurried back through the wicked tangle of abatis to the fort. Colonel Gunby's fellows, finished with their bloody work, were still charging their firelocks and so could not punish them. From the battery on the right, a lone three-pounder boomed; they saw its shot sail high over the town. The last man stopped by the gate, unfastened his breeches, bent and displayed his white rump. *Oh, for a Virginia rifleman just now,* Greene thought. But today the Virginians were posted down on the Augusta road. And it wasn't a thought that a Quaker should have. Not even a lapsed Quaker. One of the Marylanders finally leveled his piece and fired. He missed. The green-coat, his breeches at his ankles, scuffled short-stepping through the gate. "Well," said Pendleton, "*that* was a debacle."

"Hardly the first," the General archly observed. "And probably, God bless us, not the last." He showed them his tender, rueful smile. "But we must reinforce the diggers now." He nodded to Major Hyrne. "Tell Kosci, will you, Edmund?" Hyrne saluted and made for his horse. Greene called after him: "And bring me a casualty report."

The General turned back. It had been a debacle indeed. One more in the dreary succession. He set the spyglass to his eye again and watched as a detail of Gunby's Continentals went out to drag in a wounded green-coat. There were few officers in the army as efficient as Colonel Gunby, and not many soldiers finer than the Marylanders; but improbably it had been Gunby and the Marylanders who had lost him Hobkirk's, and when he thought of Gunby now it was hard not to resent him. But how could he blame Gunby without blaming himself also? Gunby had done no worse than he himself had done, not only at Hobkirk's itself but also right here at Ninety-Six, that first day, with Kosci. Blame was as universal as the original sin the Presbyterians proclaimed.

Musket-fire crackled from the parapet, making him flinch because he had not expected it; and one of the soldiers dragging the hurt green-coat staggered, dropped, then got up again and hobbled off, folding a hand over the small of his back. *That's another one dead in a few days, in this heat.* Two of his fellows stopped to return the fire, then trailed grudgingly back to the lines. The skirmish was over now—at least three soldiers slain, God knew how many of the workmen. Yet the chaps struck down in this trivial scrap were just as dead as the scores killed at Monmouth and Germantown. And each was infinitely precious; he had less than a thousand.

He lowered the glass and used the heel of his hand gently to rub the sore right eye where his smallpox inoculation had settled so long ago. The air that had carried the jubilant cries of the Tories in the ditch now bore to him the powerful stench of the besieged town as it scorched under the pitiless sun. It was a poor place, a wilderness outpost—a modest brick church, a courthouse, a jail, a tavern, a few shops, some humble private houses. It had been a trading mart on the Indian frontier, so named because it was thought to lie ninety-six miles from old Fort Prince George, which had kept watch over the Cherokee towns on the Keowee River in the western mountains during the last war.

It had been a place where common folk lived ordinary lives. Now it was an enemy stronghold, the last remaining to the British in all the South below Virginia, save only Charles Town, Wilmington, Augusta, and Savannah. The old fortifications from the days of the Indian troubles had been strengthened; there were blockhouses and barracks, a small stockade on the west to guard the meager water supply, platforms for Cruger's three light guns, then the Star Fort itself; and close to six hundred New York and New Jersey Loyalists and South Carolina Tory militia cooped up inside. The lives being lived there now were far from common and ordinary. In the sweltering heat the fetor of their accumulating waste was nearly unbearable, even to the General, standing in his nest of gabions at a distance. What a purgatory it must be within.

Yet, stink as it might, Nathanael Greene was bound to have it, and have it by force too. Since taking command, he had fought a pair of pitched battles—at Guilford, at Hobkirk's—and had lost both. While it was true that in each he had punished the British so badly that they had been forced to give up posts and ground, that he had chased them nearly out of North Carolina and now bade fair to free South Carolina too, still he longed to give them a real licking in a stand-up fight. To see them beaten, shattered, as Daniel Morgan had shattered them at the Cowpens. He wanted victory, and he wanted everything that victory could bring him. If he could get that, he was confident it would fill up the hole in him that he had been trying to fill all his life. The hole was a deep one, and much would be needed to fill it; but if victory and vindication were the same—and he was sure they were—then a victory would be sufficient to complete the shaping of the significant man he had been striving to make of himself from the beginning.

The taking of Ninety-Six would be his first triumph. After Ninety-Six, more must come. Augusta must soon fall; already Pickens and Clarke and Lee had it surrounded. Afterwards, Savannah and Charles Town must surely tumble in their turn. Perhaps he need not even wait for that. In his fancy he left his subordinates to complete the work, left Harry Lee and Sumter and Marion and Pickens to carry on; while he, liberator of the Southern country, marched north out of this wasteland to which he had been consigned, to confront his old antagonist Lord Cornwallis, conquer him, break the last of the waning confidence of King and Parliament, win the war, maybe eclipse even Washington himself. He would go from strength to strength in a procession of glory. And he would no longer be empty. No longer be the self-schooled anchorsmith's son troubled by asthma, a limp, and a blemished eye, his name clouded by vague suspicions of graft and unseemly greed. He closed the spyglass and handed it back to Pendleton and turned and started down the embankment. The air was blistering; the reek of the besieged town assailed him; he opened his mouth to breathe.

They rode along the rutted path of orange dirt in blinding sun-glare and in a sear of heat. About them spread a huge space that the several armies operating here since the outbreak of war had opened in the forest—a red plain denuded of live vegetation; clotted with dead or dying growth; covered with stumps like the boils of a ravaging disease; pocked with shell holes and scored with ditches; marred by the arrow-shaped *fleches* of the gun emplacements and the ugly pattern of breastworks, each rimmed with its rows of sharpened poles to ward off cavalry and winding everywhere like ugly, swollen worms fringed with bristles; and on every side the gaping soldiers, gaunt, worn, earth-colored now from waging this dismal contest of moles day after day after day, watching in silence as their General passed, watching him with the blankness that Greene knew was the empty stare of men drawing on their last dregs of strength, and of belief.

At last they entered the welcome shade of the open wood where a part of the army was quartered, and as he approached the encampment Greene's nostrils told him how little better his own force smelled than Cruger's. War-making was a noisome business, never more so than in summer in the Southern parts of America; and high smell was one of its many features from which his naturally delicate soul recoiled. He turned to Pendleton. "More vaults must be dug, farther out from camp."

"I'll see to it," the Captain replied, then shifted his attention to a courier—a travel-stained officer of Colonel Washington's dragoons—who arrived at a gallop with an escort of troopers, holding aloft a leather dispatch case, which he passed to Pendleton with a salute.

Greene furled his brow as Pendleton dismissed the dragoons, unfastened the buckles of the case, and sorted through the papers as he rode. In the campground the General saw again, with as much pain as if it were for the first time, its pitiful scatter of ragged tents, bowers made of pine-boughs, sheds of sticks and leaves, its little rock hearths standing idle for lack of anything to cook, and the pinch-faced soldiers and their slatternly women and filthy brats crouched like crows in the smoke of their fires trying to roast green corn and munching last year's acorns. And he felt the smallness of his army, and its want, like a pang of his own hunger. "Have we any word from Northward on our promised reinforcements?"

Pendleton, who had been reading dispatches, glanced up and gave his head a forlorn shake. "None that would give us any encouragement, sir. There are only those ninety new drafts and the three hundred Virginia militia at Salisbury that are getting ready to march, that Colonel Polk held back when Lord Cornwallis left Wilmington."

Greene felt a flush of chagrin. After the battle of Guilford he had marched into South Carolina rather than follow the retreating Cornwallis to Wilmington, expecting His Lordship to pursue and maneuver against him to protect the several enemy posts in the backcountry of the Southern Province. His aim had been to rid beleaguered North Carolina of British invaders, subsist his little army for a while in the enemy's country, perhaps lure Cornwallis into a losing battle, then snap up the British posts in South Carolina and Georgia. But instead of trailing after him, Cornwallis had turned away, and now was headed north, evidently conceding to Greene all the country below the line of Virginia. If it was an unlooked-for boon, it was also a disappointment and an inconvenience. The move had cheated him of his chance to beat in the open field the man who had whipped him at Guilford. And if Cornwallis did in fact enter Virginia, it would impede—indeed, had already impeded, as Polk's delay in sending the drafts had confirmed—valuable reinforcements meant for the Southern army.

"We've a dispatch just now from Baron Steuben," Pendleton went on, waving one of the papers from the courier's packet, "dated the fifteenth of May at Carter's Ferry on James River." His eye danced quickly over the script. "The Baron's assembled a regiment of recruits—less than five hundred—under Colonel Gaskins, but only a hundred and fifty are yet armed. They were at the Albemarle Barracks when he wrote. They were marching to the Forks of the river to guard the magazines, and then presumably on Southward, agreeable to your orders."

Pendleton folded the dispatch and gave Greene a somber look. "But with Cornwallis threatening Virginia, likely the Baron'll be forced to detain them. He longs to fly on to us—more accurately, sir, to *you*, as he's disgusted with matters there. But I doubt if he can come away now. The Virginians are afraid of a worsening invasion." If he went into Virginia, as now seemed certain, Cornwallis would join a British force already gnawing at the bowels of the state under General Phillips and the traitor Benedict Arnold.

Greene snorted. The Virginians, he sourly reflected, had shown themselves a feckless and timid race. He nursed a bleak suspicion that now, with Cornwallis headed for their own ground, the Virginians would be tempted to keep back the whole latest draft of militia—two thousand badly needed troops—that Greene had ordered to join him. He was persuaded the war could never be won so long as such partial views were allowed to supersede the general plan of operations; yet Virginians seemed always to set their selfish concerns before all else. When the army was on the Virginia border before the battle of Guilford, several prominent men of the state had complained about the impressment of horses that had been necessary to supply remounts for Greene's cavalry. They had been more worried about keeping their blooded stock than about safeguarding the liberty of the country, and Greene had told them so in stinging letters to Governor Jefferson. In this way some of the greatest names of Virginia had been added to the growing list of his influential enemies. Greene did not mind. He had been right; and he was never more certain of himself than when making judgments of right.

"And North Carolina . . . ," Pendleton made as if to continue.

But Greene held up a hand to cut him off. "You need say no more, Captain." He was well acquainted with the promises of North Carolina. So crippled was that state from its dread of Cornwallis, the depredations of the Tories, and the incapacity of its Assembly that it could scarcely govern itself, much less pay its due in troops and stores to the Southern army.

He sighed, glancing dourly about him. "The woods and pocosins are swarming with outliers and Tory militia," he remarked aloud, though it was to himself he'd meant to speak. "If not for our cordon of dragoons, they'd be picking us to death worse than they already are. We're outnumbered here five to one at least, inside the town and out. And Lord Rawdon's army likely to march from Charles Town as soon as he's reinforced." Hearing his own bitter words he was startled and embarrassed; he ceased with a blush. *Now I'm talking to myself out loud. What will the staff think? That the old man is losing his wits?*

He rode on in forced silence. But his woes would not stop nagging him. Presently Major Hyrne cantered up on his lathered bay horse. Kosciuszsko, the Major reported, had put another gang into the second parallel and doubled its guard. Damage to the trench in this latest assault had been minimal. Kosci had again revised his estimate of the time required to complete the approaches; by tomorrow night or next day morning, he pledged, the ditch of the enemy's works should be achieved. Greene permitted himself a wry smile; he took this assessment as provisionally as he had taken the others. Still, it was best to be ready. He turned to Pendleton. "Have we the powder to blow up the works?"

"I think not, sir. But General Pickens has sufficient, at Augusta."

"I must write him tonight," Greene said, and behind him Captain Pierce, secretary for the day, dutifully fished a stub of pencil—the only such precious item in the whole of the army, so far as Greene knew—from

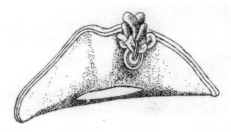

the cockade of his hat and used it to jot a reminder on his shirt-cuff. The General again addressed Hyrne. "What about casualties?"

"Three killed and four wounded among Colonel Gunby's men, sir," came the reply. Greene remembered the Marylander he had seen fall and rise; in time that one would make four killed. Five were dead among the fatigue detail.

"Were there no wounded among the workmen?" the General asked.

"No, sir."

Greene bowed his head. No quarter even for the slaves pressed into service against their will. Another grisly feature of this remorseless contest. Yes, there was much to deplore. He reckoned he was fortunate that on the whole he found more about the war that was congenial than revolted him—and he flattered himself the country was fortunate too that he loved its few allurements better than he hated its host of evils. For, given the errors he had certainly committed, and the blame he rightly bore for those errors, and given his raging ambitions and his impetuosity and the caution that balanced it, and given all his anxieties and self-doubts and his wavering between decision and contemplation, he was still the best the country had. Those above him in power knew he was the best—knew in fact that he was probably even wiser and more decisive than Washington himself—but they were afraid to advance him farther for fear of the handful of powerful croakers and belittlers in Congress and the states and the army who wished to bring him down, out of spite or envy or mistrust or plain dislike. What was it Swift wrote? *When a true genius appears in the world, you may know him by this sign, that the dunces are in confederacy against him.*

Again his thoughts went to Kosci. He turned in the saddle to Captain Shubrick, another of his aides: "Tom, somewhere in my baggage I've some copies of Vauban's works on siegecraft. Dig them out for me, please. Get one of my stewards to help you look. I'll study the texts tonight." He had relied on Kosci; Kosci was faltering. He must step in. He had taught himself strategy, tactics, the elements of command; now he would teach himself to be an engineer. *I must learn to be a mole.*

They came to the center of the camp. A squad of Delaware light infantry and a gang of Negroes were unloading a few sacks of Indian meal and some rashers of bacon from a wagon and carrying them into the abandoned plank-sided cabin that Major Forsyth, the newly arrived deputy commissary of purchases, had turned into a storehouse. The whites snapped to attention and the Major, in his new blue regimentals, which made such a contrast with the campaign-weary garb of the General and his staff, rendered a smart salute. Greene returned it with a flourish and wished them all a genial good morning. The Delawares looked up dull-eyed and spent, but with the abiding respect that Greene was always moved and humbled to see; the blacks toiled on unheeding.

The General leaned from his saddle. "I see you're settling in nicely today, Major. Allow me to repeat how pleased we are to have you with us at last. Of course we were all sorry to see Colonel Davie go; he did us great service—and I'm sure will do even greater things as our advocate to the General Assembly of North Carolina. But as his appointment here was but temporary, it's always best to set these matters in their regular courses." The truth was that Greene did not see how his force could survive now that the incredibly resourceful William Davie had departed; Forsyth, for all his sartorial splendor, did not have the cut of a man who, like Davie, was ready to starve his own mother, wife, and children in order to feed the army.

"Had the Congress and Commissary-General Pickering known the particulars of the service rendered you by Colonel Davie, sir, I'm sure they would have named him in my stead," Forsyth graciously replied. He motioned toward the wagon. "The plan of magazines and depots he labored so hard to establish only now begins to operate. We have eleven more wagonloads of meal and bacon due this day, a drove of cattle just coming into camp, and I'm reliably informed that a farther nine thousand weight of bacon is on its way to us from Charlotte, said to arrive in another week's time."

The General inclined his head and smiled somewhat in the fashion of a parent indulging a well-meaning but idiot child. "I do hope you're right, Major. But past experience with our system of supply compels me to suggest that you wait to cook your rations till you have them on the griddle." They laughed together, the Major a little nervously.

Passing on, the General noticed that all the soldiers in the commissary detail were in rags, save two who would have been literally naked had they not tied blankets about their waists for modesty. He remarked to the staff,

"It's well to have a little for the army to eat at last. But pray God we get some clothing too, before we're all as bare as Adam in the Garden." He drew rein at the door of his headquarters marquee. "Gentlemen, I think I'll take a look at our batteries and talk to the militia, who always need a word of encouragement. Thank you for your company. You may go on to your duties." He nodded to Captain Pendleton. "Except you, Nat; I'd like you to ride with me, please."

They walked their horses in silence. They did not speak because they had learned they need not; they understood each other too well to engage in needless talk. The Captain had been his aide only since December, but in that time the two had grown uncommonly close. They were much alike; the Captain shared Greene's interests in literature and philosophy, military science, and the theory of government. Like Greene, he showed the world a genial and sometimes sprightly nature; but in Pendleton that trait was appealingly wedded to a power of insight that would have done credit to one of far more mature years. Yet he also offered the beguiling freshness and promise of youth, and Greene frankly hoped his own son George might one day grow up to resemble him.

They cantered out of the camp. At the edge of the forest Greene stopped to speak to the pioneers downing trees to shape into timbers for a sharpshooters' tower. The fallen trunks lay crisscrossed amid withered tree crowns; the spot smelled agreeably of cut pine and fresh balsam. Scatters of wood chips, piles of sawdust, and slabs of broken bark lay everywhere about. The pioneers, gasping as they leaned on their axes, looked fearfully drawn from toiling in the terrible heat. The sergeant in charge gave Greene a hopeful report. All the timbers would be ready, he vowed, within six or seven days. When the time came, the trimmed logs would be carried within range of the abatis surrounding the Star Fort and there assembled into a squared tower forty feet high. Topped by a masked platform, the structure would dominate the enemy parapet and allow picked riflemen to fire down on the Provincials to deadly effect.

"Ingenious," the General exclaimed as he and Pendleton left the cutting ground. "But nothing's new under the sun, is it, Nat? The Crusaders used just such a tower to take Jerusalem."

"It's true, sir. Save the fact the Crusaders' siege tower was, I believe, mobile."

"Of course," said Greene, "you're right." It irked him somewhat to be caught in an error, even one so trivial. But he concealed his pique behind a smile—a genuine one notwithstanding the discomposure. They rode back into the scald of sunlight, quartering past the elbow of the first and second parallels to the emplacement where Captain Singleton of the Artillery Train had set up his three-pounder behind a ravine, three hundred yards from the Star Fort. Colonel Harrison, the army's chief of artillery, had chosen the spot after Cruger's sally destroyed a fleched battery closer to the walls on that disastrous first night. It was Singleton's three that had tossed the futile roundshot at the Loyalist assault earlier.

Greene chaffed the gunners good naturedly for their errant aim; crestfallen, they promised to do better next time. Singleton stood by red-faced. No angry reprimands were leveled, no one's pride injured. But the message had been delivered. The guns would be better laid when next called on. Satisfied, Greene led the way to the second battery nearby, Lieutenant Gaines's. There he used his visit simply to bolster spirits, and left gunners and officer beaming.

They rode west then, across the open ground, out of musket-shot of the stockade and its fort. He wanted to tour the camps of the Virginians and North Carolinians on the Augusta road. Militia were like flower gardens; one must tend them carefully or they would soon wither and fade. Privately he distrusted them—no sooner did they become proficient in the service than they claimed their periods of enlistment had expired and marched off homeward, sometimes to the very sound of musketry on the battlefield; and on the rare occasions when they deigned to stay to fight, they usually dispersed at the first shot like so many sparrows. Yet he had no choice but to court them—his regulars were so few, and so jaded from the endless maneuvering of the last six months, that only the periodic drafts of militia gave him the numbers he needed to keep the field.

But just now it was his own resolve that flagged, so instead of going on to spirit up the militia camps he stopped his horse in the broken shade of a scraggly oak. Pendleton, sensing the General's change of temper, turned his black mare head-to-tail by Greene's dapple gray and patiently waited. They sat their saddles for a time sweating in the dense air, listening to the whirring of the locusts in the dry grass and the screech of cicadas in the few nearby trees. In the distance some of their infantry pickets watched them curiously. From beyond the fort came a spiteful popping of musketry. Overhead one of the great turkey buzzards of the country slowly wheeled in a sky that might have been made of burnished brass.

Greene was thinking how Sterne once wrote that the body and soul of a man are like a jerkin and its lining. *Rumple one and you rumple the other*, he'd said. Laurence Sterne was his favorite author after Swift; often he consulted him. He gazed across the heat-shimmer of the field to where the far figures of the pickets stood propped on their muskets, watching back at him. He thought of the men he had ordered shot or hanged for desertion. Nearly every night he dreamed of those men; they came and bent on him their melancholy, accusing eyes. He had executed ten of the poor beggars in May alone. His mouth flattened into a lipless line. Out in the field one of the pickets raised a hand and wigwagged it to him like some husbandman hailing his neighbor across a boundary fence, till another soldier gave him a nudge with a musket-butt, recalling him to propriety, and he quit.

Surely I've rumpled the bodies of these wretches, and so rumpled their souls as well. Yet are they not stronger than I? Would I have stayed on, to be famished and naked and unpaid for months at a time, and then marched near to death and thrown into battle faint from hunger and fatigue? He drew a long breath, put the heel of his hand to his sore eye.

He knew he should not indulge such grim musings. But something in the sight of that Negro skewered on the green-coat's bayonet had loosed it, had called up in his mind all the other lives that had ended, one way or another, by his orders. He was Quaker bred; not so many years ago the East Greenwich Monthly Meeting had read him out of the Society of Friends for turning his back on the teachings of peace, and in the time since he had busied himself wholly in the awful work of Mars; yet at the root of his being he loved humanity and believed in the sacredness of life. He was a worshipper of life who dealt out death, and at times like this the shades of his dead crowded reproachfully around him.

All this time Captain Pendleton had said nothing. He'd sat patting the neck of his mare and gazing into the distance as if oblivious of the General's state of mind. But now his look came to Greene with a sudden acuity. "It isn't *you*, General," he said, as if he'd read Greene's thoughts. "It's the scoundrels stealing out of the quartermaster depots. Tories raiding our supply lines. It's the states that won't give you their due in troops and a Congress that won't provide. It's farmers that won't give wagons or provisions, and artisans in the laboratories that won't make cartridges, and clothiers that won't make clothes and cobblers that won't make shoes, all because there's no specie to pay 'em. You don't *cause* what's wrong, sir. You've tried to *ease* it. The men know that."

Greene was deeply stirred, and it was a moment before he could master his voice and ask in rejoinder, "I wonder that *any* of them stay. I wonder *why* they stay. Is it for liberty? Is it for the country we're trying to make?"

"Maybe for a few," replied the Captain, stroking the mare's mane. "Probably not for most. *We* don't know what kind of country we're making, do we? If *we* don't, how can they?"

The General gave a rueful smile. "You're right, of course; none of us knows that. But then why?"

Pendleton tipped his head aside and regarded him seriously. "I expect it's for you, General."

"But I kill them. Every day I kill more of them."

"Yes, sir," Pendleton agreed. "You do. But I think it's still for you. Most of it, anyway. Oh, some's for each other—fellows all together, keeping to it. No man likes to show the white feather before his mates. And it's shameful to run home, with neighbors and kin yet cleaving to the ranks, and the womenfolk scolding. All that's in the reasoning, sure. But mostly it's you, General." He turned up the palm of a hand like a man giving flight to a captive bird. "The ones who stay? Why, they just know what your heart's like."

That evening in his marquee the General dined with Pendleton, Shubrick, and Hyrne. It was stifling inside the tent, but they dared not raise the sides lest they admit thousands more mosquitoes than the hundreds already plaguing them or further clouds of moths to hurl themselves into the candle flames, as dozens were doing every moment, to fall flaring and smoking among the burnt husks of their fellows on the tablecloth. Greene and his staff had been in the field so many months now that the scourge of insect life had lost its novelty; they scratched their flea bites, pinched their lice between thumbnail and forefinger, swatted mosquitoes, and waved the flies out of their scuppernong wine with the casual languor of long usage.

Yet the dinner proceeded with every sign of high etiquette; the General would admit no concession in that line. They might crawl with vermin, their uniforms might be grimy, their cheeks unshaven, and their bodies unwashed, all their circumstances the most primitive; but they would take dinner like gentlefolk. Crickets were chirping merrily somewhere in the corners, field-mice scurried underfoot, and now and then in the outer darkness rifle fire crackled or there was a dull thump of artillery; but these accompaniments were now so common that they no longer seemed to clash with the decorum of a congenial meal.

When dinner was done the General leaned back in his camp chair and plucked the napkin from under his throat. The fare had been substantial but indeterminate. "What was our dinner, Owens?" he inquired of the steward, who was collecting the cups of horn, the pewter plates, and steel flatware for washing. "I couldn't quite place it."

"A local delicacy, sir," smirked Owens. "Opossum, it's called."

Greene made a surprised face. "I never thought to eat an opossum. I confess I found it somewhat greasy, but otherwise really quite acceptable. It's useful, I think, to sample the native victuals of the parts one travels in. Don't you, gentlemen?" He raised his eyebrows inquiringly to the others and was rewarded with a series of acceding nods. "I have always felt that one should take advantage of every opportunity for the improvement of one's knowledge. I thank you, Owens."

"You're most welcome, sir."

When the table was clear, Greene caught up the two thick books that had lain on the leather campaign chest beside him. He handled the calf-skin-bound volumes with the gentleness of a lover of reading, turned them, examined the gilt lettering on their spines. "Thank you, Tom, for finding these. I mistakenly recalled that I had these works in English. Lafayette gave them to me when we were at Conanicut Island."

"I gather the Marquis was the single ornament of *that* experience," Hyrne remarked, referring to the failed joint campaign in Rhode Island with the French army and fleet in 'seventy-eight.

"Indeed." Greene rounded his eyes, reliving the calamity. "I wish the Marquis were with us now. And not just for the delight of his most civilized company, either. We're in sore need of a translator. One would think our dear ally King Louis, so devoted to our cause, might furnish us a liaison officer to take on such duties." He glanced up. "Who has French?"

"I've a little," Pendleton offered, damping sweat from his brow with the crook of his arm.

The General held a book to the candlelight, which conveniently flashed brighter as a big moth plunged into the flame. "*'De l'attaque et de la defense des places.'* That seems pretty straightforward, doesn't it? *'Of the attack and the defense of places.'* Isn't that right?"

Pendleton nodded. "It's very close, sir. I think it might go a bit better as *'On Siege and Fortification.'*"

"Ah, and this? *'Traite des Mines?'* 'Treaty of Mining'? Is this warfare or diplomacy?"

"*'Treatise on Mining,'* probably, sir. Having to do with besiegement, regular approaches, saps, and the springing of mines."

"Yes, well, it might as well be in Sanskrit, for all the good it does me."

Shubrick had been paging through the other. "I find an assertion here," he announced, "with which I think we can all agree. My French is execrable, but if I've got it right it says: *'Thus our attacks reach their end by the shortest, the most reasonable, and the least bloody methods that can be used.'*"

Hyrne laughed. "Has Kosci read that?"

"Now, now," the General reproved him mildly. He turned the marble-edged leaves of his own book. "Here are some figures. They should tell us something. Here." He pointed to a page of engravings. "Here's a system of parallels and approaches."

The others rose and gathered at his back to peer at the illustrations; the close smell of dirty wool dampened with sweat grew thick about them. "They don't look at all like Kosci's," Pendleton remarked, waving away flies.

"They're much more . . . orderly," said Shubrick, tentatively.

"Very symmetrical, yes," the General agreed, turning away Shubrick's implied criticism. An impish smile came to play about his lips. "I suppose it's why they're called *regular* approaches." It was a tribute to the democracy of his headquarters that no one laughed, save Greene himself. It was but a brief laugh, for he quickly saw that his joke had fallen flat. He resumed in his earnest way, "But to be fair to Kosci, I'm sure these are representations of the *ideal* system. In practice, things are never so tidy as they appear in theory. Kosci's had much to contend with. Remember, the ground's red clay, stiff as stone. He's had to dig where he can."

He closed the book and the staff dispersed to settle again on their stools. "Well," he said with resignation, "I've probably enough French to scrape by—I *was* able to talk to d'Estaing, for Heaven's sake, not that it did any good. I'll parse out Monsieur Vauban later tonight." He called through the partition into the next chamber where Captain Pierce, who had fed somewhat earlier on a very lean squirrel, was transcribing correspondence. "Have you done with the letters, Billy?"

"Yes, General," came the tired reply.

"Let me have them. I mean to write Mrs. Greene, and I'll sign them then."

Later, behind the canvas partition that set off his private quarter of the marquee, Greene read and signed the correspondence that Captain Pierce had prepared, then dashed off a brief note to General Pickens asking him to send up the powder needed to explode the works of the Star Fort. Putting that aside, he slumped in his chair and cupped his head in his hands and allowed the tiredness to take him as it had wanted to take him all day today and yesterday too and the day before that and yes, all the days since last December when he first came South to take up the command of the disgraced General Gates. But, maddeningly, along with the tiredness came the swarm of trials that always beset him in the watches of the night, that kept him from surrendering to the tiredness and to the sleep that would have been its remedy.

Not only did he lack troops and provisions, there were feuds between his senior officers of the Continental Line and those of the militia and state lines; there were unbecoming disputes over rank among his subalterns. The soldiers had not been paid for months—Greene himself had not been paid in over three years. Hard money could not be had and no one would take the Continental paper, so most of the forage and supplies had to be seized from the country folk, who then rose up outraged by what seemed outright robbery and joined the Tory outliers plaguing his outposts. Half his men were barefoot, yet he could get no shoes. The mails were uncertain; his orders from the Congress and the Minister at War and

General Washington, when they came, were weeks out of date and bore no conceivable relation to the reality of events.

And worst of all, he himself was isolated, banished, cast out to the farthest margins of the war. He could be no more distant from the center of power if he served on the moon. It was true that Washington had sent him South because no one else in the high command could have done what was needed to rescue the war in the region. And it was true that he had garnered some laurels Southward by outgeneraling the British in strategy even as he lost the engagements he had fought; and that it even lay within his grasp to chase Cornwallis into Virginia and defeat him there. But it was also true that by sending him South, Washington had gotten him out of the way of a Congress that had come to think of him as self-righteous and opinionated and possibly corrupt, and had grown sick of him. And finally it was true that the Southern Department had always been a graveyard of reputations. Already it had crushed Robert Howe and Benjamin Lincoln and Horatio Gates. Now it threatened to crush Nathanael Greene.

Of course he would not allow that. Nothing had ever crushed him. Bent him, yes. Battered him. Lamed him, as the trip-hammer had lamed him at his father's forge when a boy. But nothing had ever crushed him. Always the iron had been in him to withstand whatever came. It was in him still. Only, these days it seemed harder and harder to call up. Yet he would summon it; he *must* summon it. He stood; he began to pace the confinement of his chamber. He thought of Caty, and as always the thought refreshed him. He brushed his teeth with a frayed sassafras twig, returned and sat staring for a time at the stained canvas wall before him, seeing the image of her face. Then he took up his pen to write to her.

He did not even know where she was. Their farm at Westerly? Maybe at her girlhood home at New Shoreham. Perhaps with friends in Philadelphia. As always, the not knowing ate strangely at him. It seemed wrong to hold someone so dear yet be unable to say with confidence at any given moment where she might be found. And Caty was a gadfly, always on the move. To predict her situation was an utter impossibility. When he pondered that, he grew annoyed with her, even angry, angry beyond all reason, as if by her frivolity she had willfully obstructed him.

He felt that anger now, sitting at his little folding camp secretary with the nib of his quill poised above the lone sheet of foolscap. Writing a personal letter was no mean undertaking in this headquarters where clean paper was so rare a thing that orders and official communications were sometimes written on scraps of wall-covering. It was a commodity too precious to waste. And he was so very weary. Yet he had the ungenerous feeling that writing to Caty just now was exactly that—a waste. Where was she? Dancing at someone's hop, no doubt. Flirting in a ballroom or a salon with His Excellency, or with Wayne or with Wadsworth, both of whom were madly in love with her—as was all the male world. Breaking hearts on every side, that was Caty. And here he sat, alone in a miserable tent in the midst of the howling waste of South Carolina, dirty, pest-ridden, surrounded by implacable enemies, a dealer in death and maiming, the chance of his soul's redemption drowning in blood sinfully spilled, the sound of gunfire continually in his ears, without reinforcements, without supplies, forgotten by all, forgotten even by Caty in her giddy whirl of self-indulgence.

He laid aside his quill, pinched the bridge of his nose between two finger ends, rubbed again at his sore eye. Having felt the old resentment, he now submitted to the guilt and regret that always followed in its train. He was thirteen years her senior; he was nearly forty, she, only twenty-six. He was more than half a father to her, she as much a daughter as a wife. He envied the heedless joy she took in a life that had brought him such vexing difficulties; he knew what pain the world held in store, she wished to know only its delights. He was jealous of the longing she inspired in men younger, more handsome, and far richer than her lame, portly husband with his flawed eye whose fortune had been blasted by bad investments, the collapse of the currency, and the inattention to personal affairs caused by the distractions of war.

He knew himself pretty well. He knew he sometimes had to shape Caty into a kind of villain, to distort her bright and fun-loving nature into one of foolish abandon. Doing that was necessary if he were to keep his sanity and hold himself to his duty. Resentment of Caty was his shield against the force of his love for her. For that love was like a great body of deep water pent up behind a dam. He must keep the floodgates shut. If he did not—if it were to breach the dam and the torrents pour forth in all their thunderous volume—the cataract would sweep him away, and with it everything by which the worth of a man was measured in this world—honor, duty, reputation, ambition, prospects. It would break him loose from his moorings, from his solemn mission of saving the Southern states and going on, against all the odds, to win the war and establish the liberty and independency of the nation. It would bear him on the breast of its mighty surge back to Caty. It would ruin him, it would save him, he did not know which. And he would bury himself in her delectable flesh and never leave her again for as long as he lived, and gather to him the young lives they had made together, George and Martha and Cornelia and little Nathanael, and devote himself ever after to their welfare, and watch them grow and wax strong in health and virtue and go on to marry in their turn and flourish and multiply; and together he and Caty would mingle again and again in their passion to make more lives just as precious and full of promise, and bring those up too in the nurture and admonition of the Lord. Yes, he would give himself over at last to the domestic bliss he had never stopped craving, and no longer cringe, as he did now, as he must now, under the spur and lash of worldly striving and aspiration.

But that would only come to be if he allowed the dam to break. And he dared not do that. It must stand. Too much—everything, in fact—remained to be done. So once again he had to search out the space in his mind where Caty was neither enemy nor refuge, where she shrank to a smaller, more remote figure in the middle distance of his thought, where the danger she posed to what he meant to be could be kept in check. It was not easy to do—it never was—but after a time he succeeded as he always did. And when it was done, when he had removed her safely to that far plane where her light and warmth had dimmed and cooled, he was able at last to take up his pen and bend to the page and begin to write. *Dear Caty*, he wrote. But even so, even as the point of the quill started its slow crawl across the page, he felt the whelming of the deep waters pressing against the wall, the wall that he had built.

Part ye' Third

In Which Baron Steuben Drills Some Recruits

THE WORST PART OF THE DRILL WAS TRYING TO understand what the Baron said. The evolutions themselves were difficult enough, but the Baron's instructions were well nigh incomprehensible. He was what everybody in the platoon called him, a Dutchman; and he spoke precious little of the King's English. Whatever he essayed in the American tongue was so heavily accented as to sound like gibberish, and when he got angry or frustrated—which was often, for they were all very awkward in the motions of the drill he was trying to teach—he quickly met his limits in that language and had to fall back on his native German, and sometimes on French or even Russian. Of course James could not tell what sort of talk the Baron resorted to—he took it on faith that those were the dialects. Captain Harris said they were.

The Captain had come down to camp the first morning after James's enrollment to explain about the Baron to the men who had joined the company since yesterday's drill. With him was a tall severe-looking officer with a hairy mole on his chin who wore a cocked hat and a brown regimental coat faced with red that was almost as pretty as the Captain's. Today, however, the Captain's person hardly matched the splendor of his uniform. His bloated face, blanched countenance, and wobbly carriage bespoke the evil effects of yesterday's excess, and it was evident from his bilious expression that he wished himself anywhere but on this parade ground under a burning sun, confronted by sixty-four privates who barely knew right foot from left.

But if his spirits had wilted, his sarcasm had not. He introduced the dour new officer as "our most high and puissant sachem," Major John Poulson, second in command to Lieutenant-Colonel Gaskins. The Major had nothing to say and betrayed no reaction at all to the Captain's ironical figure of speech, but stood examining the company in the cold speculative way of a farmer eyeing cattle at an auction—an attitude which inspired in James an instant resentment, recalling as it did that dismal day on the

Wilmington dock when Alexander Chenowith's factor stepped from a crowd of turnip-faced Carolina planters to purchase his and Libby's indentures from the supercargo of the *Edinburgh*.

Captain Harris called them to Attention and the one-eyed sergeant prowled between ranks cuffing, jerking, and prodding them into the proper stance—which was "straight and firm upon your legs, your heels no more'n two inches apart with toes summ'at turned out, your belly drawed in summ'at, but without constraint, mind you; your breast summ'at projected, your shoulders square to your front and kept back, your right hand a-hanging down the side, your left elbow not turned from the body; your firelock carried on the left shoulder at such a height that the trigger guard will set just a mite under your left breast, your forefinger and thumb afore the swell of the butt, the flat of the butt agin the bone o' your hip, and you've got to press that butt so's you can feel your firelock agin your left side; and that musket's got to stand afore the holler of your shoulder, mind you, not a-leaning towards your head nor away from it neither, with the barrel almost"—he paused here to be certain of his pronunciation—"per-pen-dic-u-lar." James had the feeling the sergeant was quoting from memory the words of some manual of instruction.

"Now, children," said the Captain as James strove to remember all these complicated dispositions of body and limb and at the same time hold steady the cumbersome musket, "some of you have already made the acquaintance of our eminent Inspector-General, the Baron von Steuben." It seemed to James that he pronounced the named *Shtoy-Ben*, which sounded wrong; before, when he had heard the Baron spoken of, the name, he thought, had been *Stew-Ben*. However pronounced, its mention now evoked a chorus of moans, whistles, and jeering laughter from the fellows who had been drilling the previous day; and James realized with a mild shock of surprise that the angry man who had ridden past him on the big white horse must have been the famous Prussian.

"For others," Captain Harris continued, miserably mopping his brow with a large silk handkerchief, "today will be the first of many delightful encounters you will enjoy with the eminent Baron, for he is the author of our drill and you will be privileged to learn its motions from the lips of the very genius of the military arts who so cleverly composed them." The moans grew louder, the laughter more contemptuous. "You must know," the Captain went on, raising his voice to quell the uproar, "that the Baron is a great and justly celebrated man."

He paused and gave a small twist of a smile that seemed to collude with their mockery. "But my natural frankness and love for my children compel me to warn you that he is a character of certain . . . peculiarities. He is, confessedly, a German—I urge you to refrain from holding that against him; he's a Prussian, not a Hessian, God rot 'em—and so the Teutonic speech, so strange to our ears, is the music of the spheres to him. He also spent many years in the Empire of Russia as an emissary of the Emperor Frederick, and in consequence is fluent in that impossible language. And, like any European of learning, he also knows his French.

"But it ought to be said—and I make bold to say it to *you*, my dear children—that the converse of America yet hangs heavy on his tongue. You will no doubt find it a challenge to apprehend him. But I beseech you to bear with him in his valiant struggles to communicate, just as I am sure you will also forgive him the fault of being a foreigner—a fault that is, after all, no more than an accident of birth, in which he in no way conspired."

But then the levity left the Captain; he advanced a step or two, removed his hat to reveal a thatch of blond hair plastered wetly to his head with the sweats of his dissipation, swabbed his brow again with his handkerchief, stood looking at them with a new earnestness, and said, "Learn what he teaches you, children. It'll kill the Lobster."

James tried to remember that injunction during most of the long day that followed; but, though he did not doubt its wisdom, the sad truth was, he often forgot it. He and his messmates went about the unfamiliar business of the manual of arms for light infantry with the best will in the world, but no amount of good intent could supply their want of understanding. And the Baron—a potbellied, bowlegged little man in his elegant wig, whose features convulsed and turned comically purple when some mistake vexed him—turned out to be hardly capable of providing it. The problem, they learned, was not just the infelicity of his English, though he did express himself in a harsh guttural that called to mind, in Sam Ham's formula, the farting of a great ox. No, it was his ill temper that undid him.

None of this was evident at first. He appeared within a few minutes of Captain Harris' queer little speech, once more mounted on his big white stallion, but trailed this time by a small band of officers, orderlies, and couriers. He checked his horse at the edge of the trodden meadow that was serving as a drill field and sat his saddle for a time examining them, surprisingly not with the displeased expression and downturn of mouth that James had seen him wear the previous day, but with an amiable and expectant air, as if he anticipated a pleasant morning's exercise.

He was dressed in the dark blue and buff of what Charlie Cooke, the mess's self-appointed fount of privileged intelligence, declared were the colors of the Continental General Staff; and he carried a brass-headed baton, which he flourished and pointed this way and that to give emphasis to his remarks. The Captain and Major Poulson were with him, and also a heavyset man in middle life with pouches under his eyes and a bevy of dangling jowls like a bloodhound's, whom Poovey Sides identified as

Lieutenant-Colonel Gaskins, "a Northumberlander," said Poovey, "but a right fair officer for all o'that, I reckon."

They were standing side by side in the first of the two ranks of the company; and James was preoccupied with a determination to keep his place in Open Order, which the sergeant had said was a span of exactly two feet between files, or the distance of an outstretched arm from one man to the other. "Some of his own fellows tried to kill him last year in the draft riots at Heathsville," Sides was saying of Gaskins, "and I think it improved his character." Poovey rubbed his chin—they were at the Position of Rest and so were permitted to move; he grinned. "Way I cipher it, it's a wise officer pays the same mind to his back as he does to his front."

James was appalled. "Draft riots? Don't the men of Virginia want to resist the British?"

"The *poor* men of Virginia want to resist the *rich-'uns*," laughed Sides. "Who d'you reckon owns most of the country? I'll tell you who, it's them Jeffersons and Washingtons and Madisons and Masons and such, the great bloated land-jobbers and monopolizers that's got us in this damned war. Why? So's *they* can get free to pile up even more goods and property, and keep on oppressing the low people. They won't part with as much as an acre of pebbly ground for a common man to try to work, nor will they take up a musket to fight in the war that serves their interests. And the merchants keep the price of bread so high the mean folk starve. But the ordinary fellow's supposed to do the fighting for all them scoundrels. I say shoot the sons of bitches. Lots of us has gone to the British, you know, and follows after 'em plundering. Or goes to pear-making."

"What's that?"

"Taking bounties from several regiments and jumping to another, and so on."

"What do you know about it?" James scoffed.

"Hellfire, I've been called up for militia four times already, ain't I?" Sides gave a conclusive nod. "*I* know what passes." He leaned and spat.

"Well," James derided him, "you can't have learned all *that* much, if you don't know any better'n to be toting a pig around in the middle of a war." Thankfully Sides hadn't fetched his shoat to the drill; it was back at camp in the care of Libby and Charlie Cooke's poor lunatic Janet. Dick Snow was back there too—he'd been excused duty on account of his lameness— and James harbored a secret hope that Dick might be inspired to butcher the beast so they could all dine on fresh pork this night.

Poovey heaved an exasperated sigh. "I done explained; that shoat's as useful as a chicken down the chimbley."

James blinked. "As a what?"

"A chicken down the chimbley," Sides testily repeated. "You know, when

48

the soot and tar clogs up the flue; when it's in need of a cleanin.' You climb up on the roof and you drop a old hen through the chimbley-top, and she flogs like hell a-going down, and that old bird'll scour out your chimbley cleaner'n a whistle."

"Why," cried James in a state of wonder, "I never heard of such a thing in all my life."

Sides gaped at him in astonishment. "No? Well, how in God's world would *you* clean a chimbley?"

"Quiet in the ranks!" bellowed the sergeant, bringing the discussion to an abrupt close before James could enlighten Sides about the more advanced methods of chimney-sweeping. "Come to Attention! Dress to the Right! Cover!" James did his best to stand at Attention and Dress to his Right, craning his head to be certain that he could, in conformity with the sergeant's instructions, *just perceive the breast* of the third man from him—all this while trying to hold the heavy musket erect and motionless.

For the next half-hour, while the Baron and his party looked on, James and his fellows straggled about the field belabored by the one-eyed sergeant's commands and oaths, learning the Right and Left Facing motions, the Right-About-Face, the Common Step of seventy-five paces a minute, the Quickstep of one hundred twenty a minute, the Oblique Step, and the March by Files to the Right and Left Wheel. It was hard, hot, and dusty work and James quickly grew tired of it. But he and his mates all knew, by way of rumor trickling down the chain of command, that the army of Corn Wallace had advanced to Petersburg, there joining a British force that had already been ravaging Virginia for weeks. This had caused the Whig General Loff Yet to abandon Richmond. Redcoat detachments were roaming far afield and might well descend on the Arsenal at any moment. The knowledge gave a special urgency to the training; James applied himself with a fretful diligence.

The company was told off into sections of four files each, and the sergeant exercised them in the wheeling movements to left and right. Concentrating hard on learning the evolutions, James was aware of little else than the tramping of feet, the rattle of accoutrements, and the sergeant's crackling voice: "By Sections of Four! To the Right—Wheel! March"; "By Sections of Four! To the Left! Wheel! March!" Mostly he saw no more than the sweat-sodden back and swaying pigtail of the file in front of him, though once he did take notice of an elderly man in a saffron coat perched on a large rock at the margin of the meadow. This was a Virginia commercial agent named David Ross, the ever-informed Charlie Cooke confided in a hushed aside, and his plantation, on whose land they marched, had been given over to the army for a campsite and drillfield. Likely, James reflected, Squire Ross was sitting on a rock and not on the top rail of a fence where a rich planter belonged, because the army had carried off all his fences and burnt them. Not to mention stealing his porkers like Poovey had done, or his currycomb like Charlie.

Presently the sergeant called a halt, put them at the Position of Rest and bawled, with a possibly menacing emphasis, "All right, you nursemaids, you butter whores, you gut-scrapers and cullies and midwives; you know as much as you need, to do what awaits you. I'm giving the lot of you to the Baron, Jesus be your help and comfort." James and the men around him were already sodden with sweat and panting like a pack of hounds. It was discouraging to think their ordeal had hardly commenced. They watched timidly as the Baron dismounted and handed the reins of his white horse to an orderly and as Captain Harris stepped down too and the pair of them crossed the space of beaten grass to stand before them, the Baron a little forward, his arms folded behind his back under the tail of his coat, his baton thrust out of the way under one arm.

Oddly he was smiling. He seemed pleased as he ran a gaze along their front; he showed no sign of the spleen James had been led to expect of him. Captain Harris lingered meekly just to his rear, much in the attitude of a butler or a valet. The subservient bearing looked ludicrous on him, and he appeared conscious of it, fidgeting with his hands and flitting glances right and left as if to spy out any who might be tempted to sneer at his predicament. He was so fearfully pale from the torments of his intemperance that James half-expected to see him swoon.

Sides once again leaned near. "Now you'll get *your* dose of the plaguey goddamn Hessian," he muttered darkly.

"He's *not* a Hushing," James whispered back. "The Captain said so. He's a Prussian. There's different kinds of Germans. Anyway, he looks kind enough."

"Far as *I'm* concerned," Poovey insisted, "he's a Hessian. You wait and see."

The Baron now addressed them. He had a rather pinched and constricted voice that sounded as if he needed to clear his throat; but annoyingly he did not, and this made James want to clear his. "*Das iss,*" he said, " . . . er, ziss iss *Der Tag* . . . er, ze day ven you become *da Zoldotten* . . . er, ze soldier off *Da Heer* . . . er, ze army off ze Unite Statez. *Oont* she iss a day off grrreat . . . grrreat . . . grrreat, er . . . *Rrroom* . . . er, *glow-are* . . . I mean to zay, glory. *Ya,* glory. Glory *oont* honor." James stared in amazement; Poovey Sides gazed heavenward in appeal. Blan Shiflet was trying to stifle a guffaw. Sam Ham grumbled under his breath. Suppressed murmurs of discontent traveled through the rear rank. "You must haff big . . . er, er *Schtollz,* er . . . pride," the Baron beamed, "zat today you bear ze armz off your . . . er, *pa-treea* . . . er, country in her big *kompf* . . . er, strifing . . . zat iss,

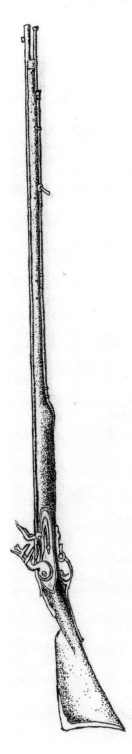

I mean to zay, *ya*, her strifing for her freedom."

Sides dipped his head close. "It's the same damned speech the son of a bitch gave us yesterday. Next he'll tell us how his heart burns."

"My heart," effused the Baron, precisely as bidden, "she burns *mit* ... er, er ... *Zoofreedenhight* ... er, vot iss dat? Vot I mean to zay, sat-is-fac-shun ... zat I am privilege to inschtruct you in ze manual off armz off ze light infantry, vich iss vot ziss battalion iss to be, ven vully traint. It hass been my cuschtom zince comink to America to inschtruct vone model company, vich zen zerves to inschtruct all ozzer companies. Zo you, *mine Zoldatten*, vill learn from me ze dizzipline, manueverz, evolutionz *oont* regulationz, *oont* zen you vill inschtruct your comradz."

James thought, perhaps out of an excess of charity, that the Baron's English improved somewhat the longer he spoke; but it had to be admitted the improvement was only by the smallest of degrees. It was still nearly impossible to make him out. Behind him, Captain Harris was seen to take a surreptitious nip from a silver flask. "Ven learnink to march," he went on, "you must take ze grrreatest painz to aqvire ze firm schtep *oont* a prrroper balance, practishink at all your leisure hourz. You must accustom yourzelvz to ze grrreatest schteadiness *oonter* armz, to pay attention to ze commants of your *offizeer*, *oont* exercise continuously *mit* your firelock, in order to aqvire vivacity in your motionz. You must acqvaint yourself *mit* ze usual beats *oont* zignalz off ze drum, *oont* inschtantly obey zem."

As the Baron concluded his remarks James detected a certain thickening of his mood. He had broken out in a profuse sweat; his smile had begun to fade; some pinch of asperity further cramped his voice, worsening James's desire to clear his own throat. James thought it possible—and reasonable—that the effort of so much talk in an unfamiliar language might have tired the Baron or perhaps stirred a measure of impatience. But these were hints only. Overall, his demeanor was as temperate as it had been at the start. He yielded his place to Captain Harris, who stepped up to give the commands of the manual of arms. The sergeant fetched a musket and took post beside the Captain to demonstrate the various movements. The Baron was to walk among the troops, study their efforts to mimic the sergeant, and correct any slips or miscues.

Till now James's big Rappahannock Forge musket had been but incidental to the business of the drill—a mere ungainly hunk of poundage to be lugged about while he learned the positions, steps, and facings. By virtue of the morning's practice it had lost some of its clumsy feel. But in spite of this degree of familiarity it had lost none of the evil portent he had sensed living in its steel and wood and brass the moment the sergeant handed it to him. In fact, the longer he had borne its cold mute weight against his shoulder, the more certain he had become that it was an instrument of wrong; it had seemed to whisper insinuating messages of lethal wickedness in his ear. Now, awaiting instruction in the manual of arms— the manipulation, loading, and firing of the piece itself—James knew that a moment of grave importance had arrived, a moment when the musket would cease to be only an inert weight and would take on an unnatural kind of potentially death-dealing life.

With the Baron standing by, Captain Harris guided the company through various exercises of Order Firelock, Shoulder Firelock, Poise Firelock, Ground Firelock, Present Arms, Advance Arms, and the rest; and in obedience to the commands, as best he understood them, James aped the actions of the sergeant and worked to shift the long, thick-throated, front-heavy piece into the various positions of the drill. He did not do as badly as he had feared he might; in fact he grew gradually more confident in his motions if he was not yet in harmony with the lethal soul of the weapon itself.

Others were less nimble. The first ones to err earned but a mild correction. The Baron would come with a smile of pitying reproach and try to explain in his halting and obscure discourse what must be done to perform the motion properly. His manner was one of amiable long-suffering. But as time passed and more and more motions went wrong, his restraint began to wear thin. The men often misunderstood him, and he grew weary of repeating the same instructions in words that came hard for him. Soon a miscarry in drill brought not a jovial correction as formerly, but a violent tongue-lashing expressed in terms none but the Baron could interpret. It soon became evident why the man bore the reputation he did. Crimson-faced, he would plunge ferociously through the ranks brandishing his baton as if to pummel the poor offender with it. "*Nick zo shnell, ze idi-owt!*" he might howl, or, "*Zee trampleteer! Swashsinnijer blodkoff!*", or, obscurely, smiting his brow with his palm in a gesture of extravagant self-pity, "*Mur-duh! Bassay luh feels doon chin key may-tawnt dan set sock-ray posee-shun!*" At least this was how James heard him; God alone knew what he actually said.

For a time James was fortunate in avoiding the fate of the others. But then—inevitably, he later came to see—calamity struck home. It was inevitable because he mistrusted his musket, and his mistrust was of the spirit; it had its roots deep in his heart. He and the piece were at odds; it was about the business of killing and he, as best he could, had always been about the business of life. Yet the musket was shaped only for the very trust that he could not give it. And if he could not trust it, then it could not give him what it must on the awful day when they entered battle together. It seemed to know this, to sense his alien mind and resent it; it fought him, it began to slip and squirm in his hands like a live thing intent on escape. Sickeningly James felt it writhe, felt himself start to lose control of it. Then, at Captain Harris' command to shift from Shoulder Arms to Slope Arms, at last the ungovernable thing shook itself loose. Mortified, he watched it fall. It struck the ground with a resounding clatter that drew to him every eye on the field.

At the noise the Baron gave a little leap—he actually left the ground—shrieked something never to be deciphered and came running on his short legs, rudely shoving soldiers out of his path the better to make his way to James. Bending to pick up the piece, James saw him approach out of the tail of an eye, saw him sweep down like fate, and realized with disbelieving horror that one of the greatest men of America—an associate of Washington, of Greene, of Sullivan and Wayne and the great Frenchman Loff Yet—had singled out for reprimand none other than his own insignificant self; and he knew for an instant the mortal despair of the creeping beetle that looks up to see the colossal sole of the boot descending.

He straightened, shaking with fright. The Baron confronted him, crowded close—so close that his hot breath smelling of cloves and the aroma of his perfume of springtime roses swept over James like the exhalation of an orangerie or an herb garden, fragrances James thought strangely delicate, even matronly, for so tremendous a figure; he thrust forward a visage contorted with the vilest possible rage. He howled something that sounded like, "*Norryture! Voo embrasseray mon anny!*" The mouth that formed the words was so finely and exquisitely shaped, indeed so suggestive of the tender and the feminine, that the ugliness it spewed seemed hideously indecent. What unspeakable anathema might it have pronounced? James was seized with an immediate and urgent desire to urinate, but of course dared not; he could only contrive to hold himself as motionless as his quaking body allowed, the muscles around his bladder tightly clenched.

This was but the first of his disputes with the rebellious musket, and so with the Baron too. In the third motion of Fixing Bayonets, the barrel of the piece fiendishly eluded him as he attempted to snap his bayonet onto the stud at the end of it; and while he stood vainly twisting the bayonet about, the Baron gave that same small leap of indignation and rushed to assail him with a cloud of oaths and once more bathe him in his implausible floral and herbal perfumes. At the Position of Recover, the top-lofty musket pitched itself backward, causing him to lose his balance and tumble out of ranks, attracting more thunders of abuse. Cruelly the wooden plug substituting for a gunflint became dislodged from the jaws of the cock and fell, of course, directly at the Baron's feet. Losing a flint was a cardinal sin, symbolizing as it seemed a careless disregard for a proper keeping of the piece, and James suffered another defaming blast for having committed it. At the order to Poise Firelock, the musket, seized with an urge of special malice, fetched him a brutal clout on the nose, leaving him ridiculously bleeding from both nostrils as the Baron once more hastened to spew on him a fountain of inscrutable swearing.

Naturally James could not have repeated or written down the expressions with any exactness. He heard only a cataract of peculiar phrases. It was bad enough to be sworn at, he thought, but to be sworn at in a foreign tongue was doubly unpleasant, for one could never say precisely to what degree one had been reviled. As the Baron poured out his curses it became a matter of utmost frustration to be unable to interpret them. One listened in a stupor of dread and never-to-be-sated curiosity. "*Slapswants! Gapissen!*" seemed to have something to do with making water, while "*Leck mick un arsh!*" sounded very much as if it referred to the paying of unseemly attentions to the backside. But one could never be sure. "*Voo shat-reneeflemownt peekure!*" could mean anything.

The only certainty was that one had been basely demeaned, and the only comfort was that before that day ended practically every soldier present had also been visited by a similar indignity. The men of Harris' company returned to camp that night smarting with peevish dudgeon. But for James, worse even than the tirades of the Baron had been the conflict between himself and his mutinous, hateful musket. He saw that conflict now as a bar to living the life of a soldier that by necessity he had chosen. The thought oppressed him. Lying weary and crestfallen by the fire, he spoke of it to Libby and the others.

"But whatever did you think, going in the army?" Libby asked in her winsome way. "All these years we've been growing up, there's been armies marching up and down, and every soul in it a-carrying a gun. We've heard them shooting, heard tell of dead folk and hurt ones on account of it. War's guns, ain't it?"

"I know," he conceded. "But someway it's different holding the piece yourself. Today we had to practice loading and shooting it. Only shot one time. Couldn't use much powder—there's not enough of it for practice, I reckon—but we shot once, and then went through the motions many and many a time, using a chunk of wood for a flint."

He stopped, remembering how he'd fired that one live shot. The bitter taste of the cartridge paper in his mouth as he tore it with his teeth, its coarse texture, the hard little grains of loose powder on his tongue. Turning his head aside to spit out the bitten part. Pouring a pinch of powder into the pan to prime the charge. Shutting the pan. Dumping the rest of the powder and the heavy ball wrapped in wadding down the barrel. Seating the load with repeated thrusts of the ramroad. Drawing back the cock, hearing its deadly metallic snick. Taking sight down the long barrel. Pulling the trigger. The flash of the flint against the frizzen. The instant's wait while the powder sizzled in the pan and ignited. The powerful kick of the butt against his shoulder, the burst of smutty smoke, the deafening *whump!* of the discharge. The rotten-egg stench of the burnt powder. A brutal, fatal force unleashed. "I could feel a little of what it might be to shoot at a man," he said. "A man like myself."

"That's it, though—he *ain't* a man like yourself," Charlie Cooke spoke up. He sat nearby wrapped in his new blanket; Janet lay curled by his side, whimpering. "He's a damned Tory, or a Bloodyback," Charlie went on. "You ever heard of spiketing? It's a trick the Tories do down in Carolina. They take a block of wood with a spike sticking out of it and make you step on it, run it up through your foot, and turn you 'round a time or two that-away. *That's* who you're a-shooting."

"The devil they do," protested Blan Shiflet. "That's a Blue-Skin Whig trick. I know, for they done it to a cousin of my brother-in-law, in Chatham County, spring a year ago."

"Some soldiers now, they don't shoot at all," Poovey Sides pointed out, from the far side of the fire where he squatted cuddling his pig. "I know some served out a whole enlistment a-shooting six foot in the air, never harmed a hair of an Englishman's head. Nor a Tory's either."

"But that ain't fighting," Sam Ham argued. "If we ain't here to fight, what's it about anyways? Ain't it about being free? If we're ascairt of killing 'em, why, they'll have us by the hair between our legs. We'll be as good as slaves. You was indentured, Jim. You and Libby. Did you like it?"

"No," they answered in unison.

Sam gave a conclusive nod. "Then it ought to be a thing to fight for."

"A damned soldier ain't free," Sides declared with a snort. "You run off from this army, see what they do to you. Stand you up against a post and shoot you, is what. How free's that? I've done told you what this war's about, and it ain't about the low man rising."

"You've got to have compulsion," Dick Snow intoned. "You reckon the British don't have it? Why're they called Bloodybacks, anyway? Because of the floggings they take, that compels 'em."

"It's a hard question," James admitted.

"You'd best quit a-whiffling over it," Poovey advised, "afore Ban Tarleton and them dragoons of his start a-coming at you with them damned big swords the sergeant talks about. You'll be shank-deep in a lot of Sir Reverence then."

"Sir Reverence?" echoed James, puzzled. "What's that, now?"

The carroty-pate gave a hooting laugh. "Sir Reverence is shit, my lad. Loads and loads of shit."

Janet began wailing and her outcries cut off any further talk; and Libby rose and went quickly to her, knelt, caught her in her arms and folded her close, the shaggy head laid against her bosom. She rocked Janet like a baby, and Janet drooled and sobbed and howled, and with Libby consoling her as a mother consoles a child, with lullabies and croons and little melodies, Janet ceased at last to scream and instead started to speak the same word over and over, a word none of them could understand, a gummy and gurgly word in her crazed mouth, but which might have been, probably was, the name of her own lost infant.

As the days wore on and the drills continued and the Baron's tantrums grew ever more frequent, ever more violently impassioned and elaborate, they at last began to take on the character of farce. In their ornamental complexity they came to seem absurd. The Baron would be degrading some poor wretch for facing to his right at the order for the company to face left, and as the soldier quailed under the assault his messmates would break first into snickers, then into chuckles, and finally into peals of hilarity; and before long, rather than cringe before him, even his victims were doubling over with delighted laughter.

Then, incredibly, it was remarked that on occasion the Baron himself might punctuate one of his diatribes with a wink of mischievous complicity, or draw the sting of an oath with an impish grin, or join the men in a burst of laughing—and then, of course, the question occurred whether his awful eruptions had been born of an impossibly irritable nature after all, or were perhaps the children of shrewd calculation instead—a means of hammering home the hard lessons they needed to learn in order to preserve their lives.

So they tramped and sweated in their innocence and ignorance and laughter and growing pride under the hot sun of June, and somehow, before even a full four days had flown, they found themselves passably Forming, Closing, Extending, Displaying From Column Into Line, Advancing and Retreating by Files, and taking the positions for Firing From the Spot, Firing While Advancing, Firing Prone, and Firing Squat; and by then they had conceived a deep fondness for their mercurial old Dutchman who smelled so oddly of roses and cloves. The very traits that had once terrified and perplexed them they now found endearing, for they could see that behind his bluster he concealed a soft heart and a love for the ordinary soldier who must be sent forth to bleed in wars whose causes might be just or otherwise; that he sought to prepare them for that pitiless fate as best he could. Naturally they were never tempted to be overfamiliar—he was too formidable a figure for that. But some few bold ones did begin to make merry with him in innocent ways, swearing loudly behind his back in imagined Prussian idioms, or barking like dogs or meowing like cats or chirping like birds, as he strutted up and down before them trying in vain to suppress his smiles.

But each day they saw less and less of him. Instead, it was the sergeant and sometimes Captain Harris who most often came to drill them. The war was worsening; the Baron's burden of command was growing heavier by the hour. Now he spent most of his time in a room on the upper floor of the big stone-and-log building conferring with Colonel Gaskins and Major Poulson and the company commanders and reading dispatches brought in almost hourly by messengers on horses covered with the foam of hard riding. The British were overrunning the country; and Charlie Cooke, who had done a turn at headquarters guard duty and had cocked a sensitive ear to the door of that upstairs room, reported the Baron was torn by conflicting demands. The government of Virginia wanted him to protect the State's stores at the Arsenal, but he must also safeguard the Continental recruits who were still too raw to pit against the British. He was under orders from General Greene to march them into South Carolina; yet, with the enemy at the very gates of Richmond, the Virginians wouldn't hear of him sending *any* troops to the Southward, not even untrained ones.

"He's a-fretting," the tow-head confided. "And I'll tell you something else—the Governor and them High Mightinesses in the General Assembly, they hates the Baron and he hates 'em back. I reckon he maligns 'em the same as he does us. Names 'em horse-cruppers and fools and shit-eaters and worse—best I can tell, anyhow; when he goes to cussing in that foreign way of his, who knows *what* he's a-saying? He's itching to go down to Carolina and join General Greene, and leave Virginia to stew in its own damn grease. They've put the Frenchman over him, y'know"—that was General Loff Yet—"and the Baron senior to the Froggie, and older. *That* gnaws him."

James shook his head. It was unsettling to hear of such distractions at the highest levels, among men who held one's fate in their hands. One ought to expect coolness and deliberation from the great. Wisdom was required, not low passion. Did they not see—or care—that mortal lives were in their trust? "I think the Baron's a good man," he remarked, "and I expect he'll look after us boys the best he can. But he needs to quit himself of jealousy and all base feelings, no matter how he's tempted."

"Tell him that, why don't you?" scoffed Poovey Sides. "Next time you see the damned old Hessian, go and preach him that sermon. I believe you can reform him."

"I'm in earnest," James insisted. "What's right's right. A man with sway over others has a duty."

"I don't believe you're no house joiner at all, Johnson. Why, I believe you're a black-coat. Ain't you a Quaker?"

James faced him staunchly. "No, I'm just a fellow trying my best, and I want them above me to do as much."

"What a babe," reflected Sam Ham in a pitying tone. "This is the *world*, Jim. Heaven's what comes after."

James knew that. He knew from sordid experience how ugly was the world and how unworthy the men in it, most particularly the ones who held high place or wielded power over the weak. But he had never been able to stop himself believing that things ought to be different, or from wishing that they were different. He wanted to help *make* them different, and he was sure that if everyone could cleave to that very same wish, and find the willingness to act upon the wish, then the world could actually *be* changed into something much better than it was, and the men in it, high and low, made better than they were. He'd heard one reason for this war was to prosecute a notion that every man had the same value. Maybe the ones who'd made the war held in mind something like what James wanted. Maybe if America won the war, it would make things better in the way he hoped. He had not joined the war for that, but now he saw it as one good reason to stay and fight it. Nor did it seem wrong to hope that great men might behave more nobly, in the service of a notion so fine as that.

On the morning of his fourth day in the army—a Sunday, as it happened, when pious folk everywhere else were bowing down to worship the Lord—a batch of three hundred Virginians marched into the compound under the command of a general named Lawson. They styled themselves the Second Virginia Militia and, like the Gaskins boys earlier, had come from the Albemarle Barracks, the place of rendezvous for the present draft. They pitched camp on what space was left of David Ross's pastures and commenced to cut and burn the last of his trees, and some lay down to rest or took pleasure of their whores while others made music with clanging banjers, wailing fiddles, and shrieking flutes and pipes, and a few began to dance with each other or with their drabs as gaily as if the war were on the other side of the world. Parties of them wandered among the Gaskins troops to make acquaintance. They were lean and rangy fellows; they had a gimlet eye and the casual but vigilant look of men who knew their business; and the callow recruits of the Battalion were somewhat reassured to sniff their mettle. Reassurance was much in need—that same evening a courier brought word that an enemy column was moving up the river in the vicinity of Goochland Court House and might be headed for the Arsenal.

Worse news was to come, and as luck would have it, James was on hand to meet it. Before dawn on Monday he was standing guard—his first experience of that consequential duty. His post was at the gap in the rock boundary wall through which he and Libby had passed upon entering the Arsenal that first morning. He was in the second hour of his tour and it was still quite dark. A steady rain had commenced at nightfall, but had ceased shortly before he took his post; now a chill mist clung about the compound. He trod his beat to and fro in a slough of mud, shivering in the wet air, the firelock pressing heavily into his shoulder. His every thought was bent to the warding off of fatigue and of the numbing urge to sleep. The soft but pervasive rumble of the joining rivers all about him muffled every sound, so that he did not hear till the last instant the thump and thud of approaching hoofbeats and was badly startled when a horseman burst suddenly out of the fog on a pale mount like a phantom rider of the Apocalypse. He remembered to bring his musket to the position of Poise, but accomplished it awkwardly and with an unseemly racket of sling-buckles. "Who goes there?" he squawked, using the words of the challenge that the sergeant had taught him, but in his upset, speaking them in a hoarse and reedy tone that did them little justice.

The rider halted in a swirl of mist. "A friend," came the brusque reply.

It was the work of an uncomfortable moment for James to rack his brains and recall the sign and countersign. "Loff Yet," he finally said.

"I don't know the goddamned countersign," blurted the stranger. "Let me pass. I'm carrying an urgent dispatch for General Steuben."

James set himself more firmly on his legs. "Loff Yet," he stubbornly repeated.

Ignoring his challenge, the rider walked his horse forward into the light of the guard fire with a jingle of bit-chains and a clatter of accoutrements. James stared; though damp from rain and spotted with mire, still the figure was like a prodigy out of myth or legend—he wore a black leather jockey helmet wrapped in a scarlet turban and plumed with a tuft of reddish-brown horsehair; his white jacket was faced with light blue; silver epaulets sparkled at his shoulders; his smallclothes were of the same blue as the trim of the jacket; he wore a crimson sash; his trousers were mud-splashed, but nonetheless James could tell they were of buff-colored leather stuffed into fine black boots with silver spurs at the heels; a saber in its leather scabbard dangled at his side.

He came steadily on, slanting down on James an expression full of haughty and dismissing contempt. Of course he was no spy or Redcoat; he was, without a doubt, exactly what he said—a dispatch rider, an American, bearing important tidings for the Baron. But there were regulations to be observed; the Baron himself had devised them. Things must be done according to pattern. Besides, the insolence of the horseman stirred something in James that had not stirred before—he cocked his musket, leveled it on the white coat, set his eye to the sights and his finger to the trigger, and shouted at the top of his lungs, "Sergeant of the Guard!"

The rider shortened his reins. "God blast you," he swore, "I'll have your ballocks for this, and feed 'em to my dogs too. I'm a major of Continental Dragoons, you goddamned little fitch." The gray horse vigorously shook its long head as if it too were angry. *A major*, James thought. He was not certain exactly where a major placed in the calendar of exalted men, but thought it was pretty far up the line. It was superior to a captain, he knew that; but then, it fell a good deal short of a general like the Baron. And since he had fared all right both with Captain Harris and—eventually—with the Baron, James did not see why he should faint away at a few sharp words from a major.

So the fellow's arrogance did not cow him. In fact, it put him in mind of his earlier musings about the ill behavior of men of lofty station. And to his own surprise he felt no need to argue, nor explain himself, nor apologize, nor to speak at all or even move; and they waited that way, the two of them, the gorgeously appareled dragoon officer on his tall steed with its roached mane and docked tail, and the private in his shabby coat and raveled stockings, the cocked musket between them oscillating very slightly but never once straying more than an inch from the row of silver buttons down the middle of the officer's smallclothes, the big mud-smeared horse stamping and shifting and chewing its bit, James no longer afraid, no longer timid, conscious now that the orders of men had entirely revolved, the wheel had turned, the meek had ascended, the arrogant had been leveled, a presented firelock had wiped away in a moment every distinction of rank and station and seemed to promise an even larger remedy, a healing of all the slights ever poured out by the mighty on the undeserving, the beatings of masters, the imposts of tacksmen, the cotter cringing before the squire, all to be made right in one blast of exploding powder—till at last the one-eyed sergeant came jogging into the firelight, identified the officer as Major Call of Washington's Horse, gave him a salute, and allowed him to pass.

With a thrust of its powerful hindquarters the big gray pushed on; a flick of the major's cold eye touched James; and he vanished into the mist with a fading squelch of hooves in the sodden earth of the compound. Now James glimpsed a cruel truth. What had seemed so significant to him had proved but a few seconds' inconvenience to the major. The great remedy that James had imagined lay within his reach had been but an illusion. He saw again what he had always seen but had allowed himself to forget in the surge of rightful wrath his musket had lent him—that the last and worst resort of the arbitrary was to deny that the poor owned any power even to trouble them in the slightest. It was the same as denying that they lived.

He turned away crestfallen. But the sergeant unleashed a roar of laughter and dealt him a hearty clap on the back. "Ah, you wee booby, you fared fine," he exulted. "Any time you can raise the hackles of one o'them pissmakers a'horseback, it's a job well done."

The praise made him feel a little better. And it was only some time later that he came to notice how, at the instant he'd leveled his musket on the officer, he and his rebellious firelock had fused at last. They had ceased to be separate and stubbornly opposed; they had attained agreement, had become one in spirit. And owing to that union, he had been emboldened, had stood firm against a high-born man—a man before whom he would have timidly abased himself but days before. It struck him then that war must be something like a mighty vise, compressing into small pockets of time, into mere minutes, things that once would have required years to accomplish. How else explain his transformation? Perhaps, he thought, this was the gift that liberty gave. If so, then surely liberty was a great prize, and worth fighting a war to win.

But he felt worse again when, after his tour, he heard the grave news that Major Call had brought to the Baron, that afterward circulated through the camps of the Gaskins Battalion and General Lawson's militia—that Corn Wallace himself, with some British cavalry, had advanced as far as Goochland, but a day's ride distant; that another enemy column was now at Louisa Court House. And that the monster Tarleton was riding hard for Charlottesville at the head of his dread Green Dragoons and might circle about and descend on the Arsenal to snare and butcher all in it. The British were closing in, conceivably from three different quarters of the compass. The war bade fair to swallow James Johnson whole, and Libby with him.

Part ye Fourth

In Which General Greene Muſt Conſider
a Deſperate Aſſault

WHEN LEE'S LEGION CAME UP FROM AUGUSTA the General sat his horse in Captain Gaines's six-pounder battery and watched the long line of riders winding out of the Southern woods, Lee himself at the head of the column, a figure so slim and compact in his fitted garb of forest green and buff that even at a long remove you felt the energy compressed in him, the spirit that lived at his core always straining to lunge out. Vigor was in the very perch of his head and in the spry and active way he kept his saddle.

Reining his bright bay thoroughbred into the sunlight of open ground, he tore off his leather helmet crested with black horsehair and waved it high; cheers burst from the men in all the batteries and breastworks around Ninety-Six and the Star Fort that offered a view of him. By ordinary, most in the army envied and some even hated him; but how could they resist him now? He looked so glorious, so much the conquering hero. Amid a chorus of their huzzas he left the column and came galloping across the Titian waste of the plain flourishing his helmet aloft like a trophy.

Looking on, Greene smiled a bit wanly. Admit it, young Lee inspired in him as much wearisome dread as pure and buoyant delight. The two emotions wavered in a fine balance, tipping now one way, now another. Sometimes he loved the boy beyond measure, sometimes he longed to give him the good round thrashing all pompous Virginia aristocrats deserved but so seldom got. But Lieutenant-Colonel Lee must be taken as he was, not as one might wish him to be. And it had to be confessed that, as he was, he could be splendid indeed.

He pelted across the pocked field drawing in his wake that rising roar of praise. He glimpsed the General mounted there between the heaped gabions at the verge of the battery, veered toward him with a whoop, surged up the low slope coaxing his horse with rapid slaps of his helmet. Greene saw the plump face redden and start to grin. It was a grin of sheer exuberance, of childish pride, and of a joy too—but a joy so fierce and finally so boast-ful as to approach the unbecoming.

The General would have been sorrier to see it had he not seen it so many times before. By now he was resigned to Lee's peculiar blend of vainglory and beguiling innocence. Harry had just taken Augusta. Before that, he had reduced Forts Watson and Motte and Granby. Augusta had been the last British post below Wilmington to fall, save Charles Town and Savannah and Ninety-Six itself, and Greene supposed the lad was entitled to gloat, so long as he shared bragging rights with South Carolina's General Pickens, who had commanded the expedition after all, and with Colonel Elijah Clarke of the Georgia militia, who had begun it. He'd had help at the other places too, and had acknowledged it, if grudg-ingly. Still, he expected everyone to understand that all of it had been his own magnificent, unaided work.

The General might harbor his reservations but could not help warm-ing when Lee's grin flashed. He adored the boy, after all. He was smiling his own glad welcome when his eye was drawn past the whipcord figure on the tall horse, yonder to the edge of the tree line where the first of the captured Augusta garrison came tramping out of the forest between files of Lee's flankers. The men in their ragged line wore the disheveled and vaguely disreputable look all prisoners seemed to take on as soon as they lose their freedom. Every soldier, Greene thought, no matter how smart or how drab he might appear when armed and in his ranks, began a pro-cess of deterioration the moment he surrendered; the spruce ones grew bedraggled, the ragged ones more ragged still. It was as if something in the spirit started to rot, which in turn rotted the body and what covered it. He saw that rot now among the Florida Rangers in their coats of rusty red and faded green and among the few Creek, Cherokee, and Chickasaw Indians in their miscellany of deerskin and shirting.

But then he noticed something else. Strutting at the head of the deject-ed column was one of Lee's infantry corporals, holding high the flag of the King's Rangers hung ignominiously upside-down; and Lee's drums were beating and his fifes were squealing an old drinking song of the British army called *"How Happy the Soldier."* Greene knew the words:

He cares not a marmedy how the world goes;
His King finds his quarters, and money, and clothes;
He laughs at all sorrow whenever it comes,
And rattles away with the roll of his drums,
With row de dow, row de dow, row de dow, dow;
And he pays all his debts with the roll of his drums.

Lee was proclaiming the disgrace of his prisoners to the world. Now as the General watched, disbelieving at first, the Legion flankers steered the poor fellows along the road leading closest to the Star Fort. He saw Harry's purpose now—the Augusta captives were to be paraded past the besieged inhabitants of Ninety-Six for no better purpose than to worsen their own humiliation and to taunt and inflame Colonel Cruger and the embattled garrison of the town.

By this time Lee had dismounted and given the reins of his mount to an orderly and was advancing afoot; the General turned back to him. He came with his rollicking swagger, his sword and carbine gear and his big Spanish spurs all a-jangle, his helmet in place again, right hand raised to an eyebrow palm-out in salute, his grin widening; and in light of what he had ordered done with the prisoners Greene now divined something more in his grin, something leering, loutish, and coarse—the pleasure of a cruel boy who has played a savage trick. A wicked fury burst in his chest like a grenade. Acknowledging Lee's salute with a curt tip of his hat, he snapped, "What do you mean, sir? Are we Romans of old, to be making a spectacle of chained barbarians? Surely you must know it no part of an officer's duty to degrade an honorable enemy."

Thunderstruck, young Harry halted with a crash of his excessive equipment—he affected a slung carbine like an ordinary trooper, perhaps in the belief it made him look more democratic than he was and more of a wrangler than some of his enemies in the officer corps believed him to be. His arm fell to his side, his countenance crumpled to a mask of shame, tears sprang into his blue eyes—a change of demeanor so abrupt that it just missed being comical. "Why, my dear General," he stammered, "I . . . I . . . only thought to demoralize the garrison here by showing them the fate of their comrades. . . ."

Before he could say more, cannon-fire belched from the gun platforms of the Star Fort—Cruger, justly outraged by what he saw, had opened on the column, heedless of the risk to the Augusta men. The noise startled Greene's horse; the big gray shied and fleered, the General fought to regain control. Pendleton stepped near to catch the bridle; poor Lee could not bring himself to stir, but only stood weeping, mortified to have been rebuked by his commander under the eyes not only of his compeers Adjutant-General Williams and Major Forsyth, but even of lesser lights like Kosciuszko, whom he considered a hopeless blockhead, not to mention the lowly Captain-Lieutenant Gaines and his gang of common artillerists. The General's horse quieted; Pendleton handed up the spyglass. Greene turned it on the column in the road.

Cruger was using roundshot. At each impact Greene saw first only the gouts of sod they threw up; then the black spheres themselves, jumping high, looking ovoid from their speed, till they bounced and began to slow and then seemed round again. If he had really wished to do damage, Cruger would have used grape or canister. His gunners were overshooting too, ranging thirty or forty yards beyond the road—by design, Greene saw, not wanting to imperil the prisoners after all. Cruger was making a statement. In the road the Legion dragoons and flankers had begun to scamper, herding the Augusta fellows along—there were a hundred or so prisoners, Greene saw as the last of them cleared the timber. In their rear, the infantry of Lee's Legion came hustling, then his three-pounder in its little butterfly carriage and an old bronze six-pounder Greene had not seen before and, finally, his baggage wagons.

Greene motioned to Gaines. "Give the Star a dash of shot, will you, Captain? Nothing serious, just enough to let 'em know we're not drowsing over here."

Gaines barked his orders. Number Thirteen fetched the shot from the ammunition cart, and Number Eight took and shoved the ugly globe of cast iron and its bagged powder charge into the muzzle of the gun, where Number Seven pushed it deep with his rammer. By the breech, Number Nine primed the vent with his goose-quill quickmatch and Number Ten stood with his smoldering portfire poised, while Gaines bent over the breech to sight the piece. He barked an order to Number Eleven, who gave the elevating screw three turns, and to Number Twelve, who grasped the handspike and moved the trail a foot to his right.

Satisfied, Gaines straightened and nodded to Number Ten, who touched his portfire to the quickmatch in the vent. Greene and the others covered their ears; the members of the gun-crew opened their mouths to keep from having their eardrums blown out, which gave them the odd appearance of all having yawned at once. The six-pounder barked, spewing its tongue of fire and dirty gout of yellowish smoke, jumped rearward onto the point of its trail, then dropped and rolled back into place down the slant of the platform with a click of wheels and a creaking of its axle. They watched the course of the black ball in its long arc till it hit the earthen rampart near one of the Star Fort embrasures and stuck there like a tick in a dog's ear. Greene had made his counter-statement. He curbed his restive horse and turned it about to face the crestfallen Lee. "Will you come with me, Colonel?"

Lee dashed away his tears with the back of a hand. "Certainly, sir." Avoiding what he rightly feared might be the censorious frowns of the others, he rounded briskly and passed back between the gabions, secured his horse from the orderly at whom he briefly glared as if to search out some simper or other sign of insubordinate scorn, failed to detect any such, mounted, and came to fall in beside the General. Together they rode down the reverse slope of the battery toward camp. Behind them, staff and officers caught up their horses to follow.

Out on the plain, the column of prisoners and Legionnaires curled past the nearest salient of the Star Fort. Cruger's guns had fallen silent; but here and there along the wall of the bastion, Loyalist muskets popped, each one making its blossom of cottony smoke that floated for a time motionless in the still air. Rifles answered from the sharpshooters' tower with the softer reports that came of their light powder charges. Narrowly Greene watched the column as it bent eastward and turned toward camp; he had seen no one fall. Relieved, he turned to Lee. "It seems we can be thankful there were no serious casualties."

But Lee rode staring straight ahead, his normally rosy hue gone a sickly white. When troubled or deep in gloomy thought, he had a habit of catching one corner of his mouth with his upper teeth, holding it askew and nibbling at it; he did that now, unknowing. The General could not help feeling sorry for him. But Lee's next remark changed that. "I shall reprimand Captain Eggleston," the Colonel announced with surprising abruptness, naming one of the troop commanders of his dragoons.

Greene was puzzled. "Whatever for, Colonel?"

Lee was as full of resolute decision as he had been faltering and downcast but seconds before. "For offering a dishonorable and unwarranted insult to the enemy," he declared, filled now with the same offended virtue Greene had just vented on him.

How very like the great child! It required every atom of restraint at Greene's disposal to keep from laughing aloud. Yet he swelled with a helpless fondness too—the poor brute had no inkling how absurd his remark made him appear. Greene mustered his coolest and most patient air. "My dear Colonel," he pointed out, "you can hardly reprimand a junior officer for carrying out your own orders."

Lee gaped, crushed yet again. "Can I not?" It was an anguished plea.

"I'm afraid it's out of the question, Harry." Lee swallowed hard and resumed chewing the corner of his mouth. His blond eyelashes began a series of rapid blinks, possibly a preliminary to more tears. Greene thought a change of topic might be in order. "Where did you acquire the six-pounder?" he inquired, trying to make idle, and safer, conversation.

"Colonel Clarke picked it up somewhere," Lee answered absently, but with a touch of surliness too. "He lent it to help us reduce this place."

"That was very generous," nodded the General. "And how did you find him?"

After a pause Harry replied, "Most enterprising, especially so for an officer of militia." But he remained morose and continued to worry at his mouth-corner. The blinking had stopped.

"I agree. And General Pickens?"

"He's indeed a worthy good man, as you told me he would be." Lee blew a thin sigh, then shocked Greene by crying out, in the sour vein of a sulking brat, "A far better man than I, most obviously."

The General jerked his reins to his chest and the big gray halted, bowing its powerful neck and champing at its bit, tired of so many unexpected alarms and checks. It stood pawing impatiently at the pebbles of the path. Lee had ridden a few steps on before noticing that Greene had stopped; when he realized he was alone, he whirled his bay about, blushing once more; but this time his color spoke not of joy but of an ugly, willful rage that he had decided to unleash. He was overstepping the bounds not of rank only but of simple propriety as well and he knew it, and for just this instant he did not care. Greene saw him—could actually *see* him—consider casting off the bonds of military discipline, of deference, of friendship, of affection; and in that one dire moment he saw Harry Lee come near to a murderous violence.

A second time that grenade-blast of rage went off in Greene's chest; he hated few things worse in a man than an ungovernable temper. But then, precisely because he hated it, he engaged it in himself, grappled with it, gradually drove it away from him like a wrestler who has found the best combination of purchase and grasp and leverage with which to overthrow an opponent. Then it was the work of some further moments to search within for the calm and decision that his outbreak of anger had submerged.

While he made that search, he and Lee sat their horses in the rutted way gazing fixedly eye to eye, the staff and other officers waiting to Greene's rear breathless with suspense. If they had not heard the exchange, they knew Lee well enough to guess its nature; but their General was a deeper mystery—that he was essentially a mild soul they knew, yet something he'd learned amid the sooty fires of the anchorsmith's forge was in him too, something hard and heavy and persisting, some acquaintance with force and how much force was necessary to bend what resisted it and the price one must pay to apply that force successfully to a certain resistance; a knowledge born of years spent shaping every kind of prodigiously intractable metal, a kind of effort so intense and thoroughgoing that the petulant force at the command of a Harry Lee looked puny against it. So none could surmise how much forbearance General Greene contained or how far he would permit Lee to trespass upon it.

Nor would they ever know what passed then between the two, for when Greene finally spoke, it was so confidentially that none but Lee could hear. It had not been easy to come by that tone, but he had managed it, and at a dear cost. "My worthy friend," he said, leaning to him, resting an elbow on the pommel of this saddle, "your temper is warm and your heart affectionate and because of this, you feel an imagined bias more forcibly than anybody." At that Lee broke his gaze away and looked doggedly at the ground under his horse's feet. Again he commenced to chew the edge of his mouth.

"No man in the progress of this campaign has had equal merit with you," Greene told him earnestly. "None is more precious to me as a soldier or as a man. But God and the Congress have placed me where I am—above you. It's not mine to say whether they were wise to place me so. But here I am. And so long as my place is high and yours lower, my duty requires me to command; and I will ever do it, till God or the Congress or a ball from the enemy remove me."

He paused. Lee continued to bite his nether lip and to study the texture of the road. On the plain, the racket of muskets and rifles began to die down. "Harry," Greene went on, "you are as near to my heart as any." Lee was, in fact, as precious as one's own child. Captain Pendleton might be the finest model of what a son could one day become, the son to be admired and of whom great deeds could be confidently expected. Harry was like the son one feared to father—a cosseted, selfish, moody, turbulent, exasperating colt, always bumbling into troubles he could not fathom yet more often than not brimfull of impetuous goodwill too, always greedy for approval, forever desperate to love and be loved, impossible not *to* love. And, one knew with a sense of foreboding, destined to end badly.

"But I implore you," the General went on, "remember that while we wear the uniform we do, you and I must stand differently one to another, however much we may claim equal merit in Heaven. Unjust as you may think it—unjust as it may well *be*—that difference must be maintained, else neither of us can command, not I at my level nor you at yours. I'm sorry to have injured you. But take thought, my boy—you have also injured me, by your heedless prank. Think, sir! I've loved you and rewarded you with so much trust and influence in this army that I've aroused the jealousy of many another good and deserving officer. You should requite me not with spite but with gratitude and with obedience and a determination to do your just duty. Do you hear me, sir? Do you understand?"

By now Lee was once more bathed in tears. His hooligan mood had melted. Miserably he nodded. "Yes, General," he answered in a voice glottal with emotion. "Yes, I do understand." He raised to Greene his long-nosed, delicately-boned face in rueful appeal. "Oh, sir," he blurted, "sometimes I hardly know what it is I think, or why. Sometimes . . . I fear I'm mad. Or will *go* mad." He spurred his mount close; he reached out, his fingers closed on Greene's arm with a grip that was actually painful. "My dear General," he sobbed, "can you forgive me?"

Four years ago, when Harry Lee commanded only a troop of the First Dragoons, it was not too much to say that during the terrible winter at Valley Forge the constant raids of his small body of horse had kept the Continental Army alive. Again and again he fell like lightning on British posts, supply trains, and depots to fetch back provisions for the starving Continentals at a time when Greene himself, newly appointed Quarter-master-General to replace the faltering Thomas Mifflin, was struggling to find horses and wagons and provender. Later, after Lee's exploits had drawn the admiration of the Congress, he was given command of the elite Partisan Legion, distinctively dressed and liberally furnished; and it was Lee who conceived and carried out the astonishing capture of the important enemy position at Paulus Hook in New Jersey.

Greene had been a younger and less seasoned man then, not yet tempered as he was nowadays. He had not immediately grasped that the Paulus Hook affair was Harry's way of throwing in the shade Anthony Wayne's similar bayonet assault on Stony Point but a short time before. It had been a bid for fame, a greater fame than Wayne's. For Lee, fame was a ladder one must climb more speedily and conspicuously than one's rivals. Of course the war had been young then too. There had been too few successes like Trenton and Saratoga and Stony Point and Paulus Hook; dreary disappointments were much more the order of the day. Dash and address like Harry's drew the eye; plodders like Greene, poring over their military texts, were seen as faintly risible, as if they were university librarians posing as officers. Greene read Santa Cruz, Frederick of Prussia, Turpin de Cressé, Grandmaison; Lee skirmished brilliantly, Greene watched from afar and coveted what came so easily to the gallant boy major.

Harry possessed the *coup d'oeil*, the priceless faculty of instantly comprehending a military situation and making a speedy and appropriate decision. Greene remembered having written years before in a letter to someone that he believed Lee's instinct was *as sure and swift as that of the eagle that drops out of the skies to snatch its prey*. It had seemed to Greene a marvelous faculty then; he had envied it. While he himself, in those days, had to study the plans of campaigns and battles before knowing what to do, Harry had but to glance at a map and in an instant all was revealed to him; raw instinct would then guide him aright. What a hero Lee had seemed then! At twenty-one years of age he had blazed like a meteor. And he was blazing still, at twenty-five.

Yes, Greene had wanted the fame Lee won; and he wanted it still. He would not be laying siege to Ninety-Six this very moment if he did not yet hunger for the praise of men and the rank and influence that came of it, as well as long to win the independency of the United States. But he thought he had learned a thing that Harry Lee hadn't. One might nurse high ambitions, but the truly great accomplishments were never wholly individual. They were never the work of one mind alone. The great man might think greatly, might exhort greatly, might lead greatly; but the greatest ends were most often achieved in concert with others. It was not that Greene knew this and Lee did not; it was that Greene made an effort to let that knowledge guide him in nearly everything, while Lee dismissed it as a trivial and easily disposable notion.

Of course by nightfall, when he arrived at the General's quarters to take the private dinner Greene had felt compelled to offer him as a salve to his hurt feelings, Lee had quite recovered his old ebullience. The General was unsurprised when he saw Harry appear at table so bright-cheeked and amiable; it was a transformation he had witnessed on many a former occasion. The boy was nothing if not resilient. Nor was this all; his spirits had not just rebounded, they had soared to such a height that he felt ready to question the very same quality in his general that Greene had found lacking in him earlier in the day.

While the stewards cleared away the remnants of the meal, he unbuttoned his waistcoat, settled back expansively in his camp chair, treated himself to a sip of wine from the engraved silver cup he carried everywhere with him as if he feared drinking from the vessels of lesser mortals might somehow degrade his station in life, and commented, "Our affairs here have hardly prospered, I collect."

The General recognized the casual but emphatic tone Lee reserved for those occasions when he felt sure his superiority would go unquestioned, and naturally as his commander Greene bristled at the implication. He also found the remark somewhat odd, since he had kept Lee advised by dispatch of every twist and turn of the progress of the siege. Still, for the sake of the amity he had intended this meal to cement, he confirmed Lee's assessment. "For each stroke of ours, Cruger has laid another on us."

Evidently Harry felt the need to pass a compliment to balance off the implied slight. "Colonel Harrison, however, has nicely laid his batteries for a crossfire of artillery upon the Star."

"Yes," the General agreed, watching him with care, waiting for whatever self-serving thrust might come next.

"I flatter myself, sir," Lee smugly smiled, "that your use of fire arrows and the sharpshooters' tower were devices inspired by my own successes at Forts Motte and Watson using the same means."

Now Greene saw where Lee was heading and the knowledge vexed him more. Furthermore, neither idea had been Lee's own; others had suggested them. But again the General thought it best not to chide. Instead he framed his answer in a way that neither confirmed nor denied Lee's claim. "The tower has won us some advantage; it keeps the enemy's head down oftener, and Cruger's efforts to fire it have failed. As for the arrows, Cruger's men stripped the shingles from the buildings of the town to prevent their burning." He paused pointedly. "As you know."

Harry seemed not to feel that chill. "And what reinforcements have you?"

Lee knew this too, but the General marshaled his patience and answered. "The ninety new Continental drafts and three hundred militia we've been awaiting have at last come in, but alas, have proved a sorry lot, untrained, ill-clothed, half unarmed." Wryly he smiled; he took this chance to slip a retributive dagger in the vitals of Lee's native state. "Of course the officials of Virginia, sir, continue to withhold the two thousand troops I've ordered Southward."

Lee allowed that to pass. Instead he inquired with astounding disingenuousness, "And the Star Fort, sir? How is it that the hundred fifty pounds of powder General Pickens sent up from Augusta to spring a mine under the outworks lie yet unused? Has a sap for the laying of a mine not yet been completed?"

Greene stiffened at the implied slur against Kosciuszko. "Again, sir, *as you know*, it has not."

To balance his arrogance Harry also owned a quick instinct for knowing when it was wise to draw in his horns; now he sensed that time had come. With a deferential dip of his golden head he hastened to make amends: "I did not mean to criticize, sir. I merely wished to comprehend fully how matters here have developed in the time since the enemy refused your summons to surrender."

The General eyed him. It would not do to dismiss his insights simply because the lad had made himself obnoxious. The penetration of Lee's mind should never be discounted; he ought to hear the boy out. "I assume, then, sir," he said, though notably without warmth, "that you wish to offer recommendations touching the improvement of our operations."

Lee brightened. "Well, sir, I *have* spent the afternoon scouting the Star and the fortified town and their appurtenances." He set aside his silver cup and bent near with enthusiasm. "Now, sir," he began, "your Muscavado is a truly good man . . ."

There was no longer any doubt that his purpose was to malign Kosciuszko. But some imp of mischief in Greene made him want to tantalize Harry by pretending to be puzzled; he interrupted, "Pray tell me, Colonel, what is a Muscavado?"

Lee looked mildly astonished. "Why, surely it's a Russian, sir."

"I believe it to be," the General concurred with solemnity. "But to my certain knowledge there are no Russians among us. May I ask, Colonel, to whom do you refer?"

"To the engineer, sir. To Kosciuszko." Harry eyed Greene with a hint of worried suspicion, as if he feared for the balance of the General's mind.

"Ah, I see," Greene nodded, amused but still showing Harry his impassive face. "Well, it happens that Kosci is a Pole, not a Russian."

"Are they not all the same, sir? Of the same . . . ilk, I mean."

"I do not believe they would say so. But now that we have established of whom we speak, please do go on."

Lee, on whom, predictably, the General's little game had been lost, was happy to resume putting his case. "The Muscavado is extremely amiable, I find, and not without a degree of professional knowledge." He held up a hand to signify the purity of his motives. "I mean no unkindness toward him." He leveled on Greene his clear blue eye. "But it must be said in all candor that he is very moderate in talent. There's not a spark of the ethereal in his composition."

The General knitted his brow. "Of the what?"

"The *ethereal*," Lee repeated, verging on irritation to find Greene so persistently slow.

The General's frown deepened. "If I may presume even further upon your patience, Colonel, permit me to say that you have quite the advantage of me. Exactly what quality do you mean when you speak of the ethereal?"

Lee colored and made a fluttering gesture in the air with the fingers of one hand. "The *ethereal*," he insisted. "The . . . the . . . that which partakes of imagination, of genius." Realizing that he had begun to stammer, he stopped, inclined his head, and scratched in agitation at the back of his neck, then seemed to decide he had embarked on too elevated a line of argument. Plain speech was no doubt best. He sighed. "The fellow's far from wise. His mind's ordinary, it's, it's, well, it's *commonplace*. Owing to his dullness, he's gravely misreckoned matters here. And unless his bungling is remedied, sir, it will lose us Ninety-Six."

The General hardened where he sat. He was no longer amused. "If Kosci has erred," he said coldly, "then so have I, for he has done nothing that I myself have not either directed or approved."

Lee shook his head in firm denial. "You take too much upon yourself, General Greene. Kosciuszko has represented himself to you and to General Washington and the Continental Congress as a master of the art of warfare, and especially of the science of military engineering as it is practiced abroad. It was but natural that his judgment would be deferred to. If you cannot escape criticism, sir, it must also be said that you have only trusted in him as others have."

Blame and condescension were so nicely mixed in the remark that it cost Greene the sharpest edge of his ire; he could not suppress a smile at the artlessness of Lee's effort to be artful. But Lee was warming to his argument. "I have made a most complete circuit of Ninety-Six this day, and I must press it upon you, sir, that Kosciuszko, though with the best of intentions, has greatly misled you. The naked truth is, sir, he has caused you to lay siege to the strongest position the enemy holds—the redoubt of the Star Fort—while the weakest post has lain all this time vulnerable to an attack which would have cost you little to make, had it been made at the outset."

"And what post is that?"

"The post on the enemy's left. The small palisade that guards their water supply. Holmes's Fort, I believe it's called."

The General sat grimly silent. Again Lee seemed to grasp that it was best to keep still; he waited, fiddling with the edges of the tablecloth. In the emptiness of the moment Greene had to consider an array of possibilities. The meanest was that by coming to him with this indictment of Kosci—and, yes, of his commanding general too—Lee was exacting his pound of flesh for the indignity he had suffered that morning in Gaines's battery. The worthiest was that Lee was so determined and forthright an officer that he was willing to risk offending his commander to expose a possibly fatal misdirection in the operations of the army.

More nearly plausible was the prospect that Lee, always the blindest servant of his own ambition, had found a way to thrust himself forward and polish the luster of his name by doing what Greene and Kosci had so far failed to do, strike on a practical method to capture Ninety-Six.

But finally the General was driven to the last and, he came to think, the soundest conclusion of any—that Harry was right. In fact, a sudden sickening revelation showed him that Lee *was* right. He had simply used the powerful insight Greene secretly envied. Now that he had exposed it, the truth stood revealed so conspicuously that Greene wanted to hide his face in shame.

He reminded himself it had been his plan at first to capture Holmes's Fort and the spring of water it protected, but from day to day he had allowed himself to be distracted by what had seemed the more pressing business of reducing the Star, till at last the need to take the lesser work had, for all intents and purposes, slipped his mind. Arriving at this melancholy certainty now kindled a burning embarrassment. Yet he remained Quaker enough to see the shape of justice in such a fate. He had imposed shame on Lee, now an equal shame must come to him. God was just. Greene breathed out a gust of air that was the very wind of surrender. "What would you have me do, Harry?"

"Give me leave to break ground opposite Holmes's Fort and use my Legion infantry to commence regular approaches. If I can take the stockade—and I'm sure I can—Ninety-Six will certainly fall."

"How long will such an operation take?"

"I would estimate twelve to fourteen days."

"A long time. Lord Rawdon may soon be reinforced and start a march to Cruger's relief. Were he to leave Charles Town this very day, he'd be at our throats before you could sink a mine under the enemy's outworks."

Lee laughed, and this time it was his old gloating laugh. "Count on me, sir," he said, leaping up from the table, once again the joyful battler. "Count on your mad, bad boy."

Bidding Lee goodnight at the fly of his marquee, Greene could glimpse a gleam or two of hope. The defenders of Ninety-Six were in parlous shape owing to exhaustion and shortages of ammunition and provisions. As soon as Pickens finished tidying up captured Augusta, he and his South Carolinians would be coming in, bringing with them their implacable hatred of all Loyalists, inspired by six years of atrocious internecine strife. This would offer Greene the double-edged sword of a resolute and disciplined militia—elsewhere in the South a contradiction in terms—which was at the same time a force for bloody vengeance scarcely to be restrained; only the good and wise General Pickens could guide them aright, and Greene thanked God for having him.

And Harry Lee's crack Partisan Legion was present now—three troops of dragoons and three companies of infantry who could be counted on to annoy the enemy almost as much as they annoyed their friends. That same evening they set about proving their undoubted worth; Harry hurled himself with a furious energy against Holmes's Fort and the water supply of the town. He commenced digging a new set of parallels and mounted his six-pounder in a battery sited to cover them. He made good progress; but on the second evening Cruger struck—not at him, as might have been expected, but at Kosciuszko's sap, which Kosci had now pushed near enough to the Star to arouse fears among the garrison of a successful undermining.

It was little more than a skirmish, but did acquire a certain notoriety. Kosci happened to be in the gallery and hurried out to direct the defense, where he was unlucky enough to receive a piece of shrapnel in a sensitive part that Shubrick cruelly named "the seat of honor"—hardly a spot the famously valiant Pole would have preferred. The wound proved a source of great hilarity among the staff. But Kosci did not have long to suffer. The following day a packet of dispatches arrived from the senior South Carolina brigadier of state troops, Thomas Sumter, that struck the laughter from every face at headquarters.

Lord Rawdon had been reinforced. British troops had debarked at Charles Town, fresh from Cork in Ireland. Rawdon, perhaps the best of the British field commanders in America, Lord Cornwallis not excepted, was even now on the march for the relief of Ninety-Six at the head of an army of two thousand Redcoats.

Greene read the message with a sinking of the bowels. The calamity he had feared, feared yet awaited with a torture of anticipation ever since investing Ninety-Six, now threatened to break over him. A reinforced enemy, a relief of the garrison, his own defeat. Another defeat. Another unmerited, unfair, unearned, demeaning defeat. A defeat forced on him by a miserly, mistrustful, and envious Congress; by recalcitrant governors and the timorous assemblies of the states, most especially that of Virginia, which had withheld the two thousand troops that might have enabled him to win a victory here; and by preoccupied superiors and incompetent underlings; by commissary and quartermaster departments that still could not be made to function; by every kind of want and penury and laggardness; by a viciously whimsical fate; yes, perhaps even by that part of his own character that preferred ease and idle speculation and irrelevant flights of philosophy to decision and prompt action; by everything and everyone save his loyal soldiers in their tatters and the few officers he could trust. In that instant he felt a confined ration of priceless time start inexorably to run. The time would run awhile, but not long. How many days for Rawdon to march the distance from Charles Town? Fifteen or sixteen, he was told—nearly the same span Lee had said would be required to lay hold of Cruger's water supply.

He must act; time was running; he could not afford to pause even to number all the features of the disaster that now bore down on him. He rapped out his orders: Pickens and General Marion with his South Carolina militia, Lieutenant-Colonel Washington and his Third Dragoons, the cavalry of Lee's Legion under Captain Rudulph, all were to march at once to join Sumter around Orangeburgh, thence to descend on Rawdon's column, skirmish continually with it, gall and harass it, slow its march, remove from its path all means of subsistence and transportation, above all give Greene the time, precious time, he would need to reduce Ninety-Six.

A breath caught wetly in his throat as if he had tried to swallow a ball of damp feathers. The soggy lump of his asthma swelled and swelled till it shut his windpipe. He felt his lungs pinch and shudder, sucking for the large gulp of air that would not come; instead he heard the high small screech of the one thread of wind that did manage to eke through, and Pendleton was by him, one arm encircling his shoulders, dosing him with the potion of rum and licorice the Captain always bore on his person in a little tin for just this purpose, speaking calmly, urging Greene to relax, promising he would soon find his breath; and the whole of the General's great world of power and station and high duty and burdensome care shrank down to the small wet and wanting funnel of his gullet and to the air that it would not allow to pass.

Much had to be done very quickly now. Before another week passed Harry had advanced his trenches far enough to gain a flanking position above the streamlet that the stockade of Holmes's Fort guarded. Nightly, as Lee pushed forward his approaches, Cruger defended the spring with savage attacks; but after Harry enfiladed the ravine, Cruger could only get water by sending Negroes out by night to fetch it from the rill, in hopes their black skins would conceal them in the dark. Sometimes they succeeded, more frequently they were shot down. Suffering agonies of thirst in the intense heat, the Provincials began to dig a well inside the stockade.

In the stillness of every night, as he listened from one of his redoubts close to the Star, Greene could hear the frantic clink and crunch of their tools. Sometimes he heard the wailing of infants too, sometimes the singing of a dirge. Once he heard a woman screaming; something lived in the sound that he dared not name, something irrevocably unmoored from all that had once been sane and secure and covered by the sheltering hand of a forgiving God. It reminded him of the squeal of the air in his own clogged windpipe when his quinsy took him; the narrow scream of the constricted wind was a miniature of this woman's scream riding upward out of Ninety-Six into the night. He listened with fascination and an abiding horror. Daytimes, he smelled the stench of ordure and filth and death that Ninety-Six offered with the rising of every sun. He knew he was presiding over mortal sin. He, Nathanael Greene, a man of tender nature and refined taste, who had once wished to do only good in the world.

He had thought badly of Harry Lee for the evil tricks he sometimes played on the enemy, such as last spring's massacre of Dr. Pyle's column of Tories in North Carolina, a piece of wickedness everyone in the army now humorously called Pyle's Hacking Match. But at least that had been committed in hot blood, amid the fever of a desperate campaign. What Greene did here at Ninety-Six was a business of coldest calculation. Each night he sat in his marquee, driven by the incessant dwindling of that small fund of time, plotting as many more exquisite miseries as his ingenuity could devise to inflict on those shut up inside the Star Fort and the stockade of the town. No outrage was too refined for him to conceive. What enormity was he not willing to attempt? Burning, starvation, disease, parching thirst, violent death in all its most hideous forms, despair, the terrible fear he had heard in the woman's scream. Not an evening descended that he did not search diligently within himself for one more unimaginable horror to visit on the sufferers of Ninety-Six—who were, after all, not just the soldiers of the enemy he was sworn to defeat but old people and women and children and, yes, wailing infants in their mothers' arms, or women screaming in the night, souls far more innocent than any Harry Lee had cut down with Dr. Pyle on that country road in North Carolina. In any mirror, Greene's own hypocrisy stared implacably back at him, and he could not look away.

Time drained on. A week after Sumter's dispatch, a courier from Colonel Washington galloped into camp with the news that Rawdon was but thirty miles away on the Little Saluda with three regiments, a corps of Guards, and a hundred fifty dragoons, having marched the nearly two hundred miles from Charles Town in three fewer days than expected. In a scant seventy-two hours his battalions could be displaying on the plains of Ninety-Six. Sumter, his force depleted by desertions, his cavalry cut up by the British horse, had retired to Fort Granby and allowed Rawdon to pass on without further let or hindrance; Washington, Rudulph, Pickens, and Marion had arrived too late and with insufficient strength materially to slow the British column of relief.

Greene heard these tidings with disgust. Sumter, whose envy and loathing of Harry Lee was surpassed only by his hatred for Greene, was in a sulk because Lee had taken Fort Granby some weeks before—a prize Sumter considered rightly his. In fact the turbulent Brigadier General of state troops seemed to consider the whole of the South Carolina war his personal property, which Greene and the Southern Continental Army had unreasonably usurped. Now, Achilles-like, he had retired to his tent to nurse his host of grudges, leaving Greene and Lee to suffer their just deserts for failing to render the fabled Blue-Hen's Chicken his proper due.

"What the devil *is* a Blue Hen's Chicken, anyway?" Greene demanded of Captain Pierce.

"The Blue Hen, I'm told, was a famous brooder of these parts," Pierce, always a source of the most recondite information, confidently replied. "She bred the fiercest of fighting cocks. General Sumter is small of stature, but is supposed to be inconceivably brave. Hence he is called the Gamecock, or the Blue Hen's Chicken."

Greene made a wry face. "Unacquainted as I am with the finer points of the main, nonetheless I do see the relevance—an abundance of valor wedded to scant wisdom."

"Yes, sir," Pierce smiled. "Others have thought so. But none, I believe, in South Carolina."

Their talk was interrupted by a popping of muskets from within the walls of Ninety-Six, an intermittent crackle that soon grew into the continuous rattle and roar of a *feu de joie* as every soldier in the town and the Star Fort and the stockade above the spring discharged his firelock in one long sequence that was then renewed and renewed again and yet again. Precious funds of scarce ammunition were going wildly up into empty air for no more reason than to speak the unspeakable joy of deliverance, Greene recognized at once, a deliverance soon to come. The fire of joy, it was called, and with good reason. Word of Rawdon's near approach must have somehow got in.

The garrison, till this moment so mortally sapped by fatigue, hunger, thirst, sickness, and unimaginable stench, so visited by death and wounds in all their worst forms that surrender itself must have come near seeming the very embodiment of redemption; those same poor, faint, and nearly expiring creatures now felt themselves filled with a surge of new life, borne high on a soar of delirious excitement. Joy indeed! One heard it in that long-continued, ever-renewing volley, and in the cheers that followed as the echoes of the firing at last died away. The General's throat swelled with regret. Now, with rescue close at hand, Cruger would not only refuse to yield Ninety-Six, he would resist with redoubled fury every attempt of Greene's to take it.

But the General had small choice. The time had run. Tomorrow was the last day. He must assault Ninety-Six. He must storm it headlong; he must capture it before the relief force came up. Knowing that he could not, knowing that Cruger and his crew of jubilant Loyalists would not let him. Then, if by a miracle his army was still an army after that, he must turn and confront the advancing Rawdon. Bring him to battle. Fight him. Fight him and beat him. Knowing that he could not do that either.

Part ye' Fifth

In Which a Young Man Muſt Croſs a Torrent

YONDER IN THE COMPOUND THE DRUMS COM-
menced an agitated beat. The moist air of morning had softened
the drumheads and muffled to a growling murmur what would ordinarily have been a terse dry rattle; but even muted, the noise carried across
the point with sufficient force to break in on James as he squatted by the
campfire of smoking damp wood recounting to Libby and his messmates
his adventure of earlier in the day with Major Call of Washington's Horse.
The persisting commotion stopped him in mid-sentence—it vexed him
too, for he had just come to the
crucial point in his tale; he was
confronting the arrogant officer
with aimed firelock, stoutly denying him passage.

But as the drums muttered
on he realized with sinking heart
that he must hold his peace for
now, that he and the others must
attend to the message the pattern
of drum-taps relayed. Not till another opportunity offered would
his sister and his messmates learn
of his bravery and presumption—
much less be moved to praise the
blow he had nearly struck in the cause of the equality of men. And when
might that be? The very sound of the drums told him it would be long, if
ever. There was urgency in the racket.

They waited in their small circle, alert to the rhythm of the beats.
James had never liked the voice of the drum; something shrill and anxious seemed to live in it, some irritant that scraped across the ends of his
nerves like a new file on an edge of iron. The irritant lingered even in this
softer, damp-dulled tone. Of course in recent days he had been forced to

surmount his dislike—the drum was organic to the life of the soldier; on occasions when spoken orders could not be heard, its different tattoos told him what to do in camp, in the field, and on the march. He had been obliged to learn these commands, and so to abide the abrasive instrument that transmitted them. Just now, though, the new note he could hear even in the dimmed rattle of the wetted drums awoke a strange resonance high in the cavity of his chest, a steep but shallow vibration that spoke edgily, importunately, and without any possibility of mistake, of danger.

"Ain't that 'The General'?" Charlie Cooke asked.

"'The General' means 'Strike the Tents,'" answered Poovey Sides, his shoat nestled in the crook of his arm, adding with pointless accuracy, "we ain't *got* no goddamned tents."

Dick Snow frowned. "It means 'Get Ready to March' too. Don it? Maybe we're fixing to take to the road, like the sergeant's been a-saying right along. Maybe we're going down to General Greene in Carolina after all."

Blan Shiflet jumped to his feet. "I expect Dick's right. Leastways, I'll bet we're going *somewhere*. We'd best get our plunder together."

James thought that wise. He too rose, began to gather knapsack, haversack, canteen. Libby's freckled face tilted up to him, her green eyes gone wide with alarm; yet he could see that she felt more wary than afraid. At that moment he glimpsed in her the shrewd attention of a creature of the wild, some wee thing that knows and fears all the world's dangers, but accedes to them too, grants them their place in the firmament and their right to hold that place, yet is determined to survive them. It made him proud to see this. *She's grown all the way up in a week's time*, he thought. "Is it the British?" she asked in a quiet voice.

"It might be," he said, excitement rising in his throat. She stood now too and quickly but deftly, without panic, busied herself drawing together their scattered possessions. The others followed her lead, but with much less composure. Dick Snow fumbled and dropped his musket in the mud; even the normally serene Shiflet, in the act of stuffing some bacon into one side of his haversack, managed to dislodge a poke of shelled corn from the other; Sam Ham, in his hurry, slipped in the treacherous footing and sprawled headlong into a mud-wallow. Sides's pig, startled by the noise and the sudden burst of activity, escaped him and fled squealing; Poovey dashed in wild pursuit. Predictably, poor mad Janet clutched her knees, started rocking to and fro and set up an ear-splitting wail. Charlie bent to her with cooing speech and reached to comfort her, but she fended him off with violent motions of her arms; and Charlie, coming to the end of his patience at last, stepped back swearing and made as if to strike her, till Libby spied him and sharply spoke his name and he relented. He slouched shamefaced as Libby ceased fetching up gear and crossed to them and, crouching, gently took Janet in her arms.

Watching her, James's pride welled higher. Moments before, he had been full of a vain desire to boast of his own actions of the morning—deeds that now looked meaningless next to Libby's grace and new courage. Smiling, he finished gathering the last of their things while she knelt in the muck to fold Janet close, stroking the matted thicket of gray hair, humming some simple nursery tune. Janet's cries diminished, became a plangent singsong, then subsided to a low groan that mimicked Libby's melody. James saw matters more clearly now. If the British truly were approaching, then the interruption of his story had surely been for the best. In the end, the impulse he had felt as he trained his musket on Major Call—the sense that a brotherhood of humankind had awaited no less than a twitch of his forefinger—had proved laughably false. It had been but a silly dream, and would have been hard to explain to the others, not to say embarrassing.

So he fetched his musket and bag of loose cartridges, then paused a moment hefting the firelock approvingly in one hand, recalling what the sergeant had told him that first day. *She'll stand up for you, so long as you do right by her.* He reflected. Yes, she was his now. She belonged to him. Furthermore, he belonged to her. They were bound as he imagined a man and woman must be in wedlock. He realized he wanted to tell Libby and his messmates about that too. But the time for such had gone.

Closer by, the company drummers were striking up their own beat now. "That's 'Assembly,'" protested Sides, returning with his muddy shoat clasped in his arms belly-upward like an infant, its little hooves curled at its chest. "Hell," he went on, shouting above the competing drumrolls, "what the bloody devil are we supposed to do? Strike the tents we don't even have and get ready to march? Or form up the Company?"

The one-eyed sergeant, approaching in more haste than they had ever seen him, provided a coarse answer. "*Fall in, you miserable catch-farts!*" he bellowed. Panting, he stopped near them and pointed emphatically to a space of miry ground before him. "Harris' Company! To me! Make yourselves a line right here. Do it quick now! And let me hear your nutmegs a-knocking while you do it!"

Obediently but anxiously, unnerved by the pandemonium of the drums and the yelling of the sergeant, they shuffled into their accustomed places, the thick porridge underfoot sucking at their every step, greasy clumps of wet earth collecting on their shoes till their legs felt sunk in balls of lead. All about on the soggy field, the other companies of the Battalion were assembling too, and James could take a new soldier's pride in having learned the name of each so well that he could call them to mind as they formed—the First Captain's, Parker's, on the right, then all the others in their proper sequence, Captain Lamb's, Captain Warman's; then Lovely's and Lewis' and Benjamin Harris' and Kirkpatrick's; next Smith's, then Woodson's and Roe's. His own company held the left flank because John Harris was Second Captain.

Opposite, Lawson's militia was also forming. They made a shuffling mass of yellow and brown, the autumnal hues of their hunting shirts. The new sun glanced brightly on their musket barrels. In the churned and trampled space between Lawson's men and the Battalion, a knot of horsemen had gathered. James recognized Baron Stew-Ben on his great stallion; the Baron was spattered to the knees with filth, and his fine mount—once a spotless silver—as sadly besmirched as a dung-cart's dray nag. The Baron spoke in lively fashion, jabbing his baton at the livid face of another rider who wore a billed helmet with a plume down the center and buff-colored britches and a short jacket of dark blue turned up with white. This officer saluted, spun his hog-maned dun, made a quick gesture to four dragoons waiting nearby, and the little cavalcade galloped off across the field toward the compound, spewing gouts of wet sod in their wake.

"That's some of Armand's Legion," Poovey Sides remarked. As he spoke, his jacket bulged and a button or two popped open, and the pig poked forth its narrow head and gazed inquisitively about, blinking its yellow lashes.

James was curious about the dragoons. He had been his master's jockey and knew horses well and had begun to wish he could ride one in this war, in place of walking. "What's Armand's ... what-you-said ... ?"

With the flat of his hand Sides pushed the pig's head back into the concealment of his bosom. He had cinched the belt of his cartridge box tight to support the weight of the beast. "Some damned Frenchie in a piss-burnt wig got it up, horse and foot," he answered. A muffled grunt issued from within the distended jacket. Poovey used a forearm to capture his load from underneath and shift it to a more comfortable position. He resembled some goodwife far gone with child. They ain't worth a handful of bum fodder, the lot of 'em," he said disparagingly, of Armand's Legion. "All them Frogs, they fancy the round mouth, you know."

James preferred not to inquire what a round mouth might be; he surmised he knew already. At his place in the ranks, he craned back to see what had become of Libby and Janet. A steer-drawn wagon—an army conveyance, by its markings—had arrived and under the supervision of a teamster in a dirty smock Libby and some Negroes were rapidly tossing the belongings of the mess into it while Janet pranced in a small circle, shaking her briary hair, alternately stooping and jerking erect, making violent gestures with her hands.

Beyond, the whole sweep of the field from the Arsenal compound to David Ross's farmhouse was a hive of confusion. At every campsite parties of perturbed women were packing up goods while squadrons of children capered at their heels frantic with excitement. Nothing official had been said about abandoning the Arsenal, yet plainly it was a common assumption that the Baron intended to march away, lest Corn Wallace or Bloody Ban Tarleton or that other British rogue—what was his name? Simcoe, that was it—snare him and his band of half-trained recruits. The lowest trollop on the point seemed to have guessed that a retreat, not a battle, was in the offing. And now that army wagons were circulating through the camp to collect the baggage, that suspicion could turn to certainty.

He faced back to the front only to gasp in wonder. It was the first time he had seen all the Gaskins boys assembled at once, with the company colors in place between the fourth and fifth platoons and the scarlet Battalion colors and the curious striped flag of the Continental Congress with its starred field of white at the head of it all, Colonel Gaskins himself fifteen paces before the colors, Major Poulson a few steps back of him, the captains and lieutenants flanking their sections and the fifers and drummers at the ends of the ranks, the sergeants behind.

They made a stirring sight gathered there in the dazzling light of morning, the air all a-sparkle, new washed by the night downpour, the hill above the point—the same hill that James and Libby had descended but a few days before to begin this strange new life—wearing a fresh crop of velvety green grass and topped by its fringe of oak woods whose leaves bristled now with new color and vitality; and the rivers flowing by on either side, widening to the point of their joining, the bigger one flowing in freshet now from the rains, speaking in a constant reverberant thunder that was the language of its incalculable tons rushing seaward, cresting thicker and higher at midstream than on the edges, an angry ridge of whirling foam and spume and spray running down its middle, a spine of turbulence, a twining of thick braids and ropes of water almost as red as fresh blood owing to the silt it had drained from the clay uplands westward; and there between them, between the two rivers, the mighty one and the smaller slacker one, the Gaskins Battalion and General Lawson's militia, motionless in their ranks, muskets at the shoulder, every man in his place, the colors snapping before them. *Why*, thought James, *I'm at war.*

But if, ravished by the splendor of what he saw, James believed war to be a spectacle of glory—and yes, for a moment he did—the next few hours would prove him mistaken. Just as so many in the camps had suspected, it was indeed the Baron's plan to evacuate the Arsenal. No sooner had the Battalion and militia assembled in such grand and eye-filling style than, instead of marching bravely forth to meet the enemy as James had been briefly tempted to imagine, they were put into column and led across the oozy field to a road—actually a slough of mud—and from thence around the northern skirt of the compound past the shot tower and the powder magazine to a boat landing at the very tip of the point, where they were permitted to disperse for the purpose, they began to divine, of embarking to the south bank of the larger river—the Fluvanna, someone called it. The retreat to join General Greene in South Carolina seemed to have begun.

They eyed with misgiving the several frail-looking vessels moored to the jetties, each straining its cables and bobbing savagely on the margins of the flood. Beyond surged the billows whose roar spoke no more to them of Nature majestically aroused, but instead of a nearly certain watery doom. While they stood about, stamping clods from their feet and contemplating their approaching end, Captain Harris appeared, dressed as ever in his finest regimentals but—as might have been expected—ghostly pallid from a night of debauchery and still as candied as David's sow. "Listen to me, children," he cried, bracing himself against a wheelbarrow, grasping a brimming tallboy by its neck. "The Baron loves you and means to keep you safe. He's sending you over because he loves you."

"Loves us, does he?" Dick Snow sneered aside. "Loves us so much he means to drown us."

But Charlie Cooke, that compassionate soul, was more interested in Captain Harris. "Poor fellow, he looks a death's-head on a mop-stick, don't he?"

"You watch," said Poovey Sides, giving the hidden shoat in his jacket another upward hitch, "he'll flash the hash in a minute."

James was saddened to see the Captain in such a state. The Captain had been kind to him after a fashion. "I believe," he said earnestly, "no man drinks to excess lessen he's tortured by some great sorrow." He wondered what woe was gnawing at the Captain and wished he owned the power to ease it.

Poovey laughed. "I'll wager a Portugee Joe *his* great sorrow's he can't find some great whore's muff to split."

"The officials of the State," Captain Harris was saying, "are hectoring our dear Baron to save the Arsenal stores first, to use the wagons of the Continent to transport out of harm's way the miscellany of truck that's the property of Virginia. But instead, you see, he chooses to make *you* safe, before all else. He'll use the wagons to bring your possibles and your sweethearts and your dear nits to the landing. And only when you and yours are safe on the other side, my children, will he send his wagons back to transport the drawers and shifts and garter-buckles of the State of Virginia." This sally drew a titter of laughter; Captain Harris improved the interval by enjoying a generous swallow from the tallboy.

"I know you dread to cross," he resumed, wiping his lips on his sleeve. "As do I—yes, I confess it. No man hates the fluid medium more than I myself. But there's no better course. We *must* cross, or we'll either meet the Lobster in battle or yield to him. Now, my nugs, you've come along right well in the last days—I am proud of you for it—but as much as you've learned, I think you'll agree you ain't ready yet to trade volleys with the Bloodybacks. And there's no question of asking quarters—most likely Tarleton's in this lot—you know what that means. So it's cross we must. And take heart, it don't look it, but the river's going down."

They peered again at the plunging cataracts of the Fluvanna, and the boldest of them raised a hoot of derision, but the outcry died when Captain Harris raised an admonishing hand. "It is," he assured them with a confident nod, "I swear 'tis. We can wait awhile yet, to let it go down some more. Meantime, the Baron wants to send some of you up the Rivanna"—that was the other stream—"to watch the fords where he thinks the Lobster'll come over to the point. And think, children, the damned Lobster has to wait for *his* river to fall, just as we do ours. His is the lesser, I grant you. But higher up, believe me, it runs deep and fast, not slow as it does here by the point, where the big one backs it up."

James was disappointed to hear the Captain say this, for one glance at the relatively placid Rivanna showed it might easily be crossed—by boat, if the enemy had any, and possibly by swimming teams and wagons—even here at its mouth, where at its broadest it still looked to be no more than thirty feet wide. How much less of an obstacle might it be a mile or so upstream, where even if it did flow more rapidly, it must also be even narrower? James would have liked to rebuke the Captain. Officers, he believed with the firm assurance of a six-day's veteran of the service, ought never resort to lies to inspire men to their duty. He was certain that honesty and straight dealing forged the most enduring bonds of discipline.

Captain Harris pushed away from the wheelbarrow and made an effort to stand erect, apparently hoping his demonstrated ability to keep from falling down in a drunken stupor would excite a general enthusiasm. "Now, children," he smiled a bit uncertainly, perhaps reading in their faces the failure of his efforts to embolden them, "I'll need a cohort of ten hearties to go stand picket, and yank the Lobster's claws. Who's game?"

Not a man moved. It was up to the sergeant then to appoint the detail. He stepped forward and set his one eye on them like a baleful beacon. "This officer here," he bawled, bobbing his head in the direction of Captain Harris, who had resorted to his wheelbarrow and was communing again with his tallboy, "he's a fine gentleman and hates to speak ill of any condition of man. That's to his credit, I say—he's as good and decent as any that wears the epaulet. But God knows, he's too easy on you silly bastards. He's pulling your sugar-sticks, saying you've done well in practice. What *I* say is this—you're hicks and chaw-bacons, the lot of you. Not a one of you's ready yet to shit the soldier's turd." He leered at them in triumphant malice. "D'you hear me? I name you craven. I call you hen-hearts, afixing to piss yourselfs for fear."

James frowned; as with the Captain, he had formed a favorable opinion of the sergeant. He was sad to see him resort to this crude effort to inspire valor through abuse, just as he had regretted the Captain's attempt to gain the same end through falsehood; strangely, in the face of so much evidence that his superiors were mishandling their duties, he began to suspect that he himself might be better able to manage men than those the army had placed over him. Indignation flooded him as the sergeant leaned at them squalling in contempt, "Do I make you mad? D'you want to prove me wrong? Here's your chance, then. I'll give you a chance to play the god-damned hero."

With that, he came among them wielding his halberd, using the butt of it to prod his choices out of the crowd and into a rank. James stood fast; though he had no wish to offer himself for a picket, neither would he avoid the service if it came. But Sides, in hopes of escaping notice, quickly turned his back to hide the pig bundled in his jacket and slipped in rear of the larger Sam Ham.

The sergeant tapped Blan Shiflet and another man and next approached James and stood looking him inscrutably up and down. For an instant his fierce black eye rested on James's face, and the look caused James suddenly to remember the Waxhaws and Colonel Buford and the severed heads bounding in the road like footballs and what the sergeant had wanted him to know of the pitiless nature of the war. And after that he thought better of the man and forgave him for what had seemed his low stratagems, which James now realized were but the simple tricks necessary to bolster the spirits of inexperienced men soon to face unimaginable dangers, tricks that James in his innocence had thought unseemly, but now saw were not only shrewdly conceived but even kindly meant. Yes, there was an elegant wisdom in the tricks the Captain and the sergeant played. Something passed then between the mutilated veteran and the callow recruit, something unspoken but consensual, something like a gift given and taken; then the sergeant broke off his gaze and, to James's unashamed relief, passed him by.

Just then Sam Ham, in nowise forgetting how gleefully and often the red-hair had ridiculed his name, made as if to bend and scratch his shins and in so doing exposed to view the crouching, back-turned Sides so that the sergeant promptly picked him. Unfortunately Sam himself was tapped next. The pair of them dejectedly joined the detail, exchanging scowls and curses, Poovey cradling his musket across his body to hide the wriggly lump in his jacket. And in this way, James imagined, surely for the first time in the whole of the war, a live weanling pig took post as an infantry picket.

The sergeant led the picket up the south bank of the Rivanna, and even before the green woodland closed behind the trudging file Captain Harris had divided his company into squads and each squad had formed a queue to wait its turn at the landing. The other captains did the same. Lawson's militia followed suit. While the two bodies of men sorted themselves out, army wagons rolled one by one down to the landing and began to disgorge the women and children, the baggage and the equipment of the State of Virginia.

At the verge of his appointed jetty, James watched anxiously back till he spied the wagon he had seen Libby loading at the campsite. Its rear wheels fastened by chains to slow its descent, it skidded down the slope plowing up coiled red sheaves of mud, the driver hauling hard at the reins, the team of steers scrambling in the deep mire to keep from being overridden by its hurtling weight. At last, heeled steeply to one side, it came to rest at the foot of the landing; and to his relief James saw Libby jump from the rear of it, raise her arms, lift Janet down, and lead her halting and cringing to the water's edge, where gangs of boatmen hustled them along a pier and into a rude dugout canoe, already crowded with other womenfolk and a gaggle of howling youngsters. At least Libby had come this far without harm or mishap. It remained to be seen if any of them could survive the crossing.

But what ensued for James and his messmates, and for Libby and Janet too, was not an immediate crossing of the river but a long and monotonous wait—a wearisome feature of military life, Charlie Cooke promised, drawing on his expert knowledge of military affairs, which James would soon learn to detest. "They always be making you line up like you're agoing somewheres," lamented Charlie, "then all that happens is you're standing around half the day a-scratching your twiddle-diddles."

Captain Harris, sensing their discontent, came by to explain somewhat sheepishly that the Virginia authorities had now prevailed in their arguments and all had changed; the stores of the State would be transported to the south bank first. Only after they had been made secure would the troops, their dependents, and their baggage be moved.

"That's another damned thing they do," growled Charlie, "tell you one thing, then do something else." But this small courtesy of the Captain's, and the candor that had prompted it, restored a measure of James's respect, which the Captain had forfeited earlier in telling his fib; but, as the poor man was now more drunk than ever, James feared he would never again be able to admire him as he had that first day, when he had presented such a splendid sight, seated at his ease under the greening maple in the Arsenal compound, shining in the sun like a god of war.

Some hours passed as the stores and other gear were loaded and borne over the river in a ragtag collection of canoes and floats and batteaux. At first the soldiers watched with keen interest to see how the vessels would fare, but when only a single craft capsized and then several more made the crossing without trouble—though they did fearfully pitch and career when they met that foaming chain of high water down the middle of the river—the event soon lost its novelty and became tedious, for all but James, that is. He did not like being apart from Libby at such a dangerous time. He was tormented by a fear that she would be cast into the deep and lost if he were not by her side to prevent it. And half-consciously behind that fear, he knew to his shame, lingered a nagging impatience with her endless stewardship. The cares he'd spent on her throughout life had sapped him, left him jaded; some dwarfish unworthy creature in a black cranny of his spirit partly hoped she *would* drown; but then at once his better nature repented and he peeped and peered amid the throng of waiting troops, anxious to learn whether she had yet set forth. She had not; she and Janet and the other women sat huddled in their dugout through the long midday, waiting in the sweltering heat even as the Battalion waited. James waited too, contemplating his guilty, selfish thoughts.

At last the delay came to an end; the Captain walked the line crying, "It's time, children! It's time," and presently they began to creep in their files toward their jetties. They would be ferried over by a fleet of James River batteaux—narrow, frail-looking, flat-bottomed, pointed at both ends, each steered by a sweep oar in the stern and rimmed with flared gunwhales which half-naked Negroes nimbly trod to and fro as they poled the vessels along. So slender and fragile did the batteaux appear that James thought they resembled nothing so much as the tiny water bugs one often saw skittering over the surface of a pond. It seemed incredible that craft so light and so unstable might be expected to carry near eight hundred men, with all their gear, not to mention the stores of the Arsenal, across a raging river in flood.

His, when it took his weight, dipped and rolled as sickeningly as if it were made of withes and reeds instead of sturdy white oak. He glanced about for a place to sit; there was none. He was alarmed to think he would be obliged to stand, he and the dozen fellows with him, while the boat tossed and heaved on the breast of the swollen Fluvanna. But he was given no time to ponder his ill luck. The boat pushed off, the Negroes drove their poles deep, the current took it, there was a stomach-dropping descent and then an appalling lurch upward, a violent shudder, and James glanced sternward in a funk of dread, thinking the tiller might have been wrenched away, but instead saw the steersman plying his sweep with such idle composure that he might have been lounging before his own hearth enjoying a smoke—*was* in fact enjoying one, puffing a long-stemmed clay pipe with a remote and meditative air.

While the steersman mused, the batteau gave a horrid lunge and slewed giddily downstream, causing the standing soldiers to embrace and clutch at each other like desperate lovers. In ludicrous contrast, the Negroes went casually to work, strolling the gunwhales with unthinking grace, artfully wielding their great poles, any one of which might easily—but never did—knock a poor soldier in the head and tip him overboard never to be seen again. Around the boat the crimson river boiled and swirled, its spray drenched them, its metallic odor was in their noses, its coppery flavor was in their mouths, the flotsam that rode it came whirling at them—uprooted saplings, dismembered boughs, great raw hunks of earth still wearing fringes of bright new springtime grass, whole dead trees, pieces of siding stripped from houses, every sort of loose log and woody trash and green tussock, once a dead donkey bloated to twice normal size, even a bedraggled rooster that floated by giving them an accusing glare of its ruby eye, as if blaming them for its misfortune.

Then, sooner than seemed possible, the batteau glided into a quiet eddy, nudged a reed-choked shore, and came to rest. Before them rose the leafy mass of the south-bank forest. Some of the troops that had been ferried over before them approached with welcoming smiles. Charlie Cooke and Dick Snow stood laughing down. James blinked. How could it be? The ordeal was done almost before it had fairly started. Disbelieving, he and the others stepped onto firm ground and wandered about in a state of bewilderment. Every twist and pitch and yaw of the slim little boat on the malevolent river still seemed to buffet and threaten them; they reeled on their unsteady legs. Yet they had come safely over.

Dick and Charlie gathered round. They spoke, but he hardly heard them. They giggled. They cuffed and poked him in fond raillery. Wanly he grinned. *Libby*, he was thinking. Dazed, he cast about. There, beached amid the river cane a short distance upstream, lay the rough canoe he had seen Libby and Janet enter at the landing. Just beyond it, someone was waving. With a raised hand he shielded his eyes against the sun; it was Libby. Emotion choked him. *How could I ever have wished her drowned?*

As the sun sank lower toward the faint blue line of the mountains to the west, the Battalion and Lawson's militia took position along the forested crest of a ridge above the south bank of the river and the Arsenal point. Owing to the force of the current, the crossing had carried them downstream for perhaps half a mile, so when they gazed toward the Arsenal they had to squint back upstream against a glare of evening light reflecting off the broad face of what was now the river James, formed by the joining of the two lesser streams. Over the course of the long day the brawling waters had quieted and fallen just as Captain Harris had predicted they would, so much so that as dusk neared it became possible for the Baron to order several of the wagons and their teams loaded onto floats and crossed to the south bank. The squadron of Armand's Legion came over too, the dragoons in batteaux, the horses swimming alongside.

By sunset, the only Americans left on the point were the fifty men of the picket, unseen in the upper woods, watching the fords of the Rivanna. Among them were Shiflet and Sam Ham and Sides, and Poovey's pig, presumably. James thought warmly of his three friends—yes, they *were* friends now, even, in a way, the ne'er-do-well Sides—and he hoped no evil would befall them yonder in those dim glades. The point itself lay in profound silence, and as daylight waned it darkened and thickened into a dense bushy wedge, assuming an aspect of threatful brooding quite at odds with the commonplace memory James kept of it. Somewhere beyond it the enemy lurked in the gathering gloom. The thought raised ripples of gooseflesh along his forearms. How would it be when they came? *How will I act? Will I be brave?*

Below, at the base of the ridge, the south bank of the big river might have been littered with the aftermath of a shipwreck, strewn as it was with boxes of clothing, bales of linen and blankets, rolls of canvas, piles of stockings, heaps of coats and britches and hats, bearskins, calfskins, shirts, barrels of saltpeter and sulphur and brimstone, an ugly little wheelless short-snouted artillery piece, five other wheeled guns also with snubbed barrels, and four bigger wheeled cannons of brass; stands of muskets, casks of gunpowder, piles of grapeshot and round shot, hogsheads of rum and tierces of brandy, bags of tea and coffee, wagons, oxen, horses, chests of carpenters' tools, kegs of gun flints.

All the watercraft had been concentrated on this side of the river too, lining the shore with an assortment of canoes, rowboats, dugouts, floats, and batteaux. When and if the British descended on the point, vessels would be sent back to collect the men of the Rivanna picket; till then, the craft would be secure from seizure by any British who might venture out by night. Looking down on the ruck, James could not but wonder what would be done with all of it, now that it had been successfully transported from the Arsenal. There did not seem to be wagons enough to move it all.

Charlie Cooke offered a cynical answer: "You watch and see, after going to the trouble of bringing it over, we'll run off and leave it for the Redcoats."

The sham of pretending to be man and wife had long since grown tiresome and unnecessary. After the first evening it had become clear that nobody in the mess posed a threat to Libby's virtue. But now that the subterfuge had lost its utility, neither she nor James could think of a way to dispose of it without awkwardness. So tonight, as on all the other seven nights they had spent in Harris' Company, brother and sister lay together under a rough army blanket by the fire, wrapped uncomfortably in one another's arms, James annoyed by an elbow in the ribs, Libby complaining that the point of his chin was digging into her shoulder, toenails disagreeably scraping shinbones, each trying but failing to ignore the mortifying shape and feel of the other's secret parts. It was indecent and repugnant, yet seemed unavoidable; to lie separately would incite gossip or questions they could not think how to answer, now that the deception had gone on for so long. Sleep would have helped, and surely both were weary from exertion; but the day's adventures had stirred the blood too deeply for either to yield to a need for rest. Talk became their means of evading a shame and embarrassment they could hardly bear to name. "Do you think Poovey will be all right?" Libby asked.

Though she had spoken largely to divert their thoughts, James heard her note of sincere concern. This surprised him. "Sides?" he repeated. "Why in the world would you care about Sides?"

Against his body he felt her squirm with discomfort; she had revealed more than she had meant to. In a voice almost too small to be heard, she confessed, "I like him."

"*That* fool? What is there about *him* to like? All he does is pass wind at both ends." Sides might be a friend, but he wasn't *that* much of one.

"Well, I still like him." She sounded stubborn now.

He grunted in derision. "I guess you like his pig too."

"That's *why* I like him," she answered sharply. "He says the pig's not a pet, that he keeps it to gather fleas. But he loves it, a-body can tell. Any man that will love a little pig's bound to have a good soul."

James pondered that. The notion did give him pause. He waited a moment, thinking how close Poovey always kept the beast, how he fondled it inordinately. Perhaps there was something more to the ginger-hackle than his busy tongue after all. "Well," he said, relenting somewhat, "I reckon he'll be all right on the picket. There's been no firing over there."

He raised his head and looked upriver. The broad brow of the point loomed blacker and more sinister than ever, framed by the ghostly glimmer of the two rivers. A pale sickle moon rode overhead. He thought of the enemy, secreted in the night. Together they listened to the rumble of the joined waters. Then Libby said, "Speak of home, James."

So he spoke. He spoke again out of the memory he held of what his Da had told him in the belly of the *Edinburgh*; he spoke of the bright winds and of the softly contoured summits of the boundless moors. He spoke of how the moors, brown and sere in winter, flushed when the heather rose, then of how they turned a deep warm purple in late summer's warmth, a warmth so quick to come, so quick to go, that it was doubly precious for its brevity. His Da had spoken the words he spoke now in his turn. His Da had spoken them in the thunderous cavern that was the dark maw of the wallowing ship, reeking of vomit and feces and urine and sicknesses not to be healed, a filthy den beset by the treacherous sea; yet they were words of beauty and of peace, words that shone with light and color, that had in them the clean crisp flavor of the Highland air itself.

Words that told of the red sandstone on the cliffs above the firth, of the rough stone *brochs* the old ones had built on the crest of nearly every hill, of the wide bogs of the strong-smelling peat, of the steep-sided narrow valley pouring its silver strand of river past Dirlot Castle on its high spire of rock, of the sound of the river falling, of the pot of gold that legend said was hidden somewhere in a dungeon of the Dirlot keep, of the champions of mighty clans who had once battled there, of Keiths and Gunns, Cheynes and Sutherlands, of Mackays, of blowing rains too and cold gales, and of skies more blue than the merciful eye of all-seeing God.

When he had done, he saw that she slept.

Part ye' Sixth

In Which General Greene Effays a Bold Stratagem

IT HAD PLEASED THE GENERAL, FOR THE SINGLE night the army encamped at Winnsborough, to pitch his marquee on the same spot his old antagonist Lord Cornwallis had occupied the previous winter. The place was in the shade of a great spreading oak in the yard of a little log Presbyterian academy called, somewhat grandly, Mount Zion College; it offered an agreeable vista across the rolling hills of the district known, for its beauty, as Fairfield. Just now that broad prospect also provided a convenient distraction: Greene could rest his gaze on the distant landscape of woods and fields and farm plots while pretending to watch, nearer at hand, the flogging of the deserters from the Second Virginia.

He had ordered the punishments and felt obliged to witness them—or, more precisely, to be present when they were inflicted. Duty seemed to demand that he at least attend, even if his sensibilities recoiled from the necessity. It was true that he believed these caitiffs had fully earned what they now suffered; but beneath that righteous wrath ran an undercurrent of unease, sprung from a well of Quaker charity that he had never found a way to stop up and that would not let him feel justified for any act that his conscience judged lacking in pity. Besides, if he hated desertion for the breach of faith it surely was, a betrayal not of country alone but of every soldier who clung steadfast to the ranks, it was still true that often in his secret heart he also forgave those who fled the army's dreary round of privation and danger, and even sometimes blamed himself when they stole away.

So as the fifer wielded his cat-o'-nine-tails and loudly counted out his hundred lashes, Greene fixed his eyes beyond the fifer and beyond the flayed back of the screaming deserter, the first of the three he must abide, and studied a faraway ridge crowned with longleaf pines, then some fields of corn and standing grain, and finally, closer by, the little village of Winnsborough straggling along its single road of white sand—half a dozen houses, a tavern and Colonel Richard Winn's plantation—all of it lit by a

94

harsh summer sun. Perhaps it was cowardly of him, this squeamish refusal to confront the consequences of his own orders. Surely it was a ridiculous failing in a commander. But there it was. He could not change it.

Scrupulously he scanned the countryside. Yonder in that ravine grew a thicket. Blackberry, he thought. Would blackberries be ripe now? No, it must be early yet for blackberries. *Fifty-eight*, cried the fifer, *Fifty-nine*. The cat whistled and cracked. *Sixty, Sixty-one*. He had heard that grapes and persimmons were plentiful in this region. Plums, crabapples. Hazlenut. What were those trees on that height? Beech? Ash? *Sixty-three, Sixty-four*. Sweet birch grew along that stream, he was certain of it; he observed the gracefully plumed crowns, the slender trunks mottled brown and yellow. Sweat poured in fat hot drops from under his hatband and rolled down his cheeks into his soggy shirt-collar. He gusted out a stale breath. He had not felt such blistering heat since Monmouth; how would the army march in it, even starting late in the day? *Sixty-six, Sixty-seven*.

Captain Pierce approached and spoke into his ear. "Your escort's here, sir."

Greene turned his head a fraction of an inch to reply; inadvertently his glance slid past the two upright posts before him, spanned by a broomhandle crossbar from which the deserter hung limp by his wrists, his back a mass of wet crimson shreds. He felt an upwelling of nausea. Absently he nodded. "Very well, Billy. Tell them to stand easy. I must attend to this first." Suddenly in the strike of the sun he felt weak and light of head; he looked back to the front, well above what he did not wish to see, set his eyes firmly on the horizon and used the undulant blue-green line as a point of reference to steady himself. He dared not faint. Not now, not here.

Seventy, Seventy-one. Pierce hesitated, then leaned close a second time. "Colonel Williams wants to know if, after the punishments are completed, we should order a *feu de joie* in honor of the day our independency was declared, this being the Fourth of July."

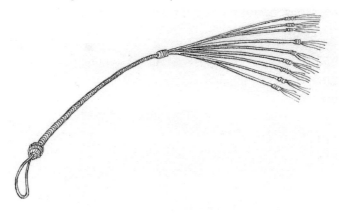

Greene could not afford to release his hold on the horizon line. He glared straight ahead. "Surely the Colonel can't be serious," he snapped, though there was a quaver in the words. "Are we to watch these poor devils whipped like beasts till their backbones show, only to turn then to unseemly displays of jubilation? With Lord Rawdon as near as the Congarees, retreating and apt to escape us lest we concentrate?"

It had been nip and tuck since the bloody failure of the storming of the Star Fort on the eighteenth of June. Contrary to expectations he had not been forced to fight Rawdon and the enemy relief column after all. The British commander, turning the Americans out of the siege lines at Ninety-Six, had left part of his force at the town and with the rest had chased Greene handily toward Charlotte. But he soon outstripped his supplies, and the sickness that simmered in the Carolina swamps began to have its way with his troops, accustomed as they were to the cool mists of Ireland. This whim of war had transformed his advance into an abject retreat. Now he hastened in retrograde with his troops dying by the dozens of heat and fever, while Greene, so recently in flight, had come about to give chase in his turn. It was known that another enemy force under Colonel Alexander Stewart was on its way up from Charles Town, and Greene hoped to run Rawdon to ground and bring him to battle before Stewart could reinforce him. Accordingly the army was under orders to draw thirty rounds per man and make ready to march by four o'clock. That was why there was no time for Otho Williams' *feu de joie.*

Captain Pierce, shaken by the unaccustomed outburst, saluted and meekly withdrew. Instantly the General regretted his intemperance. But nothing could be done about it now. Besides, Billy would understand—if not today, then in time. *Seventy-four, Seventy-five, Seventy-six.* Greene examined the pastoral scenery. Yes, it was a pretty place, this Winnsborough. There was healing in the very sight of it—he felt a little better now. Perhaps it had struck Cornwallis that way too.

Greene thought the loveliness of Fairfield spoke well for His Lordship's taste. The Modern Hannibal, as he liked to style the Noble Earl, had withdrawn here last October, after Ferguson's Tories were bested at King's Mountain, a loss that had forced him to abandon for a season his planned invasion of North Carolina. *Eighty-two, Eighty-three, Eighty-four.* Months later Cornwallis had resumed his campaign, and Greene, having assumed command in the South, met him at Guilford Court House. In that engagement the same civilized English Lord who had chosen this delightful haven for a winter post had ordered his artillery to open on his own Second Battalion of the Guards, entangled in a mortal struggle with the American troops of Gunby and Howard and William Washington. The fire had wrought an indiscriminate carnage on Briton and Patriot alike that shocked all who saw it. But it earned him the victory. A victory dearly bought, but a victory all the same.

Eighty-six, Eighty-seven. Again and again the cat whined and snapped. The deserter no longer screamed; in fact, he made no sound at all; a sidelong dart of the General's eyes revealed him hanging slack between the uprights. At every blow his body yielded languidly like something already dead. The glance skidded past, settled on the rows of faces that attended him—the deserter's comrades of the Second Regiment of Virginia Continentals, paraded at attention by their commander, Major Smith Snead, compelled by Greene's orders to observe the ordeal. Some were angry, some leering, one or two openly amused, a few expressionless; Greene wondered what those were thinking. *Eighty-nine, Ninety.*

By the time of Guilford he had seen six years of conflict; yet Cornwallis' readiness to slaughter his own troops to gain a triumph had appalled him. Here, but a few weeks later, knowing more of himself than he had known then, or than he wanted to know now, he grasped that the act had not been cruel after all. It had been merely decisive. Decisive after a fashion he feared he could never aspire to. Cornwallis was renowned as a gentleman; Greene surmised he had given his order to fire not brutishly but with the sadness and regret every gentleman had to feel, just as he himself had reluctantly presided over the horrors of Ninety-Six, and ordered men into action and deserters to be shot, hanged or, as today, flogged nearly to death. Yet still— even granting his own complicity in the more commonplace enormities of war—Greene could not imagine giving an order the like of Cornwallis' at Guilford. In a terrible way the deed seemed sublime to him.

He became aware of an odd stillness—the fifer's counting had ceased; the cat no longer spoke its whicker, its hiss, its short and narrow *pop* that sliced as wickedly through the senses as it did through flesh. He looked; men were unfastening the ropes from the deserter's wrists. He sagged muttering into their arms; they bore him away. Blood trailed behind him on the grass. The fifer, no doubt arm-weary, gave place to a drummer, who took from him the dripping cat, swabbed it dry with a rag, and stood aside impatiently waiting while other men brought the second deserter, stripped to the waist like the first, a wretch so starved and sickly that his ribs showed and his limbs were slim as reeds.

The drummer picked his nose while they strung the new victim between the uprights. The skin of this man's arms and shoulders was as white as ivory and gave an awful impression of tenderness and susceptibility, but a webwork of fine purple weals marred his back; the man had been flogged before—many times, it seemed. He carried his head defiantly high; he might have thought himself vindicated, as if he were about to be rewarded for some splendid deed rather than punished for an ignoble one. When he had been secured, the drummer stood to his work. *One, Two, Three.*

Greene turned away. He had meant to witness all three floggings, but now he decided one had been enough. Two more would be unthinkable. He started across the lawn of the school toward his marquee. He longed for the shade of the oak; his head swam from the swelter of the day. Captain Pierce fell in behind him, silent. To their rear, the drummer's voice counted on with relish, *Seven, Eight, Nine.* Mercifully though, the noise of the cat faded. And the deserter, keeping his strange air of dignity, made no outcry. Greene walked on, head down, hands folded behind.

He had once seen a circular letter of his dear friend Anthony Wayne's, addressed to Wayne's subordinate officers at Ticonderoga: "Neceſſary severity muſt be accompanied with great tenderneſs and moderation and so diſplayed on every occaſion as to appear void of all Manner of Deſign and totally the Effect of a Natural Diſpoſition—by this means you will Render yourſelves at once beloved and feared." Wayne himself was often enough a tyrant, was more readily feared than beloved, and tended to honor his own injunction more in the breach than in the observance; yet Greene had liked his formulation, and tried hard to observe it. *Necessary severity.* Yes, it was necessary. Without severity and the fear it inspired, there could be no discipline; and in the absence of discipline, an army became a mob.

Greene thought his men loved him, but he wondered if they feared him. He wondered if they feared him as Lord Cornwallis' men had learned to fear the Earl on the field of Guilford. Beyond doubt the Earl's order to take his own troops under fire had been *void of all manner of design and totally the effect of a natural disposition.* By contrast, daily it cost Greene a great deal of woe and regret and meditation to do what his duty called on him to do; and the pain of that cost was so intense for him that he thought it must also be visible to his troops, and must surely dilute the fear and discipline it was meant to inspire. Instead of fearing him, did they instead pity him? Or, worse, believe him to be weak and despise, if not him, then the weakness that diminished him?

Waiting by the marquee under the shade of the great oak as he approached with his troubled thoughts were his second in command, General Huger; Colonel Williams, adjutant-general of the army and leader of the Maryland Brigade of Continentals; Williams' subordinate, Colonel John Eager Howard of the First Maryand; Colonel Harrison of the artillery; and a knot of lesser officers, including Kosciuszko with his imperially elevated chin, Major Forsyth in his still spotless uniform, and the artillerymen Gaines and Captain William Browne. At the back, Greene's aide Major Ichabod Burnet, newly returned after a long absence on detached duty, stood grinning, happy to have his place again in the official family. A short distance beyond, the dragoons of the escort, till now taking their ease in the parched grass beneath the tree, sprang up and into the road, each claiming his mount from a horse-holder. Their officer stepped out and yelped a command; the section rattled to attention as one. *Smartly done*, Greene thought. He gave them a moment's fond and sad regard, these nimble boys in their rags.

The group by the marquee had stood to attention too. Huger, senior to everyone, rendered the salute for all. Greene returned it with a tilt of his hat. Stepping close, he was aware of Burnet's lopsided smile beaming at the rear of the crowd. How good it was to have him back. No sooner had the favored Pendleton departed to confer with authorities in North Carolina than Bod Burnet, who claimed a nearly equal share of the General's affection, returned like a blessing to fill the chasm Nat had left. In a curious parallel, Bod had been delayed in Virginia by a long spell of illness, and now Pendleton too lay sick in Charlotte. Disease was raging through Greene's whole corps of officers—Huger himself had reported but days before after lying abed some weeks at his plantation, too wasted to stir. Even yet, the General could see, the poor fellow remained far from well.

"Gentlemen," he said, the darkness of his former mood brightened by Burnet's presence, "will the army be ready to move at the appointed hour?" He wished he could take Bod with him; but Huger would need the boy's skills.

"It will, sir," Huger replied in a wisp of voice.

Dear God, thought Greene, *the man looks on the brink of death; he's as yellow as a cheese.* He had lost so much weight that the skin of his throat hung in folds like the wattles of a turkey-cock. The wattles quivered ever so slightly. Greene worried that his second in command might not last the day. "In light order?" he inquired, softly, so as not to distress the convalescent general.

"Yes, sir." Huger's eyelids drooped alarmingly; Greene stood poised to catch him should he collapse. But manfully the South Carolinian continued: "Only the ammunition and commissary equipage will start with us. Major Armstrong, with the North Carolina draftees and the Virginia militia, will escort the non-effectives, the women and children and the heavy baggage. They will move by easy stages towards Camden, as you directed, but won't cross the Wateree without further orders, unless threatened by the enemy."

"I believe we can camp tonight nearly at Cedar Creek," Colonel Williams helpfully put in, "marching in the cool of the evening, and perhaps for an hour or two after dark." Even if he sometimes had odd ideas, like treating the army to a *feu de joie* when active operations impended and every cartridge counted, it was very like Otho Williams to offer all aid in his power, large or small, which might ease another's burden. Equally at home amid his adjutant's paperwork or commanding a flying army of light troops as in the Guilford campaign, Otho was the most dependable man Greene had ever known, inside the army or out of it. His good Welsh face with its perpetual half-smile had brightened many of the General's grimmest days. Huger acknowledged Williams now with a bob of his patrician head; the Hugers, foremost among Low Country grandees, knew an act of grace when they saw one.

The name was of Huguenot origin, Greene had learned, was pronounced "You-gee," not as he had shamefully mangled it when they first met, "Hew-ger." Luckily Huger was sufficiently secure in his privileged station that he could forgive a Rhode Island ironmaster for failing to make the fine social distinctions required of every high-born Carolinian; and if he assumed, as he no doubt did, that Greene subscribed to the heretical spirit of leveling that was said to taint all New Englanders, he graciously excused that crime too. It was no ordinary aristocrat who could overlook the subversive bent toward democracy.

"Very well," Greene nodded. "I ride to join Colonel Washington and the cavalry. Do endeavor to keep the main force together and constantly ready for an immediate forced march. Once I establish the exact whereabouts of Rawdon and Stewart, I'll send word. We'll concentrate our detachments, call the South Carolinian militias to us and, if God blesses us, prevent the junction of the enemy columns and beat each in detail." He struck his fist into his palm to emphasize the urgency he felt. "But we *must* move swiftly."

He saluted, turned, and strode past them toward the waiting escort. *Main force indeed*, he thought, with contempt for his own farcical terminology. All he had in his so-called main force were two regiments each of Virginia Continentals and of Marylanders. What was that? Three hundred men? Four hundred? He did not know. The number changed daily; the only certainty was that with every return it grew smaller from sickness and desertion and the expiration of enlistments. The balance of his troops were scattered over the whole of the great wedge of land between the Saluda and Wateree rivers, trying to hold apart the enemy columns. Washington's cavalry with Kirkwood's Delawares and a detachment of South Carolina State troops were likely in the country where the Wateree and the Broad joined to form the Congaree; Lee's Legion, he hoped, was scouting westward, on the Broad near Fort Granby, or on the Saluda.

But he could have little certainty of even these dispositions. Washington sent frequent reports, but kept in such constant motion it was hard to know his exact location at any given time; Harry Lee had fallen into a mystifying silence till five days ago when, in an act of beastly insubordination, he'd defied Greene's orders, twice repeated, to send the Delawares, temporarily assigned to the Legion, back to Washington's dragoons, their proper home. Stung and hurt by this arrant piece of disobedience, Greene had instructed Kirkwood to report to Washington, bypassing the imperious Harry altogether, and Kirkwood had gone; but in deference to the emergency of the moment the General had elected not to rebuke Lee openly for his inexplicable behavior. *At least*, he thought, *I've the one malicious satisfaction that Harry still thinks he commands the Delawares, even as they serve miles away with Washington, his rival.* He could savor that irony even as he nursed an unappeased anger, mixed with his sad bewilderment. *Why must Harry play these odious tricks?*

His steward Peters waited in the road holding his favorite saddle horse, Swift, a dapple gray named for the excellent author of *A Tale of a Tub.* The gelding nickered a welcome and the General took a moment to pet him, then grasped the reins and pulled himself astride. Peters stood back. In the road behind, the lieutenant of dragoons gave another ringing shout and the troopers swung to the saddle with a crunch of leather and a clatter of sword scabbards. The young officer rode abreast and saluted. "Lieutenant Elisha King, sir," he cried in a distinctive fox-bark voice, "Swan's Troop, Third Light Dragoons."

Lieutenant King was a departure from form. In Greene's experience the dragoon officer tended toward the robust, possibly because his rank and station gave him the means to keep himself in nourishment while his troopers, poor men in civilian life now long unpaid as soldiers, more often resembled starvelings, like today's escort section. But King was as emaciated as any private and wore a dirty hunting shirt and deerskin britches with holes in them. Greene thought this evidence of good character. He returned the salute. "Good day, Lieutenant. You are freshly come from Colonel Washington?"

"Yes, sir," King replied, using that same narrow voice, holding his gaze resolutely to the front. "When I left him he was at Colonel Taylor's. He means to keep possession of the north side of the Congaree till you come down. We should reach him by noon tomorrow, sir. *If* we ride steadily."

Lieutenant King's remark seemed to imply a belief that all officers of field grade were inveterate idlers. Evidently he wished to put Greene on notice that delays would not be tolerated; Greene had fallen into the power of a martinet. He smiled. "I will endeavor to keep the pace," he promised. "Lead on, sir, if you will."

Again they exchanged salutes, and the little party struck out down the road at a canter. On both sides of the path the men of the army gathered to watch them go, and after a moment in which they seemed to weigh their affection for their General against their resentment of the ill use that had too long marked their service, they raised a cheer for him that rippled pleasantly along as he rode. He doffed his hat in acknowledgment and meted out his grateful smile. Soon they passed beyond the limits of the camp with its perpetual exhalation of dust and smoke and stench, and turned south in clear sunlight over the broad bosomy face of the land. Presently Greene felt the need of conversation. "Tell me, Lieutenant, have you seen much of this war?"

"Yes, sir, a good deal. I came up from the ranks from sergeant of infantry; I was in Weedon's Brigade, Fourteenth Virginia, Colonel Davies. I saw action at Brandywine and Germantown. Transferred to Colonel Washington's command in January. Was with the Third at The Cowpens."

Hard service, reflected Greene. "General Weedon," he remarked with nostalgia, "is a great friend of mine."

"Yes, sir, I know, sir." The clipped reply sounded impatient. Obviously Lieutenant King found Greene's information of small utility, and perhaps suspected his commander of having a hopelessly sentimental mind.

Inwardly Greene smiled. He resolved to entice the prickly fellow out. "Drawing on your wide experience, Lieutenant, I wonder how you regard the progress of our affairs here in the Southern Department?"

King answered without hesitation. "It seems to me, sir," he cried, "that matters are scarcely to our advantage." He hesitated, adding in grudging afterthought, "If I may say so, sir."

"By all means, Lieutenant. Do speak freely. I'm always interested to know the unfettered minds of my officers."

King grasped the chance as if he had been awaiting it for months. "Meaning no criticism or disrespect of my superiors, sir, but is not the Southern Army but the despised and neglected bastard child of the Continental Congress? In letters from friends to the Northward I'm told of soldiers there going about in new regimentals with lace at throat and cuff. Of troops living comfortably in tents of the most modern pattern. Hair powder is spoke of, and wigs and lip balm, and the latest fashion of wearing the cocked hat. Legs are made at balls. Feasts are spread where the most succulent delicacies are consumed and the finest wines drunk. Women are lustfully possessed whose station is as high as their virtue is low. Yet is there war to the Northward? I think not, sir. I think the thing they regard as war is an affair of perfumed gentlemen lounging about drawing rooms engaged in the tedious minuet of diplomacy and in the most minute examination of their own precious persons in gilt mirrors, or perhaps in the plucking of a conspicuous hair from the ear. The war, sir, is here with us, is it not? Yet we are abandoned, deserted, forgotten..."

"I imagine, Lieutenant, the Virginians would argue that the war has taken their Commonwealth by the throat," Greene felt compelled to remind the voluble King, though it felt strange to be defending the very persons who most vexed him.

"*They* may call it war, sir," King replied dismissively. "Yet we hear only of the enemy ranging about at will, while the civil officers of the state either take flight in panic or stand helplessly wringing their hands. Our army there, it seems, does little but follow meekly on the enemy's track of devastation."

Plainly Elisha King was a man of firm opinions, and while Greene found himself in accord with most of them, in the mouth of a junior officer of dragoons they smacked enough of insubordination, if not treason, that he thought it best to stem the flood. "Your views, sir," he remarked, with what he hoped looked a companionable smile, "are most penetrating. I thank you for them." The gentle warning was not lost on King. On the instant he fell silent, and uttered not another syllable for the next fifteen miles.

In a way Greene was sorry to have cut him off, even if it had been for his own good; the boy had said no more than Greene had often ranted to himself. He stole sidewise glances at the Lieutenant as they rode. King's lips were split to bleeding, blisters covered his nose, he had an ugly sore at one corner of his mouth, the bones of his face protruded, everything about him bespoke privation and misery. Dust and campfire smoke had reddened the whites of his eyes, and the eyes themselves, a curious shade of pale yellow, gave out an abiding, impartial remorselessness that told of anger so long held that it had seeped into every cranny of his nature. It was permanent now, and of such permanence was born the worst malignity of war. There had been a time, probably, when Elisha King was an amiable young man. That time was gone now and would not come back.

Greene did not like to contemplate what war did to the souls of individual men. So he lifted his thoughts from the personal and spread them out over the many, and in this way the damage to any single soul could be diffused and more comfortably borne. He rested his mind on the army. The whole force he hoped to collect, in all its constituent parts, numbered perhaps a thousand, surely not more than that, almost certainly less. Fortunately most would be experienced regulars; the unreliable militia and the new North Carolina draftees would be with Armstrong, going up to Camden out of harm's way.

He wished to bring to him the state troops of Sumter and Marion's militia; each might fetch as many as five hundred swords or, perhaps more likely, no more than a few score. Of their quality none could speak; they might prove as brave as lions or as craven and savage as hyenas; it would depend on whose companies chose to rally. Some, especially in Sumter's corps, were little better than banditti. Gathering them would be as easy as herding fleas—as many as might be induced to go one way, twice that number would jump contrariwise. But if fortune smiled, Greene might count seven hundred of them. With his Continentals, they would give him an army of sixteen hundred; he had fought Hobkirk's Hill with far fewer.

Against these, according to the reports of Colonel Washington, Rawdon could oppose but twelve hundred sick and exhausted men. Should Greene succeed in gathering his scattered units and striking Rawdon before that column and Stewart's met, he might actually dispose of a larger force than his enemy for the first time since the battle of Guilford. And even if Stewart's four hundred did make a junction before he could attack, the forces might still be evenly matched in numbers. Of course numbers alone augured nothing. He'd had the advantage of numbers at Guilford, but many were timorous militia and had fled; Cornwallis had defeated him with a small band of hardened regulars. And Stewart's four hundred were the British Third Regiment of Foot, the famous Buffs, certain to give a fierce account of themselves.

The day grew hotter while he rode with his deep concerns. The sun, as it sank lower on their right hand, lost none of its blinding force, though in dropping toward the tree tops it passed into a layer of purple haze that now sharply defined it, rounded it to an ominous blood-red disk. The air turned dense and steamy; the light sands of the road, more like a fine powder than a dust, whirled up from the hooves of the horses to give the riders spells of dry coughing and cover them with coats of white that made them look like some child's dolls that had been mischievously rolled in flour. Their eyes and mouths, unnaturally red and moist amid the cloak of white, gave them a vaguely hideous aspect, as if the dolls had come implausibly alive. They sweated a greasy gray slime, and when the slime ran, it darkened till their white faces were streaked with black; and as Greene looked at his companions he had a bizarre revelation: They might have been representations of the Savior's suffering, parading in some Papist ceremonial, bleeding black instead of red from commemorative crowns of thorns.

They rode through a cheerless waste of pine barrens interspersed with forests of water oak, hickory, maple, and black walnut, ancient trees all of immense height, and every few miles one of these leviathans would have freshly fallen across their path, forcing them to pick a tortuous way around the mossy monsters, through bamboo groves and briary underbrush. Stands of river cane choked every watercourse—and there were many of these, some flanked by swamps or bogs whose towering cypresses trailed beards of moss like aged mandarins. In these places pools of black standing water gave off fetid odors. Frogs sang and thrummed in the dank shallows. Parakeets the color of limes fluttered overhead. At their approach, snakes that had been sunning themselves in the road squirmed sluggishly into the sloughs. *How exotic, how strange and sinister and beautiful a place is this Southland,* Greene thought. *How different from staid and settled Rhode Island.*

On occasion the wilderness gave back to reveal an isolated cabin or a farmstead surrounded by weed-choked fields where scanty crops once had grown. Fences were fallen, roofs caved in, chimneys collapsed to heaps of rubble. Without exception the dwellings stood abandoned, the inhabitants no doubt murdered or driven away by the pitiless slaughters the war had ignited between Whig and Tory, or by the breakdown of order, which had loosed upon the population parties of outlaws who knew no allegiance or shame or mercy. Sometimes feral dogs and cats were seen, cosseted pets of farm folk in kinder days, now abandoned to run wild. Once a mad dog came at them ravening; a dragoon slew it with a pistol shot.

Greene thought of Caty, who constantly entreated his permission to come South and join him. How could he allow it? There was no safe place in this country below Philadelphia, and the fevers of the summer season would play havoc with her constitution, which was as febrile as her spirit was strong. He ached to have her with him. But it was hardly wise. He must write her at his first opportunity, urge her to wait for a more propitious time.

They camped that night at a place called Ancrum's, an empty, broken-backed farmhouse. A courier from Colonel Washington met them there. Greene despaired of reading the dispatch in the failing light till Lieutenant King, in an unexpected show of thoughtfulness, struck flint and steel to a rope's end dipped in rum and held the flame near the scrap of paper covered with Washington's loopy scrawl. The Colonel, writing from Howell's Ferry on the Congaree, had intercepted a letter from Stewart to Rawdon suggesting their junction was imminent somewhere on the lower river; Washington meant to cross the river and try to meet Harry Lee, who he thought was eight or ten miles below Rawdon's position, so together they could get between the enemy columns; General Marion was said to be approaching from the south with four hundred South Carolinians.

The General was displeased to learn that a meeting of the enemy columns might be near and hoped the information would prove mistaken. He shared the note with Lieutenant King. "I calculate that by the time we reach the Congaree," said King, "Colonel Washington may have gone as far down as Heatly's, or even Sabb's. If that's so, then he'll have left a base camp at Mrs. Motte's. Another few hours' ride will bring us there." He spoke in his shrill bark, those inflamed and angry eyes fixed straight ahead; clearly he was still annoyed with the General for first inviting and then arbitrarily cutting off his views of the state of the war. "Tomorrow we'll take the last stage at an easier gait," he added, with what Greene thought a reproachful emphasis.

Though stung that the fortitude he thought he had shown this day seemed to have escaped King's notice, he let the implied slight pass unchallenged. Instead, as was his custom whenever thrown with his soldiers, he walked among the resting troopers to sample their temper. He did this always against his most private inclination, for he found it far from a comfortable task. The truth was, he did not mix easily with the common man. It was not a question of class; his origins, while not ordinary, were neither the loftiest. It was something more elusive, a matter of mental constitution. He was too reserved, too conscious of living deeply in his own preoccupations while they moved in a realm where concrete actions alone mattered. He felt almost cripplingly grateful to them for the sacrifices they made to serve him, and then of course his gratitude was darkened by guilt when he saw that what they served was not so much his rank or his generalship as his ambition, a selfish ambition that might be close to a cardinal wickedness.

So he came among them in a manner more tentative than was probably good in a commander; but at least he was genuine in his feelings and the men sensed this and met his shy smiles with broad ones of their own. In the outer darkness, wolves yodeled in their demented way, lending the little plantation clearing in the wilderness an air of forlorn besetment; but here in the circle of firelight all was snug and companionable. They made him welcome.

On the morrow they rode again in pitiless heat, stopping often to relieve the horses. The delays drew out Lieutenant King's estimate of a few hours' journey into a day-long ordeal. Another courier from Colonel Washington met them on the way. The dispatch was dated that morning, from Howell's again; Rawdon, wrote the Colonel, was in full retreat near Beaver Creek, on the south side of the Congaree, as if inclining toward Orangeburgh. Washington intended going over the river at McCord's Ferry in hopes of falling in with Lee and Marion and getting ahead of the British commander to slow him down.

Greene was irked. Washington was supposed to have crossed last night and already come up with Lee and Marion. He felt the wastage of opportunity like the draining of his own life's blood. Not only had he wished to strike Rawdon before Stewart joined, there was now the reinforced garrison of Ninety-Six to consider. According to reports from General Pickens, whom he'd assigned to observe that post, Cruger seemed to be preparing to evacuate the place, which Greene's siege and Rawdon's retreat had rendered untenable; and his force, augmented by every Tory refugee he could gather, might soon head south down the Saluda, also aiming for a junction with Rawdon. If all three enemy columns met, Greene's strategy would fall to ruin; he would be overmatched and forced to yield up the game. The torrid weather was taking its toll on everyone, friend and foe alike; yet it seemed his own elements were marching at but a snail's pace, while those of the enemy moved, if not more swiftly, then with more art and decision regardless of the baking temperatures.

He began to rethink his plan of operations. Rather than falling on the retreating Rawdon, why not get around him with Kirkwood's light troops and the fast-moving horse of Washington and Lee, and strike at Stewart instead? That would deprive Rawdon of the fresher troops of the reinforcing column and leave his fatigued and sickness-ridden corps more vulnerable to the concentrated army of the Americans. The more the General considered this scheme the more it appealed to him. But its success, he recognized, would depend on his ability to galvanize his own. His various detachments seemed to be wandering aimlessly about the country. He must give them the vigor and focus they lacked. This was a challenge he could rise to—and once he met it, he knew it would be noticed. And yes, it was the prospect of recognition that decided him.

Full night had fallen by the time they encountered the first of Washington's videttes. Another few minutes' riding brought them to the quarter guard, whose corporal passed them on with a salute, and then into the camp proper at Mrs. Motte's. Colonel Washington, of course, was away and most of the regiment with him. Captain Swan, officer of the day, stepped forward to refresh acquaintances; newly returned from Lafayette's army, he had delivered letters to Greene's headquarters but a few days previously. He had just assumed command of Captain Barrett's troop; Barrett himself, shot through the hips at Guilford, hobbled up using a cane; he could do no duty, being both convalescent and on parole. Greene found the fellow fearfully pallid, but bearing affably the gibes of his fellow officers—they seemed to think the great swath of dressing for his wound, which made an improbable bulge under his britches, gave him a most amusing girth.

A Captain Watts next introduced himself; his troop of the First Dragoons was in camp along with Swan's men; these were orphans of a regiment shattered by Tarleton a year ago, whose Colonel, Anthony White, was in Virginia on recruiting duty. Till White returned, his remnant served as a troop of the Third. The General found Watts a vigorous, active officer, lively of spirit, quick of eye, a splendid addition, he thought, to Washington's corps.

Mrs. Motte's mansion had, of course, been rendered uninhabitable when partly burnt in May; however, she owned a modest tenant farmhouse on a nearby hill where she had taken refuge during the siege of the fortress the British had made of her confiscated home. The farmhouse stood empty now; Mrs. Motte had gone upcountry to stay with relatives. Captain Swan offered it to Greene as shelter for the night. But the General eschewed special treatment. He slept that night between the roots of a tree; no other shelter was to be had anyway, for dragoons afield spurned the tent—or would have, had there been any—as the refuge of the weak and pusillanimous; and even the humble arbor of brushwood was an object of scorn. At first Greene conceived the experience a bracing one. It seemed virtuous to undergo the spartan regimen of the private trooper. But after an hour or so the gnarled roots of the maple that cramped his shoulders and the pebbly unevenness of the ground that prodded his backbone had him tossing and writhing in wakefulness.

And presently, as he drifted in and out of a troubled slumber, a vision of that last assault at Ninety-Six formed again in his mind, as it did now nearly every night. In his dream he watched, not from Gaines's battery as he had in reality, but suspended somehow in air directly above the scene, looking down on the men of the forlorn hope as they used their axes to chop their way through the tangled abatis of the Star Fort and others with billhooks clambered past them through the fraising and into the ditch. Then in the delirium of the dream he was down in the thick of the fight too, down in the third parallel where his Marylanders and Virginians crouched among the *facines* laying on a covering fire for the forlorn hope. Their muskets belched smoke and tongues of fire, but made no sound. All around him he saw the strained, powder-blackened faces of his men; they turned and spoke to him with an indescribable urgency, but in his dream they spoke without words and he peered bewildered into their flapping, silent mouths.

He floated high again. He saw below him the tiny figures of the hookmen dislodging the sandbags that lined the bunkers of the parapet. He saw the bags tumbling into the ditch. All was eerie silence as the struggle continued. There was a tremendous moment when it seemed a breach would be opened, that the Star Fort would fall, and Ninety-Six with it. But suddenly a party of Provincials broke from a sally port on the back side of the Star, no more than sixty men with pikes and bayonets. The little band divided, half rushing one way, half another. Circling around, they fell upon the hookmen from left and right, trapping the forlorn hope between them. Down in the ditch with them now, among the fallen sandbags, Greene in his nightmare saw the slain and wounded sink across each other in gory piles. He saw their screaming faces, but could not hear them.

He waded in blood to his ankles. He was trying to cry out to Colonel Williams to stop the slaughter, but his throat would not come unstuck and his tongue refused to shape the words and he found himself unable to repeat in the dream what he knew he had shouted then, leaning out, his fists pounding helplessly on the gabions of the battery, shouting it so loud that it tore his throat almost to bleeding, *Call them back, Otho. For God's sake, call them back.*

He came awake and lay beneath the tree, wide-eyed, seeing it all again, played out before him across the starry night sky. Seeing it. Smelling it. Feeling it. Fifty-seven killed; seventy wounded; twenty missing and probably dead. Almost a fifth of his force. In suspending the attack he had acted to save lives—that was what he had believed. Surely it had been a generous and humane motive. But in ordering the assault only to call it back, had he not simply ended by wasting lives? Wasting them to no good purpose? Could he not have ordered the Marylanders and Virginians to storm the place, rescue the forlorn hope, push home an all-out assault? Had his humane impulse given rise to an inhumane outcome? Was he, as he wished to think, a prudent chieftain who knew how to cut his losses? Or was he a feckless weakling who could not bring himself to pay the cost of victory, the sublime price that Cornwallis had paid at Guilford?

He wanted to expunge the questions, wipe away the doubts that bred them. That was why he must bring the British to battle. Whip them. Hold nothing back. Rally the far-flung elements of his army—Continentals, militia, infantry, cavalry. Concentrate. Then attack. Attack with everything, attack them front and flanks and rear. Cast it all into the hazard. Come at the British with a ferocity *void of all manner of design and totally the effect of a natural disposition.* Win. Win victory. Win glory. Win the war. Win independency. Win the nation. Win greatness. Grasp the destiny that he knew was to be his.

Part ye' Seventh

In Which a Young Man Profeſſes Himſelf
Footſore and Aweary

IN THE MORNING THEY AWOKE WRAPPED IN AN impenetrable wet mist. They could hear the rush of the river and, somewhere below them, a jingle of harness, a hollow rattle of hooves on wooden decking, the neighs and snorts of horses, then a thump and splash of oars; but the fog concealed everything and they could not guess what was afoot till Charlie Cooke clambered down the slope to the unseen shore and returned, dew-drenched, after a long and anxious wait. "Some of them Frenchie cavalry's gone back over to the point on floats," he reported, "to spy the Redcoats out."

They waited another hour or so, blinded by the fog, fretful, hearing only the perpetual mutter of the river flowing past, wondering what the coming day might bring. For breakfast they chewed some greasy balls of raw bacon and handsful of uncooked peas. Lacking anything useful to do, Libby wound into her hair a strip of blue ribbon she had found lying loose among the pebbles of the riverbank the day before. Janet crouched with her skirts raised immodestly displaying thighs marred with broken blue veins; she kept picking at the grass and speaking the same unintelligible word over and over—it sounded like "Arraham." Charlie and Dick played a desultory game of five-and-forty with a pack of dingy cards.

James sat some distance apart on a flat stone cradling his firelock in his arms, trying to imagine the shape of the lives he and Libby would be living from this time hence as the war unfolded and, if the fates were willing, when peace one day arrived; and—because of what Libby had divulged to him the evening before—thinking of Poovey Sides too, wondering how it might be to regard the red-hair not as the nettlesome blusterer he presented himself to be, but as someone harboring hidden virtues that made him worthy of respect. How might Poovey figure in what was to come? James found the question intriguing and repellant in equal parts, and had to admit he was yet very far from Libby's positive opinion of the fellow.

His musings were interrupted by faint shouts from across the river and then by louder halloos answering from below. Something seemed to be happening. He stood; they all did, gazing into the veil of fog in a vain effort to penetrate it. Presently they heard a threshing of oars and the gush of a vessel breasting the waters of the river; and once again curiosity impelled Charlie to descend the ridge and serve as messenger. Within minutes he hastened back, emerging breathless from the mist to say two men of the picket had crept out to the point and called for a boat. Ferried over, they told the Baron a column of enemy troops had forded the Rivanna before dawn and were on the march down its southern bank; four hours' time would bring them to the Arsenal grounds; the picket was withdrawing ahead of them. "Was Poovey one of 'em that came over?" Libby anxiously asked.

"No," Charlie replied, "I think they were some of that militia of Lawson's." Libby sank back to her blanket sullen. "But," Charlie added, "I reckon the Baron's sending a fellow to call in the picket."

At this news Libby rose up elated. James covered her hand with his. "Poovey'll be fine," he assured her. "He's too vile a critter to get hurt, you know that." A fit of nervous giggling took her, but she nodded as though she believed him.

A few moments more and the fog began to lift, almost as if it had been awaiting Charlie's news. But it was a slow business. The cottony skeins would shred and partly dissolve to disclose a tantalizing vista, then merge again into one sea of white, only to divide in another place, offering a flash of sunlit tree-crowns or a wide span of river, then as quickly hiding that scene again under another drift of vapor. But in time the rumpled red-brown surface of the James slowly appeared, thankfully did not vanish as before; and soon the dark wedge of the Arsenal point and the bristly brow of the hill above it shouldered out of the murk, then the dark expanse of forest on either side could be seen and finally, overhead, a vast clear sky.

Newly revealed, so dazzling in the fresh sun of morning, so invitingly broad and open before them, the valley and the point and the river seemed to beckon; and at first singly and then in groups those on the ridgetop began to make their way down through the open woods to the bank to gather amid the clutter of crates and bales and weapons belonging to the State of Virginia. There they lined the shore to await what might transpire next, anxious and expectant yet vaguely apprehensive.

Providence soon rewarded them. "Yonder comes the picket!" someone cried, and sure enough, in the distance beyond the shot tower and powder magazine on the point, a file of men, like a line of ants, came winding out of the trees. Cheers, whistles, and huzzas welcomed them. Clutching Libby by the hand, James saw Baron Stew-Ben astride his white stallion, and Colonel Gaskins and General Lawson on their lesser nags, ride down through the howling mob into the reeds by the water's edge, a party of aides trailing behind. While his big horse tossed its head and pranced nervously in the shallows, the Baron pointed his baton toward the Arsenal and spoke energetically to Gaskins and Lawson; his bearing was stern and confident; James thought he looked the very picture of a mighty commander of men.

Presently the picket troops approached the boat landing at the tip of the point. No longer did they resemble ants; each face was a separate small wafer of pink or tan or even, rarely, of black; every man marched with his own distinctive gait and motion; the autumn-leaf hues of their hunting shirts and the faded blues and browns of their regimentals jostled together in a stream of many dull colors against the green background of the woods. "Do you see Poovey?" Libby, standing on tiptoe, cried to James. But he did not.

Batteaux began to leave the south bank to cross over and collect them. Now that the men of the picket seemed nearly out of danger, the mood along the south bank turned even jollier. There was laughter, singing, a jig or two broke out, a few danced a giddy reel; a fiddle scraped, a bagpipe skirled. Children scampered up and down amid the stores and cavorted in the stands of cane; one waddled bare-bottomed toward the river sucking happily on a bullet-mould no doubt filched from the military supplies. Halfway to the riverbank, the tot lost its balance and sat down in the abrupt and humorous way of all babes still learning to walk. For an instant it considered weeping for its misfortune, then decided to be brave instead and contented itself with nursing the bullet-mould. Amused, James touched Libby's shoulder, directed her attention to the child. Libby first grinned, then scowled. "Where's its mother?" she wondered aloud.

Just then, across the river, a commotion broke out in the Arsenal compound, back of the landing where the men of the picket had begun boarding the first of the batteaux. Several strange horsemen came galloping down the Rivanna road and began roaming in the vicinity of the big log-and-stone headquarters building. At first they seemed not to see the men clustered at the landing, but trotted to and fro over the compound in a way that made it clear they were looking for the retreating picket. The jubilation on the riverbank fell still at the sight. Breathlessly James and the others watched them; they wore the blue and white of Armand's Legion—the cavalry Baron Stew-Ben had sent at dawn to scout the British advance—yet their manner did not suit. What was it? At first they could not say. Then Dick Snow spied the truth. "Them ain't the Frenchies," he declared, "they've let their stirrups out too long."

James stared; Dick was right; the Legion dragoons he'd seen yesterday had ridden with knees bent; these sat their saddles straight-legged. He wondered how this could be, till Dick supplied a further answer. "Them's

Bloodybacks, by God. They've took the Frenchies, and put on their clothes." Even as he spoke, more riders swarmed into the distant compound; these were dressed in tall flat-topped caps and wore green jackets thrown over the left shoulder. "That's the hussar troop, Simcoe's Queen's Rangers," blurted a militiaman standing behind James; "I seen them bastards at Germantown." In rear of what the man had called hussars came a band of twenty or thirty sprightly-looking chaps on foot, in small peaked hats and short coats of green. "Them little buggers," the militiaman said, "they're the light company of Rangers."

Hearing him, James was astounded. "The *British?*"

"British, hell," sneered the militiaman. "Them's as American as you or me. Yorkers and Connecticut men, even some Virginians, curse 'em." He squinted and swore another time. "You want to clap an eye on a Britisher, though, here comes a pack of 'em. And not just *any* Lobsters neither. These is Red Shanks."

The soldiers he meant were infantrymen with little flat bonnets perched on the sides of their heads, garbed in vivid red coats and white overalls, who now came hurrying past the powder magazine and the shot tower and down toward the nose of the point, some hundred yards or so up the Rivanna from the landing where the men of the picket, realizing the enemy had overtaken them, were climbing ever more hastily into the waiting batteaux. Several more batteaux, already loaded with soldiers, were at midstream, their Negro polemen pushing hard for the security of the south bank. Behind, on the brow of the hill overlooking the point, the woods where James and Libby had once hidden seemed to stir as if the very trees had come alive; then the whole summit grew an implausible crop of crawling movement—more troops! Surely the enemy was there in great force.

"Red Shanks?" James repeated vaguely, his senses in a whirl, "what's them?" It was difficult to think; too much was happening all too quickly. He tried to grasp the notion that those far-off men in pretty uniforms, dodging hither and yon on the Arsenal grounds, were the same antagonists he had been learning all week long to fear and hate, and whom the Baron had been steeling him and his messmates to face in deadly battle.

"Highlanders, son," the militiaman told him. He leaned and spat to show his distaste. "Straight from Scratch Land, them is."

"Scotland, he means," said Charlie Cooke.

"Louse Land," the militiaman laughed, rudely correcting him, "Itch-land." James watched the bonneted soldiers as they crowded to the river's edge. *Highlanders.* It had not occurred to him till this very moment that fighters from his own dear half-remembered, half-forgotten homeland might come against him—maybe men of rainy Caithness, maybe men of Westerdale itself, men who knew the moorlands and the lochs and the sheltered cove and the stone cottage there even as James knew them, no, knew them *better* than he knew them, maybe playmates of his boyhood, maybe neighbors who might have loved his Da and Ma, maybe even blood kinsmen, uncles or cousins once held dear, who years ago might have dandled on their knees or tossed high in air a wee babe in swaddling clothes called James Johnson. Kith and clan, perhaps. Yet foemen he was sworn to maim or kill if he could. How came they to be enemies? Faintly he remembered his Da telling of The Forty-Five, the revolt of the Scots to set the Bonnie Prince on England's throne; he could not guess how High-landers might now don the scarlet coat and serve the same royalty that had crushed their fathers and broken up the clans. And he had also heard the contempt in the militiaman's voice. *Red Shanks. Scratch Land. Louse Land.* Highlanders, it seemed, were held much in scorn. Yet he was one. He hardly knew how to feel.

"*Janet!*" Libby's shout turned James and Charlie and Dick sharply in their tracks; they saw Libby start from the crowd, saw Janet sprinting away from her along the strand. Janet's tangled mane of gray hair flopped and swung about her shoulders as if possessed of a separate life. She ran with long, high-kneed strides, digging spouts of gravel behind her such as a galloping horse momentarily leaves on a turf track. She flung her arms wide, the fingers of her hands crooked like talons. On the shingle ahead of her sat the child James had noticed earlier, still sucking in contentment on its bullet-mould; clearly Janet had conceived an insane desire to capture it—to what end, hideous or maternal, there was no way to guess. She bore down on the infant screaming the same indecipherable word she had been mumbling earlier in camp, "*Arraham! Arraham!*"

"It's 'Abraham' she's saying!" Charlie burst out. "That's the name she meant to give her babe that died!" Even as Janet came shrieking, a bonnet-ed woman in the crowd who must have been the mother threw aside her wicker basket full of pots and kettles and gridirons and plunged frantically down the bank. Pale with fright, she scooped the infant quickly up while Janet was yet a few rods distant, whirled and mounted the slope again, la-boring in the pebbly sand, one hand cupping the child's small yellow head to her breast. When she had gained the verge of the woods, she turned back to glare down at the maniac with dread and loathing. The babe had lost its bullet mold and now began to wail. On the shore Janet dropped to her knees and began tearing at her hair; her cry ascended to a pitch of shrillness hardly to be borne, "*Arrrrrahaaaam!*"

But Libby was near; if comfort could be lent the poor loon, it lay in Libby's power to give. She was but a step or two away when, from the Arsenal compound, they all heard a noise reminiscent of the stroke of a bass drum, but so much louder and more powerful that for an instant it seemed to change the very content of the air, to compress it into something harder and more alien than air; and simultaneously one of the horses in Baron Stew-Ben's party cringed and a red corona of matter sprayed out of it and it fell kicking in the reeds, oversetting its rider; and then the cannonball that had killed it, visible now, its speed slowed by having passed through the poor beast's body, struck once on the shore in a scatter of rocks and sand, bounded high, and carried off Janet's head.

Twenty men of the Rivanna picket were able to cross to the south bank before the British descended on the Arsenal landing and took prisoner the remaining thirty. Poovey Sides, Blan Shiflet, and Sam Ham were among those saved; regrettably the one-eyed sergeant with whom James had forged his curious bond was left behind to fall into the hands of the enemy. James was saddened to conceive the rough old veteran held captive. Still, the reunion was a joyous one—or would have been, had it not been for the tragedy of Janet's death, and for a mishap that had befallen Sides.

Poovey slouched into camp bathed in copious tears. "Sergeant made me give up my shoat," he wailed, wiping his nose with a frayed sleeve. "Said 'twasn't proper, a soldier with a pig in his shirt. The poor wight's a-wandering lost and lorn in them wild woods—if the Bloodybacks ain't et him yet." His sorrow changed to rage and he cast his musket to the ground with a savage motion. "Goddamn all authority anyways!"

In this fashion James learned that Libby's generous estimate of the redhair had been somewhat accurate after all. It was a shock. How strange to think Poovey's crass ways had been but a deliberate blind to conceal a soft heart from a harsh world. James looked on him now with a measure of grudging affection as he sat weeping by the fire. But in a bitter irony, Libby, the first to have discerned Sides's true nature and to have conceived a liking for him when all others nourished only scorn, was now too distracted by grief and shock to console him in his loss or even pay him any mind at all. Her bodice spattered with Janet's life's blood, her skirts soiled with bits of Janet's brains, she could only gaze dumbly into the glowing embers, the bit of blue ribbon she had found on the beach still braided forlornly in her tresses, and James surmised she saw nothing of what lay before her, but instead saw only the scene of Janet's death endlessly repeated.

It was best, Charlie Cooke had told her by way of comfort. *Poor creature, she'd have come to a bad end, one way or t'other, soon or late. Better soon, says I. God rest her soul, says I.* Libby could do no more than give a nod of speechless assent. James suspected Charlie was secretly pleased the British had relieved him of a burden that had long since grown wearisome and embarrassing, and once again the shadow of a similar notion fell across his own conscience when he thought of Libby's care and how it wore on him. But Charlie was genuinely sad just as James knew he would be if Libby were actually lost. Charlie insisted on burying Janet's mangled corpse with his own hands, reverently he spoke a prayer over her grave at the river's edge, and afterward could be seen gently handling her few simple possessions, including the horse's currycomb he had stolen from David Ross's farm, that Libby had often used to untangle her matted hair.

There was little enough time for sentiment, though. Baron Stew-Ben gave orders to conceal the Virginia military stores in the forest and to break up the batteaux and other craft to keep them from the British; at dawn the next day the little army would march south to join General Greene. The James River boatmen took axes and sadly set about chopping to splinters their beloved vessels, while the soldiers of the Battalion and of Lawson's militia gave their attention to the secreting of the supplies.

It was the work of the balance of the day to accomplish this. They managed to conceal much of the gunpowder in the tobacco barns of several nearby farms. But the bulk of the stores were most hastily and imperfectly hidden in the scanty woods roundabout; and when nightfall brought an end to their labors, much yet remained on the riverbank in plain view of the British who, lacking boats of any kind, could only stand along the shoreline of the Arsenal point observing their endeavors, offering taunts and jeering advice—at least, after killing Janet, they had refrained from any further firing. However, others of them were busy assembling flats—the pounding of their hammers could be easily heard—and by tomorrow they would possess the means to cross the river and gather up the abandoned stores even as Charlie Cooke had prophesied. So before daybreak of the following morning the Battalion and the militia broke camp, turned their backs on the Arsenal and the British who held it, and marched away toward the Carolinas.

It was a Wednesday when they commenced, and through the morning and on past noontime they tramped upstream along a creek that gradually dwindled in size to a little brook and then to a headwater spring. They paused every hour or so for a few short minutes to catch their wind. What little they ate was nibbled during these halts or in the ranks as they

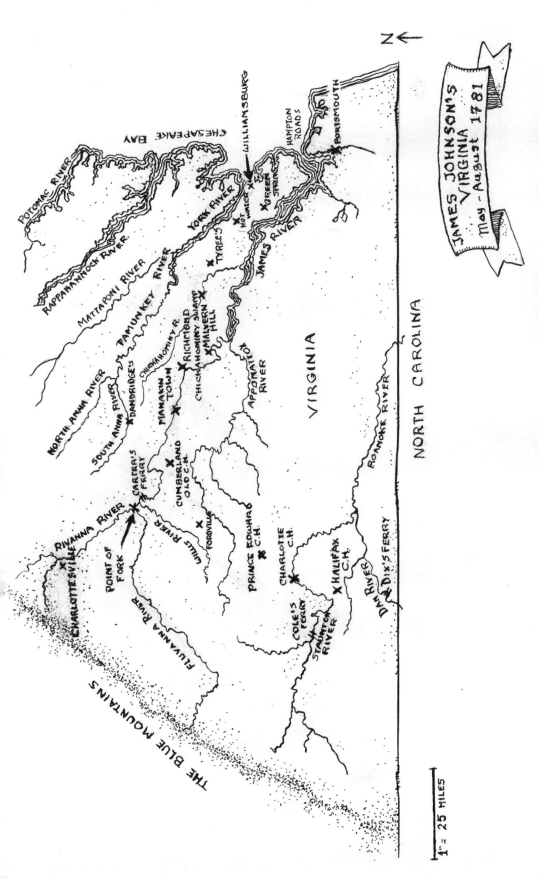

JAMES JOHNSON'S
VIRGINIA
May - August 1781

N

1" = 25 MILES

THE BLUE MOUNTAINS

CHESAPEAKE BAY

POTOMAC RIVER

RAPPAHANNOCK RIVER

MATTAPONI RIVER

PAMUNKEY RIVER

YORK RIVER

WILLIAMSBURG

HOT WATER

GREEN SPRING

HAMPTON ROADS

PORTSMOUTH

JAMES RIVER

TYREE'S

NORTH ANNA RIVER

SOUTH ANNA RIVER

DANDRIDGE'S

CHICKAHOMINY R.

RICHMOND

CHICKAHOMINY SWAMP

MALVERN HILL

MANAKIN TOWN

APPOMATTOX RIVER

VIRGINIA

RIVANNA RIVER

CHARLOTTESVILLE

POINT OF FORK

CARTER'S FERRY

WILLIS RIVER

CUMBERLAND OLD C.M.

FORDVILLE

PRINCE EDWARD C.H.

RIVANNA RIVER

CHARLOTTE C.H.

COLE'S FERRY

STAUNTON RIVER

HALIFAX C.H.

ROANOKE RIVER

DAN RIVER

DIX'S FERRY

NORTH CAROLINA

marched. They crossed high ground and near dusk came to another river, shallow enough to ford, and camped there, rising at dawn on Thursday to wade the chill waters. Here at last Libby began to put aside her grief; she paused in the river to wash the bloody stains from her clothes, a task which till now she had resisted, evidently believing the grisly smirch had been a memorial worthy of preservation in Janet's honor. Then she unwound the blue ribbon from her hair and cast it into the waters.

Soon the column was driving against a gradually rising terrain that lifted them through a thick wood of prodigious trees. Bent by the weight of his knapsack and firelock, James trudged miserably upward, the muscles in the calves of his legs twitching and cramping, his clothes sodden with sweat, the odor of his unwashed self and of his equally unwashed messmates foul in his nose. *My first march as a soldier*, he thought. He hoped to stand up to it. Not so long ago he had been a humble house-joiner, bound to a monotony of toil, each new day of his existence exactly like the last, devoid of any hope of change or expectation of relief save when his master let him ride the sorrel Patuxent in an occasional race. Now he lived a life whose only constant was bewildering and seemingly purposeless change, whose events could be boring, yes, but could be dreadful too, by immediate and appalling turns, as Janet's death had been. Yet he who had once been so simple of mind and heart had learned in a matter of days to look upon it all as commonplace, as barely meriting notice; soldiering had hardened him already. He was sorry that Janet was dead; but in truth her death had meant as little to him as had the loss of Poovey's pig. It seemed remarkable, and terrible, to have grown so coarse in so short a time.

Very soon, he noticed, the column ceased marching in the regular order the Baron had taught them on the drill square. Every man ignored the drum-tap and found the pace that suited him, so the rigorous system of rank and file dissolved into a shuffling but comfortable disorder. Though they were nominally at shoulder arms, each fellow now bore his musket as he thought easiest, this one cradling it like a loaf of bread, that one grasping his by the barrel with the stock resting on his shoulder as a laborer might tote his shovel or his hoe. As a result the column, with its muskets bristling out at all angles, presented the appearance of a walking thicket. Nor did the officers, the sergeants, or the corporals seek to correct these informalities. This was, James divined, the usual mode of an infantry march, the Baron's parade-ground injunctions to the contrary notwithstanding. The only admonitions were addressed—and sharply too—to such careless individuals holding their firelocks by the barrel as had failed to turn their pieces over with the trigger-guard uppermost, lest a dangling branch catch the exposed cock, discharge the musket, and kill the file immediately in front.

They came at last to the crest of a ridge. Beyond this high spine of land lay a forested valley with a bright thread of river winding down it. They camped on the heights amid lofty trees whose crowns met overhead to make a leafy canopy. James's feet were sore and he found his shoddy pumps had worn a blister on the ball of his right foot. Every muscle of his body ached. He lay down in a bed of leaves, drugged with fatigue. Somehow Libby had contrived to fare better. She came up from the rear of the column refreshed and seemed at last to recollect some of her old devotion for Sides, went to him, sat close and soothed with healing talk the anguish he felt for his own loss, and it was late when she joined James in his pallet.

Next day they descended into the valley and then marched two more days along poor roads in stifling heat. James's blister worsened and made him lame. Perspiring, footsore, and weary, the troops began to grumble and complain of misuse. Some questioned the wisdom—even the courage—of Baron Stew-Ben in turning tail and abandoning the Arsenal to the British. Others asked why they must go so far from home as South Carolina, which they had heard was nothing less than a desert land where wolves and wild Indians and pitiless Tories lurked in ambuscade behind every rock.

Furthermore, the Baron had cultivated an unlikely taste for the flesh of blacksnakes, and every night after pitching camp all hands were now compelled to go thrashing in the underbrush for loathsome serpents to grace the Baron's table, a chore that looked to many not only demeaning but senseless. Though James yet kept his faith in the Baron as a wise commander, even he found it marvelous to be put to such peculiar duty. But, he reasoned, the Baron *was* a foreigner; perhaps it was a custom of the Germans to dine on reptiles. James thought allowances must be made for differences of culture. He had often heard that not everyone approved of the Scotsman's haggis.

Spirits rose when the column met a wagon carrying shirts intended for the Maryland Continentals serving in General Greene's army, which the Baron appropriated for their use. Soon every man was clad in a new smock and feeling rather much the better for the change. Refreshed, on Saturday they arrived in a village called Charlotte Court House just as the sun was beginning to hide its face behind the mountains. Libby had sat late with Sides both nights, and when the column had gotten settled on the green, Poovey came sidling nervously to James. "Johnson," he began with unaccustomed shyness, "it's a damned ticklish matter, but I bound to raise it."

James was soaking his blistered foot in a horse trough. "What is?"

"Well, Sides answered, "it's concerning your Libby. I know you hold her right dear—any cully can see it. And she's your heart-o'-hearts and not just some notch you're a-grinding." He blushed then, belatedly aware the expression had been a bit crude. With a freckled hand he scratched first at his crotch and then behind an ear, all the while casting anxious looks to left and right; agitation gave him the tremulous air of a rabbit discovered in a hedge.

James examined him curiously. "What ails you anyway? You behave as though I might snap your head off. You want to say aught about Libby, go on and say it."

"You might snap my head off for certain." Poovey surmised, gazing woefully skyward, then examining the grass underfoot. "You might even jump up and kill me."

"Why would I want to do that?" James tugged at his chin and thought it best to amend that statement. "Sometimes I'd like to choke your scrawny turkey's neck till you turn purple, but not enough to kill you."

Now Sides fixed him with an earnest, not to say pleading, gaze. "Will you do me a great favor and swear a solemn vow you won't kill me if I tell you what I'm going to tell?"

James scowled, losing patience with Poovey's roundabout talk. "You ask wagon-loads without telling me a thing. Will you just speak up? What about Libby?"

"Swear that vow first."

James dipped his feet in the water several more times while giving the question some study. Finally he sighed, "All right, I won't kill you, though I can't promise we won't quarrel, or that I might not box your ears."

Poovey resumed shooting guilty glances from side to side. "All right then. I reckon that's good enough."

"Well?"

Sides moved backward three or four paces and took a stance poised to run. "Your Libby, why, she's a glory. Just a glory. A angel out of Heaven, seems to me. And pretty as a sunny Sunday, ain't she? And here's me, with my skinny shanks and hang-gallows look"—a sadness came over him—"and now, with my shoat took away by tyrants, I'll soon be crawly with cooties." He bent his head back as if in hopes of avoiding a blow. "But by God, Johnson, lessen I miss my guess entirely, the dear thing's done took sweet on me."

James gave him a look of mild surprise. "You don't say."

Poovey blinked and hesitated, evidently trying to choose between falling inexplicably silent and going on to expose himself to further risk. In the end he found the courage to undertake the risk. He spoke the next words in a rush. "I *do* say. Why, she seeks me out of an evening, and *talks* to me. Talks so dulcet and mild, I hardly know what to make of it. Now I know I'm wrong in it, Johnson, wrong as wrong can be. She's yourn and none of mine, the Lord knows it, and you can take after me with a stick if you want to—reckon I might deserve a licking, holding the bold thoughts I do. But I can't help myself a-wondering . . . well, a-wondering . . . if she don't someway *fancy* me."

He paused, ready to bolt, but when James did not act, he resumed, a little more confidently than before. "Now I surely do fancy *her*." He showed his yellow teeth in a worshipful smile. "Cute little hop-o'-my-thumb. And her behaving so winsome and sly and flirty as to bring me on, why, I swear, it torments me terrible." He raised a hand in solemn disclaimer. "Not that she's dishonored you, not in the least; nor I neither, as far as that goes. Mind me now, we've conducted ourselfs none but pure." He drew up to his full height. "But I've come to tell you straight-out, like an honest fellow ought, no matter what you may make of it, nor how you may revile me: I reckon your Libby loves me, and not you at all."

James heard Poovey's earnest words feeling regret, irritation, and amusement all mixed together. It had always been *his* part to mind Libby. How could he think of giving her up now? Her welfare was his to preserve without blemish; it wasn't some trifle to be handed over to a poxed, carrotty-pated, skin-and-bones cackler like Poovey Sides, who might fail to guard it as it deserved. Yet he had lately grown somewhat fond of Sides, and he found amusing the elaborately respectful air Poovey had summoned to present his suit, so at odds with his normally obnoxious manner. And James had not forgotten his own disgraceful truth—that deep in the lowest and most fetid pit of his soul he longed—just as Charlie Cooke had longed—to yield up the load of care that had been draining his spirit for as far back as he could remember.

He shrugged. "She *does* like you, Poovey." He stood, pulled on his shoe, and rested his palm on Sides's sharp-boned shoulder. "And it would be right agreeable to me if the two of you was to set up together."

Poovey drew back, outraged, and shook off James's touch. "What sort of a vulgar, dished-up dog are you, anyways? To be parceling your wife about like she was cockish? Why, I ought to thrash you."

"She's not my wife, Poovey. She's my sister." Sides listened slack-jawed with amazement, and presently with growing delight, as James explained how he and Libby, at Captain Harris' urging, had formed their conspiracy. "We done it for fear of such rough fellows as might mean her harm," said James. "Of course, when we saw you and Blan and Dick and the others, we knew we had little to fear. But by then, 'twas too late to call back the ruse."

"By Jesus, Johnson," Poovey exclaimed, "I reckon you've made me the gayest soul living. Libby and me's a dead match, I'm a-telling you. She's as heavenly a chuck as may be found." Then he knit his brow in thought. "'Course she's right young yet—just a lamb, you might say. And these bad times of war *is* terrible hard on a tender nature." He pondered further, then added in superior fashion, "She's some brickly yet. It may be that, in the tempering, she's been cast in the water while yet too hot." He made a dismissing motion. "But that's no great flaw; I can put it right."

Poovey's unlooked-for success had swollen him with overconfidence and caused him to let slip the respectful air he had mustered to offer his case in the best light; James frowned at the criticism, which smacked of the red-hair's former presumption. "Libby's fine just as she is," he bristled. "Seems to me it's *you* could stand some tempering. I'm granting you the right to pay court to my sister, but I'm laying on a condition, and it's flat— you'd best set about improving *yourself* and not be sitting in judgment on others. And you must stop cutting them high shines the way you do. Any man that's aiming to make a connection with *my* family has got to cultivate himself some dignity."

Poovey saw he had trespassed. Reversing course, he begged James's pardon, pledging to behave henceforth only with the most commendable decorum. And for a day or two at least, he did. He even went so far as to take upon himself the awkward duty of explaining to the mess how and why James and Libby had deceived them, and did it with such skill that most of the others greeted the news only with japes and laughter.

"Well," chortled Dick Snow, "I admit I was wondering. Either you two wasn't doing the blanket hornpipe at all, or you'd figured a way to take your flyers mighty damned shy." Only Sam Ham was downcast; he seemed to have cherished his own designs on Libby, and of course had little use for Sides in any case. Sam fell into a sulk, and it would be the better part of a week before he shook off his pall of gloom.

A shipment of shoes arrived while they lay at Charlotte Court House. The new footgear, together with the Marylanders' shirts they had donned on Friday, made them feel somewhat more like proper soldiers; and the prospect of the long march to South Carolina no longer seemed quite so grim. James, hobbled by his raw foot, was delighted to don a pair of stout hobnailed brogans that could be fastened tight with lachets; the cheap buckled pumps his master had given him had been much too large and were literally falling apart from wear.

The shoes would be needed. On Sunday they marched to a ferry crossing on a river, where they halted while couriers came and went on lathered horses and the company officers convened in solemn discourse at the Baron's marquee. Something new was clearly in the offing. The troops waited and wondered. Finally a rumor spread—the Baron had got word that General Greene did not wish them to go Southward after all; rather, they were to remain in Virginia to help General Loff Yet fend off Corn Wallace.

They began to mutter. Had they toiled all this way to no good purpose? Must they now turn about and confront the enemy from whom they had so recently flown? They had; they must—that night the orders came down; tomorrow they were to retrace their steps. Charlie Cooke nodded with his worldly-wise air, "It's what I've been a-telling you—the sons of bitches is always a-whiffling—first it's one way, then it's t'other."

It was dismal news, coming just when many had finally reconciled themselves to going into Carolina. That night several of the Battalion, impatient with what seemed the indecision of their leaders and no doubt tired of beating the brush for the Baron's blacksnakes, deserted. Next morning General Lawson and his militia marched off in disgust, none knew whither. For the next nine days the wayward Battalion tramped the countryside alone. If they had a destination at all, it was a mystery to them; perhaps they did and it was only changing by the hour as the fortunes of the war shifted; James hoped so; he clung to his stubborn trust in the Baron's judgment.

They passed back through Charlotte Court House and from there into more alien climes. They made their way over narrow pot-holed roads strewn with rocks that threatened to break their ankles, passed through dark forbidding forests and over great tracts of empty land, with here and there a rude cabin or even, on occasion, a rare plantation on its eminence or, rarer still, a crossroads hamlet offering a meeting house, perhaps a smithy, an ornery, and some few ramshackle dwellings. Country folk and Negroes gawked at them as they straggled by; dogs barked at their heels; bony cattle watched them between the rails of fences and morosely lowed; frequent thunderstorms drenched them.

At length they arrived at another ferry—and here, disconcertingly, they realized they were gazing yet again upon the wide waters of the River James, only this time some distance downstream from the Arsenal they had quitted but days before. It seemed they had traveled in an enormous and pointless circle. The British, they learned, had abandoned the Arsenal and withdrawn toward Richmond. But rather than return to that post, Baron Stew-Ben now decided to ferry the troops over the James and march them across the county of Goochland to arrive at last—after two weeks of wandering in the wilderness like the Israelites of old—at Dandridge's Plantation in Hanover, above Richmond, where General Loff Yet had his headquarters.

By now the Marylanders' shirts the Baron had given them were ragged and soiled; the soles of the shoes they had gotten at Charlotte Court House had worn thin—James's brogans had dissolved like paper in the rains and his blister was inflamed again. He and Poovey threw themselves in the grass of Dandridge's yard and lay gasping in the heat. As they did, two officers of dragoons cantered by on fine blooded horses. James gazed with envy on their brass helmets with trailing horsehair plumes, their elegant uniforms of blue and red twinkling with silver epaulets and buttons, their crimson sashes, the sabers that clanked by their sides, their gleaming black high-topped boots. With what casual authority they bore themselves! These looked even grander than had Major Call; and so changed was James by now—so weary of his own lowly, plodding, demoralized state—that he saw these proud centaurs not as agents of the oppressive power he had once thought Call served, but as heroes worthy of praise—and yes, worthy  of imitation too. "By Heaven," he declared, "I'm tired of hauling my poor shanks and marrow-bones hither and yon over the land like some lost nomad of heathen Araby. I want to ride me a great horse."

"Me, too," said Sides.

And so, in time soon to come, they would.

Part ye Eighth

In Which General Greene Taſtes ye Bitterneſs of Gall

AFTER A FITFUL NIGHT THE GENERAL AWAKENED wheezing with quinsy, and rose to find that the long horseback ride from Winnsborough had aggravated his limp. He hobbled to breakfast feeling like some latter-day Methuselah. A cup of bitter coffee, a piece of stringy salt pork, a bowl of rice, and the jovial companionship of the dragoon officers somewhat restored the physical man, so much so that he resolved to stroll about the bivouac while awaiting the escort Colonel Washington was to send back for him. As at Ancrum's the men greeted him with a warm courtesy and he strove with his reticence to return it; he chatted with two of the regiment's washerwomen, finding to his surprise that one had served under his cousin Christopher at the defense of the Delaware River forts in 'seventy-seven.

Afterward he wandered the precincts alone. But about him still clung like a dark shroud his nightly dream of the storming of the Star Fort. He walked briskly in hopes of dispelling it. But in vain. Even in broad daylight the silent mouths kept on screaming at him, the bodies fell one across the other in sagging piles, he waded to his ankles in blood. Virginia had done that. Timid, perverse Virginia. Because the state had withheld the two thousand troops Greene had ordered to him months before, his army had been too weak to capture Ninety-Six.

Now again Virginia's need had trumped his own. Before leaving the main army, he'd had to countermand Steuben's orders to bring to him Colonel Gaskins' battalion of Continental recruits. Unlike the two thousand whose lack had cost him Ninety-Six at a time when the enemy threat was worse in Carolina, Gaskins' regiment was actually required in Virginia, where Cornwallis ravaged. There, Rawdon and Stewart were seen as pygmies next to the Modern Hannibal; this time Virginia's peril could not be denied. So he must muddle on with his little force as best he could. Virginia would never satisfy her obligation to his army till Cornwallis was beaten. And no matter how powerfully ambition inclined him to it, that was not a task for Greene. His proper scope was the whole of the Southern Department. It happened that his subordinates commanded in princely Virginia, a theater replete with glory, while he commanded in South Carolina, seat of squalid civil strife and the contending of forgotten armies led by obscure men. It would be the duty of Lafayette and Steuben to fight the part of the war the light of history shone on, while he fought the part covered in its shadows.

Presently the rising sun warmed him, eased his breathing, and lifted his mood, and he ambled over the fields to see what remained of Mrs. Motte's home. The damaged house occupied the summit of a steep hill dominating a plain that rolled off in all directions, gently descending, giving a view to the southward of a long patch of vivid green that was the swamp where the Wateree and Congaree joined. There was a forest at a distance, but closer to the house only a waste of tree stumps where the contending forces had chopped down the woods for breastworks and abatis during the siege. He had not seen the house since the day the fort fell to Lee and Marion some two months before; it had looked little more than a smoking hulk then. But today, though charred and mostly roofless, it kept much of its old-fashioned grandeur, brick chimneys proudly standing at either end, fronted by what South Carolinians called, as if they were transplanted Italians, a piazza.

A giant oak and an old sweet gum stood in the yard. The British had fortified the place, dug a fosse around it, used the dirt to make a palisaded earthwork, and fringed it with abatis. In making the palisade and abatis they had spared the oak and the sweet gum; but those had been scorched in the fire that Lee and Marion had been compelled to set. Mrs. Motte had given gracious assent to this necessary piece of arson. The patriotic lady had even lent the bow and fire-arrows—family keepsakes of a friend's visit to India—needed to kindle the conflagration. It was Mrs. Motte's inspiration of the arrows that Harry Lee had appropriated as his own at dinner, that evening of his arrival at Ninety-Six.

Studying the oak, the General judged it would live; there were sprigs of new growth here and there among the burnt branches. But the sweet gum was clearly done for. The palisade had been leveled and the ditch filled in, but the overgrown lawn was littered with the trunks and branches of the dismantled abatis now beginning to shed their bark. Further down the slope the trenches of the besiegers' parallels still yawned. Fort Motte, as it was known, had been the first post of the British to fall after Rawdon won the battle of Hobkirk's Hill; but then, surprisingly, Rawdon had decided to abandon Camden. Motte's capture had given Greene his first real inkling of the triumph the fates had laid out for him. Ah, but how elusive a triumph it now seemed!

Near midday Colonel Washington came in. The distant blare of a trumpet—a sequence of golden notes floating up from the low ground by the river—signaled his approach; and presently the little platoon of sixteen troopers debouched two-by-two over the summit of one of the southern hills, a compact body of drab men on darker horses, leaving behind a red pillar of dust that did not dissipate but hung so clotted and motionless in the sultry air that it looked capable of remaining suspended there, years hence, a permanent memorial of their passing. They advanced up the undulant plain through heat-shimmers that seemed to detach them from the earth—they appeared to float suspended, soaring on nothing, breasting flat filmy waves of ether that now and then stretched their figures eerily out of shape or robbed the horses of their legs or the troopers of their bodies. Then, as they drew nearer, the distortions ceased and the column composed itself into firm, lean outlines and the General could distinguish their every detail.

No two of them were attired alike; their coats were of every dull hue; some wore little leather helmets decorated with foxtails; some wore slouch hats, some knitted caps. A few had boots, fewer had shoes, others were barefoot. They formed a jostling, motley, dust-dimmed crowd, no brightness about them save the brass trim on a few of their sword scabbards, no banner or guidon to lend them color—Colonel Washington believed fighting men were too valuable to waste carrying about frivolous rags of silk. The burly Colonel himself rode at their front on a mud-brown charger, his once-white uniform soiled to a rusty orange. *Soldiers for the working day*, Greene thought.

The sight stirred him. How could it fail to? All those slender fellows, their utter poverty on display just as surely as their hard valor. They were his Huns, his little riding warriors, spry and sinewy, easy in the saddle, eating and sleeping and scouting and fighting on their equally small and agile horses, as energetic and enduring as so many wild dogs, as fiercely loyal as dogs too, and savage in battle, resistless, without mercy, and deadly sly on the outposts. He remembered reading somewhere that in ancient times fearful victims believed the rampaging Huns kept slabs of raw meat between their thighs as they rode, feeding themselves by tearing off bits that had been warmed by no more than their horses' body heat and their own; he could almost believe that of his own dragoons. *Had they any meat, that is.* Even the barbarians had meat. But not the Continental Army.

The two walked to the scorched oak, the shorter General limping along next to the looming corpulent long-legged Colonel in his dirty regimentals that looked too small for his massive frame. They sat together in the cool grass beneath the tree. Washington removed his crested helmet and set it aside; his short-cropped hair, soaked with sweat, lay close against his head in dozens of small wet triangles, its natural rufous hue darkened now to an oily black. With his customary winning familiarity he dragged off his high-topped boots and stretched his legs straight before him, displaying without the least embarrassment all ten of his toes protruding from a pair of worn-down stockings. The odor of his feet came heavily to them.

Greene smiled. The informality was not disrespect; it was Colonel Washington's way. Billy had never lost the easy, innocent, unaffected manner of his country boyhood. Had he gotten his learning at some refined institution like Dr. Witherspoon's academy at Princeton, instead of studying for the Anglican ministry under the Reverend Charles Stuart of St. Paul's Parish in rural Virginia, it would have been easy to think him still a careless schoolboy athlete and not a grimly efficient commander of dragoons.

The General's gaze fell again on Mrs. Motte's scarred mansion. She seemed to him a remarkable woman. He fell to pondering her act. "I wonder, Billy," he inquired of Washington, "whether you or I would burn our own house for the cause, as she did?"

Washington reflected for a time before giving him a dry grin and then an even drier laugh. "Isn't that exactly what we're doing?"

Greene saw his point. Indeed, whatever they possessed might as well be going up in smoke. He nodded with a chuckle. "Yes, of course. But I suppose it's generally believed the man's part *is* to put all at hazard for patriotism, or such other great virtue as may animate him. The female, on the other hand, we exempt from this rigorous standard. We accord her the right to impartiality in our conflicts; we assign her only the delicate duties of domestic life. We expect she will enjoy peace and safety, hearth and home, the nursery and the garden. She's not obliged to play the great game of honor that is ours."

"That's so," Billy agreed after a moment's consideration, but added, "If she loves us, though, she must endure our long absences, our distraction from her affections, and—if we're unlucky—our wounding or our death. Surely that's a great sacrifice."

"It is," Greene nodded, as Caty came vividly and painfully to mind. "But we force it on them, do we not? Or our wars do. We give them no choice. They must abide what we conceive is our manly duty." He remembered with a twinge how in taking up the Southern command he'd not been given a chance to visit Caty even for an hour, to say good-bye. He knew how that must have shattered her.

"Yet," he continued, "how often she plays our own game of honor, and how well! Mrs. Motte is not alone in her willingness to pay a dear price for a great cause. Our women are often our rivals in brave and selfless action. You've seen them, Billy, as I have. Just now I spoke with a washerwoman who was at Fort Mercer. She took up a musket and helped turn back the assault of Von Donop's Hessians. Last spring when we were retreating before Cornwallis, a woman in Salisbury gave me two pouches of hard money, her life's savings, when she heard me say the army was penniless. This war may be a Devil's playground of evil, but now and then it brings up an angel too."

"Maybe," said Washington, "if it brings up enough of 'em, we can go ahead and win the damned war." He smiled. "Divine reinforcements, you might say."

They joined in a little burst of merriment. Then the General grew serious. "What's the latest intelligence?"

"Rawdon's still falling back, towards Orangeburgh most likely," Billy said, luxuriously wriggling those smelly toes. "He's taking it in very slow stages, though, on account of the heat. He's burdened by a lot of sick and dying, some of his troops are mutinous, his teams are giving out. He's got no more than eighty cavalry, all of them in bad order, horses breaking down all the time. Parsons' troop's down there keeping after him."

"And the relief force?"

The Colonel ran a big hand over his head and used it to scrub vigorously at his scanty mat of damp hair. "General Marion's coming up by Monck's Corner. He reports Stewart's column just above Four Holes Bridge, making for Orangeburgh too."

"Where is Lee? I've had no word."

Washington gave a sigh that might as easily have been a show of saddle-weariness as of the exasperation Greene knew the Colonel really felt. "God knows," Billy shrugged. "Somewhere about Fort Granby between Rawdon and Stewart, I guess." He glanced off, hating to say a word against a brother officer. His nature was to be generous and amiable, but his sense of duty was prodding at his reticence. He plucked up some weeds, absently pulled them apart, let the pieces fall.

Greene held quiet, waiting him out. You didn't force Washington to do or say anything till he was satisfied of its rightness. They sat for a time, listening to the whirring of cicadas, the jeering of a distant blue jay, somewhere a dog barking. They watched a flock of crows circling high overhead in the empty sky. Presently the Colonel drew another weighty breath, and Greene knew he had made up his mind to speak with frankness. "I've looked all over," Billy admitted, "but so far I haven't located him. I rode around half of yesterday trying to make contact. Crossed the damned river twice. He sends no messages."

This explained Billy's contradictory dispatches from Howell's. Having confessed his doubts, the Colonel now sought to put the best face possible on the turn of events. "I assume he's doing what he can to slow Rawdon down and keep him from linking up with the reinforcements." Neither of them spoke of Lee's recent insult both to his commander and to his brother officer in the matter of Kirkwood's Delawares; the subject was too embarrassing. Not only had Harry insisted in a message to headquarters that he considered Kirkwood under his own orders regardless of Greene's repeated instructions to the contrary, he'd gone so far as to demand, much in the manner of a tutor assigning a dull scholar a task, that Greene make sure Washington knew of the situation lest, in his words, "a stupid jealousy arise."

Greene could see that Billy was unhappy to have been thus slighted; the envy and vainglory that drove Lee were so far from him that the behavior must seem a cruel mystery. It was the difference between the two, the difference between innocence and worldly conceit. "If we go down," Billy added, still trying to see the bright side, "I'm satisfied Colonel Lee will appear." He paused, then launched one wistful shaft of sarcasm: "He always does."

"Yes, very well," the General nodded, choosing outwardly to ignore the pensive sally but feeling the sting of it within. The Colonel was right, Lee would spring up just as soon as there was glory to be won; but by contrast the faithful Washington was usually to be found exactly where he was needed, whether glory awaited him or only tedium and obscurity. If Harry Lee was the spoiled son one dreaded to sire and Nat Pendleton the son one wished for, Billy Washington was the brother one had never had. All the Greenes were plodding fellows with counting-house minds; one could draw little inspiration from their dullness. But Billy was a model by whose example one might shape one's character. He would never rise as high as Lee; but he was the better man, and would go to his grave justified.

"Where," asked the General, somewhat gingerly in view of their part in the difficulty with Lee, "are Captain Kirkwood and his Delawares?"

Billy displayed no discomfort with the sensitive topic. "They crossed the Congaree at McCord's yesterday and went down to Thomson's Plantation. Kirkwood put them on horses there. They've moved down toward Brown's Mills, scouting. Myddelton's state troops are roundabout Orangeburgh."

Unsurprised, Greene nodded. The immediate task was to organize the stroke he now had in mind. "Here's my thinking," he said. "First I'd planned to hit Rawdon. But now I think it best to get round him with the horse—yours and Lee's, when we can find him, and the Delaware light troops—and link up with Marion, and maybe Sumter if he'll come"—at the reference to the refractory Gamecock, Billy pinched his plump little lips into a sour trap of disfavor, unwilling to extend to the nettlesome South Carolina brigadier the same forbearance he gave Harry Lee; and Greene chose to overlook the judgment, though it matched his own— "then descend on Stewart," he continued, "with our combined strength, whip *him* and prevent the junction."

Washington frowned his misgiving, but said nothing as Greene went on. "Stewart's fresher and moving swiftly; Rawdon, I collect, is slowing down. Stewart's force will be the smaller, assuming we can succeed in uniting with the South Carolinians, so we should be able to get the better of him. In the meantime General Huger and our main army will be following on, and once we've disposed of Stewart, we can turn back on Rawdon and catch him between our two forces. We should have assembled a pretty respectable little army by then."

Washington's frown deepened. "Stewart's got the Buffs, remember."

"Yes, but Rawdon's the larger."

"Rawdon's big, yes, but weak, his men are beat out, some are ready to quit. He's the nearer of the two. Why not concentrate on him first, then go after Stewart?"

But the General was insistent. "I'm firm in my decision, Colonel," he asserted, hoping his reasoning was as sound as he represented it. It was not so much that he had shaken off all his habitual doubts as that he had grown bored with them. His desire for a victory had at last overset his usual caution. Perhaps he even hoped this bypassing of Rawdon to come to grips with Stewart would be a daring move worthy of a Cornwallis. Would be as sublime. Would draw as much praise. Would raise him as high. Whatever its prospects, its very contemplation had lent him a salutary lift of the spirits, and he got to his feet now feeling better than he had in days. And at once Billy in his negligent fashion gave up his own contrary argument. "As you say, General." He bent to pull on his boots. "Will you take a refreshment of coffee with us before we start out?"

But within a few short days Greene would have reason to wish Billy had been less compliant.

Ever since arriving at Washington's headquarters, Greene had been looking forward to what he had come to think of as The Translation, the event that divided life in the dragoon camp into two very different parts, the part when Colonel Washington was absent, and the part when he was present and his fun-loving spirit translated all. Whenever the General visited a bivouac of his horse at a time when the Colonel was away, he was welcomed by officer and trooper alike with a cordial but distant correctness, a studied formality that recognized his high station yet was touched with an agreeable warmth of personal liking that never passed over into presumption. Nor was this exquisite decorum reserved for him alone. From the most senior troop captain to the meanest private, every man treated every other with the most exacting courtesy and the nicest regard for rank. One might be tempted to think the dragoon service a model of military discipline. But when Billy Washington broke on the scene, all that changed.

This day The Translation came as he and Greene approached the head-quarters fire where the pot of coffee boiled, when with a roar Billy threw himself on a passing corporal and engaged the fellow in a wrestling match. The corporal, evidently a frequent and able opponent, would have easily bested the Colonel had not Captain Swan joined in to lend an unfair hand. Swan and Washington together were able to subdue the corporal, who complained of being ill used by gentlemen who ought to know better, but by then news of the bout had spread and a boisterous circle had formed— officers and common soldiers mixed in the most unbecoming democ- racy—and further mayhem ensued. Swan and Captain Watts fought a fencing match with stalks of bamboo. The Colonel dashed a pail of water over a private, who retaliated by pelting his Colonel with clumps of horse manure. Even the formerly dour Lieutenant Elisha King crept up behind Washington and put someone's pet ground squirrel down the back of his coat. Headquarters degenerated into a carnival of pranks and pratfalls.

Greene enjoyed it immensely. It was true that a portentous obligation remained to be discharged and such a childish diversion could be seen as untimely and irresponsible—indeed, Washington was sometimes criticized for indiscipline. And it was also true that the Third Dragoons had an unfortunate history of being surprised at bivouac—at Tappan in New Jersey, where they had been nearly annihilated, at Monck's Corner and Lenud's Ferry in South Carolina last year. But of those failures none could be laid entirely at Billy's door; others had commanded. And anyhow, all that difficulty lay now safely in the past. Greene's expedient of assigning light infantry—usually the Delaware Continentals, sometimes the light company of Virginians—to guard their camps had lent the dragoons a useful reinforcement of foot and had freed the horse to range far and fast knowing their rear areas were secure.

Furthermore, the General knew how harsh and unremitting was the dragoon's daily lot, the privations he endured, the fears he lived with, the perils he faced when he met the enemy boot-top to boot-top and saber to saber. What was a little foolish mischief when measured against so ardu- ous a service? A certain idea of discipline might suffer when a colonel and a corporal wrestled together laughing in the dust, but another kind was also forged, a kind that inspired the fellow-feeling that made men willing to die for each other, a kind that Greene deeply envied.

Colonel Washington, covered with the dirt and litter of his rough play, his moon-shaped face flushing plum-red, caught up a tin cup and poured a round of coffee for himself, Greene, and his laughing officers. Merrily he cocked a dark blue triangular eye, spat a stream of blood from a cut lip, motioned for silence, and offered a bellowing toast: "To a Meeting of Friends!" It was a labored reference to the General's Quaker heritage; Billy's humor was inclined to be somewhat heavy. He may have laid aside his studies of Holy Writ, but at times his mind still repaired to the religious; and on these occasions he liked to use the language, doctrines, and rituals of faith to illumine his discourse, though in ways peculiar to himself, as now, mingling what he imagined to be the spiritual practices of the Society of Friends with the profane ceremonies of comradeship.

The notion was rather jarring, but graciously Greene bowed and drank down the gritty brew. "Surely," he smiled, "we do meet as the very best of friends." And the disheveled circle about him broke into cheers. He was among friends indeed. In another twenty minutes the camp was broken up, and he and Colonel Washington, at the head of the troops of Swan and Watts and the escort platoon from Parsons' troop that had come up with Billy from below the Congaree, were already on the road south, back toward the river. At last the game was afoot.

After some days they did find Lee's Legion, but by then Harry had given up his attempts to delay Lord Rawdon. He was camped near Beaver Creek, much farther north than the General would have expected to find him. He was in a sulk. He complained that he had heard nothing from Colonel Washington, nor indeed from anyone in authority, and so had felt compelled to move aside and give Rawdon his road. There had, of course, been an exploit by his cavalry under Captain Eggleston, in which two officers and forty-five of Lord Rawdon's foragers were captured, of which Harry immoderately boasted. But his own silence and inactivity during the period went unexplained, as did his arbitrary action in allowing Rawdon to pass, not to mention his insubordination over the command of Kirkwood's Delawares and his slur against Washington. The behavior was perplexing. In the circumstances, which were exigent, Greene chose not to make an issue of it; but he did mark it down for later thought—something, he divined, seemed not entirely right with Light-horse Harry Lee.

General Pickens came up as promised, with five hundred of his fierce back-country militia, but Greene found it necessary to detach him again back toward Ninety-Six to watch the garrison there. He then turned his mind to Stewart's relief column; he would make a cast at it as soon as Huger reached Beaver Creek with the main army. But in the end he was no more able to fall on Stewart than he had been to get round Rawdon. The reason was simple—Stewart gave Marion the slip and made his way by unfrequented roads into Orangeburgh where Rawdon, whom Lee had left free to move unimpeded, was presently able to join him notwithstanding the weakened state of his command.

General Sumter, of course, failed timely to appear. Instead, he wrote to Greene, he had felt a necessity to tour his northern regiments; there was also a lamentable shortage of swords and ammunition and other equipments. Greene ground his teeth in impotent rage. Huger with the main army advanced to Beaver Creek on schedule. But by then Cruger's refugee column, which had abandoned Ninety-Six before Pickens could head it off, was filing into Orangeburgh, raising the British strength there to twenty-five hundred. Eventually the time did come when Greene, with all his scattered detachments at last united, even the dilatory Sumter, commanded a force equal to the enemy's. But Rawdon, with his advantage in artillery, was able to transform the little town on the Edisto into a citadel that would cost a feast of blood to carry.

Peering through his telescope at the fortified brick jail and frame courthouse of Orangeburgh crowning a low hill shaded by Pride-of-India trees, Greene once again found himself measuring the limits of his own fortitude, searching inside himself for the *necessary severity* that Anthony Wayne had invoked, aspiring to the awesome resolve of Lord Cornwallis at Guilford. His provisions were short; the men exhausted—some had marched over three hundred miles in twenty-two days; disease riddled his army; memories of the last assault at Ninety-Six hung about him like ghouls.

Someday, he thought, *I would like to meet Cornwallis. Might we not talk as gentlemen who have come to know something of one another across the rack and ruin of war?* Know and, yes, not know? Did not each harbor mysteries yet to be revealed, each to the other? Were there not questions that the bloody intimacy of conflict had still not answered? Did not the Earl wonder why and how Greene had behaved as he had during the long retreat of last winter and spring, just as Greene now sought to know whence came the Earl's remorseless power of decision? Greene longed to hear what reply the Modern Hannibal might make to such an inquisition.

But then he thought, *Perhaps he would say nothing. Perhaps there would be naught to say.* Perhaps the question itself would seem meaningless, would in fact *be* meaningless. If a man has it in him to order the unspeakable, to kill his own men as well as the enemy's, then surely it is an inherent and instinctive quality, arising not from volition, not from will, is not taught or learned, maybe is not even understood, but proceeds unconsciously, without the mediation of active thought, from the deepest place in every man, from the very seed and kernel of him, burgeoning forth unbidden, unexamined, unacknowledged, yes, bursting from him *void of all manner of design and totally the effect of a natural disposition.*

If that were true—and Greene suspected it was—then the Modern Hannibal could not enlighten him, even were they to meet in the courteous discourse he had imagined. He, Greene, could relate his own motives to the Earl, for his acts were always the fruit of his conscious deliberations; but the Earl, a man of pure remorseless martial instinct, must meet Greene's eager questions only with the profoundest silence. It would have been a mistake even to ask. *To ask,* he thought, *would be to betray weakness.*

Perhaps Billy Washington had been right. Perhaps he should have struck at the nearer Rawdon instead of the more distant and elusive Stewart. Perhaps he had been stubborn. Surely he had been impulsive. Impulsive as at Hobkirk's, impulsive as at Ninety-Six when he'd called back the assault. Impulsive in the aggressive, impulsive even in timidity. *When will I get it right?*

So he stood down from Orangeburgh and turned his back on his enemy. Rawdon and Stewart and Cruger would retreat to the vicinity of Charles Town; they were too depleted to do otherwise. Greene had freed all of South Carolina save its capital. Once more he had won by perseverance what he could not win on the field of battle. But again, he feared, he had also shrunk from the gravest of his choices.

He had been told of a place east of the Wateree called the High Hills of Santee, a chain of thickly wooded, well-watered heights locally famed for their medicinal springs and salubrious atmosphere. After maneuvering for weeks amid the scorching plains and sickly swamps of the South Carolina back parts, the General thought the place sounded like an Eden. So with the British all driven to a distance he resolved to go there and camp awhile to examine what seemed the hollowness of his achievements, to search them for meaning, to recruit his famished soul, and to allow his poor, exhausted, sun-seared troops to refresh, refit, and gather strength for the tests to come.

They crossed the Congaree at McCord's Ferry and followed a narrow causeway over the vast canebrake of the Santee bottom, the tasseled plumage of the cane-tops eddying about them like the tides of a green sea. Cypresses and gum trees loomed high above the slow toss and roll of the cane, each festooned with the draperies of moss that had become more common the deeper they penetrated into the lower country, the great trunks clustered round with holly, water oak, laurel, and gall-bush. Scarlet tanagers flickered among the boughs like tropical flowers improbably endowed with the power of flight; mockingbirds whistled at the passing columns; deer fled from them across weedy heaths; once a wildcat hissed at Greene from a low-hanging branch.

The hills themselves proved more than equal to their friendly reputation. They rose high above the foul bed of swamp that marked the joining of the rivers. Here the army tasted airs of delicious coolness. Groves of oak and chestnut gave cool shade, springs and brooks abounded, and all about lay fields of Indian corn and cotton and grain miraculously still under cultivation despite the disorders that had racked the tormented land for years. In the breezy woods the army lay down to rest for the first time in seven months. And the General, sitting in the shade of a tree, at last was able to write to Caty:

> Before this I fupofe you are at Wefterly, I wifh I was with you, free from the buftle of the World and the miferies of war. My nature recoils at the horid fcenes which this Country affords, and longs for a peaceful retirement where love and, fofter pleasures are to be found. Here turn which way you will, you hear nothing but the mournful widow, and the plaints of the fatherlefs Child; and behold nothing but houfes defolated, and plantations laid wafte. Ruin is in every form, and mifery in every fhape. The heart you fent me is in my Watch, and your picture in my bofom.

Part ye' Ninth

In Which a Young Man Witnesses a Festival of Death

TWO DAYS AFTER REACHING DANDRIDGE'S PLAN-
tation the Battalion broke camp again, and James and Poovey found
themselves marching south, this time as part of General Loff Yet's army.
It was a small army, militia mostly, reputed to be half the size of the
enemy's powerful force of regulars and Provincials. They moved by night
so it would be harder for the British to see how few were coming against
them; at least that was the account some gave. Starting at dusk, they
would march six or seven hours then pitch camp shortly before dawn
and rest till evening.

At the finish of the first stage they bivouacked at a mill belonging to a
Mr. Simms; next evening they set out for Richmond. Corn Wallace had
abandoned the capital and was said to be withdrawing down the peninsula between the rivers York and James toward Williamsburg. It looked
like a retreat, but nobody knew why Corn Wallace would want to back
away; with his numbers, he could lick Loff Yet any time he chose to stand
and fight. Whatever he was doing, they had to follow.

It had been a spring of strangely turbulent weather, parching heat one
day, piercing cold the next, violent thunderstorms sweeping over the land,
once even a freakish June snowfall blown at them on a howling wind. In
their various camps under the cover of nothing but sheds and booths of
brushwood they had felt the brunt of it all. Now they trudged down the
muddy track toward Richmond in the dark under a pelting downpour.

The rain was tepid and the air of the night hung thick about them; they
were wilting in its warm damp, their rags of clothing clung to them sodden
from the rain and from their own sweat. Steam boiled off them, the labor
of forcing their way through the glutinous mud sapped at their already
depleted energies. Their spirits drooped, and not alone from the miseries
of the march—for they had a new commander now; Colonel Gaskins had
been displaced.

"What the hell's his name again?" demanded Poovey Sides, using his
frayed cuff to wipe moisture from his face—the Maryland shirts the

Baron had given them as they passed through Charlotte County, touted as linsey-woolsey, had proved to be of the cheapest shalloon and were rotting on their backs. Nor had the sturdy-looking footgear distributed at Charlotte Court House lasted any better—many in the ranks trudged barefoot in the gruel of the road; those few still shod had used twine or hanks of cloth to bind together the separated soles and uppers of their worn-out brogans. Sides himself was shoeless, and so was James.

"Febiger," answered Charlie Cooke, one rank behind.

Sides gave out a derisive snort, blowing a spray of rainwater. "Febiger? What sort of a goddamned name is Febiger?"

"I heard a fellow say he was a Danish man," James answered with some testiness, slogging alongside the ginger-hackle. Haggard, wet to the skin, legs cramping from the toil of moving in the heavy mud, he was growing irritable.

Sides hooted. "What in the name of my two dangling whirligigs's that? Is it some damned bloody Waldecker or High German or somesuch?"

"Why," offered Blan Shiflet, from the rank in rear of Charlie, "I reckon it's somebody from Denmark."

"Where by God is Denmark, then? Is it in Virginia? If it's in *Old* Virginia, I ain't never heard of it. And if it's by the Proclamation Line, it can't be much account, and he can't neither, not even if he *is* a goddamned colonel."

"There ain't no Proclamation Line any more," Charlie Cooke announced.

Sides was shocked. "There ain't? What in hell happened to it?"

"The Congress abolished it."

"Done what?"

"Abolished it."

"Got shet of it," Shiflet explained. "The whole West's open to settlement."

"Well shit-fire," crowed Sides, "if I'd have known that, why, I'd be laying up in them faraway mountains right now, with a parcel of Injun maids playing with my pecker and trimming my toenails, 'stead of wading in this goddamned muddy road."

"It's your *pecker* they'd be cutting," Cooke pointed out. "Them Cherokee fancy the Bloodybacks."

James bristled to hear the red-hackle speak so vulgar when he was betrothed to Libby, but managed to hold his tongue, knowing Poovey's bluster to be but an ill-made cover for a better nature than he wished to show. "Still," Sides blared, "Where's Denmark?"

"Hell," put in Sam Ham, pleased to give him disagreeable news. "Denmark ain't even in America."

Poovey twisted his head backward to fix a glare on Sam, marching next to Shiflet. "'Tain't?" he exclaimed. "Then where in your mama's soppy feak *is* it?"

Sam would not answer, but only favored Sides with a smug grin. Dick Snow, from the file to Sam's rear, bowed his shoulders against the rain and spoke up instead: "Somewheres over the water, is what I heard."

Sides swung back forward, disgusted. "Do tell? Well, goddamn it, is this the Army of the United States of America or is it some kind of hidey-hole for every broke-down, cork-brained, done-up, and disgraced army officer in Europe? Why, already we got that Lafayette—he's a Frenchie—and Gates and Lee, old Redcoats the brace of 'em—and Maxwell, he's a damned Scot—hell, we got more British Generals than the British do. We had Steuben, that was a goddamned Hessian—thank the Christ *he's* gone"—the Baron, afflicted by gout and denounced on all sides for having abandoned the Arsenal stores, had obtained a leave and departed for Charlottesville, to everyone's relief but James's, who missed him unashamedly. The other men of the Battalion, having been marched and countermarched countless miles to no sensible purpose, wearied to death of beating the underbrush for the blacksnakes whose vile meat the Baron relished so unreasonably, had given up the last vestige of affection the old Prussian had temporarily won from them on the drill fields of the Arsenal. "Now," Poovey grumbled on, "we've got a damned colonel that's a . . . what?"

"A Dane," James reminded him, turning surlier now. He knew Poovey didn't care one way or another about Colonel Gaskins, or about Colonel Febiger either. The bran-face only wanted to complain. But the complaints were striking closer to James than he liked.

"A Dane, whatever that is," Sides sneered. "Febiger. Jesus Christ, is there such a thing under Heaven as an *American* officer above the rank of captain?"

James thought he would try to move the conversation in a more positive direction: "There's General Washington."

"Where's *he*?" Poovey burst out. "Is he here? Where's Morgan and Scott and all them natural-born *American* generals a-body keeps hearing about? No, we're commanded by a gang of dilapidated foreigners. That Muhlenburg, he's a Virginia general; but he ain't no more a Virginian than I'm from the Summer Islands. What in hell's he?"

"He's a Dutchman, I expect," mused Blan Shiflet.

"See," Sides whooped triumphantly, "another Hessian, to go with Steuben. And what about Armand's Legion? What's Armand? He's another Frog."

"Well, the French *are* on our side in the war," James pointed out, his temper rising. He had recently learned that France had cast its lot with

America and had thought it a fine gesture, one that merited praise and not abuse.

"*On our side?* Hell, they're in *charge*. They're running the whole concern. Why, I'll give odds one of them foreigners's presiding in the Continental Congress right while we're like to drown in this damned rainstorm."

James decided he had heard enough. He turned on Sides hotly. "Well, *I* was born in Scotland, wasn't I? And *I'm* as good an American as you are, ain't I? Or are you fixing to deny it and start a scrimmage and get your foolish head broke?" In his sudden rage he stopped dead, and the queue of troops behind him piled up against his obstruction like a collapsed squeezebox; men staggered and slipped in the mud, musket barrels clashed together ringing like discordant chimes, a chorus of swearing broke out. The whole back half of the column drew to a halt about him and stood bewildered in the dark and rain. Up ahead, James heard Captain Harris bark an angry question, and from behind came the new sergeant's answering squall of outrage. But he was too choked with anger to care. He was shaking, he felt light of head; he leaned at Sides and yelled into his face, "*Take it back, I say!*"

Poovey stood dumbfounded and uncomprehending. "Take what back? Why, why, Johnson," he stammered, "what's ailing you? I've said naught against you. . . ." He plucked at James's sleeve, he spoke in a wheedling tone, "Why, I meant no offense, Johnson; you know I never meant to slight you; why, you're my chum."

James imagined he heard low cunning and sly calculation in the words—Poovey must stay in his good graces at all costs on Libby's account—and they called up in him an awful wrath. He struck the hand aside. He heard the squelch of the sergeant's oncoming feet, heard his roar, "*What in the name of bleedin' Jesus is going on up there?*" and, as if these were encouragements instead of warnings, he threw himself blindly forward, drove the point of his shoulder into Sides's bony chest, hurled all his weight into the little man, drove himself at him with short chopping thrusts of his legs; and, entangled in firelocks and canteens and haversack straps and each other's arms, they both pitched into the muck of the road's shoulder and commenced to struggle heavily there. But weak from hunger and from marching, they flailed with no more force than two infants playing in a crib.

Their fellows, hoping for a rousing fight to break the monotony of the march, gathered expectantly; but so poor a showing did James and Poovey make that the others soon turned aside, disappointed and embarrassed by its futility. Presently the sergeant thrust his way into the dispersing group. "If this is a damned scrape," he roared, "save it for the Redcoats!" Then, seeing the two writhing vainly in the mire, he spoke an oath of contempt and fetched each a stout kick. "Get up out of that!" he bellowed. "Clean them muskets and scrape off that mud and fall in."

James and Poovey ceased their striving and unsteadily stood. The sergeant regarded them sourly. "If you was better scrappers I'd let you settle accounts some evening after Tattoo, then give you both a fair flogging. But seeing you're nothing but a pair of cunny-thumbed sister-boys, I'll have you ridin' the wooden horse, soon as we stop and make camp. You're a shame to the practice of arms, the both of you, wallowin' about like you was sodomites. If you want to play the back-gammon, it's one thing. But if you're a-going to wrangle, why, by God, *wrangle!*"

At Dandridge's, admiring splendidly appareled dragoon officers riding past, they had wished themselves astride prancing chargers. Now their longing for the mounted service had been fulfilled, but in the most absurd and degrading way: The steed they rode in tandem was a variant of the sawyer's horse, though towering three times higher than that homely instrument of James's former craft and singularly ill-made of rough boards clapped together by a detail of soldiers under the sergeant's uncaring eye. Four legs of unequal length propped it up, but at a raked angle that made it impossible for them to hold themselves erect without a continual straining for balance, and a crosspiece—a narrow plank set on edge—spanned it. This knife of wood was their saddle, and it was their torment. Arms bound behind them, feet lashed together, their heavy muskets tied athwart their ankles so as to bear their weight down harder on the crosspiece, they felt themselves so much meat being slowly split in twain for the dressing. The single lucky feature of their plight was that the rain had stopped.

They were hoisted in the yard of a place called Burrell's Ornery. Roundabout the little inn and its outbuildings lay the awakening army, a constellation of campfires dimly glowing in the dawn mists that clung to the woods on either side of the Richmond highroad, a murmurous congregation astir in the surrounding dark breathing out its constant noise—the neighs and coughs of horses, the lowing of oxen, the clatter of wagons, the talk and laughter of hundreds of men, scraps of song, even the squeal of a flute. Yearningly they eyed the distant fires and craved that warmth and company, for the humid dawn searched their bones and they shivered in their wet rags.

James sniffed the air. The morning smelled of saturated soil, of mold and mildew and every kind of foully luxuriant growth, of the everlasting wet. Poovey, hunched repulsively close against his back, gave off an odor too, clammy and rank, like the slime on the shell of an old turtle. His rancid breath blew on the nape of James's neck. The fog touched them with its veils of damp. Sides stirred and groaned. "How come you to light into me anyways?"

James was more than ready with his answer. He had been thinking about it a long time. "I'll tell you why," he cried. "You tire me out with your everlasting gab, is what. I was sore from walking, my stomach was griping, I've got no shoes, I'd stepped on a stone and bruised my foot. And you was going on about foreigners; it made me think of home. I remembered my Ma and Da, that fetched me here to this country from Scotland so we'd have . . . better'n what we had. Hell, half this army's immigrants. You was reviling that. So I lost my temper. But you *made* me. You think you're so damned clever, but you're just a silly boaster, is all you are."

"Well, I can say what I please," was Poovey's dogged reply. "I don't have to beg your leave to speak my mind, even if I *am* going to marry your sister. Why, you're a worse tyrant than this damned King we're a-fighting."

"I don't know as I like it anymore that you're going to marry my sister."

"You blessed it, didn't you? I come to you and said my piece and you give me your blessing. Are you fixing to break your pledge to me?"

"I'm thinking on it mighty hard."

"Well, you just do whatever suits you, don't you? Your word's about as good as a pinch of owl shit. You give it, you take it back. Piss on you. One of my teeth's loose. You knocked it loose."

"I wish it had been your whole head."

Sides let a deal of time pass. Then he expressed himself in a suspicious growl. "Know what I'm a-thinking? I'm a-thinking you're so partial to Libby you can't *let* her free. You want to keep her by you. You covet her so, you can't stand her liking somebody else."

"When I get off this contraption, I *will* knock your head loose. 'T'ain't Libby. It's *you*. You ain't fit."

"Not fit how?" Sides demanded.

"I don't know. It just seems that way to me."

Poovey mocked him. "*Seems* that way. Tyrant. King James. You get to say what's what, I guess."

"I'm her brother."

"You ain't her master, though. She's done *had* one of those."

The remark gave James such a turn that he forgot to be angry. He hesitated; the hateful vision of Alexander Chenowith took shape in his mind. He frowned. *Have I been holding her captive just like he did?* Then it seemed important to fend the idea off. He replaced it with another. "I can't tell if you love her."

"I do love her. I say it all the time."

"I can't tell if you know the difference between loving a pig and loving Libby. You talk about both of them the same."

"Well, goddamn it, I *do* love her. Love her till I'm fit to bust a gut." He stopped and made a small noise in his throat that seemed to come from the labor it cost him to search for exactly what he wished to say. "Why," he went on after a moment, "sometimes it comes on me so full I'm . . . like to faint. I never felt that way about that shoat. Now I *liked* that shoat. It was a right cute shoat. But Libby . . . well, I just love her. You can believe it or not."

"Well," James declared, "I don't."

But Sides didn't seem to have heard him. He went on following his line of thought as if James had never spoken at all, and he sounded unsure of himself; it was like he had no notion where his thinking might take him. "I had me that shoat. I enjoyed it to go a-rooting under my arm or in my pockets. I enjoyed to pet it. I lied to folk and said I didn't favor it, claimed I only kept it about me to fetch the lice and such. But I liked it more'n I made out. But it'd run away. Ever chance it got, it'd run. When the sergeant made me give it up, why, it run right off."

He stopped and James reckoned he was thinking some more, and this time James thought he wouldn't interrupt him or scorn him but just let him say on and see where that took them. "I don't think Libby'd do that," Poovey continued after a little spell. "Run off, I mean. I think I could take care of her and she'd not run off." Against his back James felt a faint jiggle pass through the red-hair's frame and guessed the fellow had given his head a musing shake. "I don't know," Poovey said. "Nobody much ever cared for me. Or showed me how to do, y'see? How to do . . . whatever it is. Why, if I knew, I'd do it right off."

He fell still again and there was another opportunity for James to disparage him, but James passed it by, partly out of curiosity; he'd never heard Sides go on this way before. He hardly knew what to make of it. He wanted to think it was some sort of a lie or a trick to win his sympathy, but it sounded so heartfelt he wasn't sure. So he waited, and presently the red-hair finished in a murmuring way, "I'm full, I know that. What's inside of me weighs as much as a cartload of horseshoes. And it was Libby put it there."

This time when he got quiet it seemed to be for good. In the silence James reflected. From their first meeting Sides had offered little to recommend himself. Yet at Charlotte Court House James had accepted the scamp as a suitable mate for Libby. Why? A guilty truth squirmed serpent-like in a cranny of his soul; he had been ready to give up his sister because, in the moment of the asking and the granting, the burden of her care had felt irksome to him and he had wanted to throw it off as he had seen death throw off Charlie Cooke's burden on the shore of the Rivanna. He had wanted to be free of her; he had wanted to be free and make his own way at last. He had been selfish; he had betrayed his promises to his Ma and Da, his promises to Libby herself.

But as soon as he gave his pledge to Sides he had seen again with terrible clarity the shallowness of Poovey's character and how important was his own duty to Libby and how deeply he loved her; and he began at once to regret his decision. Though he and Sides had managed over time to strike up a kind of quarrelsome, pestering friendship, still he had felt ashamed of his sordid choice every hour since. Now, improbably, Sides had spoken of love. "What's your little scrap of skimpy love amount to?" James stormed at him.

But it was Libby who gave the answer. "*I* know what it is," she declared, making her way through the tall dew-soppy grass at the edge of the yard, holding her skirts high enough to show her striped stockings that had fallen down around her ankles. She was wearing a shabby surtout and a man's felt hat with a sprig of fresh greenery stuck in the band. She stopped at the foot of the wooden horse and set her fists on her hips like somebody's old granny. "What in the world're you two doing up there?" she demanded. "Our wagon broke a wheel and we was all night a-mending it; we just now come in, and the fellows in the mess said you was both under punishment. What'd you do?"

Poovey was quick to tell. "He beat on me, is what he did. Loosened a tooth, too."

"You was *fighting?*"

James tried to make small of it. "We rassled around some. Sergeant didn't like it."

"Well, I declare. What you got to fight about?" Libby's face sharpened with suspicion. "Sounded like it was me."

"It *was,*" Sides hurried to explain. "He don't want you to marry me no more." He yelled into James's ear. "King James. Tyrant."

"That's right!" James told Libby in a flare of rage. "You can find yourself a better husband than this fool. Sam Ham likes you, I can tell. Truth is, all the fellows in the mess admire you. Why, you could have your pick of 'em."

Libby nodded with a sober air. "Sure I could. But I picked Poovey. And you gave your blessing, too."

Poovey unleashed a whinny of disdain. "He's a-going *back* on his god-damned blessing. His blessing ain't worth a tinker's fart."

Temper rose in Libby's face. "You listen to me, James Johnson. I picked Poovey on account of I wanted him. *You* ain't marrying him, I am. Poovey *needs* me. Don't you, Poovey? And I need him. I don't need Sam Ham or Dick Snow or anybody else on this earth but Poovey. His heart's right. He'll look after me as good as you."

James felt a slash of remorse, then another of sorrow. Look after her?

Had he done that? Had he shielded her from the pain of Ma and Da dying? Had he saved her from Chenowith's ravishment? From seeing Janet perish? He opened his mouth to deny what she had said of him, but she gave him no space to make utterance. "And yes," she continued, "Poovey's full of love, just like he says. I'll have the yield of that. It'll content me. And you're near played out a-doing for me. You don't say so, but it's true. And I don't want it to get worse. For if it does, one day you'll come to grudging me."

"I don't grudge you," James protested. He cast about helplessly for a way to explain what he felt. But the best he could say was, "You've been hurt in this world, and I couldn't stop it happening. If I couldn't, how can Poovey, who's less even than me?"

Libby grew solemn. "This here," she told him, "this that's happening— it's all there is. Can't nobody can stop what happens. You can't, Poovey can't, I can't. Ward off one thing; another comes. All the things that happen, why, they're just what happen. We can't stop each other getting hurt. We just make out the best we can. You and me, we've done that, all this time till now. Me and Poovey, well, we can do it too."

Poovey had held quiet while they talked. Now his patience found its end. "I'm mighty pleased you two are coming to a bargain on me," he burst out, "but if they's to *be* a wedding, and if I'm to do my husbandly offices afterwards, then somebody'd better get me off'n this damned old edgewise board, else I can't work my yard nohow." This made Libby laugh, and in another minute James was laughing too.

That day they started not after sunset but in early afternoon—word traveled along the files that Corn Wallace had sacked Richmond, and the generals were anxious to get to the capital and assess its damage: Richmond was a great depot of supplies for the army. Though his thighs were raw from riding the wooden horse, James was glad to be marching in daylight, though after the night's rain the weather did turn broiling hot and that was a trial; and the country was sparsely settled and there were few wells or springs, so they suffered for lack of fresh water as well as from the punishing sun. But traveling in the dark was a worse aggravation; you were forever tripping over unseen roots, the fellow behind you kept stepping on your heels, unexpected stops made you collide with the file in front, you were blind and helpless and vulnerable to injury from ridiculous accidents. Rather than that, James preferred the heat and dust and thirst. But before long he had good cause to wish they had moved by night after all.

Near the outskirts of Richmond they passed two Negro men lying by the shoulder of the road. At first it seemed the blacks might have sunk down there to rest from the discomfort of the burning day, but since they sprawled not in cool shade but on open ground in full blinding light it quickly became obvious they were not lounging there but had been laid low by some misfortune. The head of the column overtook the two; and James, craning out of his file to look ahead, was surprised to see the first ranks quickly veer out of line and move into a wheat field opposite where they lay, returning to the road only after passing them. "Fellows up there must not like niggers much," Poovey remarked. "But that's a hell of a long way around just to keep from smelling a couple of niggers."

James thought that an unworthy sentiment and was preparing to reproach Sides for it when a ghastly odor did in fact strike them too. "*What's that?*" Poovey gagged. "Even niggers don't stink like that." They marched on leaning against the stench much as they might have pushed at some resisting physical force. So powerful was it that as they approached the recumbent blacks it bent them out of the road and into the trampled wheat field following the same path the head of the column had beaten out. Passing the Negroes at a distance, his hand over his mouth and nose, James looked at them askance. "*Holy Jesus,*" murmured Sides.

They were naked and as bony as skeletons, and their dark skins were covered with the suppurating sores of smallpox on which swarms of flies were torpidly feasting. One lay on his side in the fixed heavy stillness of death, arms gathered at his narrow chest as if to ward off the last eternal chill; flies clustered on his open eyes. The other was alive but barely so. As the soldiers tramped past him he stirred very weakly, only enough to disturb his shroud of flies causing it momentarily to rise in a buzzing mass before settling over him again with a terrible inevitability; he sagged back with a kind of hideous languor and lay still, watching the passing troops with huge glistening eyes. Once his ravaged lips moved and with a fatal sigh seemed to ask for water. Nobody obliged him.

They tramped on, sickened. Nobody knew what to say, not even Poovey. Half a mile on, the smell came at them again and they pushed against it as before and presently neared a place where more Negroes lay lining the roadside, only this time there were two women and a child as well as several men. Most wore a few scraps of clothing, but one wench and the child were naked like the first two. The child and an old mammy lay stiff in death, but the rest were still alive, though disfigured beyond belief. The plague of flies covered them all like one dark living pulsing blanket. The sufferers peered up at them with the same entreating eyes and begged them for pity and ease with whispery voices that were so faint and frail they might have been the voices of folk already dead and pleading from beyond the grave. Revolted, the soldiers stepped gingerly around them, many swearing, some kicking out savagely to ward off their plucking hands.

There were more and more of them, some lying in orderly rows, some stacked like cordwood, a few still upright and able to stumble into the road beseeching help as the men broke formation and fled from them in terror or brutally clubbed them down with musket butts. Each wore an appalling leopard's-coat of open sores. For some reason James took note for the first time in his life of the variety of their color—cocoa, coffee, chocolate, purple-black, peach, apricot, fawn-brown, every dusky hue. *Queer*, he thought, *not one's white.* Presently Captain Harris came down the column, raw-eyed and sweating, carrying his spontoon in one hand and an uncorked bottle in the other. He explained the mystery. "Leave 'em be, lads," he was saying, "leave 'em be. 'Tis the sickly season hereabouts. The niggers of this district is all poxed as hell, and the Lobster's dragged the poor devils into 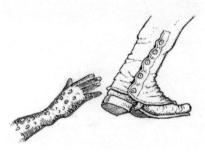 the road to infect us." He passed on, his voice like a chant, "Leave 'em be, lads, leave 'em be . . . ."

The whites of the place, they learned, had withdrawn to healthier climes upcountry, leaving their servants to the ravages of the lowland contagion. James was confounded to hear this. Who was worse, he wondered, the slave owners who had abandoned these wretches to a pestilence, or the British who had so criminally used the sick and dying as weapons against their enemies? He abhorred both alike, but could not help loathing the Negroes too. Their fingers flickered about his feet and ankles; so wasted were they that their touch felt no more substantial than the breaking of cobwebs. Their unendurable eyes followed him as he tramped by them; he shivered with horror and dread of them, and his every glance ahead revealed that the road to Richmond was bordered with more and more of the dead and dying.

Death was no stranger to him. It had entered his life when he was barely old enough to know it for what it was. It had struck on all sides of him ever since. It was as real as its opposite, living—maybe it was even more real. Death was all around, all the time, in this hard world. War had only presented him with new forms of it, like Janet's, and he had soon put that by him too. But he had never seen such a festival of death as this. He knew some folk doubted Negroes were people at all and denied they possessed any more of an immortal soul than a cow or a chicken. James didn't know about that. He'd never cared much for the blacks one way or another. But hell, it would have bothered him to watch this many cows or chickens die all at once, much less this many Negroes. And he couldn't help wondering whether Chenowith hadn't valued him and Libby about the same as a cow or a chicken; maybe in like circumstances the old bastard would have laid them out by some roadside too. It seemed like a calamity any way you looked at it, and all he wanted was to get free of it just as quick as he could and try not to think of it any more.

Part ye' Tenth

In Which General Greene Confiders
ye Difpenfations of Hiftory

REPOSE: SUCH A FINE WORD. HE SPOKE IT WITHOUT sound, his tongue softly rising and retreating, his lips touching to a brief close, then rounding to form the long fading second syllable, and finally the tongue lifting again to release a tranquil sibilance: Re-*pose*. Camp of repose—he had always loved that phrase, one of the few in military parlance that rested pleasantly in the mouth. And how well it suited this lovely spot called James's Old Field, in the High Hills of Santee.

Seated on a folding chair, he looked up from the seemingly bottomless heap of papers on his camp desk to gaze for an agreeable moment on the scene before him, which the raised fly of his marquee cut to the shape of a sunlit triangle—a sweep of rolling green meadow dotted with the brush huts and tents of the army, a grove of lush chestnuts just beyond, a patch of bright blue sky above fleeced with robust summer clouds, off-duty troops strolling at their ease, washerwomen hanging wet clothes on cords strung between saplings, children gamboling at play. As he watched, a breeze lightly stirred the tree-leaves and then the few patches of meadow grass not yet trodden flat by the soldiers; and presently it stole on to him where he sat, touching him with its refreshing coolness, stirring the ends of his hair. With a deep breath he drew in its sweet flavor.

It was a balm, this beautiful place. The army reveled in its peace and plenty. It was healing the hurts and strains of bodies abused by eight months of ceaseless campaigning. Now at last, forage could be gathered, hunger and thirst appeased, sickness treated, long-festering wounds bound up, and rest—precious rest—could begin to restore depleted spirits.

But there could be no rest for the mind of the commander of the army. He longed to yield to an indolence of thought that would comfort the brain even as the peace of James's Old Field had begun to revive the flesh. But it could not be. Too many matters pressed him. Sighing, he leaned once more to the sheaf of papers.

Atop the stack, glaring up at him like a bill of indictment, was a letter of Colonel William Davies, head of the Virginia War Office, dated June seventeenth at Staunton, wherein Baron Steuben, bless him, was bitterly complained of. The Prussian, Davies averred, had made himself "univerfally unpopular" among the sensitive Virginians. "All ranks of people," the Colonel wrote, "have taken the greateft difguft at him, and carry it to fuch a length as to talk of applying to Congrefs for his recall." Davies did concede that much of the dissatisfaction stemmed from small cause; the bulk of the State's stores, which the Baron had been blamed for losing at the Point of Fork Arsenal, had in fact been subsequently recovered. Nonetheless, he declared, Steuben's usefulness in Virginia "is entirely over."

The General took a clean sheet, dipped his quill, and sat with nib suspended, mustering his forbearance before essaying a reply. He reminded himself that Davies was but a faithful reporter of fact who in no way subscribed to the scorn being poured out on the Baron. No, it was the peevish and quarrelsome leaders of the government of Virginia—most assuredly not "all ranks of people," as Davies had been led to believe—who were enraged with the Baron, and against whose wrath Greene must now marshal his patient suasion. He pressed a curled forefinger against his sore eye, gathered another breath, and commenced to write:

> I feel for Baron Steuben who I am extremely forry has become fo very unpopular. His Letters to me befpeak his diftrefs, and indicate his fenfibility wounded by the clamour of the People. His intentions were honeft, and his zeal laudable. But he has totally miftaken the genius of the People he had to deal with. They can only be influenced by their pride and affection. They are too independant, to be drove even in matters that concern their neareft intereft. They will fooner bear the ftrokes of the Enemy than the reproach of their Friends.

He paused and smiled, thinking ironically of his own disputes with the satraps of the State over dragoon remounts and militia reinforcements. With what serenity and wise detachment he now counseled Davies to abide the same high-handed behavior he had despised and condemned in many a letter sent hotly Northward. Had he, Greene, understood the genius of the people with whom he had to deal? Had he influenced their pride and affection? Hypocrisy, he reflected, was a lightsome tool, easily wielded. Still wanly smirking, he bent again to his letter:

> The Baron from his great zeal to ferve them incurred their difpleasure inftead of rouzing their exertions. A little time perhaps will bring both parties to a better underftanding. I think the Baron from his exertions to promote the intereft of Virginia juftly entitled

to her good wifhes, and I am perfuaded after the firft ferment, and fever of paffion, is a little over, fhe will not be ungrateful. You know the Baron, and are fenfible of his worth; and I beg you as well from private as public confiderations to use all your influence to hufh into filence all improper prejudices.

He sat back to read the passage over; a hollow laugh escaped him. Was there a Calvinist divine in his pulpit in any meetinghouse of the land more apt to preach a sermon than the Quaker Nathanael Greene? The Friends were bred sooner to await the Divine Word spoken secretly within than to declaim abroad, yet each also felt obliged, in the fear of the Lord, to speak plainly for the good to men of rank; and Greene remained true enough to this belief that when he saw error he could never hold back tongue or pen.

Of course, apart from considerations of doctrine, he had always been a man quicker than most to instruct others, and he reckoned it was possible this trait found convenient company with the Quaker teaching. Many, he well knew, thought him pharisaical and full of righteous judgment, were sick of his sermonizing; he was as disliked in the Congress for this as was the Baron in Virginia for his peremptory airs and stormy temper. And like the Baron, Greene was himself; he could be no other. But he possessed a trait Steuben lacked. He owned a serpent's guile; the art of insinuation was his to command.

He continued the letter. Having satisfactorily addressed the Baron's cause head-on, he now took up his own, but with somewhat more indirection. Obscurity threatened; it must be resisted. Let Colonel Davies be certain to whom Virginia would owe her deliverance when it came, as it surely must come. "You will fee that I have not been unmindful of Virginia," he wrote.

The early application I made to the Commander in chief for the return of Lafayette from the Northward, together with the force I left him to protect your State will convince you I hope that I had forefeen the neceffity and guarded againft it all in my power. I was determined to fubject myfelf to every inconvenience here rather than leave you expofed there. My firft object was to draw Lord Cornwallis out of North Carolina into South Carolina. But finding I had failed . . . "

He paused. Was it wise to confess a failure? Twirling his quill, he examined the question. Where generals were concerned, failure—fairly earned or not—was bound to be ascribed; one's enemies brandished the slur like a battleaxe; and what general of proven ability lacked for enemies? What worthy commander did not venture into the field trailing in his wake a host of the envious, the disaffected, the conniving ambitious? Poor Charles Lee wore the ugly brand of failure, and Philip Schuyler, Horatio Gates, Baron Steuben, even at times the redoubtable Washington himself. It had been fixed on Greene too in the past; it would be again. No, it was better to admit a miscalculation rather than wait for others to accuse it. After all, unadorned frankness was at a premium in a world where vanity and self-seeking most often ruled. To utter truth was to break every normal precedent. Greene would speak truth and be hailed for his honesty.

He inked his pen and finished the thought.

But finding I had failed I thought the little force I had might be better employed here than by wafting it in an ineffectual attempt to overtake Lord Cornwallis in Virginia. Befides the total lofs of the three fouthern States which would have taken place upon my moving Northwardly, the Enemy would have had it in their power, and really had it in contemplation, to detach a larger force from this quarter than we had to employ againft them.

Let it be seen then, that instead of hurrying Northward to win the glory and fame of defeating the Modern Hannibal on the grand stage of history, Greene had chosen a course far more honorable, far more selfless and patriotic and, yes, humbly inconspicuous—to toil on against odds in a nearly forgotten theater of the war. If it was probably true that his force would have been inadequate to catch and defeat Cornwallis, and if it was also true that without his leadership Henry Lee and the others could not have held the South, still, self-abnegation was so rare in a general that men would be astonished to learn that Greene had forsworn the attempt to garner the greater renown. Most generals would have made the dash into Virginia heedless of its consequences; and of course Greene himself had dreamed of it. But in the end he had done what was right. And in doing so he had saved the South, or so he firmly believed. Now it was vital that his temperance and acumen, and the large accomplishments that had flowed from them, be duly recognized and, in time, celebrated. Every letter, like this one to Davies, would fetch nearer the day of that celebration.

"These confiderations," he wrote in conclusion, "together with the detention of 2000 Britifh troops lately arrived at Charles Town, that moft undoubtedly would have gone Northward, render the meafures I took very fortunate, given the advantages we have gaind in the reduction and evacuation of the Enemies pofts."

It was sufficient. Pleased, he put by his pen and stood, stretching his cramped muscles. More work waited—he still must write to Colonel Henderson of the South Carolina state troops and then Major McHenry in Virginia. Nearby, Major Burnet and Captain Pierce labored over more of the official correspondence that had accumulated during active operations but now demanded attention, consuming four or five hours of everyone's time each day. Bod Burnet was composing a report to Samuel Huntington, president of the Continental Congress, describing in the best light possible the disheartening events since the raising of the siege of Ninety-Six. Billy scratched out belated replies to three letters from Lafayette.

Greene sighed. The staff was overburdened. Nat Pendleton still lay sick in Charlotte, though he was said to be mending; Lewis Morris, newly returned from furlough, filled Nat's place—at least this was the pretense. As usual Major Morris' desk was vacant—ten minutes after Greene had dictated to him a message for the Commander in Chief, the careless Lewis had grown bored with the dreary business of inscribing it and had gone out for a walk. *I'm too indulgent*, the General thought, eyeing the unfinished letter. But then the lad was a scion of the illustrious family of New York patriots and statesmen, and his post with Greene was a valued symbol of their favor; and, practically speaking, Lewis was a genial soul, a quality much valued at a headquarters where every hour seemed to bring its quotient of bad news; and at times he was even a capable aide. No doubt the masters of Morrisania had grown accustomed to being indulged through several generations of privilege; why should Lewis expect anything less from a mere general of the Southern Army? And it was easy enough to give, for in his heart Greene was as doting as a parent. He smiled and shrugged away the small annoyance; he turned toward the opened fly of the marquee and its blaze of midday light.

He felt strongly tempted to follow Lewis' poor example, to forsake his bleak duties, step forth into the open and roam abroad and perhaps find some remote eminence where he might sit and meditate as of old, permitting himself the solace of the Time of Retirement the Quakers so cherished, obeying the injunction of the Psalm to "Be still and know that I am God." But silence, devotion, contemplation, the awaiting of the advent of the spirit, all these were lost to him now. His busy life had crowded them out. He did not often regret having been cut off from the community. He had rejected the Friends as they had rejected him. The country was in mortal peril yet the Friends clung blindly, stubbornly, churlishly in his view, to their pacifism while others bought with blood and toil the freedom Quakers enjoyed but refused to defend. What Meeting had not disowned those among them, like Greene, who took up arms in this mortal struggle, thus shunning the same brave souls who would save them? Cast up against the pitiless evil of this world, it was a high-mindedness that looked more like lunacy than principle. They were fools—pious, sanctimonious, glorious fools. Yet sometimes he ached for the simple truths they lived by, and for the quietude of the heart their faith inspired.

He turned back, limped to his desk, and sat. He had no leisure to consult the longings of the spirit or to ponder the Christ as the procuring cause of salvation. Worries flocked about him. The Virginia riflemen were insisting their terms of enlistment had expired and were demanding to return home. Colonel Gunby, like Nat Pendleton, lay ill with dysentery in Charlotte and his Marylanders were restless without him. A brigade of North Carolina Continentals and the militia of the Salisbury District, reinforcements so often promised but so long delayed that Greene had begun to doubt they even existed, were now said to be on the road to him at last—had been reported so for days—yet, like wraiths in some feverish dream, never seemed to draw any nearer. Obstacles of every sort impeded them—sickness, lack of shoes and arms, bad roads, wretched weather. He imagined them gloomily plodding like a corps of the damned along some phantom purgatorial track, condemned to a perpetual march assailed by the Ten Plagues of Egypt. *Even as I am condemned,* he thought, *to an eternal scribbling and dictating of letters that seem to go forth from me into a void from which nothing returns.*

He took up his pen once more to commence the report to Colonel Henderson when, to his unfeigned relief, Adjutant-General Williams ducked through the fly to interrupt the chore. "We've a dispatch from General Sumter," Williams announced, extending a tattered paper. "He was at the Rocks on the fifteenth."

"How pleasant of him to remember us as he scampers about the country," remarked the General archly. He did not accept the paper, but sat regarding it with an expression of distaste, as if he suspected some tincture of Sumter's hostility might taint it. "Has he by chance captured Monck's Corner, as he so strenuously promised?"

Williams withdrew the letter and scanned it. "Evidently not, sir. He speaks of enemy reinforcements at a church near the Corner—Biggin's Church, I suppose. A hundred . . . no, two hundred fifty, horse and foot. And a fieldpiece. He pleads he has made so many detachments that he must now move with caution."

"How melancholy for him. Have you noticed, Otho, how seldom his command is ever concentrated? One wonders what prodigies he might accomplish were his troops not forever scattered to the four winds. One may even surmise that, in such an event, he might be forced to fight the enemy and leave off the plundering he so much prefers. 'Move with caution,' he says. I interpret that to mean he intends to move not at all. Has Colonel Lee joined him?"

Williams grasped a chair, drew it close to the desk, and sat, squinting at Sumter's jagged handwriting. "He says not, though he seems to anticipate a junction shortly. He has sent Colonel Hampton to destroy the Four Holes Bridge." He read a little further, then added, "Ah, and he's made another detachment, three hundred men, to counter an enemy force at Murray's Ferry." Williams cast a glance over the rest of the note, scowling. "But then, in a postscript, it turns out the enemy is actually *gone* from Murray's Ferry. Had it not been for this diversion, he explains, he would've moved sooner."

"Very droll," Greene smiled. Pierce and Burnet worked on, pretending not to hear, selective deafness being an essential trait of the trusted aide-de-camp. "One day," continued the General, "I do hope to hear that the ferocious Blue Hen's Chicken has left off strutting about and fluffing his feathers and actually gone into the pit against the enemy." He shook his head. "He has a thousand men—General Marion's brigade, state troops, militia, Lee's Legion when it joins. He has more troops than I took to Ninety-Six—if only they were not strewn broadcast."

Glumly the General reflected. Since December his own plucky little band, outnumbered and ill-supplied, had marched nearly a thousand miles, waged three battles, snapped up nine important posts, taken three thousand prisoners and outmaneuvered two of the finest officers in the British service, freeing nearly the whole South save the immediate environs of Charles Town; and in spite of Greene's repeated pleas, General Sumter had played precious little part in any of it, preferring instead to fight the war on his own account, much in the manner of a brigand chieftain. He had even hatched a ruffianly plan to encourage enlistments by paying his men with loot, including Negroes, stolen from Tories—"Sumter's Law," it was called: Greene had approved a milder scheme, but the one the Gamecock put into practice had revolted him.

And even as Greene pursued his grueling campaign first against Cornwallis and then against Rawdon, all the while in dire need of men and matériel, the Blue Hen's Chicken had led his outlaw gang on expeditions of mindless mayhem throughout the back country—botching attacks on Forts Granby and Watson, falling into an ignominious ambush on Lynches River, trying again and failing at Granby, and then—finally, a success!—capturing Orangeburgh—all of it in contemptuous defiance of Greene's positive orders to join his force to the main army. It was flagrant insubordination, but Greene had been obliged to tolerate it because of the high regard Sumter enjoyed among his fellow Carolinians. The General's role was as much to rebuild the governments of the shattered Southern states as to make war against the British; accordingly he must strive just as diligently to keep the potentates of the country satisfied as to drive out the enemy. But now this expedition to Monck's Corner, which Sumter had pressed on him with the greatest urgency, was degenerating into farce.

Williams, the fairest of men, cocked a censorious eye. "You're wrong, sir, to question General Sumter's grit. He fights readily enough—gave Tarleton that awful drubbing last year at Blackstock's."

Impatiently the General waved a hand. "Yes, yes, you're right, of course. He's aggressive, and a capable commander in a fight, no doubt about it—but only as and when it suits him. And he's selfish—nothing's worse—and careless too." Greene ceased a moment in thought, then set his head to the side and shrugged. "Perhaps I'm only jealous that he does as he pleases while I'm as bound down by constraints as poor Gulliver among the Lilliputians. Sumter can afford his grudging and rebellious temperament, his chafing under orders; I must be forever moderate, reasonable, full of sober decision."

"It's why you're great," Williams observed, "and he's small and petty. History will say so."

"Will it indeed? I often wonder what history will say of us—of me."

"It'll depend on who writes the history, won't it?"

"It always has. Who will have power when the war ends and our independency is established? Will it be those who want the country strongly governed, or those who want it weak and divided, with the constituent states free to pursue their own ends regardless of the common welfare? If the former, perhaps I shall be remembered well, for I was always of that party. But if the latter—Mr. Jefferson and his friends, whom I have so sorely offended by my constant censure of their failure to support the army and the general interest—ah, then perhaps I shall be nothing more than the worst that has ever been said of me, that I was the venal quartermaster general who grew fat on the emoluments of office, who wallowed in corruption even as he rebuked others for their turpitude . . ."

"Those slurs are no longer believed, sir."

"No, Otho, you're wrong. Many cling to them, though I turn my pockets out to show my poverty. They insist that if I am poor, then I lost by bad investments the wealth I stole from the army."

"Your name will be held high when Sumter's is forgotten, sir."

"Do you think so? Oh, I believe not. General Sumter is one of those whom history loves—a headstrong, ruthless, turbulent rogue, hot of blood, quick to anger, nursing his grudges, revenging every slight, conquering all. His portrait will be done in high color; mine but dimly. Next to him I shall appear bland. Oh, I have my ambition, but it's a slow fire. His is a raging conflagration. I think; he acts. I'm craft; he's passion."

The General stopped and fell to pondering. Yes, Thomas Sumter was what the world worshipped—a hero. Nathanael Greene—clement, plausible, prudent, forever calculating Nathanael Greene—could never be that, at least not without the relentless advocacy he felt compelled to pursue, half ashamed of himself and half righteously justified, constantly reminding others, as he had reminded Colonel Davies just today, of what he had accomplished and why. Even so, it seemed doubtful he would ever wear a hero's mantle. Thomas Sumter did not have to remind anyone of anything; his deeds spoke for him. It was true, the General envied the Gamecock his fiery ardor.

He had met the man but twice, the second time just weeks ago when the army concentrated at Beaver Creek to descend belatedly and abortively on Orangeburgh. Till then his opinion of Sumter had been shaped mainly by the tone of the South Carolinian's letters. While he had first met Sumter at Charlotte in December, he remembered little of that interview owing to the stress and confusion attendant on assuming command of General Gates's shattered and demoralized army; he recalled only that Sumter had urged him to march on Cornwallis at Winnsborough—an impossible task just then.

In the time since, the South Carolinian's letters had been uniformly polite, respectful, even deferential at times, yet were underlain by an air of intractable stubbornness often disguised as incapacity—his force was too dispersed, or too weak, or too undisciplined, or too something, to permit him to follow Greene's orders. Back in May when Harry Lee, at Greene's direction, captured Fort Granby—a prize Sumter thought should have been his—the Gamecock had written a letter of resignation that pled, not that he felt dishonored, but that the lingering effects of the wound he had taken at Blackstock's had rendered him unfit for service. Greene had returned the letter; Sumter had continued to serve; but when the General next saw the Blue Hen's Chicken at Beaver Creek, he could feel the scorch of the South Carolinian's hate, and he knew that he and Harry Lee had made an enemy for life.

With no clear recollection of the Charlotte meeting, he had found Sumter a smallish but powerfully built man with a massive head whose size was accentuated by an abundance of graying hair brushed back from a towering brow. By gesture and motion Sumter gave an impression of heavy-boned yet supple strength, of density implausibly wedded to nimbleness; it lent his presence enormous force. A Roman nose, jutting chin and full-lipped, firm-set mouth showed his resolution and, yes, his intransigence. Everything about him spoke of physical might and manly forthrightness; and standing before him, Greene could not but be conscious of his own rotundity, his lameness, his bad eye, the wheezing of his asthma, his doughy, ordinary self thrown in the shade by Sumter's rough glamor. Yet, oddly, Sumter would not meet his gaze; the Gamecock's dark regard avoided his, settled instead on a point somewhere near the crown of Greene's head, and spoke to that; and something in the unconscious habit—for it was a habit, he did it with everyone—suggested a bent toward jobbery and deceit that reflected the inner man just as his awe-inspiring poise of body reflected the outer. Sumter was, Greene saw, as empty of virtue as he was full of primitive fortitude.

Sway and virtue rarely sat together. Francis Marion and Andrew Pickens, Sumter's subordinates, were much his betters in character—in solid accomplishment too—yet it was Sumter who enjoyed the broadest renown. Colonel Williams, sitting here by the General's side, was a finer officer than most in the Maryland Line, yet the names of Smallwood and Gunby, persons of far less worth, were more often heard. The same was true of the modest but inconceivably brave Captain Kirkwood of the Delaware Continentals upon whom everyone relied but whom no one wished to mention lest his glory outshine theirs. Vain Harry Lee outshone workaday Billy Washington. Even in the humdrum world of these headquarters, the negligent Lewis Morris basked in the unearned splendor of an illustrious name, while the more deserving Pierce, Burnet, and Shubrick labored in obscurity.

Yet Greene, who valued virtue above all else, also coveted the fame that drives virtue out; he longed to be what Thomas Sumter was. But his sense of virtue would not let him reach for the laurels without self-reproach. He might argue his merits self-servingly to Colonel Davies and, through him, to the leaders of Virginia and of the country, but he would suffer for it afterward in his conscience as a good Quaker should. That was why he said it was likely that history would fail to remember him. There were times when he thought that was true, that all his strenuous efforts to attain eminence and honors would prove barren—believed it even as he took the steps he hoped would write his name higher than Washington's. Would history know the difference between a fame wrested spontaneously from the teeth of destiny, like Sumter's, and one like his own, doggedly fashioned day after day by an effort as immense, persisting, and inexorable as the pounding of the trip-hammer that slowly and terrifically beats ancony into bar iron? As Williams had remarked, it would depend on who wrote the history. Greene must hope it would be written by men who thought well of him—or, perhaps, by himself.

After Williams left him, Greene lent his attention once more to his correspondence. The summer afternoon waned, and the triangle of light at the fly of his marquee began to dim, taking with it the temptation he had briefly felt to wander abroad in idleness. Dutifully he penned his dispatches to Colonel Henderson and Major McHenry and, after that, perused and signed Billy Pierce's replies to Lafayette and Burnet's draft of the report to the president of the Congress and, finally, Lewis Morris' long-postponed copy of the letter to General Washington.

But a hunger of the spirit ached in his vitals as he busied himself with these small duties. Victory was what he needed. If he could get a victory then history might be turned to his account after all, and the scanty gruel of virtue he fed on now be transformed in time to a feast of praise and fame. Once the army revived, once the High Hills of Santee had breathed new life into it, he would take the field again. He would seek out the enemy and fight him and win the victory that would not only raise him to the heights he deserved but make him memorable too. Such a memory as he would make would not fade or be eclipsed, certainly not by a Sumter, perhaps not even by the Commander in Chief himself.

The very prospect cheered him. Suddenly he was in a gay mood. At midnight, alone in his marquee, all his aides and stewards sent to bed, he dashed off a letter to his old friend and business associate, Colonel Jeremiah Wadsworth of Connecticut:

> When I was orderd to the Southward moſt of my Friends gave me up as loſt either by the Climate or the Enemy, and I ſuppoſe you agreed with them in Sentiment as you have never given yourſelf the Trouble to write to me; and I ſuppoſe will be little leſs ſurpriſed to receive a Letter from me than from one who had taken their Departure long ſince for the other World. But be Aſſured I am ſtill living and in good Health.

It felt fine to joke with Wadsworth, even at such a remove in space and time. One did not have to parse one's every word to be sure the proper impression had been made, one need not fret over every turn of phrase lest some innocent slip betray a hint of uncertainty or an unintended slight. One spoke one's secret mind. He and Wadsworth understood one another. He even understood that Wadsworth was in love with Caty. The understanding slept just beneath the jocular surface of their relations; it was a dragon each knew lay coiled there, but both hoped would never waken; as long as it slumbered, their old intimacy was safe.

All men loved Caty anyway; he had long since come to terms with that. There had been a time when he had resisted it, when his suspicions had got the better of him, when he had made intemperate accusations. But that time was past. Life was hard. Why should he spurn what scant pleasures it offered—the affection of an old friend, the occasional regard of a beautiful if sometimes fickle wife? Solitary in his candlelit marquee, he returned to his letter, softly chuckling now:

> Our army has been frequently beaten, and like a Stock Fifh grows the better for it. Lord Cornwallis has rambled through the great part of the Southern States, and his Tour has facrificed a great number of his Men without reaping any folid Advantages from it, except that of diftreffing the poor Inhabitants. I had a Letter fome time fince from Mr John Trumbull wherein he Afferts that with all my Talents for Warr, I am deficient in the great Art of making a timely retreat. I hope I have convinced the World to the contrary, for there are few Generals that has run oftener, or more luftily than I have done, But I have taken care not to run too farr; and commonly have run as faft forward as backward, to convince our Enemy that we were like a Crab, that could run either way.

Part ye Eleventh

In Which a Young Man Enlifts in White's Horfe

THEY SMELLED RICHMOND BEFORE THEY SAW IT
—a powerful, almost overwhelming scent of burnt tobacco, as if
ten thousand men had lighted their pipes all at once, partly a rich and
pleasant fragrance, partly a tart, bitter-edged stench that stung the nose
and made the gorge want to rise. Before long they saw the smoke too, an
inky congestion of the southern sky that resembled the piled thunder-
heads of an approaching storm. They came into Richmond under that
dark pall; ash floated everywhere and got into the eyes, soot and cinders
darkened every surface. The place seemed nearly deserted, its inhabitants
either gone into the country or cowering somewhere in secret, taught by
the British to fear any army no matter its allegiance. A few disconsolate
ones stood watching them with dazed, dull eyes as they passed. An old
woman sat on a stump smoking a pipe. A man holding a dead dog in his
arms swore at them.

At the common Captain Harris gave the company a few minutes' rest.
James wandered through the ruined, smoke-dimmed town; Corn Wallace
had abided there four days, destroying anything that might have been of
value to the army of Loff Yet. James and his messmates—famished, in-
differently armed, ill-clothed, nearly all unshod—gazed at first wistfully
and then with a growing hate on all this fiendish destruction, which had
robbed them of so much that they so badly needed. When the command
came to fall in, they were eager to leave.

Turning east from Richmond along the great bend of the River James,
the army descended from a country of hills and bluffs onto a sandy lowland covered with pine barrens and deep oak forests. Many small streams
of black water meandered hither and yon, looking as sluggish as so much
molasses. Sometimes their banks were low and marshy, sometimes they
were ravine-like and choked with wild grapevine and every sort of creeper
and ivy. In sunken spots the rains had left pools that were turning stagnant;
clouds of mosquitoes rose from these to torture them as they passed.

On the higher, better-drained lands afar off they could see level fields of new tobacco, attesting to the presence of husbandmen somewhere in what otherwise seemed a wilderness. The heat was sweltering, the air heavy with damp, yet the earth had dried out quickly after the rains and now gave up a fine dust that filled the sky and coated everyone and everything with a film of grit. In the few settled places, small clumps of country people stood gawking by the roadside: dirty boys, work-worn Negroes, poor farm folk, a few women of the better class oddly muffled to the eyes with linen wraps—to keep off sunburn, Blan Shiflet surmised. Fortunately the army was out of the poxed region and they saw no more dying blacks.

Sometimes the roiling dust would lapse, would drift and part, and then through breaks in the forests they might glimpse another file of troops marching along under a slant bundle of shiny firelocks. Now and then they might hear a sputter of musketry in the distance, or the thump of a cannon. But mostly they passed through a deep stillness that made it seem unlikely the war had actually come to such a barren place. However, near dusk, a party of horsemen dressed all in white rode out of a wood nearby to sit their saddles at the tree line, watching with leisurely attention. "Them's Tarleton's Legion," someone said. "See how they've docked their horses's tails square-off?"

James peered. They looked disappointingly ordinary—they might be no more than some commonplace fellows out for a ride. Were these the brutes who slaughtered Buford's detachment "How come they don't wear green?" he asked. "Ain't they the Green Dragoons?"

"Not in summertime, they ain't," came the answer. "Weather like this, they turns out thataway, in duck or linen, white as snow." James felt a thrill of fear as he stared at the dragoons in their dazzling garb. He remembered the one-eyed sergeant, now sadly a captive, telling of the massacre at the Waxhaws, telling of the terrible sabers Tarleton's men had wielded. *Blades ground sharp as razors. Cut through bone like it was turds.* He imagined those men yonder in their white clothes gathering their reins and charging down on him, each with a thousand pounds of galloping horse under him, each with his fine-honed sword poised to strike. *Heads bounding in the road like footballs.* Infantry could not defend against that. A man on foot stood no more chance than a puppy. James nodded to himself; he'd been a fine rider for Chenowith; he could be a fine dragoon too. What he needed was his own good horse and his own sharp sword.

Yet there was a strange indolence about this thing called war. The fearsome dragoons did not attack; they only sat observing, just as James and his messmates, some days ago, had stood on the bank of the Rivanna and watched the enemy descend on the abandoned Arsenal. It seemed to him that some part of war had that quality of sleepy casualness, a dereliction that deceptively hid its worst evils. There were those dragoons somnolently watching. There was the monotony of the troops' reasonless toil, toil for its own sake, hardship that never ended and seldom even slackened; and James thought that lulled you too, made you forget that one day the war was going to try to kill you. It was marching and marching and marching till you began to doubt there was even a destination to reach, then learning as soon as you reached one that a new one had been selected that lay even farther off than the last; marching that way then and growing weary to death from the marching, and the soles of your feet blistered and bleeding and your belly forever growling with a hunger that was never satisfied. It was thirst. It was the tiresome everlasting rattle of the drums and the whistling of the fifes. It was being grimy and lousy. It was your shirt falling to pieces and your britches wearing out and your loins raw with rash. It was murderous heat, it was dysentery, for some it was the pox.

But it had not been battle, at least not yet. Never the glory of the fight that he had heard veterans speak of. Boredom, yes. Tedium. And the weirdness and unreality of an enemy who, instead of hurtling at you in deadly ferocity, could appear and merely observe you with the detached interest of an audience at some kind of show. As if to confirm the indifference and apathy he had been pondering, the dragoons in their white smocks and overalls now appeared to lose interest in the passing column of Americans; lazily they turned their horses aside and faded into the woods; he could hear them laughing as they went.

That night the Battalion bivouacked on the grounds of a rude farm. Next day they crossed a bridge over a sluggish stream—actually a bog called White Oak Swamp, some said, or a river, others swore, the same Chickahominy River that took its rise up by Dandridge's Plantation near Hanover, whence they'd started. From this slough they turned north and east and marched to a nameless little courthouse hamlet. While they moved, firing broke out somewhere in the east; the noise seemed trivial and harmless, no more than the clatter that might be caused by children dragging sticks along a picket fence in mischief. James could not tell whether the action was near or distant, only that the faint and insignificant-sounding racket suited his new notion of war as something that seemed negligible, but in whose bosom deadly perils lurked.

That evening, seven days after leaving Richmond—or was it six? James no longer knew—they camped at a mill. It was rumored they were lying but twenty miles from Williamsburg. Corn Wallace, James heard, was there now, and must soon retreat. "We've got the damned old Earl licked," gloated Dick Snow. "We've chased him plumb out of Virginia. Pretty soon he'll be a-wadin' in the Chesapeake." How they could have achieved that, with their sorry little force, the harelip could not explain. After dark a courier reported to Colonel Febiger, and presently camp gossip spread the word that there had indeed been a skirmish that afternoon at a place near Williamsburg called Hot Water. Sure enough, poor mortals had got themselves killed and wounded in that little commotion James had heard. Those perils he'd sensed hiding in the monotony had sprung out, over there on the Hot Water, to show the other side of war.

The next few days were taken up with more pointless marches back and forth over the sweltering country. They were at somebody's plantation on the anniversary of the Declaration of Independency; the generals ordered a celebration of the great event and there was a parade and an extra portion of rum and a firing of salutes; but for common fellows like James it was a ceremony as empty as the void in their bellies that the rum only made worse by giving them cramps or making them violently sick-drunk.

How ridiculous, he thought, that he had joined the army chiefly to find food and shelter, and now endured worse hunger and exposure than he and Libby had ever known when hiding as fugitives in the wild. The most the soldiers ever got to eat in a day was some wormy bread, a handful of rice, a piece of salt pork, a swallow of rum if they were lucky—barely enough to keep them alive, never sufficient to fill the void in the stomach or replenish their waning strength. Libby, with the baggage train, received the same and suffered equally. When he remembered how he had persuaded her that the army's bounty would be their salvation, he was smitten with a black despair. How could he have been so stupid? He had reproached Sides for being a fool; now he knew himself for a worse one.

After the celebration of independency, the Battalion plodded back to their old campsite at the mill; no one in authority bothered to explain why they had ever left it. They were squatting idle in the baking heat when they heard a rumble in the distance. Later they learned another part of the army, under General Wayne, had fought an engagement with Corn Wallace at a place called Green Springs. More men were dead, more maimed; but as far as the Battalion was concerned it might have happened in China. Next day they took to the road again, going west, back toward Richmond for no earthly reason that anyone could name, and that evening they camped for the night beside yet another morass—Chickahominy Swamp, Captain Harris called it. It was here in this dismal spot that James at last resolved to change his destiny, and the destinies of Sides and Libby too. And it was here that his destiny came to seek him out.

———

Even before it chose him, he had chosen it. He discussed it first with Libby. "We can't stand it any longer," he said, and saw from her face that she understood what he meant without any need of his saying more. He was relieved. It excused him from the necessity of confessing aloud that he had been wrong to make them go down to the Arsenal that day to try to find a home in the army.

"I've been talking to some of the fellows," he went on excitedly. "They say it's a lot better in the dragoons. You ride a horse, you don't go walking everywhere toting a great musket. They give you a fine uniform. And big sturdy boots with spurs on 'em. You carry a fine shiny sword. And they feed you regular, feed you good stout rations—beef and biscuit, sweet potatoes, beans, peas, a portion of rum whenever you crave it. They don't fight much; they just ride around scouting and looking at the country and sending messages back to the army. And even if they *do* fight, why, they're up on that big high horse, with that big sword. They just go a-charging over whatever's in their way, and cut it down, if it don't skedaddle first. And you know me, I was Chenowith's jockey. Why, I can ride any horse ever foaled."

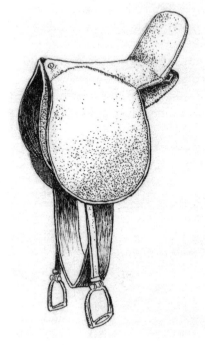

It had been a dream of his ever since the time at Dandridge's when he and Sides had watched the handsome dragoon officers ride past. Even before that, at the Arsenal, he had admired the dash of Armand's Legion. His own love of horses and of riding had roused in him a strong desire to fight this war, if he had to fight it, from the saddle. His brief sight of Tarleton's men had sharpened the desire. The monotony of the past month had not fooled him; he knew his luck must soon run out, that the menace living at the heart of the war's torpor would one day rouse itself, leap out from hiding and claim him, as it had claimed Janet and those men at Hot Water and Green Springs, unless he acted to change his fortune.

He told her of the recruiters who were circulating through the army seeking men for the dragoon service. One of them, he said, was the same Major Call he had challenged that last morning at the Arsenal. On one or two occasions in the past week he had seen the Major riding past in his splendid getup of white and pale blue and silver. Call was with Washington's Horse, the Third Regiment of Light Dragoons. Though James did not tell Libby so, he thought it best not to consider that corps. He feared

Call might remember him, take thought of their encounter, and make James pay for his impudence at the guard post. He knew it was unlikely; he was too low and Call too high, the Major would never make note of him. But his memory of Call had spread a sinister cloud over the whole of the Third; instead he preferred the other regiment whose recruiters he had watched, White's Horse, the First Dragoons.

"I've seen 'em," he exulted. "They've got grand clothes, blue turned up with red, and buttons of pewter, and brass helmets wrapped in bearskin with long crests of horsehair. Their Colonel used to be an aide of General Washington's. He's a country gentleman from the Jerseys, very rich, and he pays a bounty out of his own pocket. Pays hard money too, not Continental paper."

Libby gave him an urgent glance. "Is Poovey willing?"

"We've talked of it a good deal lately. I believe he's game for it."

Her look turned expectant. "Can *I* ride a horse too?"

James shrugged. "I reckon not. I expect you'll be with the baggage as before." Then he brightened. "But I'll see if it can be arranged." He grinned and caught her by the shoulders. "That would be something, wouldn't it? All three of us on horseback?" And for the first time since Burrell's Ornery they burst into joyful laughter.

Poovey was indeed game, though since the incident on the wooden horse he had maintained a conspicuously studied air, probably in hopes of convincing James that he was now a more mature and worthwhile prospect for Libby; he agreed, but without any undue enthusiasm. They went to their sergeant and begged leave to speak to Captain Harris.

"Sure enough," the sergeant bawled, "join the dragoons and be damned to you. Pair of bleeding sodomites, you're the worst soldiers I got. You *belong* in the goddamned dragoons. Know what dragoons do? Gallivant about looking for anything to poke their hairsplitter into—man, boy, woman, sheep, their own nag, it don't matter to a damned dragoon. Hell, dragoons don't fight. You know what that horse is for, aside from giving up its arse for a shagging? It's for running away from every tussle and whiff of powder, that's what." He spat to one side in disgust. "Whoever saw a dead man wearing spurs?"

Captain Harris, as might have been expected, was more sympathetic. Of course he was also completely corned. "Were not the distinctions of rank and station so inflexible, my children, I should bid you join me in a cup of the creature," he greeted them, brandishing a silver chalice as they came into his tent and doffed their hats in salute. "But alas," he sighed, "though we fight for the equality of man, hypocrisy prevails—I must drink, solitary in my august state, whilst you who are common must look on athirst. My apologies." He drank deep of the chalice, then banged it on the table, leaned forward in his camp chair, and fixed them with a bleary eye. "What's your pleasure then, my chicks?"

James told him. "Dragoons, eh?" he echoed, leaning back and caressing his belly. "Well, I shouldn't wonder. They do cut a damned fine figure. And you're both sprightly little bits, just the type they'll want for the saddle. The service is easy, I collect. Easier than service afoot. And with Cornwallis crossed to Portsmouth and Tarleton gone off towards Amelia, be certain the infantry'll take to the roads again quick enough; and I expect you're damned tired of going about shank's mare. Nor can I blame you; I hate it myself."

The remark seemed to send his thoughts momentarily astray. He sat reflecting, one hand lying loose on his stomach, his rosy face blank and heavy, his lips hanging slack. James was sure the Captain did not remember him and of course had never met Sides; the easy, confiding manner was simply his way with all the men of the company. But now that manner had flagged; there was a deep weariness in this pause and a distraction in the wandering of his attention that aroused James's concern. Looking more closely, he saw that while the Captain's dress was gorgeous as always, the man himself seemed oddly depleted—smaller, slighter, more fragile, perhaps even ill; the flesh about his eyes was crimped and finely pleated, gray as a bruise. The tailored uniform dangled loosely about him.

But then the Captain stirred, his features drew together again, and he sent them his brilliant smile. "They're giving us Colonel Gaskins back, though," he said, as though he expected the news to please them. He picked up the chalice and filled it to the brim from a bottle of wine at his elbow. "Did you know that?" He raised the chalice and drained it all at once, then nodded with an empty enthusiasm. "Yes," he cried, "Colonel Febiger, God bless him, has ascended on clouds of glory to some Valhalla of higher duty, and has taken with him his infernal band of musick." The Battalion had nourished doubts about the usefulness and artistry of the nine musicians—clarinetists, bassoon players, puffers upon the French horn—on whom the Colonel doted, whose tunes were inflicted nightly.

His gaze came back to them and he smiled again, and this time the smile was only an exercise of the muscles of his face; his spirit was absent from it. James thought his bloodshot hazel eyes were dark with a despair that his mocking ways could not conceal, and he wondered anew what tragedy might have turned Captain Harris to such hopelessness and debauchery. He felt a rush of sorrow knowing that he would not see this whimsical, kindly man again or ever learn the nature of his terrible sadness. "But your days of marching are done, ain't they, children?" the Captain was saying in his buoyant way. "Yes, you're bound for the dragoons. Dash and push, that's where you're headed."

He poured and tossed off another dram. "And how fortuitous that you've come to your decision just at this very moment, which is so big with promise." James wondered what "fortuitous" meant, and what large promise anyone might have made; but in the past month he had learned not to inquire into the obscure things the Captain said; usually his meanings soon enough came clear. This one did at once. "Fortuitous?" the Captain went on, arching his eyebrows. "Why, no, by God, it's more than fortuitous; it's a damned miracle." He bent toward them, nodded, gave a conspiratorial wink. "I'll tell you, lambkins, this very afternoon, *almost this very hour*, the esteemed and redoubtable Colonel Anthony White parades the Battalion to solicit recruits for his celebrated First Regiment of Continental Light Dragoons."

James was amazed. Surely "fortuitous" was another word for the finest of luck. Still, he and Poovey exchanged covert glances; Captain Harris saw this and gave them a sly grin. "You needn't fret; they've never yet turned a man down. Take 'em all, they do—lame, halt, blind, afflicted with leprosy. Gadarene swine, the woman taken in adultery, Zaccheus in the tree, the two thieves on Golgotha, the daughter of Jairus . . ." His voice trailed off and he sat for a second or two looking down at the tabletop before him, gazing intently upon it as if something there had suddenly captured his whole mind; but the table was clear of all save a pot of ink with a goose quill in it.

They waited in confusion. Then he rallied; his former mood of oddly vacant good will returned. "They're desperate, you see. The Lobster bled 'em something prodigious, down South awhile back, and they must rebuild the regiment." Then, lest they think he had slighted them, he raised a hand as if swearing an oath. "I don't mean to imply you're not the finest, my goslings, the most absolute apex, pinnacle, and epitome of heroic material, perfectly suited to service a-horse. Oh children, you'll make a likely pair of dragoons, I'm sure of it."

His laugh was like the crushing of many small sticks in the hand. He dismissed them then—somewhat curtly, James thought. They saluted and turned to leave, but as James stepped out into the light of the afternoon he heard the Captain's voice behind him quietly say, "I wish you well, Little James," and he knew the Captain had remembered him after all.

That same day—within the hour, just as Captain Harris had predicted—the Battalion was paraded under arms. James would never forget that moment. In after years he would often call it to mind, for it was the moment that turned his life out of one course and into another. He would never be able to say where his life might have taken him had he not stood in that parade and listened to Colonel White and then stepped forward when the invitation came. Where it did take him, that was going to be his life now. Years hence, he would look back on this moment of standing at parade in the sloped light of a hot July afternoon, under the tall pines, and he would remember the weight of the air, the sulphurous odor of the nearby swamp, a crackle of firing in the remote distance, his musket by his side in the position of Rest, big drops of sweat oozing from under the brim of his hat to run behind his ears, the gnats and mosquitoes dodging around his head, the itch of their bites and of the vermin that infested him, the reek of his filthy clothes and of his unwashed self and of the men he stood among, the red regimental standard four paces in front of the first rank sagging limp on its staff, Colonel Gaskins at the head of the formation, Major Poulson behind him, then the adjutant and the officers of the companies and platoons and then the drummers and fifers, all in their accustomed places; and off to the side, grandly aloof, sublime in their magnificent uniforms of dark blue faced with scarlet, in gleaming helmets with flowing white plumes, in polished boots, sabers at their sides, two officers and a sergeant and a private of dragoons waiting to lift him into their exalted world, the private holding the bridle of a splendid black charger wearing a high-cantled saddle with a pair of bearskin-covered pistol holsters slung on either side of the pommel. Yes, he would look back from the vantage of the end of the life that had begun in that moment, and he would examine it with the wisdom of all that had come after, and then, even then, knowing what had followed from it, he would not be able to say whether it had been the blighting of his life or the making of it.

One of the dragoon officers stepped before them, a man of medium size, somewhat portly, with a round face settled on a plump yoke of neck. He had a pouted mouth and a sharp inquisitive little nose and finely shaped ears. He carried himself boldly, shoulders squared, one foot advanced, a hand thrust in the bosom of his waistcoat and another resting on the hilt of his saber, a pose that lent him a powerful air of force and authority, though it also seemed a little reminiscent of an actor on a stage. James, full of ready adulation, knew this must be Colonel White.

It was. He introduced himself in a ringing voice of clipped accents. "Lads," he said, "I have the honor and privilege to command the First Regiment of Continental Light Dragoons, and when I say the first, I do mean the very first, the best, the supremest body of light horse in the Continental Army." He swelled visibly with a confident pride: James felt a surge of inspiration, gazing on that mettlesome figure. What a wise and brave commander he must be!

"Do I need tell you of the dragoon service, boys?" Colonel White asked, then shook his plumed head and smiled. "I think not. Why, I think you know. For we're famed, aren't we? Famed for the thundering charge, the bright sword, a hundred outpost fights, the blood horse, pluck and address and pistol-work. You've watched us ride by, haven't you? Watched us, up on our tall steeds, while you waded in mud? Coveted our bright raiment while you wore rags? Saw our good boots as you stood barefoot?"

As he said this, he motioned to the private standing by with the black horse. The private sprang into the saddle and began to ride the charger to and fro along the battalion front. James and the others watched with greedy eyes, noting every detail of his spotless dress and glittering equipment. The horse pranced and curvetted and tossed its great head. *Oh,* thought James, *to ride such a steed, to wear such pretty duds, to wield such splendid weapons, to be fed and shod and clean.* He was seized with an irresistible longing.

"Dragoons is grand, ain't they?" cried Colonel White. He turned sly then, bent a little toward them as if to share a secret. "And you know how the wenches favor us," he confided. This provoked a roar of laughter from the ranks. The Colonel stood wearing his naughty grin—why, he was one of them, he was a rogue too, he was an excellent democratic fellow. "Oh," he cried, as their laughter rose, "the wenches does love the hearty dragoon." He raised a finger and wagged it. "Dragoons *is* for riding, you know." Their merriment roared.

When they had quieted, he resumed in a more solemn vein. "No, I need not tell you of the dragoons, lads. Dragoons is the honey in the comb, ain't it? 'Tis the sweetmeats, the best fruit of the tree. So here's my offer, boys. All men of you who'd enlist for the war in the First Regiment of Light Dragoons, who'll ground your arms and march five paces to your front, I'll give a bounty of a thousand dollars and half pay during life."

A collective gasp passed through the Battalion. *A thousand dollars? Half pay for life?* Such a bounty had never been heard of. Could he possibly mean it? Could it be true? James stood stunned. It had shaken him to hear that the enlistment was to be for the duration of the war—he was obligated now for but eighteen months, and this confounded war had been going on ever since he could remember, indeed might never end—but the offer of a bounty of such incredible proportions soon swept every reservation away. Besides, the Colonel was obviously a glorious and distinguished man, yet had the common touch as well, would not wrap himself in the arrogance of rank and station as would Major Call, would never demean any man for the accident of his birth. Here was a gentleman to be trusted, to be admired, to be followed wherever he might lead. James took a breath, grounded his musket, and stepped forward. Poovey did too. So did forty other men of the battalion.

The new recruits formed a line before a tent where a clerk sat at a camp table filling out the enlistment forms; Colonel White and one of his officers relaxed on a fallen pine log nearby. James and Poovey, waiting their turns with the clerk, shuffled past. James felt a pinch of excitement to come so near to the estimable Colonel; he took the opportunity to observe him more closely. From this vantage, White offered a rather different impression than at parade. Something about him, something indefinite, gave him an air of excessive good keeping, like a carriage horse specially groomed to shine and glisten and draw approving looks. There was a satiny sheen to his skin that spoke of frequent bathing, a pampered softness to the hands that lay careless in his lap. He had removed his helmet to display an expensive wig carefully powdered. He gave off a mingled fragrance of snuff and perfume. All this made him rounder, more plump, softer, somehow less sharply defined than he had seemed standing before the battalion making his lively speech. He and the captain were in conversation; James could not help overhearing.

"Oh," said the Colonel in a sleepy, drawling voice very different from the crisp one he had used at parade, "'Twas a pushing school outside Richmond. I was in my altitudes from drinking strip-me-naked half the night, and got me a right biter, I'm telling you. God, the mab was a horse godmother. I laid out my chink, and we were in buttock-ball before I got my bleeders off. A hell of a goer, that one. And me so foxed I was letting cheesers the whole time and half ready to shoot the cat." The Captain chortled obligingly, but James thought it a forced and unconvincing laugh—a laugh to be used when you wished to stay in the good graces of someone you did not especially like.

Poovey leaned close. "What in hell's he talking about?"

James shrugged. "Can't say for sure. It sounds lewd to me, though."

Poovey broke into a leer and edged toward the officers, hoping to relish some bawdy morsel. "Jesus, Belfield," the Colonel was saying, "she was beating me all hollow. Then what d'you suppose? Why, by Christ, I smoked some cove standing in the door. An uppish cull, all the crack from the cut of his duds, but a beau-nasty from his smell, and fat as a hen in the forehead."

"You don't say," Captain Belfield remarked, gazing emptily into the distance.

Poovey whispered, "What lingo's that? I can't make out a thing he's telling. Is it the King's English?"

James shrugged. It was indeed like a foreign tongue. But even not know-ing what it was, he did not like it and tried not to listen. But the Colonel was too close by; it was impossible to ignore him. "'That's my lawful blan-ket you're a-knocking,' the bastard says. 'I'll not be hornified,' he says, 'I'll give you a basting,' he says. Well, I was still nazy and I don't mind telling you, it cogged me. 'Ask my arse,' says I. 'It's a nanny-house, ain't it? She's a mawkes, ain't she?' I couldn't stand such talk nohow. 'My arse in a bandbox,' says I. 'You've tongue enough for two sets of teeth,' says I, 'but I reckon you'd fight, come to that. D'you want snappers? Or the cold iron? It's all the same to me.' 'Neither one,' says he, with a laugh. 'You're done over already; the flat cock's a fire-ship.' Gave me a turn, that did; I was all aground. Then I figured 'twas a bamboozle they'd got up—him pretending the offended spouse; maybe they was Tories, out to hand the bube to the whole of the dragoon service—half the regiment was in there at clicket, after all. Any-how, 'You're burnt,' crows he, 'it's the dripper for you.' And sure enough, I've had the dropping member ever since."

Captain Belfield bestirred himself to ask, "Did you hush the cull?" But James could tell from the way he asked it that he already knew the answer and cared little in any case.

"No," answered the Colonel with a chuckle, "I've been clapped many's the time; if I'm to make some cuffin easy, why, it'll be for more than any goddamned dose of the gleet."

James and Poovey moved out of hearing then. James was vaguely troubled, but he did not speak of it to Sides. Poovey was intrigued by the strangeness of their dialect. "I never in my life listened to such canting talk," he marveled. "What d'you reckon it meant?"

James shrugged. "Maybe it's how dragoons speak," he said.

* * *

The hardest thing was saying good-bye to the fellows in the mess. James had not realized how fond he had grown of them till the time came to part. The four stood all in a row while James and Poovey moved by shak-ing hands one by one—confident Blan Shiflet, busybody Charlie Cooke, Sam Ham blushing when Poovey derided his name once more but this time not resenting it, silent Dick Snow. Then Libby passed along, giving each a buss on the cheek, pausing a little longer with the heartbroken Sam, who wept, and with Charlie, with whom she shared bittersweet memories of his lost Janet.

The next hardest thing was giving up his musket. In the beginning—was it only a little more than a month ago?—he had feared and mistrusted it, and the piece had seemed to sense his misgiving and resisted him. Now, next to Libby and Poovey and his messmates, it was the closest thing to him in the whole world. Circumstances had not called on him to fire it in battle; never had he fixed its sights on another mortal to kill, only to enforce regulations as with Major Call; he had been spared that final lethal trial. But he had come to be *ready* to fire it; and somehow that big Rappahannock Forge gun had brought him to that point. It had begun the business of making a man of him, and he was grateful. He racked it in the bell of arms with a pang.

A dragoon sergeant was to march them to Manakin Town, somewhere up the James River to the west, where it seemed there was a horse depot and camp of instruction for recruits. There, said the sergeant, they would collect their fabulous bounty of a thousand dollars. James and Poovey stared at the man askance—instead of the fancy uniform of blue and red worn by the trooper with Colonel White, he was dressed in a shabby little green coatee, a pair of mud-smeared linen overalls, and an ugly little peaked cap with a tassel on it. And he was barefoot. He did not look like a fellow who had earned a thousand dollars at any recent time.

Troubled, James tried to puzzle out a reason for the fellow's bedraggled state. His elevated rank suggested he had perhaps enlisted on an occasion—unpropitious for him—sometime previous to the offering of the Colonel's bounty. Still, James thought his looks boded somewhat ill. But it was too late now to repine; their fate was sealed. They helped Libby into one of the wagons for the womenfolk and baggage; the sergeant chained the tailgate, turned and mounted a rat-tailed nag no better than a plowhorse; and they started.

Part ye' Twelfth

In Which General Greene Wreſtles
With a Mighty Paſſion

O N A SWELTERING FIRST DAY OF AUGUST THE
main reinforcement of North Carolina Continentals under General Jethro Sumner marched into Greene's camp on the High Hills of Santee. There were but a hundred fifty of them—a so-called regiment of regulars that numbered little more than two companies. A small advance party had arrived two days before, and further contingents were promised from Salisbury over the next weeks, but Heaven alone knew whether those would actually appear or would instead keep on wandering immaterially across the dreary landscape of the General's vain hopes. A few from the Northern Province had been serving with the army since before the siege of Ninety-Six; now Greene would have this little battalion. Were the Salisbury phantoms ever to take on substance, he might command nearly five hundred North Carolina regulars—a small brigade, just as these two companies made a miniature regiment. And there would be a fresh infusion of militia. It remained to be seen what sort of troops all these would make.

He rode out to watch the regiment come in. Otho Williams and Billy Washington and Colonel John Ashe, who had commanded Sumner's forward detachment, were with him; and the four of them, backed by some of the staff, sat their horses on the break of the westernmost height overlooking the causeway from McCord's Ferry. The causeway itself was a brown ribbon laid across the green expanse of the canebrake below; the line of marching men pulsed rhythmically along it, topped by a bristling of muskets. Their dust hung in the still air. A moted light struck through it; those undulant firelock barrels twinkled in it. "A pretty sight," declared Otho Williams.

"It would be prettier still," observed the General, "were they three times as many." Then it occurred to him the comment might have sounded ungenerous to Colonel Ashe, and he repented of it. "Still," he conceded, "I'm glad to see them." He was. Yes, they were too few, and they were North Carolinians—of all his troops, usually the most skittish and unreliable—but for over half a year he had been getting by with too few and too little, and by now he knew this was to be his fate as long as he commanded the Southern army. Besides, for months now a small corps of North Carolinians, militiamen conscripted into the regular service as punishment for their cowardice at the battle of Guilford, had been redeeming themselves in his service at such places as Fort Motte and Augusta and Ninety-Six. No one knew better than Greene how readily one day's poltroon might play the morrow's Hector.

This new regiment, together with the Salisbury levies he still awaited, would be nothing if not a miscellany. Most were untrained recruits; a stalwart few were experienced volunteers—old Continentals turned out for the emergency. Greene flicked over them his practiced, not to say jaundiced, eye. At their head rode Sumner, their brigadier, on a great sorrel, a too-small wig that was turning green sitting askew on his pumpkin-shaped head, his face split by his customary jack-o'-lantern grin. His hearty spirit seemed to precede him like a bustling of air, a happy turbulence that stirred the spirits of everyone nearby. Approaching, he doffed his hat in salute; Greene acknowledged it; warmly they shook hands past their horse's heads; and Sumner swung out of the road, gave greeting to the others, and took his place by the General's side. "I reckon, sir," he boomed, "you was despairing if North Carolina would ever give over her rightful complement of troops."

Greene crooked an arm before his face against the dust now rolling over them lest it aggravate his quinsey. "I can't deny it, General. I was anxious."

"Despaired of it myself," Sumner cried, lifting the corner of his hat to his saluting captains as the companies filed past, the men panting and coughing from the long climb up from the causeway, the smell of them ripening in the moist heat. "First there was the smallpox, then we could find no shoes, nor arms, nor cartridges. Nor clothing neither, nor rum nor sugar nor coffee." Indeed, as Greene looked on, he saw many bare feet and a gauntness and variety of garb that would have done justice to a pack of

beggars. "Some of 'em was bounty men," Sumner was saying, "and no sooner was they collected than they scattered like quail. Some was deserting
to look after their families in peril of the Tories. Blount's detachment of
a hundred twenty's delayed; Malmedy's militia too. Then, goddamn him,
Armstrong got himself shot in a duel . . ."

Greene swallowed his disappointment and smiled; he had conceived
a fondness for Jethro Sumner the moment he met him, last winter during the maneuvering against Cornwallis; it was good to have him close
again. The North Carolinian was a bluff, openhearted and honest man
and a thoroughly seasoned soldier. Some years Greene's senior, he had
seen service in the war against the French and Indians and, in the present
conflict, at Brandywine and Germantown, at Stono Ferry and the siege
of Charles Town.

In time of peace he had been a tavern-keeper, and he still took pride in
the plain worthiness of that occupation and kept about him the amused
tolerance and sensible judgment earned in it, though he hid these attri-
butes behind a mask of cross-grained distemper and often bore himself so
stolidly that others were tempted into the error of thinking him dim-wit-
ted. He was one of those American generals, like the former ironmaster
Greene himself, who in civilian life had earned their bread by the sweat of
their brows and so were detested by the British as jumped-up tradesmen;
he enjoyed flaunting his supposed baseness. *I ain't no goddamned gentleman*, he liked to boast. *It's them fine rosy-arsed gentlemen's the reason the
British'll lose the goddamned war. War ain't a chamber quartet, you know. Or
boys buggering boys at Eton.*

His subordinate the unsuccessful duelist Major Armstrong, his arm
yet bound in an ignominious sling, reined out of the column to join the
party by the road. Just now Armstrong dwelt under a cloud of scandal
for his ill-timed affair of honor and his even worse blunder of allowing
himself to be shot in it. He had commanded the column of noncomba-
tants Greene had sent toward Camden during the pursuit of Rawdon in
July; and while Armstrong had done a fair job of that, had also showed
himself something of a whiner; the General had not been sorry to see
him return to North Carolina. He was no happier to have him back.
Worse, Greene loathed the absurd practice of dueling. Armstrong would
have much to prove.

Major Reading Blount, by repute a reliable officer, was to bring the Salisbury levy of regulars, when it came, though, alas, Sumner told Greene,
most of these were apt to be unarmed. The Marquis de Malmedy, who
would fetch down the rest of the militia, was a French nobleman whom
North Carolina had in its wisdom made a colonel. Malmedy was an unknown quantity—they had exchanged a few noncommittal letters—but

Greene harbored misgivings anyway. Save for Lafayette and Steuben, he had come to distrust the host of foreign adventurers who had hastened to America to escape their scandals and creditors and failed careers to remake themselves in its natal war.

That evening, on the greensward before his marquee and in the shade of a spreading oak, the General and the other senior officers of the army shared a bumper with Sumner and his subordinates. The drink was a fine Rhine recently liberated from the baggage of a British officer by a patrol of Colonel Washington's dragoons, a distinct improvement over the customary scuppernong or concord vintage or, worse, the vile grog which was always their last resort. The wine, together with General Sumner's rough good humor, lent the gathering a casual air that gave Greene more ease of mind than he had felt in weeks.

"Do you know, sir," he confided to Sumner, savoring the new serenity, "when I first came Southward, I had the devil's own time distinguishing between yourself and General *Sumter*, when I began to see your letters. Sumner in North Carolina, Sumter in the Southern Province—the name is so very nearly the same."

The North Carolinian's expression did not shift even by an atom, yet something in its very fixity seemed to betray a darkening of mood. "The name, yes," he conceded in a dead-flat tone, then added sternly, "but nothing beyond that, I *do* hope." They all conceived him offended to have been confused, even innocently, with the irascible South Carolinian; and Greene, appalled that he had vexed his friend, was jarred out of his newfound calm. A tension descended to still the gathering; then Sumner opened his broad grin and laughed his coarse guffaw, and after a moment's relieved hesitation the others joined him, all but Greene, who thought it best not to display a possibly impolitic merriment—though it did please him to learn that his nemesis Thomas Sumter, for all his valor, wore a villainous name in North Carolina too.

Still, he believed it best to choose safer conversational ground. "Many have been the days, and long the hours, sir, that I've awaited you and your troops," he told Sumner. "I give thanks to the Most High that you are among us at last." He paused then, and his mood turned gloomier. "Yet you've arrived at an especially melancholy moment; I'm sorry to tell you that tomorrow afternoon, between five and six o'clock, three of our soldiers are to hang—and sadly, one is a private of that part of the North Carolina Line that has served with me for some months. One of your very own, I fear."

As ever, any inkling of the necessity he so often faced to exact the supreme penalty wrung him with pity for the victim and with dread of the Judgment-to-Come. But Sumner only shrugged and treated himself to another sip of the Rhine. "God's teeth, we ain't all heroes, General Greene. What was his crime?"

"Desertion and the bearing of arms against the United States."

"Of course I regret it, sir," said Sumner, pleating his brow condolingly. "Yet if the whoreson's guilty, it's but justice that his neck be broke. What's his name, do you recall?"

The General reddened with guilty embarrassment; surely he should know the identities of those he had ordered to the noose. "I'm afraid I don't," he admitted, turning toward the open fly of the marquee; within, Hyrne and Pierce and Nat Pendleton—thank heaven *he* was back, and the indolent Lewis Morris gone Northward to confer with General Washington—were busy with correspondence. "Nat, how is the poor wretch called?"

"Rozier, sir," Pendleton replied.

Sumner gave another shrug. "Don't know the family, God be praised. Nothing's worse than sending home to tell a neighbor his son's turned a damned traitor and done a rope-dance for it. I'll attend it, sir, if you'll permit. 'Twill show the men I approve the sentence."

"I would be grateful. It will have a good effect, I'm sure."

"The other two?" Sumner inquired of the condemned.

"Marylanders, I believe."

"Tell me, sir, which do you hang the most of—Marylanders or North Carolina men?"

The oddity of the question startled Greene. "Why," he stammered, "I admit I've never kept account, General."

Sumner reflected. "I'll bet you hang a good deal of Virginians—a pernicious people, in my experience. Of course my own folks go to the gibbet pretty constant. Seems to me South Carolina fellows often want hanging. But I never yet heard of a Delaware man looking up a sapling. Of Georgians I cannot speak." Then, thankfully having carried that whimsy as far as he cared to, he made an abrupt change of topic. "What'll be your strategy, General, when you collect a force sufficient to resume active operations?"

Greene, now that the talk had turned to military practice, answered with confidence. "You may know, sir, there's a principle in the laws governing nations at war that when hostilities cease, the belligerents may keep any territory they yet hold. We may flatter ourselves that, as a result of our actions since the first of this year, the enemy has been forced to yield up substantial tracts of land here in the South that he once controlled. And there are whispers of discontent from London suggesting the day may be near when he will think of suing for peace."

Indeed, notwithstanding a recent refusal by Great Britain of a Russian offer of mediation, negotiations between the British and the French leading to a general settlement were rumored to be quite near, awaiting only a decision on a demand by France that the United States be a party to the talks. In the event of an armistice, it would be in Britain's interest to make whatever pretense it could of a conquest of some part of the South, preferably South Carolina and Georgia, in hopes of having those states ceded to it by provisions of the final treaty. "It's to our advantage, then," Greene explained, "to seize as much territory as we may. Yet the enemy continues to occupy much of the Low Country, and the land between that and this remains a debatable ground between us. And he holds Savannah."

"And Wilmington," Sumner reminded him; Wilmington and its small but active British garrison remained a festering sore in North Carolina's flesh. This was one of the many reasons its reinforcements had been so slow in coming to the Southward; troops were always needed to deal with forays from the city by the British and their Tory allies.

"Yes," the General agreed, "Wilmington also. I've given thought to an expedition there, which might be mounted as soon as circumstances permit; Colonel Lee especially advocates it most earnestly. But my chief aim now is to reinforce this army as much as I can, so I may march down from these hills and offer the enemy battle somewhere below the Congarees, with an eye to driving him back even further, maybe even into Charles Town itself, which of course we cannot hope to take given the paucity of our resources. But once he's mewed up there, perhaps I can, if not besiege him, keep him in his lair till peace is made. And somehow we must turn him out of Georgia too."

He took a modest draught of wine. This was the plan he was willing to speak of abroad; but what he nursed in secret was a dream of striking the enemy such a terrific blow as might cause Britain to give up the whole of the South below Virginia, a dream that might be either daring in the extreme or insane, he did not know which, but one he was determined to make real.

"What other prospects have you for reinforcement?" Sumner inquired.

"I had hoped the overmountain men of Colonels Shelby and Sevier might join us—those who drubbed Ferguson at King's Mountain last October—but I fear they may not come after all, as they have been engaged in negotiations with the Cherokees. But I trust I may still count as always on Generals Pickens and Marion, with their South Carolinians."

He did not mention The Gamecock, and Sumner acknowledged the omission with a gratified chuckle and a waft of his cup, then set on him a commiserating frown. "The presence of Cornwallis in Virginia keeps back troops that might otherwise be yours."

"Yes, nor have I begrudged the lack; the Earl is a dangerous man. Now, I hear, a French fleet of twenty sail of the line is at our coast with five to ten thousand troops, to cooperate with us as needs be—perhaps to go at New York and draw Cornwallis there. But I doubt my army will benefit in either case. If His Lordship does move to the Northward, our army in Virginia must follow him to reinforce Washington; and if he stays where he is Lafayette must keep all he has to hold him in place. Perhaps the French will sail to the Chesapeake; perhaps Washington will come there too. Whatever occurs, we here in Carolina must do what we have always done—the best we can, with the little we have."

The humble sentiments rattled emptily on his tongue. He was sick of deference and self-abnegation. No, he did not begrudge the necessity of yielding to Lafayette's greater need. Still, petty envy ate at his soul. He could not help it.

"It's known, sir," Sumner bowed and smiled, "that you've wrought miracles here. Loaves and fishes, ain't it? Bricks without straw?" He glanced roguishly about as they all laughed, but next he turned sincere and leaned to the General and said with conviction, "Your praise, sir, is in every mouth in all the country above." Greene blushed. The words moved and shamed him at once—moved him because he so immoderately yearned to hear them, and shamed him for the intensity of his yearning. In the sudden wash of feeling he barely heard what Sumner said next: "Didn't your cavalry make a wonderful stroke but a few days since?"

He had to bestir himself to reply. "Why, indeed, sir," he murmured. "Indeed they did." He motioned to Billy Washington. "Colonel, will you tell General Sumner how it came about?" Obligingly Washington related how Captain Watts of his First Dragoon troop, with an inferior force, recently made a dash at a party of twenty-odd of the enemy, took six, killed three, and wounded eight or nine more.

Sumner nodded. "Damned impressive, I call it."

Greene took fond thought of his dragoons. "In but the last fortnight," he exulted, "Colonel Washington's corps of horse have taken, killed, or wounded near forty of the enemy. I tell you, sir, the enterprise of our cavalry equals anything the world has ever produced."

"I believe," Colonel Ashe spoke up, "there was also an expedition against Monck's Corner."

The remark conjured again the dismal shade of Thomas Sumter, whose assault on the Corner of three weeks past had not only failed of its objective but exposed the South Carolinian's impulsiveness and unwisdom, two traits which, in combination, must always be fatal. Harry Lee and Francis

Marion, nominally under his command on the occasion, were now at daggers drawn with Sumter for his incompetency, which had lost them the lives of valuable men to small purpose. Greene hesitated, giving himself time to frame a diplomatic reply. "An effort was made to take the Corner," he affirmed at last. "Perhaps because we dispersed our strength it did not fare as well as I had hoped. Yet we were able to move the enemy down."

But Sumner would not let pass the opportunity to set the blame firmly on the head that had earned it. With a mischievous squint he inquired, "That was General *Sumter's* command, was it not?"

Greene could only nod. "It was."

Gratified, Sumner sank back into his camp chair. One or two of those present were seen to smirk. Major Armstrong uttered a bleat that might have been a chortle had he not stifled it. Colonel Ashe cleared his throat in the awkward interval that followed and presently offered a different thought. "You are obliged, General Greene, are you not, to concern yourself as much with affairs of state as with military matters? I'm told you are continually about the business of persuading the men of South Carolina and Georgia to reestablish their institutions of state government in the freed areas, lest the British reclaim political control."

The General nodded. "Whig and Tory have been at each other's throats so long in this country they cannot conceive how to stop perpetrating the most appalling atrocities. The place is a bloody shambles and badly wants setting right. I do encourage our friends to bring order to the recaptured places. And I appeal to the humanity of our partisans and militia to use the enemy and his adherents with justice and mercy. It seems to me an end must be put to the retribution each party wreaks on the other—else there'll be no amity among the people after the peace is made. And without amity, how can we have a nation?"

While he spoke Sumner's thick features knit in a grimace; he set his cup aside. "You have much charity, General Greene," he remarked, but with a dimming of his countenance as if he thought the quality a failing, and Greene was stung to see it. "Was it me," he went on, "I'd *extinguish* the Tory scum. Stamp 'em out like so many grubs."

He stood then, and Ashe and Armstrong rose with him. A little flustered, Greene rose too, as did the others. But now Sumner displayed his wide and homely grin. "Hell, I reckon that's why you've got the command, sir," he said, crossing to the General, extending his hand. "If they gave the power to a crude old son of a whore like me, why, we'd not be making a nation, we'd be making a damned bloody butcher shop of the place, and we'd be bashing brains out till every last one of us was dead and in Hell. But blood never gets nothing but more blood, does it? And the nation's what counts, ain't it? If we can make one." Greene took the big, callused paw;

Sumner stepped back and saluted him. "We must see to the settling of our men, sir. We thank you for the cheer."

Too moved to speak, Greene returned the salute.

The executions went well. The nooses were rightly placed to snap the neck; the victims did not unduly suffer. Greene was there with General Sumner standing on a nearby knoll, but looking just past the poor fellows as they dropped and swung—he was scrupulously watching the crowns of some oaks stirring in a breeze just as he'd done at Winnsborough, and so did not actually see them die though he distinctly heard the dry *click* of the breaking vertebra and heard it in memory again and again that evening as he worked in his quarters, and heard it that night too in fitful dreams from which he started awake, soaked in a clammy sweat.

Within ten days word came that the British in Charles Town had recently hanged a certain Isaac Hayne, a colonel of South Carolina militia who they claimed had violated his parole. This raised the ugly question whether the Americans must consider inaugurating a policy of retaliation in kind. Greene met with Otho Williams and Major Hyrne, his commissioner for prisoner exchange. They sat discussing ways and means of accomplishing the grisly business. Did they hold a British officer, equal in rank, whom they too might send to the hangman? If so, should they condemn him? Would this unleash an appalling round of militarily sanctioned murders? Had not this war's cruelties already surpassed all bounds of reason? Should they worsen the horrors just when prospects for peace were beginning to glimmer in the distance?

All the while they pondered, Greene kept hearing the small crisp noise of the snapped necks of his hanged deserters of a few days earlier. *How many now?* he wondered. *How many of my own have I hanged or shot?* For a long time he had faithfully, obsessively kept count, each new death prompting his soul, he felt, another inch down the long chute toward a well-earned perdition. But there had been so many; so many poor, famished, unpaid, and frightened fellows driven to break faith finally with the army that had long since broken faith with them. Weeks ago he had lost the tally. Now, it seemed, he would be hanging British officers too, adding captive enemy dead to the accusing host of his own condemned. The thought made him shiver with dread.

Most of that night he could not rest. He wallowed sleepless on his cot, hearing the necks break. The hundred cares of his command seethed about him; cares of subsistence and supply and equipage and manpower—how soon would Major Blount arrive with the Salisbury regulars, or Colonel Malmedy with the militia? Would they be without arms, and if not, how would he arm them? Must he now act the vengeful hangman too—he who only wanted to mend the terrible divisions of the war?

His mind spun among his troubles like a millwheel with a broken spindle turning freely in a flooded race. In his half-dreaming state he felt he might go mad if he could not stop the turning of that wheel. Then, toward dawn, exhaustion finally dragged him down into a stupor that was a kind of wakeful sleep. And Caty came to him.

It was she. Not a shade. Not a dream. It was her very self. Her own eyes—limpid, laughing, brilliant, as imperially purple as the robe of a Caesar. Her own abundance of glossy black hair; its thick, springy curls fragrant with a delectable aroma he could never persuade her to name, masses of curl that he loved to gather into his hands yielding and coiling and squirming in his fingers as if each lock were separately alive and rousing to his touch even as her body was rousing. Her own clear skin, flawless white and smooth as alabaster save on breasts and belly where a light marbling blemished it in an intimate and endearing way; soft skin, warmly soft yet with a firmness living in the softness; that warmth turning quickly to the sear of desire, the breasts risen, the nipples hardening, her plump mouth opening to his, her small lithe form twisting beneath him, heaving, her breath roaring in his ear. *Caty,* he cried. And wakened.

He lay trembling. His heart throbbed with such force that it shook the frame of the cot. She had been with him. She had come to give herself to him. The smell of her loosened hair seemed to be on his finger-ends, the scent of her essence lingered in the tent, her cry of ecstasy was just fading. He sat up bemused. Had she been but a phantom after all? How could a dream possess such shape, wield such power? He rose and struck a light to a candle and sat shaken at his camp desk.

Normally he did not dream of her. Of his reproachful dead, yes; but seldom of Caty. Dreams of her were safely pent behind the dam that held back everything he loved most. What had summoned her tonight? The executions? The ghastly prospect of reprisal hangings? He found no answer, and after a few minutes of troubled thought he was surprised to find that despite his shock he was suddenly drowsy. He fell back into bed and was instantly asleep. He slept long and dreamlessly and late; Peters had to wake him in the morning, an hour after sunrise. He arose refreshed, full of anticipation for the work of the day.

That day and the next and the next he managed his duties with renewed enthusiasm; the anxieties that had tortured him dwindled to their proper size; he handled them with his customary ease and dispatch. He wrote businesslike and well-reasoned letters to various civil and military officers seeking their views on what course to take in the matter of the execution of Isaac Hayne. He wrote a letter admonishing the militia commander in

North Carolina for not hastening to him Colonel Malmedy's contingent. He transacted a hundred of his normal tasks without the least sense of oppression. Nor did he question the nature of Caty's visitation; in fact he hardly thought of it at all.

Much later, however, he came to understand that the great troubles of his place as commander of the army were not the agents that had called up his vivid dream of her, as he had supposed. Instead they were but the signs and symbols of the real agent which had been, he now realized, his own fear. For he had been afraid. Afraid of his solitude in the void of high command. Others might advise him—South Carolina's Governor Rutledge, Otho Williams, Hyrne, Pendleton, certainly Harry Lee, who was always eager to give counsel in abundance; and Jethro Sumner might even honor him for his wisdom and charity. But in the end the General, *The General*, had felt unendurably alone. Alone with his possibly deficient judgment and with his resistless Quaker conscience.

That was it. He had wrestled in solitude with questions of high moment, yet he had doubted whether he brought virtue to the struggle or the faculty of right decision, even as that other, arrogant voice within him confidently insisted that Nathanael Greene always, *always* knew what was best to do. Those two contending selves had lived inside him and fought an unremitting war for possession of his soul. They still did; they probably always would.

So that strange sleepless night after talking with Williams and Hyrne about the need to commence the hanging of prisoners in retribution for the death of Isaac Hayne, torn by those cares, he had longed for Caty. Longed for her all unknowing. Longed for Caty who he knew believed in him, who had never for an instant doubted his virtue and wisdom and the rightness of his thought. Longed for her simple, trusting, unquestioning confidence. In his fear and loneliness and the lapsing of his strength, the wall he had built to hold back the wild waters of his affection for her had broken as it perpetually wished to break. The torrent had poured forth—the torrent he knew could carry him, if he let it, to realms so far from propriety and accomplishment and the world's mention that to return from it would be a longer and more arduous journey than he would ever wish to undertake. Caty in her fullness was a distant land; one might dwell in her forever. He had gone there for refuge, in one rush of rapture, and she had given him peace.

Part ye' Thirteenth

In Which a Young Man Affigns to His Horfe a Sacred Name

ONCE AGAIN HE HAD FOUND HIMSELF BY THE mighty River James that time after time kept crossing the path of his recent life. At evening, in the brief span of leisure between Stable Call and Tattoo, he liked to stroll down the lane from camp, seat himself on the pebbled shore, and watch the play of fading light on the broad bosom of the waters. In these few moments of peace at the end of a day crowded with wearisome duties, some of the soreness began to leave his body, some of his fatigue seeped away, and even his fear of Captain Gunn could start to lose its edge.

The last of the afternoon's heat lay briefly against him, a faint sting on his sunburned cheek; it sharpened the strong odor of his little roan and of the hay and straw of the stable that lingered in the folds of his hunting shirt. Then quickly the sting waned, the coarse smells of horsehide and fodder ebbed. Dusk was upon him. He rested content in shadow, the westward sky aflame and casting over the world a dimming glow of red. Steeped in momentary calm, he listened to the murmur of the passing river and waited for the miraculous moment when a fish would leap, flicker in air quicksilver-like, then drop back with a nearly noiseless splash.

For more than ten years another river had flowed through his world, bringing not tranquility and rest but bitterness and an abiding shame. The wide Potowmack had bounded one edge of his and Libby's persisting disgrace. Often he had crouched on its Maryland bank in evening's twilight, just as he did now, gazing across to the Virginia woods on the far shore, seeing the fish leap, envying them their freedom, dreaming of escape, dreaming of flight back to the free life, the honorable life his Ma and Da had told him about, that he himself could but dimly remember. In those times the exhaustion of servitude had been sunk so deep in him that nothing could soothe it, surely not the sight of the great river that hemmed him in. But here, now, the rolling River James gave him ease. Yet even here he was not free.

Wryly he smiled. He remembered Captain Harris' sarcasm that first day at the Arsenal: *By enrolling to fight for the liberty of your country, you have entirely yielded up your own again.* Yes, he supposed he was in servitude here too, in this dragoon camp of instruction at Manakin Town on the River James. And in some ways it was even a worse bondage than he had left behind, for if he dared fly the army, he would be shot for it. But if this new life bound him, it also offered scope; one could rise—some said the fearsome Captain Gunn had once been a lowly private just as James and Poovey were; and Captain Hughes was thought to have joined the regiment as a quartermaster sergeant. Here a kind of liberty waited within grasp. Life on the Potowmack had held out not the faintest hope of any liberty that one could shape even in imagination, for it lay so far in the future that the mind could not grasp it.

Here there was the promise of a greater freedom too—the freedom he thought they were all fighting to gain, the possibility of a freedom so large, so all-encompassing that perhaps any servitude at all would be impermissible once they won it. He liked to think that would be so. He liked to think that when the war was done there would be no more distinctions between great and mean, no more oppression by the rich and powerful, no more servitude of any degree. Of course he knew this would probably not come to pass. Whatever shape the freedom of America took when they earned it, it would naturally be but the work of men, and men must always divide humankind by their notions of who should rule and who should submit. Still, he nourished hope. Was this not revolution? It seemed to James, from what he had seen till now, that the nature of revolution was to fetch nearer a great many things that had long lain afar off; maybe the equality of men that so many spoke of would be among them.

Now, as he sometimes did when the farm on the Potowmack came to mind, he drew from an inside pocket the tattered scrap of paper he always carried. It was fragile and velvet-soft from years of handling. Gently he unfolded it. It lay limp in his hands, nearly transparent with age, the seams of its folds almost parting, the whole of it ready to fall into quarters at the least jolt. He did not read it; he did not need to. He simply sat holding it in his two palms as gingerly as if it were woven of gossamer, looking out over the river as the fish leapt, thinking of Libby and of Libby's fate, and of how that fate would not have been hers but for him.

He heard a rustle of movement on the path behind him, and Sides came out of lengthening shadows to settle nearby with a groan, laying a wrist on each knee so his hands dangled wearily limp. Poovey often joined him at the river after Stable Call, when Libby was busy with the laundering. Just now the red-hair smelled heavily of horse manure. "That damned nag of mine shits a bushel every hour," he complained. "I've not shoveled so many horse-apples in my whole life as I have these last weeks." James, lost in reverie, grunted a noncommittal reply. For a time they sat unspeaking, listening to the rush of the river and, from the rear, the mutter and distance-softened clangor of the camp. Somewhere back there a farrier's hammer sent its patient regular tapping into the dusk as a horse was shod. Presently Sides noticed James's paper. "Now and again I see you with that writing. What is it?"

James handed it over without comment. Poovey examined the flimsy with a scowl. "Why, a-body can't read that," he exclaimed. "It's all faded out."

"Don't need to read it," James explained. "'Tis fixed in my head."

"What d'you mean?"

"I mean I remember what's on it. Every word. I have it by heart."

Sides vented a disbelieving snort. "Well, that's a mighty big brag. I'd dare you to say it all out to me, but then I couldn't prove you wasn't making it up as you went." He flourished the tissue. "It's so pale, I couldn't prove you was lying, even if I *could* read—which I can't."

"This indenture," recited James, "made the twelfth day of November in the Year of Our Lord God, One Thousand Seven Hundred and Seventy, between Alexander Chenowith of the one Part, and James Johnson of the other Part, witnesseth, that the said James Johnson do hereby covenant, promise, and grant, to and with the said Alexander Chenowith, his executors, administrators, and assigns, from the day and date hereof, for and during the term of twenty-one years . . ."

"*Twenty-one years?*" Poovey exclaimed.

" . . . twenty-one years," James went on, "this being the conjoined term of himself and of Lachlan and Mariah Johnson, his parents, deceased, to serve in such service and employment as the said Alexander Chenowith or his assigns, shall employ him according to the custom of the country, of the like kind. In consideration whereof, the said Alexander Chenowith doth hereby covenant and grant to and with the said James Johnson to pay for his passage, and to find and allow meat, drink, apparel, and lodging, with other necessaries, during the said term; and at the end of the said term to pay unto him the usual allowance, according to the custom of the country in the like kind."

James paused, drew a breath, then concluded, "In witness whereof, the parties above-mentioned to these indentures, have interchangeably set their hands and seals, in the City of Wilmington, where stamp paper is not used, the day and year above written. Signed, sealed and delivered in the presence of Benjamin Harney, Esq., Ordinary."

Sides gazed at the paper in horrified wonder. "I never heard of no indenture that lasted no twenty-one years. Some's four, some's seven. But *twenty-one?*" His questioning glance turned to James. "How in hell did that come about?"

"Chenowith wrote a contract with his factor, paid passages for four—Libby, me, our Ma and Da. But Ma and Da died on the way. So he bound their term onto me. I tried to appeal it, but I was just a slip of a boy. The magistrate was some kin to Chenowith, and approved it."

Poovey passed the paper back. "But Libby..."

Carefully James refolded the delicate thing and returned it to his pocket. "She was a mere babe of five when we docked at Wilmington," he said. "So her indenture was worthless to Chenowith till she grew old enough to be put to useful work. He grumbled of keeping her but getting no gain; many's the time he relieved his spite with floggings and the back of his hand. After she turned ten, he got two years' toil out of her, then was obliged to turn her free, young as she was. But instead of leaving as she ought—as I begged her to—she chose to stay behind with me, her only living kin in all of creation, on that hellish farm. And me with fourteen years left on my time. And by then she'd grown from child to woman. And Chenowith noticed."

He hadn't meant to say that. Hadn't meant to let Sides know. He stopped, regret coursing hotly through him. Sides turned his face apart and for some time held silent. When he spoke again, hesitantly, it was of something else, something of less consequence and less pain. "Which Wilmington was it? Delaware or Carolina?"

The question was meant to turn their thinking from what neither wished to ponder and James welcomed it. "Carolina," he replied. "Chenowith had family there, and another farm. After he bought our papers he took us to his place in Maryland. Took us up by coastwise packet."

The diversion could be but momentary; Libby meant too much to each of them. Poovey gave his head a slow shake. He cleared his throat with a wet and clotted noise. "She never said naught to me of...of that."

He made the moist sound again; the ginger-hackle was weeping. Fervently James wished he could call back his words; it had been Libby's place to tell if she thought Sides needed to know. The truth had slipped out unintended, drawn from him by the melancholy of his evening mood and the memories it gave rise to. Then for an instant his old distrust of Poovey came surging back. Did Sides cry for Libby or for his own dashed hopes? Did he now brand Libby as damaged goods? Would he spurn her? Worse, would he ignobly tell her shame abroad? Why, if he did, by God, James would kill the damned fellow. But a stolen glimpse showed him the truth; his momentary gush of ire lapsed and he repented of his doubts. "Nor to me neither," he told Sides quietly, consolingly. "She never speaks about it. Not since that day . . ."

Sides looked to him quickly. "What day?"

"The day I found her standing over him with the fire tongs in her hand."

Poovey scrubbed away tears with the heels of both hands and gave him a narrower regard. "I thought *you* was the one clouted him."

James nodded. "It's how I tell it."

Sides sat with jaw agape. "It was *her?*"

"She was in the smithy laying a fire and he got at her and she grabbed up the tongs and used 'em."

"Did she . . . kill him?"

"We never knew. We lit out, and him a-laying there. He looked right dead to me."

They spoke no more as the long summer twilight deepened and the redness of the sky dimmed to a tarnish and the night settled in till the river was only a lighter tone of dark flowing through a denser one. Against the low chortle of the river's current they heard the occasional plop of still-leaping fish. Tree-frogs commenced their keening in the forests roundabout. It was nearly time for Tattoo. Presently they rose and made their way back along the now-familiar path. Before them, the last of the camp cooking-fires winked their scarlet eyes along the troop streets. The smoke of those fires came smartly to them and so did the rank aroma of scorched hoof-rind from the farrier's hut; they heard the clang of the blacksmith's hammer and, as they passed the stables, the stirring of horses and the deep wind of their breathing.

"D'you name that horse of yours yet?" Poovey inquired.

"Yes," answered James, "I'm going to call him Jesus."

Sides halted and swung to confront him. "*Jesus?* You can't give a dumb beast the name of the Blessed Savior! That's . . . what do they call it? That's . . . blaspheming. Ain't it? Why, the Lord God'll strike you down."

James shrugged. He had never been sure there was a God to strike anybody down; if there was, He seemed to pass up many a chance to lay low the evildoers, not to mention any blasphemers. "Sergeant Dangerfield said our horse is our salvation, didn't he?"

"He told you to kiss his arse too," Sides reminded him. "Did you do that, just because he said to?"

"No, of course not," scoffed James. "But I reckon he's right about the horse. If we believe in the horse, it'll keep us safe in battle. We're supposed to believe in Jesus too. So if Jesus is our salvation and our horse is our salvation as well, then they're one and the same, seems to me. So I'm calling my horse Jesus."

"Well, if you're a-going to do that," Poovey declared with passion, "I mean to keep a good deal of distance 'twixt you and me from now on." He wheeled and went stamping off. Smiling, James watched him go. He was heading for the ravine south of camp where the washerwomen laid the soldiers' clothes on the flat rocks of the streambed to beat them with battling sticks. He was going to see Libby.

James had got in but a week of drilling as an infantryman before the British forced Baron Stew-Ben to abandon the Arsenal at Point of Fork; after that, he'd gone straight to the field. But dragooning was an infinitely more complicated business than service afoot. A man might be handed a musket and thrown into the ranks of infantry with a minimum of instruction and do well enough, but a dragoon recruit had much to grasp before he could perform the basic tasks necessary for his own survival, much less command the skills he needed to gallop forth and punish the enemy. He must learn the management of a troop horse and every element of its care; must know the proper use of pistol, carbine, and sword; and must become proficient in the many evolutions of mounted drill and tactics—else, as Captain Gunn constantly warned, he was a dead man in the first skirmish.

James was confident in his knowledge of the horse. Though apprenticed as a house joiner, owing to his small size—he weighed but ten stone—he had often served Chenowith as a racing jockey. Chenowith owned a sorrel gelding named Patuxent, reputed to be a grandson of the famed Bulle Rock, and was fond of matching him against the other four-year-olds of the district. James had broken Patuxent when the colt was a yearling, and the two had shared the deep understanding that comes only when man and beast hold in common a precisely equivalent respect and trust. The same bond now pertained between himself and his little parti-colored horse; Jesus stood fourteen hands high and was what horsemen called a roan with a blackamoor's head—he had a coal-black face and legs and a mainly bay coat thickly speckled with spots of gray and white. He was spirited yet nicely biddable—a good honest horse, and a smart one.

But cavalry riding called for another order of horsemanship than was required to win purses in heats of four miles' distance on country tracks. For one thing, the seat was far different—"Lengthen those stirrups three holes!" the terrible Gunn, their riding-master, would scream, "sink your heels and sit up like a soldier; I can't have you setting like a broody hen!" For another, one had to know not only how to hold to the saddle under ordinary circumstances, but also how to maintain a steady seat in an action, when it was vital to control not just one's own motions of attack and defense, but those of an agitated mount as well. To complicate matters most of the horses, newly impressed from their owners, were as untrained as their riders and had to be taught their duties too.

Thirdly, the evolutions of the drill required a high degree of dexterity in man and horse and an intimacy of cooperation between them; without these, the formations and maneuvers upon which the operations of cavalry depended could be easily broken up. These refinements were daunting indeed; but James, relying on his long acquaintance with the good Patuxent, felt himself capable of easily absorbing them.

Day after day under a blistering July sun, Captain Gunn drilled them amid galling swarms of flies on the makeshift exercise ground which he called, for some peculiar reason, a manage. Over a period of weeks, gangs of miserably sweating recruits had pulled up enough roots and stumps and briar-bushes to make of it a nearly level field of several acres, though it still had mole-holes in it that would snap the pastern of an awkward horse. Also there were treacherous places where trees had been pulled out, leaving sinkholes of fill-dirt that subsided into the old stump-sockets and could, often did, break an animal's leg. Drilling there called for a careful eye and a smart horse, and James was grateful to have his canny Jesus roan.

At the center of this so-called manage rose a tall wooden pole; a series of shorter poles stood round its edge in sets of twos. There was sufficient space about these poles for James and the other recruits to be drilled in their sections of eight to ten men. While Captain Gunn drilled them the roughriders—the fellows who broke horses for the service—worked the untrained animals at the poles. Putting them to the rounds, it was called. Rounds, James learned, were ovals or circles worked at different gaits by the horse going about sideways, either with hindquarters toward his pillar or headwise to it. With his knowledge of horsemanship James was fascinated by the exercise, which he had never before seen, but instantly understood and approved. He could see that its purpose was to make the horse carry his shoulders and haunches compactly, without traversing or bearing to the side. He found it difficult to pay attention to Captain Gunn's instructions, so taken was he by the animation of the horses and adroitness of the roughriders correcting them with their whiplike thongs of leather fixed to shafts of cane—shambreers, he heard these tools called.

The manage lay at the edge of the tumble-down village where a band of Huguenot immigrants had settled at some pastime only to abandon it later for scattered farms in the countryside; now Manakin Town, named for the tribe of Indians it had displaced, was little more than a clutch of poor hovels surrounding a crumbling brick courthouse. While the recruits sweated and toiled, stolid French husbandmen and their skinny, work-worn women gathered to gawk. Grimy children in ragged shifts darted squealing between the ranks. Dogs snapped at the horses' heels. Behind the trampled space where they labored stood their camp—a gaggle of tents, sheds made of tree bark and straw, booths of sticks and Indian corn shocks—and their stables, forges, and horse pens. In the distance the river ran unseen behind its dense screen of willows and sycamores. Often in the broiling heat James, tortured by his thirst, would glance that way in sad longing. And in the evenings, freed at last from his drudgery, he would repair to the river to savor his interlude of peace.

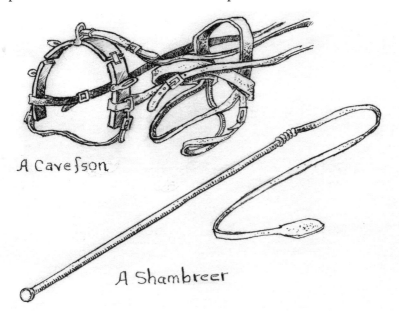

A Caveſson

A Shambreer

"Your horse," Captain Gunn had barked on their first morning, evidently reciting by rote the words of some dictionary of the art of riding, "is an animal so generally known, that to define him, 'tis sufficient to say, he's the noblest and most useful of all animals, and his sensible nature, obedience, swiftness, and vigor are at once the object and the subject of the noblest and most necessary exercise of the body.

"The art of riding," he continued in that same hortatory fashion, "teaches at once how to form both the horseman and the horse. The former it teaches a good seat upon horseback; a free, easy, disengaged posture; and the means of making his hands accord with his heels. The horse it instructs how to carry well; to take his aids gentle and fine; to fear the corrections that can fix him to a walk, a trot, and a gallop; and then to manage or work upon all sorts of airs; that thus broken and managed, he may be of use in the dangers of war."

After delivering this somewhat high-flown preliminary, Captain Gunn's bearing changed in a twinkling and he became what they would soon learn was his normal self; suddenly he seemed to be enraged. "War!" he bellowed. "That's what this is—all this shit hereabouts. War a-horseback!" He made of his face a twisted mask of what must have been the bitterest scorn. "Used to be," he bawled, "a regiment of dragoons was six troops of cavalry, plain and simple. But awhile back the Continental Congress changed all that. Now, says the swells, a-peeking out from under their Spencer wigs, there's no regiment of dragoons at all; instead, there's some goddamned thing called a Legionary Corps, which they tell us is four troops of horse and two companies of foot."

The Captain swore a terrible oath. "Well, just now, here at Manakin Town, we ain't got any of that. We've still got a regiment of dragoons. I grant you, there's some greenheads knocking about at Ruffin's Ferry and the Forks of the Pamunkey without any nags, that somebody's aiming to make into infantry and call 'em part of the dragoon service, even if they ain't—and, damn 'em, they *ain't*. You know why? Dragoons goes *a-horseback*, that's why. *Christ love me, this here, this's a horse outfit!* Any gull that claims different'll answer to me, and I don't care how high he may set. However high he is, he's still a-setting, as the fellow says, on his own arse. And the arse ain't made that I can't kick over the goddamned moon."

Then, as swiftly as he had descended into scathing invective, Gunn reverted with startling ease to his former solemnity. To the amazement of his listeners the remainder of his memorized lesson now came forth in calculated, reasonable, and measured tones: "A good dragoon is obedient to his officers, regular in his quarters, attentive to the care and cleanliness of his horses, arms, and all his appointments, and alert and exact in the discharge of every duty. It is honor and principle and not compulsion that should prompt him to an observance of these articles. Dragoons at all times carry themselves well, wear their helmets properly, and walk in a light and airy manner but with a firm, long step, which should distinguish the soldier from the clown."

Not a man in sight wore a helmet, but they attended him respectfully nonetheless. A troop, he went on to explain, was made up of sixty privates under the command of a captain, two lieutenants, and a junior officer called a cornet. A squadron—two troops—thus counted a hundred and twenty men. Whether there were to be four troops of horse and two of foot as the Congress decreed, or six of horse alone as Gunn so adamantly insisted, each comprised two units called divisions, and every division had a pair of platoons. In a platoon were two sections of eight to ten men each. Recruits, he said, were first to be trained in sections, the smallest and most easily managed unit; then by platoons and divisions. After that, they would be assigned to troops and sent into the field to learn by hard experience of warfare what they had not picked up on the manage.

No sooner had they absorbed this useful intelligence than, without warning, his coarseness broke over them again with the force of a lightning strike. "The First and Third Regiments had such bloody work in Carolina last year that both was pulled out of action and fetched back to Virginia to recruit to strength," he roared. "So any of you duck-fuckers who've enrolled thinking the dragoon service is going to be a featherbed, you've made the worst mistake of your miserable lives. You'll learn there ain't an ounce of pity in the blade of a saber or the blue plum of a pistol. We lost many a fine trooper in them goddamned swamps. And not a one of you shit-heads is good enough to kiss the dead rotten arse of the least of 'em. Hell, I've had *horses* shot from under me that was better than any dozen of you'll ever be."

James's heart writhed in his chest. His notion of easy service in the dragoons was now confirmed as wildest fancy. He could not stop himself trembling with terror. "Now," Gunn continued, "there's Lobsters all over the part of Virginia just east of here, and now and then Bloody Ban Tarleton makes a raid, and these is the very same goddamned cutthroat bastards that chopped us up in Carolina. And we've a detachment down in Carolina with General Greene too, a-fighting even more of the sons of bitches. When you're trained and equipped, by God, you'll be going one place or t'other, so you'd best pay me heed and learn fast, for ready or not, you'll be going to see the lions when cavalry's needed, and if you ain't ready when you go, well, it's your own goddamned blood that'll flow for it."

Under the lash of Captain Gunn's scurrilous tongue, and at times even under the pounding of his big fists, they began to learn what they needed to know. None of this meant, of course, that the training James and his mates received was as meticulous as might have been laid out in an official manual, which the Congress in its wisdom had yet to provide. "We're in a goddamned war," Gunn repeated, "and war don't wait on all the niceties of the riding-school, how to hold the reins and take the stirrup, nor how your goddamned hair's clubbed, nor your boots shined—if you've got any boots, which you ain't—nor if the fuzz under your horse's jaw's singed off, or if his tail's docked square or not. All that matters is staying on your nag, knowing the cuts and the guards of the broadsword, using the carbine and the pistol, keeping your place in ranks, and recognizing every bloody one of the trumpet calls."

Gunn was a redoubtable figure. James judged him to be nearly thirty years of age; he was sturdily built, long of leg but short in the body, with heavy arms and great meaty hands and a general air of crudity and belligerence that perhaps bespoke not just his stormy nature but also his humble

origins—in coming up through the ranks he had carried off an unimagin-
ably difficult feat in the aristocratic officer corps of the dragoon service. He
showed a hard agate eye in a sharp-angled face with a thin slash of mouth,
one of whose corners turned up and one down, making him look as if he
could not make up his mind whether to approve of the world or condemn
it. His skin was clear and milk-white, his hair as black as jet and worn in a
long queue hanging down his back.

A train of incriminating rumors followed him—that he had a disposition to reasonless violence, that he was a rogue of utterly debauched mor-
als, that his temperament was so unstable as to border on lunacy. None
seemed able to confirm all the dark surmises but, thanks to his turbulent
behavior before the troop, every ranker believed them—more than once
they had watched astounded as, enraged by some recruit's innocent
blunder, he hurled himself upon the poor offender and pummeled him
unmercifully. It was known for a certainty that he was a notorious duelist, though it could not be discovered whether he had ever actually killed
anyone on the field of honor. As a consequence, even his fellow officers
seemed to live in dread of him; how much more baleful must he appear
to such poor fellows as James and Poovey, who trembled powerless under
his absolute reign?

The time had quickly come, in the Gaskins Battalion, when James had
grown comfortable, even familiar, with the musket that at first had repelled him. But the cavalryman's arsenal on first acquaintance looked so
alien and so fiendishly lethal as to seem excessive and he did not see how he
would ever come to terms with it.

Each man was issued a brace of pistols—his were great cumbersome
long-handled pieces, French-made, .69 caliber, brass mounted, with nine-
inch barrels. He had never before clutched a pistol, much less discharged
one; these hung so heavily in his hands that he despaired of ever steadying
them at arm's length long enough to aim and fire. Thankfully, he learned,
the monsters were to be carried not on the person but on the saddle in the
bearskin-covered holsters that hung to either side of the pommel.

It was the responsibility of their sergeant, Dangerfield, to acquaint
them with the practice of arms. The pistols, he demonstrated, were primed
and loaded just as a firelock was. They were to be employed one at a time,
so a hand was always free to control the reins. You reached across the body
to draw the left pistol from its pommel holster first. Once discharged,
that piece was returned and the right one drawn, if needed. The pistol
was steadied for cocking by resting it against the palm of the reins-hand,
then leveled right-handed for aiming and fired with the wrist held at the

height of the shoulder, the pistol itself tilted over to the side so the prim-
ing charge covered the touch hole. It was simple enough in principle, but
James thought the pistols horribly ponderous and difficult to manipulate,
and in his small hands their great weight dragged continually downward
so he could never reliably take aim.

"Come here, son," Dangerfield beckoned in his steely voice, on the first
day of practice with the weapons he called snappers. James approached
with trepidation, bracing himself for some demeaning reproof; but Dangerfield only grasped his left forearm, bore it firmly upward, then bade
James cup his left hand beneath his right wrist so the pistol was supported
two-handed.

"Little fellows like Johnson here," he told the others, "need
to shoot any way they can, be damned to what the drill says.
Just remember, keep hold of the reins in that left hand. That
horse'll be fractious, he'll want to pull you off your aim, but
hell, nobody ever hits anything with a snapper anyhow."
With his open palm he smacked the broadsword hooked
by his side. "Remember, it's the cold iron that does the work
and spills the tripe and dumplings. The Congress gives you
a snapper, you've got to use it. Comes to shooting, point the
damned thing, draw the trigger, and hope for the best—but
put your trust in your sword."

The carbine offered a reassuring affinity, for it was very like
his old firelock, only shorter, lighter, and thus more service-
able to a mounted man. Not all recruits received one, for they
were in short supply, but nearly every man in James's section
did. His was a .65-caliber musketoon with a short forestock
that exposed most of the barrel. The happiest news was that
he need not lug it about by hand or truss it across the shoulder as he had his old firelock. It could be fastened to a leather
sling worn across the body, and when he was mounted, he might secure
it by shoving the muzzle into a small leather bucket fixed to the saddle
just ahead of his right stirrup. It was, of course, an awkward and unwieldy
piece to manage—was too long to be comfortably slung when afoot, and
when worn mounted and plugged into its little socket, it pounded the side
of the leg unmercifully with every stride of the horse. But at least he knew
how to use the thing.

The saber, though, unsettled him. At first, when he held one in his own
fist, the notion of wielding a metal blade struck James as oddly antique.
Did not the sword belong more fitly to the age of knights and fair damsels?
Yet somehow it had survived, improbably and impractically, into this
modern scientific world. At the same time, though, he knew its deadly

uses. Sergeant Dangerfield insisted it was the primitive cold steel, far more than the lead ball fired by the more advanced pistol or carbine, that gave cavalry its most decisive power; and James well remembered the carnage the Green Dragoons had wrought on Colonel Buford's men at the Waxhaws, so vividly described by his old sergeant.

It was awesome to think he too might now command that same murderous force just as he had longed to do while plodding through the Chickahominy bogs not so many days before. Many recruits were given straight-bladed broadswords with basket hilts, but for some reason James received a big iron stirrup-hilted saber with a curved blade thirty-six inches long. It had a knurled grip of cherry wood bound with woven brass wire. It was carried in a leather scabbard attached to a belt of white buff slung over one shoulder. As with the pistols, its clumsy weight frightened him. How would he ever ply it?

Dangerfield taught him, drawing on the same fatherly patience he had shown with the pistols, and as James slowly grew to understand the saber, he also came to admire the man giving him that understanding. "Your saber," the sergeant explained, "is for cutting with the edge. Some of your mates has got the broadsword with a straight blade; it's for skewering. If we was set up like they are in Europe, we'd have regiments of heavy dragoons that use the broadsword, on account of it's best in the thrust and the massed charge; and light dragoons, for scouting and skirmishing and such, that use the saber to slash and cut at the enemy when going at it boot-top to boot-top. But here in American it's catch-as-catch-can; we must use such swords as we can get. So some has got the broadsword and some, like you, the saber; with us, a dragoon's a dragoon, light or heavy or whatever's the need.

"Now, for my taste, you've the best of it with the saber. Learn the cuts and you can give a fellow, say, a Cut One and cleave his head to the chin. Down and up, in and out, you'll make a wound as clean as if you'd split a turnip, while a fellow with a straight blade, thrusting through his man in a charge, will like as not get his sword stuck in the rib cage and break his goddamned wrist."

Like Gunn, Dangerfield could wear his authority with a swagger, and at the outset James had been frightened of him; but oddly, of the two, his temper eventually proved the more refined. Gunn's smacked of the hooligan; Dangerfield's, of a serene confidence that seemed to rise from good blood, from privilege, and perhaps from a measure of learning. He bore a famous Virginia name, and the men were fond of imagining the various scandalous ways a high-born Dangerfield might have been brought so low as to wear the two blue worsted epaulets of a sergeant rather than the single silver one of a captain, as did Gunn, whose origins were undeniably mean. Though it was a mystery not to be solved, every recruit might see for himself the subtle deference every officer, even Colonel White, extended to this peculiarly misplaced sergeant, whose every word and gesture asserted a force of personality as sovereign as any general's.

———————

There was a daily routine: Reveille at dawn, then Stable Call at eight, Mounted Parade at ten, Stables at three in the afternoon, a dismounted Evening Parade at five, Stable Call again at seven, then Tattoo at ten, with drills interspersed throughout. Each duty was announced by intricate and at first indecipherable blasts of the trumpet, which Captain Gunn kept admonishing them to memorize. But often this ordinary schedule was interrupted by the need to send out parties to gather forage, or even to chase after Tarleton, who these days was said to be plundering about Dinwiddie Court House and Petersburg. Save for his rampages, the war in Virginia seemed to have fallen quiet; Corn Wallace was in Portsmouth, where he lay coiled like a serpent in its den, watched by General Loff Yet's little army. But even if the war had shrunk down to Tarleton alone, it remained a deadly enough affair; naturally no recruits were taken on any patrol that might run afoul of him. Foraging expeditions, however, did occasionally fall to their lot. Any one of the several officers on hand—Captains Hughes, Pemberton, or Nixon, sometimes Gunn himself—might command such a foray.

James disliked the work intensely, for it made him feel little better than a brigand to go dashing about Powhatan and surrounding counties stripping poor farmers of their swine, sheep, and chickens. At least they were no longer confiscating horses, a repugnant business that had aroused the wrath of the people like no other—both regiments were now at full strength in saddle mounts after weeks of ruthless impressments that many Virginians had regarded as little better than thievery. However, officers from Colonel Henry Lee's Partisan Legion had come up from General Greene's army and were now requisitioning what few private horses the First and Third might have missed, so the temper of the populace was waxing hotter by the day. The farmers and millers and merchants howled imprecations at James and his mates that followed them to their beds at night and echoed in their troubled dreams. Was it an act of patriotism, they could not help wondering, to make off with the goods of common folk?

Though James found the duty disagreeable, it was admittedly a relief to escape for a few days the confines of camp, the rigors of drill, and the abusive harangues of Captain Gunn. James and his fellows—Sides; a dour young Prince William chandler named Tom Brown; Cornelius Bussey, a fuller from Essex County; three lads from his mess called Nichols,

Baldwin, and Arthur; and always a few recruits he didn't know drawn from other sections and companies—these could revel in the now-rare privilege of ranging along under the bright wholesome sun, with a good horse between the legs, the honest taste of open air in the mouth, and the rich smells of forest and field and pasture to breathe. Those simple pleasures, after the confinement of Manakin Town, helped blunt the pangs of guilt they felt for the distress they were spreading in their wake.

Poovey alone regarded the foraging with unmixed delight. "How much more fun could a fellow have?" he would cry. "My whole life I've craved all the truck other folks had and I didn't. Well, now, by God, I can grab as much as I want of it. Besides, I been in the army all this time and ain't never been paid a farthing. And don't the damn army owe me a thousand dollars' bounty anyways, that they ain't never give over?"

Of course what they took was hardly theirs to keep; everything they confiscated went to the support of the cavalry. For Sides, the gratification seemed to be in the sheer act of taking. Part of what he said, however, was true enough—they had not been paid, nor had they received the thousand dollars Colonel White had pledged as an enlistment bounty. Though every man who had enrolled under the inducement had long been wondering when the money might be laid out, none was brave enough to raise the matter with Gunn or Dangerfield; and to mention it to the lordly Colonel White himself was unthinkable. So day after day the matter languished unresolved while the discontented recruits grumbled and swore, nursing suspicions that the Colonel had foully and selfishly lied so as to swell the depleted ranks of the First Dragoons.

Then, one evening in early August, James's bounty, at least, was paid out—but hardly in the fashion he had been expecting.

Part ye' Fourteenth

In Which General Greene Owns His Paſſion

IT SEEMED HE HAD KNOWN HER ALL HIS LIFE. Of course this was not true. He was already a strapping lad of twelve working at his father's forge at Potowomut when she was born at New Shoreham on stormy, faraway Block Island twelve miles out in the raging Atlantic. Not for ten more years, after the death of her mother, did she move to the mainland to live with her Aunt Catharine at East Greenwich.

He would have been twenty-two then. He must have seen her about that time, for he visited often; her uncle by marriage, William Greene, was his distant kinsman. She would have been but a child, one among the many who had the run of that big, friendly East Greenwich house; there was no particular reason he should have noticed her at such a tender age. Yet it worried him now that he had no memory of a first meeting. For everyone said she was an extraordinary child, just as she would become an extraordinary woman.

They called her Kitty then. The name suited, they said. They spoke of her kitten's gamboling, winsome ways, of her penchant for mischief, of her unquenchable curiosity, her boundless energy. She had come to them half-untamed, they said, having grown up on that isolated, wind-blasted, primitive island where even the womenfolk rode astride and wore britches like the men, where all the islanders were unchurched, willful, fiercely independent, and freethinking. She was little better than a savage, they said. Surely he should have remembered her.

Doubtless Hannah Ward was the reason he did not. Hannah was Sammy Ward's sister; Sammy was his great friend in those days and, incidentally, the favorite cousin of the little barbarian from Block Island. But Sammy's comely sister had laid early claim to Nathanael's heart, and for some period of time—how long, he knew not and reproved himself for the ignorance—he paid earnest court to Hannah Ward at East Greenwich while Kitty Littlefield must have peeped at them from behind the furniture or perhaps galloped past on a broomstick horse, all unnoticed by Nathanael in the blindness of his supposed love.

Then came the day when Hannah Ward gave him the mitten. He was uncertain why. That he was something of a plodder, that he limped and had a bad eye and suffered from asthma, that he had a Quaker's reticence and too-conspicuous rectitude, that he was perhaps too anxious to parade

the knowledge he'd gained from his extensive and possibly ponderous reading, and that he had a regrettable tendency to correct the grammar and etiquette of others—all these faults in himself he readily acknowledged.

But he had wanted to believe his many brighter qualities overrode the dimmer ones. After all, he was a jovial sort, women seemed to think him good-looking, his teeth were in good order, he had a wry sense of humor and could tell a humorous anecdote better than anyone, and he very much fancied dancing, to the intense disgust of the Friends Meeting. He was, by then, a middling successful merchant and anchorsmith, and he owned a sound new house in Coventry.

But for Hannah Ward all these inducements proved insufficient in the end. She loved him not, she said. She turned from him to another. Nathanael was crushed. Soon afterward the forge in Coventry burned down. The fates, it seemed, had frowned on him. It must have been then, sunk in the trapfall of his misfortunes, that he first gazed into the luminous violet eyes of the stunning young woman Kitty Littlefield had grown up to be while he was making his tedious way into stolid middle age, wasting precious years infatuated with a woman whose charms, in the blaze of Caty's beauty, now faded away like a forest flower exposed to sun.

Once that beauty burst on him, it withered all that had come before.

That was why it seemed to him now, looking back, that he must have known her from the first. His life—his truest life—had not begun till he'd been bathed in her fire. It was not alone the fire of her beauty, it was the fire of her spirit too. For in her breast the turbulent seas still surged and the howling winds still blew, the barren wastes she had grown up loving still spoke to a certain small cold loneliness at the center of her being that nothing could warm, though he never ceased believing he could warm it. The vitality of the wild was in her; the valor of her Scots forebears too, chafing against every restraint. Yes, she was wild; would forever be wild, like a creature of the forest that has consented to live with you, but whose behavior will always be subject to rules you can never understand or predict.

Yet in many ways she remained a heedless, self-regarding child. Loving the outdoors, she had neglected her studies and was, by Nathanael's lights, nearly as ignorant as a Red Indian; she spelled appallingly, knew nothing of history or political economy or literature or philosophy, though she did begin to dabble in a little serious reading after he first displayed an interest in her. She had no concept of the value of money and was a relentless purchaser of pretty but inconsequential goods.

She cared not a whit for the opinions of others, which made her seem more arrogant than she was—it only meant she wanted to believe in the invincible rightness of her every act. Too often instinct alone governed her, led her into ill-considered ventures that ended badly. She was accustomed to being pampered and abetted—yes, she was spoiled; and she was far too accustomed to the admiration of men and the resentment of women, which she relished shamelessly and impartially.

It was this child who called up the older man in him, the doting father. She was the child he wished to nurture and protect and teach and improve. But it was the woman who called up the fun-loving swain he'd never had a chance to be. Not only had he enjoyed dancing, he'd gone to parties and read novels and romances and committed a very few mild indiscretions—enough to annoy his pious father and the dour Friends Meeting of Potowomut, yet never sufficient to imperil his immortal soul—but in the main, as Cousin Christopher had once said of him, he'd been born thirty-nine years old and had the temperament of a country schoolmaster.

But beneath all that, his blood ran hot. Caty ran it hotter. They were married on the twentieth of July, seventeen-seventy-four, in Uncle William Greene's home in East Greenwich, the great house where Caty had grown up. A Baptist, Elder John Gorton, performed the sacrament—the Friends had read Nathanael out of Meeting by then because as a committed Patriot he had been attending militia drills in the belief that war must soon come. They were married in the southeast room of the house where, Caty confided, none other than Benjamin Franklin, in former times an unsuccessful suitor of Aunt Catharine's, used to sit and savor the long views over the peaceful Rhode Island hills and valleys.

He knew why he had married her. He had done it because he could do no other. He had looked into those eyes and seen in them a deep light he had never before glimpsed, a light that seemed to say, *I accept you as you are; my trust in you has no limits; I surrender to you with nothing held back; I will be faithful to you all your life.* He saw that she was going to believe in him more fully than he had ever been able to believe in himself notwithstanding all his vaulting aspirations. Once he had seen that, and once he had put his fingers tenderly into that thick mane of glistening, coiling raven-black hair and kissed that delectably plump mouth, he knew there could be no one for him but this wild, willful, child-woman in whom secretly nested, waiting for her to discover them, ambitions and powers he knew in his vitals might be the equal of those he nourished in himself.

Yet with all her strength, he would learn in time that in some ways she was as delicate as a moth. Touch a moth's wings, bring away on your fingertips the precious dust that gives them flight, and the moth will sicken; he'd always heard that and believed it. So too with Caty. Whenever life dealt out rough handling, her health would wilt as easily as the moth's wings. It was odd. How could so robust a spirit live in a vessel so frail? He could not guess; nor did he even know at first how fragile her body was. The weakness—if it *was* a weakness—only showed itself later, under the stresses of the war. Still, sick or well, Caty was going to be, now was, the only love he was ever going to have.

It was less clear why she had chosen him. Hosts of handsome young men with greater fortunes and better prospects had vied for her favor. She could have picked any one of them and risen far higher than she ever could with Nathanael Greene, that dull, lame, paunchy old fussbudget whose ambitions always seemed to outrun his abilities and whose businesses doddered along moderately well without ever really prospering. To some—on occasion, even to himself—he came off as disagreeably vain about his learning; he could not help it; his knowledge had come hard; he'd gained it against the will of a father who harbored dark suspicions about the worth of education. He was hardly a prize that a beautiful young woman might covet.

It was something she had never explained—why she'd accepted him— save to say, wide-eyed, when asked, *Why, Nathanael, I just love you.* He believed she truly did. He had believed it every moment of every day of the seven years and one month since, believed it even when he disbelieved, even in the blackest times when jealousy got the better of him and he lost faith and feared the worst and raged at her with frenzied accusations. Believed it down at the deepest footing of himself even as he reproached her

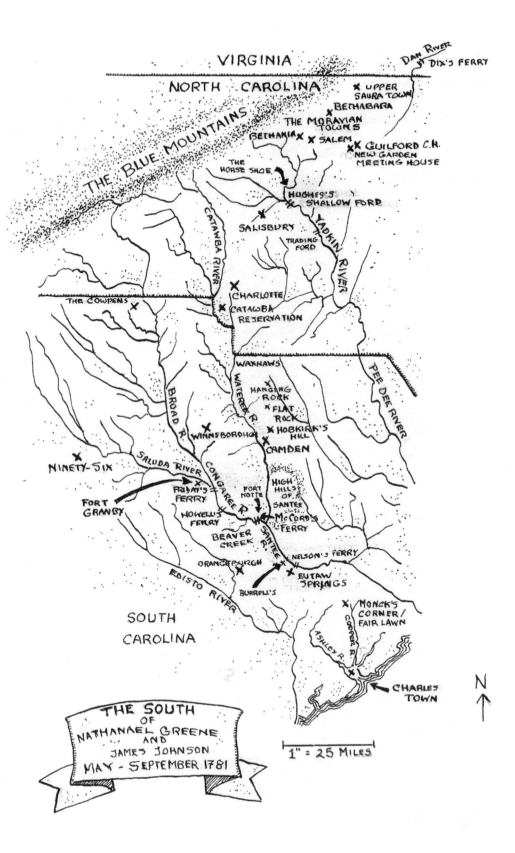

and shut out her tearful denials. There had been some appalling scenes; but there had never been a second during the worst of them when he had not known that in some perverse way he was pretending to think she had betrayed him when he knew for certain she had not. Even at his angriest, he had never ceased believing; and because he had believed so persistently, so absolutely, and because he had learned at last to trust in that belief, he did not listen now to the whispers of her misconduct that sometimes came to him.

The war he had known must come burst over them much too soon. Ten months after their wedding the minutemen of Lexington and Concord clashed with the column of British regulars General Gates had sent out from Boston to raid the munitions of the Massachussetts militia; Nathanael, till then a private in the local Kentish Guards, very quickly found himself a general of militia helping invest British-held Boston with his Rhode Islanders. Within weeks he was commissioned a brigadier in the new Continental Army.

Caty, by then, was carrying a child. Despite her condition, and without notifying him ahead of time, she undertook a day-long carriage journey up to his camp at Jamaica Plains, west of besieged Boston. He was overjoyed to see her, but much alarmed by the risk she'd taken. He obtained leave and took her back to Coventry, but was recalled on the occasion of the fight at Breed's Hill. Not many weeks later, and now in an advanced state of pregnancy, she came to him again in the camp at Prospect Hills. Once more, after an agreeable visit, he sent her packing. And presently, at William Greene's house in East Greenwich, she gave birth to a boy whom they named George Washington Greene.

This established a pattern that had held till he came Southward—long separations, letters from Caty pleading with him to come home, letters from him seeking to comfort and reassure, Caty's impulsive trips to camp, passionate reunions, tearful returns to Coventry or East Greenwich or New Shoreham, soon followed by the discovery of a fresh pregnancy, then difficulties with the carrying of the child which left her seriously weakened, and finally a birth—Martha in 'seventy-seven, Cornelia in 'seventy-eight, then little Nat just over a year ago; three in as many years.

What it cost her to be with him! But he soon learned she also drew strength from him. Her own, which he knew to be great, slept a deep sleep when they were apart. Only he could awaken it—or so she believed. At first he did not wish to think that; he wanted her to bring it out of herself. But finally he came to see it was his duty to stir her to her own possibilities. When they were together, he could rouse the powers; when apart, she did not even know she had them. It did not help that having been raised much like a feral boy, then turned over to her Aunt Catharine, who finished her off as little more than an ornament, she lacked every practical feminine art—could not sew or knit or weave or tend a garden, knew nothing of how to be the mistress of a house and everything about how to seem trivial and self-indulgent.

So during their long partings she tended to lose her bearings. Nathanael's brother Jacob and his wife Peggy lived with her in the Coventry house; naturally Peggy was appalled at what she regarded as Caty's indolence and felt compelled to usurp the duties Caty neglected. This made Caty feel demeaned; she grew surly; soon she was quarrelling with Peggy, then with Jacob, next with Nathanael's stepmother, and finally with the wives of his other brothers.

She gave in to imaginary maladies, she shopped impermissibly; and worst of all, she played the coquette with the men who were always offering to immolate themselves on the altar of her love, not excepting his own friends Varnum and Wadsworth and Wayne; his assistants Cox and Pettit when he was named Quartermaster General; even Lafayette after the French came into the war, and His Excellency himself. She set envious tongues to wagging all over New England. So rife was the scandalous talk that even her Aunt Catharine finally broke with her for fear of a disgrace that might blot the high name of William Greene.

Nathanael no longer paid heed to the rumors. He remembered what her eyes had said, *I will be faithful to you all your life*. If she busied herself with parties and hops and balls, if she flirted without shame, she did so because it was the only way to remind herself that she was desirable, the only way to warm that icy loneliness at the core of her, the only way she could make herself believe, if but for a moment, in her own strength. At those times she reverted to the wild, restless creature from rugged, sea-swept Block Island.

She was at her best in camp with him. There she withstood every hardship with patience and good humor; there her spirits flourished and her beauty glowed as nowhere else. The grimmer the surroundings, the more brightly she shone. Nathanael's troops worshipped her; his officers swooned at her feet, and though the idolatry did incite the envy and disgust of more than one officer's wife, Lady Washington became her great friend and that quieted many a complaint. The Commander-in-Chief adored her; once His Excellency danced with her three whole hours, boasting the while how he'd stolen her from her Quaker preacher. After the terrible winter at Valley Forge, Washington was heard to say that Caty Greene had done as much for the morale of the Continental Army as anyone, himself included.

But always there came the time when she must go home. And there the gloom would descend. He did his duty; he wrote often trying to bolster her spirits from afar the way he used to do at home. He took her side in the feuds with the Greenes; no one knew better than he how irritating most of his kinfolk were, what delight they took in finding fault and laying blame. He told her to disregard all gossip. He reminded her of her grace and beauty and of his love for her. *My Angel*, he called her.

But he knew his letters sometimes reproached and hectored as often as they gave encouragement. He perfected her spelling and grammar; he lectured her on the proper deportment for the drawing-room; he gave her lessons—God forgive him—on how to be as great a lady as Martha Washington and Lucy Knox; yes, sometimes his own crude ambitions crept in to hurt and humiliate her. But amid all his worries and distractions, this was the best he had been able to do. He knew it was not enough.

That was when he had begun to build the wall to hold back the massy waters of his great love that he thought, if allowed to rush forth, would bear him away from all he wished to accomplish in the world. He was tired; the energy was no longer in him, he feared, both to fight this war and give to Caty what she needed. It seemed he must choose between one and the other, between saving the country and saving Caty.

The wall he'd built to avoid that choice had stood for a long time. He had resisted her repeated pleas to come Southward to join him. The country was too unsettled, he told her. The climate was sickly and would undermine her health. And what of the children? She could scarcely bring them into this hideous abyss of fratricidal strife; and were she to leave the little ones behind, who would care for them? Each argument was a new brick in the wall. Each built it higher.

Yet each, he guiltily knew, also had its conspicuous answer—numerous friends like Lady Washington would clamor to take in George and Cornelia and Martha and Nat. If South Carolina was a stew of murder, so to some degree were Tory-ridden New Jersey, New York, and Pennsylvania. There were miasmas Northward as well as to the South; she would fall sick sooner in Rhode Island, estranged from him, than by his side in Carolina, where every day his will could speak power to hers.

Now he understood that the flow of faith had never been just from him to her; it had been reciprocal. The wall he'd built to save his energy had instead starved it of what she had once given and wanted to give again—her belief. Now the wall had fallen; Caty had breached it with her utter trust, released the cataracts it had been holding back; and rather than bear him away from his duty as he'd once feared, instead he saw how they were going to carry him upward, to meet it.

Finally he was glad. He could give back the same pledge she had given to him: *I accept you as you are; my trust in you has no limits; I surrender to you with nothing held back; I will be faithful to you all my life.*

Part ye' Fifteenth

In Which a Young Man Gains Liberty
Whilſt His Friend Loſes It

I T WAS MAINLY A MATTER OF WHAT THINGS WERE
called. Your right hand, for instance, was no longer your right hand,
it was your "sword-hand"; nor did your left hand keep its former identity,
but instead became your "bridle-hand." You might prick your horse, as
you were used to do, with your spurs, called your "bleeders" now; but you
must not on any account leave the spurs embedded in the hair of your
horse's flanks, though the reason for this prohibition remained obscure.
As any fool knew, to prick or pinch with your spurs was an aid, but to
bear hard was a correction; and a good horse always obeyed the heels.
These particular admonitions would have been easier to follow had
James and many of his fellows owned boots instead of having to strap the
spurs around their bare feet so the buckles and chains constantly slipped,
chafing ankle-bones and arches.

What James had been wont to call the carry of a horse—that is, the
motion of its legs at the gallop or any of the gaits—Captain Gunn insisted
was its "air." That sense of lively and intimate communion between the
horse's mouth and the bridle-hand, which to James had ever gone nameless, now became the "stay"; or, if it conveyed the will of the horse as well
as its answering to the bit, the "feel." The "manage," that mysterious word,
signified not just the ground set aside for the exercise of riding, but the exercise itself. Rounds were also "volts," God knew why. And so on.

James quickly learned the words for the things he had always known.
And it did not take long for his superior horsemanship to capture the
notice of the demonic riding-master. He sensed Gunn's darkling regard
resting on him, knew the Captain saw and commended his light hand and
how deftly he used the calves of his legs on the flanks, with Jesus bearing
well on them. It did not hurt that Jesus was himself the nearly perfect
dragoon mount—a little small at fourteen hands, but brisk, high-mettled,
and stately, with a raised neck, a fine motion, his mouth good and tractable,

210

champing on his bridle with a fair grace. Jesus knew his heels, fitted well on his hips, and kept his haunches low, and on the rare occasions when he went narrow, enlarged at once with but the merest touch of spur and leg and a nearly invisible lift of the bridle-hand. Some might be tempted to name him a mean breed, but Jesus surmounted every prejudice.

Gunn watched, watched man and horse alike with a close, shrewd, and practiced eye, watched with the dimmest show of approval; but he let fall no single word of commendation, not one syllable of encouragement. On the contrary, his reprimands stung James as often as any other, perhaps oftener, and James burned with resentment knowing much of the scolding to be unwarranted. It was as if Gunn perversely wished to punish him for his evident skill. Whenever their gazes met, the Captain's flat black eyes, lightless as a pair of buttons, held his for an instant of cold disdain, then flicked away in dismissal; James did not seem worthy of even a particle of respect.

One day as his section was dispersing from drill, James spied a roughrider struggling at one of the pillars with a nervous trout-colored horse whose eyes and nose were spotted white; at every flourish of the shambreer, the beast, a gelding that looked to be a four-year-old, shied back and made as if to rear, but because its head was held fast by its tether to the post, it could only twist and pull in vain. Too much of this would strain the neck, and James could see that in plunging about so desperately the animal might also damage a tendon or even snap a leg. Clearly the roughrider was an incompetent and the horse knew it; knew it as all horses know all bunglers; and it feared the injury the man's clumsiness might inflict. James watched in deepening anger as the gelding grew more and more unmanageable and the roughrider, losing patience, commenced to lash it with his shambreer.

"I'll stop that!" he suddenly cried, jumping from the saddle quick as any monkey. Tossing his reins to a disconcerted Poovey, he sped across the width of the manage to the post, where in a spasm of rage he wrenched the shambreer from the roughrider's grasp. "Can't you see?" he yelled into the man's face, "it's your damned awkward waving of this here stick that's stirred that horse up!"

"Give that back or I'll bust you one!" yelled the roughrider.

Beside himself with rage, James gave the fellow a savage push that toppled him on his backside in the dust. The villain sprang back up, and James cast aside the shambreer, squared to him, and stuck out his chin. "Bust away," he said. "See what you get."

The roughrider was half a head taller, heavier through the shoulders and bigger in the upper arms; when he doubled his fists before him they looked the size of cantaloupes. But James figured on licking him anyway. James was mad as a doused cat, and he'd always believed being mad gave a man a considerable advantage. He raised his own hands and balled them tight and set himself firm on his feet and puffed out his cheeks so a blow wouldn't hurt the inside of his mouth as much. But then he noticed the worsted epaulet on the right shoulder of the roughrider's jacket. *Confound! The caitiff's a corporal.* To fight a man who outranked you was to incur a flogging or, worse, another ride on the wooden horse. His heart sank into a trough of woe.

But the roughrider was peering at him now in an unexpected way. He seemed diffident, uncertain. He lowered his fists an inch or two. "It's a dull horse," he explained with a touch of meekness. He moved back a step. "Look at them eyes," he said, almost entreating. "White-spotted eyes means a dull-'un. Everybody knows that."

Why, James thought, *he's yellow as a stream of piss.* He bent and picked up the shambreer, whipped his snotrag from his sleeve, and commenced tying it to the end of the thong. "The vulgar may say so," he snapped back, fastening the knot, "but any man that's about horses much at all knows it's a sign of goodness, not stupidity; and ones that've got 'em are good sensible horses, and quick as hell on the spur."

He turned from the roughrider to the gelding. The poor brute was in a kind of squat, haunches down, front legs splayed, head raised back as far as the tether would allow, ears laid flat. That rope was drawn tight as a fiddle-string. Tremors ran along the muscles of the withers and down the legs. The whites of its eyes showed; its nostrils kept crimping and flaring; its wind rumbled in its throat. Sweat-lather covered its flanks like so much clabber. With the shambreer idle by his side James stood stock-still, made a quiet crooning noise, then commenced speaking to the horse in words of mellow nonsense. The gelding's ears pricked. James murmured some more, and presently the tension on the tether loosened and the gelding rose out of its squat and came flat on all fours. In five minutes more it was standing calm and steady.

Only then did James ply the shambreer with his snotrag on the end of it. Very gently he flicked the white rag an inch or two, left and right, about the toes of his bare feet. The horse's eyes followed the movement but not in fear; now there was a glimmer of curiosity in the limpid brown orbs. It stamped and snorted, ears alertly forward. It was a pretty beast, James thought as he twitched the rag a bit further from side to side—mainly a cream-colored horse with splotches of sorrel thickly mottled on head and neck, branded with an H on its mounting buttock. *Who was H?* he idly wondered. He made some more talk, some silly, some not; he told the horse how pretty he thought it was. And it wasn't long before he could move the snotrag anywhere around that gelding and it would hold still and watch the thing go flitting by.

When he was done and the gelding was standing easy, he unfastened his snotrag from the thong and turned to hand the shambreer back to the embarrassed roughrider and was amazed to find a ring of fellows gathered all about him, Sides and Bussey and Brown and all his mates from the section, some of the roughriders, others too, but foremost among them a glowering Captain Gunn. Every eye was on him, especially the Captain's, which were small and round and dense, as if the buttons they once resembled had turned now to black lead. A sinister silence reigned. Nothing stirred save the inevitable clouds of flies. Nothing, that is, till Captain Gunn took one step forward and smote the roughrider to the ground with a blow to the face. "The lad's right, you goddamned bum-fucker," he told the fallen wretch, "a white-spotted animal's a damn good-'un. And you're broke to private for not knowing it, too."

James was feeling pretty proud of himself just then. He'd done right and the roughrider had done wrong and now at last the Captain was bound to praise him for his wisdom about horses. But that was not to be. Instead the Captain wheeled and clouted him too. He lay supine gazing up at the summer sky, which was unaccountably flecked with many little dancing stars, then the Captain's broad figure leaned over him and he heard Gunn's growl, "That'll teach you to lay hands on a noncommissioned officer, you goddamned little turd."

James regretted he hadn't had time to puff out his cheeks before getting hit. His mouth felt bad inside. He tasted the gluey salt of his own blood. But even so, he knew himself to have been unfairly penalized; and injustice should always be resisted. He spat a sluice of red over himself and spoke up stoutly, "If you've broke him to private, Captain, then as I reckon it, he don't outrank me no more."

Something shifted very slightly in the Captain's scowl, and James wondered if it might have been the semblance of a grin. But he was dizzy and couldn't see very well, and he may have imagined it. "He ranked you when you shoved him," Gunn pointed out, then straightened and settled his great hands on his hips with an air of satisfaction. "But he ain't over you no more, for I've broke him." Then the smile did emerge, though it was a thin and dry one. "*Now* you can beat the dog-date out of him and I won't give a brewer's fart." He nodded shortly. "And when you're done, come see me at my quarters. I'm naming you roughrider, in place of this damned gap-stopper."

Biddable mares. Sweet ponies that had been the pets of little girls. Frisky good-humored colts. Old plow-horses that were fat and lazy and lay down to die if you tried to make them rack or canter; young plow-horses that were vicious and breachy, rebelling at any usage but that of the farm field. Stone horses bursting with vigor, ticklish, apt to struggle and fling and fall foul of the partition-bar in the stable, laming themselves and sometimes their stablemates. Fat little good-for-nothing fillies. Weary nags that had been pulling booby-hutches, hackney coaches, traps, and sulkies for God knew how many boring years.

Bays, blacks, browns, duns, blaze-faced, white-footed, pyebal'd, peach-colored, burnt sorrels, roans, rubicunds, dapple grays, dapple blacks, and every conceivable hue in between. Moon-eyed, wall-eyed, rat-tailed, long-jointed, short-jointed, wither-wrung, well-trussed, ill-trussed, beasts whose chines sagged like washing on a line and others whose backs were straight as rulers, horses well flanked and horses that were gaunt-bellied and thin-gutted whose flanks turned up like a greyhound's. Horses with a pretty motion and horses that plodded like mules. This was what the months of impressment had scoured up and delivered to the Manakin Town camp to be made into troop horses for the dragoon service. And for six days they were the stuff of all James's work.

It was true many of the animals he was to train were spoiled beyond redemption, and even more were so unfit that but a few days of hard service would ruin them regardless of his best efforts to ready them for the manage and build them up for the practice of war. But a precious few were what Captain Gunn called champers, animals that were vital and strong and full of spirit and showed their good health by constantly champing with tongue and mandible. "That white ropy foam, it keeps their mouth fresh," Gunn confidently declared. "Shows 'em mettlesome. Shoot a horse like that through the goddamned guts and he'll run for you all day long afore he drops." Working with such lively beasts was such a joy and a privilege it felt to James the way a sacrament must feel to the churchly.

He worked the horses. Worked the good horses and the bad. Worked them all and loved them all. Worked them six whole days, six wonderful days, perhaps the best six days of his life so far. He'd apprenticed as a house joiner, had practiced that dreary trade for years, had hated everything about it—the backbreaking work in the sawpit, the everlasting to-and-fro motion of the heavy jack plane, the turning of the spring-pole lathe that wore out your foot on the treadle, the tedious shiplapping of boards for wainscoting and the finishing of balisters on stairwells, the smell of raw lumber and rosin and glue and polishing wax and wet plaster forever in your nose, sawdust in your eyes and lashes and hair and in every wrinkle of your body and every seam of your clothes. One of his few joys in those cramped and sweaty days had been the freedom of working and racing with Chenowith's Patuxent in sunny spring and summer. Now, thanks to Captain Gunn and a dash of whimsical good fortune, he could spend all his time—duty time and free time too, if he wished—with the horses he had loved since he first felt his own heart begin to beat in rhythm with

Patuxent's on the turf of that little Maryland racing track six years before.

It was not easy, though, for as a roughrider he was now under Gunn's immediate and personal supervision. His purpose, Gunn had told him at the outset, was to get the horses *wayed*. "'Wayed' means backed, suppled, broke, and showing a disposition to the manage, so's when they goes to the troops they'll know the bridle and answer the bleeders."

James was puzzled by the Captain's use of the term "broke"; some might think—indeed, James thought it—breaking was the whole business of chastening the horse to saddle and bridle. So he made bold to ask, "Captain, what d'you mean by broke?"

For answer, Captain Gunn boxed his ear with a stroke that laid him flat. He got up deaf in that ear and the Captain seemed to know it, for he moved around and spoke into the other as coolly as if nothing had happened: "Broke's to make him light on the hand for the trot. Makes him fit for the gallop. Then you make him ready for running by suppling him. 'Tis a furious goddamned fatigue to run horses full speed afore they're broke."

"Yes, Your Honor," said James, to show he was wiser than the Captain thought, "I know that."

The words were hardly spoken when Gunn knocked him down again, smiting the very same ear. Of course, that ear being sore, the buffet hurt much worse than before; but then, James reflected as he got shakily to his feet, it had also spared his hearing on the other side. Maybe it was the Captain's idea of a kindness. "Get 'em wayed," Gunn said into his good ear. "My job's to turn gobs of shit into horsemen, yours is to make me the nags to carry 'em. You send me one goddamned horse that won't manage, you'll wish your mama had never let your pa give her a grinding."

The figure of speech, so disrespectful of his dear Ma and Da, hurt James and angered him—a fierce blush betrayed it—and a third time James found himself on his back. The blow had been to his temple and had addled him. Gunn knelt beside him as his head swam. "I'll say whatever suits me, you little whoreson," the Captain told him pleasantly, "and by God's balls, you'll abide it. If I want to speak of fondling your mama's bubbies or of ramming myself up your sister's cunt, why, you'll but smile, won't you? Smile and name it the grandest notion you've heard in a week."

So the six wonderful days did have their drawbacks. But Captain Gunn only cuffed him twice more that week, never again hard enough to overset him, and though the defaming language never ceased even for a moment, the abuse seemed a small price to pay for the privilege of working the horses. James would have gladly spent the balance of the war, indeed the balance of his days, doing just that. But it was not to be.

One humid August evening after Stable Call, he was at the manage working a particularly stiff-necked mare with the cavisson. The horse was a good well-formed dapple-black fifteen hands high whose only fault was that she would sooner perish than bow the neck and hold the head in subjection; in these cases the best remedy was the iron band that wrung the nose at a pull of the reins, forcing the neck to bend and advantageously suppling the shoulders too. She was responding well, and James was feeling very much like the finest roughrider in the dragoon service when, to his amazement, Captain Gunn came galloping up on his big black fetching behind him a saddled dun on a lead-rope.

"Mount up and come with me!"
Gunn commanded. There was none
of his usual bombast; just a tight-
mouthed, hard-jawed intensity.

The Captain flung the lead-rope
of the dun; James caught it by instinct with his free hand but still sat
unmoving, dumbfounded. It took
him a second or two to find his voice.
"But, I've this horse to work."

"Turn her free," snapped Gunn. "Rudge'll take the nag in. Mount up, I say! We've no time to lose!"

Rudge was the Captain's batman. The dun was Rudge's horse; James remembered it. "Captain," he felt obliged to point out, "that ain't my tack." The saddle was Rudge's too—a fine officer's saddle, nearly as fine as Captain Gunn's, made of leather and heavy brocade, high-cantled, with a roll-padded seat. James's own was a poor patchwork affair of kersey stuffed with straw, with looped ropes for stirrups. He looked with pity at the mare. "That cavisson's got to come off."

The Captain fixed him with bullet-dead eyes. "Rudge'll do that too. Now stop your yammering, get down from that mare, and mount up."

James did. Rudge's fancy saddle, after his own thin mat of crushed straw and worn cloth, felt luscious between his thighs; the stirrups hung a bit low, but he knew he could fix them when opportunity offered; and the dun answered the reins right well. James felt handsomely furnished. Though the Captain's intentions remained a mystery it was sublime to bestride a good horse in a gentleman's saddle. He resolved not to question his lot. He made the lead-rope fast to a saddle-ring, and in another moment they were moving at a canter through the dusty, sloping, and gradually dimming light.

Gunn led, James fell in behind. They passed across the camp, riding a zigzag course between huts, over each troop street in its turn; it was suppertime, the cooking kettles were going, most of the men were feeding, and but few took note of the passing horsemen. The savory smells of hot stew were in the air and James's stomach gurgled; but it looked like he was going to miss his supper. Presently they skirted the vaults, and the stench of excrement replaced the agreeable fragrances of food and extinguished his hunger; and now he saw they were headed not to one of the main gates of the camp, but toward the forest that enclosed it on the west. He had thought at first that Gunn had some special duty for him to perform, perhaps a particularly difficult horse that none of the other roughriders had succeeded in waying; but they had long since left behind the manage, the stables, the horse pens, every venue where such a service might be performed. Instead, it seemed, incredibly, they were about to leave the camp—and leave it in secrecy, for they were avoiding all the gates and sentries.

At the edge of the camp stood a worm fence grown over with creeper and ivy. Gunn jumped it smoothly on his black; after a moment's trepidation, James did the same with the dun, which also took the fence with ease. The darkening woods swallowed them. An early owl, disturbed in its tree, floated down and past them, eerily silent on white wings. The husks of old leaves rustled under the horses' hooves. James sweated in the moist heat. Was this desertion? Absence without leave? Or had the Captain arranged a leave for some purpose he did not feel obliged to explain?

None of these possibilities seemed right, for though Gunn was avoiding the main gates, not far ahead lay the western picket line of the camp, running along an old farm lane in the woods—James had ridden it many a time on vedette duty. They could not pass that line without challenge. To breach it would be to risk drawing fire, so the Captain must identify himself to the picket. Thus the secrecy of this strange nighttime ride could be but partial.

Was Gunn's a worse purpose? A darker one? James's imagination awoke to a host of fell prospects. Had he innocently offended the Captain? Instead of having his ears boxed, was he to be punished in some unmentionable fashion fit only for the depths of the woods? He remembered the awful tales of the Captain's deadly temper. Of the men he was supposed to have killed. The notion of his own death flew through his head the way the white owl had sailed over them on its quiet wings.

Now Libby came to mind, and Poovey, and his own good horse Jesus. Brown and Arthur and Bussey, Nichols and Baldwin too. Even the poor miserable filthy hut they all shared. Suddenly he missed with a piercing ache everything about his present life that had become so blandly familiar. Much that had long seemed wearisome beckoned to him now like the raptures of Paradise. Would he ever again see his sister, his messmates, his horse, his squalid little wigwam? Would he live to see the war end? See Libby and Poovey bound in wedlock? See their children born and grow? Find a woman himself, marry, sire his own young?

He considered asking the Captain for reassurance, for some fragment of information that might be of comfort—where they were bound and why; but he knew it would be useless to inquire; no, worse than useless—he'd only earn another knocking about. But presently they came to a break in the forest and the farm lane that marked the picket line; a short distance down this path to their left a picket fire burned low, gleaming in the dimness like a dollop of molten gold.

A mounted officer was advancing up the path toward them, outlined against the flicker of the fire; James recognized him as Lieutenant Glascock. Gunn stepped his black straight out of the trees into the road and turned to meet Glascock; James held back among some holly bushes, uncertain whether to show himself. From the road he heard the Lieutenant give a gurgling laugh. "Is it Thursday again already?"

"Comes oftener every week, don't it?" answered the Captain.

"It's two times this week already," the Lieutenant remarked. "That's a long ride you make."

"If you knew the wench, you'd not say so," Gunn replied with a lewd chuckle, then turned in the saddle and casually beckoned to James; and with his heart in his mouth James gigged the dun out of the cover of the hollies and followed Gunn as he crossed over to enter the woods on the far side of the path. Glascock paid not the slightest heed, just reined about and trotted back toward the picket fire. James and the Captain met in the darkness; Gunn said nothing. He turned the big black and started.

James followed, more chafed than frightened now, knowing he'd been made complicit in the Captain's notorious dissipations—and under compulsion too. Why, he could not guess. But neither could he deny a certain guilty but expectant fascination. What wantonness and perversion might await them? *I ought to be ashamed*, he thought. He was, and he wasn't. He rode on, Gunn's big figure looming ever before him, high on a horse so black that it blended into the deepening shadows, became a shadow itself, a shadow whose outlines changed and shifted as if it were some phantom that could alter its form at will, while night drew down around them like a winding sheet.

They broke out of the forest, jumped another fence, and found themselves on what the risen moon revealed to be a well-traveled road passing through broad flat farmlands. The haze and swelter of the day had not dissipated, and the air was heavy and the three-quarters moon so blurred that James could not see the bruises on the silver face of the man in it. The countryside around them lay featureless under a vast stillness. It was so quiet that he heard the munching of cows grazing in a nearby pasture; the rich odor of manure came to him, also the sweet fragrance of the grass the cows ate.

Once on the road, the Captain broke into a hand-gallop. James kept to his rear; to have ridden level with Gunn might have lifted his spirits, but he feared to make the move lest it be taken as insubordinate. He did feel a little easier to be out of the closeness of the woods. They rode for another hour, then two, then three, alternating gaits between a walk, a trot, and a gallop, saving the horses' wind. The Captain seemed in no particular hurry. The later grew the hour, the more James began to fret about getting back to camp in time for tomorrow's duties—Reveille, Morning Parade, Roll Call, and all the rest.

But Gunn spoke not a word of explanation, and James still dared not venture an inquiry. On and on they rode. James grew tired; he'd spent a long day working the horses even before they started; he could not help dozing in the saddle.

When he next came to himself, a vague gray light was seeping into the world. He jerked erect; it was nearly dawn. Slow tendrils of ground fog eddied about them. They were sitting their horses in the yard of a small frame house with brick chimneys at either end, surrounded by crepe myrtles and lilacs and, beyond it, a necessary and some log outbuildings. There were several army tents too, one with a light burning in it, and a pen where a great number of horses slept standing up, and several unhitched wagons that James recognized as the kind that carried ammunition and powder. Two great oak trees towered overhead. Under one of the oaks, a few rods off, the last of a picket fire was smoldering down to embers and a thread of smoke, and a man in a dragoon helmet and kit was standing over it with both hands crossed on the muzzle of a carbine propped before him. Though he could not remember hearing them speak, James had the feeling they had done so in the same jocular fashion Gunn and Glascock had.

He was groggy and this made him thoughtless; his curiosity, so long deferred, now got the better of him. "What place is this?" he asked, and instantly regretted the audacity of the question.

But the Captain, surprisingly, took no umbrage. He merely allowed the side of his mouth that always curled up to rise a little higher, perhaps an inch; and in the growing light James thought he detected more sarcasm in the expression than the contempt to which he had grown accustomed. "Why? You writing a book?"

"No, Captain, I ain't writing no book," James answered, more testily than he probably should have. He didn't entirely understand the import of the question, but was certain he'd been maligned and resented it. And after their long night together, the Captain no longer struck him as so formidable. Besides, he was irritable from the suspense and the fatigue of the mysterious ride. "I could if I wanted to, though," he added with truculence.

Their horses were standing side by side and he steadied himself for a blow, but strangely, Gunn did not strike. Instead he explained, "It's an ordinary."

"An ornery?"

"No, Johnson. An *ordinary*." He poked himself in the chest with a thumb. "*I'm* ornery, and you'd best not forget it." Then he pointed to the house. "*This* is an ord-i–*nary.*"

"I thought it was spoke *ornery.*"

"You're a fool, Johnson."

"If it's an ornery—*ordinary*—how come there's all these tents and muskets and powder around? And that fellow yonder—he's a sentry, ain't he?"

"This is another camp of the regiment, but it's a courthouse too. There's a cabin yonder, though," he said, indicating a small windowless hut of squared logs at some distance from the ordinary—"and *it* ain't no dragoon camp, nor any ordinary, nor any goddamned courthouse neither. I've got some private business in there. Take me twenty minutes, no more. While I'm at it, you go out by the jakes and make yourself small there, till I come for you. And mind you, make no stir. There's a reason you're here. Anybody spies you, you're done up like a dish of eels."

"What about this here sentry? He's seen me."

Gunn laughed, tossing the man a coin. "He ain't seen a goddamned thing. Have you, Utley?"

Utley was a nimble fellow, for he caught that coin in the dim light with one flick of a hand. "Not a blessed thing, Captain," he agreed.

Captain Gunn's private business consumed not twenty minutes but something over an hour. While he waited James led the black and Rudge's dun into a nearby grove of cedars where, unobserved, he might unsaddle the pair, walk them cool, and give them wipe-down. They watered at a brook, and he picketed them on a patch of good grass, then settled in some weeds behind the jakes to while away the time.

When the Captain finally emerged from the cabin the sun was fairly up, the fog burned away, the dragoon camp astir, and James was heartily sick of hiding back of the privy. He was also ashamed and chastened to concede he'd felt a certain disappointment at not having personally witnessed an example of the Captain's famed depravity—much less partaken of it. He reproached himself for this as the Captain led him covertly into the vacant ordinary and down a stone stairway to a small basement room lit by two six-light windows set high on opposite walls. His glum mood passed unnoticed by the Captain, who had every appearance of a most agreeable satiety. In the confines of the basement Gunn smelled so strongly of rut and strong drink that for the second time in twelve hours James lost his appetite for the nourishment he had been craving.

They took chairs at the single table in the little room. Gunn leaned back in his. "You've not got your bounty money yet, have you?"

"No, Captain."

"Damned few have," he laughed raucously. "Nor, by God, will you."

James stiffened with indignation. "Why not, Your Honor? That was the promise made me when I enrolled."

Gunn pulled a mocking face of exaggerated sympathy. "Was it now? Poor little noddy—somebody made you a promise and broke it, did they?"

"Yes, Captain, Colonel White did," James insisted. Then it occurred to him that he should be absolutely correct in his answers, for this was a matter of honest, or dishonest, dealing. "Leastways," he amended, "I ain't been paid *yet*."

Gunn smiled wryly. "I've just told you. You'll get no bleeding bounty."

"Why won't I?"

The Captain sighed. "You bolt your indenture, then enroll in the army with your own goddamned name, *James Johnson*, clear as day. All your plaguey master had to do was go 'round the regiments asking after a little fartleberry calling himself James Johnson. That's just what he's done and now, by Christ, he's found you out. He's come for you."

This news rocked James like a blow to the belly. Chenowith, not dead after all? Chenowith—at Manakin Town? Fear rolled through him in an icy tide. "Yes, damn you," Gunn went on while James listened in a daze, "the fat son of a whore was up at headquarters yesterday, just after Evening Parade, swilling grog with the Colonel. Why d'you reckon I snatched you out of camp so helter-skelter?" The Captain leaned close. "D'you understand? The Colonel was fixing to collect your trifling arse and turn you over."

James did not even think before he spoke. What he said shot from his heart like an arrow from its bow. "I'll not go, Captain." He straightened and set his back teeth hard. "I'll die first."

Gunn sat back. "Judging by his gab, the fellow's a goddamned Tory. Bacon-faced son of a dog says you're a Scotchman; says all Scotchmen was rebels in their own country and now are rebels in this one too." He cocked an expectant eye at James. "*Are* you a Scotchman, Johnson?"

"Yes, Your Honor, I am."

"Highlander?"

"I am."

Gunn grew solemn. The angles of his features rounded a bit, grew heavier with thought. Suddenly, at the back of James's mind, the Captain's name tolled like a faraway bell. *Gunn.* The name had not struck its chord till now. It awoke another. *Caithness*. Then, in quick succession, the changes rang, *Dirlot Castle, the Gunns, the Keiths*. Yes, it was true—the Johnsons of Strathmore had served the Gunns; his Da had often said it. The Gunns were the fiercest of the clans, the Johnsons their most stalwart retainers in their ceaseless feuds with the Keiths. And here tonight, in this ornery—ordinary—stood a Johnson and a Gunn, as Johnsons and Gunns had stood together in Caithness down all the ages. James's head swam.

The Captain was watching closely. "This master of yours, he's got a great blob of drawing-plaster on his head. Claims you tried to murder him with some fire-tongs on the occasion of your running off. Is that true?"

James strove to push aside the shock of all he had just divined, tried to concentrate— yes, Chenowith; it seemed Chenowith was ashamed of having had his skull cracked by a slip of a girl. He resisted the temptation to laugh. "Yes, Captain," he answered stoutly, "'tis."

"Well," said Gunn in a grudging way, turning his look down toward his boot-toes, "scraggy as you are, you must've took him a fine thundering topper if it's still giving pus two months after." He fixed his beetling regard on James. "And you ain't the worst roughrider I've got neither. *And* you're a Scotchman." One ham-like fist smartly smote his knee. "No, Johnson, you ain't getting no damned bounty. I'm *giving* your bounty to your master. I'm buying your time for the dragoon service."

"But that's *a thousand dollars*," James gasped. "My indenture's not worth a pittance of that."

"It's not as if I was robbing you of the Imperial Spanish treasure, you ignorant little nit," Gunn snidely assured him. "It's a thousand dollars *Continental* Colonel White talks of when he makes his enlistment speech. Comes closer to twenty dollars Proc." He paused to expel an ironical laugh. "Mind you, that bum-fodder's dropping in value by the day—hell, it's dropping by the goddamned minute. By tomorrow, you won't be worth even a farthing. Your Tory shit-sack of a master'll be content to get whatever he can for you. I'll be fetching a bargain, and you'll have cast off that indenture."

Perhaps it was unfair; perhaps it was high-handed. It certainly was not honest dealing. But that was how James Johnson, God bless him, became a free man at last, only to bind himself again, almost at once, to a Gunn, as his Da had been bound, as all Johnsons had been bound, for as long as any in the Highlands could remember.

In Which a Young Man Gains Liberty Whilſt His Friend Loſes It

The day after their arrival at the Manakin Town camp, Libby, seized by a sudden ambition, had gone to the troop quartermaster sergeant and asked to be taken on as a washerwoman. As luck would have it, one of the troop's two laundresses, the wife of the farrier, had recently died of smallpox, and Libby was given the vacant post. Hitherto, her virtue notwithstanding, she could claim no better condition than that of the lowest slattern following in the wake of the army, and so had lived more or less constantly open to mistreatment by a lustful soldiery; but now she held a proper place on the troop establishment. She received a soldier's rations—when there *were* rations—and shared a brush shed with James and Poovey and their messmates. In addition to washing the men's poor tattered clothes, she also did some mending and cooking for the mess.

Since Bussey and Arthur were somewhat rougher sorts than their genial fellows in the Gaskins Battalion, James and Poovey had thought it wise to revive Captain Harris' old fiction that Libby was a married woman, only this time, because of their betrothal, it had seemed best that Poovey play the part of the purported husband. But Sides made a poor thespian. So embarrassed was he—with James lying conspicuously and perhaps ominously by his side—that whenever he pretended an amorous advance by night, the performance was sadly unconvincing. Libby complained that in his awkwardness he often got his sharp elbows in the hollows of her shoulders, and that his moans of supposed passion sounded not like the transports of rapture but like some constipated fellow straining at a turd.

James had been resisting making a fact of what Sides and Libby were so unsuccessfully imitating. He couldn't help it—if Sides had shown himself a better character than he'd once thought, there were still things about him James didn't like. And it was hard to give up Libby's care, no matter how wearisome the duty had become. Now, however, he saw the marriage could be postponed no longer; and in a mood of blended sadness and anticipation he resigned himself. To put the matter in train at last, one day after drill he resorted to Sergeant Dangerfield. "Have we a chaplain with the regiment?"

The Sergeant confronted him with a dry expression. "What is it, Johnson? Are there black sins pressing on your soul? Do you long for confession and absolution?"

"No, Sergeant. I wish to find a parson who can make a wedding."

"Are you getting married, Johnson?"

"No, Sergeant. 'Tis my sister, Libby. She and Private Sides are to be wed."

Dangerfield looked at him askance. "Hearing that makes me question her judgment."

James shrugged. "There's arguments to both sides, I admit. But their minds are made up."

"Well," mused the Sergeant, "this being a Virginia regiment, it would be a chaplain of the Established Church—if we had one. But we don't. I'm afraid Colonel White is a perfect infidel and damns all religion. He'll have no devil-drivers near him. And anyways, like as not your dragoon's a drunkard and a rowdy and a follower after his prick, and ain't often found at his devotions. But we do have a sort of a fallen preacher, a private in Captain Hughes's troop—used to be one of them Methodist enthusiasts that goes around the back parts making folk go to twitching and hallooing. Name of Obediah Plumbley. I doubt if he's ordained; don't know if a Methodist can *be* ordained. But I reckon he'll celebrate a marrying for you, if you pay him the price of a measure of rum. Like I say, he's fallen."

Plumbley proved a great robust hulk of a fellow with the high color and bulbous pitted nose that confirmed the Sergeant's assertion about his fondness for spirits. His manner was large and vigorous, his eye bleared and bloodshot, his breath had the foulness of carrion further tainted by the vile smell of the tobacco he constantly chewed. "Yes, by God," he roared, gesticulating so violently that James fell back from him in alarm, "I was a preacher—and a hell of a good-'un too. Took my appointment at the Southern Conference at Broken Back Church in May of 'seventy-nine. The Reverend Freeborn Garrettson give me my circuit. Why, I held a horse for Bishop Asbury himself; slipped his own blessed foot in the stirrup, I did."

James thought these credentials a sufficient justification for pursuing the matter of a wedding, but Plumbley gave him no chance to speak of it. Spitting a thick stream of brown juice, he went on, pacing heavily up and down in the street of Captain Hughes's troop, extending both arms over his head and fluttering his hands aloft as if he sought to take flight into the Paradise he celebrated. "Took up a circuit on the Augusta District. Preached up the inexpediency of human learning and the practice of moral virtue, as against the great and powerful expediency of dreams, visions, and immediate revelations. Why, I conjured visions of demons and hellfire and the vengeance of the Almighty and the terrors of the Judgment till the godless fell on their hands and knees before me and wept for mercy."

He stopped in his pacing to whirl on James with such savagery that for an instant James himself considered repenting so as to save himself the torments of a Perdition he did not even believe in. "I preached to the swearers," Plumbley cried, his eyeballs rolling back to expose only their yellowed whites thickly netted with red, "the liars, the whores and whoremasters, to the cock-fighters, adulterers, thieves, card-players, to the horse-racers and the topers. Preached to Moravians and Quakers and Mennonites and

New Light Baptists and Presbyterians and Catholics. Niggers and Indians too. Preached to the beasts of the field and the birds of the goddamned air. I dwelt as among briars, thorns, and scorpions. Ah, nobody could make 'em writhe and howl and fall into trances like I could. Cling to the trees and jerk. Bark like a flock of spaniels. Foam at the mouth, pop their teeth in holy frenzy. Hallelujah! Amen!"

Plumbley's eyeballs rolled back into place and he paused to replenish his air; James seized the opportunity to speak. "Can you make a wedding?"

Abruptly the man's confidence appeared to fade; his jaw worked at his plug, and he shifted uneasily from one foot to the other, examining the distant woods with a morose air. "Well, not according to the Ordinances of the Methodist Church." Now he seemed wounded; he hung his head. "For, you see . . . ," he stammered, "well, the truth is, I was deprived of my ministry." He looked up with a defiant snap of his head and shook a finger in James's face. "Unjustly deprived, I hasten to say."

"Why was that?" James frowned.

Plumbley dropped his gaze again and watched the big toe of his bare foot roll a pebble about. "It may prejudice you against me if I say," he murmured.

"I reckon you'd *better* say," James insisted. "I want this wedding to be rightful. 'T'won't do no good if it's not."

"Oh, it'll be rightful," Plumbley assured him, bending again to spit. "All the right words'll get said. The Methodists won't recognize it, if you're couple's of that belief, but otherwise, it'll be sealed as surely as the Lord Jesus sealed the one at Cana."

But James did not want his sister in any way imperfectly wed. "Still," he demanded, "you must say."

Plumbley gave a grudging sigh. "All right, goddamn it. You see, all that mighty power I was speaking of, the power of the Holy Ghost coming over folk, all that sacramental ecstasy, all that wailing and shaking and falling down to wallow, why, it heats the loins; it unleashes the carnal hankerings. Folk can't help it, their blood gets high in the Spirit of the Lord and they goes to fornicating, and the women, well, the womenfolk, they's all a-panting and a-grunting and a-pitching on the ground with their skirts throwed over their heads, shouting praises to God, and what's a poor preacher to do but fall on 'em in the same transports of bliss—pious bliss it is, rhapsodic, exalted bliss, radiant with the love of the Lord Jesus . . ."

James softened; Plumbley seemed so helpless in the grip of his reverential lechery that the spectacle could not help but stir pity and even a bit of affection; besides, James had always been tolerant of those who confessed, rather than hid, their weaknesses. "I see what you mean," he smiled, then hurried to ask, "but you *can* make a proper wedding, too. Can't you?"

"Oh yes, son. Yes, indeed. The properest wedding you ever saw. So long as your couple don't profess the Methodism."

And a proper wedding it was, considering the constraints imposed by military life. Instead of a footrace from the groom's house to the bride's for the prize of a bottle of liquor, the groomsmen sprinted from their hut on the troop street to the place at streamside where Libby did her washing; and the winner, Bussey, had to settle for a gill of rum. The wedding breakfast was held not at the bride's home, since she had none, but on the bank of the River James; and the party dined on salt pork and biscuit washed down with spruce beer rather than the customary fare of venison, beef, chicken, and good wine. There was but a single bridesmaid, Mrs. Fletcher, the troop's other laundress, who proved so sly at protecting Libby's slipper that none could steal it and earn another gill of rum.

To James's relief Plumbley came sober to the ceremony, if well supplied with a loathsome hunk of tobacco in his cheek, and presided in more or less dignified fashion. The vows were exchanged with due decorum, though Sides did tremble as though a flogging awaited him rather than the delights of matrimony. The scant provisions having been consumed at breakfast, the evening dinner was dispensed with; and the blowing of Tattoo suspended the dancing, which had been pretty ragged in any event thanks to the lack of a fiddler.

Their hut of corn shocks, straw, and boards served as a bridal chamber; the groomsmen and Mrs. Fletcher stood with their backs turned and tossed the rolled-up stocking over their shoulders at the embarrassed newlyweds as they lay abed. Brown and Mrs. Fletcher scored the hits on groom and bride, but since Mrs. Fletcher was already married, Brown could hardly claim her. Plumbley went off evidently satisfied with the five shillings Sides and the mess had scraped together, and later in the night was heard vigorously and drunkenly preaching to a crowd in Captain Hughes's troop street.

With the hut given over to the nuptials, the groomsmen slept under the stars. The honor of being in the wedding party had not entirely appeased Bussey and Arthur, who felt themselves degraded by the mummery that for weeks had portrayed Sides and Libby as man and wife. Accordingly, at midnight they talked of breaking in on the couple and taking revenge by coarsely annoying them. But James would permit no such villainous mischief and spent the next hours till Reveille standing guard at a circumspect distance from the hut, ready to crack their ruffianly skulls should they attempt to make a rush. But they did not, and the night passed quietly.

Shortly before dawn Libby, wrapped in her surtout, stepped from the hut and crept to the vaults. James, in a fit of bashfulness, lurked in the shadows fearing to reveal himself. But on her return she spied him and approached him bristling. "What d'you think you're doing?" He made shift to explain, but impatiently she cut him off. "You've looked after me long enough. Poovey's my husband now. *He* must do the minding."

"I know, I know," James murmured. "It's just that ... well, my whole life, I've been accountable for you. Maybe I don't know how to do nothing else."

She regarded him with asperity in the slowly growing light. "Well, you've got to learn."

"And I don't mean to say I was always good at minding you. I know I wasn't, sometimes. But I wanted to be."

"I know you did. But you didn't have the power. That wasn't your fault."

"It felt like it."

"Well, it wasn't."

They waited a time in silence. He wanted to know what he had no right to know, what he had no right to ask. But he started to ask it anyway. "Was Poovey ...?"

She stopped him with her firm assertion, "Poovey's a good man. A kind and tender man."

James felt a flare of anger, thinking of all the red-hair's most annoying traits. "He'd better be good to you. He'd better always be good."

"He will be," she assured him. "You needn't worry."

He waited a long time. Then he said, "I wish you could've come to this ... different."

"Me too," she said. "But I couldn't. Master Chenowith changed me. I've got to stay changed. And Poovey, he don't mind. He loves me, changed or not."

"Still, I wish ..."

"Wishing's a waste." She moved away from him a little distance and resumed her brisk manner. "Now it's nearly time for Reveille. You've got to go and get ready."

"How'll it be now, with you and me?"

Even in the dimness he could see her smile. "I'll still ask you to tell me of home. Will you do that?"

"Yes, you know I will."

"Then it'll be all right, won't it?" He watched her smile, watched her turn and dart away, watched her stoop through the hanging deerskin into the hut. He saw that she was happy.

That same day after Stable Call, when he went out to sit by the river to enjoy the soft evening light, he took from his pocket the flimsy of parchment that was the legal evidence of his indenture and tore it into many small pieces, threw the pieces into the water, and watched them float away from him on the current.

Part ye Sixteenth

In Which General Greene Strives to Compofe
His Army for ye Offenfive

H E WAS INDULGING IN A RARE OUTBURST OF TEM-
per. He stood at the opening of his marquee shouting out into the
endless rains as if they, and not Brigadier General Thomas Sumter, had
offended him. They had, of course; but that was not the immediate point.
The dispatch Nat Pendleton had just handed him was the point. "What
can be the reasons for such an extraordinary measure?" Greene exclaimed.
"I can't conceive how he could take such a step without consulting me or
obtaining my consent!"

"Well, sir," Pendleton reminded him, somewhat abashed, for he had
never witnessed the General in such an agitated state, "he does, by this
message, direct Colonel Henderson to *seek* your permission."

In a way it was moot. The fiasco of the Monck's Corner expedition had
finished Sumter; Governor Rutledge had reprimanded him and Henderson had been given command of his troops, though the Gamecock's stated
reason for retirement was the wound he'd taken at Blackstock's ten months
before. Tarleton's people had indeed put six buckshot in his right side that
day, one of which had chipped his spine—surely a serious hurt; but by
now, Greene reflected savagely, even an amputated limb ought to have
nicely healed. Yet Sumter's convalescence lingered on. Could the fearsome
Blue Hen's Chicken be so delicate? Hardly. "Yes," the General answered
Nat with smoldering sarcasm, "*after the fact*, he seeks permission."

He glared out at the wind-blown swathes of rain and the millions of
dimples they made in the scummy puddles covering every low piece of
ground in sight. He hated them. He hated Sumter. He even hated poor
hapless William Henderson, who on taking over Sumter's band had confessed he'd never seen a more worthless, used-up crowd than the Gamecock had left him. "By the thundering wrath of Great Jehovah," Greene
bellowed with such violence that several in the marquee winced, "Sumter's
already furloughed his whole brigade and retired to his plantation, where

I reckon he'll lounge in comfort while we drown in these hurricanes. *Now* he asks my leave."

He raised his fist aloft and brandished it as if in imprecation against the torrents driving at the peak and sides of the marquee making such a din that heretofore all within had been forced to address each other in shouts simply to be heard, even if they were not enraged like the General. They had been summoned to discuss the prospects for undertaking active operations, but then Henderson's letter had arrived, and now none dared make any utterance at all, not Jethro Sumner nor Otho Williams nor Otho's fellow Marylander Colonel Howard, certainly not Kosciuszko, whose notion of giving counsel to his general was to strike a superb martial pose, nor Colonel Richard Campbell, the commander of the Battalion of Virginia Continentals, habitually a man of impenetrable silence.

Besides, in his present mood the General required no counsel. "By now the state troops are scattered to the four points of the compass," he complained, "just as I'm trying to concentrate the army to give Stewart a dressing at last—if the confounded ground will ever dry under us. Why, I might as well appeal to these everlasting rainstorms to cease, as try to gather up Sumter's men now he's sent them off." As if to mock him, a deafening thunderclap shook the immediate world.

"It may not be quite as bad as all that, sir," ventured Pendleton meekly. "The dispatch of General Sumter which Henderson appends, if you'll notice, directs 'as many of the men as the service permits' to be furloughed home 'from time to time.' He says he believes them due a respite from the hard service they've done. And he does direct Henderson to apply to you for permission."

The General did not wish to be propitiated. "Hard service indeed," he laughed in bitter scorn. "Plundering and pillaging, hanging Tories, stealing Negroes. They're picaroons, Captain—common pirates! A respite of service till the first of October! Why, if I've not whipped Stewart by the middle of *September*, it's the end of us." He wheeled to amaze them with his scarlet, congested countenance. He shook a finger at them. "Depend upon it, we must have victory or ruin."

Against the back wall, beneath one of the few spots where the tent's roof had not yet sprung a leak, Billy Pierce was taking hurried notes at his camp desk in the warm anticipation and fond hope that the General would wish to put his sentiments in an official letter. Captain Shubrick, reading the balance of the day's mail, kept a studied but transparent air of indifference through which his gratified amusement faintly gleamed. Williams sat in a corner making out strength reports and pretending not to pay attention, but his normally sly smile had broadened into a grin of open satisfaction. Greene felt their abetting force and drew a justifying strength from it; everyone in his official family had been longing for the day when he would reach the end of his patience with South Carolina's senior brigadier. Now the day had come.

He turned outward again, to the slanting downpour. "If he supposes himself at liberty to employ his troops independent of the Continental Army, then, by Heaven, it's time he was convinced to the contrary," he said of Sumter. "I've given him and his gang of renegades every possible indulgence, and given *him* far more latitude and discretion than I ever should've."

A blast of rainy wind rocked the tent; the roof shivered, bellied, and dumped streams of water from several new places; a shower of it spattered his head and shoulders. He paused, seething, and when the gale had passed, continued, "I would've thought his own ambition—boundless and monstrous as it is—and his envy and suspicion of far worthier brother officers like Marion and Pickens, would at least excite him to leave his brigade intact and able to operate in concert with us. But no! He furloughs the lot. Now he lounges in his hammock on the piazza of his mansion, the back of his wrist lain upon his brow, while some slave wafts him with a palmetto fan."

He spun from the dreary prospect outside and crossed to where Pierce sat scribbling. "Write this!" he blurted. "By a measure of this kind, the country will be left open to the enemy to ravage, and the Continental Army exposed to any attack which the enemy may think proper." He crumpled Colonel Henderson's note in his fist and cast it from him; Pendleton, ever mindful of the archives, knelt to retrieve it. The Captain tottered; he was but recently back from Charlotte after his bout with fever.

"But besides the impolicy," Greene continued as Pendleton smoothed the paper against his thigh and Billy hurried his pen along, "a great injustice is done to the public in granting such extensive license to state troops. They have more than five times the pay of Continental soldiers, who, if they're paid at all—and most, alas, are not—are confined to the field from one year's end to the other, while the state troops, who took the field but yesterday, are set at liberty to go home and see their friends."

That was the burning core of his fury: the thought of his regulars held in the ranks by compulsion—by the threat, *his* threat, of flogging or execution—for three long years or the duration of the war.

"Sir," Pendleton assured him, putting by the rescued dispatch, "I rather doubt if Colonel Henderson has actually furloughed the brigade. He himself expresses surprise at General Sumter's memorandum. I believe he's asking your opinion in the matter."

Greene no longer cared to be reasonable. He glanced down at his hands and saw with a kind of mordant delight that they were shaking with passion. A biting amusement came. *Where, Nathanael, be thy famous Quaker temperance?* What did it matter now if his words were not those that should pass the lips of a good Quaker? He was a Friend no longer. The Friends had thrown him out of Meeting. He was a soldier; he was the commander of the Army of the South. It was time he was treated as his rank entitled him. Henderson was a fool even to have considered Sumter's obnoxious order. "Colonel Henderson," he asserted, while Billy wrote, "will *not* furlough a man or an officer, but he *will* give positive orders that the whole of the brigade be collected as fast as possible, and every man at home be called to the field as soon as may be."

Now the General leaned to Pierce and came to his last and largest point, pounding the flat of one hand on Billy's desk once, twice, three times, till the ink-pot began to jump and Billy had to steady it with a deft move of his free hand lest some of its precious liquid be spilled. "I have the public good and the safety of the people of this State too much at heart to think of such a measure!"

Yes, his greatest duty was to all those persons in every part of the embattled South who relied on him; there was always that to mention—his never-flagging devotion to the work of freeing the Southern country from the despot's rule. The South must never be allowed to forget why he did what he did. How enormous it was, how disinterested. How much higher than the work of scoundrels like Thomas Sumter whom history was going to want to remember more than it might wish to remember him.

He dismissed the abortive council of officers and decided to dispel his evil humor by walking it off. In his distraction he set forth into the rain bareheaded and in his waistcoat, but Pendleton hastened after him with hat and cloak and afterward fell back to follow along several rods behind as a dutiful aide should; and presently, when Greene again glanced rearward, he saw that Tom Shubrick had come to join Nat. He smiled. Their unspeaking presence reassured and soon began to calm him. He had left the marquee borne down both by a dank sense of shame and by a burden of private worry. The shame rose out of his old Quaker moderation, which admonished him for his unbecoming tantrum; the worry was purely secular—his investments were imperiled and the furloughing of Thomas Sumter's troops had been but the fuse to that powder.

Yet it was not long before the shame abated, and the speed with which it dwindled away made him think, and hope, that the old Quaker pettifogger from Potowomut was receding from the stage of his life at last. His fury had been justified and he knew it; Sumter was an unmitigated disgrace to the cause. But his vexation with the dangerous state of his business affairs would not relax its grip. He was in partnership with his friend Wadsworth and with Barnabas Deane of Connecticut in several ventures that the depreciation of the currency had nearly ruined; and now Deane had entered into negotiations in New London for part interest in two privateers, a brig and a Bermudan sloop, for the raiding of British commerce. There were also investments in a store and wharf in Hartford, and in a lot upon which Deane wished to build a distillery. In addition, Wadsworth had been named purchasing agent for the French army in America and though an eventual yield from Jeremiah's commissions might be safely predicted, that spigot had yet to turn and the flow of profits commence.

Meanwhile, their other enterprises were big with risk. So far Greene, who'd laid out large sums in capital—mostly the funds he'd amassed as Quartermaster General—had seen not a dollar in return. Without return, and more importantly, without the foundation of wealth that profit built, how was he to maintain himself as a man of affairs? Daily he had been hoping for a letter from Deane giving him encouraging news; instead there had been Henderson's infuriating account of Sumter's perfidy.

It was not simply a matter of providing well for Caty and the little ones. Statesmanship and success in arms could raise one but so high in the world. True greatness rested on great fortunes. Every great man in America was a man of fortune inherited or made. Arnold before his treachery had enriched himself as military governor of Philadelphia. Robert Morris the Superintendent of Finance was amassing a mountain of personal wealth even as he regularized the country's currency. Nathanael Greene, the anchorsmith from insignificant Rhode Island, whatever his

excellent features and achievements in the field, would in the end be measured against Washington and Jefferson, Virginia aristocrats of immense
property; against John Hancock, Boston's richest merchant; against the
South Carolina grandee Henry Laurens; against the whole prolific tribe
of opulent Lees. A vast distance of financial attainment remained ahead of
him. Given his humble beginnings, he must go farther than any to traverse
it and grasp what his ambitions told him remorselessly he deserved.

Fretful, he slogged through the mire, his hat and the wool of his cloak
growing heavy from the rain. He passed through the ugly clutter of a camp
that invincibly resisted all his orders that it be kept aright because the
means were never at hand to keep it aright, the want made all the worse by
these Noah's floods—the rude brush bowers of the soldiers disintegrating
into miscellaneous masses of sticks that floated away at random; their few
mildewing tents no more proof against the rains than so much tissue and
soon to collapse and dissolve; the drenched cooking hearths; the wagons
sunk to their wheel-hubs; horses and mules in their pens standing in muck
hock-deep, watching him dolefully as he passed.

The men were watching too. And their lanky women and their children
as thin and big-eyed as monkeys. Watching from the dim apertures of
their wilting huts where pitiful little fires smoked, or standing about in the
open, heedless of the storm that pelted them. His Marylanders. His Delawares. His Virginians. His North Carolinians. Men who'd fought and bled
for him at Cowan's Ford and Guilford Court House and Hobkirk's Hill
and Ninety-Six. After the murderous heat of the summer campaign in the
lowlands the High Hills of Santee had given them a few weeks of delectable weather that had refreshed them and restored their vigor. But then
the rains had come. Now as he walked among them he saw again, as he'd
seen every day of this long spell of monsoon, how stolidly they abided it.

They saluted, waved, hailed him, some few came and touched their
sodden forelocks and spoke to him smiling. Now the vexations of his
private affairs no longer pressed him as they had. The strong-boned faces
of his soldiers started pushing them away. More and more of them came,
breaking down his shyness with their rough goodwill. He saw the rags
that served them for clothing, he smelled the stench of them. Yet every eye
showed its predatory sparkle. They were all as lean as whippets. The poor
fellows had so little—what did it matter if it rotted and washed away? At
least the waters flushed out the trash and offal. The thought of Sumter's
pampered, cosseted, and overpaid bandits came back to him, and his anger
came back too, and he was no longer depressed about business affairs.

Suddenly his spirit felt weightless yet replete too, plump to a round fullness like the great cloth bags Lafayette once told him of, which men of ex-
perimental science in France believed could be filled with gases and made

to rise and float aloft. That a device far heavier than the medium meant to bear it up could be made to fly seemed to him miraculous. Yet it was good to remember that if he lived in a time of horrors, he also lived in an age of miracles. Not all the world was engaged in war; some of it still bent its energies toward the advancement of knowledge and the improvement of life. He imagined what it might be like to be a passenger in such a contrivance as Lafayette had described, to break one's moorings and ascend high into light and empty air. It must very much resemble how his spirit felt at this moment. He knew the freedom that came of rising from what had restrained him. His step lightened. *He* lightened.

The men had done it. His army had done it. Sometimes, he knew, he immured himself too long in the isolation of command; it was good to come abroad and see who it was that did his will and to whom he owed whatever had been accomplished. When all was said and done, they, not he and not his kind, *were* this revolution. Without them the revolution did not exist. Without them the nation the revolution was trying to establish would never exist; and if the day ever came when a nation *was* established it would not be able to endure without them. He passed among them now in the pounding rain, thanking them, touching them, shaking their hands, laughing at their rude jokes. *They're commoner than I am*, he thought, *but perhaps, in their slovenliness and rough innocence, they're better.*

He had Caty to thank too. He surmised she was as much the reason for his renewed vitality as these indomitable men swarming about him— Caty whom he'd so long and unfairly held at a distance, all the time sinking deeper into despair and indecision and loneliness, till she'd had to come into his dreams to remind him of her untiring belief in his capacity. Yes, his temper was worse again now. He was mad again. But it was the anger and impatience of the unfettered man, the man truly free, a man whose restraints had burst and who, like Lafayette's bag filled with elevating gases, was rising high above every small and petty thing. And because his restraints had been burst he knew clearly what must be done and how it must be done and who must do it. His men had given him that. And Caty had given it too.

The army's camp was now at a place called Bloom Hills—the constant filling up of the vaults required that it be moved at intervals to fresh ground—so he and Pendleton and Shubrick had to make a longer walk than usual to find a point that gave them a view of the bottomlands. Presently they stood under an old chestnut whose leaves leapt and chattered overhead from the constant beat of the rain. Greene gnawed his nether lip as Harry Lee was wont to do when fretted. Yonder lay what used to be the canebrake of the swamps and the causeway leading over them to McCord's Ferry. But today the whole scene was one vast deep expanse of lake spreading north and west and south, its farthest reaches closed off by a clinging wet mist, its broad surface wrinkled by the blown rains. It had been that way for a week.

"The enemy lies just yonder," he said, pointing Southwestward across the face of the waters, "at Thomson's Plantation near McCord's—or so Colonel Lee reports." McCord's was on the lower Congaree above the junction of that river and the Wateree. "That's—what?—fifteen miles away?"

Shubrick and Pendleton knew as well as Greene where McCord's Ferry was, and how far the distance. But they understood the General needed to talk. Shubrick nodded. "A single day's forced march."

The British had advanced first from Orangeburgh, where they had concentrated in July, thence to Fair Lawn near Monck's Corner and now to McCord's. Two thousand men, Harry Lee said. Regulars, most of them. Also some Provincials—Cruger's garrison of New York and New Jersey Loyalists, Greene's old antagonists from Ninety-Six. Artillery.

"Maybe," said Pendleton, "they were planning to attack us when the rains stopped them."

Greene shrugged. "It's hard to say. I don't yet know how this Stewart thinks."

Rawdon was gone, called home to England—Rawdon who had executed Isaac Hayne for breaking parole, seeming to launch a dreaded cycle of reprisal hangings. Thank Heaven nothing yet had come of that save an exchange of threatening letters between Greene and the British commandant in Charles Town. In place of Rawdon, Colonel Stewart commanded in the field now—the same Stewart whose junction with Rawdon Greene had tried so hard to prevent at Orangeburgh in July.

"I doubt he's of Rawdon's caliber," ventured Tom. "If he were, he'd have moved on us sometime since."

Greene ached to come to grips with the man. Rumor said General Alexander Leslie was on his way down from New York to take command with reinforcements; whatever Stewart's merits, Leslie would likely make a more formidable opponent—Greene remembered him with a wary respect from last spring's campaign in North Carolina.

"Colonel Lee importunes me to descend at once and engage the enemy," he told his aides, "flood or no flood. But even were the causeway as dry as Jonah's bones, I still lack the force to operate with confidence. Not only has Sumter failed me, General Huger continues ill at home. Half the North Carolina Continentals we've been promised have yet to turn up; the rest of that state's militia seem incapable of leaving Salisbury. And in any event, many of them lack arms. And in another four months the terms of half my regulars will expire." Nat and Tom knew all this too, but listened as attentively as if they did not.

The General had hoped to draw together a thousand North Carolinians. Pickens' South Carolina militia were already gathering in the back country. Henderson, if he could ever scrape together the leavings of Sumter's command, was to muster at Friday's Ferry, up the Congaree. In time Marion, senior brigadier of state troops now that Sumter was gone, would be coming to him from the Low Country unless other business down there supervened. But in the absence of the rest of the North Carolina troops it would be risky indeed to try conclusions with Stewart—even were it possible to cross to McCord's on dry land.

Greene sighed. "Wouldn't it be wonderful to play the part of Moses and call upon the Lord to divide the waters before us?"

Pendleton laughed. "Perhaps you should try it, sir."

"I'll look about," Shubrick offered in mock seriousness, "and see if I can find a suitable staff for you to wield." They stood chuckling. The General supposed they spoke blasphemy. He was not Moses. *Not yet, anyway*, he smiled to himself.

"No," he said, "we must accept the part the Lord has given us. We'll march *around* the flooded lands. We'll make a circle to the north till we can strike a place upstream where the Wateree and then the Congaree can be crossed, by ferry or by ford—probably somewhere around Camden, I'd guess. Then we'll turn downriver and collect Pickens and Henderson and, eventually, Colonel Lee's Legion. And if God is kindly disposed, perhaps the missing North Carolinians will join us somewhere on the way."

He paused and took a moment's deep thought. The decision, when it came, came easily. "If not," he said, "we'll fight Stewart anyway, with whatever we have. It's as I said to the council just now—it must be victory or ruin, and it must be before the end of September. It must be one or the other before General Leslie arrives."

That evening he sat at his camp desk writing out yet another melancholy order:

> William Bayley, Daniel Cooper and Jofias Salyers are to be execut-
> ed tomorrow in accordance with the Sentences pronounced againft
> them for Defertion & bearing Arms againft the United States. The
> repeated Examples, given to the Army, of the Punifhment due to fuch
> crimes, ought to evince the Troops that no Mercy is to be expected
> by thofe who forget the Solemn Obligations, they have entered into
> by Inliftments. The Oaths they have taken, & their Duty to their
> Country: And who defert the Caufe of Freedom for that of Violence
> & Defpotism. Nothing is more painful to the Genl, than to be under
> the neceffity of taking the Life of a Soldier. But when his conduct is
> marked with Perjury & Infidelity, the Laws, both Civil & Military,
> requires fuch an atonement for his crime. No difcrimination will
> take place except where reprefentation is made of former good con-
> duct & Services; or other circumftances paliating the Offence, in an
> extraordinary degree.

The General laid aside his pen and rested his face in his cupped hands. *God grant*, he prayed, *these are the last of my own that I am called on to mur-der. If others must die, in the name of Christ Jesus, let the enemy be the ones to do the killing.*

Happily for a change, his prayer was answered, at least in large part. Proof was offered him next day that Salyers and Cooper did not in fact de-serve death and he was able to pardon them. So only poor William Bayley had to die.

This time he did not go out to watch.

Part ye' Seventeenth

In Which a Young Man Difcovers He Hath a Diftinguifhed Lineage

IT WAS SOME TIME BEFORE JAMES LEARNED THE REAL reason Captain Gunn had gone to the trouble of spiriting him away from camp to buy his time from Chenowith. For days after their return the affair remained a mystery. Poovey and Libby were wed; James went back to his duties, dividing his time between breaking horses and attending drill; the Captain resumed his place at the head of the troop and treated James with the same impartial mixture of indifference and hostility as before; and all seemed unchanged. That is, till the day James received special orders that would carry him away from Manakin Town forever.

The orders came one morning while he and his section mates were at their sword exercise in the suffocating heat of the manage. The drill was still a dismounted one; they were not yet proficient enough to perform the cuts and guards and parries in the saddle without a risk of cutting off their horses' ears, or their own. Sergeant Dangerfield stood before them acting as fugleman, shouting the commands and demonstrating the motions with his broadsword, while all about them on the manage other sections wheeled and maneuvered in mounted drill amid burning clouds of dust.

Standing next to Dangerfield was a backward-leaning wooden panel much like those used in civilian life to display broadsides, only instead of notices of public hangings, the latest news, and bulletins advertising the escape of runaway slaves and indentured servants, a large sheet of paper was tacked to it on which someone had drawn, with notable lack of skill, a large round human face divided into diagonal sections representing the six cuts of the sword. Improbably the face wore a beatific smile that seemed at variance with the fact it was split into a half dozen wedge-shaped pieces. This was their guide in learning the cuts.

They were performing the drill motions to be employed in the defense of one man against two after engaging the enemy in a mounted charge. "Carry the arm to the left," Dangerfield explained, "preserving the sword in the exact position of the guard, and cut *one* and *two*"—his blade slashed wickedly down, up and down again, making the shape of an X in the air—"then carry it to the off side, the body at the same time turning to the right—and be sure, goddamn you, to clear your horse's head—then bring your blade up to the guard again, and on the right, cut *one* and *two*"—again, this time on that side, his sword made the same invisible X of two whistling strokes which, on a man of flesh and blood and not a smiling figure drawn on a piece of paper, would have transformed his features into something that resembled a pie sliced for eating—only no one would ever want to eat it.

The recruits followed the motions, sweating in the pitiless sun. Because James had been given a saber lighter than the broadswords issued to some of his fellows, his small wrist and grasp were not at the disadvantage they would have been had he been trying to wield the larger, heavier blade; and he was proving a rather able swordsman—Dangerfield had actually told him so, kindling in his bosom a cozy warmth of pride. Accordingly the broadsword exercise was a part of the drill he had actually come to enjoy despite being soaked with sweat and near to smothering in his stable jacket; and he always, as today, worked hard to improve his skill.

Next they were to perform the defense to a near-side attack in pursuit. Dangerfield began with the now-familiar instruction, "Left parry is done in two motions . . . ," but was interrupted when a trooper cantered up through the confusion of the manage on a skewbald horse and leaned to speak to him; and next James was startled to hear the Sergeant bark, "Private Johnson, fall out and go with this corporal. They've got orders for you up at headquarters."

Questioningly Poovey glanced sideways to him, but Dangerfield pealed a rebuke and Sides quickly looked back to his front. Full of misgiving, James sheathed his saber and stepped out of ranks. Without a word the corporal reined about and trotted off at such a pace that James had to break into a trot to keep up, saber clanking at his side and annoyingly banging his left heel at every second step. By the time they reached regimental headquarters he was gasping for breath and felt as if he might faint from the heat. But he had never before passed through these sacred portals, had never ascended any higher than his own troop's orderly tent, and the thought of perhaps encountering Colonel White himself made him weak with suspense.

He leaned panting at the entrance of the marquee while the corporal dismounted and was relieved when the man motioned him to wait and ducked inside. This gave him a blessed moment to catch his breath and remind himself that if he'd survived his strange night with Captain Gunn he probably had little to fear from the likes of majors and colonels who were more afraid of Gunn than he now was. So when the corporal emerged and nodded toward the entrance, James was able to comply with an even breath and a feigned air of calm.

Coming in from the dazzling light of noonday, he was momentarily blinded and stood blinking while his nose told him things he could not see. All was heavy with the bitter smell of dead air long trapped under hot canvas, but even stronger was the reek of rum, and someone was also wearing a perfume that reminded him of the floral scents he'd sniffed on Baron Stew-Ben. He sensed a presence nearby and, in case that presence were an officer, drew himself to attention and saluted. "Private Johnson, reporting as ordered!"

"Be at your ease, Johnson," a voice told him in a clipped accent that was unfamiliar and belonged to the Northward. "I'm Lieutenant Ambrose Gordon." James did not know this name. By now the form of the officer had begun to materialize before him, seated at a camp desk covered with papers. In the brightening James discerned the glitter of a silver epaulet, and in another moment the white regimentals and blue smallclothes of the Third Dragoons. This was a shock in itself—what was an officer of the Third doing in the headquarters of the First? Finally his vision cleared altogether, and the officer was revealed to be a young man in his mid-twenties with a curly mass of brownish-blond hair, a high unwrinkled brow, a long jaw, and clear brown eyes. Though the smells of rum and perfume lingered about, the Lieutenant himself did not appear to be the offender. A partition hung at his back; from behind it James could hear the murmured conversation of a man and a woman. He deduced the lady wore the perfume while the gentleman drank the rum, hardly a lady's libation.

"It seems, Private Johnson," Lieutenant Gordon began, "that Captain Payton the clothier has a wagonload of uniforms assigned to Captain Watts's troop of the First Dragoons serving with our detachment in General Greene's army. It's an embarrassment to the Captain to have it, for it should've gone sooner, and Captain Watts has expressed urgent need of it. I, as it happens, have been given command of a train of seven wagons of clothing also due to go Southward for the use of my own regiment.

"Captain Payton, to make his absolution," Gordon went on, "has prevailed upon me to take his orphan wagonload along in my train as well." Now from behind the curtain the unseen gentleman's voice grew suddenly louder, and James recognized Colonel White's distinctive drawling tones. Next, to his amazement, the lady giggled naughtily, then cried aloud, "Shag me hard, you great ram cat," and commenced rhythmically to gasp. "Give me those diddies," the Colonel cried, "Oh God, I'm coming up like a coach and four."

"Thus," the Lieutenant continued, as if a seduction were not occurring nearly at his back, "we shall have a train of seven wagons of the Third and one of the First. Naturally, for this anomalous arrangement to be put into effect, the permission of the commander of your regiment, your esteemed Colonel White"—here he tilted his head in the direction of the scandalous noises behind the partition—"was required, and he has generously given it."

"Grind me, you devil of a mad dragoon," moaned the woman; "impale me, my divine lancer." "Oh, oh, oh," exclaimed the Colonel. The partition bulged and twitched, the ropes of a mattress could be heard madly thrumming. "There is, however, a caveat," Gordon blandly continued, raising his voice to be heard above the ruction. James did not know what a caveat was, and at this interesting moment did not really care, but the Lieutenant went on to explain: "Since a wagon carrying the property of the First Dragoons is to travel with the train, the Colonel insists that it be accompanied by a detail of troopers of the First, to act in the capacity, one might say, of supercargo. You're assigned that detail, private. You'll pack your gear and be ready to move at dawn tomorrow. That is all." Back of the partition the woman now began to wail as if unbearably bereaved. "Christ!" the Colonel groaned, "I'm coming down Cock Lane now! Christ, what a load!"

Despite the intriguing distractions James was astounded at his abrupt turn of fortune and shocked at the prospect of leaving Manakin Town. How had it come about? "Lieutenant," he ventured, "may I ask why I was picked?"

The woman's cries had begun to weaken into gratified whimpers. "There's a drove of twenty remounts going down with the train, destined for Colonel Washington's regiment," Gordon explained impassively, as her sighs at last ceased. "Your Captain Gunn," he said, "recommends you as a fair horsemaster."

James hesitated. All was quiet now beyond the partition save some low mutters. "May I ask another question, Lieutenant?"

Gordon frowned as a warning to James that he was in peril of stepping out of place. "What is it?"

"Who else from the First is going, Your Honor?"

"Private Plumbley, from Captain Harris' troop." The Lieutenant fixed him with a hard eye. "And before you ask me why, I'll tell you: Plumbley's Methodist rantings have turned half the troop into shrieking evangelical enthusiasts who go about jerking their heads and howling at the moon, while the other half have grown so sick of his endless sermons they heartily wish to hang him. He's going Southward because if he stays, he'll most assuredly be murdered by the half who've learned to hate him."

James sucked back a large breath before making his next inquiry, for he knew it would be taken as impudent. "Lieutenant, I have a sister that's married to Private Sides . . ."

Brusquely Gordon interrupted him. "No women are permitted, Private. And now, that *will* be all."

———————

No sooner had a stunned James left the headquarters marquee to stand outside once more blinded by the sun than Captain Gunn's distinctive baritone hailed him. "Got your orders, did you?"

James squinted till he made out Gunn's figure advancing on him. He saluted with truculence. "Yes, I did." Because he was angry he added with more sarcasm than was wise, "Thanks to you, I reckon." He paused for an offending second, then added, "Captain."

He braced himself to be struck, puffed out his cheeks with air, but Gunn, surprisingly, forbore. Instead the Captain laid the flat of his meaty hand on James's arm and turned him to the path that led down toward camp. They fell in stride together. "You're vexed," he remarked with an unaccustomed congeniality that James soon recognized for fiendishness, "to be parted from your pretty sister." James's eyes were now accustomed to the dazzle of the light; he turned to see the Captain leering in vulgar fashion. Gunn patted his shoulder. "You needn't worry, Johnson, *I'll* take good care of her." He captured his genitals in one paw and gave them a meaningful lift.

James flushed with a choking wrath he dared not unleash. But he did manage to twist away from Gunn's touch. "She's got a husband now," he said, as grimly as he could, by way of reminder.

"Sides?" Gunn laughed mightily. "He ain't no husband. He's a wether. 'Baaaaaa,' is what he says. She'll enjoy to have a real man's yard run up her for a change." James wanted to weep with rage, but he kept on walking, eyes pinned to the dust and pebbles of the path without seeing. "And *you* won't miss 'em, either one of 'em," the Captain ruminated with evident pleasure. "Not for long, anyhow. Little nacky fellow like you, once you get down South, why, you'll take one of them swamp fevers, your doodle'll drop off, and you'll be dead in a week's time."

James bristled but said nothing. They walked a few more steps and then Gunn stopped short. James stopped with him. They turned to stand face to face, James having to tilt his head backward to look up into the Captain's face. For that single instant the two of them might have been mortal foes, and equals, ready to fight to the death. Gunn set his knuckles on his hips. "Tell me," he demanded, "who in hell *are* you, Johnson?"

James frowned, bewildered. "Why, Captain, you know me."

"God rot you," Gunn cried, "*listen* to me. Who in fucking hell *are* you?"

James grimaced. "I don't understand. Why, I'm myself. I'm James Johnson." He even had a moment of doubt. "Ain't I?"

The Captain swung away from him with a savage look. "You're a fool, Johnson."

James was tired of hearing that, and getting mad, and before he knew it he heard himself complain, "I truly wish you wouldn't say that so much, Captain." Finally that was too bold. Gunn whirled on him, hit him on the side of the face with the heel of one of his hands, and knocked him flat on his back in the dirt of the path.

Gunn addressed him sternly as he lay there dazed. "I say it, you little dung-beetle, because it's the goddamned truth. Any man that *is* a man has got to know who in hell he is. And if he *don't* know that, then by Christ's wounds, he *is* a fool. So *you're a fool.*" He leaned over James like a menacing giant. "You want to know just how bloody much of a fool you *are?*"

"I don't know," said James, rubbing his jaw. "Maybe not. Maybe I wouldn't like it." He got unsteadily to his feet.

Gunn drew back a step or two and measured him contemptuously with his black regard. "Well, I don't give a two-handed turd whether you want to know or not. I'm going to tell you. Now listen to me. I'm a stranger to you, ain't I?"

"Why, no, Captain. You ain't no stranger. I know you well enough."

"No, you shit-licker," growled Gunn, "I mean I was a perfect stranger afore that black day when you enrolled in my troop."

"Yes, Your Honor," James nodded, eager now to find some common ground. "*That's* true—I didn't know you till then. You and me was strangers sure enough."

"All right," the Captain said, bending near and giving him a sly inquiring look. "Now how d'you reckon it is I come to know more about you than you know about yourself?"

"Well, I don't know that you *do* know that."

"What if I was to *tell* you what I know about you that you don't?"

"Well, if you done that, how would I know the difference? I mean, maybe you'd be making it up." As soon as he said it he knew it merited another blow; he filled his cheeks with air just as Gunn's fist smote him, rocked him back on his heels, and made his head ring. But he did not fall down this time and was proud of that, though it was true he staggered about somewhat ingloriously before regaining his senses and his balance.

The Captain waited a time till he seemed to think James was once more capable of listening. He resumed while James stood spitting blood and testing the fixity of his teeth between two fingers. "Pay me heed, now. Does the name of Gunn strike any meaning for you? Apart from it being my name and me being your captain and riding-master?"

James left off feeling his teeth and nodded, recalling the night when Gunn bought his indenture, when faint bells of memory had seemed to ring out the sounds of old names long lost. "Well," he answered, "when I was small, my Da told me the Johnsons used to serve Clan Gunn in Scotland, before the Forty-Five. Before the clans was broke up."

Gunn cocked his head. "And who did your Da say these Gunns was?"

"A clan that was often in feud with the Keiths, as he told it. But I never knew what a feud was till later, nor could never say who the Keiths was, nor why the Gunns and the Keiths was a-feuding anyways."

The Captain smiled with the one corner of his mouth that always turned upward. "'Twasn't only the Keiths that Clan Gunn made war on," he announced with evident pride. "'Twas the Mackays too. And even high lords like the Earls of Sutherland and Caithness."

"My Da spoke of Mackays. And our home was in Caithness, he told me. In Strathmore."

Gunn took him again by the arm and drew him roughly off the path. A ravine turned down to their left toward the stream where the laundresses worked, and they descended to the brook whose clear waters ran past flat white rocks. There were no washerwomen at their toil today, and here they were quite alone, isolated from the bustle of the camp. Overhead grew tall sycamores with mottled flaking bark and big shaggy leaves; mockingbirds whistled and chirped in the high branches. In their shade, and on the bank of the trickling stream, Gunn, rather than inflict the beating James expected, bade him sit. Surprised, he did, choosing a place in the mossy fork of some sycamore roots. He rested his sore jaw in both hands while Gunn began pacing up and down before him.

"Listen now," the Captain said, "Johnsons is a sept of the Gunns. 'Sept' means they come down from the Gunns. Two hundred years back, the greatest of the clan was a chieftain name of George Gunn; he ruled in the Caithness Highlands. They called him the Crowner, on account of a great silver brooch he wore, so big it had a name itself, *Am Braisdeach Mor*. 'Big Broochy,' that means. That brooch signified a high office he held of the Earl of Caithness. Maybe he had the right of crowning the earls, nobody knows. But they hailed him the Crowner and he was a mighty warrior, maybe the mightiest there was. By his time the Gunns had a motto: 'Stand Either Peace or War.'"

"What's a motto?" James couldn't help it; the tale had intrigued him and now he wished to know it in all its parts.

Gunn stopped his pacing. "A motto's a saying that tells folk what you're about. Gunns can stand either peace or war, makes no difference to them. They prefer war, though. Always have. Always will."

"But what've I got to do with these here Crowners and Big Broochies?"

"Hush and you'll hear." He was pacing again. "This Crowner, he had five sons that lived—survived all his wars, I mean. They was James, Henry, Robert, Will, and John. The Johnsons—*your* Johnsons—why, they come straight down from John, that youngest son. *John's son*, you see? John Gunn and his kin settled around Cattaig and Bregual, at the head of the River Thurso above Westerdale, right there in Strathmore, same place your Da told you of. And his blood ran in your Da. It runs in you too. John's blood and the Crowner's, all the way back to a parcel of Norse seafarers that founded the line. All them warriors, you come from them. You *are* them. *That's* what I know about you that you don't."

"My Da said the clans all had signs to know 'em by. How'd I know a Gunn?"

"Before the Forty-Five you'd know a Gunn by the sprig of juniper in his bonnet and by his tartan, which is a somber dark green and blue, made to blend with mountain heath and herbage, in ambuscade."

"How come you to know all this?"

"It's been told among the Gunns from the beginning. Every Gunn knows it. And every member of all the septs too. All save you. And *that's* why you're a fool."

"But, Captain, why d'you tell me all this?"

"Same reason I bought your time. The Gunns cares for their own, even if there own's a weaselly creature like you whose pelt ain't worth the skinning." He spat angrily to the side. "You needed to know what you was. What's in you to do. You'll need it in going Southward."

"You said I'd die in the South."

"Maybe so, maybe not. There's worse things than dying, like not knowing what's in you to do. I'll tell you a story that can *keep* you from dying, or if you've got to die, to die right."

"Now?"

"No, tomorrow. When you start out with the train. I'll tell it to you then."

Part ye Eighteenth

In Which General Greene, Againſt Counſel, Caſts All Into ye Hazard

ALMOST EVERYONE WAS OPPOSED TO IT, SAVE BILLY Washington and the ever-impetuous Harry Lee, whose dispatches from beyond the Congaree kept urging an immediate attack on Stewart's British force at McCord's Ferry. Harry argued Cornwallis might leave Virginia and descend on Charles Town; General Leslie's reinforcements were expected at any time so Stewart must be destroyed now lest these conjoined armies grow too strong to dispute. Greene, however, did not believe Leslie was as near as Harry thought and was even more unconvinced that Cornwallis was about to abandon Virginia and return to his old haunts in South Carolina. But he did plan to move on Stewart, if not as quickly as Colonel Lee wished then far more quickly than many of his senior commanders felt was prudent.

Seated in an arc before him, sweating in the stifling heat that the raised sides of the marquee failed to stir, they gave him their doubting countenances. Of course they were unwilling. Councils of war were forever unwilling. Not that it mattered; Greene had never much approved of the device, though he sometimes called them for appearances' sake. In his opinion General Washington had relied on them excessively and as a result now unfairly wore a reputation for indecision when in fact he only desired a consensus that could never be obtained. Left to his own devices as at Trenton, His Excellency had a stunning audacity. But seldom did he give himself such liberties.

It was ironic—Washington, the Virginia patrician, disdainful of the popular, cleaved to a democratic principle while Greene, sprung from New England, the cradle of leveling, tended to autocracy. Though on occasion he could be swayed by incisive argument, as he often was by Harry Lee, his preferred idea of a council of war was to announce his plans, give his officers an opportunity to discuss them, then ignore their advice and proceed exactly as he had resolved from the first.

Even so, he was sometimes unhappily surprised. Today, for instance, Sumner, normally the boldest of the bold, counseled a patience that sounded to Greene very like timidity. While it was true the long delinquent Marquis de Malmedy had at last arrived with the balance of the North Carolina militia of Mecklenburg, Rowan, and Orange, Sumner argued, half of these were without arms and Major Reading Blount was as near as Charlotte with two hundred more troops—armed regulars. Blount, it happily turned out, was also bringing with him three hundred stand of badly needed muskets. Till that news came, it had been thought many in Blount's contingent would be unarmed; that they now were bringing an extra store of weapons seemed wonderful. "Should not the General wait for the Major and the arms?" Sumner wondered.

Otho Williams, another disappointment, suggested waiting for the detachment his native state of Maryland had been promising to send. Greene acidly reminded his Adjutant-General those troops had been immobile for two whole months supposedly awaiting camp equipage and did not seem disposed to move ever again in their lives.

Captain Kirkwood, who commanded the Delaware scouts, said nothing, but Greene could read the doubt in even this intrepid fighter's sunburned face. Kosci stared back at him with a deep intensity, but then Kosci always stared like that; one never knew what to make of it; at least he held silent. Colonel Malmedy, with his uncertain command of English, expressed no sentiments either way, but wore a determined expression so much like Kosci's that Greene could not help wondering if it might be a demeanor taught by European military academies to be adopted whenever one's mental faculties failed. Major Forsyth, the commissary, did find his voice; he asked the whereabouts of Colonel Shelby's overmountain men, whom the General had summoned to him many weeks ago. Greene answered he now despaired of their ever coming.

No one, Major Hyrne reminded the General, had heard from Pickens. "One seldom hears from General Pickens," Greene quipped, "till he turns up just where one has been hoping he'll be." This was a bit of bravado; Greene was not as unconcerned as he pretended. In fact he had not heard from Pickens in some time and was a little worried that he might not appear when needed. But he was not worried enough to delay the movement. "And Colonel Henderson," he added, "is already in the vicinity of Friday's Ferry collecting the remnants of Sumter's brigade. Pickens will come."

It went on. Major Hardaman of the Second Maryland worried that the flooded Wateree was still deep to a horse's belly; perhaps the roads along it remained impassable. Washington, who had reconnoitered the roads, reassured him; but Colonel Ashe complained there was sickness among the North Carolina regulars. Even the redoubtable Colonel Howard of the Maryland Line questioned whether the army had a sufficiency of ammunition. Edmunds of the First Virginia questioned whether the powder stores, dampened by the long rains, had had time to dry. Greene barely heard all this. His mind was made up. He knew his plan was bold, just as he knew that in the end they would do as he said even if he could not convince them the policy was wise.

They regarded him uneasily and he returned them his supreme confidence that, once it took hold, was as strong if not stronger than the meditative turn of mind that so often made him seem indecisive. Of all the officers before him that August noonday, only Washington, like Lee down on the far bank of the Congaree keeping an eye on the enemy, wanted to fight—Billy always did—but Greene knew Billy was too modest to speak of his unquenchable thirst for action in such company for fear of seeming to boast in the midst of timidity.

The burden was Greene's alone, as was right. It was time to bring the wrangling to an end. "Gentlemen," he broke in firmly, "we've been in such a situation that I fancy few would have thought of operating offensively. But *I* think it the safest way."

He paused; perhaps *the safest way* had not been the very best formulation. It was not by any means a safe course of action. He would be setting out with but a fragment of his force, hoping the state troops of Henderson and the western militias of Pickens and the last of the North Carolina Continentals would all come to him in time, on the road, as he marched. If they did, he would have nearly man for man with Stewart. If they did not? He had no answer for that except that he would fight the enemy with whatever force he collected. He trusted in God's mercy that help would come. Even without help he would still wield an admittedly small but light, flexible, maybe even dangerous force. Stewart was better equipped and his troops more experienced. It would come down to the men. Whose were more game? Whose the steadier? Whose the more willing to die?

"Allow me to make amendment," he confessed frankly, after his moment of thought. "It's *not* the safest course. I *do* know that, just as I also know you will trust me in this as you have so far trusted me in all else. It's true that in the main I have had to play the Fabian game, and that we've all grown somewhat used to that fashion of operating. But those of you who've been with me since I first took up the Southern command have also seen that I'm willing to take a risk when I believe one is warranted. You've always taken that same risk with me. I wish you to take it with me again."

He yet rode the exhilarating anger that had buoyed his spirits when he went among his men during the rains and saw how they, not he and not his officers, were the true heart of the revolution. Neither had he forgotten how Caty's shade had visited him in the night to embolden him with her reminder of all she believed of him. He turned to Captain Shubrick, seated at a desk nearby, and gave his orders. "The army will drill by brigades this afternoon, and at six o'clock P.M., one round of blank cartridges will be fired by platoons from right to left." Shubrick snatched up goose quill and paper, dipped the pen in his pot of oak-gall ink, and began rapidly to write.

"At five o'clock tomorrow morning," the General went on, "the army will march by the left, all save Colonel Washington's corps of cavalry. Two regiments of the North Carolina brigade will lead the advance; then the battalions of the Virginia regulars; the Delaware and Maryland Continentals; Captain Kirkwood's light troops; and the contingent of North Carolina militia. Part of the North Carolina brigade will be detached to the rear as bullock guard. We will take but two wagons to carry ammunition, hospital stores, and rum. During the march, all public stores are to be committed to the care of the baggage guard."

He ceased; Shubrick's pen scratched in the silence till the orders were complete. Then Greene turned to Washington. "Two days hence," he said to the Colonel, "the cavalry will cross the Wateree at Simmons' Ferry and meet us—God willing—somewhere about Culpeper's on the Congaree in two days more."

"We'll be there," Billy pledged.

"I know you will." Greene addressed the others. "Then, all we'll require is a small blessing of Heaven"—he cocked his head in playful extenuation—"or maybe two, and then we'll give Colonel Stewart the trouncing he deserves." Though he watched hopefully, in the whole surround of faces Billy's held the only merriment he saw.

The afternoon was a bustle of preparation. The brigades drilled on their parades raising masses of dust struck through with shafts of sunlight. Watching them from the saddle of the bay horse he had bought from Colonel Ashe to replace the recently lamed Swift, Greene thought he saw a new spring in their step. The weeks of rest and refreshment had done them good; they were eager to move, eager to come to grips with the enemy again. The fifes had an extra lilt, the drums whirred smartly; the few regimental colors, faded though they were, bobbed bravely about; the rows of muskets stood brighter and straighter than the General had any reason to hope.

When at six o'clock the whole army drew up in its ten battalions of foot to fire a blank volley by platoons from right to left, the crackle of it ran so smoothly and continuously down the line that it made the General laugh aloud with pleasure. "All General Sumner's musket practice," he confided to Williams, "has made a difference in the North Carolina brigade. They sound as if they might actually kill someone."

The exercise of making ready for the march had animated the Adjutant-General at last. "Let's pray," he rejoined, "it'll be the *enemy* they kill."

"All the same," Greene joked, "we shall stand well behind them on the day of battle."

Darkness came slowly. A waxing sickle-moon drooped low in the sky. In the deepening dusk the troops busied themselves packing their gear and talking excitedly of what the morrow might bring. Their cooking fires glowed like scattered hearth-coals; the air stung with woodsmoke; the familiar odor of the camp rose to Greene, the fetor of the filled vaults, the thick smell of many men long unbathed; the manure of oxen and horses and beef cattle; and finally that indescribable essence radiated by every army, partaking somehow of its spirit, as if fear had a scent, and hope did, and trust and companionship and every other feeling men might nourish as they waited poised at the very edge of life. Greene stood at his marquee amid winking fireflies and heard the great stir of his troops in the night. From above, the sinking moon and a starlit sky cast over the world a spell of silver. Another thought took shape and he smiled. *Soon, Caty. Very soon now.*

At five in the morning when the drums began to beat Assembly there no longer was a moon. To the east a first faint hint of light was wakening, but everywhere else the grudging night held fast, the glittering dome of the heavens still casting in silver the campground and all in it. But eerily a thick starlit fog covered all the lower country roundabout them, the flooded canebrake and the swamps and the joining rivers, so they could look down from their height upon what might have been a level carpet of luminous wool stretching eastward toward the Low Country and then toward a sea so distant it lay beyond the inconceivable outer curve of the earth. *What a marvel is this world*, thought the General, watching the eye of dawn slowly open somewhere yonder above the mouth of the great Pee Dee River, above the mouth of the Santee itself, above broad Winyah Bay, above the vast Atlantic.

He could feel the ethereal beauty of that sight tempting him toward the immaterial, toward the aesthetic and philosophical, toward his bad habit of losing the focus of his mind to go wandering in realms of unwholesome speculation; he squared himself, fended off that temptation, put by all thought of Dryden and Swift, of Milton, Sterne, Pope, and Shakespeare; deliberately turned his back on the splendor of the scene to oversee the dismantling of his marquee. His baggage had been loaded; his new horse stood ready with flaring nostrils and tossing head, roused by the tumult. He himself was more than ready.

Around him as darkness began to fade the breakfast fires winked out, yielding up their last tart fragrance of smoke. The various battalions formed on their parades; the commands of the officers sounded on the humid air. At the head of the Camden road a cluster of torches flared; Kosci and Major Armstrong were arranging the two battalions of the advance and counting off the members of lead patrol and the flank guard. The quartermasters and pioneers of each battalion were taking their places.

Presently he heard the battalions called to attention. Then, one by one, the orders were given for each to take its place on the road, "By sections of four, to the right wheel, march!" And soon his little army was on the move. In open order they struck a lively pace; the drums thumped; the fifes shrilled; behind him as he took his position at the head of the column he heard them laughing; he heard scraps of song, catcalls, jeers, happy bursts of swearing. His boys were in a sprightly mood. The first of the daylight brightened the sky on their right hand behind the summits of the hills; the stars faded. The dry smell of road dust came up.

Soon enough the fog burned away and they were sweltering in the swamp country. To the west the sun glared off the surface of the flooded canebrake and dazzled them nearly blind if they dared glance that way, so they marched with heads awry and eyes asquint. Nevertheless, they made extraordinarily good time. The road had been washed out in spots, but under Kosci's supervision the pioneers quickly restored it. Several fallen trees had to be cut apart and thrown aside. A few muddy stretches had to be corduroyed. Yet that first day they made twenty miles, resting at noontime, resuming at sundown and camping for the night on Swift Creek, over halfway to their destination. The second day, which was the twenty-fourth of August, they covered the remaining eighteen miles to Camden in two stages, morning and evening, and by ten o'clock at night, having tramped three hours in the dark by torchlight, were settling at the ferry crossing. It was a propitious start.

While the army crossed piecemeal to the west side of the Wateree by means of the Camden ferry and the other miscellaneous vessels the quartermasters had managed to sequester, Greene sat perspiring in his marquee catching up on his correspondence. He wrote or dictated a dozen letters and dispatches in the two days it took to get the army over the river. He sent an indignant letter to the commandant of Charles Town protesting the hanging of the poor militia colonel, Isaac Hayne. He published a broadside threatening retaliation, but promising to execute only regular enemy officers and not any deluded Carolinians who might have allied themselves with Great Britain—Americans, he implied, knew how to show a finer discrimination.

Then, on the afternoon of Monday the twenty-seventh, with the army successfully established on the western shore and Pendleton sending over the headquarters baggage, some odd whim made him mount his new gelding, summon an escort of dragoons, and ride the two miles northward to visit his old battleground at Hobkirk's Hill.

Colonel Ashe's bay had an easy gait and covered the distance comfortably across a dismal country of piney woods and prickly, impoverished-looking thickets. They passed through the melancholy ruin Lord Rawdon had made of Camden when he abandoned it in July. Crows roosted on its burnt timbers and rose in black clouds at their approach with a heavy flapping of wings and a chorus of melancholy cries. Amid the sooty rubble of the village the folk had put up shanties rudely made of poles and vines; their dirty faces peered curiously out as Greene and his party rode by. A cur chased them barking vengefully as if they too were to blame for the devastation which, Greene supposed, they must be. *We are all complicit*, he thought, *in every enormity this war spawns.*

Beyond the village they crossed a rolling open tract and soon passed the old eroded, grass-grown British earthworks with the sharpened branches of their *abatis* still in place; and then, farther on, the blackened ruins that had once been the little suburb of Logtown. Beyond loomed the low hill itself, shrouded in its dark cloak of evergreen. They drew rein before it. The General bade the dragoons wait on the flat while he went on alone, up the sandy slope of the well-remembered ridge. Ashe's animal took the climb well at first, but presently began to struggle in the deep going, and finally Greene dismounted to give him an easier time of it and led him upward.

The tall pines of the forest swayed gently overhead, creaking in the heated breeze. Sunlight and shadow flickered over him and his horse as the trees moved. Here and there glades opened out where the full fury of the sun smote down, and tall, sharp-edged grasses grew in patches of sand before the pines closed in again. Above, robins and catbirds hopped from branch to branch with heads curiously cocked at him. He smelled rosin and the heady fragrance of the beds of dry pine needles underfoot. Grasshoppers preceded him in leaping waves. Peering about, he thought it strange that no sign of the battle remained save a few bullet-pocked trees. Scavengers must have picked it clean in the four months since. *And nature heals too*, he thought.

Soon, wet with sweat, winded from plodding in the clinging sand, he came to the crest and climbed to his saddle and rode along the pine-covered summit till he came to the path leading down the back side of the hill to the little shady spring above Pine Tree Creek and its swamp where, that morning of the battle, he'd been taking his breakfast on a fallen log when the attack burst upon the Maryland and Virginia pickets.

I may ſay with the King of Pruſſia, he had written to Dan Morgan just today before starting out, *fortune is a female, and I am no gallant. She has jilted me ſeveral times this Campaign, but in ſpite of her teeth I purſue her ſtill, in hopes the old adage will be fulfilled, that a coy dame may prove kind at laſt. I am not well pleaſed with her rebuffs; but I bear it with patience. I was content at the flogging at Guilford; but I loſt all patience with that of Lord Rawdon's. In the one I conſidered victory as doubtful, in the other, certain.*

That had been his mistake, that certainty of winning. He swung down, tethered the bay to a pine sapling. The log he'd rested on that morning was gone, but in its place someone had fashioned a rude bench by laying a rough plank across two stones. Here he sat. All was quiet. A cardinal pecked in some fallen leaves nearby. Mosquitoes whined minutely about his ears. He listened to the agreeable trickle of the spring. Glancing down, he saw a crayfish resting on the pebbly bottom, languidly waving its antennae. *How peaceful,* he thought. *How different from the last time I sat here.*

Not far to his right, he knew, the road from the Waxhaws ran through the forest, over the crown of the hill, and down onto the plain where his escort waited. Though the top of the hill hid it from where he sat by the spring, his mind's eye showed him everything as it had appeared that April morning when he hurried forward from his interrupted breakfast, the near edge of the plain clear of timber with the road dividing it, the rest covered with trees and underbrush; the impassable morass of Pine Tree Creek on the left extending southward toward the enemy works; Logtown in the middle distance, a smoldering pile of ashes; Camden itself farther on, not yet destroyed, a small brown scab at the margin of the immense green crescent of wilderness; the glint of the Santee beyond; another road passing across the plain northeastward, diagonally from front to left; the British forts spaced roundabout at intervals from east to west, the last on the river. And the red lines advancing.

He commanded sixteen hundred men that day; Rawdon, less than a thousand. The odds had favored him, but his confidence had made him careless. He'd camped the army in battle formation in hopes of being ready for anything the enemy might attempt; but even so, the wily Rawdon was able to steal a march through the woods between the swamp and the open plain and come at him on the oblique from the left front, striking with complete surprise. The Americans, at first thrown on the defensive, had quickly rallied and Greene had organized his bold counterattack. But ultimately he had failed. Why? It was true the odious Thomas Sumter had disobeyed explicit orders and failed to join him, true too that a deserter had stolen out to tell the British all his dispositions, true also that in the fight Colonel Gunby's veteran Marylanders had unexpectedly, unbelievably broken without good cause.

But it was also true that Sumter had seldom come when called; that deserters were always sneaking between the lines with information; that Gunby's misunderstood order leading to the rout at Hobkirk's was little different from Colonel Howard's at The Cowpens, which had ironically won a victory. What was truest of all, he knew, was that Nathanael Greene should not have offered the kind of battle he did, when and where he did, and might never have offered battle at all had he not hungered so fatally for a victory to rival Dan Morgan's at The Cowpens. In reporting the outcome of the battle to Congress he had blamed Gunby; then he'd court-martialed the poor man and probably wrecked his career, but now he could admit with shame that he himself had invited the calamity out of sheer vaulting ambition.

He watched the crayfish idling in the eddies of the spring. He waved away mosquitoes. He had overreached; he had ordered a risky double envelopment, believing his greater force could get around both flanks of the shorter British line, as Hannibal of old had done against the Romans at Cannae—indeed, as Cornwallis himself had done against Gates on almost this same ground a year ago. *Was this but a flight of envy in the face of the Modern Hannibal? Was it no more than a play for the admiration of Cornwallis?* At the time he had not consciously thought of that; but it seemed possible now. Perhaps he'd hoped His Lordship, up on the Chesapeake, would hear how his old adversary had surrounded and crushed the army of Rawdon in South Carolina even as Hannibal the Carthaginian had destroyed Varro in Apulia.

One wing of the movement belonged to Washington's dragoons; yes, much like Hasdrubal's heavy cavalry at Cannae, they'd charged savagely into the enemy's rear, even came close to snatching up Rawdon himself, but presently got entangled among the noncombatant elements of the enemy force and so encumbered themselves with prisoners they could no longer act with their customary nimbleness and ferocity. The confusion among the other flanking troops was too great for their maneuver to succeed. Furthermore, to counter Greene's envelopment Rawdon swiftly extended his first line and brought forth a second; and after a short but vicious fight at close range with artillery and musket and bayonet, the advancing Americans were soon forced to withdraw.

Afterward, some had faulted Billy Washington for getting his cavalry mired in the enemy rear, had named it a blunder. Not Greene. If the Maryland Line had not broken, Billy's disruption of Rawdon's rear would have been hailed as a masterstroke. But there were other complaints. Harry Lee was reported to have whispered to intimates among the Legion that "a faulty tactical plan" was to blame, and that in ordering Washington's charge, Greene had showed "the deranging effects of unlimited confidence." Of course Harry had never spoken such scathing opinions to Greene's face, had in fact loudly praised the General for his audacity and address. But hearing the condemnations rumored, Greene was stung. Whatever his flaws, Harry Lee's judgments carried weight. "The deranging effects of unlimited confidence"—the phrase conveyed a frightening implication of something approaching an imbalance of the mind. If a soldier as headstrong as Lee could think Greene deranged, then truly, every man must be a mystery to himself.

He must consider, then, whether the present movement against Stewart were itself "a faulty plan deranged by unlimited confidence." Evidently his commanders at the council of war had thought so, though on this occasion Harry had seemed not to agree; for weeks he had been its tireless advocate. But then, Greene reflected, smiling, this would not be the first time the changeling Lee would have promoted on one occasion a course of action he had scorned on another—impenetrable inconsistency being, it seemed, a trait of true genius.

Then came an intriguing surmise. Perhaps Greene had ridden here today not to satisfy a whim at all but in order to work out an understanding with himself. To solve the mystery that he now was. For he was no longer the man who had tried the tactics of Cannae at Hobkirk's Hill. Since then there had been the siege of Ninety-Six. There had been the assault on the Star Fort. There had been the failed operations before Orangeburgh and Sumter's debacle at Monck's Corner. These had changed him. Yes, he still longed for a triumph on the battlefield, so long denied him. Yes, he still wished to emulate Dan Morgan's feat. Yes, he was as ambitious today as he'd been in April, and was even more anxious now to deal out defeat to the enemy. But the mystery of who he was had changed.

When he rejoined his escort near the foot of the hill, he noticed a certain agitation among them, and no sooner had he drawn rein than one, a gaunt, hollow-cheeked lad with spikes of flaxen hair jutting humorously from under the rim of his helmet, saluted him and spoke up smartly, "Beg pardon, General, permission to speak?" Greene gave it, as he did without fail when addressed by a ranker. "General, my name's Ebenezer Minton, Parsons' Troop," the fellow hurried on. "Me and my mates here, we've been a-wondering, be it in your mind, by chance, what happened on this here same piece of ground we're a-standing on?"

The General was puzzled. To him the plain looked utterly featureless. "During the battle, do you mean?"

"Why, yes, General," Minton nodded with enthusiasm, "when we was giving the Lobsters their licking." He and the others exchanged ferocious and triumphant grins.

The General gave a rueful laugh. "It's generally believed," he reminded them, "it was *we* who took the licking."

"Well, as to that," shrugged Minton, "I reckon some of them Maryland boys got theirselves licked, and maybe some of them militia that's *always* getting licked." He wagged his head decidedly. "But *we* didn't get licked. Not at all. Colonel Billy's dragoons never got licked." He leveled a gleaming eye on Greene. "And neither did *you*, General. *You* wasn't licked nohow. I know that, for I seen it." He waved a hand at the other two. "We *all* seen it."

"Us and Colonel Billy come down from the woods where we was holding in reserve," another eagerly burst in, then realized his breach of etiquette, straightened in the saddle, saluted, and gave his name, "John Weaver, General, Parsons' Troop." He too was slender and small; his look shone as fiercely as Minton's; he wore a greasy rifle smock and a round hat with a torn brim.

"We come storming straight down this road," Weaver resumed, coloring at the recollection, "on the dead jump too—saber charge, you know, General; we was squalling like demons, and by the bloody Christ"—here he paused, made a little obeisance of apology for the blasphemy, then plunged on—"we turned the left of them Bloodybacks and pitched into their rear, right yonder where them thickets is, and broke 'em, broke 'em up bad too. Looked like somebody'd throwed a wolf in a sheep-fold; they was running ever which way. Why, you could pick yourself up a sutler, a commissary, a surgeon, a quartermaster, a wagon-driver, a whore, or whatever the hell you wanted."

Now the third man—Zephaniah Ferrill, he named himself, also of Parsons' Troop, equally diminutive, equally dingy, and equally ardent—took up the tale. "And we come smack up on that deuced lord—Reardon or Rewdon or whatever his damned name was—ugliest man I ever saw, peer or gentry or common as mud, makes no difference, he was *ugly*—him and some of his officers, all in their pretty clothes and riding their fine horses. I cut one down, and Eben here, why, he hollers to this homely lord, 'Give me your goddamned sword, you red-coated son of a bitch of an Irishman.'"

Ferrill was not as sensitive as his fellows about profanity and never thought to pause to make apology for it, just hastened on, while Minton looked modest to have his encounter with Rawdon spoken of before the General. "And the lord, he's all obliging, he makes as if he's going to give his sword over to Eben, and Eben no more'n a private and the lord commanding a whole big army, but the lord, God rot him, he plays sly on us and pretends it's stuck in the scabbard and don't give it over, and then some of his cavalry comes at us and we had to give him up. Saved his ill-made arse, they did."

"Then we heard the artillery going on the road," Minton burst in, imitating the sound of cannon fire, "*boom boom boom*, and all the commotion up thisaway, and Colonel Billy, he hollers, 'Come on, boys, they're a-needing us at the front!' So we're whirling back up the road, just all of us in one big ragged drove, wasn't no formation to it. And that's when we seen *you*, General. You and the guns."

Greene nodded. He remembered it. After Gunby's botched order, the Marylanders and some of the Virginians broke, and he'd ridden down into the lines to steady the one regiment still holding, Colonel Hawes's Fifth Virginia. But quickly the British gained Hawes's flanks, and he had no choice but to order the Virginians to retreat. This exposed Colonel Harrison's guns, two of the army's four-pounders and the bigger six, stationed across the Waxhaws road. The limber horses had all been shot down and the matrosses, seeing themselves abandoned and their teams dead, left the cannon where they stood and ran for the rear. Greene ordered forward a company of Maryland light infantry to secure the guns and take them safely off the field, then turned his attention to rallying the matrosses. While he was thus engaged, first a body of British cavalry and then a force of infantry decimated the brave Marylanders he'd sent to defend the guns.

"You run them matrosses back up to the pieces they'd left," Minton was saying. "Run 'em over all them poor dead and wounded Maryland boys in the road, the balls flying all about, redcoat cavalry prowling up and down—Coffin's dragoons, they was, them damned Georgia Tories—and their infantry coming up at you through the woods."

As Minton spoke, Greene remembered his horse, good old Swift, stepping gingerly among those fallen Marylanders, trying not to tread on the limp, blood-soaked forms in their grimy hunting shirts and overalls. Some were yet alive and squirming in their agony, but called up to him with piping voices as he passed, *You look out now, General; don't you get hurt.* The powder smoke had aggravated his quinsey and his bad eye; he was coughing, the bad eye was blind and streaming tears; he felt vaguely ridiculous, lame and portly as he was, nursing his little load of ailments, while all around him frightfully maimed and dying men were begging him to be careful. And yes, he'd seen the enemy dragoons, and a red line of infantry advancing.

"You put them matrosses to the drag ropes," Weaver said, "and pretty quick you had 'em straining to drag them guns back up the hill." The trooper's voice quieted then. "When they couldn't all move the guns, why, I seen you—we *all* seen you—get down off that gray horse of yours and take hold of his bridle with one hand and put the other to a drag-rope and give it a turn or two around your fist and commence to pulling on it yourownself, and them Tory dragoons gathering for a charge to trample you down."

Through rifts in the smoke he'd seen Coffin's horsemen forming in a column of sections, the first rank of eight with their sabers at the slope, a few still wearing their red coats faced with yellow, others in the white drill that was more common for Southern wear. He saw under the bills of their black-feathered caps the row of raw, wolfish faces of those South Carolina, Georgia, and Florida Loyalists, any one of whom would be a hero for the rest of his days if he killed Nathanael Greene. "Attention to the charge!" he heard one of their officers shout, the cry shrill above the musket fire. He remembered the rough braiding of the hempen rope wound around his hand as he pulled with all his ironmaster's strength, as he dug his heels into the soft sand, as Swift backed away jerking nervously at his bridle, as the six-pounder at last slowly began to budge.

Now Ferrill put a period to their communal account. "We'd come up on their flank," he boasted. "That's when Colonel Billy yelled, 'Come on, you sons of bitches, do you want to live forever?' And we run in amongst 'em afore they could charge and the whoresons, why, they scattered like a flock of pullets." He pointed to a nearby stump as nondescript as any of the dozens on the plain save for a single splinter rising like a knife-blade a foot or so from its center. "Right there is where you was, General, right by that same sharp stump, a-yanking on that drag rope." He sat his saddle cackling with satisfaction; all three did.

Greene nodded, far more moved than he wished to show. His vision blurred; he curled a hand before his mouth and roughly cleared his throat. "You fellows saved my life that day," he finally managed to croak.

"Maybe so, General," Minton replied, giving his head a little twist. "And maybe there *was* some of our boys licked that day, like you said." Then he showed Greene his broad and toothless smile. "But, General, you wasn't one of 'em."

Part ye' Nineteenth

In Which a Young Man Hears of His Destiny

THAT EVENING IN HIS HUT AFTER STABLE CALL he began to pack his gear. There wasn't much to pack; most of it would be carried on his person—his carbine, the saber with its sling, a cartridge box and belt, the pair of spurs he wore strapped to his bare feet, a tin canteen, his leather helmet with its iron cross-bands and plume of turkey feathers. There was the haversack also, to be slung over his shoulder to hang down his back holding his extra suit of underclothes, his tin cup, a poke of parched corn, and a bit of moldy bread.

The saddlebags took the rest of what he had. Into them he put some sacks of oats and a nosebag and currycomb for Jesus, two dozen extra cartridges, and the items needed to clean his weapons. His blanket must be rolled up ready to be fastened behind the cantle—Libby did that for him, quietly sobbing and wiping her nose now and then on a hem of her skirts. Sides and his messmates sat in the firelight looking on in silence. The news of James's orders had pretty much struck them dumb. And he was trying to busy himself so as not to feel the pain of parting.

It occurred to him as he fastened the buckles of his saddlebags that every last article of what he'd been considering his own was in fact the property of the Continental Army—save the ragged underclothes which Chenowith had been obliged to furnish him so long ago now that you could see through them as if they were made of gauze. Still, it gave a fellow a deal of pride to have in his possession, at least for a time, more fine articles than he'd ever in his life be able to own outright. He'd handled them with care as he packed.

"'Twon't be long till we see you again," Sides remarked, to break the uncomfortable quiet, but mostly to console Libby. "Soon as Lafayette licks Cornwallis, the regiment'll come South to join General Greene, I'll bet."

"I don't know if Corn Wallace can *be* licked," said James in dejection. "Seems like everybody's tried it and got licked themselves. I don't reckon Loff Yet can do it neither."

259

Bussey spoke up with sudden eagerness. "I've got to ask you a question, Johnson, been bothering me ever since we met. Seems to me like, when you say Cornwallis, you make it *Corn Wallace*, like it was two names, when it ain't."

He was making up things to say to ease the awkwardness—James knew that and it moved him—but still, the question was startling, for he'd never once noticed the enemy general had one name and not two. He put the saddlebags by and gaped at Bussey, disbelieving. "It ain't?"

"No," Bussey insisted, "it's one name—Cornwallis. And just the same, it ain't *Loff Yet*, it's Lafayette. You saying them names the way you do's been trying my nerves for weeks."

James sat staring. "Well, I'll be damned. I was just saying 'em the way I heard 'em."

"There's wax in your ears, son," laughed Baldwin.

James took sober thought with a frown. Now he recalled Captain Gunn correcting him for saying *ornery* for *ordinary*. He blushed. "What about Baron Stew-Ben?" he asked, fearing the answer.

"That's another one," Bussey confirmed. "You say it like somebody put a poor fellow named Ben in a pot to cook him. It's Steuben. It's one name, not a pair."

"'Tain't neither," Arthur argued to Bussey with some heat. "You're a-saying *Stewben*. Ain't no *stew* to it. It's *Shtoy-Ben*, way I heard it. It's a German way of saying." James remembered he'd heard Captain Harris pronounce it that German way. The issue was becoming complicated.

"Hessian, you mean," Sides declared with scorn. "I say to hell with all Hessians, I don't care how they say their goddamned names. Anyway, what I meant before was, we'll be together again pretty soon, when the regiment goes South to Greene's army."

Poovey's assurance gave James no comfort, for he'd heard a new emphasis in the red-hackle's use of the name given to German mercenaries and was crushed to learn himself guilty of yet more misspeaking. "It's Hessian? Not *Hushing*?"

They all ignored his plaint because at almost the same time Libby, responding to Sides, blurted out, "I'm afraid James'll die before that."

James threw off his confusion about who was called what, grasped Libby by the wrist, and drew her close. "I won't die. A man told me I won't die." It wasn't exactly what Gunn had said, but it was what James wished her to believe, and what he wanted to believe too.

Libby gave him a queer look. "What man?"

"Captain Gunn."

"Gunn?" Poovey whooped. "Hell, Gunn'll kill you himself!"

"No," James denied, "the Captain, he . . ." He stopped; there wasn't any way to make clear to them what had passed today between him and the Captain. So he pushed on as best he could. "I can't explain it. But Gunn said I won't die and I believe him." He turned again to Libby. "And, Sister. He's a Scot. Captain Gunn is. He knows about *home*. About Westerdale and Strathmore and all. His people and our people was . . . the same. Was together. Was one." She watched him as he talked, her sea-green eyes widening with wonder.

"Gunn?" Brown hooted, before she could reply. "Bloody murdering Black Jim Gunn? Why, you're loony, Johnson. Jim Gunn's fighting a god-damned duel this very night, somewhere in the woods over towards Cumberland Old Court House—everybody knows about it. Everybody but you, I guess. He's going to shoot down some poor bastard quartermaster lieutenant that didn't issue him the right kind of britches or somesuch. He'll kill him too, just like he's killed all them others."

The news brought James up short, not so much because of learning Gunn was on his way to fight a duel even while they sat there talking, but more because he didn't see how the Captain would have the time to kill somebody fifteen miles away and still be back in Manakin Town by dawn to tell him the rest of the story he'd promised to tell. It never occurred to him that it might be Gunn who died; Gunn was unconquerable. "We don't know for sure if the Captain ever killed *anybody*, except Redcoats," he responded in surly vein.

"He's killed a power of *them*, though," Arthur reminded them. "He's a hell-hound, that Black Jim Gunn. And who's *he* to be promising folks they won't die? More like, he promises 'em they *will*."

Disgusted with their babble, James stood and took Libby by the hand and led her from the hut. The last of the supper kettles had been scoured, the cooking fires were lapsing lower, the air smelled delightfully of woodsmoke, and the odor of many pipes newly lit as the soldiers lay back in rest from the long day. Above them the sky was darkening, and they could see the first stars and the bright crown of a full moon starting to disentangle itself from the forest tops. They walked hand-in-hand down the troop street toward the path that led to the river. The first sentinel they met knew them, and knew James's orders for the morrow, and let them pass with a nod.

As they walked on, bats swooped and wheeled overhead looking for flying insects. Squadrons of crows were lifting and settling in the broad fields on either side, sending out their unpleasant calls as they began to roost for the night. Crickets were chirruping in the broomsage and Queen Anne's Lace alongside their path; and when James and Libby got into the belt of woods fringing the river, they heard the booming belch and gulp of the bullfrogs in the nearby shallows and, higher up, the singing of the tree creatures. They reached the grassy spot where he had so often sat at the end of the duty day to watch the river pass. Upstream and down, the fires of the pickets burned red holes in the deepening dark. The warm heavy odor of the river came to them, and the fragrance of the now-dewy grass.

At this place they sank down. Great as it was, the river made little sound as it rode past them. Here and there where a fallen limb trailed its twigs in the current one heard a faint continuous trickle. But save that and the occasional plop of a leaping fish, all the immense mass of water went by them as silently as if it did not exist. James had never noticed that, and he mentioned it to Libby. But she made no answer; she seemed lost in thought. Then he had another notion. "I used to believe," he said, "that me and this river, both with the same name, was part of one big thing someway. After all, it kept crossing my path—the river, I mean—at the Arsenal, then after the Arsenal, then again at Richmond, and now here at Manakin Town. James Johnson and the River James. I figured maybe I'd never leave it."

"You'll come back," she answered, so quickly he knew she hadn't been daydreaming after all but listening with care instead. "Just like Captain Gunn said, you'll live and you'll come back. It may be this river ain't finished with you yet."

"You believe me, about what the Captain said?"

"Yes, I believe you. I doubted at first—it sounded so strange—but now I figure it to be true. Because you believe it, and I always believe what you believe and what you tell me."

"Things are fearful bad down South," James said pensively. "And I guess I'm afraid when I think of going there. But then I remember what you said when Poovey and me was on the wooden horse: Can't nobody stop nothing from happening; what's meant to happen, why, it'll happen. World just rolls right over folk. I couldn't save you from Chenowith; you can't save me from this. Me and Poovey both can't save you from sickness or hurt or whatever else may come to put you in danger."

He felt her nodding as she leaned a shoulder against him. "We can't stop what's bound to come," she said. "But we *can* do things. Like you telling me about Ma and Da and about home. And Captain Gunn, he's already told you more about home than Ma and Da did, and you'll be telling that to me now in a spell. And then, when he tells you his story tomorrow—the one that's going to keep you from dying—why, you'll write me a letter when you get South and tell me why it is he says you won't die. And when you're in the South awhile, you'll write and tell me not just about Ma and Da and home again like always, but about how it is you ain't dying when so many others about you is struck down—how the Captain's promise is being kept. And I'll write to you and say how Poovey and me are faring, and if we have a little one and what it is, boy or girl, and what it's name is. If we live.

And if we don't live, why, that's just the way of things. But the finest part is, *you're* going to live. The Captain's promised us. You're going to live, and when the war's over you'll come back to this river that's been calling to you time after time."

"You think so?"

"I know it."

So then he told her all that the Captain had related of how the Johnsons came of the warrior clan of Gunns; told her of the Crowner of Caithness and his big brooch of power and of his five sons who survived his wars; and he told her how the fierce blood of one of those sons, and the blood of all the sons of all those wild tribes before him, now flowed in her veins and in his; and how, because of all that, a greatness lived in them.

He'd never really known how to talk to Poovey except to argue with him about most every subject there was in the world, so when the time came to say good-bye to him, all James did was cuff him on the shoulder and give him the friendliest kind of nod he could manage. For his part, Sides looked relieved to be getting rid of James at last, who'd been little more than a thorn in his side from the very first. James would have felt the same if he weren't worried about whether or not the red-hair would make a good husband for Libby.

Libby herself stood hugging her elbows and watching up at James while he mounted to the saddle. Though they were satisfied no other brother and sister in all of history had ever been as close, it had never been their habit to embrace or caress—save when pretending to be man and wife, and that had been awkward beyond bearing. The most show they'd make otherwise was for one to lean a shoulder on the other as Libby had done with him the night before at the river. That, and what he'd told her of the Captain's tale, had been all the farewell she'd needed. Now her look was of confidence; she didn't dread at all what might befall him—he was fated to come back whole; Gunn had said so. So they exchanged a last smile, and with a pull of the reins James turned Jesus down the troop street and put him to a brisk canter, and that would be the last he'd ever have of her, save the letters she would write to him when he got South.

The drove of remounts consisted of several horses James had trained, and he knew them to be biddable; of the twelve beasts he didn't know, five were nicely broken already and seven were so old or in such bad condition they had not spirit enough to trouble him—in fact would likely perish even before they reached Carolina. One had a blood-spavin on the inside of his nigh hindquarter; another suffered from big itching ulcers on his croup, head and neck; one was a mere colt too tender to travel.

The mystery was why anyone in authority had thought to send such poor beasts Southward where only the hardiest of remounts were needed. Of course it was scarcely within the compass of his duty to wonder about that; and he resolved to tend the sick ones as best he could till they foundered on the road. At least it would be an easy drive.

A section of veteran troopers from the Third Dragoons, replacements destined for Colonel Washington's detachment with Greene's army, rode escort for the clothing wagons. They had come down from Charlottesville, where they had been training recruits for Major Call. Most were whip-cord-thin and burned nearly black by the sun. They cleaved to their own like dogs in a pack. The Third was more surely their religion than any that sent prayers Heavenward. They made it clear by word and deed how little use they had for members of Colonel White's despised First Regiment—James and Plumbley would be regarded as pariahs.

By default, then, Plumbley joined James as horse drover. Since the animals would be easy to handle, that was all right with James so long as Obediah refrained from preaching to him. He exacted a pledge to that effect, and afterward Plumbley seemed to make an agreeable enough companion, though he did tend to quote Scripture excessively when he thought he saw some aspect of the Divine in nature or in a human act; or if he spied the work of Satan anywhere about him, which was pretty often. And he spat tobacco juice altogether too frequently to suit James.

By the time the wagons rolled, Captain Gunn had not appeared and at first James despaired. Was he never to hear the rest of the tale of the Gunns and Johnsons? Then he remembered Gunn was to have fought his duel near Cumberland Old Court House. The route of the wagon train led west from Manakin Town; he would pass that very place and Gunn would be waiting for him there; he was certain of it. The certainty warmed his temper. Repaying the hostility of the escort, he made sure to hurry the remounts well ahead of the train so as to cover the insolent troopers of the Third with a heavy and continuous cloud of road dust.

That afternoon, within a few miles of the courthouse, James rounded a bend and, sure enough, found Captain Gunn waiting in the road on his black charger, one leg thrown negligently across the pommel of his saddle. For a man who was said to have fought a duel the evening before, he looked remarkably fresh. Certainly, as all had predicted, he was alive; nor did he appear to have been wounded. In fact, never had the Captain presented himself so handsomely. His regimentals were a royal blue turned up with the same plum-red as his smallclothes; his brass helmet shone like gold and its long white crest of horsehair blew gently in the breeze; his britches were of buff leather, his boots polished black, his spurs the shiniest. Ordinarily he went about in hunting shirt and leggings. James marveled. Was this his dueling garb? Was his careless but dandified mien that of a man newly come from doing murder?

Gunn broke up these speculations. He blared to James, "Come here!"

James gave charge of the remounts to Plumbley and walked Jesus forward. Gunn swung his horse out of the road and with a slight prick of his spurs sent the black over a low hedge that bounded it. A field of rank grass lay beyond; Gunn rode a distance into it, stopped, crossed hands on the pommel, and glared impatiently back. James jumped the hedge and rode to him again.

Gunn offered no preliminaries. His air was stern and crisp and oddly solemn. Straightaway he commenced, "There's likely as many ways of telling this tale as there is of Scots to tell it. But I mean to give you the one that came down to me through my line, for I think it's the best and truest. We've said how the Gunns and the Keiths was mortal enemies. Their quarrels the worst and bloodiest. Affrays between 'em set widows to howling and orphans to weeping from one end of Caithness and Sutherland to the other. After while both sides wearied of the struggle. So the chiefs of the two turned their minds to ways of striking a peace between the clans. And one day they met at a place called St. Tayre's Chapel, near the seat of Ackergill, to have a parley and see if they couldn't reconcile."

James sat rapt while Jesus shifted beneath him and flicked at flies with his tail. He hardly knew it when Plumbley cantered past in the road with the horse drove or when the escort from the Third passed by, though he did hear them coughing and cursing as the dust of remounts settled over them. His whole attention was on Captain Gunn. "But the blood of the clans run too hot," Gunn said of the two clan chiefs. "They'd been at each other for too long. They couldn't by no means settle all their grudges. So instead of making a peace, they reckoned to settle their affairs with a trial by combat. You know what that is?"

James nodded without speech; he knew it was important only to listen. "The way t'would go," said Gunn, "was this: Each clan would pick twelve horsemen—their strongest warriors—and these twenty-four would meet in one fight, and the outcome would decide all. Whichever band of twelve won the thing, the clan it represented would be the master of the other. The place of the fight was called *Alt na gaun*, which is said to be high in a back part of Strathmore."

The first wagons were going past now, accompanied by the jingling of the harness bells of their teams of big-haunched Pennsylvania horses. Their heavy ironbound wheels made a grinding noise on the hard-packed dirt of the road. Gunn, as he talked, held James with those black eyes that could be lightless but today had a light—a dull luster as if they had been transmuted into dark gems. Lieutenant Gordon, bringing up the rear of the train, glared questioningly into the field at them, saw Gunn's rank, saluted him; Gunn, without seeming even to see him, gave Gordon a negligent flip of a hand and kept on with his story, holding James steadily with his darkling regard.

"So," he related, "on the named day, the twelve warriors of the Gunns came riding up to *Alt na gaun* all armored and ready as agreed to do fair combat, and among 'em was the fiercest of 'em all, George Gunn the Crowner, wearing his big brooch of power, and seven of his sons and four others of the clan, all covered with plate and mail and wearing their helmets with their high crests of juniper. And carrying their spears and swords, their bows and quivers of arrows, their war-axes and daggers."

James was stirred; he could almost see the scene himself. Gunn's heavy features hardened now. "But the goddamned Keiths, they played false. To their shame they fetched along twenty-four fighters, two to each horse, instead of the twelve they'd pledged to bring. So the Gunns was overmatched by treachery. The Crowner, though, he scorned to retreat, even with the odds all against him and the dishonorable advantage of the Keiths bound to bring him down in the end.

"He sung out his war cry and oh, the fight he made that day! The twelve Gunns threw themselves on them Keiths like a whirlwind. Never was a battle more prodigious. The field of *Alt na gaun* was drenched in blood. But in the end the greater numbers told, as they had to. The Crowner fell dead of a dozen mortal wounds, and the Keiths snatched his brooch off his mutilated corpse and stole it. All the band of the Gunns was killed, save only the five of his sons I've told you of."

Appalled, James again nodded, remembering. He named them to himself just to be sure—James; John from whom his own Johnsons descended; Henry, Robert, and Will. "But the Keiths," continued the Captain, "they was sore hurt too, and lots killed—more than was killed of the Gunns, as I heard it. But they was able to draw off in triumph, taking with 'em the Crowner's brooch of power. They went off cheering and singing of their victory. Some says they withdrew to a castle of their kin the Sutherlands, at Dalraid; others claim it was Dirlot they went to—Dirlot Castle on the River Thurso, that your Da knew, and likely told you of."

"Yes," James answered eagerly, "my Da said there was a battle there, of the Gunns and Keiths."

"Well, he was right. There surely was. For the battle at *Alt na gaun* wasn't the end of the thing at all. The five sons of the Crowner who'd lived through the battle, they soothed and dressed their wounds at a stream nearby and set in to thinking how they'd been betrayed by the Keiths bringing twice the men agreed, and pretty soon they commenced to burn with an awful rage and a thirst for bloody revenge; and then the least of 'em, the youngest and slightest—a little slip of a fellow mighty like you, Johnson—he stood up and said, 'Let's go right in amongst them Keiths in their own damned house and kill all we can of 'em and fetch back my father's sword and mail and brooch of office.'

"Now there's some as contend his name, this wight, was Henry. But I always heard it was John—the one that founded your *sept*—who argued for vengeance on them Keiths. And two of his brothers that was hurt the least, they swore to go with him. So the three Gunns, with the smallest of 'em at their head, tracked them Keiths right up to the tower of Dirlot, or Dalraid, whichever place it was—and I favor Dirlot myself, for the way I'm told it sets on the river. And there was a narrow window that opened into the great hall of the castle, and this wee John, he peeked in and saw the Keiths and the Sutherlands in there all merry and dancing, quaffing ale and making sport of the Gunns they'd murdered, and handing around the Crowner's brooch of office and rubbing it in the cracks of their buttocks and such.

"So when he saw this, little John went wild with anger and took his bow and arrow and singled out the chief of the Keiths who was sitting at the high table a-laughing, and he bent his bow and sent an arrow straight into the black heart of that Keith, and then he hollered in through the window, '*Beannachid no Guinnaich do'n Chai!*', which means, 'The compliments of the Gunns to the Keiths!'

"Of course all the company of Keiths and Sutherlands rose up and come dashing at the door of the tower to kill 'em, and the three Gunns stood against 'em there and fought 'em hand to hand as long as they could, and slew a great many of 'em."

James was spellbound. "Did they fetch back the Crowner's brooch and armor?"

"Brave little John did," answered Gunn. "In the confusion of the fighting, why, he snuck in among his enemies and grabbed up the brooch and sword of the Crowner and got out with 'em. But then, on account of already being worn out from the battle at *Alt na gaun*, John and his brothers finally had no choice but to yield their ground and make good their escape. And they went back into their own country and ever after that, Clan Gunn kept up its feud with the Keiths down generation after generation, no peace ever made between 'em again, right till the Forty-Five and the breaking up of all the clans. And even in the Forty-Five, the Gunns stood with the English king, for the Keiths and Mackays and Sutherlands and all the enemy clans of the Gunns was in the army of the Stuart Prince."

James scowled. "But they was broke up anyway, just like the rest, wasn't they? The Gunns, I mean. Even after they helped the king of England."

Gunn bowed his thick shoulders and his mouth assumed a dogged weight. "They was," he admitted. "And I don't answer for the path the Gunns took in the Forty-Five. My Daddy never spoke of it, whether we was in Virginia already, or came over after the clans was broke up, or what. All I know's *I* was born Virginian." He raised a hand and shoved a big finger in James's face, and all his old coarseness flowed back into him. "Besides, none of that's my goddamned point anyways. Do you know what *is*? Answer me now, why d'you reckon I've gone and told you all this?"

"I don't know, Captain. What I mean is, I don't know why *you* told it. But I *do* know what I heard."

Gunn seemed intent. "And what in hell's that?"

"That John, the least of the Gunns, was the bravest and best, that day of the battle."

The Captain stood in his stirrups, cocking a suspicious eye. "And what d'you think *that* means?"

"That his blood's in me, and I ain't going to die, like he didn't die. And like you said."

Gunn relaxed his knees and sank back into the pouch of his saddle. The upward-turning corner of his mouth ascended another inch or two, but still without any visible hint of mirth. He spoke not a word more. He turned the black's head with a jerk of the reins and clapped his spurs savagely to its flanks and the animal squealed and wrung its tail in pain, and with a thrust of its powerful hindquarters took three long strides, bounded over the hedge and struck a hand-gallop back toward camp.

On the roadside a mile or so west of Cumberland Old Court House, James, at the head of the horse drove, came across a burial party of Negroes digging a grave in a stand of cedars under the supervision of several officers wearing the brown regimentals of the Continental Army. Lying beside the red crater was the body of a dark-haired young man with a bloody wound in his chest and the silver epaulet of a lieutenant on the left shoulder of his coat.

Part ye' Twentieth

In Which General Greene Muſt
Oppoſe Light-horſe Harry

IT SEEMED HE WOULD GET AN ARMY AFTER ALL.
Once across the Wateree, the little force he'd brought up from the High
Hills to Camden traversed the boggy lands between the two rivers, quick-
ly reached the banks of the Congaree, turned down its southern shore
toward Howell's Ferry and, on Tuesday the twenty-eighth of August on a
miry track near Wildcat Creek, at last met Colonel William Henderson's
South Carolina state troops of Sumter's old command, two hundred sixty
cavalry under Wade Hampton and a hundred ten infantry under Charles
Myddelton; together with another hundred ten mounted militia led by
North Carolina's Colonel William Polk.

A third of them were without arms, many were sickly—poor Henderson himself had been down with fever at Friday's Ferry three days previously—but at least they made a start toward the building of the force he
needed. Henderson was as yellow as an apricot with jaundice, wasted to
a skeletal thinness; and even while he and Greene spoke, several of his
troopers slid off their horses with the frailty of the very ill to drop supine
by the roadside. Hampton, at least, looked hale, and Henderson's eye, for
all its unnatural glister, was level and clear. Both men pronounced themselves ready for whatever fortune might offer, and their knotty, narrow,
hollow-cheeked horsemen looked equal to any challenge; even the sick
ones glared up with a fierce determination as the General rode by doffing
his hat in salute. They might be little better than picaroons, but just now
he was glad to have them.

Later that same day General Andrew Pickens rode in from the Saluda with another three hundred militia, most of them mounted infantry.
Greene welcomed the gangly, saturnine Indian fighter with true warmth.
The savages he had fought in the Long Canes region and the mountains
of the far northwest called him Skyagunska, or the Border Wizard Owl,
a name with no certain meaning save an inference of stealth, shrewdness,

269

and ferocity that indeed summed the fellow up right well, though it left out his Presbyterian piety and his commendably modest nature. He had fought superbly at The Cowpens, commanding some North Carolina militia as well as his own, and it was a measure of the man that the North Carolinians came to admire him as much as the troops who were his neighbors. He and his militias had served with distinction in the maneuvering leading up to the battle of Guilford, but a bitter dispute with Harry Lee had parted him from the army just before that engagement. It was a comfort to have his uncompromising virtue near at hand again.

A bit further down toward Howell's waited yet another little oddment of seventy more South Carolina horse, under Colonel Samuel Hammond, another wiry, hard-eyed set like Pickens', clad in homespun or deerskin and bristling with tomahawks, rifles, and knives. The army moved on downriver to Goodwin's Mill, where Billy Washington and his eighty dragoons, plastered with the mud of the lowlands between Simmons' Ferry and the mill, waited with the surprising news that the British had abandoned their advanced position near McCord's that same morning.

"Kirkwood reports Stewart has left his campground at Colonel Thomson's and is pulling back," Billy told the General. Captain Kirkwood's Delawares were at Culpeper's Ferry on the lower Congaree keeping an eye on the enemy while the main army descended from upstream.

"Maybe it's a retreat," Jethro Sumner eagerly surmised. "Maybe the goddamned Scotchman's lost his nerve and is scampering all the way back to Charles Town."

Greene pondered. This seemed to call into question Lee's belief that Stewart had been spoiling for a fight all these weeks. Or perhaps the British commander was withdrawing to meet those reinforcements of General Leslie's that Harry kept worrying about, to make an even better match of it on the day of battle. On the other hand, it was possible Stewart had learned of Greene's approach and was only repositioning himself for defense.

The army pitched camp long enough for the men to clean their arms, wash such clothes as they might possess, and undergo a cursory inspection, then took to the road again at six that afternoon and closed the distance to Howell's. Early on Wednesday they were at the ferry; and there the General received heartening word from another messenger that General Marion was advancing with two hundred infantry and forty cavalry and should arrive within the week. At nightfall a galloper arrived to say Major Blount and the rest of the North Carolina regulars had left Charlotte on the twenty-third and should be with him in a matter of days. He began to breathe easier.

On Thursday, satisfied that all was as ready as might be, he gave orders for the crossing. The baggage was to be left at Howell's under the care of the invalids and convalescents; soldiers were to carry only their camp kettles, provisions, and ammunition—thirty rounds per man to the Continentals, twenty to the militia. They made the crossing smoothly and in good time. Waiting on the south shore as they debarked were Harry Lee and his Legion.

<hr />

It was necessary—Lee insisted upon it—for the General to review the Legion before a council of war could be convened; Harry had promised the men they would bask under the eye of the army commander. So Greene was obliged to ride the ranks admiring the three dragoon troops and the three companies of foot, all dressed in their spotless green and buff—the only corps in the whole of the Southern force uniformly clothed and equipped, thanks to Harry's tireless efforts on their behalf with the Clothier-General, the Quartermaster-General and, of course, his intimate friend and sponsor, the Commander in Chief.

All were smart, sunburned, and sturdy-looking. And Greene could not help feeling his spirits rousing when they marched past him in a column of sections, every eye turned to him, each captain rendering his saber salute with a flourish. Yet their very smartness posed such a painful contrast with the nakedness and want of his own Continentals that he could not damp down a flare of envy—*he* had no great influence with high officialdom such as Harry wielded; *his* army looked like beggars compared to these bandbox soldiers. He found himself growing jealous and angry; he began to dread the council to come.

And with good reason. "I'm convinced," Harry declaimed in his most positive manner, strutting up and down that evening in the General's marquee before the assembled senior officers, carrying himself in the customary chin-high, shoulders-back posture that he hoped made him seem physically more robust than he actually was, "that Stewart is in retreat. While it now seems that Cornwallis will not come Southward after all, but will instead operate along the Patowmac, General Leslie has certainly arrived in Charles Town, and though my informants no longer believe he has brought substantial reinforcements of infantry, still we cannot discount that possibility." Greene was relieved to learn that Harry had given up his ridiculous notion that Cornwallis was about to come bounding into his bedchamber, but was depressed to hear, yet again, the name of Leslie, who Greene strongly suspected had yet to leave British headquarters in New York.

Lee stopped, crossed his arms, and struck a dramatic pose. "I do know positively that as recently as ten days ago Colonel Stewart had it in contemplation to surprise our main army, supposing the impracticability of crossing the swamps would have made our security lax." He gave an approving smile. It was evident he thought Stewart an enterprising fellow.

"This plan," he went brightly on, "reveals him as an officer of push and address, so I cannot persuade myself his retreat means he has given up the aggressive at all. Instead, I believe he has fallen down the country to make a junction with General Leslie and whatever troops Leslie has brought from New York. Once these forces have joined, they will return against us to achieve Stewart's original objective. We cannot know how large they may be. But with the movement we have made, we are no longer where Stewart expects us to be, and are at a temporary advantage over him, which we must press before he links up with Leslie. We must act. *We must attack Stewart at once.*"

But Billy Washington, unexpectedly for so thoroughgoing a fighter, spoke evenly and patiently to the contrary. "Kirkwood's latest dispatch tells me Stewart's drawn off from Center Swamp and only gone as far as Fort Motte. He says nothing now of a retreat. The movement seems to him an orderly one. I reckon Stewart's learned of our march and is maneuvering to counter it. In the meantime many of our own troops are sick with fever and worn down from hard marching on bad roads. A forced march would reduce us fatally. Isn't the best course to detach our horse forward to observe the enemy's motions and impede them if we can, while General Greene comes on with deliberation, tending to the sick, giving the men such rest as can be had, and continuing to consolidate his army? We've still the North Carolinians to collect, you know, and General Marion's people."

Sumner, Henderson, and Hampton favored Lee's recommendation for immediate attack. Kosci and Malmedy preserved their impenetrable masks of flamboyant but noncommittal resolve and said not a syllable in Polish, French, or English. Otho Williams and, predictably, Andrew Pickens, who detested Lee, urged Billy Washington's course. Campbell of the Virginia Continentals, usually silent in council, amazed them all by speaking out, if only to say he had no idea what was best to do.

There was a half-hour's animated discussion, from which the General abstained, sitting by carefully weighing every point of view though it was plain to him that most present, even Colonel Washington, anticipated that Harry's opinion would, as usual, prevail in the end. Greene himself half-anticipated it and was depressed to find himself drawn toward that conclusion, for he deeply disagreed with the action Lee advocated and the reasoning behind it. He believed Washington's advice to be right, but his ancient reverence for Lee's military insight had driven doubt into him like a splitting wedge hammered into a log. For all his known flaws Harry still had the power to sway him, make him question what he knew to be

his own better judgment. This was why he had been dreading this council more than he dreaded most others; he hated to throw himself across
Harry's imperious path.

But when the time came, he found he could speak against him far
more easily than he had expected. "I agree with Colonel Washington," he
quietly but firmly told them, and watched Harry's lip-corners curl down
in disgust like a spoiled child's. "We've no *positive* evidence General Leslie
has arrived."

Harry swung to him white with surprise and chagrin. Inwardly Greene
could not help flinching to see it—had not this same officer discovered
in less than a day his own mistaken dispositions before Ninety-Six? Had
Lee not come Southward deservedly wrapped in clouds of glory? Was he
not the hero of Paulus Hook and Watson and Granby and Motte and Augusta? But Greene was Greene; he was now the man he had become, not
the man he used to be. He had conceived his own strategy; he believed it
to be the right one; and as ever, once he had made up his mind about what
was right, the iron in him hardened.

"I make no doubt," he continued, gazing flatly into Harry's now rapidly
blinking blue eyes, "that Stewart has asked Charles Town for reinforcements and supplies, or that he's moving now to find a fit place to receive
them. But I believe he'll settle soon on what he deems a suitable spot to
offer me battle. Just now he outnumbers me. Colonel Washington is correct—I need to gather what force I can."

He sent Lee his gentlest and most commiserating smile though he
could see from the tautness of Harry's expression that it was lost on him.
"You know, sir, I never despair, nor shrink at difficulties. But our prospects
at this moment are not flattering. Or perhaps I should say, not as flattering as they will soon be. I've said all the while that what we do is full of
risk, that if need be, I will strike Stewart with a lesser force. But now our
reinforcement is assured—in but a few days more we'll have the North
Carolinians and perhaps General Marion's militia. I'll be a gambler, sir, if
gambling's what's required. But I won't gamble against odds if I can do it
when the odds are even."

Harry's neck swelled; flushes of crimson mottled his face, giving him
the complexion of a ripe peach. His front teeth worried at his lower lip.
He very much wished to contend with Greene. But a glance about him
revealed that the General's simple talk had won over Sumner, Henderson,
and Hampton and, to his credit, he instantly saw that his suit was now a
futile one. "Very well, sir," he murmured, straightening to attention with a
clatter of sword and carbine and spurs. "What are your orders, General?"

"At first light tomorrow," Greene answered, "I wish you to take your Legion and the corps of Henderson and Hampton, and move in advance of

the army, observing Stewart's force and sending me regular intelligence of its motions. I will follow at a deliberate pace, as Colonel Washington suggests, until such time as Major Blount's North Carolina contingent, and General Marion's militia if practicable, can reach us."

The mention of Colonel Washington was as deliberate as it was inflammatory. Though others had afterward supported his view, Billy had been the first to oppose Lee's ill considered but powerfully presented argument. It was but justice to give him the credit. But as dearly as the General loved and respected Lee and, yes, was still tempted, even yet, to defer to him, he took a certain pleasure in turning this knife in Harry's arrogant heart.

"Yes, sir," Lee said at once, his voice congested with pent-up feeling. He saluted, took his seat, and sat worrying his lip, a fire of petulance kindling in his blue eyes. Of course his pride was wounded and he was furious. But something of that fire looked unnatural to the General. Having stung Lee, he now began to pity him, recalling his surmise of last July that something was not entirely right with the boy. He frowned. If Harry had been for years the brightest comet to streak across the war's firmament, was the core of that comet now burning out, dying in a last dazzling flare of light before lapsing, consumed to a cinder by pride and rash ambition? It seemed possible. Sitting there, the boy appeared to dwindle before Greene's eyes. His high boots grew too big for him, his Spanish spurs became the size of saucers, the hands clasped about the helmet on his lap shrank till they looked small and pink and frail as a child's, his sword was suddenly enormous, his carbine ungainly, even his green jacket which had always fitted him perfectly now threatened to swallow what seemed his diminished self. It was a shocking transformation.

When, presently, the council of war dispersed, Lee, visibly shaken, stood without comment and left the marquee without tarrying to make his manners to the General or to speak with his fellow officers. Watching him go, that smaller and weaker person with all his too-burdensome gear dragging and clanging about his heels, Greene's sense of pity for the lad deepened. Then he recalled a joke Billy Washington had once told. Billy said soldiering with Henry Lee reminded him of the story of the frog and the scorpion crossing the river.

What story is that? Greene had asked.

Well, said Billy, *the scorpion asked the frog to let him ride on his back as he swam over, since he couldn't go himself. But the frog said, "Why would I do that? If I carry you on my back you'll sting me." And the scorpion reassured him by saying, "Why would I sting you? If I did that, we'd both drown. It wouldn't make any sense." So the frog saw the logic of that argument and took the scorpion on his back and they started across the river. But when they were about halfway across, the scorpion stung the frog. "Why did you do that?" wailed the* poor frog. "*Now we're both going to die.*" "*I can't help it*," the scorpion said, "*it's my nature.*"

It was something always to remember.

At dawn on the last day of August, Greene sat Colonel Ashe's bay horse, which he had decided to name Sterne in honor of the author of *Tristram Shandy* and *The History of a Good Warm Watch-Coat*, two books he most admired, watching the Legion begin its march down the Congaree. Colonel Lee, high on his bright thoroughbred, looked his usual handsome, genial, and confident self, his cheeks ruddy, his azure eyes a-twinkle, his blond hair freshly powdered and drawn back to an immaculate club. His salute was smart; the General acknowledged it with a lift of his hat. The pair of them, to all appearances fast friends now as before, exchanged their smiles and good wishes.

As was the custom of the Legion when Lee wished to cover distance quickly, his companies of infantry were riding double with his dragoons. The narrowness of the path had required them to form into a column of two's, and as each rank passed the General, four bronzed faces, two on each mount, turned expectantly his way and held their gazes on him with the mixture of familiarity and reverence that always unsettled him—was he worthy of their regard? He nodded to them, smiled, spoke an encouraging sentiment or two, doffed his hat; and hoped he was the man they believed him to be. *I pray*, he added silently, *that I am also the man I believe myself to be.*

At midday the army bestirred itself and marched as far as Beaver Creek, the old campsite where, last July, he had tried to concentrate against Stewart and Rawdon. After dark came a courier from Lee, who reported himself on the Santee near the old British position at Thomson's. The British, Harry said, were encamped near Nelson's Ferry at Eutaw Springs, a point farther down the Santee toward Monck's Corner. It was uncertain, he confessed, when they might march again. A spy had told him a reinforcement of six hundred British troops, together with fifty wagons and five fieldpieces, were on the way up from Charles Town.

So there was to be a reinforcement after all—if the spy could be believed. Harry could comfort himself that he might have been right about that. Yet he could take from the news but the smallest vindication, for it turned out that Leslie, his bugaboo, would not be coming after all. The dreaded British general, whose arrival Harry had so long and fervently prophesied would be the prelude to their doom, was now confirmed as ignominiously drowned; a frigate bearing him Southward had foundered in a storm with the loss of all on board.

The news convulsed Greene with laughter, firstly because the tale was far too improbable to be true, secondly because Harry so obviously believed it, and thirdly because he had reported it without a trace of the irony that an ordinary man with some awareness of the occasional absurdity of human life had to feel.

"Next," Greene joked with Pendleton and Shubrick, "we'll hear how Lord Cornwallis has drowned in his bath."

Part ye' Twenty-First

In Which a Young Man and a Maid Are Well Met

BY ORDINARY JAMES WAS AN INOFFENSIVE FELLOW and would stand a lot. Now he didn't feel like standing anything. Some of his new belligerance stemmed from the stories Captain Gunn had told him; he'd been thinking ever since of little John, the Crowner's youngest son, who'd shot the chief of the Keiths through the heart and then burst into that castle to fetch back his father's brooch of office. But the rest sprung from parting with Libby for the first time in their lives. Leaving her had left him mingled in his feelings, partly sad and sore but partly relieved too, and glad to be free and on his own; and of course he was ashamed of the gladness. All of it together had made him mad.

It came out in him that same evening, when they pitched camp at Cumberland Old Court House, which he recognized as the place Captain Gunn had taken him the night he stole him away from Manakin Town and bought his time. Lieutenant Gordon, he noticed, after lingering in the tavern-house long enough to toss back the several drams it seemed no officer of dragoons could endure long without, even paid a visit to the same windowless hut of squared logs where Gunn had tarried that memorable evening.

A company of First Dragoons lay encamped in the fields roundabout; but space remained in the tavern yard, so after herding the remounts into the horse pen, James and Obediah spread their blankets under one of the great oaks and struck their supper fire. Plumbley drew the camp kettle from its linen case, set it over the coals, and tossed into it their scant fare of bread, salt beef, and beans, together with a dash or two of water, to make a meager stew.

James took pencil and paper from his haversack, spread the paper on the back of his cartridge box, and commenced his first letter he had ever had to send to Libby. "Deer Libbie," he wrote, "i hav had my talk with Cap Gunn and he has give me the moſt wondrous talk yu can think of." As best he could, he related what Gunn had told him though he feared he had not the power of language to convey fully the majesty and power of the tale. "So yu and me," he scribbled on, "is cum downe frum Hi eftate & Place. We can be prowd of owr Ma and Da & Ourfelfs. and i wownt be adyein when i git south. i will liv long. So will yew i bet. Tell poovey he beft do Rite bye yu or i will take it owt of his hyde when i fee him. We hav had a eeffie day & the wether has bin good. When i am fettled i will tell yu whare to rite me. Yur bro. James."

He thought it was all right for his first one. He carried it to the tavern, left it there for the post, and returned. He was famished now and looked forward to the stew bubbling in Obediah's kettle. He lay down to savor the rich smells of the beef and beans. A few dozen paces away, beneath the other oak, the troopers of the escort had settled and lit their fire. By the roadside the eight Conestogas stood parked in a line with their tongues down. In the horse pen the wagoners were moving about in the slow and casual manner of men easing themselves at the end of a long day of work, unharnessing the teams, walking the animals, feeding and tending them; their talk and laughter floated agreeably on the night air. The warm odors of the horses came too. In the field beyond the pen the First Dragoon campfires were winking and the scent of their smoke made the night fragrant; somebody over there was playing a flute.

Presently one of the escort troopers rose and spoke to his mates and nodded and turned and crossed the yard to where James and Obediah sat watching their pot. James had heard this one called Lockett. His big skull perched low and forward in a way that gave him a slight stoop and this, together with his narrow, round, and high-set shoulders, made James think of someone who had unreasonably determined to butt headfirst through a wall. Even with the stoop he looked to be over six feet high. Close-cropped hair grew low on a forehead whose bony brow jutted like an ape's, and his arms dangled a little too long, reinforcing that resemblance. James looked up at the fellow with bright interest as he approached.

"That was some kind of shines you and this preacher was cutting on us boys today," Lockett remarked. He was talking about the dusting James had given them with the remounts.

"Is that so?" James answered pleasantly. In his gear lay a branding iron he'd fetched along in case they encountered any stray horses he might claim for the service. He seized this iron as he got to his feet and swung it with all his force against the side of Lockett's head. There was a noise like a smith striking a lick on his anvil only somewhat duller; Lockett pitched sideways into the middle of their cooking fire, overturning their kettle and spattering himself with steaming stew. He lay there scalded and with his clothes afire, but he did not stir till Plumbley hurried to roll him out of the blaze to see if he was dead. Once free of the flames he commenced to shiver as if he were chilled instead of burnt.

By then James was already walking straight to the other campfire, still carrying the branding iron, which was now bent into the shape of a drawn bow. Their ring of dark faces watched him as he came. He stopped at the edge of their light. "That fellow," he said, pointing behind him with the bent iron, "was twice my size and three times as strong. I reckon if he'd of whipped me to a frazzle like he meant to, that'd be a great feat for a Third Dragoon."

Not a man moved; none spoke to resent the insult. They sat in their half-circle as the campfire crackled and the bits of pork and salt fish made simmering sounds on the skillet they'd set on their broiler made of bent barrel-hoop. "I'd like to know," James went on in his heartfelt fashion, "what figure you boys think it would've cut if that great brute had tromped me to porridge. Seems to me it'd go to show he was too much of a bully and a coward to take on a man of his own heft, fair and square."

He stopped and waited for one of them to deny it but none did. So he cocked his head and conceded, "Now I admit I'm green as a gourd vine, and you boys is all veterans, but it don't look to me like you amount to much at all, if you think you've got to send the biggest lout you've got, just to whip such as me, small as I am and not weighing ten stone even wearing my sword."

He drew himself up then and tapped his chest with the end of the branding iron. "Well, I'm a First Dragoon, boys, recruit or not, and if you think you can make me holler, then you just keep on coming over to our fire tonight, one at a time, big or little, tall or short, and we'll see who's got the hardest regiment. And don't you fret about that preacher. All he'll do is hold my coat."

He paused to give them the chance to do what they believed they ought, but since none stirred nor uttered a syllable nor did anything but sit there looking at him, he finally decided they meant not to take the matter up just then. So he turned and walked back to his own fire, where Plumbley had doused out the flames on Lockett's clothes and now, with his stirring spoon, was scraping off him what beans and beef he could, to salvage for their supper. "He ain't killed," Odediah reported when James hunkered by him; he flicked a sidewise glance. "If you care." James gave no answer.

Over by the other fire two men now got up and strolled toward them. James was disgusted and scowled his scorn to think they were such low creatures as to disregard his challenge of single combat. It reminded him of how the Keiths had cheated the Crowner by bringing twice as many men to *Alt na gaun* as they'd promised. His opinion of the Third Regiment of Dragoons sank even lower. *These boys,* he thought, *are great ones for coming with advantage, but are mighty shy man for man.* He thought again of the least of the Gunns, his own ancestor, and of the arrow he'd put in that chief of the Keiths. Plumbley darted sharp looks between James and the advancing pair. "Your iron's bent," he pointed out by way of warning.

Casually James nodded. "I'll knock it back into shape here directly."

It was Shoupe, their sergeant, and Hudson, their corporal, who came. James met them standing with his iron at the ready. "I see one-to-one ain't good enough for you fellows."

Shoupe held out both palms to display a peaceful intent. He was short and squat, thick-necked, black as a Spaniard from the sun, and looked knotty and rough-handled like one of those old gnarled stunted trees you see on high ground that the wind has twisted. Surprisingly his gray eyes were mild, even a little sad, as if they'd seen more than they wanted to; yet there were grin-lines at their corners bespeaking, James thought, a genial disposition. "We ain't here to tussle," Shoupe assured them. He bent a look on Lockett, who was still smoldering a little and moaning and shaking on the ground. "We've come to fetch our hurt man here and nurse him."

"I dragged him out of the fire," Plumbley was quick to point out, letting them know it was only James whose nature was violent. "'Twas but Christian charity to do so."

"We're obliged," Shoupe said.

Hudson, more James's size and bowlegged, looked at their capsized kettle. "'Pears like your supper got wrecked." He was younger, maybe twenty-five, and might have been a good-looking man had a scar not given one side of his face a deep pleat from ear to jaw that made him seem to be always grinning in a terribly one-sided way; he was self-conscious about it, kept touching it with the ends of his fingers. James felt sorry for him, thinking that the girls would have fancied him once, but not anymore.

Shoupe joined Hudson in observing the ruined meal; the two seemed to ponder, then the sergeant said, "Why not come and eat supper with us?"

James shrugged. "All right. Yours looked better'n ours anyway."

There was never any telling what you might find in any bunch of fellows. One of them was an outright child, plump with baby fat, no more than fourteen or fifteen, and perhaps something of a halfwit, called Bobby Busby, who said he'd been given by his father to a pair of recruiters sometime back; they'd made him a batman guarding their papers and baggage. He claimed he was a Virginian, but had no notion what regiment he'd been with or when his daddy had put him in it. Later, he claimed, the recruiters passed him on to a Captain Coffrey of the Third, to be his waiter; but Shoupe said there had never been an officer in the regiment by that name. Nobody seemed to know how the lad had come to them, or at what time.

"Bobby was at The Cowpens, though," the sergeant laughed. "Fought like a cock in the pit. Colonel Billy's horse got killed and I gave him my nag, and was standing there wondering what to do next when this great hulking Red Shank in his bonnet and checkered britches come after me with a bayonet, and who springs up but wee Bobby Busby and pops that damned Seventy-First in the head with a pistol ball."

"That pistol," told one of the others, name of Neal, who had a wen on his neck, "was bigger'n Bobby was—one of them great long double-barreled pieces with box locks. I seen him lay that thing between his horse's ears and take aim thataway, resting it on the beast's head. Set the poor animal's mane afire and made it deaf as a post; the damn thing never was worth a fuck after that."

"We et that horse after Guilford Court House," Hudson reminisced. James had been saddened to hear Sergeant Shoupe speak a slur against his Highland kin, yet had sympathized with little Bobby in the management of his great pistol, which was a problem of his own. The fate of the horse was a little unsettling, though.

"I missed the fight at Guilford," Bobby confessed, chapfallen. "They put me to guarding a foraging party." He giggled, much as a little girl might. "I've got me a smaller pistol now."

Lockett sat opposite James holding a rag to his burned and bloody face, peering at James with truculence. "You took unfair advantage of me," he maintained.

"Ha!" cried James. "Unfair advantage, is it? If you want to fight somebody fair, why don't you go over to that horse pen and pick out a good stout stone horse and try to give it a licking?"

"You hush up, Lockett," said Shoupe with authority. "That business is done with."

Lockett spat blood into the fire. "Not for me it ain't."

Nobody said any more about that. One of the Thirds was a youngster called Reuben Griffin; he took an interest in Obediah. "What sort of a preacher are you, Plumbley?"

"Why, brother, I'm a Methodist."

"I seen a Methodist having a meeting once," Griffin exclaimed. "He was out in the woods in a brush arbor. He was a-preaching hellfire and repentance and the terrors of the Judgment, and folk was getting down on all fours just like dogs, growling and popping their teeth, barking and foaming at the mouth. They'd run foaming thisaway, then come foaming back. The womenfolk was dancing over the ground rattling their feet like drumsticks. Why, they'd shake their heads till their braids cracked like whips. People fell into trances. Dropped down in the dirt and wallowed. I never seen such a sight before in all my life. I run away from there as quick as I could, and ain't never willingly come into contact with no damned Methodist since."

"Well, Brother Griffin," Obediah answered sweetly, his big jaws working at his tobacco chew, "'twas the Holy Spirit that was moving those good people to act the way they did. They'd received the prevenient grace of the Most High, the free gift God offers to all mankind. Repenting of their sins, they'd got a glimpse of the perfection that awaits us all, if only we'll renounce the Devil and take Jesus as our Saviour."

"Ain't no perfection on *this* goddamned earth," growled Gunnell, who'd said he was an Essex County man. His mouth was wide and pouted out like a frog's, and from the tone of his speech James judged him to be an unbeliever like himself, but without the hopefulness he'd never been able to rid himself of no matter how many times life disappointed him.

"Brother," Obediah insisted with passion, "I tell you, there's perfection that *can* be grasped for, even in a fallen world. Even allowing for the failings of such poor vessels of mud as us. Christian perfection's always imperfect—that's a Methodist teaching. God's love is all that's perfect. But see, we can approach nearer and nearer to perfection as we repent. We're weak and we'll keep a-sinning even when we wish not to do it. But repentance washes us clean again. Repentance raises us up. It sanctifies us more and more. That's what them folk was a-praising and celebrating when Brother Griffin seen 'em."

"My people," announced Johnny Franklin, who'd kept quiet all this while, "is all Presbyterians, and they believe a man's fate's decided even afore he leaves the mother's womb. If God wants some son of a bitch damned, then, by Christ, his arse is damned black for all Eternity forever. And if God wants his soul saved and lifted up to Paradise, then that's how she'll be. Repenting or not repenting ain't in it nohow."

To everyone's surprise Lieutenant Gordon appeared just then. He was corned but hardly showed it, save drunkenness had the odd effect of making his eyes seem to draw closer together, like a tailor's who is trying to thread a needle in poor light. The Lieutenant gazed unsteadily at Lockett's injuries and demanded in a slurred voice to know if Lockett had been damaged on account of the disputes over religion he had overheard as he drew near. "Religion," he declared with solemnity, "is more often the cause of conflict than is cunt or political philosophy or money or any damned thing whatsoever."

Shoupe assured him they were not quarreling about faith. "Private Lockett," he said, "got hisself knocked about in a matter of regimental pride."

The Lieutenant ran his too-close eyes around their circle. An inquiring eyebrow rose. "Since no one else appears to be quite as bent as Private Lockett, am I to assume the Third was bested in this encounter?"

"Only temporarily, Lieutenant."

"Bested by the preacher or by the little roughrider?"

"By the roughrider. But we are presently at a truce. The talk of religion's been right friendly."

"It won't be if it continues," Gordon declared. "Put an end to it and turn in. We've an early start tomorrow." He started away, then paused and looked back frowning. "Next time there's a matter of regimental pride, Shoupe, I'd better not hear it's a First Dragoon that's got the better of it—and especially not if it's that damned midget of a roughrider."

Next morning they pushed west from Cumberland Old Court House a few miles over level farm country before taking a fork to the left, which led them across wooded lands, by evening, to a hamlet where they pitched camp. By then the colt had come down with strangles and one of the older remounts looked to be both foundered and chest-foundered. It struck him through to shoot them as the colt stood with slimy matter pouring from his nostrils and the other lay roaring for breath, both staring at him with their luminous eyes. Another day's journey brought the train to the banks of a river; they crossed this the following morning by ferry. The weather held hot and hazy, the air humid, and in the afternoon a short but violent rainstorm blew up, drenched them, startled the remounts with cracks of thunder and lightning bolts, but quickly passed on. James had to chase down a little dun mare the outbreak had startled, but soon got her back, and presently all the horses recovered their spirits and settled into easy travel.

After getting over the storm the remounts swiftly became road-wise and needed little tending, so James entertained himself using his horseman's eye to admire the skill of the wagoners in the management of their teams of four or five big draft animals. Their immense Conestogas fascinated him too, for he had not been much upon the roads when in service to Chenowith, to see them. The great vessels weighed, one teamster told him, nearly two tons dead empty. They had a rakish look with their undercurved bodies and steep, outward-slanting front and rear gates. The frames and running gear were of the toughest woods—white oak, hickory, and poplar; the six-foot wheels had hubs of black gum and tires of iron. Osnaburg hoods, fastened over a series of wooden bows, covered the beds and their cargoes of clothing. Tar pots and water buckets dangled swaying from the rear bolsters; toolboxes and water barrels were fixed to the sides; long feed troughs hung from chains under the high tailgates.

According to Sergeant Shoupe, the wagons belonged to a Philadelphia concern that had contracted with the Clothier General to transport the uniforms as far as Charlotte in North Carolina. At Charlotte, Shoupe said, it would be Lieutenant Gordon's task to arrange delivery of the goods

on to General Greene's army farther South. It seemed peculiar to James that the contract had not required the shipment to go straight through to its destination; but then he had no understanding of business. It would be some time before he learned that the same was also true of the Clothier General of the Continental Army.

That evening he wrote Libby again. "Yu owt to fee how thes waggoners handles ther teems. They yews what they call a Jerkline fixd to the bit of the neer Wheelhorse. They may ryde the wheeler aftraddlin him, on a pretty faddle with fhiney rivetts round the cantel, or wilft awalkin alongfide of him, or afettin on a thang they cals the lazie-bord of the waggon boxcks. The fella totes a horfewhup and can kill a flie on the year of a horse withowt anickin even a har of the year itfef. Its why such fellas is calld Crackers."

He told her how the wheelers were the biggest and strongest of the teams and their mighty haunches, thrown against the breeching gear strapped across their rumps, helped hold the wagons back on downgrades. When the steepness of a slope made this method of braking impractical, the rear wheels were chained to coupling poles to fix them in place. Then the screeching of the immobilized tires made an awful din, and if the descent was far, the tires could get worn out of round and, if not repaired, would irritate everyone with their constant loud thumping.

"All the Crackers is mitie proud of ther tak & harnes. The lether of hit feels like velvet, they work hit by hand & fow hit. They collarz is lether afprinkld with brafs that goes over collar and the hamz both and they got arn bell hoopz with little rows of bells thats always aringin. Sum of the boyz hates that I tell yu." Laboring over his letter, James wished Chenowith had allowed him more lessons to improve his writing and spelling. But then he figured he'd been fortunate to get even the little bit of learning his master had permitted him. Many hadn't. Often, though obliged by the terms of indenturement to instruct their servants, masters neglected the duty and sent their former servants into the world ignorant and at the mercy of the schooled and unprincipled.

James liked the Crackers. They were a merry crew, often putting by their whips to play on the jew's harp or to fiddle or sing. One, Obediah discovered to his delight, was actually a Methodist. His name was Flint and he owned a soaring tenor voice. Plumbley would ride alongside Flint's wagon and they would render up one of the Wesley Watts hymns—"Alas! And did my Saviour Bleed, and did my Sovereign die? Would He devote that massacred head, for such a worm as I?" or perhaps "Since I can read my title clear, to mansions in the skies, I'll bid farewell to every fear, and wipe my weeping eyes"—till James reminded Obediah of his duty to the remounts, not so much because the horses needed attention as because Plumbley's idea of song was a tuneless howling that drove everybody mad.

They camped that evening near Prince Edward Court House. Here it was necessary for James, sadly, to shoot another used-up remount. They had to linger there one day and a night while Lieutenant Gordon purchased provisions and supplies. During the next day's march they met another river, a larger one, and turned down its east bank and at dusk reached another ferry where they camped. Lieutenant Gordon retired early. After they'd eaten their scant supper—they were messing together now—Johnny Franklin, the Presbyterian, invited Obediah to preach them a sermon after the fashion of the Methodists to see if it would make them all jerk and bark and foam at the mouth. "Why, I'd admire to, Brother Franklin," Plumbley replied with a mixed look of eagerness and disappointment, "but I've been forbidden to preach."

"Who's forbid it?" Corporal Hudson wanted to know.

Ruefully Obediah spat. "Why, Lieutenant Gordon has. And Brother Johnson here also."

"Well," laughed Sergeant Shoupe, "I can see how you wouldn't want to rile Johnson here, if he's got his branding iron about him yet."

"You get Plumbley started," James warned them, "he's not likely to stop till daylight."

"If you're forbid to preach us a sermon," Bobby Busby cried, "then why not just tell us what Hell's like? Maybe *that'd* make us jerk and bark."

"Yes," Sergeant Shoupe agreed, "that ain't a sermon. It's a describing. Gordon can't fault you for giving us a describing. And we won't let Johnson stop you. But you'll need to keep it low, so as not to waken the Lieutenant. Likely he wouldn't see the difference between a sermon and a describing."

"Well," Plumbley offered, after considerable thought, "I can say what the Holy Scriptures tell about Hell."

"You ain't toting no Bible to read it out of," Bobby Busby pointed out.

Obediah favored him with an indulgent smile. "I don't need no Bible, son. I keep every last one of them sacred sayings right here in my bosom, and can fetch 'em out as I need 'em. Here's one, from the Book of Deuteronomy: 'For a fire is kindled in mine anger, and shall burn unto the lowest hell, and shall consume the earth with her increase, and set on fire the foundations of the mountains.'"

Bobby looked around him hopefully. "That don't sound so bad. It's just mountains He's a-burning up, ain't it?"

"'I will heap mischiefs upon them,'" Obediah intoned. "'I will spend mine arrows upon them. They shall be burnt with hunger, and devoured with burning heat, and with bitter destruction. I will also send the teeth of beasts upon them, with the poison of serpents of the dust. The sword without, and the terror within, shall destroy both the young man and the virgin, the suckling also with the man of gray hairs.'" He paused to confide, "That's out of Deuteronomy too."

Bobby listened with mouth agape; whether he was enthralled or his mind was wandering was impossible to know. "Then there's the Prophet Isaiah," Obediah continued: "'Therefore Sheol'—that's Hell, boys, in Bible lingo—'Sheol hath opened her mouth without measure; and their glory, and their multitude, and their pomp, and he that rejoiceth, shall descend into it.'"

Now Lockett stood up towering over James with his fists balled. "I don't care about no goddamned religion talk. Hell don't mean nothing to me, except it's the place I aim to send Johnson, for hitting me with that damned iron." The side of his face that James had struck was not pleasant to look at. It was badly bruised and was blistered up from the burning. James could see that it would not heal prettily and felt a pang of regret. Still, he was ready to fight if he must. He started to rise.

"Sit down, the both of you" Shoupe said, using his most severe tone. He took a brand from the fire and slapped Lockett's leg with it. "You asked for what Johnson gave you."

Lockett flicked a furtive look at Shoupe and sent another to James, then glanced around the circle and saw that everyone was against him for refusing to give up his grudge. He waited a moment more, flexing his fists and glaring at James in hate. Then he sat down. But by then the evening was spoiled and by common consent nothing more was said about Hell or Damnation.

In the morning the ferry bore them over the water and set them on the road to Halifax Court House, where they arrived in the forenoon. Here another horse, lamed beyond use by a severe attaint to its forefoot between the hoof and the coffin-bone, had to be killed; and they lost two days searching in vain for replacement remounts to confiscate. Not till the tenth day since leaving Manakin Town did they resume their journey.

The sun of the eleventh day was setting when they came to a place Corporal Hudson said was Irwin's Ferry on the River Dan; they made the crossing next morning, and that afternoon, according to Hudson, they left the Dominion of Virginia and entered into that of North Carolina.

Irwin's Ferry, Hudson told them, was a famous place. He, Reuben Griffin, Neal, Lockett, and Franklin had all been serving with General Greene six months before when he so masterfully retreated in front of Cornwallis—not *Corn Wallace*, James was pleased to remember. Greene had withdrawn all the way across North Carolina and into Virginia at Irwin's, said Hudson, where after a wait for reinforcements he'd turned to pounce on the Earl at Guilford. The battle there had been so terrible, Hudson averred, that even though Cornwallis won it, the Earl had no choice but to run away afterward.

They were two days and the morning of another covering the distance to Guilford Court House itself—travel was slow because the road had been fearfully cut up by the artillery of the armies during last spring's campaign. The day they arrived, Plumbley calculated, was a Thursday. They camped on the grounds of the courthouse, an undistinguished log building overlooking a crossroads in a clearing surrounded by what appeared to be an endless forest.

Hard by on the little space of cleared ground studded with the old stumps of trees and surrounded by a quilt pattern of open fields all run to seed stood a few rude dwellings and a ramshackle tavern; otherwise the country looked wholly unimproved. The great road toward Salisbury— the road they'd come in on—ran on past the clearing and dipped into a descending series of vales and hills. To the right of this road pines grew in scattered patches interspersed with tangled underbrush; to its left loomed what seemed an impenetrable fastness of giant oaks. Southward, nothing could be seen but the roadway passing over its undulant wooded hummocks slashed with deep ravines choked with wild vines. James thought it a place of pure desolation.

Lieutenant Gordon retired to the tavern, but Corporal Hudson was eager to conduct a tour of the famous battlefield for those who'd missed the fight in March—Sergeant Shoupe, Gunnell, Robertson, and of course James and Obediah. And naturally the veterans of the affair wanted to review the scene of their exploits. A few of the Crackers wished to see the place as well. James herded the remounts into the courthouse enclosure and went along because, if he hadn't, it would have looked odd. But he paid scant attention. In the last three months he'd heard far too many bloody tales from braggarts who he thought seemed far more proud of having fought and slain their fellow men than they should; besides, his mind kept dwelling on Libby and how much he missed her.

Hudson took them down the Salisbury road, whose rail fences on either side had been broken down and scattered in several places by the fighting. He showed them this spot where the Virginia Continentals had been, that ground where stood the Maryland Blues. Yonder to the right rear rose a little forested ridge whence, said Hudson proudly, Washington's cavalry had swooped down, he and Neal and Griffin and all his good mates with it. For the benefit of James and Obediah he even confessed there had been some First Dragoons in that charge under the command of Captain Faunt Le Roy, and admitted the Firsts had done a creditable job that cold March morning.

Quite a distance farther along than James would have expected, beyond a swale of fallow ground with a small creek winding through it, the corporal pointed out the densely wooded ridge where the Virginia militia brigades of Generals Stevens and Lawson had been posted, and James briefly wondered if this Lawson might be the same one who'd marched off in disgust after Baron Steuben—*Schtoy-ben*, that was—abandoned the Arsenal. Another several hundred yards along, at the bottom of the last vale, along a partly knocked-down zigzag split-rail fence, Hudson told how the cowardly North Carolina militia had deserted this forward post in a rout after firing but a single volley, though Reuben Griffin contradicted him, maintaining the Carolinians had loosed two volleys and hurt the enemy's first line severely.

He showed where the Delawares had been, the place in the road where Captain Singleton had placed his guns, the dark woods across beyond it where Lee's Legion and Campbell's riflemen had met the enemy. Ahead, on the other side of the broken fence, lay a field of shabby neglected corn about a quarter of a mile square, smothered by weeds and nearing its time for harvesting. Beyond the cornfield to the left of the road stood a log farmhouse and two outbuildings pocked with the holes made by musket balls; and then the highway plunged through a narrow defile and disappeared into the forested wastes four hundred yards on.

The British had come through there, Hudson said. *This is where it started.*

The spot looked so remote and untamed it was hard to believe anyone had ever sought it out for any reason at all, much less as a place to fight a battle, though some of the trees were broken off from cannon fire and others were partly deadened from being repeatedly hit by musket balls and here and there among the weeds a broken musket butt or half-rotten haversack testified that men had indeed striven here. Still, as Hudson talked with such enthusiasm of the bloody events that had taken place on this same ground, the normal workaday traffic was passing by them, going up and down the Salisbury highway—ox-drawn farm wagons, a chaise or two, a pack train with its jangling bridle bells, several travelers on foot with their packs on their shoulders. The commonplace was trampling the extraordinary underfoot.

James was little moved. He was tired of hearing about the valiant deeds of other men without ever having fired a shot at an enemy himself. He'd never even *seen* the enemy but once or twice in the whole of his service up to now. A fight? He'd heard a fight in the distance. But he'd never been in one. Never even been near one. He was beginning to think the war was a thing that was always going to happen to others, a thing that for the rest of his days he would know only by its repute.

The next morning before they started, James saw Lieutenant Gordon confer briefly with Sergeant Shoupe. Afterward the sergeant crossed to one of the wagons and ordered the Cracker to unchain the feeding trough and remove the tailgate so he could clamber in. A few moments later, while James and Obediah were saddling their horses, Shoupe approached them carrying a pair of new boots under each arm.

"Lieutenant says you boys've earned the right to these," he said, handing them over. "Besides"—here he cracked a crooked grin—"your dirty feet've been stinking so bad nobody can stand it when you're around. So we've filched these out of the First Dragoon consignment." The two stood stunned, handling the footwear as reverently as they might relics of the Saviour. "Johnson," Shoupe advised as he left, "you know, don't you, that you're such a goddamned little dwarf you're going to have to stuff grass in yours to keep 'em from falling off?"

He did. But even crammed with so much grass and straw that at first he had trouble keeping his balance when he walked in them, they made him feel more like a dragoon than he'd felt since enrolling. They were enlisted men's boots, nothing fancy, made of coarse black leather with high tops that folded down all around like collars, and they gave off a funny smell reminiscent of mildew. But to James they seemed very fine indeed. He strapped on his brass spurs and strutted about listening as they chimed prettily at the heels of the new boots instead of dragging on the ground behind him with a grating noise as they did when fastened to his bare feet. He wished Libby and Sides could see him now, got up so grandly. There hadn't been a real boot for the recruits in all of Manakin Town, only some poor moccasins and leggings that a few fellows—not Poovey—had been happy to get. He resolved to write Libby as soon as he could and brag.

Lieutenant Gordon told Shoupe he had business at the courthouse that day. Shoupe was to take the train on toward New Garden Meeting House, twelve miles down the Salisbury Road; Gordon would catch up before nightfall. Obediah started the remounts along the road; James reined Jesus across the green to the tavern, where he drew up to render Lieutenant Gordon a crisp salute. "Me and Private Plumbley, Your Honor, we're much obliged for the new boots."

Languidly the Lieutenant touched the bill of his helmet. His smile was small and ironic. "The boots are not so good that you should do much walking in 'em," he advised. "And when it rains, I suggest you put 'em in your saddlebags. Likely they'll come apart otherwise."

Still, having any boots at all was like a miracle.

They reached the Quaker settlement at mid-afternoon, but since Lieutenant Gordon still had not joined, Shoupe decided to push a few miles farther. James would've liked to linger at New Garden, for the good Quakers all greeted them with smiles and amiable talk and made them gifts of cornmeal and fruit and crocks of buttermilk. There were also a good many handsome young girls to be seen. James would've liked to get to know them, and Plumbley behaved as if he wished to preach to them. But Shoupe said the train must press on; a courier had come by, sent up from Charlotte to Lafayette, with word that General Greene wished to call together an army to take the offensive; the Southern troops would be in need of horses and clothing for campaigning.

It was hard to leave the peaceful and welcoming place. Hudson had told how, after the battle of Guilford, many of the wounded of both armies were given into the care of the Friends of New Garden. "They nursed 'em all the same," he said, "Bloodybacks and Americans alike. 'We're all brothers in God's eyes,' they'd say. They talked thee and thou just like in the Bible. Mighty good folk, the Quakers, I don't care what anybody says about 'em. General Greene, now," Hudson reminded them, "he's a Quaker himself."

That seemed peculiar to James, who'd always thought the Friends held rigid principles against taking up arms. But maybe being a Quaker meant Greene was a special kind of a general. He didn't mind fighting, he'd proved that. But maybe the tranquil faith of the Friends made a difference somehow, made him unlike other generals, the ones who reveled in war. It would be interesting, he thought, to find out.

A mile or so down the road they met an angry-looking man riding toward them bareback on what was, judging from its bridle with blinders and cheekpieces cut from a single piece of leather, a horse that had been unhitched from a wagon by reason of some unfortunate necessity. When the fellow saw them coming he stopped and waited, shifting himself impatiently on the animal's broad back, the too-long wagon-harness reins dangling into the dirt and trailing out several yards behind him. He looked to be in his early thirties, narrow and limby and long, with sharp cheekbones under a crop of half-grown sandy whiskers that had started to turn silver. His round hat had a turkey feather stuck in it; his britches were of deerskin and he wore an open-fronted hunting smock dyed purple. A long rifle lay balanced across the withers of the big gray horse.

Shoupe ordered the train to a halt and spoke to the man, whose countenance grew cheerful as the sergeant talked; James and Plumbley held the remounts; and presently Shoupe came jogging along the column. "Fellow here's got a broke wheel a ways ahead," he explained. "The crank on his jack's broke too. We'll stop and put our backs under his wagon so's he can get his spare on."

They found the wagon marooned on the road's shoulder, missing its near hind wheel and tilting steeply on the now useless jack. It was a plain farm wagon with a homespun hood rolled halfway back, and lying under its cover on a pallet of straw and blankets they saw a pale thin young man, his face pitted with livid smallpox scars and his left arm missing at the shoulder. "This here's my nephew," the farmer, who said his name was David Baker, told them. "He got shot at the fight at Guilford, then come down with the pox. Been sick all this time. That, and getting over having his arm lopped off. Me and my sister"—here he indicated a young girl who just then stepped out of the woods where, James supposed, she had been discreetly making water—"we come down to fetch him from them Quakers that was tending him."

Baker prated on as Shoupe and Hudson told off a squad—Gunnell, Robertson, Franklin, and Neal—to raise the back corner of the wagon box. His family lived away off on the Carolina frontier near a place called Burke County, Baker said as the boys lined up with their backs to the wagon and commenced to heave. He himself was a Continental veteran, he explained, rolling the spare wheel into place; he'd served in the Third Virginia and fought at White Plains, Trenton, Princeton, Brandywine, Germantown, "all them damned scrapes," finally mustering out in the spring of 'seventy-eight after the Valley Forge winter camp.

Bailey and Griffin helped him raise the wheel and fit it over the hub. "Ninian here," Baker went on, "he's my brother Richard's boy. Dick was kilt at Trenton." Ninian seemed too weak to do more than nod and lift a frail, leaf-like hand. While Baker continued with his history, Bailey and Griffin helped him hammer in the linchpin and fasten the nut. "My Mama's a widow-woman, on account of my Daddy dying while I was in the Line. They'd took the family down to Burke looking for new country, so after my discharge, Ninian and me come too."

But James, sitting his saddle holding the remounts along the road opposite the wagon while the others worked, barely heard the farmer's tale; he was too busy watching Baker's sister—Agnes, Baker had called her.

James had not seen a thing else since Agnes slipped out of the roadside thickets to stand at the head of the team petting the noses of the leaders. The first thing he'd remarked was her uncommon outfit—a broad-brimmed, round-crowned man's hat jammed down over a lappet cap whose ties hung free; and instead of the more normal bodice, a fringed hunting smock of soiled green linen. She wore a skirt with bulging under-pockets and an apron, which were ordinary dress, but she'd drawn up the bottom of the skirt on both sides and pinned it to herself in some secret region beneath the hunting shirt, revealing not only the hem of her shift and a pair of rough cowhide boots of the sort husbandmen wore, but also a few enticing inches of knee clad in rough woolen stockings. Most surprising of all, she'd buckled a heavy leather belt about her waist and into it had thrust a big brass-mounted pistol and a hunting knife in a leather sheath.

But he did not linger long over her vestments and martial equipment, unusual as they were. No, it was her person that captured him. She gave him a feeling no one else had given him in all his life. Although at this moment she seemed quite stern, even annoyed, he sensed something inside her like a sun whose light he could feel coming out to warm him even though he saw no actual light. He felt that if he were to come nearer to her, the light would make him warmer and warmer. And even if there was no light to see, he thought he could almost see it anyway, for she seemed radiant in some fashion he could not name. Yet she was watching him with no sign at all of favor. It was queer. What he thought was: *She's green-eyed like Libby, and has Libby's mouth; but Libby's cool like the moon, and this one's swallowed the sun.*

He was staring and she divined it and stared back now with an air verging on dislike; her lips lay flat and sour with suspicion, making harsh what should have been lovely. But he could not tear his gaze away. He savored the sight of the wisps of golden hair curling out from around the edges of her cap; of her dimples that he knew would deepen fetchingly if he could only tempt her to smile; of her finely shaped face with her brother's prominent cheekbones though modeled more softly than his. But most of all he bathed in that delicious warmth she dispensed, evidently without knowing. Suddenly he was shocked to hear himself address her, not respectfully as he should've, but with an impudent joke: "Who're you fixing to shoot and stab?"

She bristled at once. "*You*," she snapped back, "if you try and take indecent liberties with me." She left off petting the horses and stood defiantly with her boots wide-planted, fists balled on her hips.

"Why," James declared, aghast, "I never took an indecent liberty in my whole life."

She blew out a small puffing noise of disbelief. "You're a dragoon, ain't you?"

"That don't mean I'd take an indecent liberty."

"I hear that's all dragoons do," she argued back.

James was indignant to have been so unfairly judged. "Well, you heard wrong. A person ought not believe everything they hear." Then he thought it would be wise to make some concession to what was, after all, a generally admitted truth. "I expect there's *some* dragoons would do that, but I ain't one of 'em."

"Your claiming it don't make it so," she insisted.

James thought it was time to change the topic of conversation. "How'd your cousin get hurt at Guilford? Fellow told me all the Western militias was off fighting the Cherokees when that ruckus happened." Corporal Hudson had related that in his story of the battle.

"Captain Robinson fetched a hundred volunteers down from Burke and Rutherford and Over-the-Mountains when General Greene sent out his call," Agnes replied. "Ninian went along, and him but nineteen years of age."

"There's a fellow in my section that's not but fourteen," James remarked. "He's feebleminded, though."

Once more her temper flared. "Well, a-body don't have to be feebleminded to be a boy and go to volunteering."

James blushed for his ill-chosen words. "No," he stammered, "no, I didn't mean your cousin was feebleminded. I just meant there's lots of young fellows a-fighting in this war. Why, I believe I'm no older'n twenty myself."

For the first time she showed a glimmer of interest that was not guarded or hostile. "You're little enough."

Though his size was usually a sensitive subject, the relative mildness of the slight emboldened him. "Well, so're you. How old are you?"

"I reckon I'm near onto eighteen."

"I've a sister back in Virginia. You put me in mind of her. She's younger'n you, but you favor her in looks."

Agnes glanced down and to the side; it was her turn to blush. "Is she pretty?"

"I don't know; she's my sister." Suddenly he had the courage of a lion— or of little John the Crowner's son. "But *you're* pretty," he burst out.

"You'd better watch," she murmured, still not looking at him; but he knew she wasn't wrathy now. "Maybe I'll shoot you or stab you."

He thought he heard the hint of a laugh in what she'd said. "That wasn't no indecent liberty," he protested, laughing now too.

"No," she agreed, smiling up at him for the first time. "No, it wasn't." Now the whole power of the joy she'd been keeping inside her poured forth and warmed him as fully as though the sun she'd swallowed had finally risen. Her dimples deepened just as he'd known they would; her blue-green eyes blazed up like jewels turned to the light, and she changed from a girl he'd thought was comely into a woman he knew was beautiful. The sight set his heart to pounding so heavily he could barely hear his own voice.

"Have you got a husband?" he asked, and was nonplused for having asked it.

But instead of getting mad again she laughed, and the laugh made her glow even more. "Yes," she teased, "I've got me a husband who's seven foot tall and broad as an axe-handle across the back and mean as a wildcat, and I've got me ten younguns too."

He felt a momentary stab of disappointment, then saw she was fooling with him. "You don't, neither," he chided.

"No," she answered, suddenly turning serious. "I ain't got nobody." She paused and flashed him another smile that made his pulse pound harder. "Not yet, anyways."

Part ye' Twenty-Second

In Which General Greene Muſt Harden His Heart

ON MONDAY THE THIRD OF SEPTEMBER THE main army camped between Fort Motte and McCord's Ferry, having completed an almost circular march of over seventy-five miles to arrive on the south side of the river directly opposite their old campsite on the High Hills, fifteen miles away across the flooded canebrake. Harry Lee, farther down the Santee with the Legion and Colonel Henderson's state troops, reported Stewart still bivouacked at Eutaw Springs, where he had moved from nearly the same place the Americans now occupied. After the long weeks of waiting within a day's march of one another, the two armies now lay almost forty miles apart.

"Stewart's waiting for reinforcements and supplies," guessed Otho Williams. "At the Springs he's a good deal closer to his base." Once more he cast his glance over Lee's dispatch. "The Colonel believes Stewart means to establish a permanent post at the Eutaws."

The General inclined his head in acknowledgment of the possibility. With the end of a finger he tapped the torn scrap of paper where it lay under a stone on the folding table by his side; it was a rough map of Stewart's camp, which Lee had scrawled. "He may hold his position there—it's a good one, with the river on one flank and the Wassamasaw Road to Charles Town open behind him, and the way to Monck's Corner too. Or, if the fancy takes him, he might pass over to Orangeburgh. That would give him the road down to Four Holes Bridge and Dorchester. Either spot would make good ground for a fight, and leave passage for his relief."

"Fortifications at Orangeburgh, ain't they?" fretted Jethro Sumner.

Those were the works that had turned Greene back in July. He had made up his mind that he would storm them this time if he must. "Whatever ground he chooses," he assured the North Carolinian, "I expect he'll be prepared to engage." He set his jaw hard. "So will I." He would go to Orangeburgh if circumstances forced him. But in his vitals he felt certain Stewart would stand fast at the Eutaws.

Sumner nodded wordlessly. Their situation might be urgent but they had to save their talk, and so addressed one another more curtly than was normal or perhaps even seemly. The suffocating heat had sapped all energy. Torpor lay heavy on mind and body. The sides of the marquee were roped up, but not a zephyr blew; and even in the shade of the tent their sodden clothes clung to them. Sumner had cast off his greenish wig; it lay on the camp table between them like a hunk of wilted moss. His pink dome with its sparse fringe of white hair sparkled with droplets of sweat. Williams had tied about his head a red kerchief, now sopping, that lent him a piratical air. Thick-necked, big-bodied Colonel Washington seemed to suffer worst—his grimy regimental coat and smallclothes were drenched through, his ample face was beet-red and streaming—yet he sat among them seemingly at perfect ease, his boots thrust straight before him in a horseman's sprawl. No extreme of weather could reach his imperturbable inner self. He wasted no breath in speech, however.

Greene sent a somber look out over the expanse of the camp with its scatter of huts and bowers all a-dazzle with midday light vaguely softened by a thin haze of campfire smoke. Yonder in the distance the wooded country rose in long folds to meet the scarred hill where stood Mrs. Motte's house, faintly shimmering in the heat. The stench of the swampy canebrake and the contents of the camp's vaults and the manure of its animals lived foully in the still air along with the more agreeable smartness of the cooking fires. Within the camp the flags hung motionless on their poles and horses and oxen drooped in their pens of rope. Save the sentries on their rounds, nothing moved. In the open, the sun had made of every piece of bare metal a potentially searing instrument of torture; no one out there dared lay a hand on sword-hilt or strap-buckle, on collar-hame or musket barrel. Man and beast, the whole army lay panting under cover.

There was more fever among the troops now, and it was getting worse with every blistering march. Men had died of the heat too, though he'd moved them only by morning and evening to spare them the broiling zenith sun. That was why he meant to camp here two or three days if he could, to rest and refresh the army for the coming action, as peculiar as it might seem to lie in lassitude on the very eve of battle. The General himself felt faint and sick. He who had been from adolescence jowly and plump was now wizened and gaunt, and he knew from viewing himself every morning in his shaving-mirror that his color had turned as yellow as a Mongolian's. *What an infernal land*, he thought. Yet it tantalized him. In some odd way he had grown fond of it. *Perhaps if one contends long enough for an unlovely place, after a time the place can grow in some fashion to be beautiful. Perhaps one can even learn to love such a strange and sinister and finally beautiful place. But one must never forget that the place will give no love back, not even if you fight for it, not even if you free it from those who hold it against its will. It will have no gratitude. It will give back only sunstroke, contagion, and death.*

Presently a British courier rode into camp under flag of truce, escorted by one of the Legion dragoons. The Britisher carried a dispatch from Colonel Nisbet Balfour, commandant at Charles Town; the Legionnaire bore another message from Lee. The General dismissed them both back to Harry, giving no orders regarding the detention of the courier. Ordinarily the man and his flag would have been held lest he carry to Stewart some useful intelligence, but Greene did not mind now if the enemy learned of his approach; it might prompt Stewart to drop farther down the country, thus achieving much the same result as would a won battle. But he wished so heartily to fight his battle that he was unwilling to issue the order himself; he would leave Harry free to pass the courier or hold him; he was confident Lee would prefer the secrecy detention would ensure. And that would make battle all the more certain.

He opened Harry's note first and read that Lee, in passing the Redcoat through the lines, had gained an impression the enemy thought Greene might keep post at Fort Motte for some days. Greene could, therefore, by a rapid movement, catch Stewart by surprise.

The General handed the paper to a perspiring Captain Pendleton with a wry smile. "Colonel Lee," he remarked, after giving Pendleton a moment to read, "being impervious to heat prostration, hunger, thirst, fatigue, and every known disease, cannot credit the weaknesses that plague mere humans. Were my army wholly comprised of such as he—immortals in the Greek mode—why, we might indeed hurl ourselves upon Stewart at a moment's notice."

"The Colonel," Pendleton observed with a resolutely straight face, filing the dispatch in his camp secretary, "is quite plainly Winged Mercury reborn amongst us."

"And how grateful we are for it," said Greene, with a little moue of sarcasm.

"I don't reckon I could bestir myself to go and move my own bowels," General Sumner commented with his usual indelicacy, mopping his head with his sleeve. Colonel Washington marshaled a concurring grunt.

Waving away flies, Greene roused his logy faculties and bent to the papers. Balfour's note answered an earlier communication of Greene's condemning the execution of Isaac Hayne: "I am to inform you it took place by the joint order of Lord Rawdon and myſelf, in conſequence of the most expreſs directions from Lord Cornwallis, to us, in regard to all thoſe who shou'd be found in Arms after being, at their own requeſts received as Subjects ſince the Capitulation of Charles Town, & the clear conqueſt of the Province, in the summer of 1780 ..."

Dollops of his sweat fell to the sheet and blurred the ink in places as he read. He took up a cloth and wiped his face, but no sooner was he dry than he felt new moisture springing up. He puffed out a breath; even his own wind was stale and hot. Poor Colonel Hayne, captured at the fall of Charles Town, had been paroled to his plantation with the understanding the Crown would not afterward call him to take up arms against his fellow Americans. When in breach of their promise the enemy did demand such service, Hayne considered his parole invalidated and, like many another South Carolina patriot, took the field once more as a militia officer. Regrettably, he had fallen again into British hands, and they had hanged him.

"To His Lordſhip, therefore," Balfour's note continued, "as being reſponſible for this meaſure, the appeal will more properly be made ..." Rawdon had gone back to England, Cornwallis was in Virginia; yes, Balfour found it convenient to pass accountability for the crime to officers not just senior but far distant. Nonetheless Greene supposed the argument a sound one. Doubtless the Modern Hannibal was indeed the guilty party. It was to Cornwallis that he must send his next remonstrance, hoping the while to postpone the act of reprisal he so dreaded. His eye hurried over the text, pausing only to study the passage dealing with his own threat to retaliate in kind: "To juſtify Retaliation I am convinced you will agree, a Parity of circumſtances, in all reſpects, is required, without ſuch every ſhadow of Juſtice is removed, & Vengeance only points to Indiſcriminate Horrors ..."

He passed this paper to Pendleton also, waited till he had looked it over, then commented grimly, "What they name justice is to us injustice. What we call justice, they will say is but vengeance." He laughed emptily. "On one head only can we agree—what flows from this must be truly odious."

Sumner read the note in his turn, looked at the General heavy-lidded, and said, "Give *me* the rope, sir. I'll do your hanging for you. I've none of your philosophy. Justice, injustice, vengeance, horrors—they all stink like the same damned turd to me." He gave a great, jarring laugh. "But let's wait for cooler weather, can't we?"

That night as Greene lay unsleeping on his pallet in the stifling dark, repeatedly bitten by the enormous mosquitoes of the country, his mind turned again to Henry Lee and the too-bright burning of Harry's comet. He had made fun of Lee's urging of precipitate attack, yet in his heart he had felt not the humor he pretended, but a gloomy foreboding. Lee knew well enough the parlous condition of the army. His constant pressing for headlong action ran against reason. It was not the advice of a sensible soldier, or even of a rash but practiced one. Eutaw Springs lay at a distance not to be covered in less than two days' forced marching, a feat far beyond the power of his force. To reach it the fragile army needed a time of pampering and indulgence; it was weak, ravaged by sickness, its marches had already been hard and hot and long; now it must move slowly, convalescent. And even then, with all the coddling Greene could give, it could scarcely hope to meet Stewart's troops on equal terms, save by a gradual and stealthy advance ending in a short, sharp surprise assault.

Of all soldiers Harry should recognize this. That he did not was hardly conceivable. More than ever Greene had become convinced something was badly amiss with the commander of the Partisan Legion. Against his will he had begun to fear for the balance of the boy's mind. Of course because he loved him he worried for Harry's welfare; but because he depended on him too—wielded him as his right arm in the field—he was filled with dread to think Lee might no longer be what he had always so reliably been; for without Harry Lee, Greene would be crippled as surely as if his literal right arm had been lopped off.

The gloomy thoughts stole from him every possibility of sleep, and at last he got up from his cot, struck a light to some tapers with his tinder-mill, and sat at his camp desk in the wan wobbling glow of the candles, rubbing his sore eye with the heel of his hand. Presently his stewards Owens and Peters both appeared to ask his requirements, but he turned them away, preferring his solitude to their wheedling ministrations. But when Captain Pendleton poked his head through the curtains somewhat later, the General invited him in. Just then young Nat looked like the very physic he needed. They sat awhile, Pendleton in his stylish banyan and sleeping turban, Greene in his soiled shift and tasseled nightcap, two friends communing for a comfortable time without speech, listening to the small sounds of the night. Then at last the General spoke of what vexed him. "Do you know, Nat, what Alexander Hamilton once said of our Colonel Lee?"

"No, sir, I don't."

"He said the Colonel had 'not a little of the spice of a Julius Caesar or a Cromwell.'"

Pendleton considered a moment, then gave a consensual nod. "Indeed, the Colonel has always seemed to me a person of a singularly impetuous, impatient, and adamant character. I've always thought he possessed an imperial will." A slight and temperate smile crept over Nat's face, one that could never be taken as presumptuous; what small sport he made was innocent. "It would be easy," he added, "to imagine the Colonel on the throne of an Augustan."

Greene pressed a thumb against his aching eye. It was hardly proper to speak to a mere captain of the fitness of a higher officer. But Nat was no ordinary captain and Harry Lee was no ordinary colonel. Both were dear to him. Nat was that rare thing, a man who would both keep a confidence and render good counsel; and Lee was still like a son, if not a son of his mind's choosing then the son of his softest and most merciful heart. "There's a kind of tyranny in the Colonel, I do fear," the General answered with a pang of regret. "A thing is right for him when he *wishes* it to be right. For him, truth is malleable matter. He shapes it as he desires. I'm not certain he would be a good Augustan; perhaps instead he would rule as the Claudians did, were rule given him."

He need say no more. Pendleton would grasp his meaning. After the battle at Guilford, with Cornwallis marching away to Wilmington, a vigorous debate had broken out among the senior commanders about the strategy to be followed. Greene had chosen the bold course of turning his back on Cornwallis to descend into South Carolina, a move now widely hailed as a masterstroke. Yet Lee now insisted the plan was his own—he'd conjured it out of his own genius, had pressed it on a timid and reluctant Greene; thus he, not Greene, deserved the glory of it.

If this was first cousin to the truth, it was far from the beast itself. Lee had indeed urged the strategy with ardor. But Greene had been inclined to it from the first and would have pursued it without Lee's advocacy. His mistake, born of his liking for the lad, had been to flatter Lee in letters thanking him for his advice. Now Lee brandished the letters as proof of his brilliance. A falsehood so blatant served only to expose the boorishness of his motives; yet he was blind to this and only longed for the credit. He wanted the credit; therefore he should have it, and anyone who denied it him was not only an unreasonable enemy but no patriot.

Pendleton bent on his General a look of warm concern. "May I ask, sir, why does the Colonel prey so on your mind in the dead of night?"

Greene smiled a saddened smile. "Because he's my great friend, Nat. And because he's always to the front and his face is forever to the enemy. We're in the midst of the most important movement we've made since Guilford; I must depend upon him now as I do no other officer. I need him to be wise and vigilant and generous and charitable, and these are virtues he does not always display. In fact, as time has passed, he's displayed them less and less. Of charity he knows so little, yet I can think of no quality more important in an officer. You know what the South Carolinians say of him—that he'd sooner see a dozen Carolina militiamen die than one of his thoroughbred horses."

"Yes, sir. It's a saying not creditable to him, but manifestly true."

"Often he's unduly harsh," the General mused. "It's been that way from the outset, I'm afraid. Did you hear that in New Jersey he ordered a deserter decapitated and the severed head carried back to camp on the point of a pike as a warning to others who might be tempted to leave the ranks?"

Pendleton's mouth tightened, and he drew an offended breath but said nothing, only glanced aside, revolted by the image. "Last spring," continued Greene, "there was that killing of Dr. Pyle's Tories. Since then rumors have come of tortures and unauthorized hangings by the Legion. Orders of no quarter have evidently been given. You know this, Nat. We all know it. We do not speak of it, but we know it." He stopped and let his chin sink to his chest. "Perhaps the war has coarsened the Colonel more than he knows. It has surely coarsened me, no matter how I resist it. How much worse must it be for a leader of partisans operating without restraint behind enemy lines?"

A long silence fell. Somewhere in the camp they heard an infant crying. Its wails awakened several dogs, and in another moment the night echoed with a cacophony of barks and howls. Then one by one the dogs quieted and soon the baby too. All they heard now was the whirring of the crickets. Pendleton sat a long while in thought. Absently he stroked his chin. When in this meditative temper, he would not venture a comment till he had carefully crafted every word of it; Greene knew this and patiently waited.

Perhaps five minutes passed before Nat felt himself ready. "General," he said, fixing an intense gaze on Greene, his voice thick with feeling, "I don't know what I can say to relieve your fears on this account, save to express what I've seen with my own eyes and heard with my own ears, and that's this: You've given Colonel Lee the greatest freedom to operate, and he thrives in the independence of his command and works prodigies for us and is indeed a most wondrous figure. But you have also given him the most particular guidance, and have imposed upon him an exacting discipline mixed with a sincere respect for his ability and a genuine affection for his person, far beyond anything another commander would have had the patience and skill to administer. You've done all that can be done, sir. Beyond that, sir, I do not believe it's possible for you to go. None other would've gone as far. Colonel Lee will behave as he will. And whatever of wisdom and charity he shows—however much or however little—will have come from you, sir. That has been your gift to him. It will not be your burden to carry should he choose, as he well may, to set it aside in favor of the vanity and arrogance that naturally spring up in him."

"And what of the battle, Nat?"

"I need not remind you, sir, that battles take care of themselves. We may win; we may lose. The Colonel may contribute either way. One thing we've always done, and will surely do again. We'll hurt the enemy far worse than they'll hurt us."

The talk with Pendleton had helped, but when he took to his cot again, his worries did not cease. He had dared not speak even to Nat of another troubling disposition some claimed to have seen in the famously valiant young Colonel. Lee himself would have called it caution or prudence, favorite watchwords of his. Others were less kind and named it something worse. The man himself was slender and somewhat frail; no one expected him to be a lion in personal combat as was, say, William Washington. But high rank carried a presumption of common fortitude and Lee, it was rumored, had not always come up to that mark.

True, he had long since proved he could fight and fight well. Yet it did seem that all too frequently he preferred to fight only when he could be sure all eyes would be on his Legion, and when he could place himself where his Legionnaires would ring him safely about with saber or musket. And yes, there had been times, some few times, at Paulus Hook, for instance, when he withdrew from that post in what some thought was unwarranted haste, and at Guilford, when without explanation he left unsupported Colonel William Campbell's rifle corps while it was under attack first by Von Donop's Hessians and then by Tarleton's Legion—times when he had seemed to shrink from danger.

It seemed impossible. But Greene had seen enough to bring on his own dark thoughts of degeneracy. He might make jokes, as he'd done that morning, about Harry's Olympian pretense, but in fact the analogy held—the boy had been very like a gilded god of war. But now it was as though some rot had set in beneath the gleaming shell of him. Corruption might be feeding on what had seemed glorious and immortal. Irreversible decay might be busy inside that figure of gleaming gold. The ghastly vision lingered till at last the General sank down into restless sleep.

By Wednesday, when the army had rested the better part of three days, the General felt it was as strong as it would be. He ordered a day's rations drawn and cooked—by any who might still have rations—and in the cool of the evening broke camp and marched the army fourteen miles to Stoutenmire's Plantation on Maybrick's Creek, Colonel Washington's Dragoons and the Delaware scouts reconnoitering ahead, Lee's Legion miles farther to the front. There was no sign of the British save two messengers under flags of truce whom Lee sent back and Greene returned, again without instructions for detention, knowing Harry would hold them anyway. Lee reported the main body of the enemy still lying at Eutaw Springs, dull with lethargy, ignorant of the army's approach. This was pleasing news; it meant either that the screen of cavalry had, against odds, kept the movement secret or this Colonel Stewart was not the soldier he ought to be. Greene dared hope that fortune, for once, would favor him.

At Maybrick's he learned by galloper that Marion, six days earlier, had fought a successful action against a British detachment near Parker's Ferry on the Pon Pon River. He dashed off a note hailing the success, but urged the Swamp Fox to come on swiftly and make junction with the army, for he sensed the day of battle looming ever nearer. Another express went to Pickens, who was scouting toward Orangeburgh on the North Branch of the Edisto, bidding him hurry forward also, collecting any cattle he might find as he came, the army having butchered its last cow at Fort Motte.

Thursday morning he again ordered a day's rations cooked and "all arms put in the moſt perfect order, as there is a proſpect of our coming to Action with the Enemy." The portentous words, he hoped, would spirit up the troops. The army moved another six miles to Medway Swamp, but in heat so intense and unrelenting the march took most of the day owing to the many halts necessary to refresh the men, and if he had revived any spirits with the language of his order, that ordeal surely drained them again. Late in the afternoon he found a small eminence under a live oak tree and sat his horse studying them with a fine calculation as they passed. He must gauge what they had to give.

The militia was his largest concern. Likely they would feel the enemy first, thus their demeanor would shape the engagement. His experience in this respect was not reassuring, for in every action he had fought since coming Southward, more often than not the militia had behaved poorly. He wasted no worry on Henderson's state troops or on the fierce corps of Pickens or Marion, for what passed for militia in South Carolina would in another place be counted on a par with the hordes of the Khans. No, it was on Malmedy's North Carolinians, drafted men of Rowan, Mecklenburg, and Orange, that he laid a specially penetrating eye. Many of these, the Marquis had told him, were hired substitutes, old regulars, veterans of the service who knew how to stand steady in the ranks. They had been well fed before starting from Salisbury and so were likely in the best condition of any troops he had, and while many still lacked arms, Major Blount would soon be bringing them those extra muskets. But what would they give?

Greene watched them go by with their long loping stride, doffing his hat now and then to the salutes of their officers, and they gaped back openly at this new Quaker general of theirs, wondering if he knew what he was about even as he nursed his own doubts of them. The mutual misgiving amused him; he smiled and saw how it took some of them aback—clearly, in their view, a smiling general was a remarkable and not necessarily promising commodity. He decided he liked their looks. Old soldiers knew enough to take a jaundiced measure of their generals, and old soldiers were what he needed. Malmedy, who had joined him to watch the troops pass, might remain an unknown quantity behind his elegantly impassive façade, and Greene might have preferred to know the man better, but he had also come to believe good troops could trump bad officers, and so he made small his scruples about the Frenchman. They parted exchanging pleasantries.

His Continentals plodded past in sun-bleached regimentals, tattered hunting shirts, ragged overalls, and every imaginable sort of headgear—the Maryland Brigade; Campbell's Virginians; the new North Carolina brigade of Sumner, less Major Blount's battalion soon to come. Sumner's troops were well drilled and had shown themselves adept at target-practice; but how might they comport themselves under fire? Of the Marylanders and Virginians there could be no question. Together with Kirkwood's Delawares, ranging ahead of the army with the Legion and Washington's horse, they had been the beating heart of his army from the first. He knew what they would give. It would be everything. But he had asked so much of them already. How would they last?

Yet in truth one could no longer speak of his Continentals as wholly American, for British deserters filled ranks in every battalion. There was an ironic balance in the matter of desertion. His losses to the enemy he soon gained back in runaways from the enemy. So near was the exchange that he'd often joked the next battle would see him commanding British soldiers and the enemy, Americans. The Redcoats offered the food and pay he could not give, but at the cost of a discipline that was brutal beyond belief. Want and penury on one side and bloody oppression on the other had kept the traffic constant. How would the turncoats behave when the time came to level their muskets on their former comrades in arms? It was a riddle nothing but battle itself could solve.

The black iron guns rattled by on their oaken carriages painted either red-brown or lead-colored, Captain Gaines's pair of three-pounders in their gallopers and Captain Browne's two six-pounders couched in heavier limbers, each piece drawn by lathered horses with a rider astride, gunners and matrosses following behind on foot, the ox-drawn ammunition carts bringing up the rear. The Chief of Artillery, Colonel Harrison, had gone Northward on detached duty, and it had to be said his dilatory ways would not be missed; the capable Gaines, absent now carrying dispatches but due to rejoin the army any moment, would be senior and would command; his noncommissioned officers snapped their confident salutes, which Greene happily acknowledged. The guns would give all.

Yet save for the militia it was all, even the best of it, a worn and weary, famished and thirsting, feverish and ill-clad army. And farthest out to its front, probing the enemy, closing the roads, gathering intelligence, holding in his hands its whole fate, was Light-horse Harry Lee, possibly driven close to madness by a lust to win fame for himself at any cost. Greene must nurse all of this along a few days more. He must find as many ways as he could to usher it to the field of battle in shape to fight—to fight and, for the very first time, to win.

Soon, Caty, he thought, as he had thought now every day since she entered his dreams to give him back what he had lost. *Very soon now.* But this would be the last time. He would not think of her again till the battle was fought. Nor would he think of George nor of Cornelia nor of Martha, nor even of little Nat. Nor of the Coventry homestead nor of Potowomut nor of New Shoreham nor of East Greenwich. Nor of the mild Rhode Island springtimes. Nor of the smoke of the forge and its bright spew of sparks, nor of the salt smell of the nearby sea, nor of the sweet fragrance of new-mown hay in the sun nor of cool windy woods nor of evening fires on hearths nor of the pleasing heft of a good book in his hands, nor of Swift or Sterne or Shakespeare.

Now he must be, completely, the commander of men. Not the anchor-smith shamed by his low trade. Not the dilettante philosopher. Not the prating, self-taught aphorist. Not the political man. Not the obstinate, ambitious seeker after place. Not the dreamer. Not the doubter of his own worth. Not the mild, reasonable, equable man who saw all sides of every question, who fairly understood every opinion, who readily forgave every trespass, who worried lest he hurt another's feelings. Surely not the Quaker. All in him that smacked of refined sensibility was now but distraction. It was now his business to compress it to a tiny thing, priceless still but temporarily without practical use, a gem to be kept safe, to be stored deep within and fetched out once more when times were civil again. Keeping it safe he must harden himself around it, turn himself to unfeeling stone. He knew how to do it—had done it at Haarlem Heights and Trenton and Brandywine and Germantown, at the Delaware River forts, at Monmouth and Newport, and after coming Southward, at Guilford and Hobkirk's Hill and Ninety-Six. He who could never have killed anyone knew well enough how to make others kill in the mass. The trick was to learn how to keep it up, how not to turn blood-sick and lose his nerve and call back the killing at the wrong moment as he'd done at Ninety-Six. He had learned everything but that. This time he must push the attack home no matter its cost. He must divest himself of pity and his troops of mercy. He must be willing to kill not just the enemy but his own, and they in their turn must be in a mood to kill the whole world. He must drive his two thousand sick and haggard men toward the simple, terrible goal of utter inhumanity;

and to be successful in that task he must be the most inhuman of all. He thought he could do that now. He hoped he could. Victory depended on it. And he must have a victory. He could only hope that what he gave up now might in good time be recovered. He could hope that the blood he spilled would not taint to worthlessness the jewel he'd hidden deep inside or, worse, drown it in such a flood of gore that it be forever lost.

Part ye' Twenty-Third

In Which a Young Man Loſes His Heart

JAMES WROTE THE SECOND LETTER OF HIS LIFE. "Deer Libbie," it said, "i rekon i am now in the South even if they do call hit North Calina and i am yet living juſt as Cap Gunn promiſed i woud. ſo i hope hit bodes well for the Future and his Promis will keep on abein kep. i have met a Gal you would like her. Name of Agnes baker. we met on the road. She puts me in mind of You ſavin ſhe is flaxen hared whare You are dark. She is a Saucie one and i bleeve likes me ſum tho ſhe chides me a right ſmart. She has got a glo like the Sun. we have not ſpoke of One grave matter yet, hit is all fun. But i am athinkin hit might come to ſumthin or Woud if not for this Warr. The Warr is agoin on yet and i am agoin to hit for Sure but Agnes is agoin to her home wich is in a place they call Burke Court Houſe. Hit and the Warr is a long ways apart ſo hit may be i never ſee her again which i Hope not. But i will ſee You ſome time ſoon Cap Gunn ſayd ſo. Yr Bro James."

He thought it was a pretty good letter for only his second one. Lieutenant Gordon lent him some wax to seal it with, and he posted it with the next dispatch rider they met going back to Virginia. The Salisbury road was well traveled, and lots of dispatch riders were going to and fro between the army in Virginia and General Greene's army in South Carolina, so it was no trouble sending letters. There would probably have been no trouble receiving letters either, but James did not get any. Libby knew her alphabet and spelling but did not know them quite as well as James, so he reasoned it would take her longer to write a letter than it would him. But still, he wished she would send him one. He was missing her worse than he would have thought possible. And he fretted whether Poovey was treating her as well as he ought.

The Bakers were traveling now with the clothing train, and since the remount herd was down to only sixteen horses it was an easier matter for Plumbley to drive them along by himself. This left James free to ride alongside the Baker wagon and talk to Agnes as they went. Actually he did more listening than talking, for Agnes was like a magpie when it came to conversation. The second day, when he asked her why, if she was eighteen years old and pretty as a picture, nobody had ever married her, this was her reply:

"Well, they're always telling me, whenever some fellow comes around sweetening up to me, why, Agnes, you'd best tie a shuck to his tail lest he get away, for you'll soon be a old maid. You can't be so particular, they say, anyways, a man ain't all that much of a bargain, even the best of 'em, and if you wait too long you'll be a-bringing your ducks to a bad market. Find yourself a rich old man, they tell me, with a fine boundary of land and maybe some niggers to work it, and get him to wed up with you, and you'll have it easy. For if you hold out for some pretty handsome young feller, even if you fetch him, why, before you can say Jack Robinson he'll go stale on you and be no better'n a big slab of old fat meat a-laying there beside you drunk on corn whiskey, and doing you no good at all. And I tell 'em, well, I'm a-holding out for love. And they give me the horse laugh and tell me love is all right for fairy tales and such, but living is living, and living and loving ain't the same stripe atall. Loving won't fill the larder, they're always telling me. Marry yourself up to a rich old man, they say. Marry yourself a good provider and wax plump and live easy and forget about loving. Loving ain't in it, they say. Well, I say different."

"You say a lot, too," James observed.

"She always did," Ninian remarked from his pallet in the wagon-bed. "Uncle David says she come out of the womb just a-babbling."

Mr. Baker shook his reins and nodded decisively. "That's the Lord's truth," he affirmed. "She popped out of there quoting Scripture."

"I did not," Agnes flared. "I never quoted Scripture in my life." She turned back to James. "Are you a saved soul, Mr. Johnson?"

"No, I am not," he replied most definitely.

"Why ain't you? It's the decent thing, ain't it?"

"Folks say so. But I have my reservations about it."

"Well, if I was to marry somebody, and love 'em like I just said I'd have to, why, I reckon he'd need to be a man of faith. Even if I don't quote Scripture, I believe every word in it, just like Brother David and Cousin Ninian and every other Baker there ever was. All the Bakers has always been God-fearing. A man that ain't saved, well, he just ain't to be relied on."

"So in addition to love, you'd have to marry for religion too?"

"I don't know as I'd put it exactly like that. But religion'd be right important. It'd be near as important as good looks and health and a fair set of teeth and a willingness to work and not be lazy."

"Well, I never said I scorned religion. I said I wasn't a saved soul."

"What's the difference?" Ninian wanted to know.

"It has appeared to me all my life," answered James, "that religion is more a matter of sects and creeds than it is an affair of doing right by your fellow man. If I understand what Jesus taught, why, he taught us to love one another. He busted up all those creeds and sects of his time, didn't he? Said all that mattered was doing unto others like you'd want to be done to. But all these religions now, they set up their creeds and if a fellow don't follow them, why, he's consigned to hell for all eternity. I'll tell you my view of it: Most of these religions are intolerant. I think there's nothing more opposed to patriotism and republican principles than intolerance. Here we are fighting for our freedom, but at the same time the preachers all want to bind us down in servitude to creeds and sects and such. I believe a man ought to be free, and the thinking of his mind ought to be free too, and a man of faith ought to devote himself to the happiness of all mankind. I think it would show a more patriotic and republican spirit to lay aside these principles of sect and all of us work for this freedom we talk so much about but ain't willing to grant to others."

James had never said so many words all at once in his whole time on earth, and stopped now in astonishment at himself, realizing he had just said more than even Agnes ever had. He had never cared much for religion—partly because Chenowith had been so fervently pious and this had left him with a strong conviction that people of religion were all vile hypocrites—but he'd not before thought out his reservations so clearly, much less spoken them aloud. Now that he'd done so, though, he felt much refreshed, and proud of himself.

"Well, I declare," Agnes exclaimed. "I never heard such a speech made about religion. Are you an infidel then?"

James shook his head. "No, I'm no unbeliever. I believe in God all right, and I think God's created everything and wants it all to run just right. And in my heart I do honor to Him for it. What I disbelieve is the notion of God that men have cobbled together to suit themselves. And I think so highly of Jesus that I've named this good horse of mine after Him."

"Well, I declare," Agnes repeated, aghast. "That's as dire a sin as I ever heard of."

"That talk you just made appeals to me," Ninian spoke up in his thin voice.

"Me too," said Mr. Baker. "I respect a man that thinks for himself."

Agnes ignored these sentiments and augured in on what she seemed to think was a flaw in James's argument. "You're traveling with a preacher, ain't you?"

"Plumbley?" James smiled, enjoying her confusion. "Yes, he's a preacher all right. But he's also a helpless fornicator, and you'd do well to avoid him. It ain't his fault, I don't think, he's just a slave to lust. Yet I'm told he preaches a powerful sermon. I'd have him preach you one, but he's been forbid to do it, on account of he's a preacher of such ardor that he works folk up into dangerous fits. He's a Methodist, or used to be till they throwed him out. Now I know nothing of the Methodists, but by what he tells me of their creed, I believe they're a sight more tolerant than most. They teach that women are as good as men, and that a woman can testify in meeting, and that even niggers can testify too. So they strike me as right liberal, as sects go. But beware of him, for as I've warned you, he's a fornicator."

"You talk profane," Agnes accused him.

"He talks *straight*," Mr. Baker said. "I like him. Maybe you ought to marry him."

"I'd never marry *him*," protested Agnes. "He talks profane and he hates religion and he's named his ugly horse blasphemously after the Redeemer and he's puffed up with unseemly pride and he travels with a preacher that fornicates. You want somebody like that in the family?"

Mr. Baker laughed. "I think you've got a overblown idea of the tone of the Bakers, is what I think. I reckon you better marry Mr. Johnson here."

"I'd *surely* never marry the likes of him," bristled Agnes. "Furthermore I won't have the topic raised again."

"As you say, Sister," Mr. Baker said. But he turned on the wagon seat and winked at James, and James smiled to him because he knew now that Agnes did like him after all and even approved of his convictions, and might even have considered marrying him if not for the war that he must soon go to.

He tightened his reins allowing Jesus to drop back along the passing wagons, which he noticed now also gave off the same mysterious, faintly mildewy odor he'd smelled on his new boots when Sergeant Shoupe gave them to him back at Guilford Court House. He dropped back too past the escort troopers in their double file, all of whom, save Lockett, gave him a head-bob or a word of greeting. Lockett himself glared from under his heavy brows and loudly cleared his throat and spat a big gob of phlegm his way, which fortunately missed. Had it struck him or his horse or any of his gear, James would've made an issue of it. But as things stood he let the matter go; he figured he and Lockett would have to tangle up again sometime, but it would need to be over an issue larger than a wad of spit that never even hit him.

Presently he joined Plumbley with the horse herd, covered with the dust of the wagon train. Obediah was singing to the horses in his howling voice—"I'll praise my Maker while I've breath; and while my voice is lost in death, praise shall employ my nobler powers"—so James fell back even farther along the drove to take up a position at the very rear, where, dreamily watching the rhythmical swaying of the horses' rumps and their swishing tails, he could think without interruption of Agnes and her sunny glow and her whimsical way of talking and her blue eyes and shining yellow hair.

* * *

After the noon halt they resumed the journey, and Obediah, evidently feeling the need to talk, joined him at the back of the herd. "Brother Johnson," he said earnestly, "I was just in conversation with Brother David Baker while we was all a-feeding, and he said you'd spoke right highly of the Methodists this morning, and of myself in particular."

"Well," said James in quick defiance, "Mr. Baker has mistook my meaning by a long ways. It's true I did speak favorably of the Methodist sect, but I was right particular in warning him and Ninian and Miss Agnes that even if you're a preacher, you're a terrible fornicator and never to be trusted around any female, maid or matron or spinster or whatever she might be."

"Why, son, I've no objection to your describing me as I surely am," Plumbley went on expansively, not at all put out. "It's God that fashioned me that way, after all. I reckon if the Good Lord put it in me to be a fornicator, then I'm bound to be a saved and holy fornicator. Nor do I blame you for warning that delectable Miss Baker against me, for I know you've got tender feelings for her and I've taken a liking to you; and it's for that very reason that I've not tried to preach that little flaxen-haired lass into the sublime intimacy, nor even to approach her person. But that ain't my goddamned argument anyways. My argument's this: I'm convinced that my exposing you to The Teachings in these last days has brought your spirit up towards redemption by a damned good bit, and I'm proud to see you drawing so much nearer to the Mercy Seat."

"Pshaw," snorted James. "How could I have been exposed to The Teachings when you're forbid altogether to speak of them?"

"Well, as to that," smiled Plumbley, "it's by our *acts* that our goodness is known, not by our speech. Our Lord said so. So I've been a-leading you by precept and example, not by exhorting. And I spy the seed of belief a-sprouting within you, even as we ride along here looking up the arses of these goddamned nags. I tell you, Brother Johnson, you're coming nigh unto the Lord."

"What I'm coming nigh unto is knocking you over," James frowned.

Obediah turned serious then. "I know, son, I know. You're grieving that Miss Baker will soon be lost to you. Maybe she will but maybe she won't. But let me advise you to put your trust in the Almighty. Address Him an earnest prayer of entreaty. All things are possible with Him. Pray Him to look into your heart and into her heart and take notice of what He sees there, how you feel and how she feels. Pray Him to witness that pure love. Ask Him if He won't take a notion to bring the two of you together again one day, when the times is better."

"I'll do no such thing," James insisted with a burst of temper. "I'll not go through my whole life up to now refusing to ask anything of the Lord, only to drop down before him a-begging just because I've come across a thing I want worse than I ever wanted anything. That's hypocrisy, and if I was God, I wouldn't listen to a minute of it."

The evening of the third day after leaving New Garden and stopping at the Moravian town of Bethabara to take on some hay and twenty bushels of grain, they came to a place where a muddy river made a sweeping turn enclosing a broad down-sloped meadow with a log tavern at the bottom of it near the river bank. Sergeant Shoupe said the river in these parts made a great bend like an elbow and the neck of land inside the loop was called The Horseshoe; the river was the great Yadkin. A man named Hughes owned the tavern, and the place offered a good crossing for wagons; folk called it the Shallow Ford. Twenty-odd miles downstream, Shoupe explained, there were two more places to get over the water, a ferry operated by a man named Ellis and a horse and wagon ford with a good bottom called Trading Ford.

Lieutenant Gordon chose to use the Shallow Ford rather than the crossings lower down, but because the river was running a little high Mr. Hughes advised him not to make a crossing in the dimness of dusk, so they pitched camp planning to cross in the morning. Salisbury, Hughes said, was a little over a day's travel distant; and this news made James's stomach plummet like a lump of lead dropped down a shot tower, because at Salisbury the Bakers must part from the convoy and go west and north toward their home in Burke County.

He went to work rigging a picket line for the remounts at the lower end of the meadow while Plumbley tended the supper kettle. They were all messing together now, the Bakers and the escort troopers and the wagoners and James and Obediah, save for Lieutenant Gordon who always kept himself apart as befitted an officer and a gentleman, and while James worked he could look up betimes and glimpse Agnes' yellow head as she came and went from the wagon or bent to stir the Bakers' kettle. The sight gave him pain. He could summon little of his usual feeling of communion with the horses or of enthusiasm for his task, because a dank despair oppressed him as he thought of Agnes going away forever less than two days hence. He had grown fonder of her than he'd expected and hardly knew what to do about it, first because, though he believed she fancied him a little, he also knew he was very likely a long cast from the sort of person she might want to know well enough to think of marrying. Yes, marrying was on his mind. It had sprouted up there like a weed without his inviting it. He hardly knew why it was there or what to make of it. It wasn't even sensible, because he and Agnes must so soon go their separate ways never again to meet in this life. He fussed with himself about the dilemma while he tied off his ropes.

Later, while they all sat in a big circle around the communal fire having their supper, Plumbley asked Mr. Baker what it was like in that Burke County place where he and his family lived.

"It's a right good country," Mr. Baker answered, "foothill country most of it, but with broad valleys and good water and rich black dirt that'll grow most anything. My Pappy found it when he got to wandering and come down from Culpeper in Virginia some years back, and passed there, leaving my Mammy and Agnes here to fend for themselves while me and Dick was in the war. When Ninian and me ventured down—that was three years ago now—why, it was a wilderness as unsullied as the Garden of Eden in the Book of Genesis. But it's crowding up something fearful now, folk a-coming down the Wagon Road from Pennsylvania, Quakers and Dutchmen and Dunkards and Mennonites and such, more and more every day. Now I'll wager they's twenty families within ten mile of me."

"Country's filling up for sure," Ninian agreed, nodding his pale head on the pillow of his pallet that had been laid by the fire.

"I've been into the country west of me," Mr. Baker continued, and his countenance took on a radiant enthusiasm, "over the Blue Mountains, which is the great ridge that divides the foothills from the far fastnesses. Burke County claims all that country, but claiming it and putting any law to it's another question altogether. What few folk abides there gets no bother; officers don't go in. They's a road called Bright's Road, goes through it from Burke Court House up to the Watauga settlements, through the wildest land you ever saw. Great high ranges of peaks just as black as pitch with fir forest. Some of them hills so damned high they're bare on top like pasturage, or just got little dwarfy twisty trees on 'em, because it's so cold up there all year round that your ordinary trees and brush won't grow.

"And away up yonder, near side of Yellow Mountain, they's the prettiest valley, not the broadest valley, a narrow kind of valley but rich, hemmed in by mountains full of wild locust and sourwood and oak and tulip poplars and chestnut and pine, with laurel and ivy in big hells and slicks. The river that runs in it's clear and cold and rocky-bottomed, called the Toe, and they's a high place where a creek runs into this River Toe that they call Caney Creek. Grass up to your belly up in there. Hardly anybody lives there yet, and the savages has all pretty much pulled out since the treaty was signed up on the Holston. Speak of Eden, if I once thought the Burke country was Eden, why then, this Toe River country is Heaven on earth. I've got me a notion to pack up and go and settle me a place up there one of these days."

Bobby Busby looked puzzled. "Why would they name a river after somebody's toe?"

Mr. Baker shrugged. "Can't say of my own knowledge, son. But I've heard 'twas an Indian name, and maybe there was more to it than just the toe part, but on account of the white man's tongue not being able to get around it, why, it just got cut short. But the River Toe it is."

"Did you name that Caney Creek?" asked Reuben Griffin.

"I did," Mr. Baker proudly affirmed. "Named it for all the thick cane that was growing along it."

"Well," Agnes declared in a harsh voice that ruined the mood of Mr. Baker's talk, "one thing's sure, you ain't moving noplace till Mama passes." She leveled a hard eye on her brother. "Mama's said at least a thousand times she'll be buried right there on the North Fork of the Catawba River where Papa lies, or know the reason why."

She did have a sharp tongue in her head, but James liked even that. He kept watching her in his misery, but she never gave him the least glance, all during the rest of supper. It was as if she had forgotten his existence. He didn't think he could stand being ignored like that, but finally found that he could because he must, though it made his heart heavy as a stone. There was a good deal more talk around the fire, but he hardly heard any of it, and when supper was done and he rose to go and tend the horses, he sent her a beseeching look, but she turned her back to him at just that moment and he felt sure she was spurning him now from pure dislike.

He couldn't think why she would have so soon changed from seeming to approve of him, if somewhat grudgingly, to giving him the go-by as if he were the meanest villain at large. The transformation seemed beyond explanation and made him so melancholy that he couldn't sleep that night during Plumbley's watch. He tried to write another letter to Libby, but could get no farther than "Agnes don't seem to like me as much as befor and pretty soon will be agoin off and hit makes me feel rite bad that we will not be asein one another agin."

Consequently, when it was time for him to relieve Obediah partway through the night, he was tired and haggard and sore-eyed in addition to feeling as glum as he ever had. Plumbley of course, being a convivial soul, wanted to converse upon his relief. He asked if James had noticed the wagons smelling mouldy. But in his foul state of mind James lied and said no and made it clear to Obediah that he wished to be let alone, and Plumbley professed to understand and made his way back to camp and turned in; and James tethered Jesus to a dogwood tree and sat down by the rope pen with the horses all in a row looking over the rope at him and felt sorry for himself for about the next two hours.

That was why he was hardly ready when Benjamin Lockett came at him out of the dark of the woods with his ape's forehead pushed low and his narrow shoulders hunched up and his big fists knotted before him and told him to get up and take his licking like a man instead of like a weakling that settled his scores by hitting folk on the head with iron rods. "You haven't got any smaller since the last time," James answered as he stood, "and I sure haven't got any bigger, so the same principle applies now as applied then. Is a fellow that whips a puppy-dog a man, or is he just a fellow that whips puppy-dogs?"

"I aim to whip *you*," was Lockett's reply.

James was without his branding iron and in consequence was forced to defend himself as best he could. Afterward he couldn't remember much about the business, but was reasonably sure he never even managed to land a blow, whereas Lockett pounded on him without let or hindrance for quite some time. It hurt a lot and James lost an eyetooth and one of the big ones from the back of his jaw and bled a frightful amount, but he was proud of himself for enduring the entire beating without making a single sound or calling out for help, though he knew for certain Lockett's messmates would have come to save him if he had. There did come a moment, however, after he took a blow to the side of his head that stunned him so bad he fell and couldn't move, when he believed Lockett might actually cripple him or even kill him and not just settle for bruising him up. He was lying on his back in the meadow grass with Lockett kneeling over him whaling him left and right with an awful mechanical regularity when he heard the metallic snick of a pistol hammer being cocked and looked up and saw in the moonlight, through a blur of blood, the barrel of a pistol sticking in one of Lockett's ears. Lockett went still. "What's that?" he inquired.

"This here," said Agnes Baker, "is the front end of a seventy-two caliber horse pistol, and when I pull the trigger it's going to split your head open like a breakfast mushmelon. Now what d'you think of that?"

"I think," said Lockett, "I'd rather that not to happen."

"Then get off of Mr. Johnson there and go and stand back a ways. And remember, I'm as fair a shot at a distance as I am with the pistol poked in your ear-hole."

"Yes, ma'am," Lockett said with great respect. He unstraddled himself from James and stood and backed away holding both his big hands open in front of him. "I beg you not to shoot me now, Miss Baker." He meant it too. She stood there with her feet wide-planted the way she'd been standing when James first saw her that day by the roadside, but now holding that big pistol trained on Lockett's chest, holding it with both of her little hands, one folded tight over the other, and for all its length and heft that piece didn't move by as much as a quarter of an inch. She was going to shoot the son of a bitch if he didn't do like she told him. And she was going to hit what she shot at. James could see that and so could Lockett. "Please now," Lockett said again. "I won't do no more. I know I've gone wrong here. My pride was hurt to have been bested by this boy that hit me with a piece of iron. It festered in me till I couldn't stand it. I'm sorry now that I done it."

"Then you'd better make your manners to Mr. Johnson here," Agnes lectured him. "You'd better tell *him* how sorry you are. Telling *me* won't do you any good. I wouldn't hear a word of it. I'd like it right well just to shoot you, and I might shoot low too, and hit you where it counts."

Lockett hung his head and looked abjectly at the ground. "I'm sorry, Johnson. It was wrong of me, what I done."

James was upright now, though he found it difficult to keep his balance. With the back of a hand he wiped the blood from his mouth. He watched Lockett with as much pity as hate. He thought it must be hard to be large and powerful yet to have been struck down by a small man with an unfair weapon. But it was a fleeting thought. "However many days we've got left on this convoy," he said to the head-hung man, "that's as many days as you'd better keep out of my way. For if you come within twenty foot of me, I promise, I'll kill you sure." When he said this he was thinking of how John the least of the Crowner's sons had killed the chief of the Keiths, and he knew he could do as much himself.

By then George Robertson, who had been standing sentry at the wagon park, had made his way to the scene along with Plumbley and two or three of the Crackers that the commotion had awakened; and finally Sergeant Shoupe came along too, holding high a lantern of brass and horn to illuminate the scene with its dull amber glow. In another moment Lieutenant Gordon arrived wearing his sleeping shift over his britches, took charge in his abrupt way, and demanded to know what had happened.

"Well," he remarked when all had been explained, "I see Private Lockett has taken my frivolous observation of a few days ago entirely too much to heart. Surely I did not imply the wee roughrider should ever, under any circumstances, be foully murdered, most especially since the army needs its every man, even the tiniest. And it should've been taken as a sign of my favor, even by a dullard, when I gave the midget and the preacher a set of new boots. I do most especially detest a stupid man. It'll be twenty lashes for you in the morning, Private Lockett. See you bear 'em well." The sergeant took the crestfallen Lockett in charge and marched him back to the camp.

But James, feeling sympathy for the offender now that he was con-demned, made bold to approach the Lieutenant appealing for a suspen-sion of the twenty lashes. "I shamed him, the other night when I smote him with that iron. And shame's hard to bear. I know it by my own experience."

"I fear it's an emotion foreign to myself," the Lieutenant remarked dis-tantly. "But I have heard it spoke of, and never more plaintively than now. You show yourself a person of character by invoking it. I'll make it ten lashes instead."

By this time Mr. Baker had turned out, toting his own poor lantern of tin with holes punched in the sides. As a matter of fact, the little meadow was now so crowded it looked to James as if everybody in the convoy was there save only Ninian, who amid all the excitement seemed to have been forgotten on his pallet and was too poorly to shift for himself. Mr. Baker took Agnes aside to learn particulars, but she must've kept the account mighty brief for it wasn't long till she returned to James's side. Mr. Baker stood back regarding them with a thoughtful look. Obediah fussed and prayed over James's hurts till Agnes chased him off.

In time the group lost interest in the affair and one by one straggled back to resume their interrupted slumbers. James and Agnes, left alone as he had heartily wished all along, sat in the grass, where he held his sore head in his hands for a spell. Then he remarked, "I'm not the handsome prospect I once was. He knocked out two of my teeth, and one was an eye-tooth. It'll leave a space in my smile."

"I never noticed you being handsome," said Agnes matter-of-factly. "Nor your smiling all that much neither. Do you need me to nurse you?"

"No," he said, "Plumbley'll do it directly. I ain't so bad off." He took his hands away from his face and looked at her with gratitude. "It's good to see you know how to use all them guns and knives you carry. How'd you come to find Lockett a-thrashing me?"

"I'd sneaked away from the wagon," she confessed, "to come and talk to you in secret, while you was on watch with the horses."

"What for?"

"I was regretful for seeming to scorn you tonight. At supper-time I was feeling fickle and flighty, wouldn't look at you or talk to you, and I felt bad about that."

"Why'd you feel bad?"

"Because it ain't right to tease and torment the way I done."

"Why not? Seems like that's your regular way with folk."

"Well, it is, for most folk. But time's so short . . ."

"Does that matter?"

"Well, yes, it seems to matter. It matters to you, don't it?"

"Yes."

She hesitated and turned her gaze away across the Horseshoe. "Well, it matters to me too."

"You aren't about to say you fancy me, are you?" he tweaked her, and would have showed her the gap in his teeth if the moon had been bright enough for her to see it.

She made a noise of disgust. "Of course not. Whatever gave you such a crazy notion?"

"You mentioned the shortness of the time. I too have been giving thought to the shortness of time." He was solemn now. "And the reason is, I fancy *you*. And I reckon you know it too."

There was quite a long wait before she answered. "I reckon I do."

"So, I renew my question. Are you about to tell me you fancy me?"

"I ain't certain," she sighed. She sounded unhappy about it.

"Little enough in this world is certain," he observed. "But I'll tell you plain, Miss Agnes, I fancy you a right smart and the thought of parting from you when we get to Salisbury is about more than I can bear. I know we're strangers, and I'm a soldier, and women generally ought not trust a soldier, and you're headed to your home in Burke County, and I'm headed down to the war, and all those things together argue against any kind of a lasting connection. But there's one thing I do know pretty sure, and it's this: I'm going to live through this war. It won't kill me like it's killed many another. And I don't think it'll hurt me either, not like it's hurt your Cousin Ninian. So I'd like to know if it would be all right with you if I kept you in a special place in my bosom till the war's finished, and then if you'd let me come and seek you out after the peace and see if you're still there and if you still fancy me a little; and if you do, then I'd like to know if you'd let me pay you court proper-like, and get Mr. Baker's approval, and win yours, and then see if maybe you could come to think more of me than you do."

Agnes laughed. "Are you asking me to wait on you while you go galloping around amongst all them swamps and miasmas on your blasphemous horse getting shot at in battles and ambuscades, and taking fevers, and maybe using all kinds of loose women the way every dragoon I ever heard of does, for God knows how long, till everybody in this country agrees to quit fighting?"

But he didn't take up her saucy turn of speech. "No, Miss Agnes," he told her, "I'm not asking you to wait. I don't expect that would be fair of me. But maybe it just might turn out, in the normal course of things, that nobody better'n me would happen to cross your path, in the time I'm gone, so that when I *do* come back, as I'm certain to, why, I'll look right commendable."

"But if some better fellow comes along," she asked, to get the matter clear, "I can grab him right up?"

"You can," he nodded.

"Well," she declared, "that don't sound like such a bad bargain to me. Can't see that I'm losing anything by it."

"No, Ma'am," James agreed. "If there was a loser, I'd be him."

She waited another few moments before speaking again, and now she was serious too. "Some of this is in fun and some is not. Ain't that right?"

"A little's fun. But most ain't. Folk'll tell you, I ain't whimsical."

More time passed, then when she talked again he could hear her smile in it. "Are you going to want to kiss me?"

"I want to, but I ain't sure it's decent to do."

"I'm *right* sure it ain't," she chuckled. "But I'd like you to try it anyhow. We'll see how I stand it."

"What if you find it unpleasant?"

"Well, then, we'll know something, won't we?"

So, sore-mouthed and bloody as he was, he leaned close and put his lips gently to hers and held them there for the briefest time, and felt her warmth like the sunlight flowing into him. He hoped she felt something of his nature that was good flowing into her too. He drew slowly back. "How was it?"

She bounded up and ran away laughing. "Tell you tomorrow," she yelled back at him.

In the morning the first thing was the punishment of Lockett. It was not a pleasant thing to witness. Lieutenant Gordon ordered the poor lout stripped to the waist and lashed to the hind wheel of one of the clothing wagons. The Bakers and the Crackers were sent to the front of the convoy out of sight, so as not to have their civilian sensibilities offended by the disagreeable nature of military discipline. The troopers all stood in line to watch, Lieutenant Gordon on his horse to oversee it. Ordinarily a drummer or a fifer would have wielded the cat, but since there were no musicians in the party, lots were drawn and John Gunnell found himself holding the short straw. He laid on the ten lashes pretty smartly and Lockett bore them without complaint, but James found himself sickened when the blood first ran and then splattered about. Afterwards he went to Lockett and told him he was sorry and Lockett told him, "It's all right, I've been flogged many a time and it don't change my disposition at all."

"As long as you don't come after me again," James cautioned him.

"I won't," Lockett pledged. "Hereafter I'll find me somebody else to lick that ain't as much trouble as you, even if you are about the size of a shit-rolling beetle."

James scowled. "I reckon I'll take that as a joke."

The second thing was to ask about that kiss. While Plumbley took down the rope pen and gathered the remounts, James rode forward to the Baker wagon where he found Agnes sitting on the high seat with her man's hat tipped back on the crown of her head and all her golden curls billowing about her ears. She turned to him her sunny face, but he could tell by the pursing of her mouth and the little wrinkles at the corners of her eyes that she was making an effort not to seem too glad to see him. "How was that kiss?" he asked her right off.

"I won't pretend I ain't been kissed before last night, Mr. Johnson," she told him briskly, "and kissed plenty too. And I tell you truly, I've been kissed worse and I've been kissed a whole lot better." James's hopes sank. But then her look softened and she said, "However, I don't think I've ever been kissed so heartfelt and tender as I was by you."

"That there is high praise," Ninian commented from his pallet behind her. "Usually when a-body kisses her, she speaks of sour breath and drooling and such."

"I'm gratified to hear it," James said, then inquired of Agnes, "Is your brother about?"

Mr. Baker stepped around the tailgate of the wagon so providentially James wondered if he hadn't been waiting back there just to be summoned. His expression was one of faintly aroused and possibly belligerent interest. "Have I overheard mention of kissing in the night?" he demanded with a growling tone.

"You have, sir," James answered stoutly. "I confess to it. I have in actual fact kissed your sister."

"'Twasn't no blubbery kiss neither," Agnes bragged.

"Nor did he drool, nor have stinking breath," Ninian said.

"Well," Mr. Baker said, giving up his look of possible wrath with a sudden cackle of laughter, "I highly approve of kissing as a general matter. Furthermore, I approve in particular of your a-kissing my Agnes. She's been in dire need of the right kind of kissing by the right sort of fellow for quite some time."

In spite of all his bruises and aching ribs and missing teeth James felt as if he were swelling to two or three times his normal figure, and this made him bold enough to ask, "I wonder, sir, if I could beg your permission to write letters to Miss Agnes, once we're parted at Salisbury."

"You can write to her all you wish," Mr. Baker shrugged. "But she won't be able to read a goddamned word of it."

"I will too," Agnes cried. Then she sulked a little and confessed, "Some words, anyways."

"I can read it to her," Ninian offered. "I can read right well. Them Quakers taught me good." He tried to grin in his weak face. "Just don't write nothing naughty or I'll be forced to hold it back from her."

Mr. Baker extended his hand to James. "Write her all you want, Mr. Johnson," he said as they shook, "and Ninian'll read it to her, naughty or not. Hell, if you want to, carry her away with you down to the goddamned army. You'd be doing me a great favor by taking her off my hands. Life would be a good deal more peaceful about the place if you'd do that."

They all knew he wasn't serious. "No, sir," James said, "I'm obliged for the offer, but I believe I'll leave her with you good folk. But I'll thank you to keep her safe till I can bring myself back from this war and present myself proper, in my own person instead of by my writing, and see if she'll remember me fondly then, or if she'll hold me a stranger."

"You'll never be a stranger, son," Mr. Baker told him with a solemn air.

James turned in his saddle to feast his gaze on Agnes, whose sunrise glow was warming him from ten feet away. He saw something in her face that he could find no name for but that made his heart race and brought the blood rushing to his cheeks. He leaned out from the saddle and reached his hand to her, and she reached back and their fingertips touched in a flickity way, and she smiled in her saucy fashion, tossed her yellow tresses, and said with twinkling eyes, "Brother David can say what he wants about how you'll be received, but I can't promise how *I'll* regard you when you come back. First thing is, you've got to *come* back. Maybe you won't. Maybe them Redcoats and miasmas and fevers and such will lay you low. Second thing is, how good a letter you've been writing. Third thing is, whether somebody better'n you has come along to make himself known to me. That's the arrangement, ain't it?"

James nodded and laughed and doffed his helmet to her. "It is," he said, and turned Jesus about and rode back along the train of wagons that were smelling worse all the time and then along the escort column and past Lieutenant Gordon, saluting him, and finally to the little meadow where Plumbley was holding the remounts; and presently the column started down to Mr. Ellis' ferry.

The Yadkin was still flowing pretty full, three hundred yards across and pumpkin-colored with mud, but Mr. Hughes made two of his Negroes lead them over the ford on mules, the wagons first, the escort troopers next, James and Obediah and the remounts last. It proved an easy crossing, though the current buffeted Jesus a time or two and made him stumble for his footing. The tossing waters reminded him of the day he crossed the flooded Fluvanna leaving the Point of Fork Arsenal behind. That day Libby had been with him, and Poovey Sides and Captain Harris and all the boys in Harris' Company. And the next day Janet had been lost, and the one-eyed sergeant, and Poovey's pig. It seemed like yesterday and it seemed like long ago too. *I've come quite a ways,* he thought.

Six miles on, they arrived at the place where the Bakers would part from them. Salisbury Town lay in a clearing in a forest that rolled away so thick and heavy in all directions it resembled a dense-woven carpet of green. Narrow muddy creeks drained the space. Away off to the north and west on the edge of the world was a pale blue line that might have been a layer of stormy cloud or more likely a range of peaks that James wondered might be the Blue Mountains Mr. Baker had named when he talked of going over into the wilderness. They looked cool and pretty and while they did seem to beckon, they also appeared to offer many an opportunity for a man to become swallowed up and lost, and James had no wish to explore those dark chances.

Salisbury was all squared logs and shingling and mud-and-stick chimneys and tree stumps and hog wallows and stock pens full of oxen and steers and horses, and the stench of the droppings of those and every other kind of beast, and wagons parked every which way and swarms of folk all going everywhere in a great hurry, and ankle-deep dust that the breezes whipped up to afflict the vision, and pungent smoke and the smells of cooking and of the tanning of hides and of human shit and of quantities of dumped guts.

There was a courthouse and a treeless square where columns of slouchy infantry were drilling, Salisbury being a district headquarters for the North Carolina militia, or so Corporal Hudson asserted. The district was commanded by Colonel Francis Locke, commonly regarded as a fool and an incompetent, he further explained. There were taverns and ordinaries on all sides and near the middle of everything several buildings fashioned of new lumber smelling still of fresh rosin, which were, said Hudson, the depots, and warehouses, and shoe factories of General Greene's Southern Army. That shoe concern, Hudson said, was run by a Major Davidson, who was Commissary for General Greene; it fashioned the worst excuse for footwear any mortal had ever tried to lace on. These tidings were unsettling to James, who'd expected to find none but efficient officers in the army of the excellent Quaker, General Greene.

But as busy a spot as Salisbury was, and as disheartened as he felt to hear of sloth and unfitness in high places, James's strongest interest was fixed one way only, and that was on Miss Agnes Baker. Mr. Baker meant to take his road west that same day, as several hours of good light remained and he desired to reach a place he called Sherrill's Ford before fall of night; so James had to make his farewells on the public square with all the hullabaloo of Salisbury about him. He wrung Mr. Baker's hand and they wished each other good fortune, and he leaned down from his saddle to take Ninian's limp grasp, feeling certain he'd see the poor boy nevermore in this life; then he turned to Agnes and dragged off his cap and opened his mouth to speak, but found to his amazement that nothing at all would come out.

Agnes, though, did not seem surprised. She bent herself sideways out of the wagon seat and took him by the elbow and pulled him toward her, and when she'd got his ear next to her mouth she gave the edge of it a small nibble and then released him. By the time he had righted himself, Mr. Baker had spoken to the team and the wagon was rolling away, and she waved, and after that wave the last he saw of her was a flutter of yellow locks in a wind that came up.

Part ye' Twenty-Fourth

In Which General Greene Difposes
His Army for Battle

ON THURSDAY EVENING GENERAL PICKENS AND his militia caught up with the resting army in its camp by Medway Swamp. He had been able to gather but a dozen head of skinny cattle. These were instantly slaughtered and consumed, but left most of the army yet unfed. Many a weary starveling crept on blistered feet into the roundabout woods and swamps to shoot alligators, raccoons, wild hogs, and opossum, or to snare frogs and serpents, fare that in any other season would be spurned as unspeakably loathsome. Hunched over their fires, they dined on these alien oily viands while the weird wobbling howls of wolves filled the surrounding night.

In his candlelit marquee the General, planning his battle, raised his head to hear the squeals and screams of the wilderness. At another time the sound might have inspired some moody speculation, some morbid reverie having to do with what those wolves would be feeding on some hours hence. But not tonight. Tonight the cries were but the noises of the deep woods and offered nothing of the ominous or of the tragic. They were only the music of what must come. They were consonant with the new grim turn of his mind. Only that. He bent again to Colonel Lee's rude map of the Eutaws.

A wavering line ran roughly east-west. Harry's nearly illegible scrawl labeled it *Santee River*. North of the line he'd lettered *Swamp* over a series of squiggles representing wet, impassable ground. In the middle of the page another line branched south from the main one—*Eutaw Creek*, Harry's writing called it—and turned eastward to end in one large loop and two smaller ones. These loops he'd marked *The Springs*. Adjoining the two smaller loops he had drawn a square and written *Palifadoe'd Garden*; south of the garden he'd drawn a smaller square and written *Brick Houfe two ftoryes*, and south of that a bristle of triangles, meant to be tents, labeled *Cleared Ground & Britifh Camp*.

Running straight through the camp, parallel to the river, was another thick line—*River Road to Roches*, Lee had written above it. That, Greene saw, would be his main approach, with his left flank protected by the Santee and its swamps and his right by a piece of boggy ground Harry had portrayed with crosshatching that jutted up from the south nearly as far as the road. Just past the camp a path turned off the River Road leading southeast. This was *Charles Town or Waſſamaſaw Road*; a bit farther along, another way, coming down from Nelson's Ferry on the river, diverged in the same direction—*To Monks Corner*, Harry's scribble read.

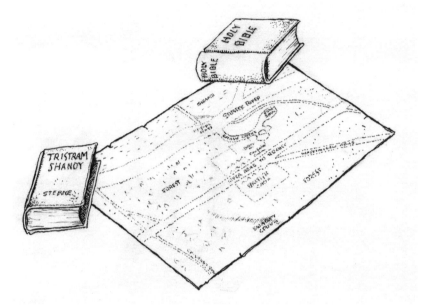

Greene nodded approvingly; these would be Stewart's routes of retreat, for he must be left an avenue of escape lest he be trapped and fight a desperate action of attrition that neither side could afford. The General scanned all the country below the river; the drawing was covered with rudimentary little umbrella shapes meant to represent trees—*Foreſt*, Harry's nub of charcoal had written. That would disturb the order of battle; formations would be hard to keep. Greene would possess the element of surprise, but the British would have as good ground to defend as he would have to attack, and both must contend with the disruption of the woods.

He mused over the drawing. To plan a battle, he knew, was purest folly. As soon as the vans of the armies engaged, a battle became a beast whose raging no man could hope to control. If God granted the time, one might come to understand a little of its nature before it was too late, and react to that understanding, and so shape a part of its outcome. But even that shaping always spawned events one did not expect, and those events yielded others, and those others in a spiral too swift to comprehend or respond to, till presently the beast was whirling and gnashing and clawing in ever more distant and unexpected quarters and in so many ever worsening fashions than one could hardly begin to grasp them, and that was the time of greatest danger, for then the temptation came to stand mute and powerless and stupefied before the continually multiplying savagery, as Gates had stood at Camden, till the beast at last turned on its author and tore his reputation limb from limb in a feast of bloody, inglorious defeat.

So it was not the plan that mattered. The plan was little more than the bringing of the army to the place where it must fight, with its troops arrayed in what seemed the best order. But one had to know the order would soon be disrupted, that the beast would go ravaging beyond control. The trick was to ride it as it grew and changed from one terrible thing into the next—became a flock of beasts, every one rabid. One needed nimbleness of mind, coolness of temperament, a watchful and discerning eye, a willingness to adapt to every unexpected turn of events. And now that he had hardened himself to the remorselessness of battle the General was confident he owned these traits and was ready to wield them.

But he knew another thing also. He knew that in order to ride the beast to victory he would need an attribute he'd begun to suspect was no longer his. It was nothing more than simple luck. Perhaps more than any feature of personality, luck was a powerful agent of victory or defeat. He'd had fine battle luck to the Northward, at Brandywine, at Monmouth, and on other fields. That fine luck had earned him fame enough that the Congress, though hating him, had endorsed his appointment as Commander of the Southern Army when His Excellency pushed it on them in the wake of Gates's ruin.

But his luck seemed to have dissipated on the battlegrounds of the Carolinas. He was not sure he could get it back, for cruelly and unfairly it was not a quality a man might develop with maturity and wisdom and perseverance, then call on at will when needed. Instead it was God's to give or withhold. Thus one did not plan one's luck any more than one planned a battle. Luck was meted out from On High, as was victory itself, or defeat. He must hope it would be given him now, in what he felt certain must be the last battle he would fight in this war. He sighed and rubbed his sore eye. He would leave the luck to Providence. He would ready himself to ride the beast.

He examined again his preference to display his first line with militia. Militia had failed him at Guilford, but had held for Dan Morgan at The Cowpens; and regulars had cost him Hobkirk's. He'd liked the cut of Malmedy's men; Pickens was reliable; and so would Marion be, when he arrived. And all the militia, in contrast to his Continentals, would be relatively fresh and well fed. His mouth leveled itself into a resolute line: Militia it would be. Quickly then he made the consequent decisions. Let the Carolina militias take the first line; let them prove their worth; Marion was senior, he would command, none better. The regulars would form the second line under the veteran Sumner. Cavalry and light troops in reserve. Lee and Henderson's people on the flanks. Yes, it was a plan.

He fetched Captain Pierce's stub of pencil and jotted notes on the margin of the map for the orders he would give tomorrow. The Legion and Henderson's state troops, cavalry and infantry, to form the vanguard. The main body to follow, militia first, then the regulars, the artillery between; Colonel Washington's horse and the Delawares to bring up the rear as a *corps de reserve.* Reaching the British position, the Legion and the state troops to divide, giving place to the infantry; the militia to display athwart the River Road, the regulars to display to its rear, then the Legion and Henderson's corps to take position on the flanks. Washington's horse and the Delawares to hold in readiness on the road.

In his newly hardened mind he superimposed these dispositions on Lee's map and watched them shift and move as he'd imagined. He saw only the lines, not the men who composed them. The lines were objects, were elements of plane geometry endowed with motion. His commanders were not the individuals he'd known, they were now but nomenclature, were the identities of objects he would maneuver. They were not Billy or Otho or Jethro. Richard Campbell was not Richard at all but the name of a brigade of Virginians. The Marquis de Malmedy, William Henderson, Andrew Pickens, Francis Marion—each of these was no person but instead a unit of soldiery, a blank blunt instrument of his will. Even Harry Lee was but a corps of infantry and horse. Any or all of these could be erased in an instant, and it might be days before Nathanael Greene would weep for them.

At dawn on Friday the seventh of September the army advanced at an easy pace to Laurens' Plantation, where it halted to wait out the blazing heat of midday. Before the molten disc of the sun had moved another hour to the west a column was seen approaching from the north and presently revealed itself as the forty horse and two hundred foot of General Marion's South Carolina militia, providentially presenting themselves just at the moment Greene had begun to despair of their arrival. The two generals sat their horses side by side as the redoubtable Low Country fighters went riding by, and watching them Greene could read in their litheness and in the rangy way they moved and in their sharp dark faces a confidence that lifted away what small doubts he'd yet nourished that on the morrow he would taste the savor of victory.

Now that Sumter had withdrawn from the field in disgrace, Marion was the state's senior brigadier of militia. Prior to the fall of Charles Town he'd been a Continental colonel, and still wore the blue coat faced with red and the plumed leather cap with its silver crescent in front that distinguished the South Carolina Line. He was small, swart, hawk-nosed, ungainly, thick-ankled, with misshapen knees, and gave an impression of singular awkwardness and ill favor—hardly a figure to suggest the hero he'd shown himself time and again to be. But for all the fierceness of his partisan warfare Greene knew Marion to be an honest, virtuous, and kindly man, and his liking for the dark little Huguenot momentarily coaxed him out of his commander's grimness; when they dismounted he came beaming to wring Marion's withy hand.

In the cool of evening the army moved on to Burdell's Tavern, hard by the farm of a man named Campton, having covered a distance of ten miles since break of day. Eutaw Springs now lay a scant seven miles farther eastward; from Burdell's, at four o'clock next morning, the General meant to launch his attack. Accordingly, agreeable to his orders, the advance elements of the army, Lee's Legion and Henderson's corps, awaited him in bivouac in Campton's pastures. The General greeted Lee with a cool detachment born of his battle demeanor, which Harry recognized from previous fields and answered with the subservience he could always marshal when he knew he must. He reported Stewart yet lying idle at The Springs, implausibly ignorant of the approach of the army. His Legion looked fit. Henderson seemed quite recovered from his fever and said the sickness among his troops had about played itself out. Hampton, Myddelton, Polk, and Hammond were lively, professing their commands eager for the most impetuous service. These expressions too the General acknowledged politely yet with a sternness that now held everyone, even Pendleton and Pierce and Hyrne, at a certain respectful distance.

Hardly had the army settled down under the live oaks and loblollies of the tavern and in the fields of Campton's farm than the long-awaited battalion of one hundred twenty North Carolina regulars under Major Reading Blount at last came marching up the same road they had just traveled. With Blount came two wagonloads of badly needed muskets, which by General Sumner's orders were quickly distributed to those of Colonel Malmedy's militia still without arms.

More small contingents arrived. At dusk a party of twenty or so Georgians rode in, volunteer cavalry under the command of a Captain Gresham; the General assigned them to Lee's Legion in the van. With these came a troop of horse, mounted infantry, from Guilford County in

North Carolina, led by one Captain Hamilton; Greene sent them to serve with Colonel Washington's corps. Then at fall of dark yet another band of horsemen appeared, just down from the Powhatan camps in Virginia. They had ridden hard from Camden. Their commander was a lieutenant of the Third Dragoons, the General was told, named Ambrose Gordon.

Part ye' Twenty-Fifth

In Which a Young Man Haſtens
to ye Scene of Battle

CHARLOTTE, WHEN THEY REACHED IT, SEEMED little different from Salisbury, save it had a better courthouse. There were the same log inns and taverns, the same new military warehouses fashioned of raw plank, the same poultry, the same mobs of folk, even the same smoke and dust and tree stumps and hog wallows, the same wagons parked everywhere higgledy-piggledy. The courthouse, though, commanded the crossroads at the center of town with conspicuous authority. It was an elongated structure of whitewashed frame with a low-pitched roof, the whole of it mounted on brick pillars bedded in a foundation of mortared river stones. This arrangement left the head-high space beneath it open, shady, and cool even in the hottest weather, providing a convenient venue for barter and trade. At each end a pair of stairsteps rose in the fashion of an inverted V to a door giving access to the interior.

James, one leg thrown across the pommel of Jesus' saddle, was admiring this fine seat of law and government of Mecklenburg County when a slim young man wearing a dragoon helmet approached and some faint shimmer of foreboding passed out of the fellow and came to James and troubled his mood so that he turned a wary eye that way.

The stranger rode a gaunt bay whose dropped ears, scarred ribs, and twisting tail told a sad history of mistreatment; he halted in the street to take frowning note of the remounts Plumbley was just then herding into a livery pen, then turned the bay with a vicious yank of the reins, dug his spurs so deep that James disliked him at once, and went cantering down the stopped train of wagons till he met Lieutenant Gordon at its tail. The two exchanged salutes, and James understood the abuser of horses to be an officer and, if the shape of his helmet could be credited, an officer of dragoons, though judging from the condition of his mount he could hardly be a decent one.

This last surmise was soon enough confirmed. Lieutenant Gordon and the new man rode two and two back along the convoy and drew rein before James, whose salute Gordon returned and the new man ignored, peering avidly past him into the livery pen where the remounts still milled about, snuffing the air and pawing at the dirt to get the flavor of the enclosure. The new man had the face of a rat—a jaw that ran back chinless, a sharp narrow wedge of nose, close-set eyes, prominent front teeth. Gordon introduced him as Lieutenant Linton of the Third Dragoons, on detachment from the Southern Army to collect horses for Colonel Washington's corps.

"Linton'll take the damned nags off your hands," Gordon announced in an airy way that somehow managed to demean not only the poor beasts and all the good care given them these last many days, but also the very worth of James and Obediah as men and soldiers. Ever since Gordon gave him his new boots James had come to think better and better of the man. While it was true the boots had started to come apart, it was also true that Gordon had warned him in a humorous and comradely way that this would happen. It had been the gesture that James approved of. It had made Gordon seem a man of easy and democratic disposition. But now, in company with another officer, Gordon had drawn back into his lofty estate to look down with drooping lids on James in languid contempt. James's throat swelled with bitterness.

Still Linton deigned not to rest a gaze on James's actual person, but kept on roaming his rodent's eye over the horses beyond. His dismissing arrogance, together with the mistreatment of his horse and the simple repulsion of his rat's face, were enough to move James to stubborn speech. "Lieutenant," he answered Gordon, but leveled his hardest look on Linton, "I've a writing signed by Colonel White, giving me and Private Plumbley the duty to deliver these remounts direct to Colonel Washington. I ain't been given authority to yield them up to nobody but him."

Now the rat's attention finally flicked to him. Its glance ran about his features as if he were no more than a bit of tasty cheese. Linton had watched the horses in the same greedy manner—he was not just a rat but a voracious rat, a rat who would eat anything and anyone. "*I'll give you the authority*," he said in an icy whisper.

"Then, Your Honor," James kept on with boldness, reaching into his bosom and drawing forth his orders, "if you'll oblige me and pardon my impudence, I'll need you to put a writing on this paper of Colonel White's, and your name too, saying you're a-doing so, and relieving me of the responsibility. Else when I get to Captain Watts, why, he may hang me for some crime having to do with their loss."

Gordon shrugged and gave Linton a nod. "He's right, John. They could say he sold 'em and pocketed the chink, or plain lost 'em. Government property, he'd swing for it."

The rat lieutenant jabbed out a clawed hand. The small, near-set eyes were without visible whites; two dull black orbs entirely filled the sockets. But if he looked like a rat, he hissed like a snake when he said, "Give me your poxy orders, you goddamned overstepping little cunt."

Though he darkened with resentment James extended the paper; Linton snatched it and turned swearing to open the buckles of his saddlebag.

The wagons of the Philadelphia shipping concern had been engaged to deliver the dragoon uniforms only as far as Charlotte. Consequently it would be necessary to unload and store them till such time as transportation could be arranged to carry them on to Colonel Washington. After making several inquiries, Lieutenant Gordon located a warehouse about twelve miles south of town, near the reservation lands of some degenerate Catawba Indians, on a farm belonging to a certain Bassett, where the deputy clothier general of the Southern Army, a Captain Hamilton, was found to be temporarily in residence.

The Captain had quartered himself in a bell tent attached to a brushwood bower in Bassett's yard; the warehouse was a rustic shed of logs perhaps twenty feet square with a backward-slanting roof and a single plank door; inside, bales of clothing wrapped in tobacco leaves and tied with twine were piled to the top, giving the place an agreeable fragrance. A pretty stream, Sugar Creek by name, flowed past at the bottom of the yard. Two sentries sat on tree stumps leaning sleepily on their muskets.

With a great deal of geeing and hawing, jangling of harness bells and lashing of whips, the Crackers maneuvered the big Conestogas end-to-end along the farm path leading up to the shed where the wagons would be emptied of their burdens one by one. While this went on, James and Obediah, freed by Lieutenant Linton of their duties to the remounts, picketed their horses in the sweet grass by Sugar Creek and waited with the escort beneath a spreading elm; they would wrestle out the bales when the time came. Meanwhile, within the bell tent, Lieutenant Gordon and Captain Hamilton, a harassed-looking individual in a dirty wig, engaged in earnest conversation, of which the men could hear but snatches.

"Greene's moving on the enemy from Camden," Hamilton clearly said. The phrase "with the greatest alacrity" came to them—alacrity, Sergeant Shoupe explained, was speed. The expression "every man'll be needed" was overheard. The phrase "more important than clothing" was spoken.

The upshot of their talk was that Gordon soon emerged grim-faced to address them. "Men," he said, "the Southern Army has commenced offensive operations. General Greene has left his camp of repose on the High Hills of Santee and crossed over at Camden to engage the enemy somewhere about McCord's Ferry. We must hasten to join him. We'll offload the clothing and leave it here for Captain Hamilton, who'll arrange its farther transport. Then we must all ride like hell for Camden, and from there to the army, wherever we may find it. If there's to be a fight, then, by God, we'll be in it."

They all raised a cheer, even James, who had no notion why the speech merited such exuberant praise. A battle did not seem so fine a thing to him. But he'd never seen one and couldn't know; perhaps there were attractive features of it he'd failed to imagine. At any rate it would be fun to move at last *with alacrity*, after so many tedious days among the trundling Conestogas. As much as any of them, James was eager to be on his way and to engage his mind with thoughts other than those of Agnes Baker and her golden ringlets, or of Libby in the arms of Poovey Sides.

Presently the wagons were in place and the Crackers, their labors ended, lounged about with a superior air, smoking their pipes, singing songs, playing their jew's harps, and swapping outrageous tales. But the jolly mood soon dissipated. The first wagon was rolled to the door of the warehouse and its feed trough removed and tailgate unchained and lowered. Gunnell, Robertson, Griffin, and Lockett arrayed themselves in a line to transfer the bales into storage; Sergeant Shoupe and Corporal Hudson stood by to supervise; James, Plumbley, Neal, and Bobby Busby clambered aboard to commence lifting down the baled uniforms. But instantly they bounded out again gasping and gagging. A sickening odor like the foul breath of some cave-dwelling monster issued forth behind them.

"Whew," Bobby Busby exclaimed, "what a stink! Did one of you let a fart?"

"That's no fart," cried James. "It's mould."

"*That's* what we've been a-smelling around them wagons," Plumbley groaned. "Been smelling it for days now."

"Them clothes," Neal declared, "has gone bad from damp."

Lieutenant Gordon, whose duty as Quartermaster for the Third Dragoons was to deliver the uniforms to Colonel Washington in good order, turned deathly pale. "*The Devil you say!*" he blurted, drawing near the lowered tailgate in hopes of disproving the calamity; then when he sniffed the worsening fetor he withdrew again hallooing, "*By God!*" thus in nearly the same instant invoking both the Deity and His opposite; but all to no purpose. Not Heaven nor Hell could change the melancholy fact that nearly the whole shipment of uniforms had fallen victim to summer's humidity.

Captain Hamilton stood by desolate as the stinking bales were dragged out. He looked close to tears. "Mouldering garments," he muttered, "mouldering garments. Fetched all the way from Philadelphia at untold toil, time, and expense. Mouldering garments. Fit but for the worms and weevils." He waved his arms at the men as they struggled to haul out the bales, the mildewed cloth disintegrating into damp lumps of scum that clung to their hands and arms like some unnatural fur. "Pile 'em here, outside the shed," he sighed. "Maybe something can be saved. I see some vests and leather britches there, some boots and socks, that look like they can be salvaged." But then he'd shake his head in woe, repeating in lamentation, "Mouldering garments, mouldering garments."

Shoupe and Hudson spoke earnestly together while the others sweated with the noisome cargo. "If we mean to ride like hell a hundred miles and more," Shoupe observed, "we'll have need of them remounts Linton took off us. Else our own nags'll wear out on the way."

"Linton never said nothing about General Greene a-moving," Hudson pointed out. "D'you suppose he knows?"

Shoupe tipped his head toward Hamilton, who still muttered in trepidation. "This here Captain knows. If he knows, Linton knows."

James had overheard all this and couldn't keep himself from stopping work to tell them sharply, "Linton knows. He just don't *care*. That's a man more interested in getting and keeping than in giving. We'll play hell getting them horses back, if that's what you're thinking."

Hudson shrugged. "It all comes to the same in the end, whether Linton takes 'em down to the army or we use 'em to get there."

"He ain't *going* to the army," James insisted, wiping slimy green film off the sleeves of his hunting shirt. "Me and Plumbley, when we drove the remounts to his pen, we heard him tell his gang they'd take 'em up to Hillsborough, where he's got a great herd gathered. I think he's more in the horse business than he is in the dragoon business."

"Oh, Linton's all right," said Shoupe, making a careless gesture. "He acts like he does 'cause he's vexed at resembling some weaselly creeping creature. Likely he's got orders to hold the nags at Hillsborough and ain't smart enough, now that Greene's a-moving, to see he ought to take 'em to the army instead. He *ain't* the brightest star in the heavens."

Lieutenant Gordon had listened closely to this exchange. Now he turned and ducked into Hamilton's tent and after a few moments came out again carrying a folded paper, which he handed to Shoupe. "Sergeant," he said, "carry this message to Linton. Take Johnson and Plumbley with you. Bring us back those remounts."

The three of them cut across country, through Bassett's land, over the Winnsborough Road and through fields of corn tasseled and ready for the harvest, James leading the way along the route he and Plumbley had followed down to Bassett's after leaving the remounts with Linton, who was camped on the farm of a family of Catheys west of town. They crossed tracts of forest and fresh-cut hayfields set about with shaggy-topped ricks leaning this way and that like loungers whose hair was in need of shearing. They crossed some roads and passed a clapboard church and then a mill that James recalled and presently found themselves trotting up the lane of the Cathey farm on Paw Creek.

Linton was keeping his herd in Cathey's stock pen. There were forty or fifty animals in the pen and James's sixteen were still huddled together in the same corner of the split-rail enclosure where he'd left them, as if they'd grown so familiar on the road from Virginia they now shunned all other company. He and Obediah rode to them; James crooned reassuringly over the top rail while Plumbley hummed a hymn tune for their edification. Shoupe turned off toward the Cathey house and the flock of tents pitched in its yard, and James twisted in his saddle to watch.

He saw Linton step from one of the tents and stand waiting before it with his arms crossed on his chest as if posing for a portrait. The other tents disgorged his hired men—two Negroes, a white, and a red man James had taken on his earlier visit for a Catawba; they loitered in a flagrant way that showed they harbored no bad intent. A Cathey female in a sunbonnet appeared in the door of the house to gape; Cathey himself was by the well giving himself a dipper of water. Shoupe drew rein and saluted; Linton, true to his rat's nature, did not honor it. Shoupe handed down Lieutenant Gordon's message; Linton snatched it away just as he'd grabbed James's orders in front of the courthouse and scanned it with the same scowl. Words passed. The words grew sharp. Then Shoupe saluted, casually wheeled his dun, and came cantering across to the pen. His mien was of calm and satisfaction. "Take 'em out, boys," he smiled.

"Is he coming with us?" James couldn't help but ask.

"That's none of your affair, Johnson," Shoupe shot back. Then he seemed to reconsider and recall it had been James who predicted the remounts would not be easily given up. "No," he admitted after a pause, "he ain't. Says his duty takes him to Hillsborough."

Plumbley's eyes rolled in his head as they did when his religion affected him. "The poor man's nature is gall and wormwood," he intoned. "He'd best repent and mend his ways, lest he be condemned to Hellfire forever."

"*You'd* best mend *your* ways," Shoupe told him, "lest I take ten goddamned lashes out of your backside."

They herded the remounts down the Catheys' lane.

335

There were ten of them, not counting Lieutenant Gordon, each riding his own horse. The reclaimed remounts gave them sixteen fresh animals to use when their own wore out or needed respite. Each man of the Third would lead a remount; James and Obediah would herd the extra six. Any horse lost or lamed on the way would be replaced out of the six—assuming the six lasted, a doubtful proposition at best owing to their sorry state.

They'd planned to leave at earliest dawn, but were delayed by saying their farewells to the genial Crackers, who were inveterate late sleepers and could hardly be roused till the sun had peeked over the eastern treetops. This annoyed the Lieutenant, who was anxious to start. Thus when Plumbley begged permission to sing, with his erstwhile companions of the road, a hymn of parting, and to say some words of benediction, Gordon refused. But Shoupe and Hudson, who'd cherished the fellow-feeling of the trip, prevailed on him to reconsider, and grudgingly he did. So as dawn broke over Bassett's fields the soldiers and the Crackers stood hats in hand while Plumbley and Flint, his fellow Methodist and songster among the wagoners, and one or two others, gave heartfelt voice:

> Thou hidden source of calm repose
> Thou all sufficient love divine,
> My help and refuge from my foes,
> Secure I am if thou art mine;
> And lo! From sin and grief and shame
> I hide me, Jesus, in Thy Name.

Then Plumbley recited from memory some words he said came from the Psalms of King David in the Bible:

He that dwelleth in the secret place of the Most High shall abide under the shadow of the Almighty.
I will say of the Lord, He is my refuge and my fortress: my God; in him will I trust.
Surely he shall deliver thee from the snare of the fowler, and from the noisome pestilence.
He shall cover thee with his feathers, and under his wings thou shalt trust; his truth shall be thy shield and buckler.
Thou shalt not be afraid for the terror by night; nor of the arrow that flieth by day;
Nor for the pestilence that walketh in darkness; nor for the destruction that wasteth at noonday.

A thousand shall fall at thy side, and ten thousand at thy right hand;
but it shall not come nigh thee.
For he shall give his angels charge over thee, to keep thee in thy ways.
They shall bear thee up in their hands, lest thou dash thy foot against
a stone.
Thou shalt tread upon the lion and adder: the young lion and the
dragon shalt thou trample under feet.
Because he hath set his love upon me, therefore will I deliver him: I
will set him on high, because he hath known my name.

At first Lieutenant Gordon was restless and impatient, but as Obediah
talked on he quieted and stood listening and finally, near the end, took off
his helmet and dropped his head. They were all rapt. Even James, who had
been a doubter all his life, found comfort in the flow of words; he thought
he heard in them an echo of the promise Captain Gunn had made to him.
When Plumbley was done there was a space of time when nobody moved
or spoke. They heard the birds of morning singing in the woods around
them, and they felt the new sun brightening over them. They saw the dew
sparkling in the grass. They smelled the lingering smoke of their breakfast
fires and listened to the crowing of Bassett's cock. It was not often, James
reflected, that men knew so long in advance that a battle awaited them,
as he and his friends did now. At such a time it was good to hear the fine
words of wise old King David.

They left Bassett's and turned down the Camden road, the troopers of
the Third in a column of two's, each leading a remount, with Lieutenant
Gordon at their head, James and Obediah following behind with the extra horses. Almost at once, however, a post rider came galloping at them
from the direction of Charlotte, doubled the column and hailed Lieutenant Gordon, who called a halt long enough to accept a pouch and secure
it in his saddlebag, then gave the order to resume. The post rider turned
back toward town, and they started again and soon picked up the pace
to a canter, and as the day warmed they rode on a mile or two, crossed a
timber bridge spanning a little creek, and presently passed over a poor and
wasted country that Obediah said was part of the reservation lands of the
Catawba Indians.

It was a place of weedy fields, sparse wood lots, humble cabins, and
dark coppery people in ragged clothes and colorful turbans who watched
impassively as they passed. James had expected to see blame in the eyes of
these wretched tribesmen whose property and lives the whites had long
ago despoiled, yet their looks were instead as blank and without feeling

as the cold unblinking stare of the lizard. He had heard they'd sided with the Whigs in the struggle against Britain, but the Tories of the region had made them pay for the choice. Perhaps theirs was the look of folk who'd given up every wish and every illusion and now knew nothing but that the world was without a trace of pity.

James knew the evil of the world too; but he could never think of giving up all hope. He could not meet those looks and was glad when they put the Catawba lands behind them and Plumbley announced they had entered the Province of South Carolina. Heretofore he had dreaded what he'd imagined would be the suffocating embrace of that alien tropical clime. Contrary to his expectations the state itself seemed barely distinguishable from its Northern neighbor, or indeed from Virginia, unless one noticed the sandiness of the soil in place of the loam and clay found Northward, and the plenitude of pine trees.

After a short noon rest they took the road again and this time alternated between a walk, a trot, and short stages of galloping, both to save the horses and make the best possible time. The weather was hot, but the animals held up well and the road was firm, and by evening they had covered over twenty-five miles of hilly tracts and forded two small creeks and the road had carried them down along the banks of a great turbulent river—the Catawba, Plumbley identified it. Not far downstream, this same river became the Wateree, Obediah said; and Camden lay on the Wateree.

They stopped at dusk and struck their supper fire to eat the salt pork and rice Lieutenant Gordon had drawn from the commissary warehouse in Salisbury. James thought he detected a certain uneasiness among the men and was curious enough to ask about it after the remounts were penned up for the night and the men's blankets spread for slumber.

Sergeant Shoupe answered his question with another. "You know where you're at, Johnson?"

"Where's that?" James obliged him.

"This here's the Waxhaws."

Gunnell felt a need to elaborate. "This here's the very ground where Bloody Tarleton hacked up Buford's boys a year ago last spring."

James glanced about at the low, forlorn-looking hills with their sparse growth of pines and felt the prickling rise of the hairs on the nape of his neck and the backs of his wrists. Nothing about the spot suggested its terrible past, but he had never forgotten the account the one-eyed sergeant gave him of what had happened here. In his darkened fancy the green-coated dragoons high on their horses lashed about with their swords while the men on the ground pled for mercy, not realizing even then, even as their limbs were severed from their bodies, what the Catwaba Indians must have long known, that the world did not offer mercy to such as they. That story—that vision—was one reason he'd joined the dragoons—to get himself up off the ground where mercy was lacking and into a saddle where he, and not the enemy, could forget the quality of mercy if he must and do the hacking of poor wretches afoot.

A breeze stirred the pines as the last of the daylight faded. "They say of a night, fellows comes out of them trees with their heads and arms lopped off," Bobby Busby told them, "a-looking for the parts they've lost."

"I never seen that," Lockett sneered, "and I've camped hereabouts more'n once."

Plumbley's eyes swelled and rolled. "Brothers, we should pray for the repose of their poor lost souls, and bid 'em rest."

"You did some grand praying this morning, Reverend," said Shoupe with a placating smile. "We all liked it a good deal. But you ought not to try us too hard. Them of us that wants, we'll pray each to ourselves, in quiet, like the Quakers do. But there's such a thing as a surfeit of praying out loud, in a dragoon troop."

Twenty feet away, propped on an elbow by the fire Bobby Busby had kindled for him and sorting through the papers from the mail pouch, Lieutenant Gordon, overhearing them, glanced up. "Praying," he declared in his lazy way, "along with preaching, is now an utterly prohibited activity, the Minister's effort of the morning having been so profound and all-encompassing, and having stirred us all with such newfound piety, as to render any farther exhortation not merely superfluous but possibly even a positive danger, lest the Almighty grow weary of our appeals too oft repeated, and recoil from us." He raised a cautionary finger. "Or," he added, "lest our continuing appeals first arouse His boredom, then His irritation, and finally His Divine wrath, so often kindled and unleashed upon an errant mankind in days of old, and He smite us for our importunity with famine, plague, and every kind of grievous misfortune."

Evidently the Lieutenant had been sampling his canteen of rum. Since no one understood anything of this speech—no one, that is, but Plumbley, who sank back sadly to contemplate the stopping-up of his fount of redemptive speech—they covered themselves with their blankets and listened to the rushing of the Catawba and tried not to think of the maimed phantoms of Buford's detachment wandering about in vain quest for their parted members, and sooner than they might have expected, they slept.

Presently, though, a nudge awakened James and he was startled to see Lieutenant Gordon bending over him in the waning firelight. "Letter for you, Johnson," he said, pressing into James's hand a small square of paper. "Damned if I know how it found you." Before James could thank him the

Lieutenant had gone as silently as he had come. James turned the sealed paper to the light and read his name in a handwriting he did not know. Eagerly he sat up, tore the seal and leaned to the firelight to read:

Dear Bro. James,
Someone is writing this for me, ſo it will be better ſpelt and reaſoned than if I was to write it myſelf. I have not yet had a writing from you but am ſure you are Safe as the Captain ſaid you muſt be and am never worried for you. We have been moved from Mannakin Towne to a place called Ruffins Ferry on the Forks of the Pammunky River where we are fattening the horſes. Poovey is well and Learning all he can of the Dragoon Trade tho I do fear he is not cut out for it as much as you are. I miſs your ſtories of Ma and Da and wiſh you would write me One or Two to raiſe up my ſpirits. I am yet waſhing clothes. We eat all right moſt of the time. Do you. I hope ſo. They tell us the fare is Mighty Poor down there. That is all for now. Poovey ſends Hello, the others too. Remember to ſend me a writing and a Tale. Yr. Siſter, Libby.

It troubled him deeply that she hadn't yet received his letter mentioning Agnes. Somehow it seemed wrong for her not to know of his happiness. All their lives till now, whatever happened that was important had happened to the both of them at once. Now something had happened to him but not to her. Surely by now she must have gotten the news. Surely this night, as he lay here by the dying fire, she knew. But it was also possible his own letter had gone astray and she didn't know.

He had a woeful sense that things were badly out of balance. He felt there was a flaw in the world that he wanted to remedy but couldn't. Misery overcame him and presently he wept. It wasn't only for Libby he wept. He wept for himself too, because he missed Agnes. After a time, though, he ceased weeping and promised himself he'd go to Lieutenant Gordon tomorrow to beg some scraps of paper, and in the evening when next they camped, he'd write to Libby, and to Agnes too. He hoped that would help to heal the flaw in the world that was bothering him.

In the morning Private Neal reported his horse sick. It was a fat old gelding of the color called peach-blossom, white with sorrel and bay hairs intermixed, and the whole way down from Manakin Town James had been waiting for it to fail; already it had lasted far longer than he'd expected. The minute he saw its bloated belly and heard its groans he knew the poor animal had taken a case of the molten grease—bad humors in the guts—and was as good as gone. He led it down into a ravine and shot it in the forehead. Neal took one of the remounts; fifteen now remained. Every other man exchanged his own horse for a remount for that day's journey, so the beasts ridden yesterday could have some ease. James reluctantly gave up Jesus and saddled the little dun mare he'd chased down in the thunderstorm after they'd left Cumberland Old Court House.

They made as much haste as they could along a rough and crooked road by the river, till the morning sky curdled up with ugly gray and purple clouds and thunder began to rumble and by early afternoon a heavy rain came slanting at them. Drenched, they made a midday halt in a grove of oaks and waited an hour or more till the storm abated, nibbling whatever fare each man carried in his haversack. With the returning sun came a damp and oppressive heat, and resuming they were relieved when the road took them down through a shadowy gorge with steep rocky sides that towered over them and narrowed the bed of the Catawba, making of it a heavy, tumbling cataract whose white water streamed frothing around masses of big black boulders. The coolness of that gorge refreshed them.

Below this, the river calmed into a pool; and farther along they passed a ferry and then the river broadened and quickened again and soon they entered a rugged rock-strewn landscape with dark forbidding woods hanging on stony heights to either side. Eventually the road turned away from the river and onto open brushlands that exposed them again to the punishing sun. They rode gasping in its glare. That evening they camped in a forest glade dominated by a weird, towering, mushroom-shaped pillar of stone that looked as if men in ancient times might have chipped it into that improbable shape, though it was hard to imagine there had ever been men enough, or tools enough, to fashion such a colossal thing.

When the horses were settled James got two pieces of paper from Lieutenant Gordon and sat by the fire composing his letters and scratching them out against the back of one of his saddlebags. This was the first:

Deer Libbie,
i hav got a writin from yu & hav wrote 2 to yu wich i ſpoſe you aint got yet. i hope yu do Drectly. in my laſt i tolt yu of Agnes Baker. well yu will want to nowe that we are now as good as Beſpoke. We had to part in Saulſbury but i hav got as good as a promis from Her. how about that. i hope yu are well. Tell Poovey he muſt do Better. All we are adoin is ridin to get to Genl Greens Army. i am well. Yr Bro. James.

The second letter, to Agnes, was harder to write. He felt strange; he reckoned he was in love with her and yet he hardly knew anything about her. He found it a challenge to write to someone who was both dear and a mystery.

Deer Mis Baker,

i hope this finds yu Well. i hope Ninyan is Well & yur Bro. too. i am in ſouthCalina now. i am athinkin of yu a rite ſmart & hope yu think of Me now & Agin. i feel Tender when i think of yu. i miſs yur yella curls & yur Blew eyes & yur Piſtol & yur Nife. rite me if yu care & make hit out to Pvt Jas. Johnſon firſt Regt Light dragoons, ſouthrn army. i am ahopin nobody better than Me has come along yit. Yr Friend, James Johnſon.

Camden, Lieutenant Gordon told them, now lay thirty-five or forty miles distant. On this the third day since leaving Charlotte they found the going considerably harder, for a great deal of military traffic had come this way in the last year, and many horses and much artillery and many trains of wagons had slashed the road with ruts that the weather had since scoured out till they were as deep and dangerous as so many gullies. In one of these ruts George Robertson's dapple bay broke its right foreleg and had to be destroyed, and as James put his pistol to the poor brute's head he realized

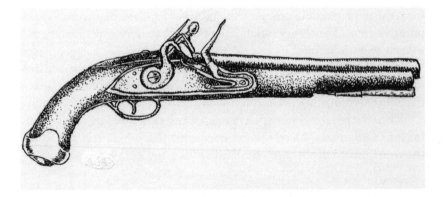

it was the sixth horse he'd had to kill since leaving Manakin Town. It didn't help that he'd known from the first that the trip would have to be a slaughter. He couldn't stop thinking what poor nags these were, or why if there had to be a war the great men who were running it couldn't manage it any better. Why establish a dragoon service only to furnish it with the worst of mounts? It didn't seem right that those in high places would commence an enterprise in which thousands of men and beasts must die, without thinking how to run it rightly.

Robertson threw his saddle on a remount and they rode on. They passed through a dreary stretch of forest and around patches of briary undergrowth and then over an expanse of undulant plain covered with dozens of boulders, and then came upon a massive slab of level stone, five hundred yards across at least, pocked and pitted with water-filled depressions that Corporal Hudson believed were once used as cisterns by the savages of the olden time. This was the famous Flat Rock, he said; but James declared it surely wasn't famous to him—he was beginning not to like the wild, stark, brooding look of his surroundings.

By dusk the road veered back toward the river again, and they saw its glint below them through a tangled undergrowth. They broke out of a belt of chestnut woods on high ground above it and looked down on its sinuous length wrinkled and gleaming in the late sun. There was a long slender island in the middle of it that resembled a great snake cooling itself in the waters, save this snake wore a thick coat of timber; closer examination revealed treetops half-drowned on all sides of the island and the bottomland covered with pools of standing water that gleamed a burnished copper color in the last of the light. The river had recently been in flood and was receding; the sulphur odor of miles of hot stagnant wetness hung heavy in the air. All across the broad valley groups of sandhills speckled with pines raised their heads above the drowned lands and little squares of farm plots were beginning to reappear as the creeks and swamps that had claimed them slowly crept back into their banks. It was a doleful scene, and gazing on it James thought of Agnes Baker and of Libby and felt ever more imperiled and lost and alone.

That night they camped with the wilderness at their backs and the river and its sodden valley below them. The darkness, when it fell, was impenetrable, and the wastes roundabout rang with strange yodeling cries and whoops and howls that made James tremble with misgiving. "Them's only wolves," Obediah reassured him. "Just some of God's beloved creatures." *Only wolves*, James thought bitterly. *Can God love a wolf?* Were there wolves left in Virginia? He doubted it. Stumbling with fatigue, he lit a pine-knot torch and went to examine the horses and found that the remount with the blood-spavin had gone lame during the day; he judged it useless and shot it. The one with the tettar ulcers was now so ravaged the poor creature spent all its time biting at its sores and rubbing itself against tree-trunks to ease the unbearable itching, and James took his other pistol and shot it too. They were the seventh and eighth he had killed. He had begun to feel like a butcher.

They rose before dawn determined to reach Camden before dark. The eight troopers of the Third each led a remount; this left but four of the original twenty for James and Plumbley to drive. The men were all saddlesore and weak from hunger; the horses were road-weary and suffered from strains of the sinews and from bruises of the fetlocks and pasterns gotten from knocking against rocks in the treacherous roads, and from various af-flictions of the hooves caused by cast or worn-down shoes and corrupted soles. But they pushed themselves and the poor beasts on, down the rut-ted and stony path off the tableland in the blazing heat, through sloughs of mud and masses of gum shrubs and cane and across the turbid pools and through a sluggish creek, over a pine-covered hill and down its farther slope to another swampy stream, then on amid more and more groves of pines and dense thickets of hawthorns and bogs of mire.

They were crossing the field of General Gates's catastrophic defeat of a year ago, but to all save James this was familiar ground and they paid little heed. And James himself was so tired and so hungry and so anxious for the relief he imagined he would find in Camden that even he gave small notice to the detritus of battle that lay strewn about; nor did he even much remark the disarticulated skeletons of horses, nor even the acres and acres of graves, dug up by wolves and wild dogs or washed out by the floods, from which human bones protruded like some grisly crop ready for harvest.

James had expected Camden to be a town much like Charlotte or Salis-bury. Instead he was shocked to find it mostly a charred ruin. The British, he learned, had razed a lot of it to the ground when they abandoned it in the spring. In spite of not being a whole town, though, it was as busy as a bee-log. But the people teeming about weren't so much living in the few remaining houses as they were dug into muddy holes in the ground like rabbits in their warrens, or crowded into sheds or shacks made of partly scorched lumber scavenged from burnt buildings. There were several large tents standing about, but after Lieutenant Gordon made some inquiries it was learned they were not meant for folk to reside in but rather comprised General Greene's hospital, which he'd set up to care for the smallpox victims who'd fallen sick on his march up from the High Hills of Santee.

James and the others kept clear of that hospital. Its smell alone was enough to hold a person at a good distance. Besides, James had never for-gotten the sight of all those poxed Negroes lying along the road to Rich-mond. He'd probably never get infected himself—the one useful thing Chenowith had done for him was get him inoculated—but that didn't mean he wanted to go peeking in on the poor wretches in the hospital and suffer their fluttery hands and whispery pleas, as he'd had to do with those dying blacks. Besides, he wasn't entirely convinced that having a doctor slash your arm and drag a dirty string through the cut and then lying half-sick with a fever for some days was remedy enough to keep a fellow from taking as terrible a thing as the pox. So instead of going to the hospital he roamed around Camden till he decided his most earnest wish was to leave it pretty quick.

A company of Continentals from various states, most of them invalids or smallpox convalescents or men still without arms, held the place, but by their looks might have been mistaken for a gang of loitering mudsills. Most of the women of the army had been left back too, and these all gave an appearance not of want alone but also of slovenliness and depravity, while their brats ranged abroad as wild as deer.

Life in Virginia had been crude enough, and James had surely housed his own person in many a brushwood hut and gone for long in need, but looking about him now he understood that in coming into South Carolina he had cast himself entirely out of a recognizable and familiar world, among a people so foreign and in a clime so grim and unforgiving that he might never again feel at his ease, no matter what Captain Gunn had promised him.

And he understood another, worse thing too, gazing askance at the swarming tatterdemalions and remembering the sorry state Lieutenant Linton had been in; he knew that what he saw was an inexcusable poverty—inexcusable because the men who had commenced this war had, by their neglect, permitted the armies that must fight it for them to sink so low as to go about like beggars. When he grasped this, he grew as angry as he was afraid.

There were, of course, no horses to be had in Camden, though Lieutenant Gordon was able to procure some few provisions. None of them wished to pass a night in the town, so as dusk fell they took the ferry over the Wateree and camped on the far bank. Even there, with the river between them, they could still smell the stench of Camden.

They made an early start next day, feeling little rested though the horses seemed to have benefited from grazing on the new grass sprouting everywhere in the wake of the flood. "General Greene crossed from Camden nine or ten days ago," Lieutenant Gordon told them as they started. "Not long after, some North Carolina regulars came over, and a set of Georgia volunteers on horseback. If the nags hold out, we ought to make up the distance between us and the main army in about three or four more days, and perhaps overtake the regulars and the Georgians even before then. Let's hope like the devil Greene doesn't fight his battle till we can get to him."

The trail of the army was easy enough to see—a swath of torn-up ground and crushed undergrowth and manure trodden into the damp earth and patches of corduroying and the stumps of the trees felled for the corduroying, all of it a hundred yards wide, turning west and southerly from the ferry. But after following this track awhile, Lieutenant Gordon and Sergeant Shoupe fell to conferring, then Shoupe called them together to say it looked like Greene had gone the long way around to skirt the flood, but now that the waters had fallen the ground was solid; so instead of going on as the General had, they would take the straighter road down the Wateree to McCord's, and so save time—McCord's, James came to understand, was a ferry over the next river west. Accordingly they turned more southerly along the river.

At first they kept together in their column with James and Obediah at the back herding along the four remounts, but by mid-morning the stronger horses had drawn ahead, the weaker ones had fallen back, and they were strung out over a distance of nearly a quarter of a mile. About noon-time James and Plumbley, still bringing up the rear, overtook Benjamin Lockett standing over his foundered horse. They drew rein and sat their saddles. "You'd best shoot it," James advised him.

Lockett raised his head and glowered at James from under his heavy ape's brow. "Tried it," he growled. "My powder's wet." Some of his old malice crept back into his face. "You're the horse-shooter of the outfit anyway, ain't you?"

"It appears so," James agreed. The task had grown old by now, and he could look down on the heaving flanks of the pyebal'd and hear the rumbling noise of its efforts to breathe and feel not so much a sadness but another surge of the wrath that kept rising to his throat stinging like vomit not quite thrown up. "Strip off the saddle," he told Lockett, and Lockett complied, having to wrestle with the horse a bit to get it loose. When he was done, James drew a pistol from its holster and cocked it and leaned from the saddle and shot the horse while Lockett looked on dully. Seating the pistol in its holster, he turned to Lockett and lingered a look on the big man with the high hunched shoulders and forward-hung head, this ruffian who would once have killed him. Lockett would never show it, but James could see he hadn't shot the horse because he hadn't been able to. James softened. "Where's your led horse?"

"It run off." James knew the animal, a worthless old dray puller—no great loss.

"Take mine," he said, lifting a leg over the cantle of Jesus' saddle.

But Lockett wagged his head. "No," he murmured, "I'll not have the favor of a man I count an enemy. Give me one of them others." Not looking up, he knelt to unfasten his bridle from the dead pyebal'd.

James settled back into his seat. He was neither offended nor surprised. Lockett would never warm to him—too much that was bad had parted them; but Lockett would never be a danger either. Hereafter they would observe a certain coolness and distance; but, as soldiers, each would always know the other could be counted on when the times called for that. In this one way, soldiering was a higher thing than just being mortal; so James was satisfied. He spoke to Jesus and rode on; and Lockett set about choosing another horse from Obediah.

Then Jesus dropped his head; his forequarters sagged; he went almost gently to his knees, tottered there, then his haunches sank too and all of him settled to the road, his four legs tucked underneath. For a long moment he seemed to wait, kneeling there, and with a pang James knew somehow that he was waiting for his master to step off, that he wanted to roll but could not without crushing James's leg and so was waiting for James to realize this; and James stood in his right stirrup and stepped off into the road, and Jesus rolled slowly over on his left side and was dead, never having made a sound from first to last. James gazed down on him. *His heart just gave out*, he thought. He wondered why he hadn't felt it coming. Then he knew it was because he was so tired.

Lockett rode past glancing down. "Good thing I didn't take him," he remarked. But he said it flatly and without a hint of gloating, and went on, leading another remount.

Plumbley came up with the horses. "It was a great provocation unto Heaven," he said with an air of sad reproach, "to give the poor innocent creature the Saviour's name."

"You reckon it was *God* killed this horse?" James demanded hotly. "Killed it on account of its *name*? I know a great many reasons this horse is dead, Plumbley, and God ain't one of 'em. I ain't even sure there *is* such a thing as God. But I'll tell you this: If there is, and if He's as you represent Him, full of forgiveness and mercy and loving-kindness and every good thing, then He can't have nothing to do with this poor horse a-dying, or with killing it for having the name it had, nor with the woes of all them poor folk back in Camden, nor with armies nor with wars nor with any of what's wrong in this miserable damned world." Angrily he bent and with savage motions got to work unfastening his saddle and bridle, having to stop now and then to dash away tears with the backs of his hands.

They were not alone in going down to General Greene's army. In fact the traffic was quite brisk. They overtook a mule-drawn wagon full of Virginia Continentals who'd left the Camden hospital in hopes of getting into the coming fight; one of them, a lad named Clark, for some reason wished them to know he'd been shot through the guts at the battle of Guilford, the ball passing entirely through to lodge in one of his buttocks, whence it had to be cut out. He was eagerly pulling down his britches and commencing to unwind his bandage to show them this symbol of his valor when they thought it best to press on. Farther down they passed a chaise full of enthusiastic whores. Soldiers—some regulars, some militia, some armed, some not—trudged on foot, a few in orderly columns, most strung out like gaggles of geese. Couriers galloped past spewing mud behind. Truculent country people plodded along on farm errands, or rode in steer carts or sledges, giving hard looks this way and that, hating the war and all that came of it.

Dispatch riders from the army frequently came up the other way, and when he could, Lieutenant Gordon stopped them to learn the latest. Greene had left McCord's. Greene had camped at Stoutemire's Plantation. The enemy had moved down to the Eutaws. Greene was at Medway Swamp. None of these place names meant anything to James, save that the Eutaws were said to be forty miles below McCord's and he did not see how the worsening horses could carry them that far. By now his mind was befogged with fatigue; images blurred one into another—dead horses on the roadside, swollen and fly-blown, their legs stiff in the air; giant cypresses trailing gray skeins of moss like the untrimmed hair of ancient crones; a broken-down wagon heeled over in a ditch; sunlight dazzling the surface of the river; a soldier squatting to relieve himself behind a patch of holly; the many bristly hues of green on a gall bush; a dead man sitting against a tree as peacefully as if asleep if not for the pair of crows pecking at his eyes; dark groves of water-oak and gum and hickory. He could not have named the things he saw, did not even see them clearly. He sagged in his saddle; his mouth hung slack; his eyes stung and watered.

The dun mare went fatally lame and he shot it. He shot a foundered bay horse. He shot a roan, but later couldn't remember what complaint it had. They camped, but he did not know how many times or where or what they said to each other. They ate the last of their food; they begged farmers for bread and ears of corn. Their bowels began to trouble them and soon they all had the flux. They weakened. Plumbley prayed aloud; nobody stopped him. James tried to remember the fair face of Agnes Baker, but only recalled her yellow locks, nothing else. He tried to think of Libby, but her features would not come, the countenance he'd held dear all his days; nor Poovey's, nor Captain Gunn's, nor even Chenowith's. He huddled behind a laurel bush straining to void a bloody stool. He shot a spotted horse. He shot Lieutenant Gordon's chestnut because it started spouting gouts of gore and mucous from its nose; it had picked up glanders at Camden. After the glanders hit them he didn't have to shoot any more horses. They started dying on their own and James was sorrowfully, wearily glad. They died and died and died, and when the winking campfires of General Greene's camp at Burdell's Plantation finally swam into view out of the dark—four days and three nights after they'd left Camden, James later learned—half the men were riding double, and two more of the beasts dropped dead the moment they dismounted.

Part ye Twenty-Sixth

In Which Is Had a Moſt Obſtinate and Bloody Action*

A WANING GIBBOUS MOON HUNG AT ITS ZENITH in a clear night sky as the army began to move. It shed a pale and tainted light over the fields around Burdell's and Campton's, over the masses of woodland crowding in on all sides, over the road and the moving columns and the muskets that the men in the columns were carrying and even over the dust they raised, making of that dust a veil of dim gossamer. But it did not give light enough for the General to read his watch as he sat the bay gelding Sterne by the roadside pressing a handkerchief to his face lest the dust of the marching aggravate his asthma.

Captain Pendleton was obliged to flash the lock of an unloaded pistol allowing Greene to glimpse the face of his timepiece. The hands showed ten minutes past four o'clock; he snapped it quickly shut, not seeing—not allowing himself to see—Caty's miniature. "For once," he remarked, "we have moved at the appointed hour." He was pleased but tense and the men gathered around him knew this and held respectfully quiet.

"The troops are eager, sir," Pendleton answered. He knew better than to say more; even so little might have been a presumption. Captain Shubrick, Captain Pierce, Major Hyrne, Colonel Kosciuszko, and Major Forsyth would never have said as much. They had not Pendleton's intimacy with the General. Furthermore, Greene knew, they were feeling the somber weight of their own responsibility; in the coming battle they must act as his messengers to and from the commanders on the field, and any single misheard order from Greene or miscommunicated appeal from the front could bring calamity. This was a duty oft performed but never comfortable. All were practiced at it, but none took for granted that he would do or say what was right, when it was right, while the musket-balls were whistling.

The van under Colonel Lee and Colonel Henderson had just passed eastward beyond sight, the infantry of the Legion and of Myddelton and

---

* Nathanael Greene to Governor John Rutledge of South Carolina, September 9, 1781

Polk leading to take down fences and clear the road, the horsemen following two hundred yards behind, advance guard out front, flankers to either
side, the darkness under the moon-tinted forest tops swallowing them all
with a suddenness that had seemed vaguely alarming.

It was a formidable advance—well over four hundred horse, half as
many foot. Still, the General had peered anxiously after them. He had
not liked the way the blackness so swiftly engulfed them; he strove with
himself to resist the onset of a blind and ignorant superstition. In him the
prospect of battle always seemed to stir premonitions belonging not to the
rational being he flattered himself he was, but to some primitive creature
cringing deep within who apprehended sinister omens in the commonplace. The tenseness his aides saw in him came in part from this striving.

Fending off his portents, he set his regard on the men before him—four
columns of South Carolina militia, the two nearest composing General
Pickens' troops, the farther two, Marion's, five hundred men altogether.
Like most back-country militia, these fellows spurned walking as the low
habit of insignificant persons, save of course when walking into battle, and
so had ridden to Burdell's, leaving their horses there under guard.

Behind them came Colonel Malmedy's North Carolinians, a hundred
eighty more militia in two columns. Whatever their prejudices might
originally have been in regard to walking, Colonel Malmedy had given
them no choice but to walk all the way from Salisbury—some from as far
as Hillsborough—and they were walking yet, and doing it with the same
cool confidence and fine humor that had aroused the General's liking on
the march to Medway Swamp.

All these were General Marion's command, and according to Greene's
plan of battle would display as the army's first line. "Ordinarily," he said to
Pendleton, "I'd be loath to assign militia to the front again. But perhaps
I've been less than fair to their class. General Morgan constantly urges me
to set them to the front. But then he always tells me to put riflemen to their
rear too, to shoot them down when they run. I've not done *that*, at least." It
was his nervousness talking; Pendleton was wise enough to offer nothing
in response.

Greene was still in hopes of catching Stewart unawares. Accordingly
orders had been passed for the advance to be conducted in silence. No fifes
played, no drums tapped. But as the North Carolina ranks passed him he
saw the white wafers of their faces turn to him; the militiamen recognized
him there by the road, even in the wan moonlight. A few smiled, two or
three spoke his name. He recalled how, on Thursday, his own smile had
bewildered some of them and was cheered to think that in the time since
they might have come to believe in him a little. In another moment he felt
their entire goodwill sweep over him like a warm breath, and one by one he

saw men start to raise their hats and caps to him and hold them aloft, and some others put their headgear on the muzzles of their muskets and twirl them high, but all in silence, nothing to be heard but the tramp of feet and the rattle of equipment. Much moved, he answered the wordless tribute with a doff of his cocked hat.

They passed on, and there was a break in the columns and the crest of feeling he had ridden soon subsided. He turned again in his saddle to gaze at the dark eastern woods that had closed around his vanguard. Presently it would engorge his militia as well. The portents returned like swarms of devil's imps. *Why?* he asked himself. If he had some reason to doubt the steadiness of Colonel Lee, and had no knowledge of Gresham's tiny troop of Georgians, there could be little question about the quality of Lee's subordinate commanders, or of the others; Hampton, Myddelton, and Polk had all proven themselves in many an action, and now Colonel Maham, General Marion's fierce cavalry commander, was in the mix as well, with his forty-man militia troop.

Their task was simple enough—to feel their way quietly to the enemy and be the first to brush against him. But it was also a delicate duty. They must brush him heavily enough to learn his dispositions and count his numbers, but not so heavily as to collide with his main body and entangle themselves in a meeting engagement that would bring on the full-scale battle before Greene was ready for it. They must whisk along his front feather-like, entice him out, make him display himself, then withdraw, continue to flick and snap and tantalize him, and send Greene word of any development that might call for last-minute changes in the American order of battle. There was little reason for worry. Such was their stock in trade, none more expert than Colonel Lee. But worry he did.

He motioned to Shubrick with his handkerchief. "Captain, have the provision wagon brought forward. I want the army halted at three miles and a gill of rum distributed to every man." Shubrick saluted and galloped westward, doubling the columns of the approaching Continentals. However the vanguard fared, the General wanted the main army refreshed. Over the past days he had given them every indulgence. The militia were mostly robust, but his Continentals—if now as strong and rested and whole as he could make them—remained malnourished and worn down from heat and sickness, and more than a few were British deserters whose loyalties were bound to be divided and suspect. The traditional dash of spirits would be his last incentive. After that, everything would be up to them. Yet when he considered them, fragility was what came to mind instead of strength; he feared they were not so much men as the husks of men, contriving to move by will alone.

They came on now, his Continentals, General Sumner riding at their head. Sumner offered no jack-o-lantern grin this morning; his great slit of mouth was clamped tight and protuberant, froglike. Solemnly he lifted his hat, Greene doffed his. Next came Colonels Williams and Campbell and their staffs leading a heavy column composed of two battalions of Marylanders, two of Virginians, and the three of the North Carolina brigade, eight hundred fifty muskets all told. These would display as his second line, Sumner commanding the whole.

Darkness still ruled; the three-quarter moon gave down the merest glow, but even in its faintness these troops knew him too and raised their voiceless cheer as the militiamen had, lifting their hats or hoisting them on musket-ends, and one of the Maryland boys leaned out of ranks to speak a hoarse sentiment to him, "Don't you fret, Your Honor, we'll give them sons of bitches a right basting." Another in the next rank spoke too, and another and then another, and soon a chorus of rasping confidences was being offered him. He heard but snatches: "make you proud today, sir"; "blow their goddamned arses back to England"; "pay 'em back for Hobkirk's"; "give 'em Buford's play."

He sat tongue-tied. He knew their condition; their bravado in the face of desperate want and weariness touched him. But it was one thing to exchange unspoken salutations—that suited his modest nature. It was easy to lift his hat and smile and bask in good regard. But to banter with the men was wholly out of his power. Not only had he, by necessity, newly garbed himself in the inexpressive armor of command, he had no natural talent for easy intimacy with the troops. Besides, though his heart was hardened for battle he still could not escape his accursed brain, which wanted to remind him that any man he addressed might well be dead by nightfall, so whatever he said should be wise and comforting, worthy of going into the next world with that man's departing soul.

Yet he must do something, however much he dreaded it. He wheeled Sterne and trotted along the column, baring his head, extending his hat toward the rows of expectant faces, his handkerchief fluttering from it like a crumpled and soiled parody of a plume. "Remember why we're here, my men," he told them in stilted fashion. "Remember we fight for freedom and honor, family and victory."

It was as much as he could think to say. Hardly a sentiment anyone would wish to take heavenward. Nods, half-smiles, and some derisive smirks rewarded him. But if he had not inspired them, he had at least made the effort and he knew generals in the army who would not have done as much, the Commander-in-Chief among them. He drew rein, turned, rode back blushing to his place.

The rear ranks went by even as the head of their column disappeared into the black woods to the east, and he peered after them as anxiously as he had the vanguard and the militia; their dust settled over him and again he covered his face with the handkerchief, coughing mildly into it as the same grim auguries came to flick at him. There was a bit more light over the woods now, not moonlight only but the first wan glimmer of dawn; he could see the bristling shapes of the treetops. But the blackness underneath was unrelieved; into its maw marched the last of his Continentals.

The guns came next with a rumble of wheels—Captain Gaines, his dispatches delivered, had joined now—and finally the reserve under Colonel Washington. These would trail the army, keep to the woods, and when battle was joined would display to form a cordon in its rear to help reform the retiring militia, detain stragglers and shirkers, see to the walking wounded, and guard against envelopment by the British. If opportunity offered, they would of course charge a shaken or broken enemy.

Washington raised and lowered his saber in salute; his eighty dragoons, wizened fellows on lank horses, went slouching past in a way that looked negligent but was instead, Greene knew, the loose, casual, yielding air of a seasoned boldness. Faces sharp-featured like those of foxes turned incuriously his way. Captain Hamilton's little troop of North Carolina volunteers passed, then Kirkwood's Delawares, loping stealthy as Indians on the warpath. Again he lifted his hat.

The gloomy eastern woods took these as they had taken the others, and again he felt the same foreboding; again he thrust it off. "Come, gentlemen," he said, and reined Sterne about and started up the road toward the blackness into which the whole of his army had now vanished. Now he too must enter it, must confront what lurked there. The staff and his little escort of dragoons came clattering behind. When he consulted his watch he found that he could read it without aid; dawn had begun to break. It was thirty-seven minutes past five o'clock.

James, numb from sleeplessness and weak from the flux, riding a strange horse, no familiar face about him save Plumbley's, and that two ranks behind him in the same file, sensed a stir in the troop, saw others look leftward, and by a great effort managed to lift his nodding head and direct his attention that way also; he wasn't too sick to be curious. There by the roadside a small party of officers sat their horses in the twilight watching back. One, the foremost, a well-set-up fellow, kept tipping his hat.

James wanted to ask somebody if that was General Greene but did not. Up to now, few of his questions had been answered by anything other than oaths and curses because he was an unknown and they were all old messmates heading into a fight and had no time to cosset a greenhead. But the hat-tipping looked to James like a thing a general would do, especially a polite one as he'd heard General Greene unfailingly was. The officer had tipped it once to acknowledge Colonel Washington's salute, but now was tipping it when nobody expected him to. This might be a Quaker custom in addition to being a sign of good manners. Whatever it was, James found it reassuring and rode on satisfied he'd seen the famous commander of the Southern Army, by a stroke of luck, here on the morning of his very first engagement, which might also be his last.

Knowing he might soon die tempered his satisfaction. He supposed it was better to die having seen General Greene than to die not having seen him; but the fact was, he'd rather not die at all, regardless of whether he saw the General or didn't see him. James couldn't think of anybody he'd be willing to die to see, except of course for Agnes and Libby. He reminded himself that Captain Gunn had promised him he wouldn't die in any case, but then he thought of all the disagreeable and frightening things he had seen since coming into South Carolina and was no longer certain he could rely on the Captain's pledge. Gunn had cut a mighty figure in Virginia, but at this very moment of a fading moon, a menacing black wood looming ahead, a battle in the offing yonder like a storm about to break, a bony horse under him with an awkward gait that jarred his bones, his bowels as squirmy as a bag of eels, fear bathing him in an icy sweat even as he drowsed bobbing and reeling on the very verge of slumber, James could hardly conjure Gunn at all, much less repose his trust in such a wraith.

He hardly knew his own circumstances, had not known them clearly since last night when he and the others rode groggy and half-blind with fatigue into the quarter-guard to be challenged, dragged off their horses and held at musket-point till Lieutenant Gordon could produce his commission and explain their presence. No sooner had they been admitted through the lines than, after a word from Gordon, one of the quarter-guards hustled James and Obediah off to the camp of the First Dragoons without the least opportunity to bid good-bye to Shoupe, Hudson, and the others, men whom James had come to regard as friends and now would sorely miss. He would have felt worse about the rudeness of the parting were he not so feeble and near to fainting, and had he not been compelled so often to creep into the weeds to void himself.

He held a muddled recollection of being thrust before Captain Watts. For more than twenty-two days he'd carried in his bosom a set of orders signed by Colonel White and addressed to this same officer, and had toiled so hard to deliver him his twenty remounts, that in consequence he felt they were somehow already acquainted, or should be. Of course they weren't. The Captain was a slender, good-looking young man, at first mild if not congenial in manner, dressed in a hunting shirt and overalls, and in need of a shave. But James's news kindled his wrath. *No remounts?* he burst out, aghast. *Not a one?* James spoke of glanders, of molten grease, and the strangles and chest-foundering. *You're a hell of a goddamned horsemaster, ain't you?* blared the Captain, leaning into his face. But James was too swoonish even to be frightened; under the flood of profanity he stood tottering, thick-tongued, heavy-lidded, half-asleep.

Luckily Lieutenant Gordon dropped by just then to intercede, and Watts relented. In the end, the full story told, he even thanked James for his efforts. *That Linton,* he laughed, *I think he keeps the nags just to fuck 'em, since no wench'll have him.* He clapped James's back. *Get some sleep, son. There'll be a hell of a tussle in the morning; that'll be your welcome to Watts's Troop, First Dragoons.* The words meant nothing just then. James heard them as if in a dream. He dropped supine by a fire among men he did not know; as sleep was taking him he heard Obediah renewing acquaintances with old mates; *Biswell* was a name he heard, and *Fitz,* and something that sounded like *Weatherawll.* He heard them but forgot them at once. The one name he held close was Agnes.

Now, this gloomy morning, Captain Watts's words assumed an appalling significance. *A hell of a tussle,* he'd said. James shifted in his saddle of rope and straw in a vain attempt to find a comfortable way to sit the razor-like chine of his runty horse. Jesus was now an even worse lamented loss; though but a common nag, Jesus no doubt had gained in stature and stamina and wisdom from the admixture of some higher bloodline. The mount given James for today was a Chickasaw of the common type most often called a tackey, small and scrawny, thick-winded, ungainly, every rib on show. James did not like it well enough to give it a name.

As they approached the woods he thought there was more light now and glanced about him hoping to spy a welcoming smile or at least a nod that would signify acceptance; but in vain. Every face was closed; no eye would meet his. Like his new horse—like the horses they all rode—they looked shrunk to the bone. Once he'd heard a tale of certain wild tribes in distant lands who took the heads of their enemies and boiled them in pots till they achieved the hardness of leather and the size of apples. These men had that compression, that hardness. Was it that they were like no other men he had known? Or was this the form all men took when battle awaited? Did he himself look that way?

He turned to the file on his right. He could not help it; he spoke. "What's expected of us today?"

The trooper showed only his hawk-like profile. He let a long silence grow between them till it became uncomfortable. Then he said with a biting sarcasm, "Why, you're expected to get your guts blowed out, or your arm tore off, or your brains splattered all over the file in back of you. Or, if the Colonel has a mind to ask you, you're expected to bend down and pluck the goddamned fartleberries off his arse. Whatever comes up, is what's expected. Maybe you won't have to do nothing but set around and toy with your pecker."

Rebuffed, James said no more. The black tangle-edged bulk of the woods swayed nearer with every jarring stride of his horse. Other than his own failed attempt and its cynical answer, no one had spoken since the orders came in camp to mount, form section in fours, and march. In his sickly state the clatter of sword-scabbards, the jingling of bit-chains and the rhythmic thumping of hooves irritated him. Meantime more light seeped in; he noticed he was the only one carrying a carbine; all others bore only swords and pistols, as sparely armed as they were sparely shaped. They were clad in mean and indiscriminate fashion and their smell reminded him of nothing so much as a flock of soiled and dampened sheep.

He rode as number two file in the first rank of the second section. To the right of the trooper he'd spoken to was Captain Watts. At the head of the column he could see Colonel Washington in his dirty white coat too small for him and the trumpeter in a blue one, walking their horses side by side. He wished he could get a closer look at the Colonel, whose renown was as great as General Greene's. But then, even as the dawn began to brighten, the Colonel and the trumpeter passed into the dark cavern of the woods and very soon the column passed in also, rank by rank, and the blackness covered them. The fragrance of pine straw and rosin came. *Agnes Baker*, thought James, *you'd better not forget me.*

Passing through the woods, Greene looked up and found he could catch glimpses between spiny boughs of a vaguely luminous sky and in a few minutes more the forest began to lose its minatory blackness and compose itself into the familiar shapes of slim pine-trunks encrusted with slabs of bark like armor plate and of towering crowns massed with bushy needles. The trees that had looked so monstrously crowded in moonlight now showed themselves spaced comfortably apart on a broad floor of fallen pine straw as free of underwood as a park; the open glades soared like the vaults of a cathedral. A bed of reddened needles covered the road, resilient under the hooves of the horses and the feet of the men, giving up its dry tart aroma as they crushed it.

The General was glad to see the sky and the light, but his nerves kept him on edge. True, no longer was it possible to think of this simple grove of pines as an evil void gulping down his army; yet even now, as it brightened, it did not seem to offer welcome. He felt an unpropitious sullenness in its heavy quiet, in the way it muffled the sounds of the passing army, in its very solitude and peace. "Let's go to the front, gentlemen," he said, and they struck spurs to their horses, galloping up the column toward its head. The faster pace improved his mood. *It's the waiting,* he thought. *I'll be calmer when it starts.*

While they cantered, the first of the couriers met them, a ragged hatless boy with a freckled face who came bounding up the road on a one-eyed spotted horse. "Colonel Henderson's compliments, General," he piped, waving a hand in vague salute. "He begs me say the state troops ain't seen nary sign of the enemy, but we're a-looking for him like hell."

His enthusiasm broke the tension; a refreshing burst of merriment rocked the General's party. "My compliments to the Colonel," Greene laughed. "Give him my thanks, and convey to him my hope that he has good hunting."

"I'll do that, General," cried the lad, wheeled his horse and dashed back the way he had come.

They rode on, buoyed by his exuberance. The forest thinned; the spaces between the pines divided the first of the morning sun into vertical slivers of light, and when a gleam struck his face Greene squinted against it and felt the promise of its coming heat and was suddenly as thankful for the woods as he had been apprehensive of them a minute before. In his planning he'd known the army would be facing a rising sun, normally a disadvantage but nullified on this ground, he'd hoped, by the tree cover as well as by the hour, which—barring an early encounter with enemy pickets—should be no sooner than eight o'clock, when the sun ought to be well up. Also, on a wooded battleground the army could fight mostly in the shade, on a day that was bound to be hot. He was relieved to find he'd thus far planned well, but drew only the smallest comfort from the knowledge—he wouldn't know till he saw the actual field he must fight on whether he'd planned well enough. Too dense a forest, unexpectedly sharp terrain, hollow ways, sturdy undergrowth—any or all of these would play hob with his dispositions.

By the time he reached the head of the army it had halted and the provision wagon was serving out the rum. He and the staff dismounted to wait in the shade of some roadside water oaks while the escort sat their horses nearby; he propped himself against a tree to flex his lame leg, stiffened by three hours in the saddle. Opposite, the South Carolina militia loitered in ranks enjoying their dram; some raised their cups in toast to the General; a few shouted thanks that Greene acknowledged with nods and smiles that were as genial as he could craft them given his preoccupations. The day was breaking clear-skied and humid; the dank fetor of the Santee swamps ripened in the still air; he began profusely to sweat and wiped himself with his handkerchief; far too soon it was sodden.

Generals Marion and Pickens came to join him and together they talked, stiffly and at awkward intervals owing to the suspense of the moment, speaking of the weather and of the mood of the troops, swatting flies, their ears cocked eastward for the sound of firing from the vanguard. But all held eerily quiet; the whistles of mockingbirds and the jeering of jays were all they heard above the murmur of the troops. Presently another courier galloped in, this one from Colonel Lee, a glittering dragoon in polished helmet and green and buff, riding a blooded hunter, much in contrast to Colonel Henderson's sprightly messenger on his speckled nag; but his news was the same as the boy's—the British were nowhere to be seen this side of their camp. Incredibly, they seemed to have posted no picket or quarter-guard.

"I do believe," Greene ventured, dismissing the immaculate Legionnaire, "we've caught this fellow Stewart napping."

"He's not Cornwallis," General Pickens declared. "Nor any Rawdon neither."

Greene sipped water from a canteen Pendleton handed him and allowed himself a narrow smile. "We'll wake him soon enough," he quipped, and ordered the march resumed.

Marion and Pickens took their places; he and his staff and the escort trotted to the front of the column. They rode on, through alternate spots where the level sun dazzled them and then crowds of trees laid shadow down. The day dampened; the temperature steadily rose; mosquitoes swarmed. For another hour they marched on the muting carpet of pine straw to the monotonous thump of canteens, the clink of sling-buckles, an occasional sneeze or cleared throat or blown nose from the column and the snort and snuffle of their horses. Though his belly ached with tension, Greene, dozy from heat and lack of sleep, began to droop.

Then a ripple of sound came from the east, hardly enough to be heard though Greene heard it, a slight crackling as if some woodland creature had stirred a pile of deadwood. He straightened in the saddle, threw up a hand; orders pealed along the column; the army stopped in its tracks. Though a nearby woodpecker was louder, they all heard it now, the strangely delicate coughing of musket fire, half a mile on, softened by the distance and the woods. "The van's engaged," said Greene. He fished out his watch, flicked open the silver case. It was twelve minutes past eight. All his anxieties vanished; he had never felt as serene in his life.

He waited for the courier he knew would come, who proved, within another five minutes, to be a lieutenant of the Legion, as splendid in raiment as his predecessor, but just now a bit disheveled from tearing through the forest, and more than a little frightened too. "Colonel Lee's compliments, General," the young man cried, saluting as his frothing thoroughbred turned and turned in the road. "Beg to report we've met a large body of enemy foot and what appears to be all their cavalry, maybe three miles from their main camp. They advanced on us, we met 'em halfway. The Colonel requests support, General, in order to drive 'em."

Greene gave him a crisp nod. "Very well, Lieutenant. My compliments to the Colonel, tell him I'm sending him Colonel Hammond's command." The officer saluted, whirled his mount, and was gone. Greene turned to Shubrick, instructed him to ride to Colonel Hammond. "Tell him he's to take his troop of horse to the support of the Legion on the right." Shubrick spurted away on his black as Greene swung to Pierce next. "Compliments to Captain Gaines, have him bring the artillery forward and hold on the road in rear of the militia."

"All of it, sir?"

Again he nodded. "The lot." Then Pierce too was gone. Greene reined Sterne about; confidently he smiled into the solemn countenances of Pendleton, Kosciuszko, Hyrne, and Forsyth. "Well, gentlemen," he teased them, "what do you say? Shall we give this villain a drubbing?"

The dram of rum seared James's gullet and lit such a blaze in his empty stomach that he suspected at once it had been a mistake to drink it down, though the morning's heat and his parching thirst, which the tepid water in his canteen would not quench, had tempted him to it—that, and his terror, and especially Colonel Washington's cheerful admonition. The suspicion soon became a certainty; his vision blurred, his brain swam heavy as molasses in a shaken jug and, worse—much worse—his bowels commenced to stir and slide in the queasy fashion that by now was all too familiar.

He did not blame the Colonel. When the provision wagon arrived, the big man in the grimy white coat had swung his homely mud-colored horse about to pass down the column speaking to them so commonly and with such fine humor that James could not resist him. "Get off, boys," he'd said, grinning in his moony face as casually as if the prospect of blood and death were as distant as the farthest planet and not as near as the next hour, "ease your sore arses, give the nags a rest. Take your gill of fortifying. She'll put the fight in you. You'll want to whip wildcats and tigers and dragons that vomit brimstone. I pity the poor damned Bloodybacks, coming up against the likes of you."

They dismounted and took their rum while the Colonel removed his helmet and tucked it under his arm so all could get a view of his ruddy countenance and rode to and fro singling out certain ones for fond raillery. "Why, here's old Shoupe. Where've you been, Shoupe? Did your wife run you off because your yard smelt of horse-dung?" "Is that Ben Clearwaters I see? Ben, was you ever shut of that dose of the gleet, or are you still dripping?" "Hello, Story; d'you learn to shoot yet—the British,

I mean, 'stead of that poor corporal of the Maryland Line you clipped by mistake at Hobkirk's?"

The hard, shrunk-to-the-bone faces split into grins as he talked, cackles of laughter broke forth from men who had previously been mirthless; one or two voices answered back with impudent sallies that the Colonel met with hearty guffaws of his own. James had never seen an exchange between an officer and his men remotely like it.

Washington spied Obediah and drew rein chuckling; plump cheeks squeezed his eyes into tiny blue crescents of sparkling merriment. "Now here's a man of the cloth come back to grace us with his odor of sanctity. I've missed you awfully, O." He darted quick impish looks about the ranks while Obediah stood beaming at him over the rim of his cup; and James noted with approval that the Colonel was joking as warmly with a First Dragoon as he had with members of his own regiment.

"Me and O," the Colonel went on, "we've had many a discussion of theology and the profession of faith, but found we differed in our means. I was set to be a minister too, you know, but missed the talent for it that O's got. I was set to go exhorting; he went the way of fornicating. By now I reckon he's thrummed all the virgins of Virginia." He turned back to Plumbley in wicked mischief. "It hurts me to tell you, O, but there's not a virgin left in all of Carolina either. My boys've plowed every damned acre of that sweet ground."

How could a-body *not* drink? James had gazed on Washington with all the wonder and admiration he'd thought had withered to a wisp in him after dealing with such roguish ilk as Colonel White, Major Call, and Lieutenant Linton, or with such a tragic wreck as Captain Harris, or even with the silk-stocking Lieutenant Gordon who, though he'd treated him fairly in the end, had also never failed to make it clear he regarded him as but a base menial. Even Gunn, tremendous figure that he was, as low in breeding as James himself, was hardly more than a lout who reveled in the tyranny he wielded over lesser men. The stamp of arrogance had been on them all; and so vast and swollen with contempt was this arrogance that they deemed everything—the army, the war, the noble ideas of democracy and liberty, even the very nation the war was trying to set up—as the just prizes of their class, which the sweating masses they disdained must win for them.

Yet here in Colonel Washington one finally saw a leader who stood not on exalted lineage or on high learning or on ceremony or on the bullying of others but on wholesome fellowship and on the notion that all men, lofty of birth and mean alike, deserved equal respect if they put themselves earnestly to the task set them. On but a few moments' acquaintance, faint from the flux, sick with fear, sore-eyed, his bottom burning and bloody,

James had given the whole of his swelling heart to William Washington.

Then the rum started his guts. The file to his right, though without any visible sign of rank, held the post usually assigned to a sergeant or a corporal; in the emergency James appealed for his permission to fall out and answer nature's call. The hawk-faced caitiff, who'd mocked him earlier, was forming an ugly and gleeful *No* when Captain Watts leaned in growling, "Go ahead, son," and James, gratefully dodging past them, heard Watts tell the fellow, "Next time *you've* got the flux, Murphy, you can keep ranks till you shit yourself, then lick yourself clean; I'll see to it myself." Crouching behind a holly bush, his britches around his ankles, a thankful James reckoned this Captain Watts possessed a set of rare and estimable qualities of his own.

Wiping himself with a handful of grass, contemplating the possibility that the best of the leadership of his regiment might well be not in Virginia where it was numerous but here in the South where it was scarce, he heard a commotion in the road and, fretful with dread, sprang up buttoning his britches. Ahead he saw the artillery pieces they had been following pull out of the column to the left, the two smaller guns in front, each drawn by a single horse; then the two bigger ones in limbers, their teams hitched in tandem, all four pieces bouncing over the tree-roots and stones of the road, the riders plying their whips, gunners and matrosses running alongside, the ox-cart that carried the ammunition following in train.

James hastened to his place next to the frowning Corporal Murphy and waited trembling with trepidation as an officer on a panting steed rode to Colonel Washington, still afoot with his helmet under his arm, but looming so large that his head reached nearly to the new rider's chest. They saluted and spoke; Washington's visage glowed as if he'd heard the best tidings of the month, the messenger spun his horse and galloped back toward the front; and the Colonel turned his bright face to them. "Fun's commenced, boys," he cried. "The Legion's up yonder playing break-the-Pope's-neck with Mr. Coffin's cavalry, looks like."

He donned his helmet, bounded astride with an athletic grace, and came trotting the length of the column, leaning out now and again to cuff a trooper's arm with rough affection. "Pretty soon now," he smiled, "I expect we'll have to go and save the Legion's pretty arses. So get on"—James thought this a remarkable way to pass the order to mount; yet every man leapt to the saddle as one, himself included, though his raw behind stung him shockingly—"and double the files, and we'll go." The blue-coated trumpeter, riding behind, put his instrument to his lips, but Washington turned and gave him a dismissive wave. "Put it away, Larry; they heard me. Anyhow, the damn thing hurts my ears."

While the General walked his horse impatiently back and forth across the road at the head of the army awaiting further word from the vanguard, the sounds of distant firing at first diminished from a persistent crackling to a few random pops and then to a prolonged and suspenseful silence that could mean either that Colonels Lee and Henderson had gained a success or the enemy had; or that the encounter had broken off in a draw. He must know which, and know soon—not only because the knowledge would inform his next decision but also because, amid the host of large concerns besetting him, he felt an especially aching need to assure himself that Lee was acting properly and responsibly, unseen yonder in the face of the enemy.

He reined Sterne to a halt and listened to the stillness with close attention till it grew oppressive and forbidding, broken only by the continued bothersome knocking of the nearby woodpecker. Then from eastward, all at once, came the sharp stutter of musketry that always spoke of volley fire, punctuated by the dull thump of a field gun. He turned to Captain Pendleton. "Colonel Lee's dispatch suggested a skirmish of horse; this smacks of a line of battle." Pendleton held his peace, though he met the General with a settled look of confirming judgment.

Just then Colonel Henderson's enthusiastic freckled lad reappeared pounding through the woods from the left on his pied nag, crowing, "General, Colonel says tell you we've sent their cavalry skedaddling, and by God, there was infantry too, a-digging sweet potoatoes, if you can believe it, and they all run like guineas, till us and Colonel Lee's boys gathered 'em up."

He plowed to a halt grinning expectantly, remembering the jolly welcome of his first visit. But his were stale tidings; save word of the capture of the rooting party, he was redundant with Lee's report and had left the van before the present outbreak. Greene dismissed him somewhat curtly and after lingering a moment, gaping and blinking in bewilderment at having failed to entertain headquarters as before, he turned his horse about and slunk off crestfallen.

A few minutes more the General uneasily waited while at intervals the British fieldpiece thudded in the distance. Then the expected messenger from the Legion materialized. He was a different courier than the last, attired in the same splendor and riding as fine a mount, but far less rattled; and his composure helped ease Greene's misgivings about the state of affairs in Lee's wing of the van. "We've drove the enemy's horse," the cornet cried, "but he's thrown out his infantry with a fieldpiece in support."

Greene leaned to him urgently. "Is it a line of battle?"

"Can't say, General. Their flanks is in the woods and brush. Artillery's in the middle, though."

"Has Colonel Hammond joined?"

"He has, General."

Briskly Greene nodded as the enemy gun sounded again in the distance. "Tell Colonel Lee I'm ordering up Captain Gaines to support him with a pair of three-pounders, and that I desire the Legion with Colonel Hammond's command to withdraw to the right and hang there amusing the enemy's line with as galling an oblique fire as may be laid down. Tell him I suppose this to be the main line of the enemy, that I'm displaying my first line at once, and that I'll advance it to fill the center." With a quick salute the cornet reined away.

Greene gave Pierce a stabbing glance. "Convey my orders to Lieutenant Gaines, if you will, Captain. And have General Sumner send a detachment of the North Carolina Continentals to support the guns." Next he swung to Kosciuszko. "Colonel, my compliments to Colonel Henderson, explain my new dispositions and say to him he's to withdraw to the left and open on the enemy's line obliquely." The two horsemen galloped off, Pierce to the rear, Kosciuszko into the woods on the left.

But he must delay a while longer till the artillery got up. Once more he commenced passing to and fro over the road, listening to the continual snap and pop of the musket fire and the occasional thud of the British gun, and in the silences between, to the drumming of the ever-industrious woodpecker. He was cool and composed, but his senses had never been more lively; his eyes saw a world whose texture was finer-grained and whose tints were more vivid than before, his nose smelled odors richer and more intensely mixed, he breathed air that was as clear and bracing as a tonic. His impatience did not sap him; it was a stimulant. The very glare of the sun lent him a hard vigor. Shubrick, Pendleton, Hyrne, and Forsyth sat their mounts in the roadside shade waiting on tenterhooks for his next orders; the escort of dragoons drew together like players in a match at football readying themselves to protect a goal.

Presently, down the road to the rear, they all heard the oncoming rumble of Captain Gaines's pieces, which soon grew to a hammering, racketing roar; then the first of the guns burst upon them, its driver lying flat on his horse's neck like a jockey, his whip snapping, the three-pounder in its little butterfly carriage jouncing behind with a crash of axles, the second horse and gun following; then Captain Gaines himself on his gray gelding already soapy with the sweat of its run, and next his hastening crews and the powder cart; and the whole train hurtled past them and on up the road toward the sound of the fighting, the commotion of its passage fading as swiftly as it had come. In its wake twenty-odd of Sumner's North Carolina Continentals came jogging, muskets at trail arms.

Then it was time. The General spoke to Sterne and crossed to the head of the waiting militia where Marion, Pickens, and Malmedy sat their horses; they exchanged salutes; Greene told them quietly, "Gentlemen, form your line, if you please. And we needn't be quiet about it." He gave them a tight smile. "I collect Mr. Stewart knows we're coming."

Moving at a walk, the dragoons advanced fifty or seventy-five yards to fill the vacancy left by the departed artillery and again halted, staring at the backs of six columns of regulars filling the road left to right, leaning on their muskets awaiting orders. Although most of these were dressed in greasy hunting shirts or simply in collections of rags, a few in each file wore regimentals, and James, in spite of his rum-bleared eyes, knew enough to distinguish, leftmost and center, the blue of Maryland and the brown of Virginia. A rustier blue prevailed rightmost; he did not know if these were the colors of another state or of more, worse-off Marylanders.

Notwithstanding the Colonel's expressed hope, the dragoons held where they stood instead of being ordered to the support of Lee's Legion in the van. But by now James was such a veteran of so many military delays that the change of plan did not surprise him. In fact he was relieved; he did not yet feel sufficiently well constituted to hurl himself into deadly danger. Stupid and sleepy with drink, drained by the flux, he watched drop-jawed as another courier came, spoke rapidly to the Colonel, and left again at a gallop, then as the Colonel called a conference of officers and as Captain Watts, Lieutenant Gordon, and five others—one no more than a child by his tender looks—rode to gather round the big man on his brown horse.

As they talked he heard from up ahead a faraway sustained rumpling noise as if some enormous sheet of parchment were being gradually crushed, then two deep booms like the strokes of a bass drum; and with a moil of nausea in his belly he recognized the sound of musketry and cannon fire, recognized it from the fights he'd heard at Hot Water and Green Springs, and knew with sudden fright that the battle had now been truly joined. The knot of officers at once broke up; each but one, the boy, rode to his place; the boy passed down the column to the rear; and Colonel Washington again took post at the head of the column to speak.

"Fellows, the Bloodybacks've run out a line of battle," he cried in his jubilant way, "and we've thrown one out too and they're engaged up there. Ours is militia, so you know what that means. Us and the Delawares'll form us a cordon right here across the road and turn 'em back when they run. I'm setting the Delawares in front. Maybe between us we can keep those Carolina boys from scampering all the way back to Halifax."

Amid the coarse laughter of the regiment James heard orders being barked somewhere behind, "Battalion, at trail arms, by files, Advance!" and on either side of the column two files of nimble-looking fellows, many in short coats of faded blue trimmed with red and all wearing the little peaked caps that designated light infantry troops, suddenly came running, their muskets sloping by their sides; the boy who'd fetched them came too.

James hadn't even known there was another corps to the rear and was surprised to see these agile chaps dashing so resolutely past. In a twinkling they formed a line across the front; an officer barked more commands, "Secure firelocks! Fix Bayonets! Order Firelocks!" James thrilled with revulsion when he saw that double row of motionless steel gleaming in the low sunlight and realized it was meant to receive on its leveled points any poor wretch who left the front. Would they actually skewer their own? He feared they would.

Then the Colonel's orders came. His voice rang above the rising clamor of battle like the trumpet he would not allow to be blown: "Close ranks to half distance, march! Halt. By sections, to left and right, display!" The formation divided, displayed; and a startled James found himself on the front rank, immediately behind the light infantry holding erect their bright hedge of bayonets. Next the Colonel shouted, "Draw swords!" and he understood for the first time that it was now to be his duty, not to contend with the fierce enemy he had dreaded but instead to cut down with his own saber such poor timorous despairing Americans as might be unmanned by the horrors of the battle and so flee to the rear for safety only to meet the remorseless cold steel of those who, on another day, should have been their friends.

Greene rode on the left flank of the advancing double-ranked battle line, turning in his saddle to gaze beaming with proprietary pride down its front—nearly five hundred yards of front and yes, crooked as a ram's horn as any militia line always was—made worse this morning by the woods that broke it into segments each trailing its little coil of men hurrying to catch up and knit the breaks—yes, a crooked line, none more crooked, the North Carolinians in the middle bulging out ahead, the brigades of Pickens and Marion trailing behind like the broken wings of a bedraggled fighting cock, but *advancing*, by Heaven, advancing to the attack against a defensive enemy for the first time in his Southern war. Never had he dreamt he could feel so proud of the militia he had so often despised and condemned.

Orders were to advance with muskets at the slope; hence, had they been regulars, every piece would have been borne at a near uniform slant. But this was militia and no two muskets stood on the same tilt; the front poked every way like the spines of a sea urchin; Greene laughed aloud to see it. Somewhere in the line, fifes were squealing and two or three drums rattled; and for the first time ever on a field of battle Greene heard militiamen cheering and hallooing, their voices echoing strangely among the pines.

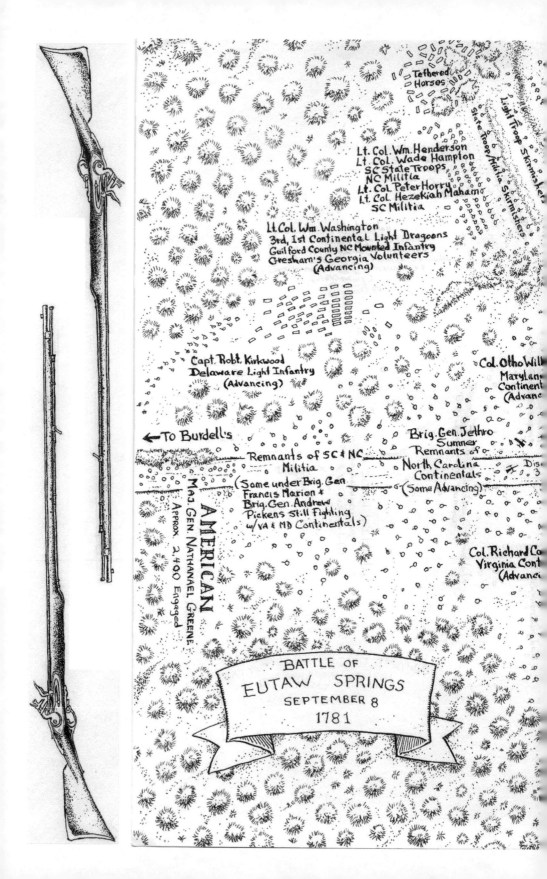

Tethered Horses

Lt. Col. Wm. Henderson
Lt. Col. Wade Hampton
SC State Troops
NC Militia
Lt. Col. Peter Horry
Lt. Col. Hezekiah Maham
SC Militia

Lt. Col. Wm. Washington
3rd, 1st Continental Light Dragoons
Guilford County NC Mounted Infantry
Gresham's Georgia Volunteers
(Advancing)

Capt. Robt. Kirkwood
Delaware Light Infantry
(Advancing)

Col. Otho Will
Maryland
Continent
(Advanc

←To Burdell's

Brig. Gen. Jethro
Sumner
Remnants of
North Carolina
Continentals
(Some Advancing)

Remnants of SC & NC
Militia

(Some under Brig. Gen
Francis Marion &
Brig. Gen. Andrew
Pickens Still Fighting
w/ VA & MD Continentals)

Col. Richard Co
Virginia Cont
(Advanci

AMERICAN
MAJ. GEN. NATHANAEL GREENE
APPROX. 2,400 Engaged

BATTLE OF
EUTAW SPRINGS
SEPTEMBER 8
1781

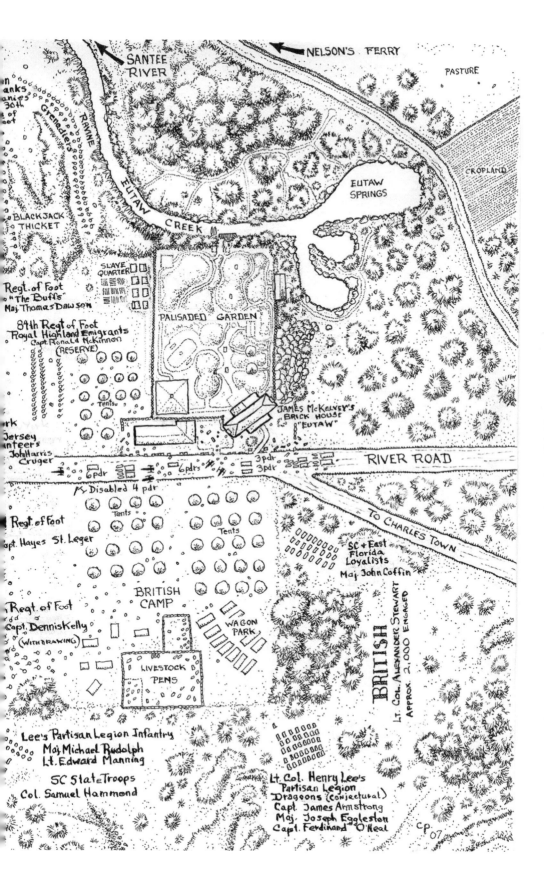

Their hurrying feet padded over the mat of pine straw on the forest floor making a noise of rushing sibilance that added to the unreality of the scene save when someone stepped on a dead branch and it snapped like a shot. He had never expected to see such spirit in the farmers and smiths and coopers and draymen who so unwillingly served their militia times; then he reminded himself some of these were volunteers or old regulars hired as substitutes rather than the normal run of peevish drafted men and poor substitutes pining for family and hearthside.

Equally unusual was the absence of the enemy, whose line of battle Stewart had evidently drawn back—nothing lay ahead now but more and more undulant pine forestland dappled with light and shade, stifling as a hothouse now that the sun was fully risen. But the rotten-egg odor of burnt powder, left from the earlier skirmishing of the van, clung to the woods, a light film of smoke still drifted in the treetops, in a glade a wounded horse struggled to rise only to tread on its own entrails and sink back, and here and there on the ground a figure of a man lay huddled in the close, flat way of the dead.

The line rolled over a hummock like the breaking of a dark surf cluttered with spindrift; and the General, from its crest, peering eagerly ahead, spied Captain Gaines's two three-pounders squatting in the middle of the road, muzzles jutting rearward, butterflies harnessed up to roll. Having disengaged from the British gun to await his own line of battle, he was ready to resume the contest in support of the oncoming militia. Unseen somewhere right and left, back in the timber, Greene knew, Henderson and Lee also hovered in wait. He glanced backward; the Continentals were driving up the road behind at a brisk pace, their column emerging from the pines rhythmically throbbing like some great millipede.

Incredibly, the battle he had planned and had believed would spin out of control almost at once was evolving on the ground just as he had imagined it while studying Harry Lee's crude map back at Medway Swamp—Henderson and Lee guarding the flanks, a powerful line of militia displayed in the middle, artillery in support on the road, Continentals in place ready to display his second line at need, dragoons and light troops in reserve, the enemy surprised and reeling. Exhilaration bore him up.

At half-past eight o'clock by the General's watch, the British line finally came into view. It was not, he saw at once, the line of battle he'd expected, but a body of foot just numerous enough—some few hundred—to impede his advance though insufficient to cover his entire front; and a field-piece, probably the same one that had contended with the van. Stewart, caught unawares by the American approach, had obviously thrown out this little force to give himself time to assemble a main line some distance farther to the rear.

At the sight of the enemy Greene's militia set up a cheer that rocked the woods, but no sooner had the British disclosed themselves than they began creeping backward through the trees behind a light screen of skirmishers. These opened a scattered fire, which the Carolina militia returned with a smashing volley that amazed Greene with its force, felled several Redcoats, and started the skirmishers scrambling rearward after their fellows. Captain Gaines ran his guns into battery on the road, loaded and engaged the British piece opposite. The enemy gun replied, then limbered up and retired in search of a better position.

Greene, elated, motioned to Pendleton and, as the militia unleashed another volley, shouted into his ear, "My compliments to General Marion, the militia is to continually fire while advancing and drive the enemy. Tell him it's not a line of battle that opposes him but an advance party; it's to be driven till the British main body is discovered."

Pendleton pelted away; the General beckoned to Major Forsyth: "Tell Captain Gaines he's to follow the retiring enemy gun and keep it under a hot fire."

Finally he called Pierce to him: "Captain Browne's to bring up his pair of six-pounders and go into battery on the road behind the first line, so as to be in position to support the line of the Continentals when it's displayed."

Forsyth and Pierce left him riding in opposite directions; he glanced about him to see that Kosciuszko, Shubrick, and Hyrne remained, anxiously looking on; those, and his little escort of dragoons. He wanted to confide in the staff but dared not; there was still his luck to consider, which had turned its back on him all too often. A vestige of superstition flickered in him yet; to speak his belief aloud might invite disaster. So he gave them a laugh and a jaunty flourish of a hand and permitted himself to think what he could not say, *I'm going to win this one.*

Drawn swords laid against their shoulders, they were moving constantly now, starting, trotting short distances, stopping, then starting again, following the army as it made its halting, hesitant but inevitable way toward the ever-louder rumble and roar of firing in the distance. To their immediate front the double line of Delaware light infantry, straddling the road with their flanks in the woods to either side, made the same truculent progress, carrying their muskets now at the position of Charge Bayonets.

Frail and sickly as he was, James could not take his eyes off that lethal row of tapered steel flashing in the intermittent sun. Twice more he'd had to plead permission to fall out with onsets of the flux; his anus was now a burning, bleeding wound; his head ached intolerably; he'd puked up the rum at last—doing that from the saddle—and still was repeatedly retching thin dribbles of bitter-tasting slime. Still, whenever he righted himself again on the thin back of his Chickasaw, that row of shiny steel slivers presented itself ever more abhorrently. He had feared and despised the bayonet ever since he'd handled one that first time at the Arsenal. To use such a terrible instrument against an enemy had always seemed atrocious enough; to plunge one into a fellow American was unthinkable. Yet the saber resting on his own shoulder had the very same purpose. *Will I use it? Should I use it? Is such a horrid thing my duty?* If it was, he feared it worse than he feared the dangers of battle.

Someone on the right flank of the Delawares yelled an order; their line came to a sudden stop; Colonel Washington threw a hand high in his turn and the dragoons reined up as well. In the road ahead the column of Continentals marched on. Puzzled, James peeked questioningly about only to confront the same stern aloofness as before; but his curiosity emboldened him; once more he addressed the formidably impassive Murphy. "Why ain't we moving?"

The hawk's features sharpened with impatience, but after a time Murphy did return a grudging answer. "We've got to open distance 'tween us and the battle lines, so's when the goddamned militia starts to run, we've room to stop 'em—and room to form and maneuver too, if we've got to charge." He twisted his head to James glaring in contempt. "Ain't you had no damned training atall?"

James knew he need not reply. Murphy swore, swiveled his head to the front with a quick twisty motion still more reminiscent of a bird of prey, and spat a stream of tobacco juice to one side as if ridding his mouth of whatever foul flavor speaking to James had left there. James looked frontward too, where the points of the bayonets stood in a shimmering row.

The General could read the signs: the day would be a bloody one. Till now it had all seemed easy, far too easy, the fox-chase through the pine groves. Three whole miles, by Greene's reckoning, the whooping Carolina militiamen had driven the British advance party and its lone cannon. Riding with the onset, bending and dipping in the saddle to peer past banks of sulphur-smelling smoke struck through with shafts of sunlight let down from the forest canopy, Greene had been lost in astonishment to see the ardor of the assault.

But for all his exaltation he'd had reason to fret. *How many rounds have they fired?* he'd asked himself each time Colonel Malmedy's troops loosed another volley from their place in the center of the line. Back at Howell's he'd issued them twenty rounds per man, thinking of what they'd need to confront a line of battle; they were using up this scarce supply beating in little more than a robust skirmish line. He'd tried to count the volleys, but knew he'd been late in starting. *Was it eight? Ten? Twelve? What will they have left for the main line?* Marion and Pickens had a sufficiency, drawn from state supplies; but Malmedy's men might well run short, with no quick way to replenish.

Yet, saving that worry, it had been easy, an easy and jubilant September morning; but now, at eight minutes past nine o'clock, with the enemy's main battle line displayed before them, it was easy no longer. There had been the merest fragment of time, no more than three or four ticks of his watch, when Greene could clearly see the British standing in two ranks across the road ahead; then a burst of musketry ran along their front and they were gone behind a boiling belt of whitish-yellow smoke all a-twinkle with muzzle-flashes. The noise startled Sterne and the gelding plunged violently away from it, almost unseating Greene, crowding back the horses of his staff and escort. The General sawed the reins to quiet the beast and in the same moment glanced to see the effect of the volley on his militia line—a dozen or more forms in homespun and deerskin dropped, some to writhe and struggle, others not. Turning Sterne's head again to the front, he leaned to yell in Pendleton's ear as the echo of the volley went crackling off into the forest, "Did you see green coats in the middle?"

"I thought so, yes, sir." Pendleton passed him the spyglass; Greene set it to his eye, Sterne shifting nervously under him. The smoke of the British volley still billowed, and as he steadied the horse and focused the lens it leapt into sharper detail, a smutty dissolving pall with bits of burnt cartridge-paper floating in it, unspent grains of powder still igniting here and there like expiring fireflies. As it cleared Greene glimpsed, behind the haze it left, a pale flick and shiver of steel as enemy ramrods were plied; and then, yes, a row of faded green uniforms—Provincials.

"Our old friends from Ninety-Six are with us," he declared. "That's Cruger's Loyalists holding the center." He wagged his head in grudging admiration. "By Heaven, that was a fine disciplined fire they gave."

"As steady as regulars," Major Forsyth agreed.

The Carolinians halted; Greene thought perhaps they wavered a little, facing not a little wobbly chain of skirmishers any longer but a stern and motionless line of battle whose first murderous volley had stung them badly, had strewn the pine needles with their dead and wounded. If they were going to bolt as they'd bolted at Guilford, this was the moment; Greene looked on with bated breath, torn between a hope they would hold and a certainty they would run—then hallooed with excitement when he saw them draw together in ranks, present their muskets as one, and answer the British with a fusillade of their own, perhaps not the well-drilled, concerted fire of the Redcoats but a powerful if irregular concussion that ran successively right to left along their whole front, having very nearly the effect, if by pure accident, of the platoon firing described in every military manual; and under its withering gale men in green and red crumpled all along the enemy line.

He shifted his glass rapidly left and right to assess the strength of the line before the next volley covered it with smoke. The green-coats straddled the road, and on both sides of them the red regimentals of regular troops shone brightly in the patches of sun, less so in the shade of the woods; and on the road itself, a little in advance of Cruger's troops, three fieldpieces—one of them a howitzer—stood waiting in battery. But from where Greene sat his horse, a hundred yards left of the road at the end of Pickens's line, both British flanks were smothered by forest and thick masses of brush and underwood, for here the forest lost its parklike openness, grew rougher and more dense; he could not guess the length of the enemy front nor determine where, or how firmly, its flanks might be anchored.

Still, it roused him to see the Redcoats so handsomely resisted. Not only did the militia stand to its work, from both flanks Lee's and Henderson's infantry sent in their oblique harassing fire—though Lee was obscured in the pines far to the right opposite him, Greene could hear the clatter of the Legion's muskets, and from the left front came the sharp steady spiteful popping of Henderson's infantry; at times the General could even glimpse a float of its smoke above the treetops yonder, though rising ground and a snarled growth hid the troops themselves. Surely the enemy's hidden flanks were taking a continuous and damaging fire.

But if he could discern little of the whole, Greene's field commanders soon discovered what stood before them, and each in turn sent him word so that, piece by piece, he could assemble in his mind the composition of Stewart's force that he could not see for himself. First came a staff officer of South Carolina militia, to say the troops opposing Marion's brigade wore facings some of black and some of dark green. *The Sixty-Third and Sixty-Fourth Foot,* Greene thought; *regiments once redoubtable, now but remnants, worn down, too long in service; good tidings.*

From Colonel Malmedy came a rangy fellow in a round hat to speak what Greene already knew, that it was Cruger in front of the North Carolinians, three battalions of Jerseymen, New Yorkers, volunteers all. *Dangerous troops, hard as tortoise shells, made us bleed at Ninety-Six, outlasted us.* The guns, he said, looked like a howitzer and a pair of three-pounders. Next a Legionnaire rode in, reported the enemy's left flank in the air, no sharp ground about, some hollow ways and brush in front but not enough for cover, and Coffin's horse posted there, and some foot—*the infantry could be Provincials, or maybe East Florida Royalists; sometimes they serve with Coffin to make a kind of a legion.* "Colonel says tell you we're a-bickering with the foot," the courier concluded. *Coffin's horse. Hard to move, he'll hurt us if he charges.* He remembered struggling with the guns at Hobkirk's Hill, Coffin's grim Georgians and Carolinians and Florida men bearing down, *any one who killed me a hero all his days.* But just now Coffin was Colonel Lee's business; *I must believe he'll be up to it; and Hammond's with him.*

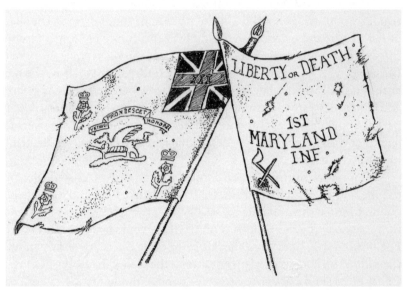

General Pickens himself trotted over. The Third Regiment of Foot was in his front, he said, the battalion companies, he thought, no grenadiers or light infantry that he could make out. *The Buffs. Stewart has none better. But they're a good deal weaker than they were when they stepped off the ship from Cork. Depleted by heat and sickness in July; had time to recover, though—refreshed at Orangeburgh and Fair Lawn and Thomson's. Not reinforced. But they'll be stubborn anyway.*

No sooner had Pickens ridden off than the familiar hatless, freckle-faced boy from the state troops arrived on his one-eyed spotted nag, all business now, hardened before his time by the stress of battle: "General, Colonel Henderson's compliments, the right of the enemy's line's posted in front of Eutaw Creek, that comes out of a ravine and runs under steep banks that's all growed up with brush and briars, and there's a big thicket of blackjack oak a-standing this side of the creek, 'twixt us and them." Greene remembered Lee's drawing, the squiggly line meant to be the creek, ending in one big loop and two little ones meant to be the springs. *Somewhere beyond that is a house. And a palisaded garden. Fortified?*

The General's heart darkened; the circumstances on that flank sounded grim. He shouted to be heard as the British artillery engaged Captain Gaines's three-pounders and Gaines replied with counter-battery fire. "What troops are there?"

"We ain't sure, General; they look like flank companies, the Colonel says. We seen facings of yellow and a kind of olive-green. Some's got grenadier hats."

The Nineteenth Foot has the brownish-green; the Thirtieth has the yellow. Came from Cork with Rawdon and the Buffs. Chased us out of Ninety-Six, died like flies on the way to Orangeburgh. Come back to serve us a pudding of revenge. "Are you engaged?"

"Why, yes, General, we're engaged like hell. But they're a stubborn set of bastards, and damned hard to get at, on account of that blackjack hedge they're in and out of; and their front runs longer'n our'n, and outflanks us." *Ominous. That flank will bear watching. God grant we don't have to assault it.*

He dismissed the lad, wheeled his horse, flicked a narrow look along the bent and uneven militia line just as the Carolinians delivered another crashing volley and received one in return that chewed viciously along its front; he saw men tumble out of ranks to go crawling in the pine straw or to sink down sodden and motionless. He feared again for Colonel Malmedy's command. *Was that thirteen rounds? Fourteen? Of course some of them will have carried their own shot and powder.* The middle of the line, where the North Carolinians stood, sagged backward some few yards; four or five fellows over there drifted loose and wandered to the rear in a bewildered way that might as easily speak of an empty cartridge box as of cowardice, though cowardice looked the more likely.

But even as the center threatened to unravel, the flanks stiffened—many of Pickens' and Marion's troops were paroled Redcoats who dared not yield to their erstwhile messmates; the noose awaited them if they fell into British hands. Some were breaking ranks to dart about the field and retrieve the enemy's cannon balls once they stopped rolling, to carry back to Captain Gaines's guns for reuse. *Fine spirit, that.* South Carolina held firm even as North Carolina appeared to weaken—North Carolina, the same stout fellows he'd admired at Medway Swamp, the same lads who'd given him that reverent voiceless salute with their raised hats but hours before in Burdell's clearing. Disappointment choked him, mingled with a smarting remorse: *I should've issued them thirty rounds, the same as the Continentals.* He did not know whether to blame them or pity them, men who might as easily be heroes who'd shot themselves empty as poltroons who longed to flee. Certainly there was himself to blame. But that would have to wait.

Whether low on ammunition or on nerve, the center of his line seemed ready to give way; he must act. He swung Sterne toward the waiting staff. *If the North Carolinians run,* he thought, looking into the ring of pinched inquiring faces, his brain awhirl with possibilities, *the enemy will come with a bayonet attack, and our chaps won't stand that; even Marion's and Pickens' people will turn tail.* In his mind, as Pendleton and Pierce and Shubrick and the others sat their horses alertly awaiting his orders, the lineaments of the dispositions he'd laid down on Harry Lee's rough map at Medway Swamp sprang again to life and commenced to move about. *Bring Sumner forward. Mend the center.*

While the lines shifted in his head a smoke-blackened courier hastened to him on a sweating mount, confirming the worst: "General, Colonel Malmedy regrets to say us boys is down to our last two or three rounds, and some of them Hillsborough sons of bitches has already broke for the rear. Colonel's got their names too, for court-martialing, by God, he says. The balance of us'll stay in the line though, long as we can. But Colonel says two more volleys'll near about dry us up." Even as he spoke, the line discharged another tremendous fire, which the enemy answered with a volley of its own, by divisions this time, a controlled, successive storm of musketry that tore appalling gaps all along the militia front.

Absently Greene nodded, gave the courier his leave; but the figures in his head kept in motion. With terrific mental force he drove his attention inward, warded off all else that crashed and swirled around him in order to watch the lines reposition themselves on the terrain of his thought. But another galloper came pounding up, broke his inward sight, made him turn outside again and listen. "Colonel Henderson's compliments, General, the enemy's outflanked us bad and has took us under fire from the left; he begs permission to charge 'em."

Outflanked. Hateful word. But Henderson was needed where he was, protecting the first line and the artillery. He would have to save his own flank. Greene looked to the road where just at that moment a British roundshot struck the galloper of one of Captain Gaines's three-pounders, dismounting the gun; a blizzard of wood splinters flew, a wheel went bounding crazily off into the woods, gunners and matrosses scattered in all directions, the horse sat back on its haunches as if amazed before toppling over dead. At nearly the same instant an enemy howitzer shell came bounding through the militia line, its fuse smoking. The Carolinians dodged and danced to get out of its path; it slowed to a roll and trundled with terrible inevitability toward Gaines's second gun, exploding just short of it in a bouquet of fire-hearted yellow smoke; pine-straw spurted up from the forest floor all about the gun, showing where the iron fragments hit; half the crew fell stricken; one headless man walked four whole steps away, his neck a red fountain, before he dropped.

The General turned back and against the tempest of noise howled into the messenger's face: "Tell the Colonel I'm sorry but he must hold his place at all hazards. He must not charge till the order is given. Tell him I rely on him to maintain his ground." The man gaped as if Greene had gabbled insanity but saluted, yanked his horse about, and hastened back. The General sucked in a scalding breath; the heat had become intolerable; his bad eye ached. But once again he strove to look into his mind, to see the lines move. *God*, he thought; maybe he spoke it; *God help me.* This was the beast at last, the beast he had been waiting for, the beast that all battles sooner or later became, that no man could ride save on the raw edge of every new moment as best he might. The lines moved. *Mend the center. Sumner in the middle; Marion and Pickens holding right and left till forced to retire. Then Williams and Campbell coming up on Sumner's flanks. The second line of Continentals restored. An attack all along the line, Lee and Henderson on the flanks, Washington's cavalry in support of Henderson against that ugly position by the creek.*

He would ride the beast. On the road, British guns threw shot after shot at Gaines's remaining piece, shaking the woods with their thunder while Gaines dashed about rallying his matrosses. The General, his decisions made, screamed his orders to the surround of anxious faces. Sterne, accustomed by now to the commotion of the fight, bent his long neck and casually began to crop sweet grass.

Beyond, where they had stopped two or three hundred paces ahead on the road, the columns of regulars in blue and brown commenced to diverge, some turning left, some right; there was a good deal of shouting of orders; drums buzzed in the annoying way that always started an unpleasant resonance in the hollow of James's chest; bugles blew; there was a tootling of fifes; and presently a line of battle shaped itself there and marched on up the road. Their tramping raised a fine brown dust of crushed pine needles that drifted back to settle over the Delawares and the dragoons, giving them its agreeable aroma of parched balsam.

The Delawares had shifted from the menacing posture of Charge Bayonets and waited now with muskets at the position of Shoulder Firelocks, bayonets standing all in a row like some improbable picket fence with palings of sharpened steel, leaving the comforting impression the carnage among fleeing militiamen James so dreaded had been postponed or at least delayed. This and the pleasant fragrance of the pine dust sifting down relieved his misgivings a little.

For some time now he had been listening to the noise of the fighting, so when the volleys started to come quicker and the cannon to boom oftener and it all got so loud he'd have had to holler right up against Corporal Murphy's head if he wanted to tell him something—though of course Murphy wouldn't have paid him any mind if he'd done that—he figured he'd been wrong a while back to think the battle had got joined then. Now he reasoned those first sounds had been but the armies taking their first nips, like two bulls in a pasture hooking their horns at one another, or like a pair of roosters billing in the main. What he was hearing now, this racket he could feel buzzing the ends of his bones and humming in his wasted belly, *this* was the battle. He'd just never been so close to one before and hadn't known how it would give the whole world a good rumpling. And it wasn't long till, in addition to hearing it, he could start to smell it too, even as the perfume of pine dust began to fade.

He already knew the smell; he'd sniffed it in Virginia from afar. It was mighty rank. That was because the gunpowder they used was made of sulphur and charcoal and human piss; he had that on good authority—Charlie Cooke had told him. He'd used a sight of powder in his time, shooting Chenowith's dinner, without giving a thought to what it was made of. He'd had to go in the army and meet Charlie Cooke to find out. The ingredients had sounded unlikely at first, but he trusted Charlie and came to believe him. It stood to reason if you mixed up a mess of sulphur and charcoal and piss and set fire to it, the damned stuff would stink like hell, and he smelled it now, the same sour odor a thousand fellows who'd eaten a supper of asparagus might give if they all made water at once.

But there was something else, something underneath all that, another smell he couldn't name but that clung in his nose like some vile snot. He wondered if it was fear. He was surely afraid, but it was hard to tell if the troopers around him were. Murphy didn't seem to be, nor Captain Watts. He glanced to his left, but couldn't read those hard-boned faces. An air of slouchy indifference prevailed; they might as easily have been waiting for the drudgery of drill as for a rush into deadly combat. He couldn't tell if what he saw in them was bravery or resignation. Certainly they did not seem afraid.

He wished Obediah were near him; he'd got fond of the scoundrel and missed him badly now. He knew Plumbley would've been able to say something out of the Good Book or the doctrine of the Methodists that would ease his fear. He even wished he could hear Obediah offer up a prayer. He turned in the saddle to catch the preacher's eye and see if at least they might exchange a wink or a smile, but before he could finish his turn Captain Watts's sharp command lashed at him, *Eyes to the front, trooper!* He swung back chagrined; Murphy slanted him a supercilious smirk.

At least he was feeling some better. His vitals weren't astir anymore; he hadn't puked in a while. The worst effects of his ill-advised drink of rum had worn off. But he was still as weak as a babe and so tired he could hardly sit his Chickasaw. So even as the tumult of battle grew loud enough to deafen him, even as the dreaded time drew nearer when he might be called on to cut down the skulkers of his own army or perhaps be cast into the fight himself to live or die or be maimed or maybe even to run away in terror as so many cowards before him had run—for he did not know if he were a brave man or craven-hearted—even as all this closed around him, the reality of it blurred over into a dream, his eyelids grew heavy and began to droop, and finally he slept the deep, sodden sleep of exhaustion, slept sitting on his horse, and amid his dream of the brazen clamor of war he dreamt too of Agnes and her golden curls, and of Libby, and of his Ma and Da, and of home.

A savage cry, close at hand, startled him awake: "Here they come, the white-livered bastards!"

Mend the center. The lines and figures Greene had imagined on the map of his fancy now moved on the ground in actual fact. General Sumner's Continentals advanced through the smoky pines at the double-quick with trailed arms; a hundred yards behind them, half-obscured by the battle haze, the General could just spy the brown and blue of the Virginians and Marylanders as they displayed. He heard the clanking din of Captain Browne's six-pounders coming up behind that line though he could not see the guns themselves.

Good, good, he thought, observing the steadiness of Sumner's advance, *he's drilled those new levies to a fine point; hard to believe they've been under ordered discipline but little more than a month.* He turned then to look into the middle of the buckling militia front, just as a small company—*those Hillsborough villains,* he bitterly surmised—commenced streaming rearward; at the shameful sight his spirits plunged from the summit of exaltation Sumner's troops had inspired. A gloomy certainty came: *That will be the start of it.* The little party of militiamen fled toward Sumner's line; grudgingly the oncoming regulars opened ranks to let them through, fellow Carolinians who were disgracing their native state; curses and taunts pursued the caitiffs as they ran.

Like a rent in a cheap garment, the hole the Hillsborough company had opened began to shred and fray around the edges as more and more troops to either side broke ranks and began straggling back. Still, despite this widening gap, for another instant most of the front held; Greene saw other Carolinians resolutely biting cartridges, spitting aside the torn paper, ramming down new loads. Then the British line opposite belched another cruel volley by divisions and the whole of Malmedy's corps staggered; perhaps twenty of them toppled. Two battalions of the enemy—*green coats and red, Cruger's people; some of the Sixty-Third*—suddenly advanced through the boiling musket smoke; the General glimpsed the glitter of naked steel, *Bayonet charge;* and just then Malmedy's command simply disintegrated, ceased to exist, swarmed back on Sumner's brigade like ants from an overturned nest.

Once more the regulars did the office of a colander and strained these through, but with the same shouts of defamation and calumny—*Unearned abuse*, Greene sadly reflected. Sumner's troops promptly filled the gulf between Pickens and Marion. Seeing this, the men in green and red sullenly faced about, withdrew. *The center's mended.* Greene slumped with relief; the beast had given him a nasty turn but he had ridden it out. *What will be next? I'll have to ride that too.*

A weeping courier came to confess the breaking of the militia, already so pitifully evident. Wanly the General smiled at this needless, mortifying courtesy. "Go back to Colonel Malmedy, son," he told the saddened fellow as kindly as he knew how, while from the road came the roar of Captain Gaines's remaining three-pounder and the responsive concussion of the enemy's guns. "Tell the Colonel he has my *permission* to withdraw. And tell him his troops have fought with a spirit and firmness reflecting the highest honor, that they've satisfied my most sanguine expectations." Even as he uttered them, the words sounded empty; he knew nothing he said now could redeem the poor wretches; all North Carolina would soon condemn them.

The courier rode off sobbing. *My fault,* Greene berated himself, *My fault. This morning they hailed me, trusted me; but they had not a sufficiency of ammunition. Now they'll be named cowards for all time. My fault. My fault.* Yet he must turn it away from him. It had been a mistake, yes. But nothing could change it, not now, not later. It was done. He could not let it crack the steel of his battle mood.

He trained his glass on Sumner's line, saw a flash of fire and burst of smoke run from flank to flank, felt the dull shock of the volley in the air about him; saw enemy soldiers in scarlet and green blown down like autumn leaves. The British answered; the noise of it, full-on, struck the ear more sharply than had Sumner's, heard from the side and rear; a ghastly number of Continentals withered before the gale of musketry. But even as these fell, their messmates were plying ramrods, taking aim, and firing again; and the smoke of that volley was still rolling when the enemy replied with yet another even more terrific. The ground on both sides was strewn with the fallen. *Never an exchange more tremendous,* Greene thought, *never more fierce and determined.* He did not know which to admire most, the gallantry of the officers or the bravery of the troops. *Their obstinacy would do honor to the best of veterans.*

The freckle-faced messenger from the state troops emerged through the woods on the left, this time riding a brown colt. His hunting shirt was spattered with blood, evidently not his own, for he seemed whole. "General," he cried, saluting with his new sense of gravity, "sorry to inform you, but Colonel Henderson's got shot down. Colonel Myddelton too. Colonel

Hampton's taken command. Them Bloodybacks keep rushing out of that damned thicket no matter how much we beat 'em back, and their line wraps round our'n on the left by a right smart. Colonel Hampton, he says tell you the going's mighty hard over yonder."

The General winced inwardly to hear this—the more he learned of that position on the left, the more dangerous it seemed; also, he'd known Henderson better than he knew Hampton and he hated to rely on a man whose quality he could not judge by personal acquaintance. But he held firmly to his outer show of calm. "Very well," he nodded. "Go to Colonel Hampton and say to him he's to hold that flank against all odds. If he thinks he can't hold, he's to send me word immediately. Colonel Washington's cavalry and the light troops are in reserve, and if necessary can come to his support."
The boy saluted and wheeled the colt to go, but Greene called after him. "What is Colonel Henderson's condition?"

"Thigh-bone's broke, I fear. They've done toted him off the field."

The General nodded, dismissed him, then again summoned him back with a shout. "What happened to your old one-eyed horse?"

The lad shrugged and hung his shaggy head as if from guilt. "Got kilt, General. Some goddamned son of a bitch over there put a big ball through that poor brute's neck, and he bled to death with me a-riding around on him. Hell, I never knowed it, till he fell right out from under me." He dashed away a tear and added with an air of deep remorse, "My Daddy'll skin me for it too. 'Twas his own good plow horse."

There was nothing the General could say to ease that small tragedy, feel it piquantly though he did. Brusquely he bade the child go and was swinging about to view the continuing stubborn fight on Sumner's front when, most strangely, a galloper arrived from Colonel Hammond, reporting an advance of the enemy's left flank, a battalion of the Sixty-third and some Loyalists—*those Provincials or East Florida troops with Coffin*, thought Greene. These had taken a position threatening to the right of Marion's line, Hammond's man affirmed. The Legion infantry and Hammond's troops had engaged them. *Stewart's itching to attack; first he's probed the center, now the right, he's pounding hard at the left*. Still, he raised a puzzled eyebrow. "Why is Colonel Hammond reporting to me and not Colonel Lee?"

The messenger shifted his gaze from side to side, the unvarying sign of a subordinate unwilling to incriminate a higher officer. "Can't say, General," he yelled above exchanges of musketry and the slamming of the guns.

Greene's temper rose. "If you please, sir, go back and thank Colonel Hammond for the information, and say to him that he and Colonel Lee must hold our right if it costs them every man. But also tell him," he added with fierce emphasis, "*that he must report to the commanding general in the proper fashion, through his superior officer*."

The fellow saluted, crimson-faced. "I will, General." As Greene watched after him, ire receded and a creeping unease took its place. From his observation he did not deem Hammond the sort to ignore protocol. *Is something amiss on the right flank?* Till now he'd thought all was well there, had even felt safe in detaching Gresham's Georgians from Lee, sending them to join Washington's reserve. His troubled gaze and Pendleton's met, but neither saw fit to speak, though the same question bedeviled them both. What was Lee up to; or, more ominously, *not* up to? *Has my mad, bad boy gone astray after all?*

What came, to James's amazement as he jerked awake, was not the mob of *white-livered bastards* he had dreaded confronting; not at all a crowd of cowardly fugitives so addled with terror they must be given the point of the bayonet or the edge of the saber to bring them again to a discipline they had forgotten amid the horrors of the battleground. No, what came, as the Delawares and the dragoons looked on perplexed, might have been a mass of fellows angrily debating some profound disagreement.

It was true they had lost any semblance of order and approached in one great unruly gaggle; but they came not in a stampede of panic but at the deliberate, stolid pace of fellows who have put in a hard task of work that has failed to turn out satisfactorily. Most retained their arms, every mouth was smeared black from biting cartridges, many were bloody and limping from wounds or were worse hurt and getting borne along on the arms of their fellows; they brought with them a heavy odor of sweat and burnt powder. In fact, far from appearing craven or demoralized, they showed every sign of having been heavily and stubbornly engaged. And all seemed in the grip of the same towering rage, disputing violently with one another as they came trudging down the road toward the waiting cordon.

Though the whole bunch seethed with a dozen arguments, one poor wretch—surprisingly a field-grade officer by his pair of silver epaulets— appeared to be a special target of fury for many of the angriest. Hatless and bedraggled, his bald pate scratched and bruised, the poor wretch was stumbling along at the front of the mass, three or four friends gathered round him to fend off blows from the angry militiamen, while imprecations of every sort rained down on him from all sides: *Turd-eater, wait'll Ruthy hears; you'll not see her oyster basket again; goddamned chicken-hearted cunt. You damned yellow cur; you're done up in Orange County after this. Bitch-booby. Piss-pot. Colonel ought to hang you by your goddamned doodle.*

So intent were they on slandering the officer they hardly noticed the arrayed bayonets of the Delawares and swords of the dragoons—paid them so little mind that James, no longer facing the necessity he had dreaded to cut them down as skulkers, took some offense at their utter dismissal of the danger he and the others in the cordon presented; after all, he might've had to kill some of them, and not a one seemed the least grateful. He watched in disgust while the disputes continued and their company officers at last appeared and took control. Colonel Washington gave the order to Return Swords; Captain Kirkwood put the Delawares at rest; and presently the wrathful militiamen, still hurling recriminations at the hated offender, were passing between files toward the rear.

They went by on either side of James, some brushing lightly against his knees, others shoving at him or at his Chickasaw with spiteful intent; the heat of their bodies, which also seemed to be the heat of their scorn, lifted thickly to him. They were engorged with passionate feeling. "Fuck them Hillsborough cock-suckers," one man growled. "One fine day on the banks of the Eno I'll shoot that yellow bastard Farmer where it'll hurt the most."

A degrading thing seemed to have happened to them; the man called Farmer must be at fault. Humiliation and shame congested every countenance. Their anguish was so painful to witness that after the first few had passed him James could no longer set eyes on them. But some of the dragoons spat down on them or spoke cutting slurs, and of course this only provoked them worse and caused savage outbreaks with the offending troopers; Colonel Washington hastened to quell these with the flat of his saber.

But after these quarrelers something different glided at them from the smoke. A boy dressed in deerskin was the first, no older than fifteen, dragging his musket by the barrel, sobbing and calling out a name. "Nancy," he wailed, "Nancy." Next, two fellows came stumbling with their arms wrapped around a third, who hopped lopsided clutching to his bosom a pale white foot torn off at the ankle. The weeping boy passed between the files to the rear, "Nancy, Nancy." Helped by his friends, the man holding his foot slipped by after him; James heard him humming some country tune; his eyes were blank and fixed like the eyes of a stuffed raccoon.

More emerged. Wanderers, shufflers, limpers, crawlers; a blood-soaked man in a hunting shirt, half his face gone leaving a red hole with a pale wedge of cheekbone showing, his jaw unhinged on one side and dropped down swaying loose by some cords of sinew—*odd to see that line of teeth hanging thataway*; he seemed uncommon cool, looking up to James with a grave and ceremonious nod. "Nancy," the cries faded behind, "Nancy."

"Defeat ain't pretty," the Colonel told the regiment, riding the ranks as the maimed and mangled Carolinians kept coming at them from the smoke. "Sometimes the enemy whips us, sometimes we whip ourselves, like those boys've done. However it happens, it's the ugliest damned thing there is. Don't let it happen to us today." He pointed his saber toward the front, where the commotion of the fighting was waxing louder and louder by the minute. "The Continentals have gone in. I figure we'll be next. When we go, make damned sure, every one of you, it's the Bloodybacks get whipped today, not the Continental Dragoons."

The beast the General sought to ride kept pitching and rolling and blaring, ever more intense, ever more frenzied, its continuous snarl and rumble traveling to and fro along the front and shaking the flanks the way a terrier shakes a rat in its jaws: it gave up a massed concatenation of noise no bugle or drum or fife could penetrate, a volume so terrific that Greene and his officers had to screech in each other's faces like demented persons so as to be barely heard. By now the form of the beast had no form at all, but was instead an immense shapeless fog of stinking smoke in which indistinct figures swam and the flashes of muskets and artillery flickered like the coals of Hell. The air itself consisted not of the soft sweet familiar ether one was accustomed to breathe, but had hardened into a medium made of shocks and blows that, rather than nourish one's body, assailed it, battered it with the clout of the contending guns, the stiff staccato of musketry, the yelling and cheering of men maddened by a carnival of blood and death, and the screams of the injured and dying. *Yes*, thought the General, *this is Hell indeed, and for my sins do I sink into it.*

He could see nothing; he knew only what a ceaseless succession of grimy, perspiring couriers screamed at him, that General Sumner remained heavily engaged; that the enemy had brought up his reserve and was pressing Sumner's right; that the Legion infantry and Colonel Hammond's command were picking away at the flank of this enemy force—though, vexingly, no word had lately come to him direct from Colonel Lee himself, only from Hammond, his subordinate. He knew that the British to Sumner's front and right were double the North Carolinian's strength and had inflicted appalling casualties—two captains and two lieutenants killed and six other officers wounded, God knew how many troops. But he also knew Sumner's line was holding; that his musket practice was, as one messenger proudly put it, "goddamned fine"; his ear told him Sumner's controlled volley firing had given way to the more effective *feu de billbaude*, each man firing at will, that sooner or later came to dominate every extended action.

And he knew the brigades of Marion and Pickens, out of ammunition at last, had been compelled to retire; that Sumner had extended his line to replace them along the front as best he could; that after a courageous duel with the British artillery Captain Gaines's remaining gun had got dismounted owing to its trunnions breaking; that Captain Browne's two pieces had gone into battery in advance of the main line; and that at the first exchange Browne had succeeded in disabling a three-pounder of the enemy. On the left, Colonel Hampton still battled desperately with the flank companies of the Nineteenth and Thirtieth Regiments and the Buffs; the enemy there had just advanced a battalion and was threatening to envelop Hampton's open flank.

It was time to send in the rest of the second line of Continentals, Colonel Williams' Maryland and Virginia brigades, and to bring up the *corps de reserve* to aid Colonel Hampton—that was the remnant of his battle plan yet remaining regardless of the derangements of the beast; but before he could give the orders Colonel Hammond's beleaguered messenger emerged from the haze and, shamefaced, shouted to him, not daring to meet what he knew would be the General's disapproving glare, "Compliments of Colonel Hammond, General."

"My dear young man," Greene blurted, "why the devil do I keep hearing from Colonel Hammond and not from his superior, Colonel Lee?"

The fellow—he was a captain of state troops in a white coat turned up with dark blue—ducked his head as if to dodge a missile, bending his gaze on the mane of his gray horse and fixing it there in a dogged, persecuted manner. "Colonel Hammond, General, he begs to report a weakening in the enemy's left flank. It's as if they come up by mistake and then got ordered back and don't want to withdraw or something; they behave confused. Colonel Hammond thinks they'll break under a spirited charge."

Then the captain looked straight into Greene's face; his dark eyes glittered; he colored and at last vented the surge of temper he'd long held in check. "But he can't find Colonel Lee, General," he cried, "and the commander of the Legion cavalry won't move without him. Colonel Hammond begs me say to you, sir, with all respect, sir, and meaning no reflection on Colonel Lee, sir, *but goddamn it, the only force he's got's his own little company and the damned Legion infantry.*"

With each new twist or lurch or pounce of the beast the General had felt its colossal power spinning out from under him, and shaken by these tidings he knew with his first sink of fear that he no longer rode it, that it had passed beyond his grasp and compass, that now he was not its rider but its helpless, futile witness. He stared like an idiot. "Cant *find* Colonel Lee?"

"Nary a whiff of him, sir," was the defiant reply. The General's jaw tightened with alarm. *Could my precious boy be killed or hurt?* But no sooner had the suspicion come than its bleak answer followed: *Someone would've reported it. No, he's well. He's very well. He's himself.*

Hammond's captain waited scowling. Greene took pity on him; how could he not? He closed a consoling hand on the fellow's sleeve. "My good young man, please go back to Colonel Hammond. Give him my most cordial thanks for his persistence, and for his valor in opposing the enemy with so little force. Say to him I'll send an aide to find Colonel Lee, and another to Captain Armstrong of the Legion cavalry ordering him to obey Colonel Hammond's instructions. Regardless of Lee's whereabouts, tell Colonel Hammond I concur that a charge should be made at once on the disordered enemy."

The General yelped his orders—Pendleton to locate Lee; Shubrick to ride back with Hammond's captain, wreathed now in grim smiles of vindication. As they vanished into the murk two streams of feeling poured into Greene's heart, one of tartest venom, the other bittersweet with regret. *Harry Lee. Light-horse Harry Lee. goddamn your arrogance and vainglory. Where the deuce are you, you pompous self-seeking little pup? Looking for some other part of the field where you and your Legion cavalry may distinguish yourselves? Or hiding behind a tree or in some ravine, paralyzed with fear? Which is it, my dear sublime and terrible, insubordinate rogue? My son. My splendid, my calamitous, my beloved son. Because of you, this damned beast may devour us all.*

Then, ironically, even as he began to yield up his last notion of turning any part of the beast to his smallest advantage, another galloper came to him through the smoke, drew up grinning, screeched at him as he leaned eagerly near, "General Sumner's compliments, General. The enemy's numbers will compel him to yield ground. But he says tell you he's pretty damned sure if he draws back, the enemy's center will advance on him, and if they do, why, they'll derange their line; and if you bring up the Virginia and Maryland brigades at once, why he thinks you can break the bastards and set 'em to running like the devil."

The plan of the battle, knocked to a shambles by the ungovernable beast, *no, by Harry Lee, damn his inconstant soul,* now improbably resumed its former pattern on the landscape of his thinking—the advance of the Maryland and Virginia Continentals under the command of Otho Williams, *dear Otho; yes, I may shed my shell of battle sternness and say his name now, Otho my valiant friend,* poised now in line of battle in Sumner's rear. An advance of the cavalry to drive back the troops on the left now threatening Colonel Hampton. *A charge all along the front, maybe even on the right as well, if Hammond can induce Eggleston to charge*—the figures in his mind leapt into motion edged with points of steel. He turned to Dr. Clements of the medical department, who had volunteered his services as an aide but moments before. "Go to Colonel Williams, Doctor. Tell him to advance and sweep the field with his bayonets." Clements pounded off.

Next he summoned Captain Pierce, seized his shoulder, drew him close. "My compliments to Colonel Washington," he shrieked above the uproar. "The dragoons and the Delaware Light Troops are to make a rapid advance, take post on the left flank, and reinforce Colonel Hampton. Tell Colonel Washington he's to assess the situation there and, if practicable, contrive to dislodge the enemy from his position, which endangers our left. Colonel Hampton is to support."

Kosciuszko next steered his mount close; the General howled at him; he nodded and turned and rode hard to the left toward Hampton. *God will aid us after all*, Greene thought, just as a musket ball struck Sterne in the forehead and the animal's legs crumpled under him and Sterne plunged heavily sideways with a crash of harness; and the General rolled free on the soft, fragrant bed of pine straw.

Part ye' Twenty-Seventh

In Which ye Moſt Aſtoniſhing Efforts
Are Made to Diſlodge ye Enemy*

*H*OW LONG HAS IT BEEN NOW? FIVE HOURS? SIX?
It felt long—as long as the eternity the preachers harangued
about, a timeless time where time itself had no meaning or being but was
just the lack of anything else but time; where time didn't begin or end;
where time was a void but somehow had also come to be so full that it
was everything too. The preachers said your condemned soul endured
that in Perdition, that little and that much. Absence and presence all in
one. *That's where I am.*

*Scared at first so bad your teeth go to rattling in your head like dice, scared
just to get up in the dark of night with the moon leaning low at you, scared to
mount up and ride into the black woods, wondering about dying and whether
Captain Gunn had seen matters wrongways or right. Saying Agnes' name,
seeing Libby's face. Watching some new fellows riding up to take post in the
rear, Gresham's Georgians, somebody said. Then more waiting. Waiting and
waiting and waiting. Waiting so long you finally forget to be scared and start to
remember how bad you feel, how your guts are all a-bubble, how your bunghole
hurts, how your head aches, how tired you are, so tired you fall a-drowsing even
with the noise of the fighting in your ears.*

*Then somebody jerks you awake saying you're apt to have to cut up a bunch
of your own good American boys on account of them running; but then the
Americans you're supposed to be cutting up don't need cutting up after all. Instead you have to sit your horse and watch the poor hurt ones straggle back from
the fight, folk you've never in your life seen hurt so dire, not even those poxed
blacks on the Richmond road. You don't want to see them but you can't stop
yourself either, leering down at their misery like a ghoul, wanting to know how
many ways a mortal man can get broke and tore, but ashamed for your leering*

---

*Nathanael Greene to Thomas McKean, President of the Continental Congress, September
11, 1781

390

even as you do it. Then finally even the horror of that gets tiresome. You're hungry and dozy and you've shit blood till you're weak and you've puked your guts dry and you're too sapped down even to feel pity for the hurt ones or to feel your own fear any more. How long has it been now?

He sagged. *I'm give out*; his head drooped forward onto the Chickasaw's rough mane; he lost himself again in sleep.

He heard a command, "Form by Sections! The Regiment will advance; Forward, at the Trot, March!" They were moving. The shout and the hard gait of the Chickasaw rudely roused him; he righted himself in the saddle even as Captain Watts called across, "Goddamn you, Johnson, wake up!" Corporal Murphy swore and fetched him a blow on the side of his head with the heel of a horny hand; it knocked off James's helmet and James looked dully back to see the helmet roll in the road and then the horse of the man behind him mash it flat with a hoof. He resented the unfairness of having to lose his helmet, but felt too frail to protest to Murphy of it; instead he yawned. *I reckon I could sleep for a year.*

They were going up the road in column, twelve ranks deep; again he found himself riding as number two file in the front rank of the second section. Yet now that the sun was well up and they had resumed what the Colonel and everyone else in the regiment seemed to believe was a section formation that he could now see the whole of, the arrangement looked foreign to him—far too broad, oddly misshapen. In Virginia a section had always formed up in two even ranks of four troopers, or five at the most, a sergeant on the right of the first rank and a corporal on the right of the second. Here, the front of a so-called section was twice as wide, eight or more men—what Captain Gunn would have named a platoon front. Furthermore, in some sections the second rank was a man or two shorter than the first, in others the width of both ranks was identical. And while the sergeants and corporals still held post on the right of each rank, the officers, instead of leading ahead of each section on the right front, rode level with the front rank, to the outside of the sergeants.

James wanted to inquire into this difference in practice, but by now knew better than to indulge his curiosity. Instead, after thinking the matter over he decided the conditions of service in South Carolina, so different from those in Virginia, must have dictated changes better suited to the rougher terrain of the country and to what Shoupe and Hudson had told him were Colonel Washington's more aggressive ideas about using cavalry as a fighting force on the battlefield. To the Northward, the dragoon service most often performed only outpost work and reconnaissance—the lighter duties that had at first tempted James to enlist in White's Horse. Rarely, if ever, had it been called on to play a role in combat. James, as he reflected on this difference, which set him so at hazard, disapproved of it.

The Delawares had drawn off to the flanks. A white mist of smoke hung in the air. It stung the eyes and nose; its bitter flavor was in his mouth; the tall slender trunks of the pines hovered in it like brooding ha'nts. The rumpus of the battle up ahead beat a low pulse against him as if it were something living in the air and not just some force giving the air a tremor. The horses blew and snorted, shook their bridle-chains; a rangy chestnut in the file in front of James squeezed out three or four big clods of manure that the Chickasaw stepped in; the warm grassy odor, redolent of cozy stables and peacetime, rose to him. He thought of Patuxent and the Maryland track, the dark turf spewing into his face from the lead horse on the rail as he and Patuxent rounded the last turn, Patuxent giving that bold toss of his head that meant he was going to give the best of his speed now and pass the leader on the outside and go on to the finish. *Patuxent, what a great heart you had.*

"Draw swords!" came a ringing cry from the front—James knew that tenor note by now; Colonel Washington's. Awkwardly he dragged his sword grating from its scabbard. "Slope swords!" He laid the top edge of the sword to his shoulder. "Dress right, square the files." He glanced to Murphy on his right, then to his front, touching his spurs to the Chickasaw to even himself in the rank and align himself in his file, then glanced left and saw the six faces there all in a row as on a string of silhouette portraits cut from paper, each as impassive as the other. "Quick Trot, March!" The Chickasaw's sharp spine jiggled his crotch and racked his bowels. He reckoned he should be afraid now, but all he felt was a tiredness that pulled down at him as if he were a sack of stones.

All this time they were passing more of the hurt ones. But these had lost their novelty now. He hardly gave them a glance, except for one that was special because his scalp was gone and a loose raggedy cup of hair flapped behind, exposing a bulb of skull as smooth as a peeled onion save where it had a big half-moon dent in it with a small pink nib of brain peeping out. James didn't know how this one could still be walking, and just as he mused this, the man's eyes rolled up white and he pitched over dead on the side of the road. He fell right in front of a fellow who was scooting along with pushes of his hands, dragging the rest of him behind like he was some new type of two-tailed creation; maybe both his legs were broken, or his back. "Goddamn," the dragging man hollered at the corpse, as if by dropping across his way it had insulted him on purpose.

James remembered feeding Patuxent apple slices out of the hollow of his hand. *The soft nibble of his lips, the crunch them apples made, the cidery smell.* He remembered turning balusters on his spring-pole lathe in the joiner's shop, the white shavings curling off the shaped wood in thin coiled clean-smelling ribbons. He remembered giving Agnes a bashful kiss. Writing

Libby two letters. Poovey Sides with his shoat pushing its nose under his armpit. Captain Gunn. Little John the Crowner's son. *Remember that for certain*, the least of the Gunns but the bravest of all. *Will I be brave? Will I live as Gunn promised me? If I live, will I live whole, or will I live tore and hurt and broke like that two-tailed man pulling himself along on the ground?*

A riderless horse burst out of the smoke, its head twisted to the side to keep from stepping on its trailing reins, its saddle covered with blood. It galloped past; James had an instant's look into its mad black eye, then began to shoot sharp worried glances all about him. *Shoupe, Hudson, Bobby Busby, Neal, Lockett, all them boys. Where are they? Why don't I see nobody I know?* It didn't seem right to stare all this danger in the face with no friend by him. He turned to the rear, knowing he'd spy Plumbley there, and yes, he saw Obediah yonder in his place, but saw him blankly glaring, not seeming to know him, maybe not seeing anything now, maybe not even looking at this world at all anymore but looking into the next, into that eternity preachers like himself knew about that was time and not time and all the time there was or could ever be. Far behind now, James glimpsed the Delawares forming a line of battle across the road.

The Chickasaw's hard trot was giving James a worse joggling than ever, pounding his stung bottom against the sparse padding of the saddle, banging the ends of his bones, making his head jar and wobble on his neck and the barrel of his carbine knock against the shin of his right leg. The smoke thickened, the tempest ahead got louder, he heard the bray of a bugle and the beating of drums and the throb of cannon fire and a noise he'd not heard before and at first couldn't name—a high hollow howl like a big wind will make sometimes, and then all at once he knew what it was, *Why, them's the men all a-fighting, all of 'em together in the struggle, squalling out their fear and fury.* The smoke parted, showed him a brown line of men weaving among the pines; then another line beyond, wearing red and green. He saw the flash of bayonets.

The regiment veered off the road to the left, passing through the piney woods. The hooves of the horses thumped a soft thunder on the deeper carpet of pine straw. It was blistering hot, *that's not only the hot of a summer day, that's the hot of burnt powder and spilt blood and scalding sweat and fellows all a-blowing out their seared breath at once*; the bouncing gait of the Chickasaw sent James's own sweat flying off him in showers. He longed for a drink, but his canteen flung and flew so hard he couldn't capture it and dared not try anyway, for Murphy kept yelling, "Align to the right, goddamn it, align to the right. Watch the line, keep it straight, you sons of bitches." At Murphy's side Captain Watts rode with his face set firm, his chin low and held a bit to the side, as if one eye had gone bad and he must cock his head to see aright. He was looking into eternity too, maybe looking all the way over the edge of eternity into whatever might be on the other side of it, if anything was.

The ground under the horses rose, dipped, rose again, and with every change of surface the ranks of troopers rolled and sank as well, in succession, like the rows of waves James had once seen pushing themselves ceaselessly onto a seashore, one after another. Off to the right, musketry rippled, starting near and loud, then fading away further that way. Somewhere over there horses were screaming. Fifes played. *Please*, he thought, *let me live.*

The General, covered with pine needles from his tumble, watching with fierce intensity as Colonel Williams' second line of Virginia and Maryland Continentals advanced, was holding lightly in one hand the reins of the fallen Sterne; and though his battle temper still plated him, a stray shred of pity escaped to let him hope the poor animal might yet recover and rise, though absently he knew the hope was vain. *A great slaughter of men encompasses me and for them I can have no pity; yet I'm sorry for this loyal, innocent brute.*

He did not like having had this thought and thrust it away, just as yonder amid a swirl of smoke the surging regulars plunged into a hurricane of the enemy's musketry and grapeshot; he looked on stolidly unfeeling as scores of men in blue and brown were scythed down. And when his steward Owens approached leading a fresh mount he relinquished Sterne's reins and pulled himself into the new saddle and forgot at once that the good bay had ever lived.

Forty yards from the enemy's front Williams' and Campbell's Continentals halted even as howitzer shells came bouncing at them like badly rolled bowls to explode in dingy clouds tossing bodies to all sides, even as savage blasts of grape tore bloody holes in the ranks, even as the British gave them a stuttering volley of platoon fire. Under this assailment the regulars steadied, *Look at that, look at that composure, my Continentals.* Even above the turmoil he could hear the piping screams and ululations of their wounded, dead and dying; but still he could not pity them. Admire them yes, *but pity is for another day, a day without this sin.*

He leaned forward in his saddle eagerly watching; they leveled their pieces, vomited forth a sheet of fire; the British line writhed and fluttered like wind-blown washing on a line; tatters of red and green gusted rearward in that gale, others littered the forest floor as might remnants scattered from a ragpicker's cart; then, as the crackle of that volley faded, a remarkable, improbable stillness fell like a stroke across the whole scene. Not a shot was fired, not a wheel creaked, not a horse whinnied, not a man spoke. No creature of the woods stirred. It was as if every living being on that deadly ground now sensed the advent of some tremendous thing and turned to look, transfixed, expectant. Volumes of smoke silently rose.

The General held his breath. *Now,* he thought, *Now. Pray God, this is victory.* Then came an insistent patter of drums, a bugle's wail, Otho Williams' unmistakable whoop, "At Trail Arms! Charge!" and with a mighty cheer the regulars hurled themselves like a thunderbolt at the enemy line, every musket carried at the trail, bayonets aslant. The two lines, the rushing one and the standing one, nearly met; bayonets of both sides clashed and rang; then the left center of the enemy front shattered and the greater part of Cruger's Loyalists and the Sixty-Third and Sixty-Fourth Foot crumbled away in disorderly fragments. Through this 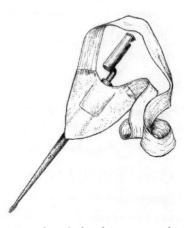 enormous rift the Marylanders and Virginians hurtled, taking up a jubilant pursuit. In the next moment, their left flank compromised, the Buffs too dropped back, grudgingly at first, then in quickening haste; and what had once been a stout British line of battle now became a fleeing rabble.

Greene shouted a huzzah of joy; but the cry stopped in his throat when he spied, deep in the smoke-hazed pines on the far right, a pack of men in red more stubbornly and reluctantly withdrawing. *Those troops aren't licked; they're in some disorder, but they'll fight a rear-guard action, cover the retreat.* He heard a smatter of musketry over there; it had to be Hammond and the Legion infantry, slashing at them. *But where's Lee and the Legion horse? Part of the enemy line's routed, part remains. A charge of horse will break that damned flank, there'll be an utter rout. Where's Harry Lee?* He pounded his fist on his saddlebow. *Oh, damn you, my boy; oh, where's my boy?*

There was no knowing; Pendleton had not returned with a report, nor had Shubrick or Colonel Hammond's captain. Quickly he motioned to Major Hyrne, snapped at him as incourteously as if he were Lee himself, "Find Colonel Lee. Find him and say to him I've assumed direction of the Legion horse and he's under my express orders to take them in hand and charge the enemy's left flank." Hyrne saluted, white-faced and tight-lipped, spun his horse and rode away. Greene looked behind; no sign yet of Colonel Washington's dragoons and the Delawares. But unlike Lee, he knew Washington and Kirkwood would be coming. *Crush the enemy's right with Washington, his left with Lee, and the battle's truly won.*

It was time to go forward with the victorious Continentals. Reining to the front, for the first time he looked down and recognized the new horse Owens had fetched him, a large dun with black points. *Cruger,* he realized with a twisting, ironical smile. *It's Cruger's horse.* Colonel John Harris Cruger, commander of the New York Loyalists; Cruger, who'd turned him back at Ninety-Six; Cruger, who just now was running for his very life. During the siege the dun had got loose from the Star Fort; Colonel Washington had captured it, identified its owner by the contents of its saddlebags, and presented it to Greene. *A nice turn of fortune, this. To chase the very man who beat me—now ignominiously beaten in his turn—and on his own horse too.*

He spoke to the beast, laughing, perversely savoring the name in his mouth, *Cruger*; he struck his spurs and started forward, staff and escort following behind. The new steed had a smooth gait, a soft mouth, and a biddable air. They rode through the thinning smoke, in and out of the pine groves, sometimes having to jump trees that had been downed by cannon fire or to waft aside dangling boughs shot half-loose; as the stench of powder dissipated, the woods began to smell pleasantly of fresh rosin flowing now from all the shattered and bullet-pocked trees. Very often they had to step their mounts carefully around the stricken, some crying piteously for water or for a doctor's care or for their mothers or for a preacher to hear their last prayer. Many lay babbling and squealing from wounds the General did not allow himself to see. *I pity you not,* Greene insisted, *for you are the price we must pay.*

On the road Captain Browne was limbering up his six-pounders for the chase. The General hailed him, exhorted him to hurry; presently the guns were rattling ahead. The last smoke drifted, opening a view of what lay beyond—a last belt of pines, then a broad sunlit clearing covered with orderly rows of tents, *The British camp,* the road running through the middle, commanded on the left front by a large house. *The house on Harry's map, with the palisaded garden in its rear, the creek to the side, the springs beyond—one big loop and two little ones.*

The clearing teemed with intermixed and contending British and American troops; random musket fire popped. Large bodies of the retreating enemy were disappearing into the woods on the far side of the field; others milled about the camp in confusion; but still more made for the house and the General looked hard at it, scowling. In the drawing it had been a small, irregular, insignificant-looking blob; but yonder at the edge of the clearing, looming higher on its promontory of rocky ground than one might expect in so featureless a country, stood a strong structure of pinkish brick, double-chimneyed, two stories high, with garret windows that would answer for a third, backed by a barn, a warren of outbuildings and that palisaded garden, which in Lee's sketch had seemed a fragile picketed domestic affair, but in fact better resembled a stockade designed by military engineers; and already, as Greene watched, all the windows of the mansion bristled with muskets, even as more and more men in red poured in through its several doors. *They'll make a bastion of it.*

Instantly he thought of the stone house at Germantown. Fortified by the British, it had drawn about it nearly the whole of the American army, had resisted their every effort to breach it, had turned their victory into a draw if not a loss. *Battered at that damned place the whole day long.* He and his division, lost in the fog, entangled with other troops in appalling confusion, had not gotten up that day; but he remembered Stirling's and Sullivan's dead lying in grisly heaps around the Chew house afterward, and now he felt a chill of foreboding. Captain Browne was wheeling his guns about to unlimber and take the brick citadel under fire. Once more the beast the General believed he'd tamed for the moment commenced to spin away from him; once more it defied his puny schemes; once more, with a pang of despair but with an inward shrug of resignation too, he saw he could not nudge it one inch from whatever mad path it now wished to take.

Suddenly he felt an exhaustion like a deep numbing. He was hungry; thirst burned his throat—he begged a swallow of scalding water from Owens' canteen—his quinsey brought on a fit of choking. Heat suffocated him; he realized with stupid amazement that his smallclothes and even his coat were wringing wet; his nose told him that he stank like a drowned dog.

Then he heard a mutter of many hooves behind and glanced back just as Washington's column of dragoons burst from the woods and passed at a hammering trot diagonally across the rear, a thick rectangular block of horsemen, swords at the slope, burly Colonel Washington at its head, Gresham's and Hamilton's little troops trailing at a short distance. Behind them at a steady run came the Delaware Continentals in a straggling arrow-shaped crowd that must once have been a line of battle, but now had lost its cohesion in the race to support the impatient Washington. The tread of the dragoon horses made the forest floor tremble; Greene felt it in his legs and rump. He whipped off his hat, brandished it aloft; Washington, grinning in his round face, replied with a happy wave of his saber. *Never happier than in an advance.* On they thundered, raising a great clangor of sword-scabbards and harness, bearing down on that difficult left flank Greene had not yet seen, where Colonel Hampton still fought the grenadiers and light troops of the enemy around their tangled thicket of blackjack.

James glanced to his right, spied a man on a dun horse flourishing his cocked hat, recognized the sturdy form and the solid seat in the saddle, thought, *Why, that's General Greene again, the second time today.* Surely it was remarkable to pass by the commander of an army twice on the same day of battle; maybe it was an omen for good. He hoped it was. He watched wistfully back as the figure of the General dwindled behind; they trotted on. In another few moments an officer mounted on a blaze-faced black horse approached from the left front. On his head was a little billed cap with a silver crescent fixed to it. He turned about to ride abreast of Colonel Washington and the trumpeter as the column continued its advance. The two officers spoke with some animation; the unfamiliar one, who wore a white coat somewhat like the Colonel's though much cleaner and with facings of a darker blue, kept pointing ahead with his straight-bladed sword while the Colonel vigorously nodded. Then the Colonel twisted rearward in the saddle to shout an order James could not distinguish amid the din, and the column came suddenly to a halt.

The horses stood blowing from the long trot, stamping and shaking their heads. Now the Colonel and the strange officer cantered off through the same patch of woods by which the white-coated fellow had approached. Though the noise of battle still raged roundabout, the regiment dwelt for a time in what seemed a peculiar stillness born of the ceasing of the pounding of hoofbeats and the clatter of equipment. James found the island of quiet eerily disconcerting.

But it did not last long. "Dress to your right," Murphy bellowed. "Straighten the goddamned line. You whoresons, you're supposed to be in open order; get them fucking ranks sixteen feet apart, head to croup. Swords at the slope." Obediently they shuffled about till Murphy declared himself satisfied; all this while Captain Watts said nothing, only sat his horse gazing moodily into the distance. Soon there was nothing else to do but wait, sweating some in the scorch of the sun and some in the damp fug of the tree-shade, swords still laid against their shoulders, the tails of their horses whisking at flies, while in the distance the woods resounded with artillery fire and the tattoo of musketry.

Every moment of the advance James had thought the Colonel would order a charge, that they would throw themselves upon the enemy and he would be lost in the lethal whirl and cut and thrust of a fight for life. His nerves had been pitched for that, his muscles had been tensed for it, his brain had been emptied of all but an expectation of blind, immediate, fatal action. Now this wait, as abrupt and unexpected as having run full-tilt over a field only to fall without warning into a hidden well, seemed cruelly unjust. He chafed under it. *Why'd we stop? What's going on? Where'd the Colonel go?* To be prepared for the worst then immured in pointless inaction was irritating in the extreme.

He squinted questioningly about him to see if any of the others felt as he did, but no one else appeared to share his unease; every face was impassive. Watching them, James was reminded of the deep, endless, unquestioning patience of dogs, who may drowse about for hours, complacent in utter idleness, then spring up at a single word, ready for the chase. Perhaps this lassitude among veteran dragoons was a habit arising from the same acquaintance with oft-postponed consummation.

Actually, though, the wait was not terribly long. Betimes the Colonel returned, the officer in the white coat no longer with him. He rode across their front showing them his confident grin. "Well, boys," he cried, "there's a nasty piece of ground ahead of us, some blackjack scattered about that gets denser the farther you go into it, and the Bloodybacks've got grenadiers and light infantry in amongst it, who've been trying all morning to outflank the army. The South Carolina boys've held 'em back the best they could, but they're outnumbered and the enemy keeps pushing around their left. So we're going to go in there and break those Lobsters up. The South Carolina troops'll be in support, and Gresham's Georgians and that Guilford troop, and the Delawares. So, what d'you say? Are you ready to pitch in?"

All but James cheered him; James was glancing back over his shoulder to see if the Delawares had yet appeared, for the idea of infantry support had for him a great appeal. He thought he might have spied the blue flicker of their uniforms among the trees some distance to the rear, but could not be sure before the Colonel's orders came to resume the advance. The regiment moved, and in rapid sequence, in answer to the shouts of the Colonel, changed its gait from the walk to the trot, then from the trot to the quick trot, and finally to the gallop.

Soon—far too soon for James's taste—he heard the Colonel bawl, "Swords at the Point! Charge!" Finally now the trumpeter was allowed to blow the calls, but the notes of his horn sounded so tinny in the suffocating air that they were hardly as rousing as was the simple sight of the Colonel when he turned his big self in the saddle to show them his laugh and flourish his saber high over the crest of his helmet. Even James was roused, if only for a moment. He wondered, *What would it be like to love battle so?*

He didn't know if he could ever learn the savage joy the Colonel felt, even if he was well enough to try; but he did know he was far from any such delight just now as the regiment changed gaits with a sudden lurch and the Chickasaw bounded into its run which, to James's relief, finally grew fluid and easy on the loins. He lowered his saber from his shoulder till it pointed straight ahead, where naught seemed to wait but piney woods and skeins of dirty smoke. He saw no growth of blackjacks, no enemy position, nothing to attack. The saber was too heavy for him; the point drooped. "Get that sword up!" Captain Watts hooted at him. He strained to raise it, but it only sank lower; he was too frail to hold it in *tierce* as Sergeant Dangerfield had taught him—wrist supple, sword hand above the level of the shoulder, arm extended, elbow bent well back. Ashamed, he laid the thing along the Chickasaw's scrawny neck hoping Captain Watts wouldn't notice.

The commotion of the charge was a muffled rumble of hooves on the spongy forest floor and the coarse breathing of the tiring mounts and a clamor of every sort of gear and the repeated barking of orders, "Close up, Dress to your right, close up!" Every sword but James's was on point, a shimmering wave of steel. The other men were shrieking or howling like wolves or gobbling Indian war-whoops; he looked to both sides; theirs were not the faces he'd come to know in the last hours, but contortions of faces—worse, were not the faces of mortals at all, but the masks of beings not human, beings whose traits and dispositions he could not guess. With every stride of his horse the barrel of his carbine slammed at his shin; *I'm going to get a bad bruise there.*

On they ran, through more drifts of smoke, through more pine woods in flickers of sun and shade, past standing bodies of cavalry and foot, some of whom called out to them, maybe the South Carolinians the Colonel had mentioned who were supposed to charge in support; James thought he saw their cavalry start to move, *That's good, we'll have horse to help us, even if we've outrun the Delawares;* then over a slightly rising terrain, cresting a low ridge, bursting into the open; a dazzle of sunlight. In the glare, an awful scene—bodies of men and horses, some struggling to rise, others asquirm, more lying in the untidy composition of death, the pine straw under them so soaked with blood the hooves of the horses passing over splashed red.

A dazed white face turned up to James like a blooming flower, a wounded man; the Chickasaw's foreleg struck him and he was gone. The place stank of burnt powder and the sickish reek of gore. Pounding through, several troopers steered to miss the fallen, but some made as if to ride straight over them, "State troops," a voice jeered; but, as James knew from the Maryland track, horses don't like to tread on flesh and they commenced to shy and stumble and double-step to avoid the trampling and this disordered the column and there was a great shouting of officers and sergeants and corporals to realign the ranks. Murphy was yelling, "Align to the right. Keep up the pace, goddamn it, watch the line. Get that sword on point."

James felt faint. Though the Chickasaw's gait was smoother at the gallop, still the agitation of it fatally loosened his bowels; to his mortification he shat anew, shat a mess of blood and feces that his bottom must sit in as he rode and fought and maybe even died, all the rest of this long day. A shroud of smoke rose in front. He heard Colonel Washington's jubilant shout, "There they are, boys! Let's go at 'em like hell!" The breath caught in James's gullet.

The last of the smoke blew off. His vision cleared and he saw more viv-idly than he'd ever seen anything. *Oh, Lord.* It was ugly ground. First a few scanty clumps of darkish growth, *must be that blackjack stuff,* then more and more of it, a matted, twisty brush standing higher and denser till as they pressed deeper it closed about them knee-high to the horses, caught at their stirrups with a wicked stubbornness, then, on beyond, visible now as they came hammering at it, a hedge of cragged shrubbery that looked like a dwarfish, black-leaved kind of oak, tough-rooted, thick-branched, the separate bushes all knit together so as to make one briary wall about breast-high to a man—a man a good deal bigger than James Johnson. On horseback, coming at it now at a dead run, peering between the files of the first section, you could see over the top of it, and see behind it the red uni-forms and the bearskin-trimmed, steeple-shaped hats of grenadiers and the little peaked caps of light troops all packed together, and the glitter of their waiting bayonets.

He only had time to sweep one glance beyond that, where the ground was all hummocks and low swales, the hummocks thinly grown with pines and thorny shrubs, the swales marshy and reed-choked, with here and there sharp ravines and deep hollow ways cutting through. The whole of it lay on a long tilt so slight you could hardly make it out, from right to left to-ward a far glint of water, creek or river, there beyond the last of the foliage; the thicket with the Bloodybacks behind it closed off the biggest part save the lowest and wettest and roughest, and the enemy's line extended farther that way than the hedge did. In the distance, like a dream, floated a vision of a pretty mansion of pink brick.

James saw Colonel Washington swerve left along the front of the bar-rier, seeking a way through or around it, then turn to holler back a com-mand; the trumpeter blew a call; but at the same instant the Bloodybacks behind the thicket let go a blast of musketry and nobody knew what the Colonel had said or what the horn was telling them to do, and James heard the torn-silk *pzzzzzttt* of musket balls going past his head while, just in front, amid the roiling smoke of the volley, most of the first section in its blind momentum squarely struck the hedge. There was a crunch and smash of gnarly boughs; horses squealed and plunged, some floundered in the body of the thicket, others repeatedly tried with heaving hindquarters to plunge over, one or two actually broke through amid fluttering showers of small dark leaves, but more turned aside to follow the Colonel or simply struggled to back out and free themselves from entanglement.

Captain Watts and Corporal Murphy, unable to rein about in time, collided partly with the confusion of horses at the hedge and partly with the hedge itself and were lost to view; but the Chickasaw, *Why, the damned nag's got some sense*, whirled to the left and did it so violently James nearly lost his seat, in fact saved himself from falling only by letting go his sword so it swung free by its wrist-cord in order to hold fast to the Chickasaw's mane with both hands. The little beast drove its bony shoulder into the barrel of the pyebal'd horse of the next file, forcing it to the left; squealing, the pyebal'd brutally stumbled, then recovered its footing, but not before throwing its rider directly in the Chickasaw's path, who leapt adroitly over the fellow; James heard the trooper squall, saw him roll among the roots of the hedge, saw him no more.

The pyebal'd pushed the next horse leftward, and it the next, and then much of the front rank of James's section was wheeling along the face of the hedgerow, away from the piling-up of the first section's men and horses, and looking back James saw the rest of his section, with horses pitching and bucking—and the rest of the column too—wheeling with them in a curling stream. Another storm of musketry blew from behind the hedge with a deafening shock; more bullets wickedly ripped the air; and James would've escaped unscathed had his saber, flailing at the end of its wrist-cord, not struck him a stunning blow on the right temple. Blood gushed, blinding and enraging him; he'd been unfairly assailed, *First I'm mired in my own shit, then the Lobster tries to shoot me, now I'm cut by my own damned sword.*

Scrubbing away blood with the forearm of his rein-hand, with his right he regained his grip on the handle of his sword. His Chickasaw hammered close along the thicket's edge; the stiff boughs of the ugly little trees lashed at his right side, snagged at his slung carbine as if they wanted to steal it from him, tore off and kept the outer half of the boot Lieutenant Gordon had given him at Guilford. Up ahead, the Colonel on his mud-colored horse, standing in his stirrups, leaned out to hack over the rim of the hedge with his sword; bayonets stabbed back at him. James rose in his own irons, bent to his right, raised his sword too; a big man in a grenadier hat, back of the squatty shrubs, gnashed yellow teeth while furiously pumping his ramrod up and down the barrel of his musket; James, without thinking, aimed a stroke at him. There was an impact precisely the same as sinking a hatchet into a soft wood like poplar; the Chickasaw ran on; he looked—there was blood on his blade, but he couldn't say if it was his or the yellow-toothed grenadier's. *Have I killed a man?*

He was aware of an oddly suppressed but insistent hubbub *wump bump, wump wump bump* and it was only when he saw the darts of flame and gouts of smoke spurting over the hedgerow at him that he knew the shooting had dulled his hearing and he dwelt now in a nightmare world of queerly rustling quiet that beat faintly against him—musketry suppressed to a stifled mutter, the yowls of men to a mewing such as kittens make, the hoofbeats of his Chickasaw to a distant patter; the loudest thing in his ears the beating of his own heart.

Behind the thicket a succession of grenadier hats flowed by; bayonets poked out at him, withdrew; flushed faces howled at him without sound. The riderless pyebal'd, still running with him, bore against his left leg, forced the Chickasaw rightward deeper into the clutches of the hedge; the sharp twigs gashed at James's deerskin britches and at the flesh of his knee and thigh, tore off the rest of his boot; *Goddamn*, he struck the pyebal'd's nose with the flat of his sword; it sheered off; another turmoil of musketry flared from the hedge *wump wump bump wump bump*, something hit the pyebal'd, a small spray of red, its head dropped, it somersaulted; and in its place, impossibly, rose Obediah Plumbley, lying forward on the ewe neck of a gray horse even skinnier and more ill-made than James's own, his drunkard's plum-colored nose as red as a beacon, his sword still at point. He yelled something that came to James only as a wordless yammer; James stared back bewildered.

On Plumbley's left another rider surged into view—big ape-browed Benjamin Lockett, his mouth stretched wide with a war-cry that, to the deafened James, his old antagonist, might as well have been the cooing of an infant. *The sections're mixed up now. What's behind?* A jockey's swift glance, backward under his left armpit, showed him, galloping close on the Chickasaw's heels, Captain Watts and Corporal Murphy, unhurt after all, and two troopers he didn't know, all four of these in a gathered bunch; and coming on behind, a churning flood of more men and horses, the troopers nearest the thicket leaning out to beat with their swords at the Bloody-backs. *By God, the regiment's held together.*

He flicked a second look to the rear. *Where's all those spry little Delaware fellows; wasn't they supposed to help us?* He saw no sign of them, though a party of horse—*maybe Gresham's, maybe them state troops we passed, that hallooed at us*—moved at a brisk canter through the woods two hundred paces behind and to the left, as if to converge; sunlight sparkled on the sword-blades they brandished.

Turning to the front, he had a vision, darkened by the blood pouring from the cut in his temple, through a simmer of musket-smoke—Colonel Washington on his brown horse angling away from the thicket, circling back to face the oncoming regiment, his small mouth in his round face repeatedly flapping open and shut in a way that on any other occasion would've looked absurd; he shook his saber at them in imperative fashion. *He's giving orders. What are they?* Nearby him the blue-coated trumpeter set his horn to his lips, his cheeks swelled as he blew—but to James all

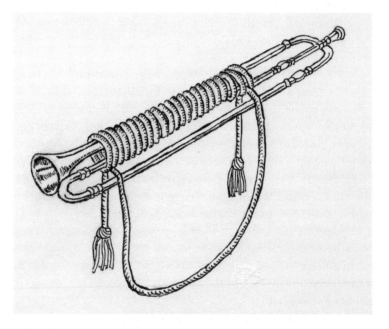

sound had by now swirled together into the gently rumbling susurrus a seashell gives when put against the ear, the notes of the trumpet no more than a seagull's cry.

Colonel Washington pointed his saber toward the enemy position in short, straight jabs. Bearing down on him, James could see he was pointing past the lower end of the hedge where it straggled out to a few stray scrubby bushes, and where—back of this, a line of red uniforms and shiny muskets, near a hundred at least, stood clustered along all that rough ground, all those piney hummocks and reedy swales slanting down to water. *Their flank's open down there*, James divined—how, he knew not; perhaps in a glimmer he'd spied the gap without knowing it, a small space between the end of the enemy line and the creek or river or whatever the water was. *Yes, open, but not by much—a mighty little space. He wants us to go around 'em, go through that slot, get in their rear. A bolt of fear shook him. But first we've got to ride across their front.*

The beast Greene knew would one day be called the Battle of the Eutaws now executed one immense pivot, turning on the hinge of its left flank where Washington's dragoons assaulted the blackjack thicket, the main line of Virginia and Maryland Continentals gradually swinging like a great door closing, turning its face from eastward to northward, right edge sweeping in an arc from the woods where Hammond's horse and the Legion infantry had so equivocally contended with Coffin's cavalry, over the Charles Town road, coming shut at last against the Eutaw Springs themselves in their grove of cypresses, the whole of his army fronting now on the brick house and its palisaded garden, into which the remains of several battalions of Provincials and British regulars had now withdrawn.

Of course he could not see any movement so composed and orderly as to suggest the closing of a door, not from where he sat the new horse Cruger at the northern edge of the captured enemy's camp, the embattled house before him, chaos reigning on all sides, Captain Browne's four six-pounders—his own two and a pair seized from the enemy—throwing roundshot after roundshot into the citadel, musket fire popping from every window of the house, British baggage guards and commissaries frenziedly wrecking or setting afire the army's stores, sutlers' wagons dashing off down the Charles Town road while pioneers felled trees behind them to impede pursuit, bodies of enemy troops lingering stubbornly in the tree-lines now and then unleashing a ragged fire, others shamelessly retreating, deserters flying in every direction, camp followers and batmen and miscellaneous retainers streaming into the woods, his own regulars hastening to display opposite the mansion and its compound, parties of prisoners being marched to the rear. *The beast possesses no single shape to be seen. It can't stay the same long enough to hold any one pattern; it's a succession of forms and forces and whims, each more startling, more ambiguous, more destructive than the last.*

The simile of the closing door could only be a cruelly tantalizing illusion, for as the successive couriers came to him he learned that at the door's hinge the impetuous Washington—*Oh, Colonel, would to God you were not so bold!*—had charged without awaiting the support of the Delawares and before Colonel Hampton's state troops could organize to come up and now struggled at the blackjack hedgerow to get at Stewart's grenadiers and light troops. He knew that along the reforming main line—the face of that figurative door—his casualties, particularly among officers, had been impermissibly high, *Colonel Campbell killed, several captains and lieuten-*

ants down, the Virginians wavering; Colonel Howard of the First Maryland wounded, two of Colonel Williams' captains dead.

And finally, maybe worst of all, he knew the outer edge of the door, his right wing, to be still an infernal pandemonium of charge and counter-charge between Hammond and Coffin, only transferred now to new ground around the springs, Colonel Lee still nowhere to be found—though, incredibly, one rumor had him appearing among the Virginia Line to dispute with the officers of the fallen Campbell for command of that brigade. Pendleton, unable to find Lee, had at least prevailed on Captain Eggleston to charge the disorganized enemy with a part of the Legion horse, but alas, to little effect.

All this Greene had from his array of howling messengers, and from it he took his illusory battle-portrait, a semblance only, an imperfect reflection, a distortion, probably even a mistaken likeness, of the beast whose true nature and proportions none could know. He seemed to have won a victory—the army of Stewart was broken; the evidence of its breakage lay everywhere about, its remnants sped pell-mell from the field. Yet there was something sinister in the intractable way those troops at the hedge stood against Washington on the left. Something ominous in that towering edifice of brick with its three levels of windows each belching musket-smoke and in its stockaded garden and its maze of outbuildings. Some ill harbinger in the inexplicable muddle on the right. He remembered his premonitions of the morning, the portents that beset him as the black maw of the forest swallowed up his army. Now, surrounded by every sign of triumph, he sensed the palpable nearness of an evil fortune. Even as the tumult of the enemy's rout worsened, he felt calamity drawing closer like Banquo's foretelling ghost. Its cold breath began to blow on him.

As the regiment in its tumbling cascade approached the thicket's end where Colonel Washington impatiently waited on his pawing horse, a rider pushed between James's Chickasaw and Plumbley's gray, forging ahead of them and of Lockett too—a lean man in a yellow hunting shirt and a full-crested helmet, lashing the withers of his roan horse with the flat of his saber to urge the beast to greater speed. Two other troopers brushed past too, following in his wake, *Who's that?* Lockett's mouth stretched unnaturally wider as he hurled at their backs what James imagined must be curses; he was mystified, *Lockett acts like this is nothing but a damned horse-race and he don't want to get outrun.* Bearing down on the Colonel, the three unknown troopers formed a sort of truncated front rank with James, Obediah, and Lockett crowding close on their heels and then Captain Watts and Corporal Murphy and the balance of the regiment strung out behind like a river in flood.

The thicket on the right disgorged another volley—to James another series of blunted concussive beats of air, more jets of flame, more gouts of smoke—and yonder the Colonel's horse twirled on its haunches in the blast like a top. Then they were on him and he twisted his horse's head to the front again and struck his spurs and resumed the lead; and the regiment stormed past the last of the hedgerow and made a sweeping turn half-right along the face of the longer British line. James gathered himself. *God save us.*

God's answer was to let those Bloodybacks raise their firelocks all at once in long shivering sheaves of steel and train them level on the regiment and commence to firing right to left by platoons—James saw through his smear of blood the explosions of white smoke start at one end of their line and run along their front to the other like kernels of corn popping on a hot skillet, and if he could hear no more than a suchlike popping he could surely see the effect of it—the full-crested helmet of the trooper on the roan horse leaping skyward as if yanked by a string to leave behind a little plume of red floating as if by magic, which James rode right through and found to be wet and warm and tasting of salt; then the riderless roan swinging wide out of line. Saw too Lockett's horse cringe, hurl itself head-long into the ground, hindquarters high and kicking, Lockett rolling over and over, his mouth still wide with its yelling. Saw with relief Obediah ducking lower on the neck of his nag, unhurt. And though nearly deaf, heard from behind a vague din and clamor that he knew spoke of more men and horses struck.

Following Plumbley's example, he laid himself flat along the Chickasaw's mane, tried his best to make himself even smaller than he already was, turned his gaze anxiously toward the Bloodyback line; over there the fellows in their short red coats and peaked caps were biting their cartridges, ramming down their loads, *Another one coming.* He glanced ahead; Colonel Washington pounded on, inclining more and more to the right, leaning that way in his saddle, sword poised, headed for the gap between the end of the enemy's line and the span of bright water now revealed to be a shallow creek behind a high-banked ravine.

The Bloodybacks presented their reloaded pieces; James took a last hungry look at the world as he had known it till now, saw its azure dome of heaven, a hawk soaring aloft, the morning sun mellowed with haze, the soft crowns of pines; saw the world's beauty even as battle soiled it; saw the different shades of red of the coats of the British, their row of heads all neatly atilt at the same angle, aiming; the slight tremor of sunlight on the barrels of their muskets; the dreamlike vision of the pink mansion beyond seeming to swim free of earth on a veil of smoke. Then he shut his eyes tight so as not to witness what he knew would be his death or terrible wounding, heard with his dulled ears the confined mutter of the volley; and sure enough, a savage blow smote him.

He rose out of a bloody litter of fallen men and horses. He heard a hushed screaming. Bewildered, he looked about. *Chickasaw's down; look at them holes, that leg bent wrongways; and him yet a-trying to get up.* Obediah. *Where's he at?* Mostly all he saw was a pile of horses and sprawled men. Some were moving, some weren't. Dozens of nags were running wildly about with empty saddles and trailing reins, many bleeding from wounds. Captain Watts was nowhere to be seen that he could tell, nor the hateful Murphy. He didn't think he himself was hurt, as much as he'd expected it; he seemed to be getting around all right. *That smack I got; must've been the Chickasaw getting shot.* His right boot, ripped off by the sharp twigs of the thicket, had left that foot bare so that he teetered off-balance on his shod one. His britches had been torn to shreds on the right side; he bled freely there. He scoured blood from his eye too. His carbine was still in its sling, but a twisty bough from the hedge was caught in its trigger-guard and another between the ramrod and the muzzle. He yanked these out, then noticed, lying on the ground before him, somebody's detached hand; one of its fingers kept crooking as if it beckoned to him. He smelled the mashed shit in the seat of his britches.

Off yonder to the left a line of mounted troops shaped themselves vaguely in the smoke like a train of ghosts, *Who's that? Them South Carolina troops? Gresham's?* Others rode about singly or in small bands, aimlessly, as if they knew not where to go next. Ten or twenty were reforming nearer by. *Is that the regiment?* Wobbling, he turned to look behind; some of the fellows seemed to have stalled at the thicket's end; on horses that reared and shied they were thrashing with their swords at clusters of grenadiers who shoved bayonets up at them. He reeled back, in the direction he believed he'd been riding before the Chickasaw fell; smoke drew away like the curtain on a Punch-and-Judy box, showed him fellows in red coming at a jog, a wriggly line of them, splinters of shining among them, *Them's bayonets.* Plumbley appeared, fell against him; the two nearly toppled till James got his feet steady under him, wedged the preacher up; Obediah's tart breath blew on him, *Where'd he get ahold of peach brandy?* With great agitation Plumbley spoke something to him that was lost in the seashell thunder of his deafness; James only shrugged. Lockett stood by, stooping his sloped shoulders, giving the onrushing Bloodybacks a frown of his ape's brows.

The three of them leaned on their swords, panting. *Damn, it's hot.* The advancing British slowed a bit, the way folk do when they're gathering strength to make a strong effort. A sudden urgency stirred James. *Where's the Colonel? Wouldn't want to fight these fellows without him.* Frantically he turned this way and that, began yelling at the others, his voice a deadened booming inside his skull as if he'd hollered with his head under water, "Where's the Colonel?"

The next second gave him his bad answer. Yet another banner of smoke trailed off, opened a little distance; and a dozen yards on he spied the Colonel, still high on his charger, surrounded by a mob of Redcoats all jabbing their bayonets up at him, the horse whirling on its hindquarters round and round and round while the Colonel's saber rose and fell and rose again, its blade a deeper red each time it rose, sparks flaring whenever it struck a musket barrel or a bayonet, blood spouting when it found flesh, at every stroke a Redcoat falling away fearfully slashed, others pushing in, a whole mass of Bloodybacks swarming about him with the fierce eagerness of a pack of hounds tearing at their prey.

The sight fetched James right out of himself. He thought, *I'll drive 'em back, I'll free him.* It was as if seeing the Colonel in that fix got hold of something in him he hadn't known was there till now and yanked it loose from whatever it was bedded in and brought it up to the daylight; he imagined for an instant it was what Captain Gunn had told him lived in his blood, the spirit of wee John the Crowner's son, the hero of *Alt na gaun* and Dirlot Castle. *"Let's go and help the Colonel!"* he cried, the sound rumbling in his head like a thunderclap.

But he could not. The line of British came weaving at him, cut off his path to the Colonel. A pair of them leaned to skewer him, and seeing in memory the sketch of the human face on Sergeant Dangerfield's board at Manakin Town, a face divided into wedges showing the six cuts of the broadsword, remembering the Sergeant's instructions, *Cut Two*, James slashed the nearest snarling visage diagonally from top to bottom, right eye to left jaw; recovered; then gave the second man the opposite stroke, *Cut One*, and both gushed blood all over him, slid crumpling to either side.

Obediah stepped in, stuck his saber in a Redcoat's neck; Lockett hurtled into their midst; also, surprisingly, the two troopers who'd been with the man in the full-crested helmet, who'd all of a sudden conjured themselves out of nowhere; at this onset the British line drew back a few yards and the five put their backs together and made a little fort of swords; and then the Bloodybacks came at them again in one big flock fringed with bayonet points.

It seemed they battled a long time, but it must have been moments only. In after days James could never recount to anyone what he did then, or how he did it, or what any of the others did or how, not because he wished to disremember it so as to put away from him forever its ugliness, but for the simple reason he kept almost nothing of it in his mind. What little he did keep was a flashing of different images, much as if somebody took a deck of playing cards such as are used in the game of fair chance and quickly spread them out, swept them together, then spread them out again, over and over, yet never twice in the same order, so the faces of cards before him constantly changed. He could not have said what any single image was; all he remembered was how fast the changing came, and how the muffled roar of his deafness made the changing all the more unreal by giving him the odd sense it was far from him and not near.

The one sight he did keep, clear and crisp like a dark jewel in his mind, there beyond the genadier hats of the enemy crowding in, was of Colonel Washington's horse falling, pierced by a dozen wounds, yonder across the distance none of them could traverse, the Colonel too toppling with the horse like some great tower undermined, going over slowly and with the terrible inevitability of all things of prodigious size and weight finally, impossibly brought down, then man and horse were covered over by the ravaging pack of Redcoats. That vision would never leave him all the rest of his days.

He had failed to act, failed to save the Colonel, failed to emulate the Crowner's son; yet the Bloodybacks kept coming and he must fight them; and he fought on but with a deadening sense of woe, for he had not answered the call of the clan, had not proved worthy of everything fine Captain Gunn had offered him or of all that his lineage demanded. It was a desperate fight, and afterward he did not know if they'd fought skillfully or without art, if they'd killed men or not, if they should be proud of themselves or not; he would recall how hot they'd been, how thirsty, how arm-weary; he would remember they'd been too few, that presently the crush of Bloodybacks had got too great and breached their little fort of swords. But mainly he would remember his shame.

At some point he was knocked down, he knew that; and while he grov-eled in a daze the crush of the fighting happened to part, affording him, as if by a miracle, a last view over those few tantalizing but impassable yards of Colonel Washington. Though trapped beneath his dead charger, the Colonel had somehow compelled his tormenters to withdraw from him a space and now, lying on his back, right leg caught fast, left foot braced against the cup of his saddle for leverage, never more alert yet never more composed, almost implausibly comfortable, as if the turn events had taken quite satisfied him, he held them at bay, deftly warding off Redcoat bayo-nets with expert cuts of his saber.

James looked on helplessly. From the dust and smoke an American dragoon he did not recognize leapt in to defend the Colonel as he himself had wished to do, bestrode the neck of the Colonel's horse, wielded his saber against the bayonets, acted the hero James had longed to play, was cut down quickly in a bright flurry of steel points. Then again the Bloody-backs plunged hound-like upon their victim. A Briton stabbed, Washington fended off the bayonet as before, the Redcoat stepped aside, measured him, tried again with a lunge, and this time sank his blade partway in the Colonel's chest. Then a British officer shouldered in, knelt to the Colonel, waved off the bayoneter. *Took him prisoner.*

The sights sickened James with regret. He was no longer sure he wanted to stay alive badly enough to keep on fighting. *What sort of warrior are you?* he demanded bitterly of himself. Then a strong hand grasped his arm, dragged him to his feet; he looked; his Samaritan was one of the two troopers who'd helped make their fort of swords, a broad-chested fellow with dark eyes, the seam of an old scar along one jaw. The scarred man spoke, but again James heard only a slurred babble. Obediah was by them, the other strange trooper, and Lockett. Yonder the British pack swallowed up the Colonel and the officer who'd taken him captive; another line was advancing behind a shiny quilling of bayonets.

The scarred man tugged James backward; the others started away with them; but in his rage and disgrace James stopped, turned, drove the point of his saber into the ground, seized his slung carbine, brought it to his shoulder drawing back the cock with his thumb, drew dead aim on the nearest Redcoat in the approaching line, a brawny fellow, bowlegged, slitted eyes, face pitted from pox, mouth open in a yell, a missing front tooth; and wondering if there was powder enough left in the pan of the damned carbine after the rumpus it had been through even to catch fire, he pulled the trigger *Hell, it went off anyways* and the poxy Bloodyback stopped, staggered, James lost him in the smoke of the discharge, then found him again a moment later, sitting on the ground just as his line marched on and left him, closed the space he'd left in the rank. *By God, I reckon I've killed that one.*

He threw off his sling, cast it and the empty carbine aside, pulled the point of his sword out of the ground, turned his back on the enemy *Shoot me now if you want to, you sons of bitches,* and left that place. He didn't hurry, he walked at his contemptuous leisure, followed the others up, limping first on his bare foot and then on his shod one.

They came to the spot where the Chickasaw lay and James saw the skinny nag was dead now. *Better horse than I gave it credit for.* He stooped, unfastened the set of bearskin-covered pommel holsters from the saddle, and threw the rig over his shoulder, one pistol hanging before and one behind; he'd need them when he found another mount. Obediah said something that boomed in James's deafness and pointed off; they all craned that way, saw a battle line of the Delaware Continentals come tramping at them through the woods, bayoneted muskets at the trail. *Them spry little fellows after all; guess we way outran 'em.* The Delawares swept past—a glimpse of grim faces, pointed caps, short blue coats, a whiff of sweated clothes and fresh shit, *Reckon I ain't the only one a-fluxing*; these hurried on, closed with the oncoming Redcoats.

A quake of ground underfoot spoke of horsemen; a column of cavalry hammered up, two or three in front wearing the same caps with silver crescents on them and white regimentals faced with dark blue that James had seen on the officer who'd talked to the Colonel before the charge, the rest garbed in a motley of coarse cloth and deerskin. James thought he heard, in what might be a fading of his deafness, the rumble and clangor of their arrival. In the ranks he recognized with an upwelling of relief Bobby Busby, John Gunnell, Sergeant Shoupe, also a number of others he knew for men who'd ridden in the charge on the thicket; *somehow the regiment and these others must've got together.*

The crush of champing mounts drew to a halt; one of the men in white hallooed down to them, and James's ears gave a dry click and at last he heard, sharp-toned and distinct, what the officer bellowed, "I'm Colonel Hampton, commanding South Carolina State Troops. You boys fetch yourselves some horses and join up. We've got to drive those Lobsterback sons of bitches!"

Greene had never witnessed the eruption of an actual volcano though of course he had read of Vesuvius, Stromboli, and Aetna and had seen engravings purporting to illustrate the spectacle such a marvelous occurrence might offer. He could not know whether the engravings gave an accurate representation. Current fashion required that any phenomenon of the natural world be rendered in the most ornately embellished style; accordingly the volcanic action one viewed in books tended more to resemble a display of petrified ostrich plumes than any explosion of ash-clouds and molten lava. Still, if one discounted the influence of artful manner, the mansion of pink brick, looming before him on its stony mound, venting musket-fire from every orifice, wreathed in shrouds of powder-smoke, favored the likenesses uncannily—enough, at least, to inspire in him a moment's awe and apprehension, a hint, perhaps, of what he might have felt if presented with the colossal reality.

The reality of the mansion was baleful enough. Even as its similarity to a volcano occurred to him, the edifice dealt out a measure of destruction no less shocking, no less lethal, than the prodigy of nature whose image it evoked; a concentrated blast of musketry struck Captain Browne's battery of six-pounders; leaden balls rang on the iron and bronze of the guns like hail on a slate roof, it pocked with ragged holes the carriages and limbers, felled all the horses, smote down at a stroke nearly every gunner and matross. Such a universal wilting and withering, such a chorus of screaming, such a sudden welter of blood, shocked him; from a scant twenty yards away he looked on speechless as the whole of his artillery was demolished in a moment.

Till then he had mostly succeeded in staving off what had seemed his earlier unfounded divinations of doom. Amid the rack of battle, welcome word had come that Captain Rudulph's Legion infantry, on the far right, had driven the remains of the Sixty-Third and Sixty-Fourth Foot, had gained the cover of the mansion's barn, and a party under Lieutenant Manning had almost broken into the house itself, then, when turned aside after a desperate struggle in the very doorway of the place, had fallen back to take the main building under a flanking fire. Though Colonel Lee's whereabouts remained an impenetrable mystery, Captain Eggleston, spurred on by Captain Shubrick, had essayed a second charge of the Legion dragoons on Coffin's horse, driving those intrepid Loyalists off the fringes of the campground and into the woods near the Eutaw Springs with the help of Colonel Hammond and his state troops.

The successes had brightened the General's hopes and chased to a distance his darkest auguries even though, as he sat his horse in the middle of his reforming line of Continentals, he knew from his couriers the enemy had repelled Colonel Washington's attack on the left, which first the Delaware scouts and now Colonel Hampton were renewing, had in fact brought down the gallant Washington himself, bayoneted him, taken him prisoner, calamitous news whose import he absorbed as a commander must, but whose pain his hauberk of battle temperament deflected to some later, more convenient time, when pity would again assume its accustomed place.

Now he gazed to the front and saw for himself another troubling sign—elements of the Buffs and of Cruger's Provincials reassembling opposite along the base of the height where stood the deadly volcano of the mansion and its appendages. *Many of the enemy have run, but these have not*, he thought sternly to himself; *Stewart's rebuilding his center; be careful now*—hundreds of the enemy's fugitives lurked in the forest roundabout, beaten for the moment, yes; but possibly able to rally if given cause. His battle might seem nearly won, but he dared not forget the whorish caprice of his luck.

Just as he cautioned himself against overconfidence Greene cast a critical eye left and right along his front, thinking to send an aide to recruit replacement artillerists from the ranks of his Virginia and Maryland Continentals, yet liked not what he saw—the main battle line still unformed, officers racing to and fro frantically calling on the men to fall in, troops milling about in disorder, an improbable unsteadiness among his regulars, an unimaginable hanging back from the very brink of victory, a wavering in their ranks as the fire from the mansion tore at them, then—he perceived this with a stab of horror—a thinning of their mass caused not alone by the casualties they were taking but also by a gradual turning away of soldiers to the rear, first singly and then in larger and larger groups, a withdrawal so resolute, so willful and determined as hardly to be believed, till what had almost displayed as a line of battle became instead a sullen and formless multitude turning its collective back on the dangers of the front to roll rearward not in riot or rout but with a settled determination, a sadness too, an evident regret that fate had made it necessary for them to give up their duty. With slow tread they made for the refuge of the captured enemy camp. The General stared disbelieving. *By God, they're breaking up!*

Yet the dissolution that struck him so forcibly as unutterable, even unthinkable, surely had its melancholy precedent—the Maryland Continentals giving way at Hobkirk's Hill—and while he rued it, he was hardly taken by surprise; it was not as if his regulars had never quit him. Furthermore, in his deepest heart he knew the collapse to have been tragically predestined. He opened his watch; it was a few minutes past one o'clock; they had been persisting four long hours, giving and taking the worst kind of carnage, straining every nerve the whole time in intolerable heat, weakened by unappeased hunger, parching with thirst on this hellish ground where the enemy controlled all access to water.

This is no fickle prank of the beast none might predict; this is what my black demons of the morning whispered to me; this is the truth I knew from the first, the truth I would not let myself see. He recalled how they'd marched past him so confidently in the moonlit dawn of this same day—so long ago now!—calling out to him their raucous encouragement, *Don't you fret, Your Honor, we'll give them sons of bitches a right basting; make you proud today, sir; blow their goddamned arses back to England*, while in his saddle by the roadside he'd glumly pondered the weakness he knew lived at the core of them, sensing even in their boasts how weary they were, how depleted by sickness and endless marching, how they came nearer being the empty shells of men than the men themselves, an army of fragile husks temporarily galvanized by a common illusion of victory. Now it seemed that illusion had glimmered out as exhaustion and want leached the last of their energies.

The fault is not in the stars, he thought, recalling his Shakespeare, *it is in myself.* He had led into battle an army incapable of victory. *Nor was it but simple fault, it was sin. I fancied I partook of sin by hard compulsion, but no, I partook of it by choice.* Was it not the part of a commander of armies to partake of such a sin for the greater gain—a triumph over the enemy, the ultimate independency of the United States? *But had I in mind the nation's good, or my own? Was it patriotism? Or was it an ambition as naked and unlovely as Harry Lee's?*

He knew no answer. But the questions cracked his shield of composure, admitted at last the pity he'd so long held at bay; and he wept now for Billy Washington and wept even more bitterly watching his poor fellows straggling away, fellows he'd beguiled into thinking they were invincible, who now must taste the mortification of defeat. He recalled his old insight—in this struggle the worst of them was in most ways better than he. *Lord*, he prayed, *let them blame me and not themselves.*

But he must know for certain. He sent a tear-blurred glance behind him for an aide to send to Colonel Williams, but found himself attended by none but his little escort of dragoons—Pendleton, Shubrick, and Hyrne were all somewhere on the right tending to the mysterious business of Lee's disappearance; Kosciuszko had hurried off on some errand of his own; Major Forsyth was on the left with Colonel Hampton's corps; even Dr. Clements, the volunteer from the medical department, had departed to help minister to the wounded.

He found it oddly disconcerting to be bereft of the whole of his official family; he did not think it had ever happened before. *Generals aren't often left to themselves.* Even in the grip of his sorrow and remorse—or perhaps because of them—another, ironical notion came: *Nor should we be, lest we commit even worse mistakes.* A laugh rattled through him; he dried his tears on his sleeve. *Hasty Billy Washington. He at least won't blame me. Nor himself either. He'll say,* They were there, and by God I made a run at 'em. He pressed the heel of a hand against his aching eye. *What was I doing? Oh yes, Otho Williams.*

Providentially Colonel Williams rode up that very moment, sweat-soaked, smoke-blackened, his face a portrait of dejection. "My dear General Greene," he leaned near and shouted above the crash of musketry, gravely saluting, "I regret to inform you the troops under my command have got into irretrievable confusion. When our officers had proceeded beyond the enemy's encampment, they found themselves abandoned by nearly all their soldiers, and being so exposed, have been frightfully cut up by the parties pouring fire from the windows of the house. The few men who accompanied them have likewise suffered as they attempted to display. But most of the second line, perhaps thinking victory secure, seem to be falling back to avail themselves of its spoils."

Greene gave the good Colonel a wistful smile. "I fear it's not victory they apprehend, Otho."

Williams was round-eyed with despair. "Whatever actuates them, sir, they're dispersing among the tents, fastening upon all the liquors and refreshments, and have become utterly unmanageable."

While Williams made this confession the freckled, tousle-haired courier from the state troops came racing up, this time on a foaming black;

evidently he'd had his second mount of the day shot from under him. The loss of his father's plow-horse had been forgotten; nothing remained of his ebullience of the morning; blood-spattered, hard-jawed, he spoke now in clipped accents as the nearly ridden-down black stood shivering, its wind rasping in its throat, "General, Colonel Hampton's compliments, he says tell you Colonel Washington's dragoons is fought to a frazzle, most of their officers is killed or wounded. Colonel Hampton's took what's left into his command and made two charges on the Bloodyback sons of bitches, and us and the Delawares has finally drove 'em out of that goddamned nest of withy shrubs. But now they've took up a new position with their arses to the creek and their left on that picketed garden, and Colonel says tell you his command's near fought out—his'n and the Delawares both."

This is the fate I know so well; there's even a certain comfort to it. He nodded, understanding everything now. "My compliments to Colonel Hampton. He and Captain Kirkwood are to hold where they are, refrain from further attacks, keep the enemy under observation and, if he essays any movement, report it to me at once and resist it as effectively as may be practicable, pending my orders."

When the courier had whirled away he turned to rest a hand tenderly on Colonel Williams' shoulder. "We must endeavor now to gather the Continentals, and prepare to make good our retreat."

At these words Williams' countenance, in better times so often beatifically half-smiling as if all in the world contented him, wrinkled with woe. "Retreat, sir?" Tears sprang into his dark eyes.

The General nodded, leaving his hand where it was, on the shoulder of this good and honest man who had led the army within reach of victory only to see fortune snatch it away. Gently with his grasp he swayed Williams to and fro in his saddle, almost as one might rock a weeping infant in its cradle to give it comfort. "The enemy troops on the left are unbeaten," he explained, and though he must yell to be heard above the uproar of musketry from the mansion he hoped the Colonel would hear his words as he meant them, as patient and consoling, compliant with the manifest will of God. "So too are Coffin's cavalry on the right. Colonel Lee has vanished; the horse of his Legion is ineffective without him. Stewart is reorganizing the middle of his line. Meantime, our main line's in chaos. Shortly the enemy will launch a counterattack. It's no longer a question of beating him; we must keep from being beaten ourselves. We'll give up the field and be satisfied with having given Mr. Stewart the drubbing of his life." Again he smiled. "It's another draw, Otho. We've fought another draw."

Everybody said they made two more charges on the British behind their damnable hedge. But the unwilled forgetfulness that in later times kept

James from remembering how he and the others had fought the Bloodybacks behind the hedge only deepened when he tried to summon up memories of what transpired immediately after Colonel Hampton took them
into his command. Much later, first on the picket line after the battle, then
back at Burdell's, he heard some of what had happened from his mates
both old and new—the new ones being the troopers who'd helped him and
Obediah and Lockett make their fort of swords, a pair of brothers from
the Rapidan River country of Virginia, Bartlett and Benjamin Hawkins.

Curiously he remembered well the events of later in the afternoon when
they'd covered the retreat of the army. But the two more charges the fellows spoke of were mostly a void. What he did recall with a terrible clarity
was the thirst that burned his throat and the heat of the day that parched
and shriveled him till he hadn't a drop of wet left in him to be sweated out
or pissed out or even shat out, leaving him so dry his lips split open and
his eyeballs rolled as burry in their sockets as chestnut pods. So withered
did he feel that he wondered if he could even bleed; thought maybe if he
got shot, nothing but a dry red grit would come pouring forth. He knew
if he didn't soon get a drink of water he was going to die, yet all the canteens were empty and the woods roundabout as dry as tinder; the British
had the water—the springs, the creek, the river; he even envied them the
marshy spots he'd glimpsed behind their thicket, scummy, stagnant, and
probably stinking; he'd have lapped those up like a dog. He'd never forget
that torture.

But beyond the thirst he could recover very little, when older, of what
had passed when Colonel Hampton led them twice more against the
Bloodybacks. Whenever he tried to imagine it, and his part in it, it seemed
so far off and so peculiar that he half thought it a falsehood, as if it were a
tale told by another that he'd somehow taken up—by intent or by mistake,
he didn't know which—as his own. Yet a self that was undeniably him did
dwell in it, did act. But the self didn't seem to be him as he'd come to be over
the span of his life, or anything like him. It was as thin and twisty as the
flame on a candle and just as lacking in substance—it was apt to blow out
in the least air. But unlike a flame, that self was dark; and he knew its darkness for the shadow of evil.

The Hawkinses had told him. Obediah told him and afterward was
good enough to say many a prayer in his behalf. The boys who'd made the
trek from Manakin Town told him too; by a miracle, every single one had
lived through the fight. All these recounted the same dark matter, so when
he got older and looked back to that day, after recalling his pangs of thirst
and heat, he always had to peer through this darkness they'd seen but he'd
been blind to. For him, behind the darkness all was broken and piecemeal.
It was as if that part of the day had been a picture painted on a mirror that

someone suddenly smashed; he glimpsed only its flying shards. After that, though, about the time the Delawares at last drove the Bloodybacks out of their hedge and back to a stockade in rear of the mansion, the pieces of the shattered painting all at once rejoined, the dismal veil of darkness cleared, and he would always own a vivid memory of what came next.

He remembered feeling oddly refreshed, which seemed unlikely considering his earlier state, and indeed the others seemed to watch him with an air of suspicion as if they too found the change unaccountable. They were drawn up in back of the thicket watching the Delawares skirmishing at long range with the British in the stockade. Everywhere around them in bloody heaps lay the dead and wounded of both sides and the mutilated horses shot down in the mounted attacks on the thicket. All the hurt men and horses trying to move or get up made the whole field look as if it had grown some kind of living crust that was making an effort to crawl away to a less terrible place. The noises they were making were unlike any noises James had ever heard.

Though he'd so uncommonly revived, these surroundings depressed him. And while he rejoiced to have found Plumbley and the Hawkins boys and the others whole, he fretted over the faces he didn't see around him. Captain Watts was absent, and Lieutenant Gordon, and the trooper in the full-crested helmet that charged past him at the thicket whose spume of blood he'd ridden through, tasting its salt on his tongue. *Surely that one's dead.* But he held out hope for Captain Watts, if only because Watts had shown himself a gentleman and James thought the type so rare that Providence, if there was such a thing, must certainly favor them. *Strict but considerate,* James thought approvingly of the Captain, *Worthy of respect.* Lieutenant Gordon too—a pompous ass, yes; negligent and vain. But generously he'd given over those boots, and spoken up for James when Watts doubted him—how long ago was that? Ages, it seemed. *No, it was just last night.*

Conversation was difficult because of the fighting around the stockade, so for the most part they sat their horses and kept quiet, gathering strength for whatever was coming next. As a replacement for the Chickasaw, James had picked up a short-jointed whitish mare whose tack was as fine as she was ill-made, though the blood of her former owner clotted the roll-padded saddle and stained its good woolen blanket. He must've worked her hard in the two charges he couldn't remember, for she was panting heavily. He couldn't say how she'd performed, whether she was an honest horse or otherwise, and this small mystery rankled him. Nearby, Plumbley sat an unhandsome roan similarly bloodied and winded. Obediah, and everybody else James knew or recognized, looked ten years older than they had that morning.

The company they were keeping depressed him further. Colonel Hampton had scooped up whatever bands of horse he could find roaming the field after Colonel Washington got taken—Gresham's company of Georgia volunteers, the Guilford County band, some parties of militia, what was left of the Third and First Dragoons. But the bulk of what he had was South Carolina State Troops. During a lull in the skirmishing Neal had confided they hailed from the back parts of the state where living was rough even without a war going on, and it was true they looked as wild and stony and inhospitable as those frontier uplands must've been. Some carried tomahawks and long knives in their belts, and from the bridles of others dangled twists of what looked like human hair. Evidently they'd fought well enough in going at the thicket. But afterwards James saw them fondling such trinkets as cut-off fingers and ears, and brandishing bloody scalps. One kept a severed nose, continually fitting it over his own, going about asking, "Don't that make me look better? Don't I look like a Lord?" Laughter followed him.

All this while the racket of musketry had persisted around the stockade, inhibiting most of their talk, but suddenly the fighting over on the right in front of the pink brick mansion, which for some time now had offered but a desultory and inconstant mumbling, burst into such a volume that no speech at all could have been understood above it. The air vibrated with the concentrated multiple shocks of musketry; artillery laid on them its broader, duller strokes. At the same time the tussle around the stockade broke from a skirmish into a full-scale engagement that girdled the place with dingy billows of smoke and a sparkling of muzzle-flashes; and presently the Delawares emerged from the smoke and came trotting back toward the hedge in their customary Indian file, firelocks at the trail, no longer moving as spry and nimble as they once had. That did not seem promising to James; he thought, *Could be they're whipped.*

Colonel Hampton rode to meet the Delawares' commander, a Captain by his epaulet; the two saluted, bent together, twined arms as if in intimacy but in fact the better to screech into one anothers' ears; the Captain nodded, grim-faced, turned his horse away; the Delawares passed on toward the rear. The Colonel motioned to his miscellany of officers; they gathered about him in a craning, inward-leaning circle, Carolinians with their crescent insignia on their caps, militia fellows in every sort of rough garb, one in a hunting shirt that Hudson pointed out as Captain Parsons of the Third, the only dragoon officer anybody had seen still in the saddle since the first charge on the thicket. Looking on this muddle of strangers that he knew he must follow as soon as they agreed on what to do—strangers not only to him but to each other—James reflected glumly that he'd preferred it better when his allegiance was to the dragoons alone, even if they were mostly the Third Dragoons and not the First, with Colonel Washington leading them.

But then he thought of how he'd fallen short of his duty to clan and sept and homeland, how he'd let the British take Colonel Washington when a real warrior like John the Crowner's son would've found a way to save him; and then he knew he'd shown himself too frail a vessel to hold an honest allegiance or even to keep a preference about anything at all. Mixed with the feeling of renewal that had so strangely come over him after the two unremembered charges, this lingering shame yielded up a queer ferment: James grew vexed and quarrelsome.

He was nursing these sour feelings when a courier came pounding through the woods and pushed his way into the conferring circle of officers. There was another moment of discussion over there; then the cluster disbanded and all the strangers scattered to whatever parts of the command they figured they belonged to. The officer Corporal Hudson had pointed out as Captain Parsons rode up on a limping horse and called together the little remnant of dragoons, thirty or forty tired-out fellows of the First and Third on winded nags. He was a slim young fellow, fine-featured and fair-haired, who'd most likely given a splendid appearance leaving Burdell's that morning, dressed as he was in his turbaned helmet, a pretty fringed plum-colored hunting shirt, buff britches, and high boots. But now in his soiled and tattered state he resembled a misfortunate person who might've fallen all the way down a long and rocky hill, and in his dirty face a pair of pale green eyes, inflamed and sunken, stared vacantly. Against the sputter and thump of the fighting in the distance he told them in husky tones the Delawares had given up trying to dig the enemy out of the stockade and now the Bloodybacks there were preparing to make a sally.

"Horse alone can't stop 'em," he went on, weariness thickening his words, "so we're licked on this end of the line. And judging from all that uproar"—he dipped his head toward the worsening clamor in the distance—"looks like the enemy's fixing to come at us all along the line. That courier says the Buffs have captured our artillery, the firing from the house has disrupted our center, there's disorder in our rear, and Coffin's cavalry's threatening the right." He stopped and heaved a sigh. "So, boys, General Greene's ordered a retreat. And we're to cover it—us and the state troops."

Licked? Disorder in the rear? Retreat? The words fell like hammer blows. It was true they'd had the devil's own time getting at the Bloodybacks behind that cursed thicket and now at the stockade. It was true they'd suffered fearful losses—every officer save Parsons seemed to have been struck down, maybe as many as two sections' worth of rank and file, untold numbers of poor innocent horses. And it was true the ones who remained were bone-tired and cooked to a crisp by heat and thirst. But licked? In his nettlesome state James's hackles rose. *We ain't licked.* He for sure wasn't licked. *Look at all them Lobsters a-laying there. We've killed plenty. Why, they've got to be wore out too.*

But Captain Parsons spoke grimly on even as James denied to himself the import of the words. "We'll pass through the rear of the army," the Captain said, "so as to get between it and Coffin. It's likely we'll have to light into Coffin. We've seen him before, so you'll know what to expect."

I ain't seen no damned Coffin. What in hell's he? James shot defiant glances side to side to see who else's spirits might be ruffled up, but the rest seemed not to share his rebellious temper. You could tell they hadn't liked hearing the battle was lost, but save for a few like the Hawkinses and Lockett, Shoupe and Hudson, and even loony little Bobby Busby, who seemed as mutinous and determined as James himself, there was a good deal of slumping and slouching in the ranks, and many a face with eyes as sore and deep-sunk and empty as Captain Parsons'. They looked as if the least squabble might finish them. They looked beaten.

How could that be? Was this defeat? He'd imagined defeat to be a rabble of fellows all running around in a panic with a triumphant enemy shooting them down like dogs or spearing them with their bayonets like trout in a brook. But the Bloodybacks hadn't even ventured out of their stockade yet to start shooting them or bayoneting them, and nobody was running away, and nothing much seemed to have changed that he could tell. Yet they were beaten. Not just them, the dragoons. The whole damned army. General Greene too, he was beaten. *America's beaten.* Captain Parsons had said so. James wanted to argue against it. He wanted to exhort the others. But gazing about him he could tell the effort would be wasted.

But then they've seen and done what I can't even remember happening, and something's borne me up whilst they've gone without. What was it? That missing piece of time when Colonel Hampton led the two charges—is that what's made the difference? Is that why I'm full and they're empty? The possibility quelled his turbulence. *Maybe it's best to hold still. I fell short once today, failed the Colonel when he needed me. I ought to practice the humility of the shamed. Let the fates have their way.* It wasn't done anyhow, not yet. Even if they were licked, they still had this Coffin and his cavalry to hold back at sword's point while the balance of the army retreated. *That's something, ain't it? Even if dragoons get licked, they're still good enough to go boot-to-boot with this Coffin, a man whose very name speaks of death and burial and the worms to come. That's a thing to be proud of in itself, ain't it? And mightn't I redeem a measure of my own shame if I put up a good enough fight?*

It wasn't long till they started moving off, turning away from the hateful stockade that had defied them, skirting the ugly thicket where so many had been lost, passing over the corpses of the dead of both sides and of the fallen horses, trying not to heed the whimpers and wails of the wounded or the squeals of the still-suffering beasts, heading back again into the smoky pine woods toward the noise of the fighting that got continually louder and more ominous. Riderless and wounded horses roamed everywhere; many hurried anxiously near, pressing close in answer to some vague memory of their training, pitifully trying to align themselves in ranks. The men beat at them with their swords to drive them away. Meantime the strange officers rode about sorting the state troops into one gang, the militia into another, the volunteers into a third; Captain Parsons put the dragoons into a column of twos; and with all right distinctions finally made and order properly restored, James felt better satisfied.

Still, it was coming clear to him that, in a battle, no arrangement was without its defect, for when the state troops finished forming up, to his disgust he found them plodding right alongside, scant yards away. He and Bart Hawkins, the brother with the scarred face, were the two files in the third rank of the column, and some of the Carolinians rode nearly abreast of them—stringy, long-necked fellows, hanks of greasy hair coiling to their shoulders, lop-brimmed hats jammed low on their heads with foxtails or turkey feathers stuck in them; they smelled like game hung far too long. Though the noise of the fighting waxed ever more intense, James and Bart had no trouble hearing the closest one remark bitterly to his neighbor, in a honking voice that penetrated like a goose's, "Here we are, about to get killed, and I ain't even got my nigger yet." He leaned out, pressed a finger to a nostril, blew a blob of snot to the ground, then turned a gimlet eye on his mate. "D'you get yourn?"

"Naw," the other replied with equal contempt, "I ain't got no nigger. Nor no farmstead nor no bound'ry of land neither. Signed up for ten months' duty and ain't got shit to show for it." He spat aside a scornful stream of tobacco juice. "Sumter's Law, my arse."

Bart, like the others who'd earlier fought by James's side, had lately been holding a distance from him that smacked of some small misgiving, no doubt owing to whatever it was that had lapsed from his memory during those two charges on the hedge. But now Bart broke his restraint, bending to confide that Colonel Hampton had only got charge of the state troops that same morning after its real commander, a Colonel Henderson, took a musket ball. And this Henderson, in his turn, had but recently got it from a South Carolina officer name of Sumter.

"Sumter," Hawkins explained, "he's no better'n a plundering damned thief. Enrolled these fellows promising to pay 'em in loot stole from the Tories, specially slaves. They all put their names down figuring to get 'em a passel of blacks and set up for rich planters and go down to Charles Town after the war and get in the Assembly."

"Only the Governor revoked the damned law," Ben sniggered from the rank behind. "Now I reckon they won't get no pay atall."

Derisively James snorted. "Like us?"

Bart straightened in his saddle; some of that misgiving crept back into his mood. "Continentals may not get paid any more'n a damned dirt-eating villain. But at least a Continental's a *soldier*, and not any scavenging thief." It was an important distinction; James was compelled to agree with it. He'd be mighty relieved when the time came for the dragoons of the regular service to part forever from so degenerate and contaminating an influence.

Now the piney woods got scanty and they saw ahead of them a break in the timber, what looked like a big clearing, not an empty glade but a field cluttered with indistinct shapes half obscured by a film of pale gray powder smoke. In several places rose heavy pillars of another kind of smoke, dark and curdled, and at the foot of each you could see the glimmer of fires. They rode closer. The vague shapes they'd seen sharpened into crisp ones—row after row of tents, some still standing neatly white and triangular, more collapsed to the ground, most serving to feed the dark-smoked fires. Yonder on the furthest edge they saw a place where a number of wagons had been run together and set alight. Ash and soot floated everywhere; the smell of burning stung the nose. *Bloodybacks' camp*, somebody said.

The place was strangely astir. Something circulated through it and among the tents in a broken and irregular way like a stream swirling and tumbling and dividing around the stones that interrupted its course, only the movement couldn't have been water because it wasn't fluid, and James saw now as the column came nearer that it was a throng of men in blue and brown that passed and repassed through the camp, in and out of the tents left standing, knocking others down and setting fire to them, carrying off their contents, pillaging the place as if they were no longer civilized soldiers of the noble Continental army but some tribe of vulgar barbarians of the olden time.

Nearby on the left bulked the pink brick mansion; four enemy field guns stood wheel-to-wheel before it; British troops had massed left to right around the camp; and all these were laying down a blistering fire on the teeming mob. But not even the lethal rain of musketry, grapeshot, canister balls, and howitzer bombs seemed to deter the sacking. James saw two fellows shot down lugging a camp trunk between them; saw a man with an armload of candelabra and table service blown in half by a round-shot that sent his treasure of silverware flying fanwise; saw another drag a harpsichord from a tent, return inside to fetch a stool, sit down before the instrument, and begin to play.

Oafs hunched amid piles of hams, roast turkeys, and sweet potatoes gorging themselves, swilling wine and rum, oblivious of the leaden missives that whistled past and sometimes struck them down even as they ate and drank. Some found prostitutes and drew them into the open to have their way with them; lines formed to wait turns; fellows in those lines were killed even as they fumbled at their britches to bring forth their members. Soldiers fought each other over heaps of spoils. A few hapless officers hastened about waving their swords vainly hoping to rally the rioters; the men jeered at them. Every face James saw was coarsely flushed with drunkenness. The sight made him turn away in shame. If there was a single thing on this earth he knew for certain, it was that he would never stoop to such abhorrent acts; nor would any of his dragoon mates.

But no sooner had this certainty come over him than he was amazed to see Captain Parsons sternly double the column on his lame nag, a cocked pistol in his hand, his red-rimmed eyes fixed on them like the stare of the dead. "First man of you drops out to join this rabble," he told them in his clogged voice, "I'll shoot him in the brains. Don't any of you sons of bitches think of falling out. Keep your goddamned places; Coffin's up ahead."

James gave a dry incredulous laugh; it was folly to think any dragoon—even the worst, even Benjamin Lockett, bully and brawler, who'd bravely fought in their fort of swords—might be tempted to join in this unholy frenzy; he shifted in his saddle to share his amusement with the others. But to his shock he found them all, even Obediah Plumbley, leering with the same wanton relish that seethed about them; and he was sickened further still. At least none yielded, though they enviously eyed the few state troops who did, till Colonel Hampton galloped up and herded these back into line roundly cursing.

At least, he thought, glaring at his mates in disgust, *I'm better'n them. Even if I ain't as good as John the Crowner's boy, even if I didn't go to save the Colonel, I'm better'n these.* Again he scoffed at the melee roundabout. *Better'n that too.* Of course he didn't want to think too highly of himself; that wasn't in his nature; he was a modest soul, and usually a charitable one; and it was true he'd fallen short of the glory he'd hoped was in him, that Captain Gunn had assured him was. Besides, unseemly pride was one of the faults he disliked most in others. *But by God, I know what I'll do and what I won't do. A-body has a right to be proud to know for sure he's above doing evil.*

Off to the right rear, in the woods, a semblance of an infantry column was forming up—other men in blue and brown still carrying their firelocks unlike the scapegraces in the camp; they must be the part of the army that hadn't got caught up in the madness of rapine. General Greene must be over there trying to organize a retreat. James felt a moment's pity for the General, then a swelling pride to think how earnestly he must be working to rally what seemed past rallying. He remembered riding past the General two times that day, remembered how the General had politely tipped his hat to the passing troops that morning, and how he'd flourished it again that afternoon when the dragoons set off to hold the flank, remembered believing the General must be a fine and thoughtful Quaker gentleman. He regretted having suspected him of pursuing private ambitions like the meanest of the mean.

"Attention!" Captain Parsons suddenly yelled. "Form section!" Just opposite, seventy yards or so distant, a column of horse was approaching, black-capped riders in red and green, sabers at the slope. *Coffin's cavalry,* James thought, *Coffins, caskets, crepe, falling clods of turned earth, eternal sleep, decay.* He and the two Hawkinses and Obediah swung into line.

Part ye' Twenty-Eighth
In Which a Young Man at Laſt Grows Wiſe

BART HAWKINS WAS THE FIRST TO TELL HIM. THEY were patrolling back and forth between the pickets and the videttes the night after the battle, and from time to time during their rounds James would take to disparaging the troops of the army who'd forsaken their duty to go rampaging through the British camp, letting their greed and gluttony and lust turn victory into defeat. He condemned them for their lack of republican virtue and patriotic principle. He named them scavenging robbers. He asserted that he himself was far above such beastly behavior.

Finally, the fourth or fifth time he resumed the same harangue, Bart turned on him in exasperation. "By God, Johnson, you give yourself some awful high and mighty airs for a damned fellow that stole water from poor dying men and snatched food out of the mouths of the wounded whilst they pled with you for mercy."

James drew rein gawking in disbelief. He couldn't see why Bart would falsely accuse him of such heinous doings. There was a space of time in which he couldn't think what to say. In the distance, yonder in the British camp beyond the vidette line, they heard bugles and drums and what sounded like a lot of wagons beginning to move. Presently he recovered his voice; he grew indignant. "I never done that."

The look Bart gave him was so superior he could make it out even in the dark and drizzling rain. Bart had unwrapped the turban from about his helmet and let the ends hang down to keep the rain off the back of his neck, and the whole contraption gave his head an odd new outline that resembled a pyramid. "When we get off this here picket," Bart declared, "we'll ask the other boys and see what they say."

James was hurt and deeply offended. It was true he hadn't known the brothers before this day and might have misjudged their character, but on the other hand the three of them had been through a great trial together and he'd come to consider them friends and brothers in arms. Now he could think of no just reason why Bart would want to lay on him so false

426

and terrible a charge. "Why," he persisted, "I'd never sink so low as to do those things."

Bart gave a derisive laugh. "Oh yes, you would. You done it, all right." It was as if he felt defiled to find himself in such low company as James constituted. Nobody else had ever felt that way about him, though since the incident of Colonel Washington behind the thicket he'd often thought it of himself, and he was at a loss as to how he should receive this new attitude of scorn coming from without. Most people he'd met, save for Chenowith and Benjamin Lockett and of course the officers and noncommissioned officers of the army who were required by their rank to demean him, had not found in him any qualities worse than were normal.

Bart would tell him no more while they walked their horses through the black piney woods under the soughing rain, to and fro between the poor lonesome videttes on the farthest outposts near the edge of the Bloody-backs' camp and the pickets huddled over their fires five hundred yards westward, deeper in the forest. Nor would Bart take up the subject even later when they got to rest a bit with the other fellows of the grand guard. It hardly mattered anyway because James was too shocked and mystified by what had been said to pry into the matter. He tried to think over the events of the day for any memory that might comport however roughly with what Bart had claimed of him. But nothing came to mind.

He remembered fighting Coffin's cavalry to cover the army's retreat—riding like a whirlwind at all those fellows in their little black caps, trying to cut with his saber though his arm felt so tired and his grip so weak he feared any blow he struck would do no more damage than a river reed, yet his blade crossing others, turning them away, edges clanging and grating, sparks flying, the horses wheeling and rearing and stamping, men showing their teeth like cornered rats. He didn't think once of Sergeant Dangerfield's admonitions about executing the cut straight-armed, from the shoulder, by a flexing of the fingers and wrist. He'd hacked like a butcher. He'd killed one that he knew of, middling-sized with gold hair as fine and pretty as Agnes Baker's and drawn back to a club tied with a green ribbon; he'd cut him across the base of his throat so his blood shot out in a long curling stream, six or seven yards out, pulsing with such force it might've been squirted from a hose. He could call up lots of thoughts like that, and they were plenty ugly in themselves, maybe even shameful, and would probably return to haunt him in later times; but he didn't think they were any worse than what the rest of the boys had done, Bart Hawkins included. It had been a fierce and bloody struggle.

But later, at Burdell's, after they'd been relieved from patrol duty and the whole outpost drawn back, he learned different. He and Bart had to ask their way through a confusion of mixed commands till they found the camp where what was left of the First and Third Dragoons had fetched up to lick their wounds, in a pasture of Campton's farm. There James was relieved to spy Lieutenant Gordon still among the living, propped on a stick talking to Captain Parsons with his leg swathed in bandages. He saw Shoupe and Hudson, Neal, Griffin, Gunnell, Robertson, Bobby Busby, Lockett—all unhurt. It seemed the dragoons had suffered their greatest loss not among privates but among the corps of officers, who'd all been posted on the right of the column when it turned left in front of the hedge, exposing them to the worst of the enemy's fire.

They came to a brush hut where Ben Hawkins and Obediah hunkered over a little blaze of twigs that hissed now and then as the rain dripped into it between the woven withes overhead. "Maybe you'll believe Plumbley if you won't believe me," said Bart in a surly way, dropping into a crouch over the small flicker of warmth.

James eased himself down gingerly and sat. Every part of his body had its strain or bruise or scrape, and the cut his flailing saber had given him over his eye earlier in the day was swollen and achey. The seat of his britches was still soiled and what laid in it had dried and hardened and had left his bottom raw and itching. He'd never felt so filthy or so used up. But he'd also never been accused of an atrocity and just now that was his worst worry. He searched Plumbley for some sign of the preacher's old good will, but Plumbley didn't seem to want to look him in the face; instead put his gaze on the fire and vigorously worked his chew of tobacco with his big jaws.

The fact was, none of them, not the Hawkinses nor Plumbley nor Lockett either, had acted right to James after those two charges Colonel Hampton led against the blackjack thicket—the occasions that for some reason seemed to have slipped his mind. He grew restless and anxious, casting wary looks first at Ben and then at Bart and finally at the preacher. At last he had to appeal to Obediah, "Is it true what Bart says? Did I do things I shouldn't have?"

Plumbley turned his head, spat, pulled at his bulbous nose, and surprised James by bursting out, "You're claiming you forgot, I reckon. All right, claim it. But I want you to know, ain't a one of us here hasn't done the same or worse'n you done, some time or other." He shot James a penetrating bloodshot glance. "Only *we* don't prance about afterwards bragging how we're too much of a Christian or a republican or a patriot to stoop to such. For that's *hypocrisy*, is what that is."

The word took James unawares. He leaned back baffled. *Hypocrisy!* Why, he'd never once thought himself a Pharisee or a Holy Willie. He wanted to remonstrate, but Obediah gave him no opportunity. "By God, Johnson," the preacher suddenly bellowed, shaking his big head, "'tain't what you *done*, it's what you've been *a-saying!* I'll tell you, Brother, you've a failing that sorely tries the patience of them about you. For you're a fault-finder. A carper and a caviler and a smellfungus. A-wagging your finger at them you say fail to do right, as if you're bettern'n the common run of humanity and know best how folk ought to act." He spat a jet of tobacco juice into the fire; it sizzled angrily.

"These past hours we've all had to listen to you impugn and revile them poor fellows that went rummaging through the Bloodybacks' camp today. Well, it's true they done shameful. But they done it on account of suffering hunger and thirst and sickness, with the temptation thrown in their path of all them eats and drink and snatch and goods. But it's *war* that's the shame, Johnson, not the miserable heartsick buggers a-fighting it. You want to go reproving and rebuking, go and defame war itself, and leave off vilifying the misfortunate goddamned wretches a-toiling in the ranks. Hell, every man here's done as much as those boys did today. And you've done it yourself."

He ceased his hectoring then and seemed to turn sadder and more thoughtful, and when he spoke next, it was in a fashion more subdued. "But we're mortal. We're disposed to sin and be weak. But we don't *always* do wrong of our own will. We can't *always* answer for what the body does. For sometimes the flesh gets its own mind, overcomes what the spirit would want us to do if times was otherwise."

He stopped again and the sadness in him deepened. "You know, Brother," he went on after a moment, "of my own carnal failings, which caused my downfall amongst the Methodists. Now I pray constantly to resist temptation and refrain from sinning, and I think the Almighty hears and absolves me when I come to Him repenting. But I don't deny my own offenses to myself, whether they're willful or not; nor do I go about blaming others for the evil they may do. It's as the Savior enjoins us: 'Cast out first the beam out of thine own eye, and then thou shalt see clearly to pull out the mote that is in thy brother's eye.'"

Plumbley gave a curt nod as if to show he was done preaching, if a sermon was what he'd been giving. But the sadness didn't leave him. "Now," he said, "I'll tell you what was done—what you done," and James, exhausted and pained as he was, tensed in dread of what he might hear. "When Colonel Hampton led us against the thicket that first time," Obediah continued, "some of us—you too—finally got through them damned stiff stickly briary tangled-up shrubs and broke the Bloodyback line, and for a minute or so we was in the rear of 'em, hacking down at them grenadiers and light troops. And there was a big oak tree back there where they'd dragged all their hurt and dying ones so's they could lay in the shade and the surgeons could tend to 'em. You'd been a-perishing of the heat—hell, we all was. And there was this Lobster drummer-boy a-laying there with

429

a big hole through his middle, had a wooden canteen full of water, and he was a-drinking from it, only you jumped off your horse and run over and snatched it from him, and turned it up and drained it, and him pleading with you the whole time, plucking at your ankles. And a Bloodyback surgeon came and made as if to stop you, and you stuck him with your sword and I expect you killed him, the way the point come out the other side. Then you stabbed the boy too, for grabbing at you."

Strangely it was not altogether a surprise to hear the revolting words; two murky visions flitted by—hands, delicate as cobwebs, grasping at his legs much as had the hands of those poxed Negroes on the Richmond road; and a pale-faced man in a snowy wig opening his mouth in amazement as a shaft of curved steel sank into him. James blinked; the images fell away.

"Then the second time we charged," Plumbley was saying, his voice even gentler now, "we got in there again, only this time you didn't do no fighting atall, you headed straight for that damned tree where the hurt ones was piled up and you jumped off your horse and commenced to paw through them poor whining wounded and dying Redcoats till you found one that was eating a piece of bread, and you snatched it away and gobbled it down, and then you stripped the haversacks and canteens off of two or three more of 'em and throwed 'em over your shoulder and got back on your horse and rode back to our lines with 'em while we was all still a-fighting; and when we come back after the Bloodybacks drove us off, you was a-setting on the ground under a pine tree wolfing down all the eats you'd dug out of them haversacks and guzzling all the water in them canteens."

Obediah hung his head and gazed once more into the fire as if to grieve. "Now, Brother Johnson, I reckon God in His mercy would want you to look back on them acts not as willful sins but as the work of the weakened flesh. Your body was in torment and required appeasement. Your soul wasn't in any part of what you done. God knows what your soul's like, knows it's mostly good and gentle and meaning no harm to anyone—save when you go to blaming and reproaching other folk like you do. I believe He's already forgive you for them acts, and for being a goddamned pettifogger too, if you'll only repent of that too, which I know you'll do. He's redeemed you."

Then he raised up and nearly frightened James to death by pushing his head toward him and hollering into his face, at the same time searing him with his breath of peach brandy, "But in the Holy Name of the Resurrected Christ, will you please quit telling us how you'd never do this, nor never do that, nor how better a patriot and a democratic man James Johnson is than any other son of a bitch alive?"

He'd been so worn down and given out that Plumbley's account, appalling as it was, probably hadn't stirred or meekened him as it should've. It wasn't that he disbelieved the preacher. No, Obediah was an honest man; what he'd told could on no account be doubted. Nor could James dismiss those visions that had come to him while Plumbley talked, the cobwebby fingers plucking at his ankles, the man in the white wig with the sword going in him; cloudy images of something real that maybe he'd covertly wished hadn't been. He recalled the sensation of peculiar freshness he'd felt just before they charged into Coffin's cavalry, when he'd gone, without any reason he knew, from near fainting with heat and thirst to a new vigor that made him able to fight passably well even given the puniness of his arm. He guessed that had come of the food and drink he'd taken in the loathsome way Obediah described.

Of course as the days passed he grew more and more despondent, mortified both by the terrible deeds he'd done and by the censoriousness his mates all complained he practiced, which had only deepened the dejection he already felt for having failed to grasp the heritage of the Gunns and Johnsons when Colonel Washington fell. Yet he was still a willful soul. True, his acts against the British wounded were terrible indeed and he felt sorry for having done them, but as a confirmed unbeliever he had no intention of falling to his knees, as Obediah urged him, to pray to be forgiven. By his lights, forgiveness was one's own personal business. He'd always tried to live his life in a fashion that met his own standards, not any rules written down in a supposedly sacred book, and if anybody needed to forgive him, or not forgive him, that person was himself and not God. And he wasn't sure yet whether he *should* forgive himself. What he'd done to those suffering British was unspeakably bad; perhaps it was even past forgiving. For what he *hadn't* done—rescue the Colonel—there was no forgiveness at all; he was certain of that.

Yet, as foul as his crimes were, it had been almost worse to learn he was not the tolerant person he'd always believed himself to be. It was ever his custom to expect folk to do the best that was in them, just as he expected that of himself. When they fell short, or when he fell short, he was disappointed, and he reckoned he did express that disappointment right readily—maybe too readily. His expectations were high, and he'd believed this to be a positive and admirable trait. He wanted the world to improve. *Maybe I want it so much,* he thought, *because life's been so hard on Libby and me, and on Ma and Da. Good folk too often get trampled down; I've wanted them raised up. I've hoped this liberty we're fighting to get would get to be a pure and perfecting thing, and might improve the world, and raise folk up. Has it been too much to ask?*

After a time the army turned around and took to the road back the way it had come till it arrived at a ferry, and there crossed the river and marched along a causeway over a canebrake to a pretty spot on some wooded heights overlooking a big swamp—the High Hills of Santee, the place was called—and all during this march and during the time they were settling into the new camp, James kept turning matters over in his mind. He stayed distant from the others as much as he could, and his mates, sensing how his thoughts were working, left him pretty much alone, though he could tell by their looks they were harboring no more ill will against him and only wanted him to mend himself. He was grateful for that.

Then one day a corporal rode up while he was washing his hunting shirt in a creek and handed down two sealed packets of paper—letters, he realized with a surge of joy. Eagerly he tore them open. This was the first:

Dear Privt Johnſon,
I inſcribe this letter on behalf of yr Deere Siſter Elizabeth who deſireth me to ſay ſhe is well enough though ſomewhat ſickly & wiſhes you to knowe She has got your laſt Writing & is moſt Cheered to learn of Miſtreſs Agnes Baker as the Object of your Affectionate Intereſt. She ſayeth hit is High Time. She deſireth me alſo to ſay She thinks often of Home and how you uſed to tell Her of it but Miſſes you aDoing hit. Her huſband Mr Sides is All Right tho he frets a good deal. She will ſend You another Writing preſently.
By hand of Margaret Hackley, Laundreſs, 1ſt Regt Light Dragoons

He felt a twinge of worry for her sickness—*goddamn that Poovey; he'd better quit thinking of himself and go to taking good care of her*—but he sensed no dismal portents in the tone of the letter. She sounded like herself—sensible and humorously bossy yet full of warm sentiment, longing for his tales of home. It pleased him that she knew of Agnes Baker and favored his intentions. But her mention of his stories brought a mist to his eyes. He thought he might commence a new habit of telling her a story of home in his mind every night after Tattoo, in hopes she might somehow grasp it out of the air in her sleep and be comforted.

The second letter said:

Friend Johnſon, This is writ by David Baker who I am confident you will remember as Bro. to ye Saucey Agnes my Siſter. She has got yr Letter & liked it Better than She will Admit to & has aſked me to give Anſwer. She wd prefer me to write Clever & Canny & Whimſical but I wont, for I have taken a Liking to you and refuſe to be a Party to her Pranks. You ſaid in yr Laſt you hoped Nobody better than You wd come along. Well ſuch is not Poſſible in my opinyon nor in Hers neither if She will only admit it. You are Moſt welcome amongſt us when this War is over which Pray God will come to paſs ſoon. You muſt guard againſt Sickneſs & keep Well in all ways moſt eſpecially in Battel. We aſk ye Lord daily to Preſerve you Safe. Sadly Ninian hath died. Yr. Friend, David Baker.

Under this, in another hand, blocky and irregular like a child's, came a single line: "i rite this my ſef i keep my piſtol loded & my nife cleen ſo look out, agnes."

The more he pondered his offenses during the battle the more he gave thought to Captain Gunn and what the Captain had told him of wee John the Crowner's son—how the lad had fought at *Alt na gaun* just as James himself had fought at the Eutaws, fighting till he was little more than a leached-out hull the same as James, doubtless tortured as much by heat and thirst and tiredness. But how, unlike James, he'd bound up his wounds and slaked his thirst honorably in a stream and insisted on going to avenge the death of the Crowner and fetch back his father's brooch of office. He hadn't rifled the dead or stolen from the wounded or committed any such outrages. He'd taken up his bow and arrow and urged his brothers to come with him, and they'd trailed the treacherous Keiths all the way to Dirlot Castle, and there he'd perched himself in a window and shot the chief of the Keiths through the heart in the midst of his ignoble revels.

Captain Gunn had offered that example for James to follow. Valor was in his bloodline if only he would be equal to it. Let him imitate John the Crowner's son and he would play the hero and survive this war. But Captain Gunn hadn't prepared him for what the war would be, for what it would demand of him, for what it would take from him. Now he knew that nobody, not even a figure as mighty as Captain Gunn, could do that. There could be no adequate preparation. War was a thing so enormous it was beyond preparing for. Before its evil every man was alone and power-less, must confront the part of war that sucked out the essence of the soul. It had been easy to blame others whose souls were drained till he'd learned how his had been. Now he recognized there could be no right judgment of conduct in any war. Nor any just way of measuring patriotism.

He considered all the various reasons men gave for being in the army. Those state troops who so repelled him with their longing for Negro slaves; weren't they no more than poor bad-luck wretches who hoped fi-nally to enrich themselves and have a life of ease? *Didn't Libby and me join the army thinking to find food and shelter, even if we didn't get it? Didn't we join the dragoons because Colonel White offered us a bounty, even if he didn't pay it? Didn't we long to better ourselves too, just like these Carolina clay-eaters?*

Poovey Sides and Charlie Cooke and Blan Shiflet and those other fel-lows in the Gaskins Battalion, some had got drafted and had no choice but to serve; many had sold themselves as substitutes to men of property who preferred not to offer their own flesh on the altar of their country; some few, he knew, had volunteered, though not so much to serve the country as to get shut of nagging wives or hounding creditors or failed farms and trades or, like himself, were throwing off indenturement. Some indentured wretches had been forced into the ranks to serve in place of their cowardly masters. Many had enlisted because if they didn't, their sweethearts would've spurned them for cowards, or because all their neighbors had enrolled and if they didn't too, they'd be shamed. A very few, maybe like Captain Gunn, might've gone in the army because they had a devil in them that made them love to fight. There were all kinds of reasons, good ones and bad ones, for folk to take up the musket. But he didn't know a single soul who, if you asked him, would say he was in the army to fight for the liberty of men or the independency of America.

Maybe General Greene would say it. Probably he would. It was what men in high places were supposed to say. On the day of the battle James had thought the General too great and disinterested a figure to let low ambition move him. But now he reckoned even General Greene must nurse in his bosom reasons no less selfish than the desire of those shaggy Carolinians to possess a Negro, or his own and Libby's wish to eat and sleep in comfort or to get a bounty and a pension to smooth their way in life.

But is a person no more than his meanest wish? No better than the worst thing that ever moved him? At the Arsenal he'd sensed a greater space around him than his lowest expectation could ever fill, a space that gave him room to be larger in. Ever since, even in the confinement of the army, it seemed he'd been growing into that space, and because of the growing he was wiser and stronger and freer now than he'd ever been. Maybe that was what they were all doing—him, Poovey, General Greene, the Hawkins brothers, South Carolina riffraff hankering to be men of property, everybody in the war; they were all growing into whatever space they could fill. One person's space might be mostly foul, reeking with greed and ill intent, while another's might be brighter with a lot of good promise, but probably nobody's space was all one thing or all the other. What mattered was that you could grow into whatever space it was. Maybe that was what the British didn't like—so many people having so much space. So maybe that private space was what men meant when they spoke of liberty. If it was, then maybe the sum of all those separate spaces was what they were fighting for without really meaning to. Maybe by fighting for what each wanted most for himself, all of them ended up, by accident, fighting for America too.

Part ye' Twenty-Ninth

In Which General Greene Closely
Examines ye Nature of Truth

LONG PAST MIDNIGHT, BACK AT BURDELL'S, THE General bent wearily to the candlelit paper on his camp desk, squinting to read the words he had dictated to Pendleton in a voice so torn and raw from screaming orders on the battlefield that he could barely speak above a whisper. But Nat seemed to have captured everything accurately despite the General's raspings, had in fact improved on some of the unhandiest of his formulations. "The Genl prefents his moft grateful thanks to all the Officers & Soldiers of the Army," Greene read, covering his aching right eye with one hand, "for their extraordinary exertions in the well fought battle of Yefterday. He has infinite pleafure in acknowledeging himfelf fatiffied in the higheft degree with the troops . . ."

The rain that had begun at nightfall drummed lightly on the roof of the marquee, a soothing, peaceful sound; its clean scent enlivened the air. It was not hard to think of it as cleansing a world that men had fouled. He read on along Nat's neat lines of script, his good eye burning with fatigue. He made his way doggedly through the litany of compliments he had seen fit to mete out to the various officers and commands—"behaved with gallantry & firmnefs;" "exhibited lively examples of intrepidity;" "deferves the higheft applaufe"—each passage provably factual at least in part yet each more telling on his candor than the last. He paused to ponder Pilate's unanswerable question. *What is truth?* Was truth what had happened, or what one said had happened? There had been intrepidity, gallantry and firmness aplenty; there had also been a repugnant riot and a rout and, in the case of Harry Lee, both a measure of good service and something very like dereliction of duty. Yet both were truths.

Political sensitivities were truths too. In some ways they were the most important truths, for upon them hung the continued active participation in the war of the several states. "The Cavalry Cmd by Lt. Cols Wafhington

435

& Lee supported in the most courageous Manner that high reputation Which they have acquired by repeated & gallant services." Virginia being foremost among the Southern provinces, and no family of that state being more highly placed than the Lees, Light-horse Harry, possibly meriting a court-martial, was instead held up for equal notice with heroic Billy Washington who, though a Virginian too, came of somewhat lower condition than the Lees. Still, if Virginia would have reason to be proud of both her sons, Harry would be irked to find Billy named first and the two of them held at par, and would regard himself as damned with faint praise. *Thus even a partial truth may sometimes nicely cut two ways,* Greene reflected, feeling a certain sly gratification.

Every state came in for its share of credit. The North Carolina Brigade "discovered a Confidence which does honour to Young soldiers." No distinction was made between Colonel Malmedy's militia, which had broken—albeit for good reason—and that of Pickens and Marion, which had stood fast. All, in Greene's order, had "ansered the most sanguine expectations." He would not forget his own part in the breaking of Malmedy's corps; nor would he mention it either. The Maryland and Virginia Brigades had demonstrated "Military perfection which is seldom Equald by the Oldest Troops." Kirkwood's Delawares and Colonel Henderson's South Carolinians were lauded for extraordinary service. He hoped he had struck a satisfactory balance among the provinces; it seemed to him that he had.

If truth and reality are the same, he thought, rubbing his eye, *is it not also, somehow, equivocal and ambivalent—in the end, a paradox, a contradiction. Isn't truth relative, different for every actor or witness; isn't it a collective of impressions, biases, results hoped for as well as outcomes gained? Or is it but a lie so cleverly dressed that it passes for truth?*

His mind whirled; he hoped he would not faint away as he had done after the battle of Guilford. He moved his hand from his eye, made a cup of it, sank his brow into its palm; his forehead felt as clammy as dead flesh. Conjectural, hypothetical, ever-cogitating Nathanael Greene had sprung unbidden out of the dank pit of his exhaustion; he heard himself utter a husky embittered laugh. *Suppositional Nathanael, get thee behind me!* Pendleton bent near, scowling with concern; the General waved him off. "I'm all right, Nat. I'm just tired."

"You should try to sleep, sir."

"I will, Captain. As soon as I finish this." Pendleton stood back to wait. Again Greene peered at the wanly lit paper. "The very great advantage of the strong Brick House was the only cause of preserving the whole british Army from Captivity. And tho the want of Water made it requisite after the Action to retire to this place, Yet the Victory is Complete & We have only to Lament the lofs of feveral of our brave Officers & foldiers whofe glorious death are to be Envied."

The Victory is complete. Yes, he would claim a victory. So of course would Colonel Stewart. And each, in his way, would be justified. Each had indeed won his battle, Greene in the morning, Stewart in the afternoon. Each had also lost it—Stewart in the morning, Greene in the afternoon. It was a fact that Greene had been driven from the field, but it was also a fact that his pickets now held the woods along the western edge of the battleground and there was little question that Stewart would commence a retreat toward Charles Town come the morrow. *Truths. Relative truths.*

He had lost all his own artillery, bringing off only a single captured piece of the enemy's. Nearly sixty officers of all arms, including the indispensable Colonel Washington, had fallen, and one, Colonel Campbell of the Virginia Brigade, was dead. Blood had flowed freely among the officers of dragoons; Captain Watts and the acerbic Lieutenant Elisha King, whose sharp tongue he'd had to curb last July while riding down from Winnsborough to Mrs. Motte's, were badly hurt and not expected to live; three other subalterns were injured; a young cornet had perished.

Out of the whole army of about two thousand, over five hundred seemed to have been killed and wounded. But he had also taken as many British prisoners as he'd lost in casualties; Stewart had taken but forty of the American wounded and had seen the flower of his army cut down, six hundred men, a fifth of his force, most of them irreplaceable regulars. Barring large reinforcements, which were unlikely, he could never again undertake active operations.

Greene's eyelids drooped; his head sagged. He jerked himself awake again, forced his brain to surmount the spreading numbness. *Taken altogether*, he thought, *it means the Battle of the Eutaws has been a disaster for both sides; I make no doubt it will prove one of the bloodiest actions of the war for the numbers engaged. But it's a worse disaster for Stewart than for us. That, perhaps, is the part of the truth that counts.* Now the British would be confined to Charles Town; they could no longer argue in negotiations for a settlement that they held the whole of South Carolina. Peace had come one step nearer.

He sat back and stretched, wincing from the pain of the bruises he'd got falling when his horse was killed. A question floundered in his mind. *What was that animal's name?* He couldn't recall it. His head felt stuffed with cotton. He pushed himself to his feet; agony shot through his lame leg. Lesser pains sang in every nerve and muscle; he'd been pitched as tight as a fiddle-string all day long; now he felt that cost. He reeled; Pendleton stepped in to catch him by the elbow. "Please, sir," said Nat, "please try to take some rest."

Not knowing how he'd come there, he found himself lying in his cot. His boots were off; he stank appallingly. His right eye throbbed. He listened to the patter of the rain. Somewhere out there in the wet and dark Harry Lee, with the cavalry of the Legion and the commands of Hammond and Maham, was passing through the country to the left of the enemy to fall upon the Charles Town road and push on for Monck's Corner in hopes of cutting Stewart off from his base. The knowledge stirred his conscience, made him toss and turn on his mattress in guilty discomfort.

It had been wrong to give the boy so consequential a commission after his inexplicable behavior of the day. But with Washington and Henderson both lost to the army and Hampton's command fought out, Harry was senior and, having materialized after the battle as suddenly and mysteriously as he'd vanished at its height, had volunteered with his usual exuberance to lead the expedition. It was, after all, precisely his kind of mission. Greene had seen no choice but to accede. He'd hoped Colonel Hammond, who in the course of serving under Lee but a single morning had learned to loathe him, and Colonel Maham, Marion's levelheaded commander of horse, would act as halters to the boy's more immoderate urges.

Still, it had been a mistake to send him. Harry had offered no plausible explanation for his lapses during the battle. "Oh," he'd airily declared, "I was organizing a *corps de reserve*," as if such a corps had not already existed in the form of Colonel Washington's horse and Kirkwood's Delawares. "I was bringing order to the Virginia Brigade after Colonel Campbell's death deranged it," he'd claimed. "I was in quest of more advantageous terrain. I was maneuvering upon the enemy's outermost flank." Outermost indeed. The General sighed. He felt sleep coming. *Don't start counting the mistakes,* he told himself. *They are too many.* His eyes closed. *Count them later. But not tomorrow. Tomorrow we must pursue the enemy, renew the action if we can, impede his retreat. Tomorrow will bring its own mistakes.*

A line from his general order came to him: "Whofe glorious death are to be Envied." As sleep took him, he saw it written before him as it had appeared on the paper, saw the grammatical slip; he frowned. *Deaths, that should be. Plural, not singular. Whose glorious deaths are to be Envied.*

Perhaps he'd said more than he meant to, envying the dead. *Another truth,* he thought, and slept.

The whole of the next day, in a drizzling rain, he drove his battered and weary army south and east, out of the pine woods at last, around the edge of a great sinister pocosin some called Ferguson's and others Hell Hole Swamp, angling toward the route of Stewart's retreat, the road through Monck's Corner to Charles Town. But the hope he'd nourished to strike the enemy another blow waned by the hour as report after report came to him, first from Lee, then from Hammond and Maham, explaining how the British rear guard had warded off their attacks and Stewart's force had successfully passed beyond reach.

Lee's dispatches spoke of a persistent pursuit, sharp and desperate actions, brilliant charges of cavalry turned away by overwhelming numbers. Those of Hammond and Maham, conspicuously sent direct to headquarters rather than through Lee and suffused with a chagrin and ill humor their circumspect language could not disguise, instead gave the clear impression that Lee had refrained from assaulting Stewart's rear with sufficient force over the vehement exhortations of his subordinates. Worse, the same rear guard elements that Harry would not attack were reputed to be the very ones conveying the wounded Colonel Washington into captivity.

The General's glum certainty of the previous night was confirmed. *Today's mistake. Yet another. Let it join the already weighty catalogue. Blunders vividly foreseen yet not to be avoided. One knew Harry would prove unequal to the challenge; but there was no officer else of rank to send. That fault is mine. Even if no acceptable alternative was on offer, still I must bear the blame, and bear it I will.* But for Lee to leave Colonel Washington a prisoner when it seemed within his power to free him? Was that a valid military decision justified by circumstances? Was it a miscalculation? Incompetence? Cowardice? Or was it something worse? Was it no more than envy? Was it, as Billy had once joked, the scorpion stinging the frog at mid-river?

Whatever explained it, the problem of Henry Lee, like so much else, must be temporarily laid aside. At dusk Greene halted the army at Martin's Tavern at the head of Ashley River, and that same evening—the campaign now to all intents and purposes having come to an end—he invited his senior officers to a valedictory dinner at his headquarters. Now he could unleash his old affections, which the rigors of battle had forced him temporarily to eschew. He could shed his armor plate of unnatural reticence and give forth the warmth of his gratitude and love for Otho Williams and Jethro Sumner, his respect and awe for Francis Marion and for dour Andrew Pickens with his injured arm bound in its still bloody sling. He could regard these stout fighters once more not simply as holders of military rank representing this or that brigade, as mere pawns to be shifted about on the chessboard of his plan of battle, but as men of flesh and blood and mostly admirable qualities, as good friends and gallant comrades-in-arms. Now he could speak their names.

One by one as they filed into his marquee he passionately wrung their hands—Malmedy the Frenchman whom he had long distrusted but whose militia had fought as obstinately as any veteran regulars till, owing to the shortage of ammunition, they had broken; now they bore an un-deserved infamy. The General closed an arm about the startled Marquis, apologized for leaving him and his brave troops liable to unjust recrimina-tions, expressed deepest admiration for their steadfastness, promised to write to Governor Burke of their fine service. At last the Marquis's mask of imperturbable and impenetrable calm slipped away; he beamed, bowed, and with exquisite courtesy professed himself honored to have served, however imperfectly, with Major-General Greene, most esteemed and ac-complished of all American commanders.

My champions, Greene thought as they passed before him. Colonel Howard of the First Regiment of the Maryland Line, bandaged and limp-ing from his wounds, arm in arm with Otho Williams and Major Harda-man of the Second Maryland. The bereaved Virginians Major Snead and Captain Edmunds, mourning the loss of poor Richard Campbell. Ashe and Blount of the North Carolina Brigade; even Colonel Armstrong who had redeemed with exceptional leadership in action his unseemly inclination toward dueling. Harry Lee, strutting in his finery, so aglow with self-assurance Greene could almost, for the moment, forgive him all his failings. Valiant Kirkwood of the Delaware scouts. Hampton and Myddelton of the South Carolina state troops. Colonel Polk, saddened by the death yesterday of a son. Gaines and Browne of the artillery. Dear reckless dashing unwise Kosci. Forsyth, Hyrne, Shubrick, Billy Pierce, Nat Pendleton.

For the most part the mood of the gathering was agreeable but subdued as befitted the end of an operation whose cost had been high and its re-sults mixed. Conversation at dinner naturally turned to reminiscences of Saturday's battle, but sorrow for the loss of so many fellow officers kept its tone largely hushed and reverent. Harry, though, was the exception. He seemed not to have read the general order insultingly equating him with Colonel Washington; he was in his glory of fitted green and buff, boots agleam, his cherry-cheeked face radiant with pride; if he'd noticed a cool-ness in the General's greeting he did not show it, nor did he seem to feel the solemnity of the occasion. Instead, flushed with wine and self-regard, he set about boasting of the exploits of his Legion.

The General heard his blaring tones above the hum of other talk. To those about him Lee spoke of what most understood to have been the light skirmishing of the van, prior to the main engagement, but in terms that called to mind not a quick clash of outposts but some grand incident out of Homer. He'd laid an ambuscade, he maintained, luring the unsus-pecting van of the enemy into a cunning trap. "Our horse under Captain Eggleston," he cried, "made a rapid movement into the enemy's rear; their infantry was destroyed, and about forty taken with their captain; their cavalry, flying in full speed as soon as they saw the Legion dragoons press-ing forward, saved themselves."

Fulsomely Lee claimed credit for hurling his infantry against the brick house on the left of the enemy's line, though in fact this had been the unaided inspiration of his subordinates Rudulph and Manning and had transpired while Lee himself was nowhere to be found. When Stewart was reforming after the Americans fell into disorder, Harry insisted, he'd placed the Legion horse at the head of a ravine "whence we might readily have broken up the incipient arrangements of the rallying enemy." But, he explained, an unspecified "discomfiture on the left some time before" de-layed the arrival of Captain Armstrong's troop, which rendered a charge impracticable. This Greene knew for an utter falsehood, for Pendleton and Shubrick were searching in vain for Lee at the very time and place spoken of.

While Harry spouted this grandiloquence, his subordinates, Eggleston of his dragoons and Rudulph and Manning of his infantry, flanking him, sat mortified. Hammond and Maham glared in open contempt. There was a general stir of discomfort among all the officers. Yet Harry did not sense this chill. "Every battle I've gone into," he now gloated in his most absolute and positive manner, speaking of his employment, or misemployment, of the Legion horse in the battle, "has more and more confirmed me in the opinion of the usefulness, and even the necessity, of keeping up a respect-able corps of reserve."

Greene heard this. A faint wintry breath of his disapproval blew across to Lee; he leaned to the boy and told him in crisp, sharply etched but still congenial language, "I too, sir, have always understood the propriety and necessity of such a disposition, and have upon all occasions taken it into view in forming the commands for battle." The talk around the table ceased at a stroke. Not a fork clinked. Every eye went to Lee. "But it is always to be understood," Greene continued coolly, "that *no one ought to take upon himself that duty who was not specifically charged with it.*"

Lee colored and fell still. The remark had come so deftly wrapped in the guise of polite discourse that he could find no way to resent it; yet at the same time he knew himself to have been severely reprimanded. Everyone else knew it too. Nor was the General finished with him. Turning now to Otho Williams, Greene casually remarked, "I never have, in all my experi-ence, been so fully satisfied of how much could be accomplished by a few brave and determined men as I was by the charges made on yesterday *by Colonel Hammond's little command and the two companies of Legion infantry under Rudulph and Lieutenant Manning.*"

With that, he smilingly raised his cup to Hammond, Rudulph, and Manning and drank, the deliberate omission of Lee's name more fatal than any bullet, and though he still loved Harry—loved his wayward, turbulent, impossible son as only a helpless father could—his unquestioning trust in the boy was at an end and he knew the emptiness of that loss like a sudden sickness.

Later in the evening, alone in his marquee at last, he commenced a letter to Caty.

> My Angel, many weeks have passed since I last wrote you and for this Lapse I am deeply sorry, offering only in partial Exculpation the excuse that we have been constantly upon the March in an endeavor to put the Enemy at a Disadvantage sufficient to bring him to Battle. Now we have had a most costly & desperate engagement & I flatter myself we have emerged Victorious.

He went on to describe the events of the campaign, then paused, took thought awhile, and bent again to his paper.

> My Dearest I feel now a Deeper and More Affectionate Obligation towards you than I ever have before, and feel your Absence more Sensibly than at any time since the Outbreak of warr Separated me from your loving arms & from the embraces of our dear Children. This may not have seemed to You to be the case Owing to my apparent Reticence & even Aloofness & Indifference to yr Entreaties to join me here. I must make to you a painfull Confession, & in doing so Must Beg yr Forgiveness & Understanding, that since coming to the Southward I have, out of a sort of Blind Perversity, held you unfairly at some Distance, not acting from any Absence of Love but from its Opposite, an Affection so Intense as to Derange my thoughts & actions as I mistakenly supposed. Now I make to you my Sincerest Apology & Profess to you my Eternall Love & Now beg with the Most Genuine Affection & Longing that you commence to make Arrangements to Come to My Side, never again to Leave it. For it is to you More than to any other Person or Circumstance, or even to the Blessings of Heaven, that I owe Whatever Success, Happiness & Repose I have thus far gaind or that my Life hereafter may Extend to me, However underserving of such Rich benefits I may surely be.

The army lay several days at Martin's. While there, the General prepared his report to the President of the Congress on the Battle of the Eutaws. In it, near the end, he wrote, "Our loss in Officers is considerably more from their value than their number, for never did Men or Officers offer their blood more willingly in the ſervice of their Country." After writing the line, he laid his quill aside and sat studying it.

The beast had had its way with him. He had ridden it as best he could, but in the end it had got the better of him. Of him and of Stewart both. But as commanders of armies what they had lost to the beast was nothing more than what Shakespeare called the bubble reputation. Now that he was open again to his gentler sentiments Greene felt the loss to the beast of something infinitely more precious than his name—the lives of those he'd put in harm's way.

He nursed no illusions about human nature. If he'd needed proof of the low impulse that lay coiled in every man aching for release, the sacking of the enemy camp by his troops gone wild with indiscipline had provided it. Further, he knew that any military force, however fine its cause, harbored its share of rogues—his own, perhaps, more than most, consisting as it did of so many British deserters, bounty jumpers, and secret Tories under compulsion, not to mention the rapists, cutpurses, footpads, and other villains evading the just punishments of civilian life common to every army that had ever marched.

No, the Continental Army of the South was no band of angels. Yet many also served who were nothing more or less than good and simple and honorable men. And it was he, driven by his ambitions, who'd pushed them all, saints and devils alike, every one weak and sick and hungry and athirst, into a battle he'd known them unequipped to fight, and so had himself loosed the worst that was in them; and had afterward, as he struggled in the woods to rally them against Stewart's counterattack, felt tempted to judge them, find them wanting in character, blame them, recoil from them in disgust.

Yet these were the same men he'd seen were in some ways better than he and were the true makers of the revolution. Better because they were honest—caitiff or hero, they did not pose as high patriots, did not pretend to personal dispassion while striving for station or riches or the mention of the world, as he did. The revolution they made was simply a matter of more often than not serving in the ranks, following orders, doing as much or as little duty as they were disposed to do, complaining of the hardness of the service, enduring every sort of privation and want, sometimes resisting or malingering or fomenting mutiny; yes, sometimes even giving way to dissipation and rapine. Now and then deserting, some to return, some not. Surely not perfect. Human. But never posing or pretending. And in the storm of battle, ready to give up their lives and limbs. Why? Fear of the lash and firing squad played its part of course, but did not explain all. If asked, they would not say they risked themselves for the vague ideals of revolution or independency. Certainly not—as Nat Pendleton had once assured him—because they knew the noble heart of Nathanael Greene. Why then? He would never know why. Perhaps they themselves did not know. In the end it was a mystery. Whatever their reasons, good and bad, they had offered themselves into his hands and he had delivered them to their fate. And now he felt that burden.

Part of the future's gone, he thought. *Something that might have been now will never be. Part of the nation we wish to make will not now come to pass because Nathanael Greene chose to ride the beast at a place called Eutaw Springs on the eighth of September, seventeen eighty-one. Who knows what statesmen we've lost, what healers, what men of science and literature, what divines, what philosophers, what excellent husbandmen? What was our gain, to balance such a loss?*

He'd told himself the prize he sought was the liberty and independency of the United States, and surely that was true in part. *But what is truth?* he asked again. A part of the truth was that he had hungered for victory on the field of battle, had longed unbecomingly for fame and fortune, had wished to rise to a peak of worldly power, had wanted history to remember him as a mighty figure. He had even prayed for such baubles. *Can there be a worse sin than to pray for one's own fame to be purchased at the cost of the lives of others?* The familiar passage from the eighth chapter of the Gospel of Mark came to him: *For what doth it profit a man if he gain the whole world and lose his own soul?*

God had denied him the fruit of his most sinful ambitions yet had granted him his best and highest. Nathanael Greene would not wear the hero's laurels, would never eclipse General Washington, would not govern or legislate, would not be remembered well in after-generations. He would not amass wealth, would not know the adoration of men, would not wield vast powers. But the country would be free.

Afterword

I WROTE *NOR THE BATTLE TO THE STRONG* BECAUSE of the events of September 11, 2001. Something about that terrible day and the effect it has had on the America I have known and loved all my life made me wish to travel back in imagination to the beginning of our country, to a time even before the beginning, before there was a Constitution or a Bill of Rights or even a unified and recognized nation, and try to understand what it was our ancestors hoped to create.

Even after the years it took me to research and write this book, I still find it hard to explain precisely what I hoped to accomplish. Perhaps I wished to escape from the difficulties of the present and retreat into the past to meditate on what the men and women who founded the United States aspired to create, in an age that was at least as bitterly divided and dangerous as our own. Perhaps I wanted to see whether they had behaved any better under those stresses than we have. In the novel I have portrayed the people and the time as fairly as I could, so it is for you, the reader, to decide: Are we the unworthy inheritors of a noble legacy? Or are we—and were they—merely human; and is it the purpose of history to put our humanity constantly to the test?

When I began this project my intention was to write a partly factual, partly imagined account of the activities of my maternal ancestor, James Johnson, in the Revolutionary War. I obtained Johnson's pension records from the National Archives and from them learned of his service in the Continental Army under Major General Nathanael Greene in South Carolina and Georgia from late 1781 to early 1783.

I realized that in order to understand my ancestor's experiences I also had to learn about Greene's campaigns during that time, which until recently had been among the least known of the war. Accordingly, I read the relevant volumes of *The Papers of General Nathanael Greene* (University of North Carolina Press) and a number of primary and secondary accounts dealing with his operations in North and South Carolina and Georgia.

I came away from my research profoundly impressed by Greene both as a man and as a commander. As my friend Seabrook Wilkinson has pointed out, Greene was not just a fine general who was, amazingly, self-taught; in mental acuity and subtlety of thought and expression he was also one of the most considerable intellectuals of his time. He could, and did, correspond as an equal with the foremost men of Enlightenment America—John Trumbull the historian, Thomas Paine the polemicist, educator and Presbyterian divine John Witherspoon, Thomas Jefferson, John Adams—and in the process showed himself a writer and thinker of remarkable style, wit, and penetrating originality.

In making his acquaintance, the feelings I had were perhaps best expressed by the General's grandson, G. W. Greene, who in 1871 published a biography of his illustrious forebear and quoted on its title page these lines of Homer, from Book Four of *The Iliad*:

> After this manner said they, who had seen him toiling; but I ne'er
> Met him myself, nor saw him; men say he was greater than others.

Toil Greene did. Few have toiled harder, been more scantily rewarded or more undeservedly forgotten. History has all but misplaced him. Yet a fair case can be made that it was he, more than any other field commander, who won the War of the Revolution. Certain it is that he saved the Southern states from British dominion. As all this came clear to me, Greene began to claim a larger and larger share of my contemplated novel, though at first I could not see how to include him, the commanding general, in a book whose other chief character was a lowly private of dragoons.

As is so often the case in my work, it was my wife Ruth whose insight resolved my dilemma. The book, she said, should be equally Johnson's *and* Greene's, the General's point of view giving the reader a top-down perspective on the war as an exercise in command; Johnson's, a bottom-up look at the same war as seen by the ordinary and usually uncomprehending soldier in the ranks. So this work owes its present form to Ruth. If it succeeds in its purpose, the credit is hers. If it does not, the fault is mine for failing to capture the pattern she so clearly saw. Since we have been together I have dedicated all my books to her, and it is with great reluctance that I depart from this practice now, especially since her support for this project has been so unflagging.

But in fact *Nor the Battle to the Strong* could not have been written without the generosity of important friends who have helped me: the late John T. Hayes, author-publisher of *The Saddlebag Almanac*; Sam Fore, former archivist with the South Caroliniana Library in Columbia, Special Collections Librarian at the John D. Rockefeller, Jr., Library at Colonial Williamsburg, and now curator of a private historical collection in Dallas, Texas; C. F. William Maurer, author of *Dragoon Diary: The History of the Third Continental Light Dragoons*; and my principal researcher on all things having to do with Revolutionary War cavalry in the South, Dr. Lee F. McGee. It is with deep gratitude that I dedicate this book, in part, to Lee.

I am also deeply grateful to Dennis and Carol Conrad, Seabrook Wilkinson, and Stephen Kirk; and to Third Dragoon reenactor Daniel Murphy for reading and commenting on the manuscript and saving me from several embarrassing blunders; to Judy Geary for helping me understand the beliefs of the Society of Friends; to Ed Sheary, Peggy Weaver, Charles B. Baxley, David P. Reuwer, Paul and Trudy Evans, and Ron Rash; to Lacey Presnell for conforming my bizarre text format to accepted standards; and most especially to Frederic Beil for seeing in this work the merit I had long hoped it possessed.

Space will not permit me to list here all the sources I consulted. Suffice it to say, my research was as broad and deep as I could make it. However, I do wish to explain that many of the words spoken by General Greene in the novel are taken directly from his published letters or from other primary sources which quote him. Also, the texts of all letters attributed to him in the novel are in fact his own save the very last; that one is my composition. Henry Lee's opinion of Kosciuszko, as well as certain other statements, are his own words from his memoirs, or are attributed to him by contemporaries. James Johnson's views on religion, which he expounds so forcefully to Agnes Baker, are borrowed, in slightly altered form, from James Collins' *Autobiography of a Revolutionary Soldier*, a delightful memoir well worth the reading.

The battle of Eutaw Springs, long one of the most neglected general engagements of the Revolutionary War, has recently come under welcome scrutiny by researchers and forensic archaeologists. As this book was going to press, these studies were yielding exciting new interpretations, especially of the cavalry actions under William Washington. We must all wait to see whether the traditional accounts will be confirmed by these studies or be radically changed. I have had little choice but to adhere to the received record. I have striven to be faithful to it, save in a single particular: I have given the British a howitzer, an advantage history does not accord them, because I wished to acquaint the reader with the effect of this fearsome artillery piece on the eighteenth-century battlefield.

I acquit all those who have assisted me of any responsibility for errors of fact or interpretation I may have made.

❊❊❊❊❊❊❊❊❊❊❊❊❊❊❊❊❊❊❊❊❊❊❊❊❊

The text of this book was set in Adobe's Jenson Pro
by the Nangle Type Shop in Meriden, Connecticut.
The type was designed by Robert Slimbach, of Adobe
Systems, who took inspiration from Nicolas Jenson's
roman and Ludovico degli Arrighi's italic typefaces.
The use of the medial, or long, "s" (ſ) in the part titles
and correspondence follows the style of eighteenth-
century compositors, who also would have had
to use a "y" as a substitute for the "th" thorn
contraction (þ) since thorns were not
available from any typefounders
overseas on the Continent.